AF334158

# Freedom's Children

## BOOK 4 OF THE GUARDIANS

# E.R. PASKEY

# Freedom's Children

**BOOK 4 OF THE GUARDIANS**

E Minor Press

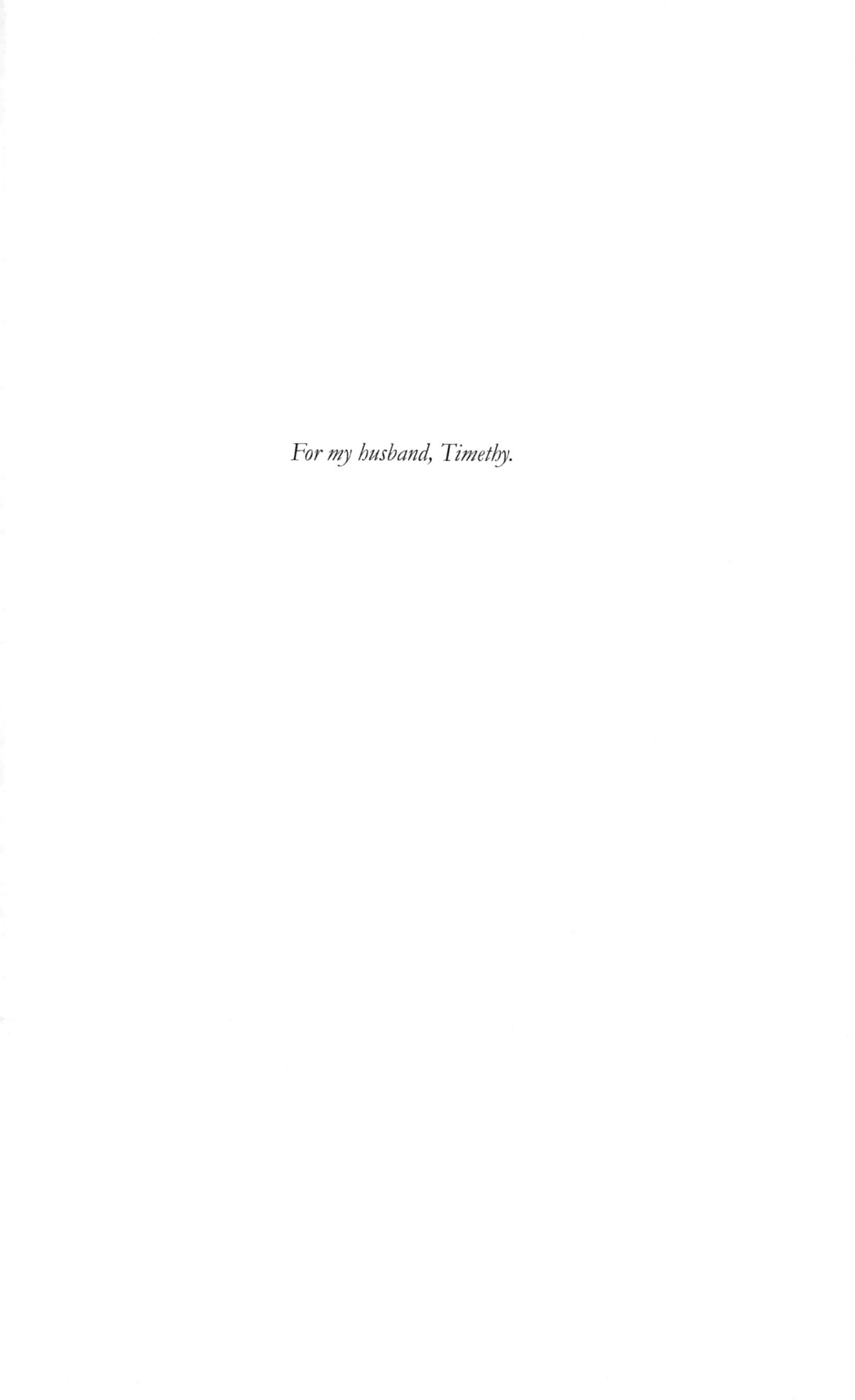

*For my husband, Timethy.*

# CHAPTER 1

COLD, dehumidified air flooded the featureless back halls of the Cuomo Convention Center, sending a chill through Lilia Strong and raising goose bumps on her skin. Her heart thudded in her chest; chilly air was only a minor inconvenience compared to the real problem facing her. This section of the convention center was also empty.

Empty enough that had she been anyone else, Lilia might have been concerned about just…disappearing.

Her palms were sweaty inside her elbow-length navy blue gloves, but there wasn't anything she could do about that except scrunch her fingers in her evening gown's matching shimmery skirt. She immediately let go; the gown was too pretty to ruin. A slim sheath that flared out from her knees, it had short, filmy sleeves to hide the scar on her left upper arm from a fight with a would-be assassin a few months back.

Her heels made sharp clicking sounds against the smooth white floor, a counterpoint to the steady, thudding footsteps of the squad of security officers escorting her through the convention center's back halls. Lilia was tall and slim, with angular features, violet eyes, and chin-length dark brown hair pinned away from her face. Her heels made her taller than several of her escorts, but that didn't seem to bother them.

Everyone else in the building was gathered in the ballroom to celebrate the Tri-World Tournament's Closing Ceremonies Gala. It was a massive celebration; the city of Atalia in Sta'Gloa's Sector 8 was thronged with people from all three inhabited worlds in the Sta'Gloan system. Only a few people even knew Lilia had left the ballroom.

Fortunately, she had two major things in her favor. One, her grandfather was a Representative sitting on the Triumvirate that governed the Sta'Gloan system, otherwise known as the Coalition. And two…she was part of the Nanotech Coalition Defense Corps, NCDC for short, a special civilian defense group whose members were called Guardians.

Guardians' bodies were infused with millions of nanites. Some of these facilitated mental Guardian-to-Guardian comm channels, while others formed several different kinds of highly effective body armor. At the moment, Lilia had a layer of stealth-armor beneath her lovely evening gown.

So, no, she couldn't just disappear. Not tonight.

Even if she *was* under arrest on charges of high treason.

A slow-burning bubble of panic lodged in her throat, but Lilia held her head high and did her best to swallow it down. *We did the right thing.*

She and two of her brothers had done the only thing they *could* do, given the circumstances.

Narrowing her eyes at the black ponytail of the man leading their little procession, Lilia broke the stiff silence. "Where are you taking me?"

Alan Birch spared her a look over his shoulder and the ice in his green eyes almost gave her frostbite. Every centimeter of his tall, lean form radiated smug satisfaction mixed with cold fury—a strange combination, if ever Lilia had seen one. Also a Guardian, Birch ranked high enough at the NCDC to have become a provisional officer with the authority to arrest people.

"You'll see soon enough," he said dismissively.

Lilia wanted to scowl at him, but forced herself to maintain an impassive expression. *He can't be taking me out of the building. Not when I haven't even spoken to the Triumvirate yet.* She had no doubts she and her brothers would be giving an account of themselves soon enough.

After two more turns—one right, one left—they stopped in a hall lined with numbered doors on both sides. Birch opened one of these doors, revealing a large mahogany conference table surrounded by matching chairs, and beckoned to Lilia. "Have a seat."

Lilia eyed him warily for a second, but she knew she really had no choice. *Either I enter of my own volition, or they bodily shove me inside.* She bit the inside of her lip. *I'd prefer the more graceful route.*

Reluctantly, she entered the conference room, sliding past Birch without touching him. The walls were a rich burgundy, and the air in here felt stuffy and humid compared to the hall. Edging around the large table to put some space between them, she watched in alarm as Birch waved the security officers away and closed the door. The hair on the back of her neck prickled; they were alone. "What do you think you're—"

Birch pulled a small, silvery device from seemingly thin air and shot her before she could finish.

A ball of electricity the size of her thumbnail hit Lilia squarely below the v-shaped neckline of her evening gown, just between her breasts. Searing pain exploded in her chest and traveled outward in a starburst along every nerve-ending. For an instant, she felt frozen— her diaphragm unable to expand to allow her to draw a breath.

Then the sensation passed, leaving a strange sort of numbness in its wake. Her knees chose that moment to decide they were off-duty and would no longer bear her weight. Staggering, Lilia grabbed for the nearest chair and leaned heavily on it, trying to convince her-self she could still *breathe.*

"I did tell you to sit down," Birch chided.

Lilia ignored him. *That felt like it burned straight through my armor.* She was almost afraid to look at her chest, but she forced herself to glance down. Instead of the charred spot she expected, her bodice only bore a faint singe mark.

That did not make Lilia feel better. *He has to know I'd materialize stealth-mode nano-armor in a situation like this.* Swallowing with an effort, she lifted her gaze to Birch. "What do you think you're *doing?*"

"Restraining you." Birch gave the device in his hand a look of deep satisfaction. "You're a Guardian, Miss Strong, a Guardian un-der arrest, and we can't take the chance that you'll escape."

Her heart sinking into her stomach, Lilia gaped at him. She *had* wondered why he hadn't bothered to place her in restraints earlier. "What *is* that thing?"

His expression turned cold and smug again. "Try Nancomming your brothers. Tell them I just shot you."

*Okay, he's starting to scare me.* Lilia swallowed again, eying Birch distrustfully. *I really don't want to be alone with him.* She also didn't want to believe a word he said, but *telling* her to contact her brothers was… strange…given the circumstances.

She tried to open a Nancom channel to her twin brother Kevin …but nothing happened. Her mind remained silent; she could no longer feel the channels in her mind connecting her to her brothers, who were also Guardians. It felt like her mind had been closed off, the mental connections she'd grown accustomed to having since she became a Guardian amputated. A cold chill skittered down her spine. *What did he do?*

Eying Birch defiantly, she attempted to open a channel to him. Still nothing. Her grip tightened on the back of her chair. *Oh, no…*

Birch was smiling now, and it did absolutely nothing to reassure her. "Disconcerting, isn't it?" He folded his arms across his chest, still smiling.

Horror flooded Lilia; for a second, she thought she might be sick. *That electricity…*She'd seen something like this before.

Once.

*Azaren Carn.*

That was *not* a good sign.

Azaren Carn was a Guardian who had been the sole survivor of a failed rescue mission on Lanx, the third inhabited world in the Sta'Gloan system, right after Galactic Union Admiral Chesnee blew a hole through Lanx's planetary shield and captured her capital city. Lilia and her brother Kevin had been part of a second team sent in to rescue a trio of scientists responsible for inventing a machine capable of opening wormholes for instantaneous travel. When they'd encountered Carn, they had learned that high voltage electricity could render a Guardian's nanites inert.

They'd also learned that the loss of her nanites had *not* been good for Carn's mental health.

Lilia tried to dematerialize a section of her stealth armor, but nothing happened. She might as well have never undergone the infusion process. This part, however, she had experienced before. *That's not something I can tell Birch, though.*

Through dry lips, she said, "You just fried my nanites."

"Yes, I did."

Terrible scenarios began racing through Lilia's head, each one worse than the last. It took a tremendous amount of effort to keep her voice even as she asked, "Permanently?"

Birch's lips twisted into a cruel smile, but then he shook his head. "It's not permanent. You should be grateful for that."

She was, tremendously so, but this was hardly the time to savor her relief. Instead, she nodded to the device in his hand. "What *is* that?"

Shrugging, Birch held it up. It was cylindrical, and reminded Lilia of a too-short silver drumstick. "The NCDC calls it an 'impactor'." He nodded to her. "You'll notice nothing else works either. No armor, no ISF, no Nancom."

"I've noticed," she said dryly.

Birch gave her a sharp smile. "Guardians are entrusted with a great deal of power. We have to be able to control rogues like you and your brothers."

Lilia wanted to roll her eyes at him, but a large part of her was afraid he'd simply shoot her with the thing again. "That was unnecessary. I'm not going anywhere, and I've certainly not gone rogue." As if to prove her point, she yanked the chair she was holding onto out from the table and sat down in it.

"You've proved you can't be trusted."

*Like you trusted me before*, Lilia thought tartly. Aloud, she said, "How long has the NCDC had those things?"

Birch made a scoffing noise in the back of his throat. "You don't think the NCDC would give people—even *vetted* individuals—access to technology like this without putting some kind of fail-safe in place, do you?"

Lilia wet her lips. She'd never really thought about it before, actually. *Fine, next question.* "How long will it last?" She lifted her chin. "I need to use the ladies' room."

Birch gave her another unpleasant smile. "Long enough for me to transport you back to Sonela for a disciplinary hearing."

Lilia blanched. *That…sounds like it'll at least be a couple of hours.* She hadn't exactly counted on not being able to dematerialize her armor the rest of the night.

Birch held out an imperious hand. "Your comlink."

Lilia barely suppressed an incredulous snort. *He should have asked me that before he shot me.* "It's in my ISF."

An interdimensional storage field—known simply as an ISF—was a byproduct of the infusion process she'd undergone in order to become a Guardian. An electromagnetic field surrounding her body capable of holding an amount equal to her body weight in weapons and gear, no one else could see it or access it, and no mechanical scanner would register its existence. She'd slipped her comlink into it for safekeeping earlier in the evening.

"Is that so?"

Lifting her chin, Lilia held Birch's gaze and slowly extended her gloved arms to either side. "Does this dress *look* like it has pockets?"

Birch gave her a long, hard look before he apparently decided she was telling the truth. "I hope you enjoyed your exploits this evening, Miss Strong." His voice dripped icicles. "It'll be your last evening as a Guardian."

An unexpected peal of laughter bubbled up in her throat. *If only you knew!* She choked it down with an effort, eying Birch's tall, disapproving form. "What makes you so sure?"

"You honestly think the NCDC will keep you after you just helped your brother smuggle a Tarynian Ambassador onto Sta'Gloa?"

Words rose to the tip of her tongue; Lilia held them back. Her oldest brother Michael's voice echoed in her mind. *Don't say anything.*

Instead, she folded her hands in her lap—to hide their sudden trembling—and fixed Birch with what she hoped was an impassive look. "I want to see my grandfather."

"You're not in any position to demand anything. The NCDC will be dealing with you."

It was Lilia's turn to give him a sharp smile. "Not before the Triumvirate wants to see me, I'm sure. I can't imagine *that* will go over well."

Birch slammed a hand down on the conference table, making her flinch, but he stopped himself before speaking. His eyes took on a distant cast Lilia recognized. Somebody had Nancommed him.

*I'm not sure if that's a good thing or not.*

Slowly, Birch straightened. "I suggest you take this opportunity to reflect on a few things. Remember tonight——" he nodded to her gown, "——it'll be the last time you wear something like that anywhere for a long time."

With that parting shot, he whirled around and stalked out of the conference room.

Lilia wanted to slump in relief that he had *finally* left her alone, wanted to slump down on the table and just *breathe*, but she didn't dare. If there were cameras in here monitoring her—and there probably were—she didn't dare show signs of *anything*.

Instead, she straightened her back just as her grandmother had taught her so many years ago and sat primly in her chair. She knotted her fingers together in her lap, willing herself not to twist them together, and prayed. Without access to Nancom, tendrils of panic curled through her; she felt alone and adrift.

*In all the furor of figuring out how to get Ambassador Kedis in to see the Triumvirate, we didn't exactly think about what would happen afterward.*

In hindsight, that might have been a mistake.

# Chapter 2

AFTER the warmth of being in the ballroom with hundreds of other people, the drop in temperature in the Cuomo Convention Center's back halls was a relief. Kevin Strong breathed in slowly and deeply, belying the way his heart pounded in his chest. He was taller than his twin sister, but they shared the same angular features, dark hair, and violet eyes.

*You expected this,* he reminded himself. *You knew there was a good chance you'd probably wind up arrested on charges of treason.* Kevin had hoped it wouldn't come to that. He'd hoped that there would be enough confusion and astonishment over Ambassador Kedis's unexpected arrival at the Gala and their brother Lon's resurrection from the dead that no one would immediately make the connection to him and Lilia, but he had known it was a possibility.

He hadn't expected to be arrested by Guardians.

Shortly after Lon introduced Kedis to the crowd in the ballroom, three men—one clad in a tuxedo and the other two in security uniforms—had quietly confronted Kevin. They placed him under arrest and spirited him out of the ballroom. He didn't know any of them.

A muscle tightened in his jaw. *Outside of my family, the only Guardian I know here tonight is Alan Birch—and he went after Lilia on purpose.*

"In here." The tallest of his three escorts stopped in front of a numbered door and opened it to reveal a dimly lit conference room.

Kevin glanced between them. "What are we doing here?"

The man didn't answer, but held out a hand. "Comlink."

Reluctantly, Kevin fished it from his breast pocket and dropped the device into the tall man's outstretched hand. "I'd better get this back."

"Talk to Alan Birch," the shortest man said, before he and his companions shoved Kevin none-too-gently through the door.

Kevin started to turn around, started to demand to know exactly why he was being held here—

—and that was when the tallest man shot him in the side.

A brief—but intense—explosion of pain radiated out from the spot; Kevin barely had time to react before the conference room door slid shut, leaving him alone, wide-eyed and stunned. Astonished, he looked down at his black jacket-clad side. *He* shot *me. If I hadn't been wearing stealth armor...*

He had no idea what weapon the man had used; he hadn't seen it clearly enough. *And,* he fingered his jacket, *it didn't leave a hole, so it wasn't a laser bolt.* His forehead crinkled in a frown. *What was the point of that?*

Kevin started to open a channel to his sister, but nothing happened. He tried again; still, nothing. For a split-second, his heart stopped beating. Lilia wasn't answering—and she should have. Her mental voice should have flooded his mind, they *should* be debating their next move.

Various scenarios raced through his mind—everything from Lilia lying dead in a room somewhere to her lying on the floor unconscious because of Birch—but Kevin forced them back. Drawing a deep breath, he tamped his panic down. *There has to be a logical explanation for why she's not responding—and one that* doesn't *involve her being hurt.*

Birch wouldn't *dare* break the law—not with their grandfather a Sta'Gloan Representative sitting on the Triumvirate. That was too bold, even for him.

*Okay, then.* There had to be another explanation. Kevin attempted to Nancom his older brothers instead, but, again, nothing happened. He stilled, a seed of suspicion sprouting in his mind, rapidly taking deep root. *Wait a minute...*

Focusing on the nanites that comprised his stealth-mode armor beneath his tuxedo, he tried to dematerialize them back into the pores of his skin.

Nothing happened.

Swallowing heavily, Kevin pulled out a chair from the conference table and sank heavily into it. *This…this is not good. Somebody's figured out how to weaponize freezing a Guardian's nanites.*

He shook his head, staring blankly at the no doubt locked door. *No wonder they didn't restrain me. They knew I wouldn't be able to do anything.*

If he had never experienced anything like this before, Kevin knew he probably would have flipped out. To have control of his nanites ripped away, to be cut off from all of the Nancom connections he had…it was definitely disconcerting. *Probably also part of the purpose*, he thought grimly. *You don't realize how much you rely on this stuff until it's gone.*

As it was, he and Lilia both had an edge over most Guardians and knew how to handle that loss.

Kevin glanced down at his watch. *Only thing to do now is wait for somebody to come collect us.*

That could take a while. *In the meantime…*

The room was hot and stuffy, like its connection to the rest of the convention center's heating and cooling system had been shut off, and beads of sweat had already broken out on Kevin's forehead. He loosened his tie and shed his jacket, before settling down in his chair again and shoving another chair out from the table to prop his feet up on. *Might as well be comfortable.*

His stomach was in knots, but he kept his expression nonchalant. *Can't wait to see how this is all going to play out.*

He and Lilia had taken a huge gamble…he just hoped they weren't about to lose everything.

# CHAPTER 3

HIS head had not spun like this since that terrible day two decades earlier when he and his wife learned they had lost their only child and her husband in the first wave of a Tarynian invasion. But this time, instead of the horror and terrible, aching grief pressing down on him, Sta'Gloan Representative Aiden Monroe felt only deep joy welling up inside his newly-healed chest.

Joy—and relief so intense he half-suspected he might simply float up out of his hoverchair.

*Lon is alive.*

Aiden held onto that thought, cradled it protectively in his mind like an ephemeral flame that might wink out at the slightest breath of air. *Thank you, God Almighty.* He had not failed after all. His middle grandson was *alive.*

He drew in a deep breath and felt life surge through his old veins. It filled him with an energy and purpose he had not felt since the fateful holocall two months before that had upended his world.

*Lon is alive…and he brought a Galactic Union Ambassador through Sta'Gloa's shield.*

The latter part of that statement *should* have filled Aiden with trepidation—if one man was smart enough to figure out how to smuggle Tarynians through the shield, then it stood to reason others might have already attempted such a feat—but if pressed, he would have had to admit that all he felt was a deep swell of pride.

His grandson had done the impossible—in more ways than one—and now? *Now the Triumvirate will have to listen. Kedis is here, and there is no undoing his arrival.*

All the money and power in the Coalition could not stuff *that* genie back into its particular bottle.

Granted, Aiden was *not* pleased his youngest two grandchildren had just been arrested on charges of treason. He could not say it would surprise him to learn they'd had a hand in this—Lon, Kevin, and Lilia had always been close, and the twins had taken his death hard—but that someone from the NCDC had already arrested them?

His green eyes narrowed in distaste. *This will require untangling. One would think certain parties would have more sense than to allow petty grudges to prevent them from making diplomatic choices.*

He knew, of course, of the grudge Alan Birch bore his grandchildren. It had never been significant enough to warrant special consideration, and they had previously handled things well, but Aiden made a mental note to revisit the issue later.

"Perhaps I shouldn't ask this of you, old friend, but I can't help myself. Did you know?"

Aiden glanced sideways at Glo'Stean Representative Martin Hollowell, who was keeping pace with his hoverchair as they hurried through the all-but-deserted off-limits halls of the Cuomo Convention Center. He was a decade younger than Aiden, with close-cropped curly white hair. His friend's wrinkled brown expression was a strange mix of delight, disbelief, and something that looked like cold fury.

"I did not." Aiden swallowed a sudden lump in his throat as painful memories of the past two months crowded to the forefront of his mind. "I buried him, Martin. He was *gone.*" He swallowed again, rubbing his short white beard. "Until I speak to Lon myself, I am afraid I find myself unable to quite believe it."

"Not to mention the fact that he brought a damned G.U. ambassador through Sta'Gloa's shield."

Aiden tried for a wry smile to deflect the maelstrom of thoughts and emotions swirling inside him. "Now *that*, Martin, I can believe."

Seeing the astonishment on Hollowell's face, Aiden could only shrug. "Lon has always been bold enough to do whatever he sets his mind to. Did I ever expect him to embroil himself in something like this?" He shook his head. "No. But does it surprise me?" His wry smile deepened. "Not particularly."

Hollowell still looked like he did not quite believe Aiden, but he inclined his head in a gracious nod. "For your sake, Aiden, I am glad the boy survived."

"Thank you, my friend."

Hollowell cast a grim look over his shoulder in the direction of the frenzy they had left behind. "The media will have a field day with this. A G.U. Ambassador, here?"

Aiden was still far too relieved he had more or less received his grandson back from the grave to be anything more than mildly concerned, but he inclined his head in agreement. "Undoubtedly."

His fingers tightened on the arms of his hoverchair; he wished fervently he could make the blasted thing go *faster*. It frustrated him that he still required the chair, but he *had*, after all, nearly been killed in the explosion that rocked the Tri-Global Tournament's Opening Ball. In many respects, it was a miracle he had survived.

"What of Lilia and Kevin?" Hollowell glanced over his shoulder again, this time to consider Michael and Derek, Aiden's oldest grandchildren, who flanked them along with Hollowell's aide and the Representatives' respective security teams. "Do you think they're involved?"

Aiden looked back at his grandsons as well. Their faces remained impassive.

The elder, Michael, was his head of security. He had taken the position a little earlier than planned; his predecessor and old family friend, Will Graves, had died in the bombing attack at the Opening Ball that had nearly killed Aiden himself. Michael took after his Tarynian father in appearance—blond hair and startling violet eyes. The twins had inherited those same eyes.

Derek, his second-eldest grandson, worked as his personal aide. Of all his grandchildren, Derek most resembled Aiden himself, both in appearance and in disposition. He was tall and lean, with dark brown hair, angular features, and keen green eyes.

"That," Aiden said at last, "will be a question I put to the twins when I see them."

Hollowell gave him a strange smile. "I don't envy you the scrutiny you'll be under as a result of this, old friend."

"If it means my grandson is alive, Martin, I will take it." Aiden tightened his fingers on the arms of his hoverchair again. "You of all people should understand that." Hollowell had lost his entire family to the Tarynians the same day Aiden lost his daughter and son-in-law.

"Oh, I do. It does not, however, change the fact that the next few weeks are likely to be…rather unpleasant for your family."

Aiden merely inclined his head. *It will be worth it.* He could weather any storm that followed tonight's events. In the meantime…they needed to deal with Ambassador Kedis. Where had Dion Pamos and Shane Briscoe taken him?

At that moment, Derek's comlink buzzed. "Grandfather, Representative Briscoe would like you to meet him at Conference Room Warrington, on Sublevel 2."

"Excellent," Aiden said briskly.

The group of them took the next accelevator they found down to Sublevel 2. They turned down two more corridors, and then Derek, who was striding along with one eye on his comlink, suddenly faltered. "Grandfather…"

His voice sounded odd; Aiden stopped his hoverchair in the middle of the corridor to look at him. "What is it?"

Derek swallowed, his eyes flicking to Hollowell and his aide before focusing on his grandfather. Taking a deep breath, he nodded to his comlink. "I've just received word someone activated a number of shield generators in occupied territory. Glo'Stea's planetary shield is now completely intact."

For the span of a heartbeat, his words made no sense. Aiden heard each one, but the picture they formed was an unfathomable jumble of syllables strung randomly together. That picture then abruptly rearranged itself, snapping reality back into crystal clear focus.

One word escaped him. "*When?*"

"Less than fifteen minutes ago, near as anyone can tell." Derek jabbed his comlink with a finger. "Communications are a mess. All G.U. forces stationed in occupied territory have been completely cut off from the rest of the Blockade Division."

"What happened?" Michael demanded.

Derek shook his head. "The only info anyone has yet is that every single Glo'Stean city that was supposed to host a shield generator is now contributing to the planetary shield."

Utterly astonished, Aiden looked at Hollowell, who was nodding as his aide spoke quietly in his ear. He had also just received the news. "Martin, how in the galaxy did your people manage to build shield generators under the Tarynians' noses?"

Hollowell smiled grimly. "Too early to say for sure, but I will say we Glo'Steans are a very resourceful lot when we choose to be." His eyes narrowed into brown slits. "Does Kedis know yet?"

Derek shook his head. "He can't know. Not yet. Not unless he's got a comlink capable of contacting Admiral Chesnee."

"Which he may very well have." Hollowell's face settled into stern lines.

Derek hesitated for a fraction of a second—Aiden was sure Hollowell had missed it, not knowing his grandson as he did—and Aiden suddenly knew Kedis did *not* possess such a comlink. *That is one good thing, at least.* They would be able to control *when* the Ambassador learned of this latest bombshell.

*Hopefully.*

It also meant that Derek—and probably Michael as well—knew a good deal more about this affair than they were letting on. *We will be having a chat later.* Aiden narrowed his eyes, thinking of the twins. *All of us.*

"We can't tell him," Hollowell said forcefully. "Not yet." He resumed traveling down the corridor at a brisk pace.

Aiden glided forward, catching up in a matter of seconds. "Nor can we withhold that information from him very long." He shook his head, already filtering through all the possible scenarios that could arise as a result of this latest turn of events. "It will be practically impossible to keep it from him."

Hollowell tilted his bushy white eyebrows in an expression that clearly asked, *Even if he's safely locked away?*

Aiden merely frowned.

They turned left and encountered Glo'Stean Representative Shane Briscoe, surrounded by a bevy of security guards—probably not all his own, Aiden surmised, though it was difficult to know who else was involved just yet. He was tall, with brown hair and electrifying hazel eyes.

When he caught sight of them, Briscoe's face was for a few seconds a strange blend of relief and concern. Regaining control of himself, he strode forward. "Representatives. Good. I'm glad you're here."

"Where's Pamos?" Hollowell looked around, as though expecting the shorter Sta'Gloan Representative to materialize out of thin air.

A smile curved Briscoe's mouth, but it was short-lived. "Have you heard the news?" When both Representatives nodded, he spread his hands in a little, *what do you expect?* gesture. "Our esteemed colleague was quite torn over which direction to jump." He nodded over his shoulder at the closed door behind him. "He assured the Ambassador the Triumvirate will take good care of him and left him to me."

Aiden blinked. He had anticipated Pamos to have glued himself to Kedis's side. "That is…unexpected."

"Not particularly," Hollowell said curtly. "You know Dion as well as I do, Aiden. No doubt he's already calculating how best to turn this to his advantage." His upper lip curled. "Wouldn't surprise me at all if he's comming Chesnee as we speak."

"Without even speaking to the Ambassador first?" Briscoe's hazel eyes tracked back and forth between the two older Representatives.

Beyond Derek, Michael, and Hollowell's aide, their respective security teams maintained a close, but respective distance.

Hollowell smiled; it was not a pleasant expression. "He never bothers to inform the Triumvirate." He abruptly shifted to fix Aiden with a piercing stare. "Kedis doesn't need to know about Glo'Stea's shield." He included Briscoe in his stare. "Not yet."

"With all due respect, Martin, I disagree. He'll find out eventually." Briscoe shook his head, his face uncharacteristically grim. "There will be no hiding something of this magnitude for long."

Hollowell waved a hand. "His access to the ComNet and the media can be restricted."

"Not for long," Aiden said. "And not, Martin, without drawing attention. The Ambassador seems an intelligent man; I doubt a ploy like that would make him anything but suspicious."

"Best to offer the information as a peace offering of sorts, I think." Briscoe sighed, looking for an instant much older than his thirty-six years. "It is in our favor, at any rate, and it sets the stage for the negotiations we will inevitably face once he's standing before the Triumvirate."

"Besides," Briscoe offered Hollowell a grim smile, "we'll need him to call off Chesnee, won't we?"

*Oh, yes*, Aiden thought. *The Admiral has proved himself quite adept at doing his job.* Aloud, he said, "For the sake of our people, it would be most helpful to avoid any further loss of life and property."

"Especially since we now have a number of Lanxians and Glo'Steans temporarily stranded on Sta'Gloa," Briscoe said.

He did not have to say more; they all knew how delicately balanced the situation in the Coalition was at the moment. The Tri-

Global Tournament had quelled a fraction of the rioting and unrest that had plagued them since Admiral Chesnee upset the status quo and not only breached Lanx's shield but cut several of their mining worlds off from the rest of the Coalition, but tonight's events could only stir everyone up again.

Hollowell's expression could have been carved from granite.

"We can't hide this from him," Briscoe reiterated, shaking his head. "*That* would be a political disaster greater than anything we've dealt with lately. One wrong word at the wrong moment…"

"I see your point," Hollowell said at last, holding up a hand. He eyed Briscoe keenly. "And will you be telling the Ambassador this yourself?"

"No." Briscoe smiled again. "I intend to tell Lon and have *him* pass the news along." He shrugged. "He is, after all, Kedis's Coalition liaison."

Hollowell absorbed this, and then rounded on Aiden. "No offense, old friend, but is your grandson up to the task he's set himself?"

Aiden exchanged a wry look with Briscoe. "He has apparently managed up until this point."

He had never considered Lon—his bold, adventurous middle grandchild—as one much for politicking. He had always thought Lon lacked the patience necessary to deal with tedious people and tedious situations. This business with Kedis, however, shed a different light on things.

"What will you tell him, exactly?" Hollowell asked abruptly.

Briscoe's smile held a little more humor this time. "The facts, Representative—as could be gleaned from any media source at the moment."

Looking mollified, Hollowell bent his head in a nod. "Then I will leave you to it. Good night, gentlemen."

"Good night, Martin." Aiden waited until Hollowell had set off, security team in tow, before he looked at Briscoe. "I am afraid I must leave as well."

"Understandable." Briscoe offered him a bow. "Go home and get some rest, Aiden. You've had a shock tonight, and you're still recovering."

Aiden's bearded face creased in a small smile. "Yes, well, as far as shocks go, this one is better than the alternative." He wheeled around in his hoverchair—Michael, Derek, and his security detail flanking him—and added over his shoulder, "We are in for an interesting day tomorrow."

"That," Briscoe said to their retreating forms, "is an understatement if I've ever heard one."

Once they were out of earshot of the Glo'Stean Representative, Aiden addressed his grandsons. "Kevin and Lilia. Where are they?"

Michael and Derek exchanged glances. "We don't know yet," Michael answered, an undercurrent of frustration lacing his voice.

"Birch won't tell us anything," Derek added.

Aiden narrowed his eyes. "He knows you work for me."

"Oh, he knows." Derek looked disgusted—and tired. "I think he's actually waiting to hear from you in person."

*Of all the petty, vindictive…*Aiden pressed his lips together until the urge to say a few choice words passed. At last, he said, "I can only assume the twins' comlinks were confiscated when they were arrested. What of…other forms of communication?"

His grandsons exchanged another grim look. "They've all failed," Derek said flatly, "and we have no idea why."

Michael's expression said he had a couple of ideas—none of them good.

"I see." Aiden digested this, his concern for his youngest grandchildren deepening. *That they cannot even be reached via Nancom…*

He did not speak again until they had taken the accelevator back up to the convention center's main floor. His mind whirled, sifting through and prioritizing all the scenarios likely to arise in the next few hours, and his white eyebrows knit together in a frown.

His grandsons guessed the direction of his thoughts. "Don't worry about the twins, Grandfather," Michael said abruptly. "We'll find them. The most important thing right now is that we get you out of here before things turn into any more of a madhouse than they already are."

"We can deal with everything else from the spaceport." Derek managed a wry smile. "Including the statement you'll have to release about tonight's events."

Aiden exhaled slowly, before nodding. If the NCDC was behind the twins' arrest, they would not dare do anything with them before the Triumvirate had their say. *Even Alan Birch.* "Very well. Get me back to the ship."

He had work to do.

# CHAPTER 4

THE Tri-Global Tournament Closing Ceremonies Gala was still going strong, but as far as anyone in the large conference room in the lower depths of the Cuomo Convention Center was concerned, the party was over. Despite the late evening hour, work had begun. *Because,* Lieutenant Jasper Wright thought wryly, *politicians never really stop working, do they?*

Clad in tuxedos instead of uniforms, he and Corporal Victor Renner stood flanking Ambassador Kedis, motionless statues, save for their sharp gazes roaming around the room, constantly assessing everything. The conference room was interior and therefore windowless, but the walls were covered in floor-to-ceiling holopanels that reflected various scenes from what Jasper assumed was the Sta'Gloan city of Atalia around them. At the moment, they were showing a stunning view of the evening cityscape from out on the water.

Jasper was a head taller than Renner, with golden hair and sharp gray eyes set in a lean, tanned face. Renner was a decade older, in his mid-thirties, and much stockier, with brown eyes, sandy brown hair, and a face that had seen its share of fights. Both of them spoke Sta'Gloan, which was how they had ended up being assigned to Ambassador Kedis as his translators and protection detail.

For his part, the Ambassador sprawled comfortably in a chair, completely at his ease. Also dressed in an expensive tuxedo, Kedis was bald, with olive-toned skin, and was probably the same age as Renner, but looked younger. His expression was amiable, but Jasper noted it never quite reached his dark eyes.

Lon Strong stood leaning against the heavy ebony table in the center of the room, one foot propped flat against a table leg. He was currently tapping a stylus restlessly against his thigh, his green gaze dancing around as though he didn't know what to look at. He was shorter than Jasper, with sandy blond hair. He had discarded his tuxedo jacket and had rolled his white sleeves up to his elbows.

Jasper wished he could do the same. Catching the Sta'Gloan's eye, he tilted an eyebrow in a silent question.

"The honor guard didn't take us very far," Lon answered in Tarynian, gesturing with the stylus. "I was expecting them to at least get us out of the building." He quirked a lopsided smile. "Guess I overestimated how fast the Triumvirate would move once you got here, Ambassador."

Kedis looked amused. "You expected an immediate emergency convening?"

"More like immediate transport to Sonela." Lon resumed tapping his thigh. "Cuts down on the possibility of someone making an attempt on your life between now and when you speak to the Triumvirate. Not that it's likely," he added hastily, catching the darting glance Jasper exchanged with Renner, "but we *did* just introduce you to the entire Coalition, and there are a *lot* of people holding grudges against the G.U. and everything it stands for."

"I am aware of the possibility," Kedis reminded him. "Believe me, I took that into consideration a long time ago."

Lon glanced at Jasper, as if to say, *Of course he did*, before giving his head a minute shake and turning his attention back to the door.

Renner just folded his arms across his chest, his expression grim.

Jasper exhaled slowly. It had been a whirlwind of an evening and he still had adrenaline coursing through his veins. His thoughts turned to Lilia Strong. She had smuggled him into the Gala as her escort, and the last time he'd seen her had been right before Lon introduced Kedis to the entire ballroom. *I wonder how much trouble she and Kevin are in right now.* It wouldn't take a genius to connect the dots.

Less than fifteen minutes later, they all started as the door opened to admit one of the Triumvirate Representatives who had escorted them here—Jasper thought his name was Briscoe; the man was younger than he had expected of a member of the Triumvirate—and another man, probably Briscoe's aide. Briscoe beckoned to Lon.

"Representative?" Lon unfolded from his position and crossed to join the Glo'Stean as he moved toward the center of the conference room.

For a politician, there was something about Briscoe Jasper liked. He seemed…genuine. The other Representative they had met moments after Kedis introduced himself at the Gala—Pamos?—struck Jasper as more akin to Kedis. *They'll get along just fine.*

Briscoe turned to Kedis, encompassing Jasper, Renner, and Lon in his warm nod. "I am sorry for the delay. We've set up accommodations for you and your men in Sonela, Ambassador, as well as procured a security detail to see you safely there."

"Excellent." Kedis returned the nod. "I thank you, Representative."

Briscoe wore an autotranslator; there was no need for Lon to interpret. The Glo'Stean gave Kedis a cordial smile. "As much as we would all love to sit down and officially open up negotiations, we might be served best with a good night's rest first."

"As you say." Kedis offered him a quicksilver smile in return. "I look forward to enjoying further Coalition hospitality."

He and Briscoe both looked at Lon, who gave a slightly sheepish shrug. "Did the best I could."

"I can't wait to hear the story." Briscoe clapped a hand on Lon's shoulder. "Nor can your grandfather, I imagine."

Lon's expression tightened. "He didn't know about any of it."

"Oh, of that I am quite sure." Briscoe's face shifted, his expression reminding Jasper of an older brother. He wondered suddenly just how well Lon and Briscoe actually knew each other. "I attended your funeral."

Lon froze. After a long pause, he swallowed. "Wasn't much I could do about that, Shane."

"So it would seem."

Out of the corner of his eye, Jasper saw Briscoe's aide check his comlink. He then leaned forward to murmur something to his boss.

Briscoe gave him a quick, startled look and reached for the comlink. He read the display and handed it back, frowning.

Every nerve in Jasper's body snapped to attention. *What has happened now?*

Lon raised his eyebrows at Briscoe. "What's the matter, Representative?"

Jasper half-expected the older man to demure, but instead, Briscoe turned to face Lon. His expression was an odd mix of concern, resignation, and something Jasper wanted to call pride. "I've just learned your youngest siblings have been arrested on charges of high treason."

*Already?* Jasper's heart skipped a beat, imagining Lilia and her brother in handcuffs, but he kept his face impassive. Kedis shot him a blink-and-you'll-miss-it look before turning his attention back to Lon and Briscoe.

Instead of looking shocked at this news, Lon threw back his head and laughed. "Of course they have. Bet I know who arrested them, too." He turned away, shaking his head. "I'd be under arrest too, if I wasn't Kedis's liaison." He grinned cheerfully at Briscoe. "I have no doubt everything will be straightened out later."

Briscoe canted his head to one side. "I admire your confidence."

Still grinning, Lon waved a hand. "The Ambassador's here to open peace talks. I'm pretty sure the treason charges will be dropped when the Triumvirate hears the story."

"It sounds like it will be a fascinating tale."

"Oh, it will," Lon assured him.

They exchanged a few more words, but Jasper was barely paying attention. His thoughts had traveled to Lilia—and Kevin. *Where are they?* His eyebrows knit in a frown. Would they have been sequestered here at the convention center, or had they been dragged straight to the local jail?

The door slid aside again to admit a stocky man with a buzz-cut in nondescript evening clothes, and Jasper wrenched his attention back to the here and now.

"Ah, here he is." Briscoe nodded to Kedis. "Ambassador, this is the head of your new security team."

Lon was the first to step forward. "Lon Strong." He offered the man a short bow, before straightening and jerking a thumb over his shoulder. "I'm Ambassador Kedis's Coalition liaison."

For a split-second, Jasper could have sworn the man's eyes widened in shock. But it passed, and he returned Lon's bow. "Corran. Timon Corran." He had a milder voice than Jasper would have expected coming from a man as stocky as he was. His skin was a golden medium brown and he had liquid dark eyes. "You Sta'Gloan?" he asked Lon. "You sound it."

Lon nodded. "Oh, yeah." He cleared his throat. "And if you haven't already heard, my grandfather's on the Triumvirate. But don't let that scare you."

"I've heard. And I won't." Corran then approached Kedis. "Ambassador, my team and I will be responsible for your security while you're in the Coalition. Where you go, we go."

"Your service is much appreciated," Kedis replied in Tarynian, which Lon translated, before Corran tapped his ear to indicate he had an autotranslator.

Kedis then waved one long-fingered hand to Jasper and Renner and Lon introduced them. "They speak Sta'Gloan," he added.

The assessing look in Corran's eyes sharpened. "That so?" He eyed both Jasper and Renner. "Makes our job easier." He then gave Kedis a short, perfunctory bow. "If you'll follow me, Ambassador, I'll take you to the rest of our team and we'll head out."

Kedis gave him an acquiescent nod.

"One moment, Corran. I need a word with Lon." Briscoe looked at Kedis. "I will see you tomorrow, Ambassador." He glanced at his wrist and smiled. "Well, later today, to be precise."

"We shall have much to discuss, Representative."

"Yes, we shall."

"I'll be right back," Lon said, before following Briscoe out into the corridor.


A group of men—Corran's men, no doubt—stood waiting in the hall with Briscoe's own security team. At a look from the Representative, they backed up a discreet distance. Dropping his voice, Briscoe said without preamble, "Lon, Glo'Stea's planetary shield is completely intact."

"What?" Lon blinked, staring at Shane Briscoe, and then he shook his head. "I'm sorry, could you repeat that? I don't think I—"

"It's true." Briscoe regarded him steadily, though Lon could see the fatigue pulling at his muscles. "In fact, we're fairly sure it happened while you were in the midst of introducing the Ambassador to the Coalition."

Lon rocked back on his heels, the implications of this racing through his tired mind like a fleet of souped-up Piranhas. For the span of two heartbeats, he saw the future of travel between Glo'Stea and the rest of the Coalition stretched out before him in all its glittering glory. Then he blinked and the vision was gone, replaced by images of death and ruin and destruction as trapped G.U. forces clashed with the Glo'Stean Resistance.

"How—"

Briscoe shook his head. "We don't know. Assure Kedis of that, if you would."

Tired though he was, Lon heard the unspoken implication behind those words. *Telling you anything at all is a courtesy.* He raised sandy eyebrows. "Nice of you to tell him anything."

"We don't have much of a choice." Briscoe smiled wryly. "It's that or lock you all up somewhere with no access to the outside galaxy—and don't think that thought didn't occur to certain individuals."

Lon nodded sagely, shoving his hands into his trouser pockets. "And *that's* not suspicious at all."

"Oh, no."

"Smart."

"We do try." Briscoe clapped him on the shoulder. "As I mentioned earlier, it's good to see you back among the living. Try to get some rest—I have a feeling tomorrow will be a long day."

"And today isn't exactly over yet." Lon inhaled and then blew it out all at once. "Thanks for the heads up."

"You're welcome."

Briscoe departed, and Lon braced himself to return to Kedis, Renner, and Jasper. *He* was still reeling from the news; he couldn't imagine how *Kedis* would react. *Glo'Stea's shield is* intact. *How in the galaxy did they pull that off under the Tarynians' noses?*

Lon tried to school his expression into neutrality as he re-entered the conference room, but some of his shock must have bled through, because Kedis took one look at him and his dark eyes narrowed.

"What is the matter?"

*Where do I even start?* Lon opened his mouth, closed it, and considered a few seconds, before he shrugged. "I've just received some rather interesting news."

"Oh?" Kedis did not move, but his entire aura seemed to sharpen. He looked at Corran. "Leave us a moment."

Corran nodded and moved toward the door.

Once it had slid shut behind him, Lon glanced at Jasper and Renner, who were both looking back and forth between him and the Ambassador, before focusing on Kedis. "Yeah…So, apparently, in the middle of all the excitement tonight, a number of shield generators were activated on Glo'Stea."

He took a breath. "Glo'Stea now has a fully functioning planetary shield, which means all G.U. forces have been cut off from Admiral Chesnee's Blockade Division."

Kedis stood perfectly still, absorbing this. For a few seconds, his expression took on a faraway cast…and then he focused on Lon again with a laser-like intensity that had him itching to take a step back. "This happened tonight?"

"Yes."

"And you were told to inform me?"

Lon glanced at Jasper and Renner again. "I was." He half-shrugged. "It's all over the news, apparently. They didn't see the point in trying to keep it from you."

"That would have been suspicious," Jasper agreed.

Kedis waved an impatient hand. "*That* could have been explained away easily enough." He tapped the fingers of his other hand on his thigh. "They're hoping I'll be able to influence Admiral Chesnee and keep him from some sort of retaliation."

Lon wasn't surprised Kedis had reached this conclusion; it wasn't much of a leap. "Can you?"

Kedis smiled indulgently, belying the razor-sharp look in his eyes. "I've done it before."

Jasper caught Lon's eye; his expression seemed to say, *The Admiral will* love *that*. Clearing his throat, the lieutenant asked, "Will this have a significant impact on what you planned to say to the Triumvirate tomorrow, Ambassador?"

For a moment, Kedis did not answer. He then raised one tuxedo-clad shoulder in an insouciant shrug. "It changes a few things, yes. But on the other hand…" he trailed off thoughtfully.

Lon and the other two men waited a moment, but the Ambassador did not elaborate. Instead, he headed for the door.

Corran and his team were waiting for them in the hall outside. Corran briefly introduced his men. "Ambassador, this is Carl Denisk, Omri Lutz, Wyatt Swift, and Javier Torres." He pointed to each man in turn.

Denisk was bald, tall, and broad-shouldered, with tan skin and a bushy brown beard that seemed to be doing its level best to make up for the lack of hair on his smooth head. Swift was equally tall and broad, with dark brown skin, curly black hair, and a goatee. Lutz was Lon's height, with a wiry frame, olive-toned skin, and dark hair pulled back in a low ponytail. Torres was shorter than Lutz, with short dark hair and light brown skin, but he moved with an easy grace that told Lon he'd be devastatingly fast in a fight.

Introductions done, Corran motioned for his team to form up around Kedis. "This way, Ambassador."

As they set off down the corridor, Jasper leaned closer to Lon. "You think it will be that easy?"

"Easy? Heck, no." Lon shook his head. "It won't be easy at all. What it *will* be is *simple*. There's a difference." His smile had a feral edge. "Triumvirate won't have much of a choice about *that*."

Jasper spent a few seconds digesting that before he asked, "Will they be all right? Lilia and Kevin?"

"Oh, yeah." Lon waved a hand. "This'll be the one time being related to Grandfather will actually come in handy for something." He grinned sheepishly. "Besides using our connection to him to actually get into the Gala in the first place."

They rounded the corner and Lon gave an almost imperceptible jolt as he felt the tickle of an incoming channel request in the back of his mind. A Guardian he didn't have a connection to was trying to Nancom him. *That means…*

Lon glanced around at Kedis's new security team and his gaze met Corran's. The shorter man raised his eyebrows, as if to say, *What are you waiting for?*

Lon allowed the channel request and Corran's voice flooded his mind.

[They said you were a Guardian.]

*'They' being the NCDC, I wonder?* Lon kept his expression neutral. [Yeah. Nobody told me Kedis's team would have a Guardian, though. Makes sense,] he added, lest Corran think he was being critical.

[This team got pulled together pretty quickly. NCDC must have figured they'd let me tell you.]

Lon nodded shortly. [It'll make protecting Kedis easier.]

[That's the theory.]

[Any other Guardians on the team?]

Corran could have been carved from granite. [Just you and me.]

[Good to know.] And it was—at this point Lon could see the NCDC keeping that information from him until they figured out what was going on. *I'm glad Corran told me.*

His eyes flicked to Kedis. *I have a feeling that when it comes to keeping him alive, we're going to need as much of an edge as possible.*

# CHAPTER 5

AS far as Admiral Giles Chesnee was concerned, the situation facing him made no more sense now than it had when it first broke. A lanky man with a craggy face, blue eyes, and graying blond hair, Chesnee stood in the center of his Flag Tactical Command Center with his hands clasped behind his back, frowning down at the smooth holographic sphere representing Glo'Stea while his subordinates bustled madly around him. To all outward appearances, he seemed calm—the eye of the storm preparing to break aboard his flagship, the *Chironex*-class battlecruiser *Winds of Change*—but his thoughts whirled and tumbled inside his head.

*How in the galaxy did they do it?*

Thanks to the Glo'Steans' inability to build and activate all of the shield generators they needed for complete planetary protection before the invasion began, G.U. forces had occupied nearly a quarter of Glo'Stea's surface for over twenty years. The rest of the planet had been protected, but the borders along the shields were hotly contested. G.U. troops had clashed with the Glo'Stean Resistance countless times through the years.

In all that time, there had never even been a hint of anything that would suggest the Glo'Steans were planning to pull off something of this magnitude. Chesnee didn't even see how it was *possible*. Glo'Stea was predominantly a water world; their many islands and small continents lacked the manufacturing base for many basic necessities, let alone the parts needed for something as complex as a bevy of shield generators.

And while the Coalition might be able to bypass his blockade and smuggle many things in and out of the shielded portion of Glo'Stea, Chesnee was relatively certain they were not smuggling things back and forth between shielded and unshielded territory onworld. Records would indicate that—and he kept up on records.

Knowledge was power, after all, and he had realized the moment he was assigned the Blockade Division that he would need as much of an edge as he could get to thwart the Sta'Gloan Coalition on one hand and deal with his superiors in High Command and the Galactic Union Senate on the other. The Blockade Division was supposed to be a career graveyard. Everyone knew that. He, Chesnee, had single-handedly changed that when he successfully breached Lanx's shield a few months before.

But for the Glo'Stean Resistance to have actually built shield generators in G.U.-held territory without anyone noticing? *Heads will roll for this*, Chesnee thought grimly.

Though it was late, there would be no rest for anyone until they had a handle on this.

"Sir." Lieutenant Darkon, his comm officer, interrupted his thoughts. He had curly black hair shorn short, chocolate eyes, and looked perpetually tanned. "You have an incoming transmission from General Deam."

*That was only a matter of time.* General Ira Deam commanded the Blockade's ground divisions; he was currently overseeing things in newly-held G.U. territory on Lanx, the third and largest of the Sta'Gloan system's habitable worlds. Chesnee pursed his lips. *I'd almost rather he'd been on Glo'Stea for this.*

He turned to Lieutenant Darkon. "Patch him through to my office. I'll have to contact High Command afterward. This may take a while. Keep me apprised of any new developments."

"Aye, aye, Admiral."


Chesnee's office occupied a spacious compartment inside his quarters, which were adjacent to his command center. It was not always convenient to travel back and forth, but discretion was important these days. Chesnee let himself in, ignoring the indigo carpet, the glossy walnut-paneled bulkheads, the random collection of ancient and abstract fiber art tied together by the same somber colors, and the strange tapestry in the corner he was half-convinced possessed beady eyes. He kept meaning to redecorate—one of his predecessors had had truly abysmal taste—but had yet to get around to it.

Settling himself behind his desk, he tapped the comm embedded in his desk and the holographic head and shoulders of a stern-faced man with blue eyes and graying brown hair bloomed in front of him. "General Deam, what in the galaxy is going on down on Glo'Stea?"

The lines in General Ira Deam's face deepened. Over the months Chesnee had known him since taking command of the Blockade Division, Deam had proved himself both competent and in control. He was not in control now, and they both knew it. "The Glo'Steans have managed to activate shield generators in occupied territory."

"Yes, yes," Chesnee waved a hand testily, "that much is obvious. I want to know how they *did* it."

"I don't know." A muscle twitched in Deam's jaw. "I've heard from my second-in-command, who is in charge of things on Glo'Stea while I'm here on Lanx, and he said they had no warning. One moment the sky is clear, the next, our territory is completely boxed in, and some group called Freedom's Children is announcing they're responsible. They're calling it a 'liberation'." He said the word distastefully.

*Freedom's Children?* Chesnee frowned, puzzled. "I've never heard of them."

"Neither have we."

"Have you located these shield generators yet?" Even as he asked the question, Chesnee knew it was too early for Deam's people to have made any real progress.

The general's answer confirmed this. "Not yet, Admiral. We're working on it."

Chesnee nodded. "Nothing has happened on Lanx?"

"Nothing at all."

Out of the corner of his eye, Chesnee glimpsed a flashing light. He had another incoming comm call. A glance at the attached details told him the call originated from Sta'Gloa. His eyes narrowed. *I know that frequency.*

Why was Sta'Gloan Representative Dion Pamos comming him *now?*

"Admiral?"

Chesnee wrenched his attention back to Deam. "Apologies, Ira. I have another call." Deam didn't know about Kedis's crazy venture—unless his people had broken confidence and scuttlebutt had traveled from the *Winds of Change* out to the rest of the Blockade Division—and telling him was not a priority just now.

He nodded to the other man. "What are your plans?"

"My plans?" Deam made a derisive sound. "I plan to find those shield generators and destroy them. Preferably before occupied territory dissolves into chaos and I start losing my men."

"Contain the situation," Chesnee ordered. "Don't exacerbate it."

Deam raised an eyebrow. "With all due respect, Admiral, this is an act of war."

Chesnee shook his head. "Be that as it may, I want you to contain things. There's more going on here than you realize."

The light was still flashing.

"Let me guess." Deam gave him a shrewd look. "The Ambassador? He's cooked up some kind of scheme, hasn't he?"

In some respects, Deam was more intelligent than High Command had ever given him credit. "Our orders from High Command are to cooperate with him." Chesnee grimaced. "The Senate might think he's lost his mind, but he's still their golden boy right now, Ira. There isn't much we can do at the moment *but* cooperate with him."

He reached for his comm panel. "I've got to go. I expect regular updates."

"You'll get them." Deam snapped the palm of his right hand to his left shoulder in a salute and then his image vanished.

Taking a bracing breath, Chesnee tapped a button on his comm panel and found himself face to face with the holograph upper half of a trim little man with sleek black hair and a general pervasive air of oiliness. "Representative Pamos. This is an unexpected surprise."

Pamos's dark, beady eyes narrowed for an instant, as if he doubted that, before he gave Chesnee a polite smile that was nonetheless strained around the edges. "Admiral Chesnee."

"It's been a while." The last time they had spoken, Pamos had offered him a massive bribe to let Coalition ships bypass his blockade unmolested. He, Chesnee, had refused, and subsequently breached Lanx's shields and gained a foothold on a planet that had not received non-Coalition visitors in two decades.

Chesnee was rather proud of that.

"Indeed it has."

Chesnee wanted to ask about Kedis, but he restrained himself. One couldn't appear too eager when dealing with someone like Pamos—and one certainly couldn't go about handing out information without getting something in return. Instead, he simply looked at the politician, waiting, until the short man let out an irritated huff.

The Admiral barely kept his surprise from showing on his face. *His nerves are more frayed than I would have expected.*

"Let's not beat around the proverbial bush, shall we, Admiral?" Pamos's holographic form leaned closer. "I've just met Ambassador Kedis in person."

"The Ambassador is still alive, I trust?"

Pamos scoffed again, waving a hand. "Of course he is. This is unprecedented, you understand. The Triumvirate will be holding a special session to open negotiations tomorrow."

"But that's not why you commed me." Chesnee couldn't help himself.

"No. It is not."

Pamos exhaled audibly; beneath his calm façade, Chesnee caught glimpses of extreme agitation. He held his peace, waiting, and the politician did not disappoint.

"I've just heard about Glo'Stea. Has anyone claimed responsibility for the...situation?"

"You mean the Glo'Stean Resistance isn't behind it?" Chesnee took great delight in the frustration that momentarily flashed over the other man's face. "Hasn't Glo'Stea been attempting to rectify its errors for the past twenty years?"

"One can hardly blame them for attempting to reclaim their homes, Admiral," Pamos said smoothly, "but, no, that was not their operation."

"You're sure of that, are you?"

"Quite."

Chesnee leaned back in his seat. "Why did you comm me, Representative?"

Pamos did not blink. "I've just told you why."

"That's not the real reason. If your people have no idea who is behind the attack, no doubt they will soon enough." Chesnee gave him a grim smile. "The Coalition seems competent enough for that."

Pamos ignored the dig. "Perhaps I was also hoping for some kind of...reassurance...that the Blockade Division will not do anything...foolish...while the Triumvirate and the Ambassador begin negotiations."

"Shouldn't that be something you discuss with Kedis?"

"Oh, it will be discussed, never fear, Admiral." Pamos gave him a thin smile. "It is simply my wish to keep bloodshed between now and then to a minimum."

It sounded good, but Chesnee did not believe for a second the Representative was that altruistic. "The Ambassador is well, I hope."

"Perfectly fine. On his way to Sonela now."

"What about his bodyguards, Lieutenant Wright and Corporal Renner?" Chesnee hesitated. "And Captain Strong?"

A strange look filled Pamos's dark eyes; he seemed torn between frustration and satisfaction. "They are also on their way to Sonela with the Ambassador." He raised a hand, as though anticipating Chesnee's next words. "You have no reason to believe me, of course, but then, I have no reason to lie." He turned his hand palm up.

Chesnee didn't know where his next words came from. "I imagine Representative Monroe was happy to see his grandson."

"That would be one word for it," Pamos said thoughtfully. "'Stunned' might be more apt." He looked askance at Chesnee. "Why do you ask?"

"No reason."

"I see." Pamos surveyed him sharply for a few seconds. "They are a curious family," he said at last. "Given past history, I must confess I am surprised Captain Strong acted as he did." He smiled; it was edged with razor blades. "Perhaps that is simply the Tarynian in him coming through."

*I doubt it*, Chesnee thought, but he held his tongue.

Pamos inclined his head. "I must take my leave of you now, Admiral. I implore you again to refrain from doing anything…foolish while we sort things out." He waited for Chesnee to give him some indication that he agreed, but when Chesnee merely looked at him, he ended the call.

The Admiral sat for a moment, processing the hidden layers and subtexts of that conversation, before heaving a sigh. High Command would have to be informed of these latest developments. He did not particularly *want* to deal with Fleet Admiral Joseph Tyler yet—not until he had a better grasp of the situation—but he would not be able to delay long. Too many things had just happened.

A moment later, he received a text-only transmission from Sta'Gloa. This one, he knew was from Kedis. It was only six words.

*Made successful contact. Wait for instructions.*

Frowning heavily, Chesnee stared at those words. *I wonder if Kedis has any idea what the Glo'Steans have just done.*

As much as the idea of listening to a group of politicians dance around each other with veiled insults bored him to death, Chesnee almost wished he could be a fly on the wall for the inevitable showdown between the Ambassador and the Triumvirate.

# CHAPTER 6

S AVE for the ever-present and inescapable faint hum of electricity in the background, the stillness of the conference room was deafening. It rang in Lilia's ears, behind the steady throb of her own heartbeat. Without access to her comlink—which was trapped in her ISF because she'd put it there for safekeeping when Birch arrested her—she had no way of knowing how long she'd been locked in here.

It felt like an eternity, but was probably closer to an hour or two.

*Long enough for me to get both sleepy and impatient.* She turned that over in her mind. *Sleepily impatient, or impatiently sleepy? Which is it?*

Realizing her thoughts were now turning into nonsense, Lilia leaned forward to prop her elbows on the table and pressed the heels of her gloved hands into her eyes. *Get a grip. Stay awake. Focus.*

*On what?* asked a little voice in the back of her mind, a voice that sounded a lot like Erik Holt, a fellow Guardian and friend. *On what you're going to tell the Triumvirate? Or the NCDC?*

Neither of those upcoming prospects filled Lilia with anything other than an impending sense of doom. *Can't say I'm looking forward to talking to either of them.* Dropping her hands to the table, she frowned at the door. *They're going to have a lot of questions—and we can't answer all of them.*

She froze as one of those questions materialized in her mind, and her mouth went very, very dry.

*Questions like how we managed to use the transporter without Cait or Jayce knowing about it.*

Lilia swallowed, with an effort, faint tendrils of nausea beginning to churn in her stomach. *Or how we even knew where to find them.*

They had used wormholes to smuggle Kedis into the Gala—

—but those wormholes hadn't been connected to any machine the Triumvirate knew about.

Lilia took a deep breath in an attempt to quell the nausea, and tried opening a Nancom channel to her twin.

Nothing.

*Didn't really expect it to work yet, but it was worth a try.*

Her violet eyes snapped to the conference room door as it abruptly slid aside. Birch marched back inside, looking grim and displeased. Behind him, she caught sight of two men standing in the hall.

Birch motioned impatiently to her. "On your feet. Let's go."

Lilia did not move. "Where are we going?"

He gave her a dark look. "You're being remanded into your grandfather's custody for the trip back to Sonela. You're to appear before the Triumvirate, and then," he smiled unpleasantly, "then you're mine."

*That* sent a fine shudder of dislike coursing through Lilia's body. She knew what he meant, but his implications were disturbing. *They're supposed to be*, she reminded herself. *He's just ticked off that we're going to Sonela with Grandfather.*

She arched an eyebrow at him as she rose from her seat. "We'll see about that."

Head held high, Lilia rounded the table and crossed the conference room. Just as she stepped through the door, Birch's long fingers closed over her upper arm and squeezed hard enough to be painful.

"You won't be getting out of this one unscathed," he said in her ear, his voice low and malicious. "None of you."

Her heart thudded in her chest, but Lilia shot him a scathing look. "Unhand me this instant."

"Would you rather wear restraints?" Birch did not release her arm. Instead, he bent closer until his face was centimeters from hers. "By rights you should have an NCDC escort from here on out to make sure you don't do anything else illegal, but thanks to your dear old grandfather, that's been nixed."

*Thank God*, Lilia thought, fighting the urge to either put several meters between them—or else haul back and punch him in the nose. "Mr. Birch, if you don't let—"

"You'll be receiving a summons to the Cramer Building. If you don't show…" Birch gave a slow shrug and released his hold on her arm.

Lilia gave him a narrow, tightlipped look, and turned away, tossing her head. "Never fear, Mr. Birch. I'll be there." She glanced back over her shoulder at him. "Are you escorting me to my grandfather, or is one of these gentlemen?" Her gaze flicked to his two companions, who had shifted nervously and avoided looking at either of them during Birch's little intimidation display.

Ignoring her, Birch stepped across the hall to another conference room door, opened it, and made a curt gesture. "Out."

"It's about time," said a familiar voice.

Lilia's heart leaped as her brother appeared in the doorway. Kevin caught sight of her immediately and lifted his eyebrows in a silent question. *Are you okay?*

Giving him a minuscule nod, she quirked her own eyebrows. Kevin returned the nod.

Oblivious to the quick exchange, Birch addressed one of his companions. "Take them to Representative Monroe and then report back to your normal station."

The man—young and dark-skinned, with a mop of wiry black curls and a slightly nervous expression—nodded and motioned to the twins. "This way."

Lilia started to follow, but Kevin did not budge. He narrowed his eyes at Birch. "I want my comlink back."

For a few seconds, the two men stared at each other. Then Birch's mouth twisted in a sneer and he fished in his pants' pocket. Withdrawing a comlink, he tossed the little device to Kevin and then wordlessly stalked away down the hall. His remaining companion fell in step behind him.

"Thanks," Kevin said to his retreating back. He glanced down at his comlink, hefting it in the palm of his hand. "No telling what he did to it." He glanced at Lilia, his expression wry. "He's in charge of Triumvirate Tower security, after all."

"I don't know what to tell you." Lilia shook her head, wrapping her arms around her torso and curling her hands around her elbows. She looked at their guide. "Who are you?"

"Roan Pallmer." His dark eyes slid past her to the corner Birch and his entourage had just disappeared around, and his expression turned abashed. "Ah, you wouldn't happen to know *where* Representative Monroe is, would you?"

When the twins both blinked at him, Pallmer made a face. "He disappeared off the security grid over two hours ago. So did a bunch of the other bigwigs."

Lilia arched an eyebrow. "So ask Birch."

"Ah…" Pallmer cast a nervous glance up the corridor again. "I don't think he knows either. It's been a crazy night and he's not in charge of Gala security."

The twins exchanged looks. "Not for lack of trying, I'll guess," Kevin said dryly. "Bet that's been killing him all night."

Palmer laughed, and immediately coughed to cover it.

Kevin grinned back wearily, and held up his comlink. "Hang on a sec; I'll call my brother."

Michael answered immediately; in the quiet hall, Lilia and Pallmer could hear his voice on the other end. "Kevin! Are you all right? Is Lilia with you?"

"Yeah, she's here. We're both fine." Kevin glanced sideways at her. "Birch just turned us loose into Grandfather's custody."

"Good." Michael sounded fiercely relieved. "I was afraid he was going to be difficult. Again."

"Oh, he's not happy about it, that's for sure, but he let us go. Where are you?"

"Spaceport. We left Oppelt in the parking garage to wait for you; I'll tell him to meet you at the side entrance. We're taking off as soon as you get here."

"Great. We'll be there shortly."

"Also…" Michael paused. "Grandfather wanted me to tell you he can't wait to hear this story."

Kevin swallowed, his eyes darting to Lilia. "I'll bet not. Tell him we'll fill him in on everything when we get there."

"Will do." With that, Michael ended the call.

Sliding his comlink back into his pocket, Kevin turned to Pallmer. "We need to go to the side entrance. Somebody's picking us up."

"No problem. This way." Pallmer started off down the hall. After a moment, he glanced sideways at Kevin and Lilia in turn. "Did you really sneak Tarynians past the shield?"

"*We* didn't," Kevin said, "but we did help get Ambassador Kedis into the party tonight."

Pallmer eyed them both again, as though they had morphed into some kind of strange alien life form right before his eyes, and then shook his head. He said nothing for the remainder of their trek through the side halls of the convention center.

"Thank you," the twins told him in unison when they reached a set of wide plastiglass double doors separating them from the parking garage level beyond. A sleek black skimmer waited outside. Pallmer just nodded curtly and disappeared back the way they had come.

The question of how they would deal with the scientists and the transporter burned in Lilia's mind, but she knew better than to discuss it with Kevin here and now. She gulped anxiously as Kevin pushed open the door and motioned for her to precede him into the parking garage. *It won't be safe to talk in the skimmer either; we'll have to wait until we get back to the spaceport.*

She wasn't sure she could hold everything in that long; she felt it building pressure inside her, threatening to make her explode.

Kevin picked up on her anxiety—it was hard to miss—but he understood the danger. "It'll be fine, Lil. Honest." He gave her a reassuring look as he opened the skimmer door for her.

Nodding, Lilia slid inside and scooted across the seat to make room for him. "Thanks for waiting for us," she told their driver breathlessly.

"Not a problem." Oppelt glanced over his shoulder at them; the shadows under his hazel eyes gave evidence to the fact that this had been a very long night. He had short blond hair and extremely broad shoulders. "You two okay?"

"Tired," Kevin said, "but other than that, we're good."

"Glad to hear it." Oppelt began winding through the parking level toward the exit. "Did Michael tell you we'll be taking off as soon as we reach the spaceport?"

"Yes, he did," Lilia answered.

"Okay. That's everything."

As Oppelt merged into Atalia traffic, the twins tried to settle back against their seats, but they were too keyed up to relax. Their driver said very little, for which they were thankful. Both of them were wondering how they would explain their actions to their grand-father—and the Triumvirate!—without mentioning the not-so-inconsequential tidbit that they had *transporters* embedded in their nano-armor.

It had been over three months since they had made this discov-ery, thanks to a request from the scientists to test their transporter that had triggered a secret program created by their colleague, Dr. Banx, who had not survived the rescue mission. Banx's coordinate strings had resulted in the twins being bounced all over the Coalition. Lilia still sometimes found it hard to believe they could open up portals to different places and simply step through. She and Kevin had adjusted quickly to the freedom their transporters gave them, but it did mean they would have to fabricate part of their story. Even Kedis didn't know how they'd really gotten him into the Gala.

Though traffic was still somewhat congested, Oppelt made fairly good progress through Atalia. Lilia stared at the dark city streets flashing past without seeing them; her thoughts had now traveled to Lon, the Ambassador, and his two bodyguards. For all her reluctance to smuggle a Tarynian soldier into the Gala as her escort, she had ended up genuinely enjoying the evening with Jasper. And after spending two solid weeks around him, she was startled to realize she would actually miss him a little.

Overwhelmingly, however, the primary emotion surfacing amid the jumble inside her was relief. They'd gotten Kedis in, and nobody had died. *That was the hard part. Now it's just a matter of figuring out our story.* It came down to details, really.

Beside her, Kevin suddenly choked. She glanced at him, alarmed, and her heart began to pound at the ashen look on his face. Her eyes dropped from his face to the comlink in his hand. "What's wrong? What happened?"

Kevin looked at her, his violet eyes wide with shock and…was that remorse? Wordlessly, he handed his comlink to her.

Lilia accepted it with trembling fingers. Torn between the burning desire to know what was wrong and the equally strong conviction that she was not going to like whatever she saw, she looked down at the display. One glance at the news headline and the color drained from her face as well.

"They did it." Her free hand flattening against her chest, she snapped her gaze to her brother, to find him staring back, his face still chalky.

Kevin nodded jerkily.

"They actually *did* it." Lilia scanned the rest of the article. "Have you read this?"

"Not yet." Kevin tried for a smile; it emerged as more of a grimace.

Lilia handed his comlink back. "It says it happened around eleven-thirty this evening." Her brow furrowed. "That's—"

Kevin abruptly drew a finger across his neck, his eyes darting meaningfully to Oppelt. *Not here.*

"—interesting," she finished, with an oblique nod. She'd have to wait, but the words burned on the tip of her tongue, anxious to be spoken.


When Oppelt finally pulled into the Atalia Spaceport, it took a few moments more to pass through the assorted security checkpoints that lay between them and their grandfather's private ship, a slender *Butterfly*-class yacht called the *Vinka*. By then, Lilia and Kevin were all but vibrating in their seats from a combination of anxiety and anticipation. Oppelt stopped beside the yacht long enough to let them off before he drove the skimmer into the cargo bay with Aiden's other skimmer, and the twins lost no time in piling out.

Tossing "thank you"s over their shoulders to Oppelt, Lilia and Kevin hastily greeted the two men standing guard at the foot of the landing ramp.

Juan Engle and Booth Imlay had been members of their grandfather's security detail for years; both usually worked the night shift. Engle was short and wiry, with medium-brown skin, curly black hair, and a newly-grown goatee. Imlay was taller, with brown hair, brown eyes, and rather nondescript features—something he often took advantage of when Aiden had to travel. Both men nodded to the twins as they bounded up the ramp into the ship.

Skidding around an alabaster corner into the main living compartment, Lilia and Kevin found their grandfather, his chief of staff, Felix Mouta, and his wife, and their brothers all gathered together. The living compartment was decorated in pastel blues, greens, and golds, with comfortable chairs and couches scattered around.

Aiden was seated in a chair, deep in an earnest discussion with Mouta, a wiry olive-skinned man  in his mid-forties, but he broke off when he caught sight of the twins, looking profoundly relieved. "Excellent. Are you all right?"

"Yes, Grandfather," they replied together.

"Good." Aiden looked at Michael. "Tell Tanata we are ready to depart now."

"Yes, sir." Rising to his feet, Michael disappeared from the compartment. He returned a moment later with Engle and Imlay in tow; Lilia and Kevin had already sunk down on a pale gold couch and strapped themselves in for take-off.

Derek leaned toward them from his chair near their grandfather. "In case you were wondering, we already packed up everything from the hotel."

Lilia hadn't even given that a thought, but she nodded. "Thanks." Twisting her gloved hands together in her lap, she glanced sideways at Kevin. *I don't know what to do now.*

They needed to talk to their grandfather, true, but she hadn't taken into account that they might have an audience. Her eyes traveled from Mouta and his wife, Elena, to Engle and Imlay—Oppelt had not appeared yet—before coming to rest on Aiden himself.

Her grandfather looked exhausted, no doubt about it, and yet… Lilia squinted at him thoughtfully. *There's a spark about him that hasn't been there for a while.* She bit her lip, hope stirring in her chest. *Maybe that's because of Lon.*

As though feeling her eyes on him, Aiden turned his head to meet her gaze. He held up a hand to forestall further conversation. "Felix, I am aware there are a thousand things requiring my immediate attention before we return to Sonela, but at the moment, it is imperative that I speak to Kevin and Lilia."

"Certainly," Mouta said at once. He had vibrant black hair and soulful brown eyes. He half-glanced at his wife, who was a head shorter and several shades paler, with a riot of dark brown curls. "Would you like us to—"

"That will not be necessary, thank you." Rising from his seat with an effort, Aiden held out his hand to Derek in a silent request for assistance. "We will be in my cabin."

# CHAPTER 7

AIDEN did not speak again until Derek had helped him prop himself up in a sitting position on his bed. His cabin—white bulkheads with silver and blue accents, something his late wife had selected—was large enough to accommodate a desk, several silver-and-blue plush chairs, and a matching loveseat facing the bed. He motioned for Lilia and Kevin to take seats there. Derek and Michael sank into chairs.

"Now," he said shortly, "we do not have much time. Tell me everything. Start with how you determined Lon was alive."

His tone made it clear this was not a request.

This required a bit of tricky phrasing, but the twins managed to string together enough of the story to make a cohesive whole without mentioning *they* had transporters.

By the time they finished, their grandfather's face had paled again. Slowly, Aiden shook his head at them. "Am I to understand you actually used the transporter to get Kedis into the convention center?"

Lilia and Kevin exchanged glances, before nodding. "We didn't exactly—"

"—have much of a choice."

"Plus," Kevin said, "it's not like the Ambassador didn't—"

"—know about it already," Lilia finished.

Aiden studied them for a brief span, before turning to encompass Michael and Derek in his reproachful gaze. "I understand why you kept this from me, but I wish you had not."

"Plausible deniability," Derek reminded him. "You have it." His expression turned apologetic. "Albeit at the cost of looking like you don't know what's going on with your own family—"

"And we're *very* sorry about that, Grandfather," Michael interjected.

"—but in your defense," Derek continued, "you *were* in the hospital recovering from severe trauma."

Aiden fell silent for a long moment, long enough that they could see the fatigue tugging at his muscles when he finally roused himself. "Kevin, Lilia, you will be defending yourselves to the Triumvirate tomorrow." A slow blink. "Today, rather. Later this morning. There will be no avoiding it."

The twins exchanged glances again. "We understand," they said together.

Lilia shrugged one shoulder, dropping her eyes to her skirt and resisting the urge to pick at the beautiful fabric. "We knew that was a possibility."

"Whatever happens, it was worth it, Grandfather," Kevin said earnestly. "There's been enough blood spilled on our worlds."

Aiden looked as though he agreed, but his expression remained drawn.

Heavy silence filled the cabin…and guilt began to wriggle in the pit of Lilia's stomach like an overactive worm.

They hadn't told their grandfather what they knew about Freedom's Children.

Granted, he hadn't asked, but Lilia knew that was only because he didn't know he *should*.

Her heart began to pound in her chest; her palms grew sweaty. She scrunched the skirt of her dress anxiously, her eyes flicking sideways to Kevin. *We have to tell him.*

They'd put off mentioning Freedom's Children long enough already; now she could only hope it wasn't too late.

Lilia cleared her throat, gathering her courage in the process. "Grandfather, about the shield generators—has anybody claimed responsibility yet?"

Aiden's face grew more drawn. "Why do you ask?"

Ignoring the way her brothers were now all staring at her, Lilia wet her lips. "Because I know who's responsible."

"*We* know," Kevin interjected, frowning.

"Is that so?" Aiden regarded both of them with a mixture of surprise and concern, before motioning for them to continue.

They shared a look. This was it. "It's a group called Freedom's Children," Lilia began and saw a flicker of shock pass through her grandfather's green eyes. "They've—"

"—been building shield generators in occupied territory," Kevin continued. "We found out about it the week we spent—"

"—being bounced around Glo'Stea a few months ago. We don't know—"

"—how long they've been working on them, but they—"

"—were close to being finished then." Lilia shook her head miserably. "We were going to tell you, but—"

"—we weren't sure how." Kevin spread his hands. "We only knew of a couple of them for certain."

Aiden was silent for a long time, regarding the twins as though they were strangers. When he finally spoke, his voice was quiet. Too quiet. "How did they get the materials past the Tarynians?"

The twins exchanged glances again, carefully refraining from looking at their older brothers. "This..." Kevin said slowly, "...is partly why we didn't tell you anything at first."

Lilia began twisting her gloved fingers together in her lap. "They used a transporter."

Visible shock washed over Aiden at this. He straightened in his bed. "*How?*" All of them flinched at the sharp command in his tone. "Have those scientists been working with them this entire time?"

Lilia's mouth was dry, but she forced words past her tongue. "We think Dr. Banx was working with them before he died, yes. He must have helped them build one, and they've been opening portals in occupied territory the same way the Triumvirate delivered supplies to the mining stations." She shook her head. "The other scientists don't know about it."

Aiden frowned. "How can you be so sure?"

"Because after we brought them to Sta'Gloa, somebody broke into their lab and stole a bunch of Banx's data," Kevin said. "Cait and Jayce *still* aren't completely sure what's missing." He opened his mouth to say something else, but hesitated and closed it again.

Their grandfather did not miss this. He gave Kevin a sharp look. "Well? This is not the time to hold back any further information, boy."

Kevin met Lilia's eyes and she knew exactly what he was thinking. *Dover.* She widened her eyes in alarm. *Don't.* She wasn't ready to handle *that* revelation yet. *And I don't think Grandfather is either. Not tonight.*

"We told you the transporter was glitching," Kevin said instead, "but that's not exactly true. Turns out Banx programmed a specific string of coordinates into the transporters he, Cait, and Jayce built, and—"

"—our nanites tripped it," Lilia interjected quickly. "That's why we were being bounced all over the Coalition."

Kevin took a deep breath. "I think one of those places is Freedom's Children's headquarters."

Another wave of shock passed over Aiden. He gathered himself with an effort. "It would seem there is a great deal you have been keeping from me."

Guilt gnawed at Lilia's insides. "We had good reason," she said meekly.

"It's this little island on Glo'Stea," Kevin continued, "and somebody has basically built a fortress on it."

Aiden passed a hand over his face. "That does not prove anything."

"No, it doesn't," Kevin admitted freely. "We…came to that conclusion based on the fact that in practically every place in occupied territory on Glo'Stea, somebody was building a shield generator, and then—"

"—most of the other places we were dropped on Sta'Gloa, Lanx, and free Glo'Stea had something to do with Freedom's Children." Lilia swallowed. "Including Kyman."

"Kyman?" Aiden asked, startled. "Why that medcenter?"

Lilia shook her head. "I still don't know what the connection is."

"I see." Aiden pressed his fingers into a steeple and swept his tired—but still piercing—green gaze around the cabin at his grandchildren before he returned to the twins. "You took a tremendous risk revealing the transporter to Kedis."

Kevin's mouth twisted into a grimace. "I told you, we didn't exactly have much of a choice."

"He knew about it anyway," Lilia said. "He saw the press conference."

Aiden's gaze was relentless in its intensity. "You revealed that you have—or at least had—access to it. How did you explain that to him and his men?"

"We didn't," Lilia said simply.

"For that matter," Aiden continued, "how *did* you get access? The joint Departments of Internal Affairs have ensured that both transporters have been heavily guarded."

The twins both froze. Neither of them wanted to lie again…but they couldn't tell him the truth now, could they? On top of everything else? What would he say? What would he *do*?

Kevin finally waved a hand. "We rescued the scientists, remember? And we helped them test the transporter because they asked us to." He let Aiden draw his own conclusions.

Unease sat heavily on Lilia's shoulders, but she didn't know what else to do.

Michael solved the moral dilemma for them. "Tell him the truth," he said, his voice heavy. "*All* of it."

Betrayed, the twins both swung to gape at him. "Mike—"

"He's right," Derek said. "It's time Grandfather knew." He ran a weary hand through his dark hair. "There's too much at stake, especially now, and we should have mentioned Freedom's Children a long time ago."

Aiden regarded each of his grandchildren in turn. "I suppose I should not be surprised you are all in on it," he said at last. "And given that you have grown up with me as a grandfather, I suppose I should not be surprised at your adeptness in keeping secrets, either." Bracing himself, he looked at Lilia and Kevin again. "What else is there?"

Lilia sidestepped his question—and the faint trace of disappointment in his eyes—to fix Michael and Derek with a challenging stare. "*All* of it?" She would have preferred to use Nancom, to keep this conversation private, but it couldn't be helped.

"All of it," Derek confirmed wearily. "It's time."

Biting down on the inside of her cheek hard enough to draw blood, Lilia looked at Kevin. He stared back at her, the same battle waging in his violet eyes, and then together they turned back to face their grandfather.

"We didn't use the scientists' transporter—"

"—we used our own."

Despite their best efforts to keep the story short, it was very late by the time the twins finished telling their grandfather everything—including the fact that the NCDC had developed a means of controlling wayward Guardians and their nanites were currently frozen.

Aiden took it better than they had expected—they had all envisioned him keeling over—but his face still turned a few shades grayer. "My God." He drew a long, shuddering breath. "I would advise you to continue to keep this to yourselves."

Lilia and Kevin exchanged worried looks. "It wasn't that we wanted—"

"—to keep it from you all this time, we just—"

"—didn't want to give you more stress on top of—"

"—Lon's funeral and everything else."

After a long pause, Aiden gave them a small nod. "I understand your reasoning. It does not mean that I do not wish you had made a different decision, but I do understand."

A tiny fraction of Lilia's anxiety dissipated.

"What about the Triumvirate?" Derek looked from Lilia to Kevin and back. "Have you figured out how you're going to explain how you used the transporter to sneak Kedis in?"

They still hadn't worked that part out. Lilia gulped, feeling her stomach begin to twist itself into knots again.

Kevin just shrugged. "We'll think of something."

"You've only got a few hours left in which to do it," Michael reminded him.

Kevin threw his hands into the air. "This was always going to be the sticky part, Mike. We knew that from the start." Leaning forward on the loveseat, he rested his elbows on his knees and locked his hands behind his head. "I don't know what we're going to say yet, but we *will* say something."

"You don't have a choice," Derek said sharply.

A wry smile curved Kevin's lips. "Well, we *could* always open a portal and just disappear. Mind you, it wouldn't be easy, living on the run, but—"

"That's not funny." Michael's tone could have frozen molten lava.

"Not in the least." Aiden agreed. He looked from Lilia to Kevin. "I am afraid I cannot help you with this."

"We never expected you to," Lilia assured him. Beneath the navy blue gloves covering her clasped hands, her knuckles were white.

"You can't tell anyone," Kevin said abruptly. It was his turn to fix his grandfather with a steely look. "Not Uncle Martin, not Shane Briscoe, or Kane Fenton, or anyone else. We don't know why Dr. Dover gave us the transporters when she coded our nano-armor, but we're working on finding out, and we can't do that if you—"

"Believe me," Aiden interrupted, "I have no intentions of telling anyone about this." His expression grew more troubled with every word. "The outcome of a revelation like that at this particular junction could only result in me losing two more grandchildren to the NCDC and the Department of Internal Affairs."

His eyes sharpened again. "How are you investigating?"

"We have…friends." Kevin made an apologetic gesture with one hand. "I would prefer to leave you out of that part, Grandfather. Just in case."

After another long pause, Aiden inclined his head. "Very well." He glanced at Derek, and a little of the stern, grandfatherliness seemed to drain out of him. In that moment, he looked like an old man—an exhausted old man still recovering from a near-death experience. "We will be arriving in Sonela shortly. In the meantime, I suggest you get what rest you can. I am afraid to say that dealing with the Triumvirate will likely be an ordeal."

"I expected that," Lilia muttered, rubbing her eyes. Her stomach twisted again; dealing with the NCDC wasn't likely to be any better.

"By the way," Aiden said abruptly, as though he had come to a sudden decision, "the answer to your original question is yes."

Startled, three of his four grandchildren looked at him.

"It has not yet been publicly broadcast, but shortly after the shield generators were activated, the Triumvirate received a transmission from the group claiming responsibility."

"What?" Michael asked, shocked.

"Freedom's Children?" Kevin asked.

Aiden inclined his head. "Yes."

Before anyone else could speak, Michael rounded on Derek, who was the only one of them who had not looked surprised. "You knew. You knew and you didn't say anything."

Derek gave a little shrug, as though the gesture took all the energy he had. "He didn't give me permission to say anything."

The twins gaped at him. "But—" Kevin began.

"Enough." Aiden cut the impending argument off at the knees. "This is not the time. You are all aware of how things work." He motioned toward the door, fatigue written in every wrinkle on his face. "Get some rest now. All of you. And, Derek, send Mouta in, please."

"Yes, Grandfather."

As she unfolded from her seat on the loveseat, Lilia tried her nanites again, but they were still frozen. She grimaced. *Great.*

They filed out of Aiden's cabin into the corridor, and Derek jerked his head toward the cabin he and Michael shared. "In here. All of you. I'll be right back."

He disappeared in the direction of the living compartment, leaving his baffled siblings staring after him. He returned a moment later, Felix Mouta on his heels. Mouta stepped into Aiden's cabin, while Derek joined his siblings and shut the door.

"What's going on?" Kevin asked, leaning up against the bunks stacked two high along one bulkhead.

Derek looked between him and Lilia. "Nob has been trying to contact you two all evening."

Lilia and Kevin darted glances at each other. "I'm not surprised," Lilia said.

"He Nancommed me when he couldn't raise you, and I explained that you'd been arrested, but that I didn't know why you weren't answering. He sounded fairly agitated."

"Freedom's Children activated those shield generators," Kevin said dryly, "and we knew it was a possibility."

"But why tonight?"

They all turned to stare at Michael. He was frowning, his blond eyebrows knit together in sudden concentration. All his earlier pique with Derek had vanished. "Why tonight?" he asked again.

Derek glanced from him to the twins and back as though he expected to find the answer written in neon letters on their foreheads. "Why not tonight?" He shrugged. "God only knows what their timetable is."

"*Think* about it." A note of urgency slid into Michael's voice. "The Tournament's Closing Ceremonies were tonight. Thousands of people slipped past Sta'Gloa's shield to attend and none of them are flying home until at least tomorrow. Why would they do it *now*?"

A faint glimmer of understanding began to dawn in Lilia's mind, but the exhaustion setting in made it difficult to grasp.

Kevin drew in a sharp breath. "Some of them are going to be stranded for a while. Shield Control isn't going to let *anybody* in or out until we figure out how Chesnee's going to react."

"Exactly." Michael checked his comlink. "We got word that the shield generators had been activated within fifteen minutes of Lon introducing Kedis." He looked around at his siblings. "That's awfully coincidental timing, don't you think?"

"Wait a minute, Mike." Derek held up a hand. "Are you saying what I *think* you're saying?"

Lilia stared at her oldest brother as realization finally unfolded like a flower inside her mind. She sank down onto the bottom bunk; her knees had given way. "You think somebody in the crowd tipped them off."

For a moment, her words hung in the tiny cabin. Then Michael nodded and spread his hands. "That's exactly what I think. How else would they have known so quickly? *Why* would they have picked *now* to act?"

It made a terrible kind of sense. Lilia's mouth went dry again.

Kevin looked horrified. "That would mean somebody at the Gala is working for Freedom's Children—and is pretty high up in the ranks, to boot."

"Yes."

"Hold up, hold up." Derek held up both hands this time. "That's a great theory, Mike, but you're forgetting one thing. There were media cams there tonight. Reporters. We've both seen the footage—as soon as they realized what was going on, they started broadcasting. Kedis's little introduction speech is all over the Coalition."

He looked around at his siblings. "Somebody involved with Freedom's Children was probably watching the Gala coverage, saw Kedis, and immediately contacted their higher-ups. Wouldn't take long for it to reach whoever's in charge. He or she moved the timetable up, gave the order, and boom." Derek mimed a shield sphere blossoming around a planet. "Glo'Stea's got an intact planetary shield for the first time in two decades."

Michael shook his head doggedly. "There isn't enough *time* for that. Whoever's in charge made that decision *fast*, like they didn't have to be convinced there was actually a Tarynian ambassador on Sta'Gloa."

"Or they just didn't want to take the chance they were wrong," Derek shot back.

"Mike's got a point," Kevin said slowly. "That's an awfully big chance to take, Derek. I met some of these people—a *lot* of planning went into this operation. Somehow I don't think they'd risk blowing it on a whim."

"I agree," Lilia said from the bunk.

Derek blew out a breath. "Well, that's my theory, and I'm sticking to it." His face was somber. "Maybe it doesn't matter right now."

Lilia and Kevin exchanged glances.

"Oh, it matters," Kevin said. "We just don't have enough information at the moment."

Somber silence fell over the four of them. After a long moment, Michael roused himself. "Get some rest. It's going to be a long day."

# Chapter 8

LON stood by the wide window in the spacious living room of their hotel suite, staring out at the early dawn cityscape glittering with a multitude of different-colored neon lights. They were on the top floor of the Beliana Hotel, which stood in the middle ring of Sonela's downtown business district and provided a spectacular view of the city. Corran and his team were stationed in the hall outside and in the suite next door; the entire floor had been cordoned off for Kedis's protection.

He should be asleep, he knew that, but Lon was still too keyed up to relax. Even though they'd managed to pull it off, part of him had been half-expecting to be blown out of the sky the entire flight from Atalia to Sonela. It didn't help that he hadn't been able to contact the twins since he introduced Kedis to the entire Coalition.

He had eventually talked to Michael and Derek, who assured him the twins were fine, but they couldn't explain why their siblings were incommunicado. That worried him. Their involvement wasn't likely to go over well in certain quarters.

Sensing movement behind him, he said, "This is one of the swankiest hotels in Sonela."

"It's nice," Jasper agreed, coming to peer out the window as well.

This particular suite featured color scheme of silver, white, and various pastels, with tan couches, and glass-topped tables built from matching wood. They had performed a thorough sweep of the suite after Corran and his men withdrew outside the door, but had come up empty. Lon had even—discreetly—used his own NCDC-issue scanner to double-check their rooms were neither bugged nor booby-trapped.

Kedis had retired to the master bedroom as soon as they cleared the suite, citing the need to be as rested as possible for his impending meeting with the Triumvirate. Renner claimed first watch, since Lon was likely to have to speak to the Triumvirate as well.

Now that the bulk of the excitement was over, mundane things like luggage came to mind. Lon rubbed a hand over his face, feeling the faint prickle of stubble. *Didn't think about luggage.* "I'll have to ask Kevin to fly to Marina and pick up our bags." He flashed Jasper a wry smile. "Although yours is already aboard the *Talia*, isn't it?"

Jasper nodded, his gray eyes sweeping over Sonela. He was still dressed in his tuxedo shirt, though he had loosened the collar and rolled the sleeves up to his elbows. "Do you think your brother and sister will be in much trouble?"

"Honestly?" Lon shrugged. "I have no idea." His gut twisted faintly at the admission. "I'm betting the Triumvirate lets them off, though."

Jasper's gaze flicked to Renner, before he dropped his voice. "Earlier, when you were speaking to Briscoe, the Ambassador ordered us to say nothing of your use of the transporter to anyone."

Lon glanced at him sharply. "Really?"

"Yes." Jasper clasped his hands behind his back, falling into an easy parade rest. "I believe he wishes to keep that knowledge very close to his chest."

"Big surprise there."

Jasper's words lifted some of the weight off of Lon's chest, however, and he found himself breathing a little easier. If Kedis had no intentions of mentioning he had traveled to the Cuomo Convention Center via wormhole, then the twins no longer needed to invent a plausible explanation for their use of the transporter. *Problem solved.*

It didn't erase the future potential for a sticky situation, since they'd still have to explain how they smuggled Kedis in, but it would take some of the pressure off.

Lon tried Nancomming the twins again, but they were still unreachable. He frowned at his reflection in the plastiglass window. *Something's wrong. I don't know what it is, but something is definitely wrong.*

They should have Nancommed him long before now to make sure everything was okay.

He opened channels to Michael and Derek again as well, but neither of them responded either. A glance at the time, however, informed him that they, at least, had an excuse. *Okay, it is pretty late. They're probably asleep…which is where I should be too.*

Looking at Jasper, he jerked a thumb over his shoulder. "I'm turning in now."

Jasper inclined his head in a nod.

"If we need you," Renner said from a black leather armchair in the corner, where he was engrossed in a datapad, "we'll shout."

"Do that."

A loud chiming woke Lon six hours later, just before eleven AM. Blinking in his room's blessed darkness, he rubbed his eyes—which felt glued together—and rolled over in bed to fumble for his comlink on the nightstand. He didn't bother with the lights. "Hello?"

"Hello, Liaison Strong? This is Marissa Benko, from Chief Minister Koen's office. The Chief Minister would like to extend Ambassador Kedis an invitation to speak with the Triumvirate in Triumvirate Tower this afternoon at three PM."

"Three PM?" Lon rubbed a hand over his face. "That's great. The Ambassador will be delighted to accept."

"Also," Benko continued, "The Triumvirate wishes to speak to you at two PM."

"Me?" Lon could have smacked himself immediately for sounding so inane. His residual sleepiness fell away as a surge of adrenaline began to pump through his veins. Of *course* the Triumvirate wanted to talk to him. He knew that. "I'll be there, Ms. Benko."

"Thank you." Benko provided him with instructions on what to do once they reached Triumvirate Tower and then cut the connection.

Curling his fingers around his comlink, Lon sat up in his bed and braced himself for an onslaught of daylight. "Window, open."

Behind the curtains, the window melted from opaque to transparent, flooding the room with cheerful morning light. Lon squinted while his eyes adjusted, ignoring his surroundings—he'd drawn the short straw and had ended up with the most girly-looking room, which boasted silver, turquoise, pale blue, and lavender stripes—and lost no time in climbing out of bed and pulling on his black trousers and white dress shirt from the night before. They'd have to do something about their clothes before they met with the Triumvirate, but for now it could wait.

Shoving his comlink into his pocket, Lon headed out to tell Kedis the news.

He found the Ambassador sitting in the suite's breakfast nook with a cup of tea, also dressed in his tuxedo from the night before. Several breakfast trays were spread across the table. Renner and Wright were both drinking coffee; Renner was absently dipping a piece of toast into his mug.

Kedis paused with his teacup halfway to his lips when he spotted Lon. "You've had news?"

"I have," Lon said in Tarynian. "The Triumvirate wants to see you at three today." He watched the faint beginnings of a frown form on Kedis's olive face and added, "They want to see me an hour earlier."

"I see." Kedis sipped his tea thoughtfully, before glancing at Jasper and Renner. "Well, we'll all join you."

"Probably for the best, Ambassador."

"I think so." Setting down his teacup, Kedis reached for a bowl of cut fruit. "By the way, Lon, I intend to say nothing of the transporter." His dark eyes watched for Lon's reaction. "There will be no doubt some who desire to know all the particulars, but I think it will be best for everyone if we leave that bit out."

"I see." Lon regarded him shrewdly. It was impossible to say exactly what Kedis intended to do with that bit of leverage, but he could hardly complain. "That will be fine with me."

*Speaking of which…*He attempted to Nancom the twins again. *It's after eleven—surely they'll be awake by now.*

# Chapter 9

THE impactor took six hours to wear off. By this time, Lilia, Kevin, and the rest of their family were home, back in Sonela and the penthouse that had stood empty—other than a few quick visits Lilia had made via portal—while Aiden was in the hospital. As soon as she realized she could dematerialize her nano-armor, Lilia made a beeline for the hygiene unit. Kevin was waiting when she emerged.

They flipped a coin to see who would get a shower first, and Lilia won. She emerged fifteen minutes later, clean and dressed in pajamas, and went straight to bed.

After the combined pressure and exhaustion of both preparing to introduce Kedis to the Coalition at the Gala and keeping everything secret, she should have passed out cold. Problem was, thoughts of the transporter still fluttered madly around her brain. She still didn't know what they were going to do.

Lilia lay staring up at the ceiling for a long time, before sleep finally found her.

At nine AM, she jolted awake, suddenly remembering it was Sunday morning and they were going to be late for church if they didn't hurry. Sliding out of bed, she threw on a robe and staggered out into the hall. Her bare feet made no sound on the burnished hardwood floor.

Zoë, their humanoid housekeeping 'bot, greeted her with a nod and a cheerful, "Good morning, Lilia." She had silver skin, black hair, and a crisp, navy-skirted uniform.

Even in her groggy state, Lilia could tell that the penthouse was unusually quiet. "Morning, Zoë. Where is everybody?"

"Still in bed. Master Aiden requested me to inform you that since the media is currently encamped outside Ferndale again, he thinks it best if you stay in this morning."

Dread rolled over Lilia in a clammy wave; her grandfather did not like any of them to miss church. "Is it that bad? The news, I mean."

If Zoë could have pursed her mechanical lips, she would have. "I believe the answer to that is yes and no."

*Great.* Lilia rubbed her eyes, which felt like she had sand in them. "I'm going back to bed."

"A sensible idea."

This time around, it did not take long for Lilia to fall back asleep. She slept for another hour and a half. When she woke again, it was to a familiar channel request niggling in the back of her mind.

[Finally.] Erik Holt, a former Sonela police officer and fellow Guardian, sounded both relieved and borderline annoyed. [Do you have any idea how long I've been tryin' to reach you two?]

[Sorry.] Stifling a yawn, Lilia sat up in bed. [It's been a rough night.]

[I'll bet. Did you know there are media crews pokin' around your ship?]

[What?] The last vestiges of sleep vanished in a surge of adrenaline. While they attended the Gala, she and Kevin had left Erik aboard their *Ceratina*-class freighter, the *Talia*, which was berthed in Sonela Spaceport.

[They can't get in, an' I haven't talked to 'em, but they're bein' awfully nosy.]

[Great. Kevin's going to love that.]

A pause. [Tried to contact you last night to make sure you were okay an' I got nothin'.] Erik's Nancom voice was deceptively light, but the fact that he had been worried about them bled through.

[Sorry. We…were indisposed.] A bitter taste filled Lilia's mouth. [The NCDC has got something that freezes Guardians' nanites and they shot us with it last night to keep us from 'escaping'.]

[What?] Erik sounded stunned; Lilia could imagine the look on his face.

[Yeah. Birch called it an 'impactor'. Took about six hours to wear off.]

[Birch was there?]

[Oh, yes.]

[But you're okay now? Both of you?]

[I'm fine, and I'm assuming Kevin's fine.] Lilia smothered another yawn. [Just woke up.]

[I see.] Erik digested this. [What happens now?]

[Now?] Lilia shrugged, even though he couldn't see her. [I have no idea. According to Grandfather, the Triumvirate will want to talk to us sometime today, and Birch assured me we'll be hearing from the NCDC.]

One corner of her mouth curved into a wry smile. [He's convinced the NCDC will kick us out.]

[I can see why they'd want to, after the stunt you pulled.]

[Thanks a lot, Erik.]

[You're welcome.] He abruptly switched subjects. [What do you want me to do? Stay here?]

Lilia hesitated. [Only if you can stand being by yourself today. I don't think we're going to be able to make it to the spaceport.]

A snort carried through Erik's Nancom channel. [Wouldn't advise it. Probably make 'em think you're gettin' ready to skip town.]

[Thanks.]

[No problem.]

[I'll tell Kevin to Nancom you when he wakes up.]

[Be careful, kid.]

[Will do.]

Closing his channel, Lilia emerged from her room and headed down the hall to find Derek and Michael gathered in the living room. The room was full of light; the walls were white with silver swirls, making the navy blue-and-dark-wood furniture stand out. Derek occupied one corner of a navy blue couch, Michael sat in a matching armchair. Their grandfather was nowhere to be seen.

"Where's Grandfather?" she asked without preamble.

Derek nodded in the direction of Aiden's master bedroom. "Getting ready. We've heard from the Triumvirate; they want to see you and Kevin at one."

Lilia's stomach fluttered; she bit her lip. "Okay. Is Grandfather all right?"

"He's fine," Michael assured her wearily. He was nursing a cup of coffee, his comlink in one hand.

For his part, Derek looked like he hadn't slept well either. He was managing triage on Aiden's incoming messages. His comlink buzzed again; he ignored it. "Hasn't stopped ringing since Kedis showed up on Coalition news last night." He rubbed a hand over his face. "Looks like a madhouse outside."

Lilia stepped over to the wide windows running the length of the living room, which were framed in gauzy silver and navy blue curtains, but she couldn't see anything. Ferndale's main entrance was on the other side of the apartment building. "They didn't just send cams?"

"Oh, no. They're hoping we come out." Derek gave a little shrug. "The regulars know Grandfather's routine. They know we usually attend church, and they were hoping to ambush us when we left this morning."

*That reminds me.* Reaching into her ISF, which was functioning just fine now that the impactor had worn off, Lilia withdrew her comlink. She took one look at the number of missed messages she had and winced. She didn't recognize most of the comm details—though she would have to check them later to make sure they weren't from potential clients—but she had several messages from people she *did* know…including her best friend.

Her heart sank. That was not going to be a pleasant conversation. Not when she'd lied to Alexis and made her think that Jasper Wright was her brand-new boyfriend, instead of a G.U. soldier she was helping smuggle into the Tri-World Tournament's Closing Ceremonies Gala.

Speaking of Jasper…

Her thoughts drifted to him; she wondered how he, and Lon, Kedis, and Renner were doing. Though she had Jasper's comm details, she wasn't about to actually *use* them. For one, she had no idea if he actually still had a comlink or if it had been confiscated, and for another…well…what was she supposed to say?

They might have formed a tentative friendship over the course of the weeks they were trapped in the Mansion and she was teaching him to dance, but that job was done. In the cold, groggy light of day, the erstwhile magic of the dance floor the night before seemed like it belong to a distant dream.

*Besides,* she told herself a moment later, settling down on the other end of the couch from Derek with a cup of coffee after she made a trip to the kitchen, *it's not like you're probably going to hear from him. Why would you? They're not stuck in the Mansion, he knows how to dance, and Kedis has an audience with the Triumvirate. There's no reason for him to contact you.*

Lilia frowned down into her coffee, remembering Derek's words of caution several weeks before. He had warned her against getting too comfortable around Jasper, lest people assume the wrong thing later on. At the time, the idea of people across the Coalition thinking she was involved with a Tarynian soldier had made her shudder.

Now, it was easier to see Jasper as the man behind the uniform...but she still didn't like the idea of people thinking she was involved with him.

*Unlike Alexis, who I deliberately* made *think we were involved.*

"What's the matter, Lil? You look like you just swallowed a raw egg."

She looked up with a start, to find Michael gazing at her in concern. She bit her lip and held up her comlink. "I've got to explain things to Alexis."

"We haven't got time now." Derek did not look up from his datapad. "You and Kevin need to eat something and get ready to go. Grandfather prefers to be early."

"Right." Lilia knew that, but it didn't ease the guilt she felt. Shoving her comlink back into her ISF, she went to rouse her brother.

Halfway to Kevin's room, another channel request niggled in the back of her mind.

[Thank God,] Lon said as soon as she allowed him access. [I've been trying to get a hold of you two since last night. What gives?]

Lilia pursed her lips, even though he couldn't see her. [It's a long story.]

[Did you open a portal? Go off-world?]

[No.]

A pause. [Then what happened? Condense it for me.]

Lilia debated it for two whole seconds before she went ahead and gave him a brief rundown.

At the end, Lon said, [You've got to be kidding me. Impactors?]

[Nope.]

[Okay, well, we'll worry about that later. You heard from the Triumvirate yet?]

Lilia reached Kevin's door. [We're supposed to be there at one.]

[Interesting. They're seeing us after you. Anyway—] she could almost *see* her brother shaking his head, [—just wanted to tell you that Kedis is keeping his mouth shut about the transporter. One less thing to worry about. At least for now,] he added darkly.

A huge weight lifted off Lilia, its removal so sudden that she sagged against Kevin's door. [Really?]

[Yeah.]

[Well, that definitely…simplifies things.]

[Thought it might.]

Pressing a hand against her chest, Lilia closed her eyes. *Thank you, Jesus.* After a few seconds, she said, [Kevin was going to tell them about his transporter, if it came to that.]

[Now he doesn't have to.]

[Praise the Lord.] Lilia straightened up. [Are you doing all right?]

[Dandy. They've got us in the Beliana.]

[The Beliana?] Lilia blinked, impressed. [Wow.]

[Yep.] Lon abruptly switched subjects. [Is Kevin okay? I still can't reach him.]

[That's because he's still asleep.] Lilia rapped sharply on her twin's door. [I'm actually in the process of waking him up now. We've got to get ready to go.]

[Okay.] Lon sounded relieved. [Well, I'll see you later then.]

He closed his channel just as Lilia knocked on the door again. After a moment, it slid aside to reveal a sleepy, rumpled Kevin.

"Time to wake up," Lilia said brightly. "I've got some good news."

The twins were finishing brunch—or attempting to finish; neither of them had much of an appetite with their impending interview before the Triumvirate looming over their heads—when a sudden thought made Lilia jolt in her seat, nearly spilling her iced tea. She looked across the dining room table at Kevin and opened a Nancom channel to him. Zoë was in the kitchen, but this wasn't anything she wanted the 'bot overhearing. [We've got to tell Nob about the impactors.]

Her brother's violet eyes widened in comprehension. [Yes, we do. Because God only knows—]

[—what'll happen between now and our NCDC hearing,] Lilia finished.

They opened a joint Nancom channel to their fellow Guardian. They had met Nob Farr, a computer programmer by trade, on the NCDC mission to Lanx to rescue the transporter and the scientists responsible for inventing it. At the end of that mission, Nob had determined that he, Erik Holt, and the twins were all nano-genetic anomalies—Guardians who would be unable to have their nanites removed in order to leave the NCDC. He had also been helping the twins with research into Freedom's Children and the connections between that group, the NCDC, and Dr. Banx.

Nob answered immediately. [I was wondering when I'd hear from you. Seen the news?]

The twins shared another glance across the table. [If by news you mean, have we heard about—]

[—Glo'Stea, then, yes. We've heard.]

Nob took that in stride. [Have you talked to your grandfather?]

[Did that on the trip back to Sonela this morning,] Kevin said.

[Why?] Lilia asked. [Have you learned something else?]

[Nothing of note.] Nob sounded mildly frustrated. [There's a lot of comm chatter coming from Glo'Stea, most of it from the Tarynians. To say they're not happy would be an understatement.]

Lilia took a half-hearted sip of her tea. [That's not surprising.]

[Guess it's a good thing you got Kedis in when you did. According to the media, he's speaking to the Triumvirate this afternoon?]

[As far as we know, yes.] Lilia pinched the bridge of her nose. [We're speaking to them before that.]

[They want to interrogate you?]

[Yeah,] Kevin said, [but that's not—]

[—why we Nancommed you.] Lilia pushed her half-finished plate aside. [See, the thing is, Nob, we found out last night that the NCDC has developed something that can basically—]

[—neutralize a Guardian's nanites,] Kevin said flatly. [Alan Birch shot Lilia with it, and some other Guardian shot me.]

[Birch called it an 'impactor'.] Lilia twisted her fingers together on the table. [It looked like he shot me with a little ball of electricity. We timed it—our nanites were frozen afterward for six hours.]

[Have you heard of these things?] Kevin asked.

Nob was silent for a moment. [No,] he said at last. [I've never heard of an impactor before. But—]

[But, what?] Lilia prompted, when he did not immediately finish.

[I've been wondering lately how the NCDC keeps rogue Guardians under control. It shouldn't be much of an issue for them—they're far too careful in choosing who's allowed to join—but... that's interesting.]

[If we hadn't already had experience with our nanites freezing thanks to opening portals,] Kevin said bluntly, [I'd have been pretty scared.]

Lilia snorted softly. [You and me both.]

[Speaking of the NCDC, have you heard from them yet?]

The twins exchanged grim glances. [Not yet, but—]

[—we expect to.]

[I don't know what to tell you, other than to not let them know you know anything.] An apologetic note slid into Nob's Nancom voice. [Even though you successfully managed to keep your Guardian status from the Tarynians, I suspect they'll attempt to dismiss you.]

Lilia bit the inside of her lip. [That—]

[—doesn't surprise us.]

Derek poked his head into the dining room. "You two ready to go?"

"Yes." Lilia pushed her chair back from the table.

[Look, we've got to go now,] Kevin told Nob. [We'll keep you apprised of any new developments.]

[All right. Have fun with the Triumvirate.] His Nancom voice was very dry. [I'm glad it's you and not me.]

The twins exchanged wry looks. Together, they said, [You're too kind.]

# Chapter 10

T HOUGH their grandfather had been a Representative of Sector 4 their entire lives, the twins had only ever visited the seat of Sta'Gloa's government twice. The last time they had set foot in the Four Towers, they had been twelve.

[It's a little different when you're getting ready to face the Triumvirate,] Kevin said via Nancom, as their skimmer pulled into the underground VIP parking bay beneath Triumvirate Tower behind their grandfather's. He looked a little pale around the edges, but his jaw was set.

Lilia could only nod; she felt like they were marching to their doom.

Aiden led the way across the parking bay to the accelevator bank that swept them up to the ground-floor lobby, where the twins were issued visitor's badges. Aiden then steered his hoverchair through the semi-crowded halls to one of the triangular plastiglass accelevators that would take them all the way up to the Chamber, which occupied the top three floors of Triumvirate Tower.

No one spoke as they ascended level after level, whizzing past the glittering, spoke-like plastiglass corridors that connected Triumvirate Tower every tenth floor to the three shorter, also triangular Towers housing the Departments of Finance, Security, and Internal Affairs surrounding it. Aiden's face had settled into a calm, serene expression that hid whatever doubts and fears he might have been battling. It was his politician's face, and his grandchildren knew it well.

At last the accelevator door opened on a long, tall corridor known as the Hall to the myriad aides, bodyguards, and other staff who waited there during Triumvirate sessions. Standing as tall as the Chamber and running the full length of the top floor, the Hall was lined with floor-to-ceiling windows, elegant chairs and couches, and the occasional potted plant. Another triangular accelevator stood at the opposite end of the Hall. Dozens of men and women were milling around, and the twins noticed more than one military uniforms mixed in for good measure.

As they neared the massive double doors that led into the Chamber, Aiden stopped his hoverchair and wheeled around to face the twins. "This is where we part ways for the time being." He glanced from Kevin to Lilia in turn. "I will be praying for you to find the right words."

"Thank you," Kevin said.

Lilia remained silent; the words had stuck in her throat. She was acutely aware of the stares and whispers that erupted as a result of their entrance. By now what they had done was all over the ComNet. A few of the stares were curious, but most of them held cold derision, scorn, and, in a few cases, fury.

While Aiden continued on into the Chamber, Derek took them aside. "You'll wait out here until they send for you." He paused apologetically. "I have no idea how long that will take."

"We understand." Kevin tried for a smile. "We'll be all right."

Derek's green eyes, so like their grandfather's, flicked to Lilia. She couldn't summon a smile—she was far too nervous for that— but she nodded with as much encouragement as she could muster.

"You'll be fine," Derek assured them, before hastening after their grandfather.

Lilia and Kevin sank into unoccupied seats on one of the long dark gold couches. Michael did not join them, but remained standing, leaning up against one of the walls separating the windows and keeping an eye on the length of the Hall.

A little while later, the accelevator doors opened and disgorged one of the last people the twins wanted to see at this particular moment—Alan Birch.

[There's no escaping him,] Kevin muttered resentfully to Lilia and Michael via Nancom.

[Not when he works here.] Lilia tried to keep her expression neutral as Birch swaggered up to them.

Michael went very still, but did not move from his spot. [Don't let him rattle you.]

Lilia half-expected Birch to broadcast his reason for seeking them out to the entire Hall, but he surprised her by keeping his voice low.

"I see you made it."

Kevin regarded him coolly, raising both eyebrows. "You doubted we'd show up? To a summons from the Triumvirate?"

Birch ignored him. "Your NCDC disciplinary hearing is at nine AM tomorrow morning, at the Cramer Building." He smiled, but it held only frost. "Don't be late."

Lilia finally found her voice. "You came all this way just to tell us that in person?" She frowned at him. "Don't you have anything better to do?"

"Unless," Kevin put in quietly, "you're planning on *shooting* us again?"

"Don't tempt me." Birch's fingers twitched, as though he was itching to reach into his ISF for his impactor. "It's occurred to me that the two of you might get your story…straight…if you can't communicate via…other means."

Kevin lifted his chin, as though daring him to try it.

Michael chose that moment to intervene. "That'd be a great move, Birch. Shoot them in front of all these witnesses." He allowed himself a smile. "You'll be under arrest before anybody realizes they're not hurt."

Birch's upper lip curled in a sneer. "You're all traitors, and I hope you get what's coming to you."

Lilia narrowed her eyes at him, but before she could say anything, Birch touched the tiny comlink he wore in his ear. "Understood." He gave Michael and the twins one last scornful look and departed, skirting around another cluster of people who had just disembarked from the accelevator.

Lilia recognized the short, black-haired man in the forefront as Dion Pamos and her heart sank. *Oh, don't look at us*, she prayed. *Just walk on by and don't pay any attention to us.*

It was not to be.

Though Pamos was obviously running late, his sharp, beady eyes fell on the twins and his steps slowed. His entourage slowed with him. "Ah, yes. The Strong twins. You'll be telling us all about your part in this little coup shortly, won't you?"

It was not a question.

Pamos smiled, and unlike Birch, he seemed genuinely cheerful. "Oh, this will be an interesting tale."

A fine shudder worked its way down Lilia's spine, dancing from vertebra to vertebra. [He is entirely too happy about this.]

[He *wants* the Coalition to join the G.U., remember?] Michael reminded them.

"We will see you shortly," Pamos promised, and swept onward.

Lilia and Kevin exchanged dubious glances after the double doors swung shut behind the Sta'Gloan Representative on noiseless hinges.

Less than ten minutes later, both of them received incoming channel requests from a familiar Guardian—Riley Callahan, their handler at the NCDC.

[You two have managed to land yourselves in a fine mess,] he said by way of greeting.

Kevin barely restrained a scowl. [Good morning to you too, Mr. Callahan.]

[I'd ask for the details, but I'm going to get them soon enough. You're both required to appear before the NCDC disciplinary hearing board tomorrow morning at nine AM.]

[We know,] Lilia told him. [Alan Birch just informed us.]

[Birch?] Callahan sounded startled. [I only just received the news myself.]

[Apparently, he's—]

[—got connections.]

[Apparently,] Callahan repeated dryly. [Where are you now?]

The twins exchanged glances again. [Triumvirate Tower.]

[What?] For an instant, Callahan sounded taken aback, but then his Nancom voice turned sage. [Ah, yes. You have some explaining to do to the higher-ups.]

[Something like that,] Kevin agreed.

[The NCDC wants to see your brother as well,] Callahan continued, [but from the look of things he'll be tied up for a while with this liaison deal.]

Kevin caught Lilia's eye. [Can you tell us anything about this hearing tomorrow?]

[Unfortunately, I can't. The only thing I know for certain is that they will be determining whether or not you are allowed to remain Guardians, after…well, after the events that unfolded last night.]

Lilia went very still. They'd figured as much, after all of the hammer-heavy hints Birch had dropped, but to have it confirmed… She swallowed; her mouth had gone bone dry. [We didn't reveal anything about our Guardian status to Kedis or his men.]

*Other than our connection to the transporter*, she added silently.

[That's what they'll be investigating.] Callahan paused. [While I am glad to hear it, I regret to say that it probably won't make much of a difference. This kind of hearing almost never ends well.]

[Thanks for the heads up,] Kevin said. [Will you be there tomorrow?]

[I will. As your handler, I am required to attend.]

[Well, we'll see you then,] Lilia said.

After Callahan closed his channel, they looked at each other again, the same thought running through both their minds. *What will the NCDC do when they find out we're both nano-genetic anomalies?*

As far as they had been able to discover, the NCDC preferred to sweep little embarrassments like them under the rug and pretend they didn't exist. No one knew why some people ended up being anomalies…and while the NCDC could tell after infusion that someone was an anomaly, they had no way of fixing the problem. Nob Farr had been investigating for months, but all his time and effort hadn't turned up much in the way of helpful information.

An hour later, the twins were still sitting in the Hall waiting to be summoned. "I wish they'd just get it over with already," Kevin muttered.

"You and me both." Lilia stood for a moment to stretch her legs. She still felt shaky and nauseous; the anticipation of speaking to the Triumvirate was killing her.

Her comlink vibrated in her pocket; she almost ignored it. She didn't particularly want to talk to anyone right now. However…it *was* a temporary distraction. Sighing, Lilia pulled the device out of her pocket and glanced at it.

*This is Jasper Wright*, the message read. *I have a comlink now. Hope you are well after last night's events.*

Her heart promptly stuttered in her chest; she sank back into her seat. Jasper had a comlink—and hadn't he assured her just before Lon announced Kedis at the Gala that he'd memorized her comm details just in case?

Lilia pursed her lips, willing her heart rate to return to normal. *I'm fine, thanks*, she sent back. *Kevin and I got arrested, but every-*

*THING'S GOOD NOW.* She cast about for something else to say, but her mind had suddenly gone blank.

Her comlink vibrated again. *I ASSUME YOU'VE HEARD THE NEWS ABOUT GLO'STEA?*

*I'VE HEARD.* She snorted softly. *IT'S IMPOSSIBLE TO ESCAPE IT.*

*HOW DID THEY DO IT?* Jasper asked.

She barely had time to frown at that before another line of text appeared.

*THAT'S A RHETORICAL QUESTION. I DON'T EXPECT YOU TO KNOW. BUT THIS IS HUGE.*

*TELL ME ABOUT IT,* she replied.

*DO YOUR PEOPLE HAVE ANY IDEA WHAT KIND OF CHAOS THIS IS PROBABLY ALREADY CAUSING?*

Lilia's breath caught in her throat. A dozen different grim scenarios played out in her head—all the terrible things that could be happening on Glo'Stea right now. Her eyes flicked involuntarily to the Chamber doors, which were still closed.

*WE DO,* she sent back. *THAT'S WHY THE TRIUMVIRATE IS HOLDING AN EMERGENCY MEETING TODAY.*

Struck by a sudden thought, Lilia bit her lip and stared down at her comlink. *Two can play at this game.* If Jasper was fishing for information, that is. *Which, given his proximity to Kedis,* she thought grimly, *is not entirely outside the realm of possibility.*

Sitting here in the Hall, it was harder to remember that she halfway trusted Jasper. She almost thought he'd be disappointed in her lack of faith, except that she wasn't sure now how much he trusted her either.

Swallowing, she tapped out, *WHAT'S GOING TO HAPPEN ON YOUR END? WHAT WILL YOUR SOLDIERS ON GLO'STEA DO?*

Other than panic and start killing Glo'Steans, that is.

It took Jasper a long moment to reply, longer than the pause she'd just taken. When her comlink finally vibrated with an incoming message, all it said was, *I DON'T KNOW. THIS IS NEW.*

"That's an understatement if I ever heard one," Lilia muttered under her breath. Irritated, though she wasn't entirely sure why, she shoved her comlink back into her pocket and glared at the floor.

Kevin glanced sideways at her. "Did you say something?"

"No."

Her brother lifted an eyebrow at her terse reply, but returned to his own contemplation of the floor.

*THIS IS NEW,* Jasper had said.

Lilia snorted softly. *Of course it's new. Glo'Stea has never managed to pull off something like this before.*

Her thoughts turned to the islands that had, up until just last night, occupied the fringes of free Glo'Stea. Some of them—most of them, really, if she thought about it—had secondary shields. Her mouth twisted. Places like Kyman, the Christian medcenter where she'd worked up until the NCDC recalled her for that rescue mission to Uva. Those secondary shields would still protect those islands, but everything beyond them was vulnerable, open to attack from angry, terrified Tarynian soldiers who'd been stranded on-world.

For a second, she toyed with the idea of opening a portal to Kyman and paying her friend Greg Bhar a visit when they finished with everything at the Four Towers. Thanks to Banx's coordinate string, she knew she'd land on the beach, away from most prying eyes. And though Greg might bat an eye at her sudden reappearance—after she'd told him when a portal unceremoniously dumped her there that something was malfunctioning—she was sure she could come up with a good excuse.

*Except he's still probably not happy you left him in Tashjian*, a small voice in the back of her mind commented.

Lilia scowled. *Surely he's over that by now. It was for his own good; he has to have realized that.* Greg had made the insane choice to follow her through a portal; she was just happy she'd managed to leave him somewhere in free Glo'Stea before she got him killed. *I didn't need his death on my conscience.*

It was bad enough what she'd gone through in Challa.

A cold chill settled over Lilia like a whisper of icy air. She swallowed thickly, her mouth suddenly dry. She didn't want to think about Challa.

Challa was where she'd been arrested by G.U. forces who had thought she was part of a drug deal. Challa was where she'd nearly been raped…and shot her would-be rapist to escape. Challa was where she'd met Jasper for the first time, though she would deny that until the day she died.

The lieutenant had recognized her at the Mansion and confronted her, but she couldn't tell him the truth—for all sorts of reasons, only some of them having to do with portals and transporters and Guardians.

"Lilia?"

She looked up sharply to find Michael staring at her, his blond eyebrows knit together in concern.

"Are you all right?"

"I'm fine." Lilia straightened in her seat, gathering cool diffidence around herself like a cloak. "I was just…thinking."

Her older brother offered her a reassuring smile. "It's going to be all right."

Lilia smiled wanly back, but didn't reply. *I sure hope so.*

A moment later, Lon Nancommed them. [Am I interrupting anything?]

[Boredom,] Kevin replied. [We're still waiting to speak to the Triumvirate.]

[Where are you?]

[The Hall.] Lilia's eyes flicked hopefully to the doors again. [Just outside the Chamber.]

[Where are *you*?] Kevin asked in return.

[Level below you, I think. Somebody's office.]

[You made it here in one piece,] Lilia observed.

[Yeah.] Lon sounded amused, though it wasn't funny. [Listen, I—]

The twins lost whatever else he had been intending to say; at that moment, the Chamber's massive doors swung open far enough for a tall, dark-skinned woman in a midnight blue wrap dress to slip through them and emerge into the Hall.

Touching a mic at her throat with one hand, she glanced down at the datapad she held in the other and looked around the Hall. "Kevin and Lilia Strong, the Triumvirate will see you now."

A hundred butterflies exploded in Lilia's stomach. [Lon, we've—]

[—got to go,] Kevin finished. [They're calling us in.]

# CHAPTER 11

R ISING jerkily to their feet, the twins strode over to the woman with more confidence than either of them actually felt. Ignoring the dozens of curious eyes now fixed on them, they showed her their visitor's badges. After scrutinizing them, she affixed tiny mics to both of their collars and allowed them to step past her through the double doors.

Lilia's breath caught in her throat. The Chamber was *enormous*. She had seen holos, but that did not prepare one to see it in person. Three stories high, the massive triangular room was glassed in from ceiling to floor on two sides to provide a stunning view of Sonela. Sunlight streamed through the plastiglass windows.

Her attention immediately zeroed in on the semi-circle of glossy cherry chairs and tables fanned out around the center of the celadon marble floor, facing the north point of the Chamber, where the three Chief Ministers sat at a table. Her violet eyes widened; she darted a glance at Kevin. [They're all here in *person*.]

Because of the danger the blockade posed to interplanetary travel, usually only the Sta'Gloan Chief Minister attended Triumvirate sessions in person. The Chief Ministers of Lanx and Glo'Stea—along with many of their respective worlds' Representatives and Directors—attended via holograph. Today, however, the entire Triumvirate occupied the Chamber in bodily form.

[They've been using the transporter,] Kevin said wryly.

Together, the twins moved forward. They saw their grandfather and Dion Pamos seated in the Sta'Gloan section of the semi-circle of chairs in the center, and Martin Hollowell and Shane Briscoe in the Glo'Stean section on the left, but their gaze slid past all of them to rest on the dark-haired, coppery-skinned man standing at a small podium off to one side of the Chief Ministers. He was beckoning them forward, rather impatiently.

*Quin'lan Dunn, Chairman*, Lilia thought, recalling the brief run-down of Triumvirate members Derek had given them over brunch. Thanks to the media and Aiden's passing comments over the years, she and Kevin were already familiar with many of them by name, if not necessarily by sight.

Passing through the semi-circle of chairs into the center of the floor, they approached Dunn. The Chairman motioned for them to stand off to one side of his podium, where they would be visible to everyone.

He tapped a gold bell. "State your names for the record."

The twins complied, their magnified voices echoing in the silence of the Chamber. Lilia swallowed; she could *feel* the keen interest swirling through the atmosphere in here.

Dunn then leaned forward, his dark eyes intent on them. "It is our understanding that you two were directly involved in helping your brother, Lon Strong, smuggle three Galactic Union citizens past Sta'Gloa's shield and into the Cuomo Convention Center last night."

Kevin cleared his throat. "With all due respect, sir, we only helped Ambassador Kedis get into the Closing Ceremonies Gala so he could introduce himself and set up a meeting with the Triumvirate. We had nothing to do with getting him through the shield."

A murmur rippled around the Chamber at this. Lilia let her eyes dart over the rows of faces, but she didn't linger.

Dunn tapped his bell for silence. "You admit, then, that you knowingly aided and abetted three Galactic Union citizens on Sta'Gloan soil."

Internally, Lilia bristled, but she managed to keep her expression neutral. "We helped Ambassador Kedis and his escorts once we found out they were on Sta'Gloa, yes."

"In the interest of opening peace talks," Kevin added, lest anyone forget that important fact.

In the Sta'Gloan section, Dion Pamos rose to his feet, almost lazily. He represented Sector 1, which, incidentally, included Sonela.

Quin'lan Dunn tapped the bell again. "The Triumvirate recognizes Representative Pamos."

"Miss Strong, Captain Strong…" Pamos's voice carried an innocently curious lilt that immediately put them on edge, "I think we would all like to know how you became involved in this, and why you would willingly risk treason charges."

Lilia and Kevin exchanged glances. [Here—]

[—goes.] Kevin cleared his throat. "Some of you may know this already, but Lon, Lilia, and I spent the past two years on the fringes of free Glo'Stea. Lon and I worked as supply runners, while—"

"—I worked in medcenters," Lilia said. "We've seen firsthand the death and destruction this blockade has caused—"

"—and we thought this was an opportunity to stop the bloodshed." Kevin spread his hands. "The Ambassador was already on Sta'Gloa when we discovered our brother was still alive and he introduced us. What were we—"

"—supposed to do?"

"You should have called the authorities." Malik Thane, the redheaded Sta'Gloan Director of Security, regarded them frostily from his seat.

Pamos glanced over at Thane, before turning back to the twins and cocking an eyebrow.

"I considered that," Lilia said honestly. "But things were in such an uproar following the Opening Ball bombing and I know how much people in the Coalition hate the Tarynians for everything they've done." She took a breath. "I've hated them too." The words were hard to say. "But if there's a chance that things could be different, that we could stop our people from being killed—"

"—we had to take it," Kevin finished.

"I see." Pamos locked his hands behind his back, his dark eyes glittering. "Even though according to the laws of the Coalition such an act would certainly be viewed as treason?"

Lilia and Kevin exchanged darting glances. They'd had to ask themselves that same question.

"Yes," Kevin answered, his spine ramrod straight.

"It was the right thing to do," Lilia added, her heart pounding and her palms sweaty. "We thought it was a chance to help end the bloodshed, so we—"

"—ran with it."

Pamos offered them a tiny bow, practically radiating smug satisfaction. "Thank you for your honesty."

While the Sta'Gloan Representative resumed his seat, Quin'lan Dunn glanced around the Chamber. "Does anyone else have questions for these witnesses?"

Lilia did not dare relax. [That was—]

[—surprisingly easy,] Kevin agreed. [Too easy.]

Malik Thane stood and was recognized. For a second, the Director said nothing; he merely regarded the twins as though they were complex security algorithms he intended to puzzle out. Other than Shane Briscoe, he was the youngest member of the Triumvirate—and from a few of Aiden's comments, the twins suspected he was arguably one of the most ambitious as well.

Finally, just when the atmosphere in the Chamber started to shift into something approaching restlessness, Thane drawled, "I suppose one might say you've given ample, even admirable justification for your actions. However," his voice grew colder, "it falls to me to ask perhaps the most pertinent question."

He straightened, his brown eyes boring holes in them, and the air in the Chamber electrified. "*How* did the three of you manage to smuggle three Tarynians past the Gala's considerable security?"

*This is it.* Lilia's heart began to pound in her chest again.

Kevin glanced at her before shrugging casually. "Well, it helped that they had flawless Sta'Gloan identcards."

Startled, uneasy murmurs greeted this announcement; they heard several loud "What?"'s in three different languages.

Quin'lan Dunn tapped his bell for silence and leaned forward on his podium. "What do you mean?"

"I mean that the Tarynians have the ability to forge Sta'Gloan identcards." Kevin shook his head. "I don't know how they do it, or how long they've been doing it, or if they can do the same with Lanxian and Glo'Stean identcards, but when we met the Ambassador, he had identification that enabled him to pass as a Sta'Gloan citizen."

He cracked a wry smile. "Except, of course, for the fact that he doesn't actually *speak* Sta'Gloan."

Malik Thane did not look amused. More murmurs rippled around the Chamber.

Lilia picked up the narrative. "We decided I would bring Lieutenant Wright to the Gala as my escort, and then—"

"—I slipped the Ambassador and Corporal Renner in with me," Kevin finished. It was vague, but they couldn't be any more specific.

"You slipped them in with you?" Thane's voice dripped disdain. "Just like that."

Kevin gave a half-apologetic shrug. "There were an awful lot of people in attendance that night, and I was looking for an opportunity. Gala security had no reason to think any of them were threats, and so it all worked out."

*Please believe us*, Lilia prayed.

Thane looked like he didn't quite buy it, but after a long pause he sat down without another word.

Quin'lan Dunn looked around the Chamber again. "Any other questions?"

In the Glo'Stean section, Martin Hollowell rose to his feet.

Dunn tapped his bell. "The Triumvirate recognizes Representative Hollowell."

"Are we to understand that your grandfather, Representative Monroe," Hollowell motioned to Aiden across the row of seats, "knew nothing of any of this?" His expression narrowed. "It would certainly have made your task easier if you had his help arranging things." He nodded to Aiden. "No offense, Representative."

Aiden turned a hand palm up, his expression calm. "None taken."

"He didn't know a thing," Kevin said firmly. "He was in intensive care when we first learned Lon was alive and we—"

"—weren't sure if he was going to make it." Lilia resisted the urge to twist her fingers together; it was difficult. "Then, later, we were afraid the shock would—" she hesitated.

*Kill him*, was what she wanted to say, but he was sitting right there. Neither she nor Kevin could look in his direction.

"We were afraid the shock would be more than he could handle in his condition," Kevin finished diplomatically.

"I see." Hollowell offered Quin'lan Dunn a slight bow. "I have no further questions, Chairman."

Quin'lan Dunn tapped his bell again. "Anyone else?"

The twins fielded a few more probing questions and then, after a glance in the Chief Ministers' direction, Dunn dismissed them. "You may leave the Chamber. Do not leave Triumvirate Tower. The Triumvirate will summon you when we reach a decision in your case." He rapped the bell sharply; the sound seemed to echo throughout the Chamber with a foreboding sense of finality.

Hardly daring to breathe, Lilia and Kevin bowed to the Chief Ministers and Quin'lan Dunn before turning to face the rest of the Triumvirate and bowing again. Straightening, they marched across the celadon floor to the double doors without meeting anyone's eyes.

Neither of them wanted to see the disappointment on their grandfather's face…or that of Martin Hollowell.

They escaped into the Hall, but neither of them relaxed. Almost every eye had turned to watch them emerge, though the quiet chatter of dozens of conversations still filled the air. A quick glance up and down the Hall netted them their brother's location; Michael had not moved.

"How'd it go?" he asked quietly as they approached. "You look a little pale."

"It went fine, I guess." Kevin raised one shoulder in a shrug. "They told us—"

"—they'll call us after they decide what to do with us." Lilia forced herself to keep her body language open and confident. It was difficult; she wanted to wrap her arms around herself and disappear. *What will they do to us?*

Michael switched to Nancom. [No questions about how you smuggled Kedis in?]

[Director Thane questioned us, but they seemed to buy it.] Kevin shook his head. [Either that or they're not really concerned about *how* we got into the Gala right now.]

[Bigger things to worry about,] Lilia agreed. Aloud, she said, "In the meantime, we're stuck here."

Kevin groaned, just barely resisting the urge to run hand over his face. "We could be here for *hours*."

"That's probably not a bad thing," Michael said soberly.

Lilia's stomach churned uneasily. "Why?"

"Because the second you two set foot in the lobby downstairs, you're going to be swamped by the media."

Kevin shrugged, looking nonplussed. "We can handle that, Mike."

"Maybe so, but Derek just told me that in the past few hours Grandfather's gotten a lot of angry messages and threats that now involve you two." Michael's violet eyes, so like the twins', filled with concern. "It's just as well you can't leave for a while. You can wait this out in Grandfather's office and then we'll all brave the media storm and head home together."

Lilia blanched.

"But what if the Triumvirate reaches a decision this morning?" Kevin protested. "I don't want to be stuck here all day."

"Trust me, they won't," Michael said bluntly, shaking his head. "They don't decide anything that quickly. Especially not something involving high treason." He gave them both significant looks. "This is better than winding up dead."

He did not have to mention that someone had already tried to kill their grandfather several times now; they remembered. Lilia had been injured during that first assassination attempt. And now that they were in the middle of everything?

[Even so, we're *Guardians*,] Kevin said stubbornly, switching to Nancom. [I think we could handle it.]

Michael just raised a blond eyebrow. [Do you want the entire Coalition *knowing* you're Guardians? Because if there's an incident, the entire Coalition is going to know about it by the end of the day.]

*I definitely do* not *want that.* Lilia bit her lip. [I hate to say it, but he's got a point, Kev.]

After a long moment, Kevin blew out an impatient breath. "Fine."

"Good. I'll walk you down." Michael straightened, but at that moment, the noise level in the Hall spiked.

They all glanced toward the other end of the Hall, where a large knot of people had just emerged from the accelevator and were now striding up toward the Chamber's entrance. Lilia recognized the security team for what it was, and as they drew nearer, she recognized the four men in their midst: Lon, Kedis, Renner, and Jasper.

"Show time," Michael murmured under his breath.

Kedis wore the same tuxedo he had worn to the Gala the night before, but it had been cleaned and pressed. He looked calm and confident. Catching sight of the twins, he offered them a brief nod and a flash of a smile before his security escort came to a halt in front of the double doors.

Lilia's eyes skipped involuntarily from the Ambassador to her brother, who wore a cocky expression she knew too well, before settling on Jasper. Their eyes met; he gave her the barest of nods before facing forward and schooling his expression into impassivity as the tall dark-skinned woman in the blue dress slipped out of the Chamber to greet Kedis.

"Pity we can't sit in on that," Kevin remarked, as he and Michael turned to leave.

The curious eyes following them made the hair on the back of her neck prickle; she swallowed uncomfortably. *I can't* wait *to get out of here.*

# CHAPTER 12

THE trip from the Beliana hotel to the Four Towers went smooth-ly; Corran and his team and Triumvirate Tower security did an excellent job coordinating everything. Lon half-expected something to go wrong, but nothing did. He, Kedis, Jasper, and Renner were escorted to a secure office one level below the Hall to wait until the Triumvirate was ready for them.

When a team of Triumvirate security officers arrived to escort Lon up to the Hall, Kedis rose from the comfortable leather chair he had been occupying behind a desk made from glass and twisted black metal. "We will all go," he announced breezily.

They all stared at him. The security officers exchanged dubious glances, indicating they, too, had been outfitted with autotranslators. "Sir," one of them began, a beefy man with a flat face and sharp brown eyes, "our instructions are to bring Captain Strong and Captain Strong alone."

"I beg to differ." Kedis waved a hand, smiling easily. "I cannot be parted from my liaison. You understand, I'm sure."

The glint in the Ambassador's dark eyes warned Lon the Taryn-ian was planning something, but Lon wasn't entirely sure what to expect. He glanced over at Jasper and Renner, but the two soldiers seemed equally in the dark. *Okay, then.*

Lon squared his shoulders. Seconds were slipping past; they didn't have time for an argument.

But before he could speak, Corran said dryly, "I wouldn't argue with the Ambassador. This is above our pay grade." He nodded to the ceiling. "They can sort it out upstairs."

The security officers exchanged glances again and then shrugged.

It took only a few moments to traverse the halls separating them from the nearest accelevator that would whisk them up to the top of Triumvirate Tower. When they stepped out of the triangular accelevator into the Hall, Lon thought he glimpsed familiar figures in the distance. As they drew nearer, the figures resolved themselves into Lilia, Kevin, and Michael.

He did not have time to speak to them, however. Kedis, surrounded by Corran and his men, marched straight to the Chamber entrance. A tall, dark-skinned woman in a dark blue dress had just emerged from the double doors.

Looking up from her datapad, the woman asked in an amplified musical voice, "Captain Lon Strong?"

Lon raised a hand. "That would be me."

"The Triumvirate will see you now." The woman swept a hand toward the double doors.

Before Lon had even taken a step forward, Kedis offered the woman a charming smile. "I will be accompanying Captain Strong." He held out a hand. "Ambassador Leo Kedis."

After barely a second's worth of hesitation, the woman shook his hand. "Ambassador." She had no difficulty understanding Kedis's words; she, too, wore an autotranslator. "The Triumvirate will be receiving you shortly."

"Oh, I am aware of that," Kedis said pleasantly. "But Captain Strong is my Coalition liaison, and I prefer not to be separated from him."

To her credit, the woman maintained a pleasantly neutral expression. "One moment, please, Ambassador." She slipped back through the double doors.

Lon glanced sideways at Kedis, but the Ambassador said nothing. He merely smiled and locked his hands behind his back, waiting. Lon then looked at Jasper, whose face was expressionless, but the Lieutenant gave his head the tiniest of shakes.

Lon pasted a cordial smile on his face, belying the unease he felt. *The Triumvirate might have decided when they want to talk to Kedis, but the Ambassador's going to play by his own rules.* He wondered what impact this would have on his own interview with the Triumvirate. *It'd be nice if I got out of it entirely.*

A moment later, the woman returned. "Ambassador, the Triumvirate will see you now."

Kedis's face showed none of the triumph he must have been feeling. "I thank you." He strode into the Chamber and Lon followed. Jasper, Renner, and Corran and his security team would remain in the Hall with everyone else.

Lon had to restrain a whistle as he took in the magnitude of the Chamber, but if Kedis was impressed, he let none of it show. *Wonder if his palms are sweaty too*, Lon thought sourly, discreetly wiping his hands against his trousers. He resisted the urge to shift on his feet. *I think I'd rather take on a pack of Piranha fighters than face this lot.*

Fleetingly, he wished he was back aboard the *Star*…but the *Crimson Star* was gone. The twins had the *Talia* now—which he had yet to set eyes on—but his era was gone. He felt it in his bones; the strangest sense of mingled finality and foreboding.

When the Chairman tapped his gold bell, Lon expected him to run them through some sort of formal opening before things really got started, but to his surprise, Quin'lan Dunn only glanced solemnly around the Chamber before intoning, "This special convening of the Triumvirate will come to order. The Triumvirate welcomes—"

A low wave of murmurs greeted this.

"—and recognizes Galactic Union Ambassador Leo Kedis."

Absolute silence met this pronouncement. From his spot beside Lon, toward the rear of the Chamber, Kedis glided forward. He strode purposefully into the space between the semi-circle of Representatives and Directors and the three Chief Ministers at the north point of the room and took the position Dunn indicated. From here he could address the entire Chamber.

Lon stayed where he was. *Everyone should have autotranslators, so he won't need me to interpret.*

Kedis offered the Triumvirate a sweeping bow, before straightening and smiling broadly. "Ladies and gentlemen of the Triumvirate, on behalf of the Galactic Union, I thank you for welcoming me here today. It is my dearest hope that our two sovereign powers may find common ground and a way to work with each other."

The silence in the Chamber was so complete Lon thought it a wonder they couldn't all hear each other breathe.

"The magnitude of this historic moment aside—" Kedis spread his arms to encompass the entire Chamber, "—may I congratulate you on another historic achievement, a technological marvel that is already changing the galaxy as we know it?"

*He wouldn't.* Lon's eyes widened. *Surely he's not going to lead with—*

"The Coalition has invented the galaxy's first teleportation device." Kedis's dark eyes glittered. "This is incredible. Truly, the magnitude of this achievement takes my breath away."

Lon wanted to tell him that flattery would get him nowhere with this crowd, but then he reminded himself that they were politicians, so all bets were off.

"I must also," Kedis continued, "congratulate you on successfully implementing the remainder of Glo'Stea's planetary shield. That was a masterful stroke, and I am not too proud to admit that our Blockade and ground forces on Glo'Stea were caught unawares."

*Wait for it.* Lon narrowed his eyes. *Wait for it...*

"However, even you must concede Admiral Chesnee has shown great aptitude for succeeding where his predecessors have failed" Kedis spread his hands. "It would be a shame for more loss of life and property on either side when we have such a momentous opportunity such as this before us."

Hugh Koen, Sta'Gloan Chief Minister, glanced sideways at his fellow Chief Ministers. He was a stately middle-aged man with silver-streaked dark hair and sharp features. "What exactly are you proposing, Ambassador?"

"At this precise moment?" Kedis inclined his head in a respectful nod. "Another cease-fire, Chief Minister. And after that? I propose the Coalition and the Galactic Union open negotiations for peace."

Low murmurs rippled around the Chamber.

Lon cast a discreet glance left and right. *They can't have* not *seen that coming.* It was a good move—really the only opening gambit Kedis could make. *I can't imagine Grandfather and the rest of the Triumvirate would open negotiations with the G.U. while our people and our ships are being destroyed.*

It would be suicide—political or otherwise.

*And, doing it this way enables the Triumvirate to save face, since they don't have to immediately demand a cease-fire themselves.* Lon glanced toward the Sta'Gloan section, where his grandfather sat, wishing he could see faces. All he could see from this vantage point were Kedis, Dunn, the Chief Ministers, and the backs of everyone else's heads. *Wonder what Grandfather thinks of all this.*

For his part, Aiden was thinking about the last time Kedis had proposed a cease-fire. At the time, the Ambassador had been addressing the Triumvirate via a hologram transmitted from Admiral Chesnee's flagship—and the Triumvirate had not allowed him to see the chaos that had accompanied voting on that proposal. *Now, what choice do we have? Politely toss him out?* He restrained a snort at the thought.

He glanced left and right along the semi-circle of chairs without moving his head. He could not remember the last time the Triumvirate had met on a Sunday—even in the midst of Chesnee's successful breach of Lanx's planetary shield. *Given our circumstances, however, we had little choice.*

They now had a Galactic Union Ambassador on their hands… and Glo'Stea's now-intact planetary shield meant blood would soon be staining her oceans red again.

If conflict between the Glo'Stean Resistance, the G.U. occupation forces, and the so-called Freedom's Children hadn't already begun.

Communication with the quarter of Glo'Stea under G.U. control was questionable at the moment, that much Aiden knew for certain. The Tarynians had been jamming Glo'Stean communications for years, which had not completely succeeded, but with the added chaos of panicked messages being sent back and forth by citizens and soldiers alike, everything was a rather tangled mess.

A glance toward the Chief Ministers showed them leaning their heads together, hands over the mics attached to their collars, deliberating in voices too low for anyone else to catch.

Resignation mixed with a prickle of irritation settled over Aiden. *We* must *vote on this cease-fire.* Unless all three Chief Ministers attempted an unprecedented executive override of the Triumvirate's customary procedure, there would be no getting around it. *And that would reveal far too much about our state of affairs to Kedis than any of us would like.*

Before anyone could respond—or object—Kedis spread his hands in a gesture of cooperation. "If you would prefer, members of the Triumvirate, I can step out for a moment?" He trailed off politely.

Aiden's eyebrows rose a fraction; he was impressed, despite himself. *Very adroit.*

"That won't be necessary."

All heads whipped toward the three Chief Ministers. Glo'Stean Chief Minister Devlin Vance had risen to his feet. He had light brown skin, dark eyes, and a pointy chin. He looked older than his fifty-two years; being Chief Minister of a world under attack had aged him prematurely. His limp black hair was streaked with gray.

Aiden was hard-pressed to keep his surprise from showing in his expression. Vance did not tend to speak as often as the other two Chief Ministers; he favored silence over blustering in the face of his world's weaker position in the Coalition. *This business with Glo'Stea's shield seems to have emboldened him.*

Dunn tapped his bell. "The Triumvirate recognizes Chief Minister Devlin Vance."

"Put the cease-fire to a vote," Vance said unexpectedly, drawing himself up to his full height and sweeping his gaze around the Chamber. "We Glo'Steans are the ones who bear the brunt of the loss of life and property the Ambassador mentioned. Every moment we delay, more of my—our people—suffer."

Aiden thought Dunn handled his surprise well. The Chairman tapped his gold bell. "Chief Minister Vance has made a motion to vote on Ambassador Kedis's proposal to negotiate a cease-fire. Do I have a second?"

Several hands shot up, Dion Pamos's first and foremost, and several voices spoke at once. "I second that."

"Motion passed." Another peal of the bell.

"Chairman, a word?"

Dunn glanced toward the Lanxian section, where Representative Zane Chas had risen ponderously to his feet. "The Triumvirate recognizes Representative Chas."

"I believe we require a stipulation as part of this cease-fire." Chas looked from Kedis to the Chief Ministers, and then around at his colleagues. He was tall and broad-shouldered, with short brown hair pulled back in a ponytail and a neatly-trimmed beard. He also had ties to one of Lanx's largest manufacturing companies. "Obviously at this point it is too great a concession to ask that all G.U. forces be withdrawn from our system, but I would propose that the mining stations be freed."

"I second that proposal." Nolan Snyder, also from Lanx, rose to his feet as well. He was the Representative of Sector 4, where Uva, one of the cities G.U. forces currently held, was located. Already a beefy man, he had gained a good deal more weight over the past couple of months from stress. He wiped his flushed, sweaty forehead with a handkerchief. "In fact, I think that's quite reasonable, given the circumstances."

All eyes swung to Kedis, whose expression remained affable. He considered for a moment—or pretended to consider, Aiden was not sure which—before inclining his head. "I believe we can arrange that."

"You *believe* you can, or you can in fact arrange this?" Snyder asked shrewdly, pale eyes narrowing.

Kedis allowed himself a slight smile. "I can—and will—arrange it, Representative. You have my word."

Snyder scrutinized him for a few seconds before nodding to himself and resuming his seat.

Dunn glanced around the Chamber again. "If there is nothing else…" He waited a few seconds, but no one else spoke. "Very well. Ladies and gentlemen of the Triumvirate, please cast your votes."

As he touched the panel on the table before him to indicate his choice, Aiden wondered if any of his colleagues would be foolish enough—or prideful enough, or angry enough, in Martin Hollowell's case—to actually oppose this cease-fire.

He need not have wondered. All along the semi-circle, green bars flared to life to indicate the Triumvirate's unanimous acceptance.

"Well, Ambassador," Hugh Koen said, "you have your cease-fire. All hostilities between our peoples must come to an immediate halt, and the airspace around Xana 5 and Sapriske 6 must be cleared."

"I will be most pleased to see it happen." Kedis offered the Triumvirate a slight bow. "Thank you."

In the Glo'Stean section, Shane Briscoe rose to his feet. "Ambassador, when will you contact Admiral Chesnee?"

Dunn tapped his bell. "The Triumvirate recognizes Representative Briscoe." A touch of asperity colored his words; Aiden knew the Chairman would have preferred Briscoe to follow proper protocol in front of Kedis.

*Not that we always follow protocol anyway*, he thought wryly.

Kedis turned one hand palm up. "This very moment, Representative, if the Triumvirate will be so kind as to allow me the use of a secure comm channel to the *Winds of Change*. Provided," he added lightly, "the Triumvirate sends out its own notification of the cease-fire to the people of the Coalition, particularly the Glo'Stean Resistance."

A low murmur of agreement rippled around the Chamber.

The three Chief Ministers exchanged glances, and then Vance gave Kedis a decisive nod. "Consider it done."

Kedis's answering smile had a self-satisfied tinge. "Excellent."

# CHAPTER 13

*T*HIS, Admiral Chesnee thought darkly, glaring out through his office's wide viewport at the expanse of Lanx hanging in the distance, *can all be laid squarely at a certain ambassador's feet.*

Were Kedis less of the Senate's golden boy, High Command would hardly be breathing down his, Chesnee's, neck, demanding to know if Kedis was unharmed. And if he'd made any progress yet with the Coalition.

Chesnee suppressed a snort. *As if I would know.* Kedis barely saw fit to tell him anything. His last communiqué had been comprised solely of the fact that he had successfully made contact with the Triumvirate. No other details, and he had sent nothing since.

*Granted*, Chesnee admitted grudgingly, *it's been less than twenty-four hours.*

He had dutifully passed that information along to High Command, pleased to finally have something to report. A small corner of him had hoped it would allay some of the Senate's fears, given them a chance to go back to the much larger issues facing the Galactic Union at the moment. The rest of him knew it was a foolish, vain hope.

The idea of opening peace talks with the Coalition after two decades of enmity was beyond newsworthy.

*Not to mention the money to be made in some quarters.* Chesnee half-smiled. *Not that I'd call myself a cynical man.*

When the comm panel on the corner of his desk lit up with an incoming high-priority message a few moments later, the Admiral was not at all surprised.

Schooling his face into impassivity, he touched a button and the holographic head and shoulders of Fleet Admiral Joseph Tyler appeared on the other side of the desk.

"Good afternoon, Admiral." He discreetly reached for the volume control; Tyler had a voice like a foghorn. "To what do I owe the pleasure?"

"Chesnee." Tyler gave him a curt nod. His round face was redder than usual, making his silver hair stand out. "Any further news from Ambassador Kedis?"

"No, sir."

"Nothing?"

Chesnee raised his eyebrows a fraction. Tyler almost sounded… anxious. "Is the Senate putting more pressure on you, Admiral?"

Tyler huffed. "You have no idea, Giles. It was bad enough when all they had was the *hope* of him making contact. Now that he's gone and *done* it…" he trailed off, shaking his head grimly.

"Even Kedis can't work miracles, sir. It's been less than twenty-four hours. Someone should remind them of that fact."

"*I* know that, and *you* know that, but the *Senate* appears to operate in a time zone of their own choosing."

Watching Tyler pull a limp white handkerchief from his breast pocket and wipe his perspiring forehead, Chesnee felt the briefest stirrings of pity for his superior officer. As long as he'd known the Admiral, he had never seen him in such a state. *Certain members of High Command and the Senate must really be bearing down on him.*

Which of course meant that Tyler in turn bore down on Chesnee, but Chesnee sensed his success with the Blockade Division gave him a little more leverage. He cleared his throat. "Admiral, you have my word. As soon as I hear anything from Kedis, I will immediately pass it on to you."

"Good, good." Tyler looked only slightly relieved. "I'd make it an order, if I had to Giles."

"No need, Admiral."


Hours later, Chesnee sat in his Flag Tactical Command Center, sifting through what little data was available from Glo'Stea. His comm officer drew him out of his contemplation.

"Admiral?"

Chesnee glanced over at the young man. "Yes, Lieutenant?"

Darkon swiveled in his chair to face his commanding officer. "You have a high-priority incoming transmission from Sta'Gloa."

"Excellent. Let's hope it's the Ambassador, calling with good news." Chesnee doubted Pamos would be calling him again. "I'll take it in my quarters."

Leaving his seat, Chesnee marched out of the compartment and down the corridor to his quarters. Striding to his office, he seated himself behind his desk and tapped the comm panel. To his surprise, a full-size holograph of Leo Kedis appeared on the other side of his desk. The man was impeccably dressed in a tuxedo, which struck Chesnee as slightly odd, and wore a humble expression that—as far as Chesnee was concerned—completely failed to mask the smugness practically radiating off of him.

"Good afternoon, Admiral Chesnee."

Something in his voice warned Chesnee to be on his guard. *And there's the matter of the holograph. The Triumvirate has given him access to a secure comm channel.* He inclined his head. "Ambassador."

"I am calling you from Triumvirate Tower to tell you that the Triumvirate has agreed to a cease-fire between our forces, to be implemented immediately."

This did not surprise Chesnee at all. Having managed to smuggle himself onto Sta'Gloa, Kedis accomplishing everything else was only a matter of time. "That is…excellent news, Ambassador."

Kedis smiled. "I thought so." A beat and then, "This cease-fire includes, Admiral, the removal of our ships from around the two mining stations, Xana 5 and Sapriske 6."

*That* did surprise him. Chesnee knew he should have seen it coming, but still…"Are you quite—"

"Oh, yes." Kedis waved a hand. "I believe it is a necessary concession."

Chesnee took a breath, before inclining his head. "I will withdraw them immediately."

"Excellent."

"Are you well?" It was a reasonable question…and there was the nagging matter of the fact that Chesnee had no idea who else was listening to this conversation. He recalled where and what Triumvirate Tower was, but Kedis had offered no specifics as to his precise location.

"Oh, quite well. The people of the Coalition so far have proved to be excellent hosts." Kedis turned to offer a smile in another direction—

—and Chesnee knew. *He's with the Triumvirate now.* Only long years of experience enabled him to keep his expression under control. "The Senate will be glad to hear it."

Kedis's smile took on a bland cast. "I'm sure they will. You may also inform them that we will be discussing opening peace negotiations. Send me word when all of our forces have received notice of the cease-fire."

"Understood, Ambassador."

"Thank you, Admiral."

The holograph dissolved as Kedis ended the transmission.

For a moment—just a moment—Chesnee drummed his fingers on the edge of his desk, his brain working at light speed, filtering and sorting this new information and its implications. Then he sprang into action, sending the order to each of his subordinates, General Deam and others. They in turn would relay the cease-fire to the troops under their command.

That done, Chesnee braced himself and prepared to contact Admiral Tyler.

Predictably, Tyler wanted more details than Chesnee possessed. "That's all he said?" he pressed, for the fourth time in the past six minutes.

"Yes, sir." Chesnee clamped a tight lid on his mounting frustration. Once he had realized their conversation was no doubt audible to the entire Triumvirate, several of the questions he had wanted to ask died unsaid. Tyler either had no concept of that, or else he had descended into panic mode.

*Even on a good day, that's a toss-up.*

"Do you think things are going well?"

"I…had that distinct impression, yes, sir. The Ambassador seemed very sure of himself."

Tyler digested that. "It's logical," he boomed after a moment. "Can't very well expect to deal with anything else when our people are still shooting at each other."

"There is that," Chesnee agreed. He hesitated, reluctant to unleash this particular expectation, but felt duty-bound to add, "It's likely that Kedis will either contact me with more information at a later date to relay to the Senate, or else he will use the *Change* as a relay station to contact them directly." The latter was the more likely scenario, in his opinion, but Tyler looked like he desperately needed to be thrown a bone.

"Good, good. I think you're right. He'll want to keep everyone updated on his progress."

*Particularly if things go well*, Chesnee thought, but he kept it to himself. A sudden thought occurred to him. "Admiral," he leaned forward slightly in his seat, "I've been meaning to ask. How goes the investigation into the Blockade Division command history?"

He suspected he knew more than Tyler realized, given his position, but he wanted it from a more official source.

Some of the redness faded from Tyler's cheeks. "It's ugly, Giles. The media has made such a fuss over things that High Command is still talking trials, when before they would have just considered reversing honorable retirements and benefits. And there's the not-so-insignificant fact that several of your predecessors made enough money to retire and live in rather…connected social circles."

Chesnee nodded; none of this surprised him. *Ethics and morals be damned; they got what they were after. Power and money.* Given the ignoble, inglorious history of the Blockade Division, he fully understood the temptation, but he disagreed with his predecessors' succumbing to it. *They lacked vision—all of them.*

"Still," Tyler looked a fraction more cheerful, "this news has put a serious dent in their reputations. You've already emerged from this as the G.U.'s shining hero—if Kedis pulls this off, the both of you will be absolutely golden."

Chesnee couldn't help himself; he liked the sound of that. He'd set out to prove he could do the impossible—and he'd succeeded. Kedis's involvement was an unfortunate—but inescapable—downside. *The politicians always sail in once someone else has done all the hard work.*

"Well, Giles, I shall pass this on to High Command. They'll be relieved."

"I'm sure they will."

"I don't have to tell you to keep me apprised."

"No, sir, you do not."

Tyler nodded. "You're a good man, Giles, and a damn fine officer. None of this would have even been possible without you—and I'll make sure High Command doesn't forget it."

"Thank you, sir."

Chesnee waited until the transmission ended before he allowed himself to slump back in his seat and give into the frown that had been building throughout the entire conversation. In all of this—Kedis's arrival, the weeks of patiently waiting for him to make contact with the Triumvirate—he had never really taken into consideration what would happen if the Ambassador actually *succeeded*.

For the first time, Chesnee glimpsed his future—and found it more than a little horrifying. He could just see High Command parading him around the Galactic Union arm-in-arm with Kedis. *Instead of commanding troops, they'll have me giving speeches to roomfuls of politicians, their spouses, and other high rollers in society.* His expression turned bleak. *Who knows how long it'll be before I see any real action again?*

Chesnee shook his head, forcing the visions before his mind's eye to dissolve. *With any luck, I'll come out of this with more leverage than that. After assigning me to a dead-end career position where I overcome the impossible, I'll be damned if I let High Command sideline me now.*

A slow smile spread over his face. He'd use Kedis if he had to. *It's the least he can do.*

# CHAPTER 14

THE cease-fire negotiated and his request to open peace negotiations received, Ambassador Kedis was politely dismissed for the day. He passed through the semi-circle of tables and chairs to rejoin Lon in the back of the Chamber and Lon fell in step beside him. Faint tendrils of relief began to curl through Lon. *I guess the Triumvirate doesn't need me.*

It seemed crazy, but he might escape this without an interrogation after all.

The thought had barely crossed his mind when Quin'lan Dunn called out, "One moment, Captain Strong."

Lon froze mid-step. Slowly, he and Kedis turned to look back at Dunn.

The Chairman glanced toward the Chief Ministers. "The Triumvirate has a few questions for you before you depart."

Kedis started to retrace his steps, but Chief Minister Hugh Koen said dryly, "We will not take up any more of your time, Ambassador. We will send Captain Strong out to you when we are finished."

"I would prefer to remain with my liaison, Chief Minister," Kedis said smoothly.

"I'm sure you would." Koen raised a hand. "However, he is a citizen of the Coalition and the Triumvirate requires a word with him. In addition, we have already rearranged our schedule once this afternoon to accommodate your preferences, Ambassador."

For a split-second, Lon thought Kedis would argue the point. Instead, the Ambassador inclined his head in polite acquiescence. "As you say, Chief Minister. I thank you for your time and consideration."

He exited the Chamber into the Hall while, heart pounding, Lon moved to the center of the Chamber to face the Triumvirate. He cast a quick, appraising look around the semi-circle, noting the assorted Representatives' and Directors' expressions. Some were blank, others—like his grandfather—politely neutral, while several looked downright unpleasant.

*Oh, this should be interesting,* he thought grimly. *They weren't about to let me off the hook.*

Granted, he *had* smuggled Tarynians past Sta'Gloa's shield—something that had never been done before. *Or if it has, nobody's ever admitted to it.*

And he had known he'd have to face the music eventually.

The back of his neck warmed under the combined scrutiny of every single person in the Chamber, including his grandfather. Lon met Aiden's eyes briefly; his grandfather gave him the barest of encouraging nods.

To Lon's surprise, Chief Minister Koen himself took the lead. Peering thoughtfully at Lon from his seat with the other Chief Ministers at the north point of the Tower, he shook his head. "Captain Strong, I hardly know where to begin." He glanced around the Chamber. "In fact, I believe I can safely say that none of us sitting here today know precisely where to begin."

Out of the corner of his eye, Lon saw several Representatives exchange looks. *Oh, I think a few of them know where to start.*

"Your supposed 'death' was a tragedy a few months ago, and yet here you stand before us, a liaison to a Galactic Union Ambassador." Koen's dark eyes gave nothing away. "The Triumvirate would like to know how that happened."

Flickers of anger stirred inside Lon's chest. *You want to know how it happened?* He drew himself upright. "As I'm sure you know, Chief Minister, as well as the rest of the Triumvirate," he spared a nod for the Chamber at large, "when Admiral Chesnee's forces attacked the convoy I belonged to, Sta'Gloan Shield Control closed the shield on us."

He swallowed, remembering the shock and horror he had felt in that moment when he realized his fate had been sealed. "My ship wasn't the only one stranded outside of Sta'Gloa for the Tarynians to tear apart."

"Standard operating procedure," Malik Thane said from his seat.

Quin'lan Dunn shot the redheaded Sta'Gloan Director of Security a look, but did not tap his bell.

"The Tarynians blew my ship to hell." Lon shook his head, unable to keep a note of bitterness from his voice. "I only barely made it out in an escape pod, and I would have died out there like everyone else if one of Admiral Chesnee's ships hadn't picked me up."

Dion Pamos rose to his feet and was recognized. He regarded Lon with half-lidded eyes. "Is it just me, or does it seem strange that the only survivor of that attack was a half-Tarynian? Do you really expect us to believe that was just a coincidence?"

A hot wave of anger pulsed through Lon, making his green eyes flash. *How dare he?* He took half a breath and tamped his fury down. "Are you accusing me of somehow colluding with Admiral Chesnee's forces?"

Pamos's serene expression did not change.

"I lost my *ship*." Lon's hands clenched into fists. "I almost lost my *life*. I know you," he nodded to the semi-circle of faces, "know how valuable starships are. Why in the galaxy would I do that?"

He threw his arms wide. "Go ahead, dig into my life—if you haven't already." He was betting they had. "You're not going to find anything connecting me to Admiral Chesnee or any other Tarynian before Shield Control abandoned my convoy to die."

His words rang through the Chamber, eliciting a few murmurs.

Dion Pamos resumed his seat, and Chief Minister Koen waved a hand to Lon. "You may continue."

Lon proceeded to detail how he had awakened in the *Winds of Change*'s Med Bay, how he had met Kedis…and the moment he realized he was aboard a G.U. ship. He then gave the Triumvirate a brief overview of how Kedis had finally talked him into helping him gain an audience with the Triumvirate.

"I didn't know if it could even be done," he said boldly, "but at that point I didn't have much to lose. My entire family already thought I was dead. I figured if blockade runners could get past the blockade to trade with the outside galaxy and then return, we had a chance of getting in."

The silence in the Chamber was almost deafening. No one spoke; the members of the Triumvirate were so intent on his story they hardly even seemed to be breathing.

Lon took a deep breath. He wasn't sure what the reaction to the next part of his story would be; he knew it would probably shock most of them. "The only hitch, of course, was getting past Customs." He gave a nonchalant shrug. "Turns out the Ambassador had that covered—the Tarynians are capable of forging flawless Sta'Gloan identcards. Lanxian and Glo'Stean ones too, I'd wager."

He expected this to send a shockwave rippling around the Chamber, but the reaction he garnered was more contained. He blinked, taken aback. Didn't they *care*?

Then realization washed over him. *Kevin and Lilia must have already told them about the identcards.* The Triumvirate had already had time to wrap their minds around this revelation.

Movement out of the corner of his eye drew Lon's attention to the Sta'Gloan section, where Malik Thane had shot to his feet. Dunn tapped his bell, and Thane leaned forward slightly, his face just this shy of murderous. "Your siblings mentioned these identcards, but could offer no further details. We've been waiting for an explanation, Captain."

Lon met his furious gaze head-on. "You heard me, Director. I have no idea how long they've been doing it, but Kedis was able to procure identcards that got us past Customs when we landed on Sta'Gloa. No one even batted an eye at them."

"Where did you land?" Thane demanded through gritted teeth.

Lon shook his head. "I don't think that's relevant."

"Oh, it is *entirely* relevant," Thane snarled.

They locked eyes, and briefly Lon thought of Captain Geary, the blockade runner who had flown them to Sta'Gloa. He didn't want to ruin her life, but…what was he supposed to do? *Of course, without more detail…Thane will have to do a* lot *of digging to find anything.*

"We landed in Rizwan."

Lon raised his voice to be heard over a round of fierce murmurs. "It wouldn't have mattered *where* we landed. Those identcards were too good." He pointed to the floor. "They'd even pass security here."

"From there…" He shrugged. "The rest of the story is pretty simple. I took the Ambassador and his men to my grandfather's house in Marina, because I knew my entire family would be in Sonela."

Thane had regained control of his expression. "And then your youngest siblings arrived on the scene."

"Yes." Lon flashed the Chamber a self-deprecating smile. "I had to talk Lilia out of shooting me and calling the police—" this was met with a few flickers of amusement, but not many, "—but once she got over the shock, she and Kevin both realized what an important opportunity this was for the entire Coalition."

Lon straightened his spine. "Don't get me wrong—I'm still angry that Chesnee's Piranhas blew my ship up. And I've seen how much damage Tarynian forces on Glo'Stea have done over the years, how much pain and suffering they've caused. But if Kedis—" he stabbed a finger in the direction of the Hall, "—can help us find a way to stop people from dying? How could I not take that chance?"

Silence greeted these words, a different silence. It seemed to carry a thoughtful edge instead of the fury he had felt earlier.

In the Glo'Stean section, Shane Briscoe rose to his feet and was recognized. "Is that what led you to become the Ambassador's liaison?"

"It is." Lon smiled ruefully. "I'm a starship pilot, not a politician." He waved a hand to indicate the Chamber. "This is the last place I ever thought I'd be standing. But I've gotten to know the Ambassador over the past couple of months, and my goal is to help keep him aware of the Coalition side of the story while he negotiates with you."

Briscoe shook his head. "I would say you have your work cut out for you."

*Oh, I do*, Lon wanted to tell him, but he kept his mouth shut and only inclined his head.

"Are there any more questions?" Quin'lan Dunn looked around the Chamber, but no one responded. He tapped his bell. "Captain Strong, you are dismissed for now."

Lon bowed to them all. "You know where to find me should you need anything else."

Straightening, he marched out of the Chamber with his head held high. He spared a glance for his grandfather his way out, but Aiden's face was impassive. *Doesn't matter. I said what needed to be said.*

Now he had Kedis to deal with. *He's probably going to want a blow-by-blow replay…and I'm not sure he needs to know everything.*

Lon felt a headache forming behind his eyes, but resisted the urge to pinch the bridge of his nose as he stepped out into the Hall. The lines between what he knew and what Kedis and the Triumvirate should or shouldn't know were already blurry; they would only get worse from here.

His own words came back to him: *I'm a starship pilot, not a politician.*

He shook his head to himself. *What am I doing?*

# Chapter 15

THEIR grandfather's office suite was on Level 27 of Triumvirate Tower. Michael ushered his youngest siblings inside and closed the door. The outer office was spacious, featuring a black leather couch and matching armchairs, a holoprojector mounted discreetly in the corner, and a glossy black desk by a door leading deeper into the office. The cool air smelled faintly of tropical flowers.

Aiden's secretary was fielding calls, but as soon as she disconnected, Michael approached her. "Holly," he motioned to the twins, "you remember my youngest siblings. Kevin and Lilia."

A curly black head liberally streaked with gray lifted and a pair of keen brown eyes set in a dark face peered at the twins. Holly DuBerg, as the name written in holographic letters across the front of her desk read, set her datapad aside and smiled. "You've grown a great deal since the last time I saw you in person." Her smile widened. "The holos Representative Monroe shows me periodically don't quite do you justice."

"Holly." Kevin extended a hand to her. "It's been a long time."

"That it has." Holly inspected them both, still smiling. "I'm glad your brother is alive."

"So are we," Lilia said.

Michael nodded to the door beside Holly's desk. "I'm taking the twins back to Grandfather's office. They'll be staying here until we're done for the day, although the Triumvirate may summon them at some point."

If Holly was curious, she didn't show it. She waved a hand. "That will be fine."

Michael tapped an access code into the keypad beside the door and stepped through into a short hall. Several small rooms stood to their left; Michael led them to the only door on the right. Keying in another code, he opened the door and motioned for them to precede him inside.

Lilia caught her breath; she had forgotten how stunning the view was from here. Their grandfather's office faced out toward the obsidian mirror-like plastiglass windows of the Department of Security Tower, which provided a reflection of Triumvirate Tower's obsidian surface in return.

Aiden's desk stood in front of the wide expanse of floor-to-ceiling window. Several brown leather armchairs and a matching sofa were clustered off to the left, while to the right a beautiful oak sideboard took up the length of the entire wall. The walls were pale patterned gold, complementing the rich emerald green carpet.

"Grandfather's office has a hygiene unit, so you won't need to use the one out in the reception area." Michael pointed to an almost invisible door beside the sideboard. "I swept for bugs and hidden cams this morning, but feel free to sweep again."

"That bad, huh?" Shoving his hands in his pockets, Kevin strolled up to the window and peered out.

"You know how Grandfather is about taking unnecessary chances."

"Have you ever found anything?" Lilia glanced over her shoulder at her oldest brother.

Michael shrugged. "Uncle Will said every now and then he'd find something, but from the way he talked, he never found out who was behind it." He toed the carpet with his boot. "Personally, I have yet to find anything. Overall, security's pretty tight."

Kevin settled into one of the armchairs. "That's good."

"Not if you have to explain in detail how you bypassed it." Michael cut him a sideways glance; they'd filled him in briefly via Nancom on the trip here. "The Lord was with you two this morning—Derek and I thought for sure they'd grill you about that."

Frowning, Lilia folded her arms tightly across her chest. "It surprised us too."

"Well, as long as they have more important things to worry about, you should be fine." Michael offered them a smile.

"Yeah," Kevin said wryly, "we're only charged with treason. How bad can it be?"

Michael did not respond, but turned back toward the door. "I'm serious about staying here. There are drinks and some snacks in the sideboard, or you can go down to the café, if need be, but make sure you tell Holly where you're going. Otherwise, don't talk to anybody and definitely don't leave the building. That will *not* go over well with the Triumvirate."

"We're not going anywhere, Mike," Lilia assured him. *As much as I'd love to go home*, she added silently.

"Good. Sit tight. The Triumvirate will figure things out, and by the end of the day, hopefully the media will have bigger things to talk about than your involvement in this production." With a curt nod, Michael departed the room.

Once the door slid shut with an almost inaudible whisper, stifled silence descended on the office. Lilia pressed her lips into a thin line before unbending enough to say, "Well, Grandfather's office hasn't changed much since we were last here."

She nodded to the artwork hanging against the pale gold walls— holos of Marina's coastline and tropical flowers interspersed with the occasional abstract painting in muted colors. "I remember Grandmother helping him pick out some of these."

"If it ain't broke, don't fix it." His armchair was a recliner; Kevin proceeded to kick it back. He stretched out, lacing his fingers behind his head. "You think we could sneak over to the *Talia* for a little while?"

Lilia shot him a look.

"Hey," he shrugged. "As far as Holly will know, we haven't left the office, much less the building."

"I don't think it's a good idea. Where would we be if the Triumvirate calls us back?"

"At the Sonela Spaceport."

"Kevin."

"Lilia." He mimicked her dry tone. "I don't want to be stuck here all day."

"I don't either, but we really don't—"

"—have a choice? Sure we do." Kevin jiggled one foot restlessly. "If we both open the portal, it'll only be a half an hour before we can come back."

That…was a good point.

Before Lilia could agree, however, Kevin's dark eyebrows knit in a frown. "The only hitch, of course, is if part of Triumvirate Tower's security system involves thermal imaging. And, given we basically committed treason, I could see somebody keeping a close eye on us while we're here."

"Somebody like Alan Birch?" Lilia asked, her mouth twisting.

"Exactly." Heavy disappointment filled Kevin's voice. "Guess we're stuck after all. I don't want to take that kind of chance."

Lilia finally sank down on one corner of the sofa and curled her legs beneath her. She bit her lip and then voiced the question that had been preying on her mind. "What do you think they'll do to us?"

She'd tried not to think about that during the weeks they'd been helping Lon plan how to smuggle Kedis into the Gala. It had been easier to focus on the task at hand—particularly with everything else going on. Failure hadn't been an option.

"I don't know." Kevin huffed up at the ceiling. "And thinking about it is driving me crazy. I just wanted things to go back to normal, you know?" He raised his head long enough to give her a wry smile. "Guess we didn't do a good job of factoring fallout into our equation, did we?"

"No, we didn't." Lilia pulled her comlink out of her pocket and took it off silent mode, but did not do anything else. She wasn't sure she wanted to know what the media was saying right now.

"Part of me wonders if they'll convict us of treason and throw us in prison. Or ground us in Sonela and keep us from running our business."

Lilia grimaced. Neither of those options sounded good. "I guess if I had to choose, I'd rather be—"

"—grounded than imprisoned."

They shared a grim look.

"I hope they figure something out today." Lilia exhaled shakily. The thought of spending the next few days or a week or even longer living in suspense made her sick to her stomach.

"You and me both."

Lilia started as her comlink chimed with an incoming holo-call. She pulled it from her pocket and glanced at the display.

"Who is that?"

"No idea. This is my personal comlink."

"Don't answer it," Kevin advised. "Let them leave a message." He frowned. "People shouldn't be able to get a hold of our personal comm details, but—" He sat bolt upright as his own comlink vibrated in his pocket.

Yanking it out, he stared at it for a few seconds before slowly turning to meet Lilia's wide violet eyes. "Incoming holo-call."

"It could be a coincidence," Lilia said, but even to her own ears the words sounded weak.

Kevin tipped his head toward her. "Did they leave you a message?"

Biting her lip, Lilia glanced at her own comlink. "Yes." She tapped it, and a familiar face filled her screen—a man with red hair and brown eyes set in a boyish face. She sucked in a sharp breath. *Dr. Jayce?*

"Who is it?" Kevin demanded. "What's wrong?"

Lilia swallowed, with an effort. "It's Dr. Jayce."

# CHAPTER 16

IN less than no time, Kevin had scrambled off his brown leather recliner and dropped into the seat next to Lilia on the matching sofa. Tapping her comlink, she played the recorded message from the beginning.

"Miss Strong, I understand you're in the middle of a…rather large mess at the moment, and as such you're probably screening your calls." Jayce half-smiled. "God knows I would. You won't recognize my comm details because this is a comlink I procured especially for this conversation."

The twins exchanged startled sidelong glances. What was *that* supposed to mean?

"I need to talk to you and your brother. I have…recently discovered a piece of my former colleague's research that has shed a significant bit of light on the events of our disastrous experiment not long ago."

Lilia's heart began to pound heavily in her chest. Her mouth was dry; she couldn't speak. *That can't mean what I think he means, can it?*

Jayce's face was very earnest. "Even before I found it, I'd come to the conclusion that you and your brother did not tell us everything about your adventures. And in light of last night's events…I am *sure* you didn't. I have spent *hours* and hours going back over every bit of data we have, and I keep coming back to the same conclusion."

He paused. "I know you know what I'm referring to. I'd rather not say it now, but I need to meet with the two of you." He paused again. "And just in case you decide to ignore me, let me just say that I also know Mr. Callahan and the NCDC would be *very* interested in what I've discovered."

Jayce scrunched his face in apology. "You saved my life, and you saved the transporter, and I'm very grateful, but this goes beyond that. Call me. Please."

The message ended.

Lilia felt frozen, as though she and her seat had become one. She drew in a breath slowly; it felt studded with tiny razor blades.

Kevin wet his lips and compared his comlink to Lilia's. The comm details were the same. "He called me too."

The air in the office seemed to grow heavier and more oppressive. A rush of nervous energy flooded Lilia, but she felt too shaky to move. It took two tries before she found her voice. "He's figured it out."

"Maybe not all of it, but, yeah, it sounds like he's on to something." Kevin exploded into motion in one swift movement, rising from the sofa and taking off across the office at a brisk pace. He waved his arms in the air, still clutching his comlink in one hand. "What do we do?"

Dropping her own comlink onto the sofa beside her, Lilia clasped her fingers together so tightly that her knuckles turned white. Her stomach felt like a mass of writhing snakes. "What *can* we do? We'll have to talk to him, find out—"

"—how much he actually knows." Kevin nodded, still pacing. "If he's really found some of Banx's missing research and put everything together…" He gave her a significant look. "We're probably screwed."

"What can he *do*, though?"

"No idea. Use us for test dummies, maybe. Or blackmail us into…well, something. Who knows what?"

*Blackmail*…Cold shivers danced down Lilia's spine; for a second, she felt dizzy.

"But we won't know until we talk to him." Kevin stopped pacing and whirled around to face her. "Do we talk to him now, or wait until later?"

Lilia laughed weakly. "What, you want to drag out the suspense?" She shook her head, before squaring her shoulders. "Let's get this over with."

She reached for her comlink, but Kevin stopped her.

"Wait. Let's talk to Nob first."

"What? Why?"

Kevin just looked at her. "Don't you want a second opinion?"

Lilia frowned, but nodded, and they opened a joint Nancom channel to Nob. [Sorry to bother you again—]

[—but a new wrinkle's just developed.]

[What now?] he asked immediately.

[Well…] Lilia glanced at Kevin. [Dr. Jayce just called both of us and—]

[—wants us to call him back. He's apparently found a piece of Banx's research—]

[—and he's put the pieces together. He *knows* we've got transporters.]

[Or at least he's really sure he's figured it out,] Kevin said.

Nob digested this for a moment. [And he wants to talk to you?]

[Immediately,] Kevin replied. [Or else.]

[Or else what?]

Lilia shrugged, even though Nob couldn't see her. [No idea, but probably involves him going to the NCDC.]

[Or worse,] Kevin added.

[Where are you now?] Nob asked.

[Still at Triumvirate Tower. We're in—]

[—our grandfather's office. The Triumvirate isn't—]

[—finished with us yet,] the twins said together.

[Does Jayce want to meet?]

Lilia and Kevin exchanged glances again. [Possibly.] Lilia shrugged again. [He wants us to call him for sure—he's gotten a hold of a comlink his handlers apparently don't know about.]

[He's hiding things from his handlers?] Nob's Nancom voice sharpened. [You'd better find out what he wants.]

[Oh, we will. I just don't know what kind of a mess we're heading into.] Kevin shoved his hands into his pockets. [It's been long enough that I thought he'd forget about us.]

[Apparently not. Keep me updated.]

After promising to do so, the twins closed Nob's channel and it then was Lilia's turn to jump to her feet and begin pacing across the office. "I don't like this."

"That makes two of us." Kevin's eyebrows drew together in a deep frown. "But we can't exactly risk *not* talking to Jayce."

"And he knows it." Lilia stopped in front of the wide window, hugging her arms around her torso. She thought of the transporter components embedded in her nanites and shuddered.

Behind her, Kevin stirred. "We might as well get it over with now, while we've got time and privacy. Do you want to call him, or shall I?"

Lilia swallowed. "I'll do it." Walking back over to the sofa, she picked up her comlink. "If it comes to it, I'm not above reminding him I saved his life."

Jayce answered immediately, his face filling her comlink display. "Miss Strong, I was hoping you'd respond quickly."

Glancing sideways at Kevin, Lilia put the scientist on speaker. "That was the point of your message, wasn't it?"

"Yes, it was. Is your brother with you?"

"I'm here," Kevin said.

"Good." Jayce sounded faintly relieved, though his next words were full of confidence. "I need to meet with you."

Kevin leaned forward so Jayce could see him. "Why?"

"You know why. I suspected during that portal fiasco that you weren't telling us everything you knew, but now I *know* you didn't tell us everything."

"What do you mean?" Lilia tried to keep the nervousness she felt from showing in her voice.

"I told you, I found a chunk of Dr. Banx's research. It gave me the last couple of pieces I needed to solve the puzzle."

Lilia looked at Kevin, the same thought mirrored in both their expressions. *Great.*

Rightly interpreting their silence, Jayce said, "I *could* have taken what I've discovered straight to the NCDC, but I wanted to talk to you first."

"For research purposes," Kevin said.

"That, and the fact that you saved my life—and the transporter." Jayce paused. "Not to mention the fact that I'm calling you from a new comlink so nobody else knows. If what I suspect is true…"

*We'd be in big trouble*, Lilia thought.

Kevin exhaled quietly. "Where and when do you want us to meet you?"

"Tomorrow evening would be preferable."

Lilia bit the inside of her lip. "I don't know if we'll be able to do that. We have a hearing with the NCDC tomorrow. And that's if the Triumvirate doesn't throw us in prison."

"Oh, really?" Jayce's voice sharpened with interest. "Why?"

Kevin rolled his eyes heavenward. "Why do you think? We helped our brother smuggle a Tarynian Ambassador into the Tri-Global Tournament Closing Ceremonies Gala last night."

"Oh. Right. And you think the NCDC might kick you out?" Real concern slid into the redheaded scientist's voice, though the twins both suspected it was because Jayce was afraid they'd get their nanites stripped before he had a chance to meet with them. He seemed oddly unconcerned with the Triumvirate.

"They might," Lilia said cautiously. *For all the good it will do them to try.*

"They don't know, do they?" Jayce asked.

"Know what?" Kevin asked.

For the first time, Jayce sounded impatient. "You *know* what I'm talking about."

Lilia looked at Kevin. [We're going to have to tell him *something*.] When her brother just shook his head stubbornly, she said, "It's a long, rather complicated story, Dr. Jayce, but I think the answer is, 'not exactly'."

"I want to hear this story."

"What about Cait?" Kevin demanded suddenly. "And your friend Dr. Lang? Have you told *them* about this?"

Silence fell—a rather guilty silence, in Lilia's opinion.

"…no," Jayce said at last. "I haven't said anything to them."

*Bingo.* Lilia raised her chin. "Why not?"

Jayce, who had looked quite tense throughout the conversation so far, suddenly looked very tired. "Because of what I found in Dr. Banx's research."

The twins traded tiny sideways glances. "What did you find?" they asked together.

Jayce shook his head. "I can't tell you. Not yet." He cast a furtive glance around him. "It's not safe."

"Well," Kevin said, "if you're going to hold this over our heads, the least you can do is—"

"—give us a hint." Lilia frowned at her comlink.

This seemed to rub Jayce entirely the wrong way. He threw his arms up into the air. "Do you not know what *happened* last night?"

Lilia and Kevin traded glances again. [He's found something linking Banx to Freedom's Children,] Lilia said via Nancom. [What do you want to bet?]

[No takers.] Kevin cleared his throat. "Ah, Dr. Jayce—"

The scientist wasn't finished yet. "We've barely introduced the transporters to the Coalition and yet somehow *somebody* has managed to reproduce the machines and build them on a scale massive enough to repair Glo'Stea's shield." He kept his voice low through sheer dint of effort, but there was no mistaking his intensity. "That is *not* an accident."

Well. He was right on that front. The twins exchanged glances again.

"No, it's—"

"—not."

Keeping his eyes on Jayce, Kevin addressed his sister via Nancom. [Maybe this won't be as bad as we thought. Clearly, he's—]

[—found something.] Lilia was still frowning. "Okay, Dr. Jayce, we'll come see you."

"Can't make any guarantees yet on *when*," Kevin warned him. "Like we said, we have an NCDC hearing in the morning."

"Understood." Jayce gave a short, sharp nod. "What about Tuesday?"

Kevin shook his head. "Have to make a run to Glo'Stea for a client."

Jayce's mouth took on an unhappy slant, but he nodded again. "Fine. Just—we need to meet as soon as possible."

"We understand," Lilia said.

"Good." Jayce glanced over his shoulder. "I have to go." With that, he ended the holo-call.

Lilia felt a chill that had nothing to do with the temperature in their grandfather's office as she slid her comlink back into her pocket. "This just keeps getting better and better."

"He's found something major and now he doesn't know who to trust," Kevin said shrewdly.

"So you don't think he's going to sell us out for experimentation?"

"Nah. He wants to know what's going on." Kevin held up a hand. "Don't get me wrong, it's still a possibility, but I think in light of the Freedom's Children issue, it's a very *remote* possibility."

Lilia considered him a moment, before shaking her head. "I hope you're right."

Kevin shot her a grin. "I'm always right. Right?"

They both laughed, though it did not dispel the sense of foreboding swirling through the office.

# CHAPTER 17

KEDIS was as good as his word. Within two hours of the Ambassador's holo-call to Admiral Chesnee and his departure from the Chamber, the Triumvirate received word that the G.U. ships around Xana 5 and Sapriske 6 had retreated. Aiden's colleagues greeted this news with applause and muted cheers. They then promptly returned to hashing out everything that had happened in the past twenty-four hours. More details—sketchy in some areas—were coming in from Glo'Stea via her Directors of Security and Internal Affairs.

In the back of his mind, however, Aiden kept a single thought. *I cannot be the only person here who noticed Kedis said nothing to Chesnee of the transporter.*

The Ambassador was no doubt withholding that information for a later conversation with the Admiral—he had complete control of his situation and lacked an audience.

It struck Aiden as odd, however, that none of his colleagues had said a word about this admittedly strange little wrinkle, even Martin Hollowell. Perhaps they considered it a minor point at the moment, something not worth of discussion until they had dealt with more pressing matters. He was not sure.

The transporter *was* a massive enough revelation that Kedis might not have been sure of the Admiral's reaction to it—or how quickly the news would spread from there. Aiden could see how the Ambassador might want to keep such information out of the Galactic Union Senate's hands for a short while. *But it will be revealed eventually*, he thought grimly.

Not surprisingly, one of the day's biggest arguments revolved around what to do with his youngest grandchildren.

The topic gave Aiden a strange, surreal feeling. He almost felt like he was detached from his body, floating up near the Chamber's high ceiling and watching the proceedings from there. *My grandchildren, charged with high treason.*

At the far end of the Glo'Stean section, Egan Ashford rose to his feet. Grasping his cane, he waited for Quin'lan Dunn to recognize him. His sallow face was set in grim lines.

"The Triumvirate recognizes Representative Ashford."

"With all due respect to Representative Monroe," Ashford nodded in Aiden's direction, "we the Triumvirate cannot let Lon, Kevin, and Lilia Strong go unpunished. Regardless of the sincerity of their motives, they deliberately aided and abetted G.U. citizens who entered the Coalition illegally."

Ashford tapped his cane lightly on the marble floor. "I propose that the Strongs be found guilty of treason and sentenced to life in prison." He glanced around the room once, nodded sharply, and resumed his seat.

Apparently, he seemed to think that was all he needed to say on the subject. Under different circumstances, Aiden might have been tempted to smile.

A wave of mutters swept around the Chamber. Some were pleased, others were dissatisfied.

At the other end of the Glo'Stean section, Martin Hollowell stood. Aiden's attention snapped to him; he had not expected Hollowell to get involved already.

Once he was recognized, Hollowell held out his hands. "My esteemed fellow members of the Triumvirate. You all know my stance on the Tarynians." He shook his head. "I have never made a secret of it. And, as most of you also are aware, I have known the Strongs since they were children."

By the sudden stillness in the Chamber, Aiden knew he was not the only one listening with bated breath. *Martin, where are you going with this?*

"When Kevin and Lilia said they did not tell Aiden about Lon or anything else that was going on, I am inclined to believe them."

Hollowell smiled wryly. "I have noticed they are quite protective of their grandfather, you see."

"What is your point?" Malik Thane demanded from the Sta'Gloan section.

Quin'lan Dunn shot him a dire look.

"My point," Hollowell continued calmly, "is that I believe Representative Monroe to be innocent of any involvement in this matter. Furthermore, I wish to state for the record that though I believe a prison sentence to be the general response to treason, in this particular case, I believe a different response is warranted."

All along the semi-circle of tables and chair, Representatives and Directors alike exchanged glances. Aiden did not move a muscle—he kept his gaze fixed firmly on his old friend.

Hollowell's mouth twisted again. "It is unfortunate, but I believe it is necessary to exempt Lon Strong from punishment for the time being, given his involvement with Ambassador Kedis."

*Ah, that was clever.* Aiden gave Hollowell a mental approving nod. He had effectively silenced any protests about Lon escaping punishment by slipping in that little caveat.

"In the same vein," Hollowell continued, "the Ambassador will likely take a negative view of our convicting Kevin and Lilia of treason and sending them to prison." He scowled. "It may well have an adverse impact on any further interaction he has with the Triumvirate."

*Oh, Martin.* Aiden sat back in his chair slightly; he knew how dearly those words must have cost his friend.

Quin'lan Dunn voiced the question on everyone's mind. "What do you propose?"

Hollowell straightened further. "I propose a flight ban." Restless muttering greeted these words; he held up a hand to ward them off. "Kevin and Lilia Strong run a small interplanetary shipping business. Banning them from leaving Sta'Gloan airspace for a time and perhaps—" he shrugged, "—even banning them from leaving Sonela itself will be punishment enough."

Aiden flicked his gaze to the right and left. Some of their colleagues were nodding in agreement, while other shook their heads.

Having stated his mind, Hollowell resumed his seat without another word.

"I disagree." Nolan Snyder, a portly man with rosy cheeks and sweaty brow, ponderously heaved himself to his feet at the inside end of the Lanxian section. He was the Representative for Sector 4, which Chesnee's forces had been occupying for several months now.

Quin'lan Dunn tapped his bell. "The Triumvirate recognizes Representative Snyder."

Snyder stabbed a meaty finger in the air. "We must show the G.U. that we are not afraid of them. Actions have consequences and treason *must* be met with the strictest punishment." His voice grew louder with each word. "The Ambassador must be shown that we are not a force to be trifled with."

Silence greeted these impassioned words. Aiden wondered if he was the only person who recognized that the severity of Snyder's response was probably fueled in part by his frustration at his inability to do much of anything about the Tarynian forces occupying his sector—despite the protests and pleas of his constituents.

Several, "Hear, hear"'s echoed through the Chamber.

At the other end of the Lanxian section, Zane Chas pushed back his chair and stood.

Snyder remained standing for a moment, breathing heavily, but when he did not say anything else, Quin'lan Dunn tapped his bell. "The Triumvirate recognizes Representative Chas."

Snyder finally took his seat, and Chas cleared his throat. "While I understand where my colleagues are coming from," he nodded to Snyder, who was mopping his face with a handkerchief, and Ashford and Hollowell, who both remained calm and collected, "I must respectfully disagree with all of them."

A jolt of surprise shot through Aiden. He had expected most of the Triumvirate to side with one or the other.

"Grounding Kevin and Lilia Strong and effectively killing their business is certainly an approach, as is sending them both to rot in prison." Chas turned one hand palm up. "But how is that any different than the hell the G.U. has put us through for over twenty years now? How many businesses have been crippled or destroyed?"

Chas swept his gaze around the Triumvirate. "We have an unprecedented chance to change the course of the Coalition, potentially restore our system to full access to the galaxy, and we're sitting here discussing how best to punish the people responsible for risking everything to bring us this chance?"

Shaking his head, he raised his voice to be heard above the loud muttering that had broken out. "Personally, I think we ought to be pinning medals on them."

Cries of outrage greeted this from several quarters. Chas nodded to Quin'lan Dunn and coolly resumed his seat. He looked remarkably unaffected by the chaos he had just caused.

The resulting argument went on for what felt like hours. Aiden's head was pounding by the end of it. He would have loved to crawl under his table and clamp his hands over his ears like a child, but even under normal circumstances that would hardly have been appropriate.

*Oh, Lord Jesus, help us.* He just wanted it to be over.

Eventually, Lanxian Chief Minster Pryce Gammick broke through the noise to address Aiden directly. "Representative Monroe, what would you see done in this situation?"

In the time it took Aiden to stand, the entire Chamber fell so quiet he could almost swear the sound of his heart thudding in his chest was echoing out across the marble floor. He drew a deep breath. "Chief Minister, as much as I would like to think I can remain logical and detached in this particular situation, I think it best that I recuse myself."

He smiled sadly. "This is too important a matter for the outcome to be tainted by any claim of nepotism." Bowing slightly, he sank back down into his seat.

Pleased murmurs rustled around the Chamber. Out of the corner of his eye, Aiden caught more than one approving nod. He forced himself to sit motionless. It was done; the matter was out of his hands.

Not that he had really expected to influence anyone in this particular respect.

Within seconds, the Triumvirate had resumed arguing. It raged on until at last Shane Briscoe rose to his feet in the Glo'Stean section. This had a quieting effect on the Chamber—probably, Aiden suspected, out of sheer curiosity. Briscoe had said absolutely nothing so far.

Quin'lan Dunn sounded just the slightest bit relieved as he tapped his bell and intoned, "The Triumvirate recognizes Representative Briscoe."

Briscoe swept his electrifying hazel gaze around the Chamber, briefly encompassing every member of the Triumvirate. "My esteemed colleagues, these are not light matters we have been wrestling with today. Whether we wish to admit it or not, there is a great deal of emotion tied up in all of this."

Aiden inclined his head in a fractional nod. *Truer words have not been spoken today.*

Briscoe held out his hands. "If I understand the gist of the past several hours correctly—" he smiled wryly, eliciting tiny answering smiles from several quarters, "—most of us believe that some form of punishment is warranted for Captain and Lilia Strong." He brushed a hand through the air. "I agree with Representative Hollowell that we must temporarily exempt Lon Strong."

"I also agree," he continued calmly, "with my colleagues that some form of punishment is required." He lifted his voice to be heard above a chorus of groans. "Coalition laws were broken and we cannot overlook that fact. However," his voice sharpened, "I also agree with my colleagues who stated that a prison sentence or being rendered unable to conduct their business are both punishments too harsh, given the risks Captain Strong and his sister undertook to benefit the Coalition."

A wave of confusion swirled though the Chamber. Briscoe had just agreed with *everyone*.

Aiden merely sat quietly, anticipation thrumming in his old veins. He was looking forward to seeing where the younger Representative went with this.

"I offer a solution." Briscoe glanced around the Chamber again and smiled. "It is quite simple. We convict the Strongs of treason—" he paused for effect, "—and promptly pardon them."

Dead silence greeted him as these words sank in.

*Convict them…and pardon them.* Aiden exhaled slowly, his mind already racing to weigh the pros and cons.

Briscoe held out his hands to quell a sudden swell of uneasy mutterings. "It is by no means a perfect solution, but I think it is the best shot we've got." His hazel eyes drilled into everyone again. "Please take that into consideration." He sat down without another word.

Aiden fully expected the resulting argument. Briscoe's solution was one of those ugly little things that satisfied everyone and no one at the same time…but at this point Aiden doubted anyone could propose anything that would not send at least part of the Triumvirate into hysterics. Heated words were flung back and forth across the semi-circle of Representatives and Directors.

"Order! Order!" Quin'lan Dunn called out, striking his bell, but no one paid him any attention.

It was a full ten minutes before the Chairman could get the Triumvirate back under control. Smothering an exasperated expression, Dunn looked at the three Chief Ministers before addressing the semi-circle of tables and chairs. "I believe we have…thoroughly exhausted this topic. Perhaps it is time to put these three proposed solutions to a vote."

A brief, weighty silence descended on the Chamber as everyone digested this. Aiden counted his heartbeats. He was up to seven when Zane Chas rose to his feet again and was recognized.

"I make a motion that the Triumvirate put these solutions to a vote," he said formally. He darted a glance at Aiden, something akin to sympathy flickering over his face.

"I second that motion." Helen Urquart raised a hand from the Sta'Gloan section.

"Motion passed." Quin'lan Dunn tapped his bell.

The delicate peal sounded entirely too ominous to Aiden's ears.

"The Triumvirate will put it to a vote." Dunn nodded to Aiden. "Representative Monroe will abstain."

Aiden nodded in response. He then folded his hands in his lap and began to pray.

# CHAPTER 18

L ILIA was starting to feel like their grandfather's office walls were closing in on her. The air felt heavy, weighted with all the stark, ugly, and shadowy possibilities swirling through her mind. Her stomach was a churning mass of butterflies; she felt hot and cold by turns.

Kevin had investigated the selection of snacks in the oak sideboard that took up the entire right wall, but the thought of eating anything made both of them feel sick. The smell of the tropical flowers air freshener was bad enough at this point.

They'd been taking turns pacing the office; the carpeted floor was Kevin's now. He strode back and forth with jerky motions, his mind clearly elsewhere.

Lilia sat curled up in a corner of the brown leather couch, resisting the urge to chew her fingernails ragged. She played with the end of her still-too-short dark hair, another pang of loss shooting through her at the memory of her braid.

They'd tried reading the Bible out loud to each other and had spent some time in prayer. Both of those things had helped, but as the minutes and hours wore on, both of them lost the ability to concentrate on anything. Lilia had tried playing a game on her comlink, but had given it up as temporarily impossible.

Now the office was silent, save for the steady fall of Kevin's footsteps and their quiet breathing. The silence, too, seemed heavy.

They hadn't heard anything from their brothers in almost two hours—and there hadn't been any reason to chat anyway. Nobody was in the mood for idle small talk.

The twins both jumped when Michael's voice came through his Nancom channel. [Heads up—I'm coming to get you. You're being summoned by the Triumvirate.]

Lilia and Kevin looked at each other, wide-eyed, the same thought reflected in both their faces. It had been hours since the Triumvirate dismissed Lon and Kedis and sequestered themselves for deliberation.

"Is the fact that it took them—"

"—over three hours to reach a—"

"—decision a good thing—"

"—or a bad thing?"

Neither of them knew.

Lilia unfolded herself from the couch, wincing as the circulation returned to her feet. Her knees felt wobbly, and if anything, her butterflies were worse. She pressed a hand to her stomach. *Oh, God, please help us.*

Kevin didn't say anything; he just looked grim and nervous.


They were waiting for Michael when he opened the door to the inner office. He gave them encouraging pats on the back as they headed through the outer office, but he didn't speak. Holly watched them go from her desk, her dark face solemn and concerned.

The trip back up to the Hall was a blur. All Lilia was really conscious of was the turmoil in both her head and her stomach. Her palms were sweaty.

The triangular plastiglass accelevator disgorged them into the Hall and they marched toward the Chamber with the same grim determination they might have used to march toward their execution. Up and down the Hall, heads turned to watch them. Michael noticed, his grim expression tightening further, but the twins were both oblivious. At this moment, the elegant walls could have been lined with actual eyes and Lilia and Kevin would not have given them a second glance.

The dark-skinned woman in the midnight blue dress stood at the Chamber entrance, waiting. As soon as she saw the twins, she waved them forward. She reaffixed tiny mics to Lilia and Kevin's collars and slipped through one of the Chamber doors. A second later, she reappeared. "They're ready for you."

Lilia and Kevin exchanged glances. This was it. *Our future hinges on this moment.*

Kevin took the first step toward the heavy double doors. Lilia sucked in a deep breath and felt a rush of inexplicable peace flood her mind. Whatever happened, they would make it through. She discreetly wiped her palms on her pants and followed.

The Chamber was just as imposing as it had looked a few hours earlier, but Lilia did not pay much attention. Her focus was on the semi-circle of chairs and tables facing the three equally imposing forms of the Chief Ministers at their table at the north point of the triangular room.

She and Kevin crossed the celadon marble floor to the place they had stood earlier, off to the side of Chairman Dunn's podium and turned to face the Triumvirate. The sun had shifted.

Lilia flicked her eyes across the sea of faces, briefly registering a mix of nothingness and dissatisfaction. Their grandfather's face was impassive, as was that of Martin Hollowell. Swallowing, Lilia straightened her shoulders.

"Captain Strong, Miss Strong," Quin'lan Dunn began, his coppery face stern. "You stand before the Triumvirate accused of treason."

Lilia half-expected him to ask them how they pled, but Dunn did not.

"After hearing your testimony and that of Ambassador Kedis and Lon Strong, and reviewing the evidence, the Triumvirate has reached a decision."

Lilia stood perfectly still, her heart slamming painfully against her ribcage. Beside her, Kevin resembled a living statue.

"Given that you willingly and knowingly aided and abetted Galactic Union citizens who had illegally entered the Coalition, the Triumvirate finds you guilty of treason." Dunn's voice seemed to echo through the Chamber.

*Guilty of treason.* The words hit Lilia like a sledgehammer. For the span of a few heartbeats, she couldn't *breathe.*

"The sentence for your crime," Dunn continued, "is life in a maximum-security prison. However…"

During that pause, the entirely galaxy seemed to hang motionless. The tiniest flicker of hope flared to life in Lilia's chest, but she couldn't bring herself to grasp it. Not yet.

"However…" Dunn repeated, clearing his throat, "the Triumvirate has also taken into account the fact that your actions were taken out of a patriotic desire to serve the Coalition." His gaze swept around the Chamber before coming to rest on the twins again.

*Just get on with it!* Lilia pleaded mentally.

"Therefore, Captain Strong, Miss Strong, the Triumvirate pardons you for your crimes. You are free to go."

*Free to go…* The twins stood frozen, unable to believe their ears. They'd just been convicted of treason…and now they'd been pardoned?

It almost seemed too good to be true.

Lilia had to clear her throat before she could speak. "We're—we're free to go?"

"That is correct." Dunn paused, and when he spoke again, his voice was very dry. "Certain quarters of the Triumvirate proposed we sanction you with a flight ban."

Lilia's heart sank; she knew Kevin felt the same. A flight ban would almost certainly kill Three Cords Shipping.

"That said," Dunn continued, "after much deliberation, we decided a permanent record of conviction for treason was punishment enough and no further sanction need be imposed."

The twins concluded they weren't dreaming at the same time. They shifted to face the three Chief Ministers and bowed respectfully, before turning to face the rest of the Triumvirate and repeating the gesture.

"Thank you—"

"—very much."

Chief Minister Hugh Koen spoke from the head of the room. "We would suggest you…refrain from engaging in any further illegal activities."

Lilia could have laughed out loud at that. *We have* no *desire to get in trouble again.*

Kevin's smile was full of relief. "On that point, Chief Minister, we are in complete agreement."

He and Lilia bowed again, and then moved to exit the Chamber on legs that were just the slightest bit shaky. Lilia darted a glance at their grandfather as they went. His impassive expression softened a fraction; he gave her the tiniest of smiles. Behind him, Derek mirrored his expression.

Relief flooded Lilia, spreading through her body in a warm rush, but as they neared the massive double doors, it ebbed a little. A tiny voice in the back of her mind whispered that wouldn't it be a terrible joke if Dunn abruptly called them back and said the Triumvirate had changed their minds?

She tensed as Kevin pushed one of the heavy doors open, but no one called their names. They escaped into the Hall—and freedom.

Dimly, Lilia registered the way the attention of every single person in the Hall immediately snapped to them, but at the moment she couldn't bring herself to care. *We're free. Thank you, Jesus!*

They weren't going to prison. They weren't being banned from running their business.

Michael rose from the chair he'd been occupying and came forward to meet them.

"Well," he said quietly, "that didn't take long." His voice was light, but his violet eyes were concerned.

"We're fine," Kevin said in a dazed voice. "They—they convicted us of treason—"

Michael's blond eyebrows shot up in alarm, though he quickly smothered the expression—there were far too many eyes on them.

"—and then they pardoned us," Lilia finished. "No sanctions."

Michael exhaled in a rush. "I am *so* glad to hear that."

Kevin grinned, though he still looked dazed. "Not half as glad as we are."

Lilia nodded, too overcome for words. Tears of relief picked the backs of her eyes. *Thank you, Lord. Thank you so much.*

Michael put a hand on both their backs. "Head back to Grandfather's office." Kevin started to open his mouth; Michael shook his head. "No argument. There'll definitely have to be a press conference after this."

"Come on, Kev." Lilia looped her arm through Kevin's. "We'll be fine." She switched to Nancom. [The worst is over, remember?]

[I just want to get out of here,] he grumbled, but he went.


When they reached Aiden's office suite, they shared their news with Holly and then returned to the inner office. Michael Nancommed them the access code. The first thing they did was Nancom Erik.

The blond Guardian sounded as relieved as they felt. [I was not lookin' forward to visitin' you two in prison.]

[It's sweet you would have visited us,] Lilia teased.

[Yeah, well, you have a habit of growin' on people.] Erik paused for effect. [Kinda like a fungus, if you think about it.]

[Ha, ha,] Kevin said. He told Erik about the flight ban they'd almost received.

[Glad that didn't happen either. Although...]

The twins exchanged dubious looks. That...did not sound promising. Together, they asked, ['Although', what?]

[You *do* realize this may have an impact on your business anyway,] Erik said slowly. [Bein' convicted of treason, I mean.]

Lilia and Kevin looked at each other again, some of their relief and elation beginning to fade. [But we were—]

[—just pardoned.]

[Doesn't matter.] They could almost see Erik shaking his head. [It'll still be on your official record—an' some people care about that kind of stuff.] He paused again. [Not to mention all the press you're gettin'.]

Lilia collapsed into the brown leather recliner Kevin had occupied early. [I *have* thought about all the press driving some of our clients away.] Her throat felt tight; it was a good thing she didn't have to speak aloud.

[Hey, it may not be that bad,] Erik said bracingly. [Just wanted you to be prepared.]

[Thanks,] Kevin said. [We—]

[—appreciate it,] Lilia finished.

[You still stuck there for the rest of the day?] Erik asked.

Kevin made a face, even though Erik couldn't see him. [Unfortunately.]

[Well, let me know when they let ya out.]

[Will do,] the twins promised together, before closing Erik's channel.

They Nancommed Nob next, to give him the news. The older Guardian had almost the same reaction as Erik. That done, Lilia and Kevin settled down to wait.

It was easier this time, now that they no longer had all those ugly possibilities dangling over their heads. Every so often, Lilia just closed her eyes and whispered, "Thank you."

The hardest part was behind them now—they could deal with a press conference and everything that came next.

# CHAPTER 19

AIDEN watched his youngest grandchildren stride out of the Chamber, relief and gratitude swelling his chest, though he did not show it. There would be ramifications and complications resulting from their treason conviction—it was inevitable—but they were not being escorted from the Four Towers to spend the rest of their lives in prison.

For that, he was profoundly grateful. *Thank you, Father God.*

The atmosphere in the Chamber was an odd blend of dissatisfaction and resignation. Briscoe's proposal had passed by the slimmest of margins—but it *had* passed. The majority of the Triumvirate had recognized that it was the best solution they could hope for in these circumstances.

Consequences for Lon's involvement had been officially tabled, and now the Triumvirate was free to move on to the next pressing matter facing them—

—what to do with Kedis's proposal of peace negotiations now that they officially had a cease-fire.

The Triumvirate had not made much headway on that front when they finally dismissed for the evening. Aiden and Derek departed the Chamber along with the rest of the Triumvirate and their aides and found Michael waiting for them in the Hall.

Michael did not ask how things had gone—he knew better. Instead, he tipped his head in the direction of the front of Triumvirate Tower. "Brace yourself, Grandfather. The media's been waiting all day for an official update."

Aiden restrained a sigh. "I can imagine."

He could not blame them; if he were a regular citizen, not privy to the Triumvirate's dealings, he would want answers as well. They joined the flow of traffic streaming to the right and left down the Hall toward the accelevators and veered left. "Where is Felix?"

"In your office," Michael answered. "Kevin and Lilia are with him. We can pick them up on our way down."

Aiden started. "They are still here?"

"Convinced them it was for the best that they wait for you." Michael grimaced. "I don't think they'd have been able to escape the media. Especially not after what happened today."

"Not via conventional means, no," Aiden agreed softly. He did not miss the nervous glances his grandsons exchanged—or the way their eyes flicked around them to see if anyone had overheard. He caught Derek's eye, conveying in a look that he intended to say no more on the subject.

His colleagues gathered around the accelevator bank in clumps as they awaited their turn to descend into the main part of Triumvirate Tower, either conversing with each other or with their aides. They were all aware of the media storm awaiting them when they emerged from the Four Towers. The Chief Ministers were preparing to release an official statement, but many of the Representatives would be required to speak to media crews as well.

"Mouta's preparing a statement based on info I sent him," Derek said as they descended to the next level and emerged from the triangular accelevator to join the queue forming in front of the Tower's internal accelevator bank. "It should be ready for you to review shortly."

"Excellent."

Aiden did not speak again until they set foot in his office suite on Level 27. He nodded to his secretary, who still occupied her desk in the outer office. "Go home, Holly. It's been a long day."

Holly did not move. "Representative, are you sure—"

"Quite." Aiden smiled kindly. "Tomorrow will be another long day. Go home and get some rest. Have Security escort you out, just to be on the safe side."

"Yes, sir." Rising from her chair, Holly set about gathering her things.

Michael keyed in the access code for the door leading into the inner hall and Aiden strode down the hall into his office, where he found his Chief of Staff, Felix Mouta, muttering to himself and pacing back and forth, his attention on his datapad. Kevin stood leaning up against one of the windows, staring blankly at the mirrored plastiglass of Security Tower, while Lilia lay stretched out on his brown leather sofa, propped up by her elbows, staring at her own datapad.

All three of them turned to look at Aiden and Michael and Derek as they entered behind him.

Kevin pushed off the window; Lilia sat up. "Grandfather," they said together.

Aiden acknowledged them with a nod, but the bulk of his attention was for his Chief of Staff. "What do you have for me, Felix?"

"See for yourself." Mouta handed him the datapad.

Aiden scanned the short speech, before nodding in approval. "Thank you." He turned to his grandchildren. "We will get this over with and get something to eat on the way home." He was not particularly hungry, but he recognized that his body needed sustenance and he knew his grandchildren needed to eat more than usual because of the nanites in their bodies.

His comlink buzzed with an incoming call. Aiden glanced down in a little surprise; only a few people had these comm details and most of them were standing in this office with him. He glanced at the display and his mouth tightened. *Carson.* After weeks of stony silence, his brother finally wanted to talk.

*I will have to get back to him later.* Aiden shook his head slightly; he still had work to do.


The press conference went more smoothly than Aiden had expected. The bulk of the crowd of reporters and cams gathered around the Chief Ministers and their unprecedented appearance together at the ground-level entrance to Triumvirate Tower, but others targeted individual Representatives for interviews. Aiden gave his official statement, which included the announcement about Kevin and Lilia's conviction and immediate pardon, and answered questions with as much patience as he could muster.

His grandchildren stood behind him. Aiden did not want the reporters asking the twins questions directly; he wanted everything funneled through him. He could tell this annoyed more than a few of the reporters, but he did not care. His youngest grandchildren had been through enough without adding a media interrogation on top of everything else.

Aiden finally ended the interview, giving the reporters a smile and saying, "That is enough for tonight, I believe. We will be back tomorrow."

The media crews gradually dispersed, and Michael and the rest of Aiden's security team hustled him down to the secure parking garage. Mouta bid them farewell there to return to his own home. Lilia had already called in an order for food from a restaurant near Ferndale that served all manner of stir-fry; they picked it up on the way home.

The family ate together, but Aiden finished quickly and excused himself to his study, which was next to his bedroom. His brain was still much too full to be able to relax yet.

And there was still the matter of his brother to deal with.

Carson had left him a brief message, asking him to return his call as soon as possible. The fact that he asked for a return call in-stead of demanding Aiden comply was a good sign, but Aiden would have rather ignored him tonight. Dealing with his older brother re-quired a good deal of both patience and energy—and right now Aiden was in short supply of both.

Closing his eyes, he rubbed his wrinkled forehead with the pads of his fingers. *Lord, grant me the patience to treat him kindly.* The only thing Carson could possibly have to complain about now that the mining stations were free was the fact that he was related to three people who had helped a G.U. Ambassador.

His study held two comfortable dark green armchairs in one corner, with a cherry end table between them, and matching book-cases in the other corner. His desk, also made of cherry, sat in front of a wide window. Sinking down into the dark green chair behind his desk, Aiden tapped the comm panel mounted on one corner.

A moment later, his older brother's holographic head and shoulders appeared in the air before him. Aiden inclined his head. "Carson."

"Aiden. Thank you for returning my call so quickly." Carson Monroe, an older, stockier, slightly more wrinkled version of Aiden complete with a full beard, seemed to hesitate. "I know you've had a great deal on your plate today."

Aiden did not let his surprise at this unusual graciousness show. "That is an understatement." He did not wait for his brother to get to the point but said, "I trust you have heard the news?"

"Yes." Carson hesitated again, as though his words were sticking in his throat. He cleared his throat gruffly, looking decidedly uncomfortable. "That would be why I am calling. I would have come in person, but the media presence around you is a little heavier than usual—and it has spilled over to envelope my family as well."

Aiden raised an eyebrow, waiting for a snide comment about his grandchildren's half-Tarynian blood, but to his surprise none came.

"I wanted to say—that is," Carson cleared his throat again, "Medea and I wanted to say…thank you." He paused, as though waiting for Aiden to speak, but when his younger brother remained silent, he continued, "We spoke to Pietro this evening, after the Tarynian ships left and stopped jamming their communications, and he said that the Triumvirate arranged for supplies to be sent to the mining stations via that…transporter…some weeks ago to keep the Tarynians from starving them out."

"We did." Aiden allowed one corner of his mouth to tilt in a wry smile. "None of us wished any harm to come to the miners and their families."

Carson nodded. "I was…too harsh with you in our last conversation, little brother. The thought of losing my son…" He trailed off.

A few weeks before, he had accused Aiden—and the rest of the Triumvirate—of doing nothing to help the beleaguered mining stations. At the time, there had been nothing the Triumvirate *could* do. The joint Department of Internal Affairs' revelation about the transporters had changed everything, but if Carson had known about the supply shipments sent to Xana 5 and Sapriske 6 prior to today, he had kept quiet.

*It does not matter now*, Aiden thought, mentally waving the thought away. The important thing was that the workers and their families aboard those mining stations were safe now—and they were back in full operation. This was particular important when it came to Xana 5; the bulk of the Coalition's material to make torpedo cores was mined there.

"I am just glad Ambassador Kedis was amenable to freeing the mining stations while we consider opening negotiations," he said at last.

Carson nodded again, but frowned. "What *is* the Triumvirate's position on opening negotiations?"

Something crystallized inside Aiden, a heavy weight settling in his stomach. "Surely you have seen the news, Carson." He held up a hand. "We held a press conference not long ago."

"Oh, I've heard the official line." Carson waved a hand. "I wanted to hear your thoughts."

"My thoughts." Aiden took a breath and exhaled slowly. "I do not know what to tell you yet. There are too many factors at play here. We have only just begun."

"But negotiations *will* happen," his brother pressed. "You won't cut them off before they can begin?"

"There are some who might prefer that route," Aiden conceded, "but at this point I believe we are beyond that." He hesitated for a moment. "I see only one path before us, Carson. We must negotiate *something* with the Galactic Union." He shook his head. "I do not wish to see us join them—"

"No," Carson agreed quickly. "Not join them. They'd swallow us up."

"—but we must do something."

"We don't want another twenty-year blockade."

"No."

The two brothers shared a look of grim understanding.

*It is strange*, Aiden thought, *to be on the same page with Carson about something after all this time.*

Carson's mouth puckered and then he said, "You must be ecstatic about Lon. I know—I know I would be, in your situation."

For the first time, Aiden felt a flash of humor. "What, no jibe about the fact that he is half-Tarynian?"

Carson's green eyes flashed and he drew in a sharp breath, but he restrained himself from answering. After an awkward pause, he said, "I suppose I deserve that. I still don't know what to think about what he and your other grandchildren did, but…I *am* glad he's not dead. For your sake."

"Thank you." Aiden inclined his head.

The silence between them grew awkward again. "Well," Carson said brusquely, "I trust you'll do the best thing for the Coalition in this whole Kedis business."

"That has always been my goal."

"Take care, little brother. I'm sure we'll speak again."

*Perhaps*, Aiden thought. *If it is on your terms.* All he said aloud was, "I am sure we shall."

Just before Carson severed the connection, he said, "We can't actually *join* them, Aiden. Trade with them, yes, but not join them. Not with their lack of a sound currency and their identchips and everything else."

"I am well aware of that. Give Medea my regards."

Carson gave him one last piercing look and then his holograph dissolved.

With a sigh, Aiden sat back in his chair. *A thank you and a not-so-subtle discussion on my stance and where Carson wants me stand.* He had expected the latter, but not the former. Curious. He had never expected his older brother to actually acknowledge the Triumvirate—and by extension he, Aiden—had done something productive.

*There is indeed a first time for everything, I suppose.* He allowed himself a small smile. *Even for an eighty year-old like Carson.*

# CHAPTER 20

THE shrill beep of an incoming high-priority message roused Chesnee from the middle of his sleep cycle late that night. He opened his eyes, stifling the first few words that came to mind, and rolled out of his bunk. Wiping the sleep from his eyes, he padded out into his office and hit his comm panel with a little more force than usual.

*If it's Tyler again, wanting yet* another *update…*

It wasn't.

Leo Kedis's head and shoulders greeted him. The Ambassador looked slightly rumpled—he was *still* wearing his tuxedo—but he looked as pleased with himself as any politician who had just negotiated a cease-fire had any right to be.

"Ambassador," Chesnee said in gruff surprise.

"Admiral." Kedis actually had the grace to look apologetic. "I do apologize for the late hour, but this is the first time I've had the chance to contact you since we spoke earlier."

Drowsiness fell away immediately; Chesnee's back straightened as he took a seat in his chair. "What has happened? Has the Triumvirate changed their minds?"

"No, no, nothing like that." Kedis trailed off thoughtfully, as though he wasn't quite sure where to start. Threads of fatigue showed in his face, but beneath the weariness Chesnee glimpsed the keen calculation he had fully come to expect from the man. "Let's just say I have come into possession of some rather startling information and go from there, shall we?"

"Startling information?" Even as he spoke, Chesnee's mind began to race with possibilities.

"Yes." Kedis gave him a slow nod. "Information of such a sensitive nature that though I came into possession of it a week ago, I could not safely relay it to you until now."

Chesnee leaned forward. "Consider my interest well and truly piqued, Ambassador."

"I thought you might say that." Kedis's lips curved in a slight smile before he shook his head. "Even given the advances human civilization has made thus far in the galaxy, it hardly seems possible, and yet…"

Realization washed over Chesnee, as cold and sudden as an unexpected bucket of ice water dumped over his head. He *knew* what Kedis was about to tell him. *It's real.*

"Somehow, despite the handicaps they've faced being cut off from the rest of the galaxy for twenty years, the Coalition has managed to invent an actual teleportation device." Kedis shook his head again, this time in bemusement. "They call it a transporter."

Chesnee was profoundly grateful he was already sitting down. He had spent the past few months wondering, had debated with himself many times whether or not he should inform High Command of the possibility of a transporter, and yet without *proof* all he'd had was speculation. He had to clear his throat twice before he could speak. "A transporter?"

"Yes."

"You're, ah, you're quite certain this thing is real?"

"Oh, yes." Kedis waved a holographic hand. "I've seen it in operation. It's real. The Triumvirate announced it to the entire Coalition last week. I saw it on the news."

*It's real.* Chesnee sank back in his seat, his eyes sliding past Kedis as a great many puzzle pieces fell into place inside his mind. "The mining stations. That's how they did it."

He did not realize he had spoken aloud until Kedis quizzically cocked his head to one side. "The what?"

"The mining stations." Chesnee snapped his focus back to the Ambassador. "Xana 5 and Sapriske 6. I've cut their supply chains off for the past several months, hoping to starve them out. By my people's calculations, they should have capitulated already." It still irked him that he'd had to remove his ships.

Kedis was already nodding. "You think the Coalition used this transporter device to send them supplies."

"Well…yes. It's the only logical conclusion I can draw, unless they've started eating each other." He gave a humorless smile, but Kedis was scrutinizing him with a sharp air he did not like at all.

He resisted the urge to squirm in his seat. *Admirals do not squirm.* "Is there something else, Ambassador?"

"You're not as surprised as I thought you'd be."

Chesnee blinked at him. "I beg your pardon."

Kedis's dark almond-shaped eyes narrowed further. "In fact, all things considered, you're taking the news rather well."

"I could be in shock," Chesnee said dryly. "It'll take some time to process all the implications of this."

"True…but I doubt it." It was Kedis's turn to lean forward. "You *knew*, Admiral." He sat back, looking positively dumbstruck. "How could you know?"

They stared at each other for a second. That's *not the real question you want to ask*, Chesnee wanted to say.

"And if you knew, why did High Command never mention it?"

Chesnee inhaled. He found himself at a crossroads. He could deny Kedis's allegation, which would be a lie, or he could tell the Ambassador the truth. *One can only hope he won't find a way to turn it into a weapon.*

He doubted it, but he had little choice.

"I had no proof," he said at last, spreading his hands. "I've heard scuttlebutt through General Deam, who is in charge of Ground Division, that the Coalition was developing something like this, but all we had was a dead man's word that it existed."

Kedis continued to eye him, waiting for the rest of the story.

"Given the almost certainly inflammatory nature of such a revelation, I chose not to pass it along to High Command until I had actual proof."

Silence fell between them for a long moment, and then Kedis nodded. "That would make sense. Naturally, somebody in High Command would leak it to the Senate, and then we'd have full-scale pandemonium on our hands, all based on a 'maybe'."

"That's what I was trying to avoid." Chesnee cleared his throat again. "Of course, now, with full confirmation that the machine exists, High Command will have to be notified."

"Oh, undoubtedly." Kedis's face suddenly split with a predatory grin. "And then, no doubt, we'll be inundated with yet more politicians and hangers on attempting to cash in on our discovery."

Chesnee tried to suppress his grimace at this, and was mostly successful.

Kedis abruptly changed the subject. "I expect you'll be hearing from me again shortly. I'll need to arrange the transfer of my staff from your flagship to Sonela." He grinned again; the expression held more humor this time. "If I'm lucky, I might even be able to talk the Triumvirate into letting me use the transporter. As a show of good faith on their parts."

*I wonder how your staff will feel about that.* Chesnee inclined his head. "I'll be happy to send shuttles to Sta'Gloa if they don't cooperate."

"Thank you, Admiral."

"Are my men still in one piece?"

Kedis chuckled. "Of course they are. I applaud your choices, Admiral; they've both done quite well. I think Lieutenant Wright, in particular, will be of good use as negotiations unfold."

Chesnee was not quite sure what to make of that, but he let it slide. He had a few other things to cover. "And Captain Strong?"

"He's proved very useful as well. He's now my official Coalition liaison, and I have a feeling his family relations will come in quite handy."

Nodding, Chesnee moved on to his next question. "Do you think you stand a chance of succeeding?"

"At the risk of sounding arrogant, I do. The Coalition is as tired of this strife as we are, and they are ready for a change."

"Even with Glo'Stea's shield now intact?"

Kedis's smile was shark-like. "*Especially* with their shield intact. They think they have the upper hand now."

"And you don't agree?" Chesnee raised his eyebrows in feigned disbelief. He wanted to know what was going on inside Kedis's head while he had the chance.

"Of course not." Kedis swept a hand through the air. "We still control a quarter of Glo'Stea's surface. Our ships—your ships, Admiral—still control this system. Yes, our ground forces on Glo'Stea are currently facing a sticky situation being cut off from the rest of your forces in space, but they are *still there*. The Glo'Stean Resistance's paltry efforts won't dislodge them without a fuss, and besides," he shrugged, "the cease-fire currently prevents any further conflict between them. We've reached a draw—but we still outnumber and outgun them."

"I see. Well, I thank you for your honesty, Ambassador."

Kedis's answering smile was genuinely amused. "Didn't expect it from me, did you, Admiral?"

Chesnee only shrugged. "My experience with politicians has not led me to think much of their integrity."

"Oh, honest politicians do exist." Kedis's expression turned considering. "I do believe several of them sit on the Triumvirate. Captain Strong's grandfather would be one. A man called Briscoe would be another, from what I understand."

He rubbed his hands together. "I must say, I'm looking forward to doing battle in this arena."

"If you would, Ambassador, keep me apprised of developments." Chesnee smiled wryly. "The Senate is putting pressure on High Command, and Fleet Admiral Tyler, in turn, is putting pressure on me. If you could feed them a bone periodically, I think it would go a long way to keeping both of us from being inundated with unwelcome visitors."

Kedis laughed. "I believe I can do that." His expression grew smug. "I expect to have good developments to report."

"I hope so."

"Well, Admiral, I will let you get back to your sleep."

"Wait." The word slipped out before Chesnee could help himself.

Kedis glanced at him, his eyebrows raised in a silent question.

Chesnee had a furious—but brief—debate with himself. *To hell with it*, he thought savagely. He'd been curious for months, and if the transporter was real, perhaps…just perhaps… "It's my turn to say something startling, Ambassador."

"Oh?"

"Yes. Have you by any chance heard anything about individuals called Guardians?"

When Kedis finally ended the transmission, Chesnee was no closer to solving the Guardians mystery than he was before, but he had a new ally. Intrigued by the possibilities, Kedis had promised to keep his eyes and ears open for any information. Chesnee could only hope the Ambassador, with his new social network, could either prove or disprove the myth.

*In the meantime*…He rubbed his dry eyes. *Best to call Tyler.* A small smile curved his mouth. *He did say to keep him apprised.*

# CHAPTER 21

THE next morning dawned bright and clear, promising to be a beautiful late spring day. Neither of the twins was in the proper frame of mind to appreciate it. They had escaped Ferndale without too much trouble, and had done their best to lose any possible tails on their journey to Sonela's downtown district. Their hoverbus had dropped them off several blocks from the Cramer Building; they walked the rest of the way.

Their steps slowed as they crossed an enclosed steel and plastiglass four-way pedestrian bridge spanning a broad thoroughfare. They could see the Cramer Building from here; an angular skyscraper with a slanted roof. Skimmers and other traffic streamed above and below them, a constant flow of motion.

Kevin looked faintly green. "I think I'm more nervous about this than I was about facing the Triumvirate."

Lilia flattened a hand over her stomach. "I know exactly what you mean."

Sharing a grim look, they stepped off the bridge and crossed the last block separating them from the Cramer Building. The lobby was decorated in rich tints of burgundy, forest green, and gold against a burnished dark wood background. A 'bot floated toward them—nothing more than a floating bronze head wearing a matching top hat with a pair of arms protruding from what should have been its neck—but they waved it off and headed for the accelevators. They knew where they were going.

They rode the accelevator up to Level 23 in nervous silence. Just before the accelevator doors slid open, Kevin caught Lilia's eye. "Whatever happens, Lil, we did the right thing."

She blew out a breath. "I know that."

The Sonela NCDC branch office occupied the entirety of Level 23. Tan chairs and couches were arranged on one side of the crisp white waiting room, leaving a broad walkway of lustrous green tile between the accelevator bank and a reception desk up against the right-hand wall. At the end of the room, a hall led deeper into he office.

The receptionist, Willard Travis, a pale young man with a shaved head and an inscrutable expression, regarded the twins from behind his desk. He must have commed the twins' handler as soon as they emerged from the accelevator, because Riley Callahan immediately came striding out to meet them.

Callahan was a slender, smooth-shaven man in his early thirties. He had brown hair, and there was nothing particularly remarkable about his features except for his eyes, which were the color of old ice. They cast a cold pallor over what would have otherwise been a pleasant demeanor.

"Good morning." He returned the bow the twins gave him, before eying them wryly. "Well, you're nothing if not prompt."

Kevin tried to smile. "We'd like to get this over with."

"I don't blame you." Callahan motioned for them to follow him toward the hall that led in the direction of his office, past a wall covered with interlocking gold rectangles bearing the names of Guardians who had died in the service of the NCDC.

Lilia glanced at Kevin, the same thought running through both their minds. That wall also now bore the name of Sheena Azif, a Guardian who had died near the end of the Lanx rescue mission.

"Never a dull moment for you two, is there?" Callahan glanced between them.

The twins just shrugged.

"Congratulations on your official pardon," Callahan continued. "I assured my supervisors that an armed escort was unnecessary."

Lilia barely kept herself from making a face at that. "Thanks."

"You're welcome."

"You mean 'armed' as in armed with impactors?" Kevin asked. When Callahan shot him an astonished look, he smiled humorlessly. "Alan Birch has already introduced us to those."

"Birch." Callahan looked faintly disgusted. "I should have known."

"We didn't know they existed until he shot us with them," Lilia said.

Callahan pursed his lips. "Guardians aren't supposed to know. Not until they cross the line."

Lilia and Kevin exchanged glances out of the corners of their eyes. [Well, *that* makes—]

[—a lot of sense.]

Callahan led them around a corner, but instead of turning left toward his office, he led them to the right and then halted in the middle of the hall to face them. [I'm sorry about this,] he said, opening a joint Nancom channel to them. [Unfortunately, given the magnitude of what you two accomplished, a hearing is unavoidable. The Board will be deciding if you have a future in the NCDC. There isn't much I can do about that, other than to give them my assessment of your characters, which I've already done.]

Lilia raised an eyebrow. [You don't want to see us kicked out?]

Callahan smiled, but it did not quite reach his eyes. [Certainly not. You two have too much potential.]

[Do you think we stand a chance?] Kevin asked.

[I hope so. The fact that you're not locked up on treason charges should help.] Aloud, Callahan said, "This way." He led them deeper into the confines of the NCDC offices, until they came to a set of double doors with a sign above them that read, *Conference Room Beta.*

Lilia's heart began to beat faster. *This is it.*

"Are you coming in with us?" Kevin asked.

"Yes, but we won't have any interaction." Callahan reached for the door panel. "Are you ready?"

"Ready as we'll ever be." Kevin squared his shoulders.

"That's the spirit. Remember why you joined the NCDC in the first place."

A rush of bad memories flashed before Lilia's eyes; she blinked them away. *I'm not likely to forget.*

The doors slid open to reveal what looked like a tiny courtroom. Rows of seats lined the walls on either side and fanned out behind a small table with several chairs that stood facing a much longer table in front of the far wall. Five stately-looking individuals—three men and two women—were in the process of seating themselves behind this table, facing the twins and the door. They were all older, ranging from their fifties to their sixties.

Lilia swallowed. *The Board.* She'd never thought much about who oversaw the NCDC until today.

Callahan approached the long table. "Ladies and gentlemen, as requested, Kevin and Lilia Strong have arrived for their hearing."

The man in the middle, probably ten years younger than their grandfather but just as wrinkled, with sharp, dark eyes and bushy gray eyebrows set in a deep brown face, gave the twins an intense once-over. "Excellent." He motioned to the small table. "Have a seat."

Callahan moved off to a chair on one side, while Lilia and Kevin sat down at the table. At first Lilia folded her hands on the table, but she thought the better of it and folded them in her lap instead.

The man in the middle nodded to the woman who sat to his right. She was a little younger, with slanted almond-shaped eyes, dark hair pinned up in a topknot, and delicate, papery skin. She cleared her throat. "For the record, please state your names and the date you became Guardians."

Lilia and Kevin both dutifully recited this information.

The woman proceeded to run them through a few more basic questions before she cut to the chase. "You are facing this hearing today because it has come to our attention that you were…recently…involved with smuggling Tarynians through Sta'Gloa's shield and then smuggled those same Tarynians into the Tri-Global Tournament's Closing Ceremonies Gala."

The twins exchanged glances. "We didn't smuggle the Tarynians *through* Sta'Gloa's—"

"—shield. They were already on-world when we found out about them."

All five members of the Board stared at them. Lilia fought the urge to shift uncomfortably under their unstinting scrutiny.

"You admit your involvement, then?"

*Like we can deny it when we're on holo-cam and there are hundreds of witnesses,* Lilia thought. *Not to mention the Triumvirate just convicted us of treason and then pardoned us.* It was hard to keep from rolling her eyes in exasperation. Behind them, she thought she heard the door whisper open again, but she didn't dare turn around to see who had joined them.

Kevin raised his chin. "We helped Ambassador Kedis gain an audience with the Triumvirate, yes. *Without* revealing our status as

Guardians," he added quickly, as the members of the Board exchanged glances. "And, as I'm sure you've heard, the Triumvirate issued us an official pardon yesterday."

The man on the far end of the table regarded them with narrowed eyes. He was the youngest of the five, with dark, curly hair, pale skin, and wide features that made him look younger than he was. "Why would you do this? What possible motivation could you have for risking so much?"

Lilia took a deep breath. *Here we go again.* "As we explained to the Triumvirate yesterday…" she began.

The members of the Board listened to their story, and then asked them all kinds of probing questions before dismissing the twins into the hall while they decided their fate. The twins both rose from their chairs and bowed in the members' direction. "Thank you for your consideration," they said together.

As she turned around to head for the door, Lilia caught sight of an unwelcome figure seated near the back. Her stomach twisted. *What is* he *doing here?*

Beside her, Kevin stiffened.

They marched toward the door, barely noticing Callahan rising from his seat and falling into step behind them. Birch wore a faint, sardonic smirk. He motioned for them to precede him out of the door, which they did so, reluctantly.

As soon as the doors were shut, Kevin rounded on Birch. "What are *you* doing here?"

Birch shrugged. "Just thought I'd see how things were going." He glanced past the twins at Callahan. "Riley."

"Alan." Callahan's eyes looked more like chips of old ice than ever. "Come to make sure the Board makes the right decision?"

"Oh, unlike the Triumvirate, I know they'll make the right decision." Birch smiled. "There isn't much question about that."

"That's what you think," Lilia said tartly.

Birch's green eyes slid to her. "That's what I know, Miss Strong." His expression suddenly tightened. "It's a shame your brother can't be here."

"Even if he could," Callahan said abruptly, before Kevin could respond, "I think it unlikely that the Board would revoke his Guardian status."

All three of them—Lilia, Kevin, and Birch—stared at him in shock.

Callahan shrugged. "Think about it. Guardians were intended to be a discreet backup layer of protection for our society. Lon Strong is currently serving as liaison to a Galactic Union Ambassador attempting to open peace talks with the Triumvirate. Who better to help protect Kedis and prevent all-out war than a Guardian?"

"You can't be serious," Birch said at last, distaste dripping from every syllable.

Callahan shrugged again. "At least now it's one less Guardian the NCDC has to worry about discreetly assigning to Kedis."

His eyes met Lilia's as he said this, and the half-wry, half-resigned expression in them jolted her right down to her toes. *They'll try to kick us out precisely because they* can't *punish Lon.*

It was a horrible, petty thought…but…if the NCDC had to make an example of someone…

An acutely uncomfortable silence fell in the hallway. Neither Lilia nor Kevin felt like talking, Callahan had lapsed into silence, and even Birch seemed to have temporarily run out of insults.

Almost ten minutes later, Callahan abruptly stirred. "They've reached a decision. You're to go back in now."

Lilia and Kevin traded looks—which did not go unnoticed by either Birch or Callahan—and headed back into the conference room.

The Board waited until they were seated again to address them. The man in the middle knit his bushy eyebrows together. "Mr. Strong, Miss Strong, we have reached a decision in your case This was by no means an easy decision, given the Triumvirate's decision yesterday as well as your exemplary performance in your mission to Lanx. For being as new to the NCDC as you are, you have more experience than many Guardians, but we must address this grave breach in NCDC protocols."

*What breach?* Lilia wanted to demand. *We used being Guardians to help us, sure, but we didn't tell the* Tarynians *about it.* She bit down on her tongue, however, and remained silent.

[I've got a bad feeling about this,] Kevin said through his channel. [You and me both.]

"It is with great regret that we inform you that your status within the NCDC as Guardians is hereby revoked."

Lilia's breath caught in her throat. *They actually did it.*

"You will proceed from this hearing to the Infusion Wing, where our doctors will reverse the infusion process and remove your nanites. You will be required to return all NCDC-issued equipment—including your nanoblades." The man looked down his nose at them. "Do you understand?"

Kevin did not flinch. "We understand."

Lilia had to suppress the hysterical laugh that suddenly bubbled up in her throat. [Do you think they'll take our nanoblades and equipment before or after they figure out that we're nano-genetic anomalies?]

[Hopefully they'll figure that out *before*.]

The man's expression held genuine regret. "This is an unfortunate set of circumstances. We are truly sorry to be faced with this decision."

[I think he means that,] Kevin said. [Probably pressure from other sources.]

[Like the person responsible for putting us on the Uva mission?]

[Exactly.]

The man held up a hand. "You are dismissed. I trust you will both cooperate?"

Lilia and Kevin both rose from their seats. "We will," Lilia said, before bowing stiffly and turning away. Birch, she saw, had resumed his seat in the back, and he looked extremely pleased with himself. *Just wait until you find out the joke's on you*, she told him silently.

The twins departed the conference room and stood blankly in the hallway outside. Lilia half-expected to be facing an armed escort when they left the conference room, but it was empty. The door open behind them; she suppressed a groan. *Oh, no. It's Birch.*

It was not.

Riley Callahan exited the conference room. "I'm to be your escort to the Infusion Wing," he said heavily.

"Thanks," Kevin said unenthusiastically.

Callahan regarded them both for a moment. He looked like he wanted to say something, but changed his mind at the last second and only shook his head instead. "Follow me."

He led them back toward the main office, before cutting to the left toward a set of double doors at one end of a hall. A holographic sign bearing the words 'Infusion Wing' stretched across the doors. They passed through the doors and found themselves in a tiny reception area where two nurses—one male and one female—awaited the twins.

"Lilia and Kevin Strong?" the woman asked. She was a mid-sized woman, with peaches and cream skin, light eyes, and hair so blonde it looked silver.

Kevin offered her a bleak smile. "Here we are."

The male nurse nodded to Callahan. By contrast, he was a hulking tower of a man, with dark skin and close-cropped black hair. "Thank you for bringing them in, Mr. Callahan."

"You're welcome." Callahan nodded to the twins in turn. "It was good to work with you, however briefly." His icy eyes flicked back and forth between them as he suddenly said via Nancom, [Don't hand any of your gear over until they test your nanites first.]

With that, he departed the Infusion Wing.

Lilia darted a tiny glance at her brother, to find him looking back at her, the same confusion and suspicion playing in his eyes. [Why would he tell us that?]

[I don't know. Unless… he knows about Michael.]

Lilia bit the inside of her lip. Michael was the only one of them who had been officially declared a nano-genetic anomaly by the NCDC. *I suppose it's possible Callahan is thinking we might be affected too.*

She and Kevin didn't have time to discuss it further.

"I'm Myrtle, and this is Naveen." The female nurse waved to her companion.

"First things first," Naveen said in a deep voice. He pulled a familiar small, silver device from a pocket of his pale blue scrubs and motioned for Kevin to hold out his arm. He touched the tip of the tester to Kevin's skin. "Okay, you can drop your arm."

Lilia's heart jumped into her throat as Myrtle performed the same test on her. The blonde nurse then motioned to a door leading out of the reception area. "Come with us, please."

"Will you keep us together?" Lilia blurted out. She knew they would be fine, *knew* they'd be walking out of the Cramer Building with their nanites intact, but a flicker of fear still stirred her insides. "Please?"

The nurses exchanged looks. "You underwent the infusion process together, didn't you?" Myrtle asked.

"Yes," Kevin answered.

Myrtle shrugged one slight shoulder. "No sense changing anything. Not to mention," she added over her shoulder, "they prefer to do defusions in pairs too, if it can be helped."

"Oh, that's good to know," Kevin said dryly.

Lilia just bit her lip.

Myrtle and Naveen led them to a small room that was empty save for a table standing in the center of the room. On the table were two long plastic boxes. Myrtle waved to the boxes. "Go ahead and start emptying out your ISFs. You'll be able to keep your personal effects, of course, but anything that's NCDC-issue has to stay with us." She made an apologetic face. "Company policy."

"Right," Lilia murmured, approaching the table. She glanced at Myrtle over her shoulder. "What happens if we don't clean out our ISFs?"

Short of torture or threat of bodily harm, they couldn't be forced to return everything—after all, the only person who could access an ISF was the Guardian to whom it belonged.

Myrtle and Naveen exchanged glances. "Well, we hope it won't come to that."

"Everything disappears," Naveen said bluntly. "The storage field collapses when the nanites are removed."

"Or when somebody dies," Kevin muttered, and froze.

From the look on his face, Lilia knew he hadn't meant to say it out loud.

Myrtle and Naveen both looked at him. "Yeah." Myrtle looked strangely troubled. "ISFs disappear when a Guardian dies. How did you know that?"

Kevin shrugged awkwardly. "We were on a mission a while back and we lost a Guardian."

The two nurses exchanged glances again.

"Anyway," Myrtle said, "Start emptying the boxes. We'll give you a few minutes—it can take a while."

"You are fortunate you have not been Guardians long," Naveen said. "You shouldn't have as much trouble adjusting to being regular civilians again."

"That's…great." Lilia didn't know what else to say. She knew what he meant—just being cut off from Nancom, her ISF, or her armor for a couple of hours was torture. To be permanently cut off from everything? She swallowed. *Not a pleasant prospect.*

Across the table, Kevin was staring down into his empty plastic box. [We need to delay until they check their findings.]

[Start with the non-essentials, I guess. Like protein bars.] Lilia suited action to word and reached into her ISF by her right knee. She brought out a handful of protein bars and dropped them into the box with a clatter that seemed to echo in the otherwise empty room.

She bit down hard on the inside of her lip. *How long can we stall?*

# CHAPTER 22

**W**HEN the door opened five minutes later, neither of them had made much progress. The twins both looked up, hearts in their throats, as Myrtle and Naveen reappeared.

Kevin indicated his box. "We're, ah, not quite finished."

"Don't worry about that at the moment. We need you to come with us." Myrtle exchanged a strained look with Naveen, even though it meant craning her neck up to look at him. "We have a couple more tests to run before we can prep you for defusion."

[Here we go,] Kevin said via Nancom.

Lilia did not look at him. [They've checked the data from the testers.]

[Yep.]

"If you don't mind…" Lilia reached back into the box and began stuffing things back into her ISF. It'd be a pain to sort out later, but she didn't have time to return everything to its proper spot just this moment. "I'd rather not leave anything here."

"Me either." Kevin shoved his belongings back into his ISF as well. "We'll take it out again when you bring us back here, I promise."

Neither of them expected that they *would* be back in this room, but it didn't hurt to continue playing ignorant.

Myrtle and Naveen wore matching grim looks, but they allowed the twins to return what little they had removed from their ISFs before ushering them out of the room and down the hall to a lab.

The twins cast a curious glance around—this lab bore a remarkable resemblance to the lab in the NCDC headquarters in Jamal, Glo'Stea—but they did not have time to fully study their surroundings. A tall, dark-skinned woman wearing a white lab coat, with a riot of curly platinum blond hair pulled back in a loose ponytail, met them at the door. She had sharp cheekbones and wide-set brown eyes.

Myrtle handed the woman a datapad. "Dr. Mareaux, Lilia and Kevin Strong."

"Thank you. That will be all for now, I think." Dr. Mareaux scanned the datapad before scrutinizing the twins. "I'm Dr. Mareaux. I'll be overseeing your defusion process."

"I'd say it's nice to meet you, but under the circumstances..." Kevin gave a one-sided shrug.

"Understandable. They sent me your case files."

*That's interesting.* Lilia gave the doctor a sharp look. "So you know *why* we're being kicked out of the NCDC?"

Dr. Mareaux spared her a glance over the datapad. "Yes." She motioned to several chairs in front of one of the computer consoles. "Have a seat, please."

The twins complied. Kevin couldn't resist asking, "So, Myrtle and Naveen said you have some more tests to do?"

"Yes." Dr. Mareaux slid the datapad into one pocket of her coat and withdrew a silver tester from what looked like thin air, but the twins knew had to be an ISF. "Hold out your arm, please, Miss Strong."

Lilia obeyed. Once the doctor had transferred the information to her datapad, she performed the same test on Kevin. She then took a seat at the nearest computer console—hers, by the look of it—and proceeded to study the results.

*Nothing will have changed,* Lilia wanted to tell her, but she kept her mouth sealed shut.

A full five minutes passed before Dr. Mareaux straightened in her chair and swiveled to face them. Her expression was a curious blend of frustration and resignation. "Well," she said coolly, "looks like today is your lucky day."

Lilia and Kevin glanced at each other. "What do you—"

"—mean?"

Dr. Mareaux pinched the bridge of her nose. "I mean you won't be losing your Guardian status today." She flung a hand in the direction of the datapad lying on the desk beside her. "Or any day, for that matter."

Kevin lifted his eyebrows. "The Board won't be very happy about that."

"The Board doesn't have much of a choice," Dr. Mareaux said in clipped tones. "I'm afraid the pair of you are what we call nano-genetic anomalies."

Though Lilia already knew all of this, hearing it from an actual NCDC doctor still sent chills down her spine. She cleared her throat. "What does that mean, exactly?"

"It means that we can't remove your nanites." Mareaux stood up, propping her hands on her hips as she surveyed them grimly. "Which in turns means that you can't leave the NCDC."

Kevin looked at Lilia before turning back to the doctor. "We weren't exactly planning to leave any time soon anyway."

"How did this happen?" Lilia figured that was a logical question. Nob had his information sources, but anything they could glean from an NCDC doctor couldn't hurt.

Mareaux shrugged, though the motion looked like it cost her. "We don't know. The running theory is that certain individuals react differently to the infusion process than others, and something changes for the worse. They make it through just fine, but the process cannot be reversed."

She looked back and forth between them. "You have family who are Guardians as well, don't you?"

"Yes." Lilia debated telling the doctor about Michael, but decided Mareaux had to have access to that information already. "One of our brothers was just in for recertification and found out he's a nano-genetic anomaly as well."

Dr. Mareaux did not look surprised. "Of course." She lapsed into thought, her dark eyes drifting past them to bore holes through the wall.

After a moment of rather uncomfortable silence, Kevin ventured to inquire, "Now what happens to us?"

Dr. Mareaux snapped her attention to him. "I've just informed the Board of my findings. They're sending your handler to collect you." She waved a dark hand toward the door. "Feel free to wait outside."

Exchanging wide-eyed looks, the twins traded the lab for the hall.

[That was nice and abrupt.] Kevin leaned against the wall, propping one foot flat against it.

[No kidding.] Lilia settled in beside him, her arms folded across her chest. [Mareaux acts like she's encountered nano-genetic anomalies before.]

[She probably has. After all, she works for the NCDC.]

They both straightened as Riley Callahan opened a joint Nancom channel to them. [Stay right where you are. I'll be there to collect you shortly.]

[We'll—]

[—be here.]

True to his word, Callahan rounded the corner a few minutes later. "Come with me," he said brusquely. He led the twins back through the Infusion Wing to the hall beyond and ushered them into his office. The last time they'd been here had been after they returned from Lanx with the scientists and the transporter in tow. Nothing had changed in the interim.

His office was small and windowless, but its sparse decorations gave it the illusion of being much bigger than it was. A few pieces of art, including a diagram of the cross-section of one of Glo'Stea's luxury cruise liners, hung on the wall, while a narrow set of dark wood shelves held boxes of datachips.

"Mareaux told you the news?" Callahan asked without preamble, throwing himself into his office chair.

"Yes," Kevin said as he and Lilia settled into chairs with leathery green cushions.

Callahan surveyed them both across the surface of his dark wood desk. "If I were you, I'd keep my head down for a while. The Board had to make an example of you, but now they've lost the chance."

Lilia fought a sudden, sharp-toothed smile. "Alan Birch will have a fit."

"Let him." Callahan waved a hand. "He's not important." He abruptly leaned forward. "The important thing is that *you* two not draw any more attention to yourselves. You don't want to end up like Azaren Carn."

The air in the office changed. Kevin narrowed his eyes at Callahan. "I thought Ren got in trouble because she was unhappy about being stuck in the NCDC."

"She did. She drew attention to herself." Callahan's icy eyes bored into them. "Doesn't matter what kind of attention it is—don't draw any. I can't help you if somebody higher up decides to send you off on a suicide mission or something."

A mirthless smile twisted his mouth at the looks the twins shot each other. "Oh, yes. It's happened. I'd rather not see it happen to you two. You've got potential."

"Potential for what?" Lilia asked coolly.

Callahan met her gaze and held it. "Potential to make a difference." He cracked another smile, this one a touch warmer. "Other than succeeding in helping the Galactic Union and the Coalition open up the first peace negotiations in twenty years."

"We try," Kevin said flippantly, but his tone immediately sobered. "Mr. Callahan, did you know?"

"Know what?"

Lilia leaned forward, catching the drift her brother's question. "That we are what we are?"

Slowly, Callahan looked back and forth between them. "I know your older brother was in not long ago and he ended up being an anomaly." He shrugged. "Genetically speaking, the odds were good that you were affected as well."

It made sense, but Lilia couldn't shake the sudden, nagging feeling that Callahan wasn't telling them everything. Before she could probe further, however, he said, "The Board will have to rescind your dismissal; I suspect they're already working on it. You should be able to walk out of here just like you would on any other day."

"And if that's not the case?" Kevin asked dryly.

"Then I suggest you materialize nano-armor to protect yourselves until everything is sorted out."

"Thanks. That's very helpful." Lilia was unable to keep the sarcasm from her voice. "Anything else we should be aware of?"

"Actually, yes." Callahan regarded them soberly. "This isn't exactly a topic for casual conversation. The NCDC would prefer it if you refrained from discussing nano-genetic anomalies with other Guardians."

"Even if those Guardians already know?" Kevin asked shrewdly.

Callahan shrugged. "They're trying to contain the chaos."

"Because they have no idea what's causing it." Lilia shook her head.

"It's a theory."

"Right." Kevin drummed his fingers on the arm of his chair, frowning. "None of this makes sense."

"How long has this been happening to Guardians?" Lilia asked.

Callahan shrugged, leaning back in his chair. "A few years, at least."

Kevin shook his head. "And nobody's made any progress in figuring out why?"

"Not that I know of." Callahan's gaze drifted past them. "And there's no way to test for it beforehand." He cracked a grim smile. "It's driving our scientists a little batty, that's for sure."

"I can imagine." Lilia glanced at Kevin, but a niggling channel request in the back of her mind made her snap her attention back to Callahan in surprise. *We're sitting right here; why does he need Nancom?* She allowed it, however, and formed a joint channel to Kevin.

[Have you talked to Dr. Jayce, Dr. Cait, or Dr. Lang recently? Have any more strange things happened with portals?]

Understanding flooded Lilia like a rush of cold water. *Oh.*

Kevin gave his head a minute shake. [No, we haven't heard from the scientists.]

Lilia maintained a straight face. Technically, that was true— they'd only heard from one scientist, not all of them. *And Callahan doesn't need to know about anything else.* [We haven't had any strange portals open or anything, either.]

Also true—because any portals that opened up around them, *they* were responsible for creating.

[Good. I'm glad to hear it.] Callahan shrugged. [I was just wondering.]

Lilia darted a glance at Kevin. [I would imagine Jayce, Cait, and Lang have been really busy since the Triumvirate unveiled the transporters to the Coalition.]

[Oh, undoubtedly.] Callahan tapped the fingers of one hand against the surface of his desk, before pinning both siblings with a sharp look. [The Tarynian ambassador knows about the transporter, doesn't he?]

Kevin nodded. [Saw it on the news. Wasn't anything we could do about that.]

Callahan digested this. [No, I suppose not.] He shook his head. [It'll be all over the media for weeks, any way.] He suddenly stilled, his eyes taking on a faraway cast.

Lilia's heart leaped into her throat. *It's the Board.*

A moment later, Callahan cleared his throat and swiveled in his chair to face them fully. "Well, that was the Board. Good news is, they've decided to let you remain in the NCDC."

*How magnanimous of them.* Lilia barely managed to keep her expression politely neutral.

"And the bad news?" Kevin asked.

Callahan shrugged. "You're stuck with the NCDC, I'm afraid. I'm tasked with monitoring you for the next few months."

"Monitoring us?" Lilia asked. "Why?"

Callahan spread his hands. "Several reasons, one of which is that you were just involved with something Alan Birch is cheerfully calling high treason."

"And the other reason?" Kevin asked, raising an eyebrow.

"You remember Carn," Callahan said simply. "We're discovering there's something about permanently remaining a Guardian that sometimes messes with people's minds."

The twins exchanged dubious glances. "I think we're—"

"—going to be just fine."

"That's my assessment as well, but I still have to monitor you." Callahan stood, and the twins rose to their feet as well. "I'll be in touch."

"Okay." Kevin nodded to him. "See you around."

"I hope not," Callahan said mildly. "When I said to keep your heads down, I meant it."

"We will," Lilia said. "Trust me, we have no desire to attract any more attention."

As they exited Callahan's office, Lilia thought she heard him mutter, "Let's hope so."


On their way down to the lobby, Lilia looked at Kevin. "Where to now?" She shouldn't have even asked.

"The *Talia*," he said without hesitation. "Erik's been stuck there by himself for a couple of days."

They picked up lunch for three on the way to the Sonela Spaceport, and were soon hurrying through the line of ships berthed in the commercial section to their *Ceratina*-class freighter. Kevin hummed happily as he caught sight of the *Talia*'s sleek gray lines. She was shaped like an isosceles triangle, with upper and lower decks.

As they approached, the landing ramp lowered, to reveal Erik Holt standing at the top of it. "'Bout time you two got back."

He was, Lilia was happy to see, clean-shaven and clear-eyed. His platinum blond hair had recently grown out a little from the buzz cut he usually sported, and he wore his usual brown vest over a white shirt, tucked into brown pants.

"Trust me," Kevin said fervently, bounding up the ramp, "it feels like an eternity since we were here last."

Erik surveyed the two of them. "Well, looks like you made it through your interview at the Cramer Buildin' this mornin'."

Lilia rolled her eyes, following Kevin up the ramp. "Just barely."

Once they were aboard the ship, Kevin raised the landing ramp and set off for the main living compartment. "It's official. We're nano-genetic anomalies. The NCDC was going to kick us out—"

"—because they can't touch Lon," Lilia said.

"—but they found out they can't. So…Callahan is going to 'monitor' us." Kevin made air quotes with his fingers.

Erik leaned up against a bulkhead, his arms folded across his chest. "Did you expect somethin' different?"

Shrugging, Lilia collapsed on the couch. "I didn't know *what* to expect."

Kevin abruptly grinned. "I wonder if Callahan gets to tell Birch, or if he finds out some other way." He rubbed his hands together, imagining the look on Birch's face at the news.

"It'll just give him another reason to hate us." Lilia shook her head, before glancing at Erik. "Anything interesting happen today?"

"Nah. Been pretty quiet." Erik tipped his head toward the viewport. "Couple of reporters nosin' around earlier, but they eventually gave up an' went away."

The twins made identical grimaces.

Erik shrugged. "Hey, you two are the ones who ended up plastered all over Coalition news for helpin' Kedis. I think the only reason you're not under more scrutiny is because of Glo'Stea."

"Probably," Kevin agreed. "Any word on when they're opening shields back up?"

"Not a clue." Erik shook his head. "They might have agreed to a cease-fire, but so far, nobody's comin' in, an' nobody's goin' out."

Lilia frowned. "Hopefully that will change soon." She looked at Kevin. "I'll let Sulamon know that we'll be there as soon as Sonela Shield Control starts letting ships through again."

Nadia Sulamon owned a fruit plantation in Redesh, on Glo'Stea, and the twins made regular cargo runs every Tuesday to bring produce back for high-dollar restaurants in Sonela.

Kevin scowled. "Honestly, I think they're overreacting. The only thing that's changed about that quarter of Glo'Stea is that it's got shields now. Chesnee still doesn't have enough ships to hold the entire world hostage—and thanks to Kedis, he couldn't do that anyway."

"Guess we'll find out," Erik said.

Lilia's comlink chose that moment to buzz in her pocket. Pulling it out, she stared down at the display and a tiny jolt shot through her.

Jasper.

*Good morning, dance partner, hope things are going well. I think we will be on Sta'Gloa for a while; sounds like it's going to take time for the Ambassador and the Triumvirate to find common ground beyond a cease-fire.*

She messaged back. *Morning. Can you honestly say that surprises you?*

*No,* Jasper sent after a moment. *It doesn't surprise me. On another note, your grandfather seems to be doing well.*

Lilia nodded to herself. *He's stronger than we thought he was.*

"Lil?"

She glanced up with a start, to find both Kevin and Erik staring at her. "What?"

"I said your name twice." Kevin looked bemused.

Lilia shrugged. "I wasn't paying attention."

"Clearly," Erik said.

Her comlink buzzed again. *It's strange to be staying at a hotel instead of the Mansion.*

She tapped back, *I'm sure Kedis is thrilled to have room service.* She could imagine the smile that would no doubt elicit from the blond lieutenant.

"Who are you talking to?" Kevin nodded to her comlink. "Alexis?"

A pang of guilt shot through Lilia. "No." She bit the inside of her lip. "I haven't…exactly…explained things to her yet." Her temples pulsed with the beginnings of a headache at the very thought. "It's a mess."

Erik regarded her for a moment. "It's not *that* complicated, kid. You just explain what happened, an' tell her you're sorry for lettin' her think Wright was your boyfriend."

It sounded simple, when he put it like that, but Lilia couldn't shake the feeling that it was much more involved. "I lied to her, Erik."

"For a good cause." His brown eyes were sympathetic. "She's your friend; she'll understand."

*I hope so.* Lilia kept those words to herself, however, and headed to her cabin.

Taking a deep, bracing breath, and praying for the right words, she commed her best friend. Alexis was in the middle of the lunch rush at her family's café and didn't answer, but Lilia expected that. She left a message instead.

"Hey, Alexis, it's me. I'm sorry I haven't gotten back to you sooner, but things have been crazy." She took another deep breath; her head was thudding in her chest. "I'm sorry I lied to you. Jasper isn't my boyfriend. It's a long story, but Kevin and I found out Lon was alive a couple of weeks ago, and that he'd smuggled Ambassador Kedis onto Sta'Gloa. We were pretty upset about it, but we helped him get the Ambassador an audience with the Triumvirate. That involved getting Kedis into the Gala…which involved me smuggling Jasper in as my date."

She twisted her hands together. "I'm really sorry. I couldn't tell you about it. We didn't even tell *Grandfather* Lon was alive because we didn't want to get him in trouble. We weren't sure if it would work or not. Anyway," she managed a smile, "I'll talk to you later."

Lilia ended the holo-call with trembling fingers. Now all she could do was hope her best friend understood.

# Chapter 23

ALEXIS called her back an hour later. She was short and slender, with light brown skin and big brown eyes. Purple highlights streaked her black curls. "I'm not mad," she said in a rush. "Your brother is back from the dead—I can't—I can't even imagine how you must feel about that." She swallowed. "And even if he *is* a Tarynian…I'm kind of sorry Jasper isn't really your boyfriend. I've never seen you talk about anybody like that before."

Lilia squirmed uncomfortably. "Alexis—"

"No." Alexis held up a hand. "Let me finish." She took a deep breath. "What you did was really, really dangerous, and I wish I'd known about some of it so at least I could have been praying for you." She looked at Lilia with wide eyes. "I mean, on the news, they're saying you were arrested and convicted of *treason* and then pardoned?"

Lilia made a wry face. "Well…we *were* arrested that night, but they released us and let us come back to Sonela with Grandfather. And yesterday, we had to face the Triumvirate."

Alexis gasped.

"Yeah…it was a little scary." Lilia pressed a hand to her stomach to quell the butterflies that erupted at the memory. "But…they seemed to understand why we did it, and with Ambassador Kedis here and willing to talk to them…" She shrugged. "I think they had to convict us so it looked like they were doing something, and then they had to pardon us because of Kedis, so…we're off the hook."

"Wow." Alexis digested this. "Well, we've definitely gotten a ton more business in the past two days. There have been a *lot* of people around."

"I'm not surprised." Lilia sighed. "The media's been hanging around Ferndale again, trying to catch us off guard."

"I thought your grandfather had a system for dealing with them."

"He does." Lilia grimaced. "The problem is that they want to grill Kevin and me."

"Hmm." Alexis considered this for a moment. "Why don't you just pick one of them and give them an interview?"

"And draw *more* attention to ourselves?" Lilia grimaced again. "We're trying to avoid attention, Alexis."

Her best friend gave her a flat, disbelieving look. "Lilia, I love you, but are you really that dense? Do you really think that you and Kevin can help Lon—who was supposed to be *dead*—smuggle *Tarynians* in to see the Triumvirate and then *not* have the media swarming you for details?"

*Well, when you put it like that…*Lilia blinked at Alexis, crestfallen. "We were hoping to avoid it?" she ventured sheepishly.

Alexis just shook her head. "Even *I* know it won't be *that* easy."

"But, Alexis, seriously. We're trying to minimize our involvement as much as possible. We've got a business to run."

"You're kidding yourself if you think that's going to happen. Besides, this much publicity could be good for your business."

Lilia stared at her. "How? Everybody in the Coalition knows we were convicted of treason—even if the Triumvirate immediately pardoned us."

Alexis sketched in the air with one hand and intoned in a dramatic voice, "Three Cords Shipping successfully delivered a Tarynian Ambassador to the Triumvirate. What can we do for *you*?"

In spite of herself, Lilia laughed. "Alexis…"

"I'm serious. Maybe you should give an interview."

"Maybe." Lilia bit her lip. *Except we can't control what questions get asked…and there are things we* can't *explain.*

"Anyway," Alexis glanced over her shoulder, "I've got to go. I'll talk to you later, okay?"

"Okay."

Lilia dropped her comlink onto her bunk and flopped backward to stare up at the gray metal overhead. *We were idiots to think our involve-*

*ment would end with getting Kedis to the Gala.* She pressed the heels of her hands into her eyes. It felt like a curtain had just been yanked aside, giving her a glimpse of a bottomless pit full of tar—and she and Kevin had one foot mired in it.

"Feel better?" Erik asked when she emerged from her cabin and rejoined them in the main living compartment.

Lilia shrugged. "You were right—she's not mad. I think she's too stunned to be mad." She looked over at Kevin. "She thinks we ought to give an interview to get the media to stop bothering us."

Kevin's reaction was about the same as hers had been. "I don't like that idea at all."

"Neither do I, but…" Lilia perched on the arm of a chair. "The more I think about it, the more I think she might be right."

"We'll worry about that later." Kevin waved a hand. "Don't have time to mess with that before we fly to Redesh tomorrow." He made another face. "Besides, we have to deal with Jayce first."

"Which might be easier if you don't have cams trailin' you everywhere you go," Erik pointed out.

Kevin shook his head. "Not worried about that." He nodded to his wrists. "We can evade them."

Erik nodded, conceding the point.

With the cease-fire temporarily reinstated, interplanetary traffic resumed, but out of Sta'Gloa at least, it was heavy—and slow. Very, very slow. A large number of Tri-World Tournament attendees from Lanx and Glo'Stea had been stranded on Sta'Gloa the night of the Tournament's Closing Ceremonies Gala, and now they were all trying to get home. Every passenger cruiser in every convoy for the next two weeks was booked solid.

Lilia suspected the only reason the *Talia* was being allowed to leave more or less on time was because their freighter made regular weekly commercial runs.

Further slowing traffic was the fact that, cease-fire or no cease-fire, Shield Controls across the Coalition were taking no chances on giving the Tarynians the slightest opening for an attack. They continued to operate under the stringently overhauled safe zone method. They kept convoys small and their departure times random, using an ever-changing array of coordinates constantly calculated by computers tracking both planetary rotations and the movements of Chesnee's forces to pinpoint windows of opportunity for ships to make safe, precise microjumps between the Coalition's worlds.

The safe zone method worked—but it had never been designed to handle this much traffic. It would be days before some people made it back to their homes.

Once their convoy dropped out of hyperspace outside of Glo'Stea and they were allowed through the planetary shield, Kevin settled the *Talia* into an airlane to Redesh to pick up their usual cargo from Sulamon. A massive island located toward the western edge of Sector 4, Redesh boasted a number of large fruit plantations as well as a coffee plantation. The largest pocket of civilization had a spaceport, but most of the plantations, including Sulamon's, used an off-shore landing pad.

From Redesh, the twins flew to back to Yuta, the closest safe zone city. They had a two-hour wait there before their convoy was allowed through Glo'Stea's shield and made a micro-jump back to Sta'Gloan space. By the time Kevin finally set the *Talia* down in their berth in Sonela Spaceport, it was after 10 PM.

Lilia was too tired to deal with Jayce; she waited instead until the next morning to send him a message asking where and when he'd like to meet.

The response came less than an hour later—a string of coordinates, and a time, 8 PM that evening.

Some of the blood drained from Lilia's face. She showed the message to Kevin and Erik. "He sent us a coordinate string."

Kevin glanced from the comlink to her, the same thought running through her brain reflected in his eyes. "He *expects* us to use the transporters."

Lilia nodded. Why else would he give them a coordinate string?

"I don't like it." Erik folded his arms across his chest. "Even if he's figured it out, that's awfully ballsy of him, expectin' you to confirm everythin' like that."

Kevin exhaled heavily and ran a hand through his dark hair before nodding to her comlink display. "Where will that take us?"

Lilia looked up the coordinates and Kevin and Erik crowded around her.

"That's in the industrial part of Sonela," Erik said thoughtfully.

"Yeah." Kevin frowned. "It's not where their lab used to be."

"Well…" Lilia bit the inside of her lip. "Internal Affairs probably moved everything to Sonela once they got the transporters up and running."

Erik leaned forward again. "Zoom in."

Lilia did so.

"That's some kinda nature conservatory thing." Erik looked from the comlink to Lilia and Kevin and back.

"In the Industrial sector?" Kevin looked askance at the blond.

"Oh, yeah." Erik stabbed a finger in its direction. His nails were ragged. "This is on the edge, where things are a little more high-tech an' definitely more expensive." He shot them both a sober look. "Especially if Internal Affairs is involved."

"I'm asking him why we have to meet there." Lilia tapped out the message, sent it, and then returned to the map. "That place is bound to have security cams. There's got to be somewhere else we can meet."

The response came almost instantly. *Can't leave the complex.*

"That sounds about right." Kevin frowned. "Ask him about cams."

Lilia did so, and when the response came, she matched her brother's frown. "Jayce says he's taken care of them."

"Without his handlers knowin' about it?" Erik looked skeptical. "I don't remember this guy bein' that smart."

The twins exchanged glances. "Well, he really wasn't in his—"

"—element when you met him. He's smart. The real question is—"

"—whether or not it's—"

"—a trap."

"Not to mention you're revealin' you definitely have transporters," Erik said.

Kevin's frown deepened. "Yeah. There's that too."

Lilia waved a hand. "We're past that. He's already figured it out."

"But he doesn't have *proof*, Lil," Kevin reminded her.

She raised her eyebrows at him. "You think he needs proof to go to the NCDC and tell them that they need to check our nanites for a little something extra? And you think they wouldn't do it?"

Kevin and Erik looked at each other. "Well, when you put it like that…" Erik shrugged one broad shoulder. "Don't think you've got much of a choice." His mouth slanted unhappily. "Could still be a trap."

Kevin slowly shook his head. "I think we're gonna have to risk it. Jayce knows about our nanites freezing when we open a portal, though he doesn't know *why*, but he *doesn't* know they're frozen for less time when we open a portal together. Right?"

"I don't think he knows that." Lilia closed the map. "Do I tell him we'll be there?"

Kevin nodded.

"You better pray he doesn't have friends from the NCDC there with impactors," Erik said darkly.

Lilia messaged Jayce and then shoved her comlink into her pocket, feeling queasy. "Let's hope."


The rest of the day slipped past with alarming speed. The twins did not return to Ferndale, but remained aboard the *Talia* with Erik. Kevin found some repairs to make, with Erik's help, while Lilia caught up on some bookwork. Late that afternoon, they Nancommed Michael and Derek to inform them they wouldn't be back for dinner, and that they were meeting Jayce.

Their older brothers were understandably concerned, but understood exactly why they had to meet the scientist. All they did was make the twins promise to keep them in the loop if anything went wrong.

"I'm goin' with you," Erik said casually, as the appointed meeting time drew near. He was stretched out in a chair in the living compartment, quite at his ease, but sudden tension seemed to have pulled all his muscles taut.

Lilia and Kevin glanced at him, startled, and then at each other. "Erik—" Kevin began, but the blond former police officer held up a hand.

"Nope. No arguin'. I've been cooped up in this ship for days an' I need to get out. Not to mention, you two could use some backup."

"Jayce will freak," Lilia said.

Erik gave her a sharp-toothed grin. "He knows me. Not as well as you two, obviously, but he knows me. Besides," he shrugged, "if somethin' happens, three makes for better odds than just two."

The twins looked at each other again, before scrutinizing Erik.

"You realize this'll mean that Jayce knows you know." Lilia raised an eyebrow at him.

"Anybody with half a brain will assume that, if they know what we know," Erik shot back.

"Could be a good thing." Kevin spread his hands. "If we're supposed to 'disappear', it'll be harder to kidnap all three of us."

Lilia shook her head. "I don't think he's planning on kidnapping us, Kev."

Both men gave her flatly disbelieving looks. "Wouldn't put it past him to lock you up in a secret lab to figure out your transporters," Erik said.

"He'd have a hard time doing that by himself." Lilia was still shaking her head. "And the way he was acting…I still say he doesn't trust anybody else with what he's found."

"An' *I* still say he could be lyin'," Erik retorted, "but since we all know you don't have a choice about this, I'm goin'." He folded his arms across his chest. "I *need* to get off this ship for a while."

"Okay, fine." Lilia gave him a wry smile. "I'd hate for you to get cabin fever on us."

Erik returned her smile. "You would, you really would."

Kevin glanced at his wrist. "Show time."

The three of them materialized stealth armor beneath their clothes. Erik recommended materializing their visors and facemasks as well—just in case somebody besides Jayce was waiting for them.

"You don't need 'em gettin' a good look at your faces right off the bat," he said seriously.

"Good idea." It felt a little odd wearing the facemask and visor without the helmet, but Lilia had no desire to draw any further attention. *Besides, our heads aren't affected by the transporters, so we'll be able to dematerialize the facemasks at will.*

Next, the three of them pulled hoverdiscs from their respective ISFs. They were metal discs twelve centimeters in diameter and two centimeters thick, and their smooth surfaces changed color to reflect their surroundings. When two buttons in the center were depressed, each device expanded with a faint hum into a small circular platform large enough to comfortably stand on.

As they hopped aboard their hoverdiscs, Lilia materialized her nanoboots and activated her magnetic boot soles to anchor her; there was no telling how they'd emerge from this portal. Most of the time, they came out right side up, but since their transporters lacked directional stabilizers, they had no guarantees. She'd emerged from portals upside down before.

Kevin looked over at her. "Ready?"

Lilia nodded, and they both concentrated on the coordinate string Jayce had given them. Seconds later, a portal sphere bloomed between them, rapidly expanding until it was big enough for them to pass through. The rush of displaced air wafted past them.

"I'll go first." Erik suited action to words, dropping into a crouch and flying through the portal without any hesitation.

Kevin nodded to Lilia; they couldn't keep the portal open long. "I'll go next." He glided into the portal sphere and Lilia followed.

Erik's voice sounded in her head. [Look out—]

Lilia knew something was wrong the instant she emerged on the other side. She had half a second to realize she was looking at a copse of upside-down trees before a buzzing in her mind reminded her she had to close this portal *right now*. All the blood rushed to her head.

[—we're upside down,] Erik finished.

Intensely grateful for her magnetic boot soles, Lilia helped Kevin collapse the portal.

"Well, hello, Dr. Jayce," Erik said evenly, still upside down.

A short, choked sound was his only response.

# Chapter 24

LILIA twisted her head around to see an upside-down Brian Jayce seated on an upside-down decorative metal bench. He was staring at them, his jaw slack in his thin face and his brown eyes wide with shock and something that looked suspiciously like hunger. She suppressed a resigned sigh. *Oh, boy.*

Clutching the sides of her hoverdisc with both hands, Lilia shot forward in a short, steep loop that brought her right-side up. Beside her, Kevin and Erik performed the same maneuver. All three of them remained crouched on their hoverdiscs, staring at Jayce.

"Well," Kevin said, "you're alone. I suppose that's a start."

Jayce jerked a little, as though coming back to himself. His red hair was disheveled; he'd been running his hands through it. "And you are not." He stared at Erik. "Who are you?"

"I was part of the team that rescued you." Erik tipped his head toward the twins. "Wasn't about to let 'em come alone."

Casting a sideways glance at Kevin, Lilia pitched her voice very low. "Is this a secure location?"

Jayce gave his shoulders a nervous twitch. He clutched a datapad in one hand. "As secure as I could find, given the circumstances." He tapped the datapad. "Officially, I'm taking a break. Soaking up nature—as close as I'm allowed to come to it at the moment."

"Guess there is a downside to being an inventor who changed the galaxy," Kevin said.

Jayce snorted softly. "You have no idea." He nodded to the plastiglass windows across the little park. "Can't even walk down the street alone right now. Internal Affairs doesn't want anything happening to us until they're sure they can build transporters without us."

Lilia and Kevin exchanged glances again. [He's got the—]

[—measure of them.]

Aloud, Kevin said, "You said you found some of Banx's data?"

"Yes." Jayce's fingers twitched, as though he wanted to get up but thought the better of it. "Would you mind taking those masks off? They're making me nervous." He correctly interpreted their hesitation. "Trust me, no one knows you're here, and the cams don't cover inside this group of trees. I checked; I needed to talk to you alone."

Silently, Lilia, Kevin, and Erik dematerialized their facemasks and visors.

Jayce gave Erik a sharp look that softened with recognition, before he turned back to the twins. Awe colored his voice. "You have portable transporters in your nanites." He shook his head slightly. "I thought you must—I ran the data hundreds of times, went over every possible angle, and it was the only conclusion that made any *sense*. What happened to you isn't possible any other way. I just couldn't figure out *how*."

"And then you found Dr. Banx's data," Lilia said. Out of the corner of her eye, she saw Erik pull a scanner from his ISF. *Oh, good. He's going to keep an eye out for company.*

"Yes." Jayce's thin fingers tightened on his datapad. He looked like a spring coiled tight, ready to explode into motion at any second. "Just a fragment on a datachip that had gotten mixed in with some of my research, but it was enough."

He looked back and forth between the three of them. "Banx posited it was possible. He and Cait had debated the idea a long time before I came on the scene, but never got anywhere."

His brown eyes began to burn. "*How* did he do it? We'd only just finished fine-tuning the transporters—how in the galaxy did he shrink them down to something smaller?"

Jayce shook his head. "And how did he get involved with the NCDC and *nanites*?" He stared at the twins. "Did you *know* you had transporters all along?"

Lilia and Kevin both shook their heads. "Not until we were in the middle of being bounced all over the Coalition," Kevin said. "We're pretty sure something—"

"—was activated when you sent us through the transporter as a test." Lilia started to sit on the grass instead of crouching on her hoverdisc, but thought the better of it. The grass would show signs of being trampled. She settled for sitting on her hoverdisc and letting her legs dangle.

"But *how* did you *get* them in the first place?" Jayce demanded. "It's been driving me crazy for *weeks*."

Lilia and Kevin glanced at each other again. "Banx was working with someone in the NCDC."

Jayce nodded. "That's only logical."

"Someone he'd known a long time," Lilia said carefully.

Jayce's expression froze. "Someone he'd known a long time," he repeated. "Someone also involved with the NCDC. That can't be a long list."

"What else is botherin' you, Doc?" Erik's tone was lazy, but a steel thread ran through it. "Somethin' else has been drivin' you crazy, or you wouldn't have called the twins in such a panic."

"Ah…well…" Jayce's chest heaved as he sucked in a breath. "You've, ah, heard about Glo'Stea's new shield generators, haven't you?"

All three Guardians nodded solemnly.

"Well…" Jayce set his datapad on the bench beside him and began twisting his fingers together. "It's going to sound crazy—I *know* it's going to sound crazy—but the first thing I thought when the news broke was that somebody had used a transporter to build those generators right under the Tarynians' noses."

Lilia was hard-pressed to keep her jaw from dropping. "*That* was your first thought?"

"Based on what?" Erik asked.

"Call it a hunch." Jayce shrugged. "And then I heard some of the places where new shield generators had been built and they sounded familiar." He shrugged again. "So I went back to the list of places the transporter had dropped the pair of you—" he nodded to the twins, "—and wouldn't you know, half of them were *there?*"

Ice trickled down Lilia's spine.

"So then you started puttin' pieces together," Erik said.

"Exactly." Jayce nodded. He looked like he wanted to jump up and start pacing, but was restraining himself. "*Exactly*. Banx, the transporters, all the strangeness that happened with you two…" He fixed the twins with a sharp, keen look. "You were *there*."

He swallowed. "And Dr. Banx was working with Freedom's Children."

*Yes, he was*, Lilia wanted to say.

Kevin shifted on his hoverdisc, his shoulder brushing a branch. He immediately stilled. "I think that's pretty obvious, when you look at everything."

"What we don't know," Erik said, regarding Jayce steadily, "was if Banx was sellin' the transporters to 'em, or else donatin' 'em to the cause."

Jayce rubbed his hands over his face; clearly, that was not a difficult choice. "He didn't care much for causes. But the chance to create something new? To make history? I could see him taking it." He abruptly straightened, his mind shifting gears. "Why did you come out of the portal upside down?"

Kevin snorted. "According to a friend of ours, it's because we lack a 'directional stabilizer'."

Understanding lit Jayce's features; he began to nod, and then looked alarmed. "A friend? What friend? Who else knows about this?"

Erik and Lilia both shot Kevin looks; he shrugged sheepishly.

"Dr. Jayce," Lilia extended a placating hand toward him, "trust me, we've kept this quiet. We have no desire to be turned into lab rats."

Jayce looked as though he didn't quite believe her, and then his mind latched onto the directional stabilization problem. "Phillip and I fixed that not long before we asked you to test the transporter for us."

"Well, it wasn't in the schematics that got coded into our nanites," Kevin said.

Jayce blinked. "Surely whoever was responsible for checking your nanites at the NCDC had to have *noticed* you had a few additions?"

Lilia and Kevin exchanged wry looks. [Do we tell him?] Lilia asked.

[Might as well. She's in the wind anyway.] Kevin cleared his throat. "Oh, she noticed. We're pretty sure she was in on it."

Lilia leaned forward. "Are you familiar with the name Dr. Dover?"

"Dr. Dover…" Jayce let that roll around in his mind for a few seconds before snapping his fingers. "Yes. She's an old colleague of Banx's from years ago—I believe he mentioned her a few times."

"Well…we're pretty sure she works for Freedom's Children as well." Lilia held out her hands. "She took a leave of absence and nobody's seen her since."

"Really?" Jayce asked. "You don't have any idea at all where she's gone?"

Kevin hesitated just a fraction—only someone who knew him as well as his sister would even catch it. "None."

Lilia did not risk looking at him. [What was that?]

[It just occurred to me.] Kevin did not look at her either. [Remember that island I found with a fortress on it?]

[Vaguely.]

[Well, if it's connected to Freedom's Children like I think it is, maybe that's where Dover is. Not that we can tell *Jayce* that.]

Lilia didn't have time to contemplate that further; Erik was talking.

"Dr. Jayce, what is it exactly that you want from my friends here?"

An artificial breeze ruffled the leaves above them; the atrium had quiet fans hidden in strategic places.

"I wanted confirmation that Kevin and Lilia have portable transporters—"

"You've got that," Erik said, his arms still folded across his chest.

"—and I wanted to talk to you about the places you went." Jayce shook his head. "Did you encounter *anyone* who knew anything about the transporters?"

The twins traded glances. "A couple people knew enough to expect a portal," Kevin said slowly. "I have no idea how they thought it was supposed to be opened."

Lilia shrugged. "As far as we know, we're the only Guardians with transporters—and we don't even know why we have them."

"The only reason we even know is because you and Cait asked us to test your transporter." Kevin pointed a finger at Jayce. "Otherwise, we'd be living our lives in complete oblivion."

Jayce considered that a moment. "I suppose it's fortunate Dr. Banx coded that string of coordinates into the transporter, then." He shook his head. "I realized he had to have been responsible for it—no one else could have done it. He must have been expecting to *test* it at some point, but who could have foreseen Chesnee breaking through Lanx's shield?"

Another cold chill made Lilia shiver. *Who* was *Banx going to have test that coordinate string?*

"Yeah," Erik said grimly, "an' he clearly expected whoever it was to have ties to Freedom's Children."

Jayce abruptly slumped forward, resting his head in his hands. "This is insane." His voice was muffled. "The man managed to shrink a *transporter*. God only knows how many Guardians are walking around with them in their *nano-armor*. Chaos, absolutely chaos."

"They're not perfect." Lilia tightened her fingers on the edge of her hoverdisc. "If you open a portal by yourself, your nanites are frozen for an hour. You can't open another portal, dematerialize anything, or even access your ISF until they unfreeze." She indicated the range of the effect.

[Lilia…] Erik's Nancom voice was sharp. [What are you doin'?]

She darted a glance at him out of the corner of her eye. [He needs a little reassurance that it isn't as bad as it sounds.]

[Don't tell him anythin' else. Not until we know for sure what side he's on.]

"An hour?" Jayce lifted his head, sounding dazed. "They're… frozen?"

"Yeah. Remember? We told you about it when we were getting bounced all over the place." Kevin folded his arms across his chest. "It's a pretty freaky experience. And, as you've seen, no directional stabilizer."

Jayce glanced back and forth between the three of them. "So if I had intended to trick you, you'd essentially be trapped here."

"Something like that," Kevin said.

"But you came anyway."

Lilia inclined her head in a nod. "We did."

Jayce's face scrunched up; for a second, all three of them were afraid he was actually going to cry.

Alarmed, Erik floated forward half a meter. "Okay, so you got 'em here, and you got confirmation that you're not crazy. They've got transporters. Now what?"

Jayce sucked in a deep breath and exhaled slowly. "I—I don't know. It would be good to know the extent of Banx's betrayal—whether or not they've got the schematics for an actual transporter instead of—" he cut himself off, a strange light coming into his brown eyes. "How *do* your transporters work?"

Lilia and Kevin traded glances with Erik before Kevin extended his wrists. "The machinery is coded into both wrists; the portals open between our arms."

"Fascinating," Jayce breathed, peering intently at the gray nano-armor covering Kevin's arms. "I'd like to study that at some point."

"Well, it won't be today." Kevin withdrew his arms. "We don't have time for that."

Jayce raised his eyebrows. "Not even if I could help you with the directional stabilizers you're lacking?"

For a few seconds, the only sounds to be heard in the atrium were the rustle of leaves. Then Lilia stirred. "You'd have to be able to re-code our nanites." She shook her head. "That's not possible without the NCDC's equipment."

"I'm sure Callahan would be able to—" Jayce began, but all three of them shook their heads.

"Not a chance." Kevin gave him a stern look. "We don't even know why we were given these." He held up his hand. "Until we have more information, the fewer people who know, the better."

Jayce didn't look happy about it, but he nodded. "I understand."

"Good," Erik said curtly.

Lilia froze, struck by a sudden thought. "Dr. Jayce, you said you and Dr. Cait fixed the directional stabilizer issue not long after we rescued you. Does that mean that even if Freedom's Children had an actual transporter machine, any portals they opened would be as iffy as ours are?"

Jayce nodded.

"Bet that made supply drops interesting," Kevin said.

Jayce cast a glance at his watch and then shot to his feet. "I've got to go." He waved a vague hand. "I have a—that is to say, Dr. Lang and I are meeting to discuss the future of the transporter."

Kevin narrowed his eyes at the scientist. "You're not telling her about us, are you?"

"I assure you, she has her doubts about your story as well, but, no." Jayce grimaced painfully. "I don't know who to trust anymore." He scooped up his datapad with trembling fingers. "You do realize the *implications* of this, don't you?"

Kevin looked sideways at Lilia. "We think we do."

"If there are more unregulated transporters out there—whether other Guardians are carrying them or not—things could get ugly." Jayce's voice grew intense. "Just *think* about it. Assassinations, thefts, disappearances…there's no telling how much trouble this will cause."

"Trust us," Erik held up a gray gloved hand, "we're thinkin' about it."

Jayce turned to leave the little grove. "I'll be in touch. Don't draw attention to yourselves." He gave them one last intense look, and then he was gone.

Kevin glanced back and forth between Lilia and Erik before shaking his head and materializing his facemask and visor again. "That was interesting."

Lilia, however, remained petrified on her hoverdisc. Jayce's words rang in her ears. *Assassinations, thefts, disappearances...*She took a short, shallow breath, recalling the would-be assassin she had battled at the Mansion a few months before. An assassin who wore nano-armor and had seemingly appeared from nowhere.

An assassin who would have had to work for...

"Lilia?" Erik's voice shook her from her reverie. "What's gotten into you?"

Startled, Lilia jerked her head toward him. Her mouth worked once, twice, and then she shook her head. "I'll tell you when we're back on the *Talia*."

[We *do* have Nancom,] Kevin reminded her dryly, but she just shook her head again.


Five minutes later, they had opened a return portal to their freighter and Lilia had spilled her revelation.

"It's a good theory," Erik said at last, drumming his fingers on the arm of his chair. "But it means that—"

"Freedom's Children, or at least somebody working for them, wants Grandfather dead." Lilia hunched forward in her seat, twisting her fingers together.

Kevin ran a hand through his hair. "Well, Grandfather's known all along it had to be somebody who severely disagreed with his political stance."

"Freedom's Children would fit the bill," Erik said, then frowned. "The assassin wouldn't necessarily have to have a transporter himself though—they could have just opened a portal to your house."

"They could have." Lilia nodded. "It's possible Banx sold them—"

"—or gave them," Kevin said.

"—the schematics for the actual machine instead of just working with Dover to shrink them down." She shrugged helplessly. "We have no way of knowing that, however."

"No, we don't. Pure speculation." Erik spread his hands. "But it's a start."

# CHAPTER 25

THE Triumvirate invited Ambassador Kedis to appear before them again a few days after his initial introduction. Aiden had no doubts that even if they had not invited Kedis, the man would have simply shown up at the Four Towers anyway.

Aiden settled back in his comfortable seat, wincing minutely as his right leg twitched beneath the table. Beyond the Chamber's floor-to-ceiling windows, the sky outside was overcast. It was not supposed to rain, but that meant nothing. Weather was weather—unpredictable.

Aiden thought he would have preferred sunshine to cloudy skies today, however. The sky seemed to reflect the general mood permeating the Chamber—a blend of unease, resentment, and wary anticipation mixed with a dash of excitement. Low conversation rumbled in the air as his colleagues conversed with each other. They were all seated, regally waiting to receive their visitor. The usual mix of expensive perfumes and colognes scented the air.

Beneath the table, Aiden stretched his legs a little. He had no doubts today's session would be enthralling…but he also had no doubts it would be a long day. A very long day, indeed. He glanced over his shoulder along with most of the Triumvirate as the Chamber's double doors swung open to admit the Ambassador.

Kedis moved toward the center of the massive triangular room with confident, easy strides, his expression calm and collected. He wore a new suit today, a green so dark it was almost black; it enhanced the olive tone of his face and smooth-shaven head.

Aiden's gaze slid behind Kedis in search of Lon, but his grandson did not appear. His green eyes narrowed slightly. Either Kedis did not require his services today, or Lon had received orders from Chairman Quin'lan Dunn to remain in the Hall unless specifically summoned. *Probably the latter*, Aiden surmised.

Kedis took his position off to the side of Dunn's podium and bowed slightly to the three Chief Ministers at their table, before facing the rest of the Triumvirate and offering them a bow as well.

Quin'lan Dunn tapped his gold bell. "This session of the Triumvirate will now come to order." He looked at Kedis. "The Triumvirate welcomes Ambassador Kedis."

"Thank you." Kedis inclined his head. "I am delighted to stand before you again."

Beside Aiden, Kane Fenton made a faint sound in the back of his throat. Without moving his lips, the Sta'Gloan Director of Internal Affairs said in a barely audible voice, "I am sure you are."

Aiden suppressed the faint smile that threatened to twitch at the corner of his mouth. *My sentiments exactly.*

Dunn and Kedis ran through a few formalities—polite, almost meaningless exchanges—and then Kedis said, "I would like to address the Triumvirate, if I may."

Dunn's dark eyes flicked to the three Chief Ministers before he responded, "The floor is yours, Ambassador."

Kedis straightened, looking earnest. "Ladies and gentlemen of the Triumvirate, I thank you for allowing me to appear before you today. I will not take up much of your time."

Aiden huffed slightly to himself. *That would be a small miracle.*

"My aim today is simple." Kedis spread his hands slightly. "On behalf of the Galactic Union, I ask that the Triumvirate officially open peace talks with us."

Dead silence greeted these words; everyone had expected him to say something like this.

"We have taken the first steps to peace by implementing the cease-fire," the Ambassador continued, "and now I wish to continue that forward progress." His face was still earnest as he swept his gaze around the Chamber. "There is much the Triumvirate and the Galactic Union can offer one another. The removal of the blockade and the restoration of travel and free trade are just the beginning."

All along the semi-circle, Representatives and Directors alike traded minute glances. These points, too, were expected.

Kedis opened his mouth again, apparently warming to his subject, but Lanxian Chief Minister Pryce Gammick cut him off. "I am sure you could no doubt wax poetic about all the possible benefits, Ambassador," he said dryly, from his seat, "but until the Triumvirate agrees to open said peace talks—*if* the Triumvirate agrees—it is pointless to continue."

Beside him, Glo'Stean Chief Minister Devlin Vance nodded his gray head. "Pointless," he agreed. "Best to save your eloquence for a later date."

For the briefest moment, Kedis looked taken aback. Clearly, he had not expected to be cut off so abruptly. Aiden wondered if anyone else had caught the flicker of frustration that flashed through his dark eyes before Kedis smothered it.

The Ambassador recovered quickly though, and inclined his head in a gracious nod. "As the Triumvirate wishes." His voice firmed. "My request, however, still stands."

"And the Triumvirate will consider it." This from Hugh Koen, Sta'Gloa's Chief Minister. He regarded Kedis with piercing dark eyes for a few seconds before raising a hand. "You may leave us, Ambassador. We have much to discuss."

A pleasant smile on his lips, Kedis bowed once more. "On behalf of the Galactic Union, I thank you for your consideration."

Quin'lan Dunn tapped his gold bell. "Ambassador Kedis, you are dismissed."

Kedis departed, smile and confidence intact.


It seemed to Aiden that as soon as the Chamber doors closed behind the Ambassador, the Triumvirate seemed to take a collective breath. He mentally braced himself. *Here we go.*

Cease-fire in place, Kedis had made the expected next move. Now it was up to the Triumvirate to respond—

—and respond they did.

In the Lanxian section, Representatives Cy Bali and Zane Chas both rose to their feet. At the same time, Dion Pamos stood in the

Sta'Gloan section, and Akiva Taft and Martin Hollowell stood in the Glo'Stean section.

Aiden's eyebrows lifted a fraction. He glanced sideways at Kane Fenton, who mirrored his expression.

Quin'lan Dunn blinked, but gamely plunged forward. He tapped his bell. "The Triumvirate will recognize you in alphabetical order. Representative Bali, if you please." He tapped the bell again.

Bali represented Lanx's conservative Sector 8. He was rail-thin, with ebony skin and a flat face. He had also been injured in the Opening Ceremonies Gala along with Aiden and several others, but had made a full recovery.

Drawing himself up to his considerable full height, Bali motioned to the spot Kedis had just occupied. "You all heard the Ambassador. We cannot pretend we did not know this was coming."

Aiden doubted anyone in the Chamber would claim ignorance on that front.

"As chairman of the Merger Trade Agreement Research committee, I would like to state for the record that I believe it is now in the Coalition's best interest to open peace negotiations." Bali shook his head. "With a few minor exceptions, our constituents are either strongly in favor of a trade alliance or else they are strongly in favor of a merger."

He held out his hands. "It is true that both options have the potential to provoke a backlash, but we now find ourselves at a crossroads. What is the harm in opening peace talks in the hopes of finding common ground? I do not believe it cannot hurt us."

Bali resumed his seat amid a rumble of muttered conversation, and Dunn tapped his bell. "The Triumvirate recognizes Representative Chas."

"I agree with Representative Bali." Chas's smooth voice echoed through the Chamber. "Opening negotiations does not commit us to anything other than a quest for peace. We have nothing to lose and everything to gain here." He held out his hands. "Think about what the removal of the blockade will mean for our economy."

*Oh, it will impact the economy.* Aiden pressed his lips into a thin line. The differences in the Coalition's economy and that of the Galactic Union were part of the entire reason the Coalition had ended up cut off from the rest of the galaxy in the first place.

Chas sat down and Dunn tapped his bell again, recognizing Hollowell.

"I am sure I do not need to remind my esteemed colleagues," Hollowell cut a glance toward Bali and Chas in turn, "that in every successful negotiation, both parties win *and* lose. You say we have nothing to lose—" he shook his head, "—I must respectfully disagree. We have *everything* to lose."

In the silence that greeted these words, Hollowell continued, "Some of you are too young to remember this, but the difference in our currencies has been an issue since the Galactic Union first came knocking at our door requesting we join their little band of worlds and systems. We have a gold standard." He shook his head. "They do not. If we were to do anything as foolish as actually *join* the Tarynians, it would completely disrupt commerce throughout our entire system."

"We would adjust," Chas said loudly. Quin'lan Dunn sent him an admonishing look.

"In addition," Hollowell went on, as though the younger Lanxian had not spoken, "the fact remains that no matter what we choose, the Galactic Union will never be satisfied with anything less than swallowing our system whole. We are too close to Taryn; they want our allegiance and our resources."

He shook his head again. "We must send Ambassador Kedis back where he came from—we have no need of him."

*That is a bit shortsighted, Martin.* The corners of Aiden's mouth pulled into a frown. His old friend was letting his hatred of the Tarynians cloud his better judgment. *Sending Kedis away will only prolong our stalemate—or give the G.U. an excuse to let Chesnee continue to whittle away at our worlds.*

Given what the Admiral had managed to accomplish in only the short time he had been in command, Aiden had no desire to see what the man could do in the long run.

Representative Taft, of Glo'Stea's Sector 7, said much the same as Hollowell, once the older man sat down and Dunn recognized her. She was a slight woman bronze skin and a sheath of glossy black hair, but her voice was strong and steady.

Aiden glanced at Dion Pamos more than once throughout this entire conversation. Also a member of the Merger Trade Agreement Research Committee, Pamos patiently waited his turn, his expression pleasant—but determined. Aiden already knew where his colleague stood, but he was curious to hear how the shorter man would justify opening negotiations.

"The Triumvirate recognizes Representative Pamos."

Pamos took a second to look around the Chamber before he spoke. "I understand completely where Representatives Hollowell and Taft are coming from. The state of our respective economies is one of the many vital issues at stake here."

He locked his hands behind his back. "That said, these issues can only be dealt with if the Triumvirate agrees to open negotiations with the Galactic Union—and I agree with Representative Bali and Representative Chas that it is in the Coalition's best interest to do so."

"Yes, we may lose something in the process." Pamos nodded to Hollowell. "However, I think it is clear that we stand to gain far more than we stand to lose—and *we will never know unless we try*." His voice rang through the Chamber.

"I cannot be the only one who recognizes that we stand on the edge of a precipice," he continued. "We cannot go back to the way things have been the past twenty years, and thanks to Admiral Chesnee, we cannot remain where we are. Our only viable option is to move forward by agreeing to open negotiations with the Ambassador."

Pamos paused to let that sink in. "On that note, I move that the Triumvirate vote on whether or not to open peace negotiations with the Galactic Union."

Aiden barely had time to take a breath before Nolan Snyder's pudgy hand shot up in the Lanxian section. "I second that motion."

At these words, the Chamber erupted in a cacophony of protests and cheers.

"Order!" Quin'lan Dunn bellowed, banging on the gold bell. "We will have order in the Triumvirate!" He cast a helpless look toward the three Chief Ministers, but they were leaning their heads together, engrossed in an urgent conversation.

Aiden's leg was still twitching. Partly to ease it, and partly because there were words burning on his tongue, he pushed back his chair and rose to his feet, gripping the edge of the table for balance.

It took several minutes before the Chamber quieted enough for Dunn to say tightly, "The Triumvirate recognizes Representative Monroe."

Aiden cleared his throat. "Before we deal with the motion that has been made and seconded, I would just like to remind the Triumvirate that if we were to open peace negotiations, we would have a great deal of leeway. If we enter these negotiations and decide at a later date that it is impossible for us to find common ground with the Galactic Union, we certainly have the freedom to end them and send Ambassador Kedis on his way."

"Hear, hear," Shane Briscoe said from the Glo'Stean section. He was the third and final member of the Merger Trade Agreement Research Committee. A few other murmurs of assent rippled along the semi-circle of Representatives and Directors.

Smiling wryly, Aiden looked around at his colleagues. "Of course, we shall then be forced to face the repercussions of such a move, but we will find ourselves dealing with Admiral Chesnee regardless."

He took a breath. "As things stand, I personally do not see that the Coalition has any way around opening peace negotiations at this present time." He nodded to Dunn and eased himself back down into his seat. The royal blue cushion immediately contoured to his body.

Dunn scanned the Chamber. "Anyone else?" His voice held just the faintest waspish note. When no one did, he continued, "Representative Chas made a motion to vote on opening peace negotiations with the Galactic Union and Representative Snyder seconded it. The motion is therefore passed." He tapped his bell. "The Triumvirate will now put it to a vote."

The vote passed almost unanimously. Only a few holdouts refused— among them Martin Hollowell. Aiden had no doubts the Triumvirate would decide to move forward; his colleagues fully understood the position they were in.

Tension filled the Chamber as Quin'lan Dunn tapped his bell. "Ambassador Kedis will be informed of the Triumvirate's decision. We will officially open negotiations the beginning of next week, after we have all had time to prepare ourselves."

Aiden smiled slightly. *And our constituents.*

"The Triumvirate will now adjourn for lunch," Dunn concluded.

The sound of his gold bell carried through the Chamber, and just like that, the majority of the tension in the massive room dissipated. The main emotion reflected on everyone's faces was *relief.*

In the Lanxian section, Nolan Snyder sagged in his seat, mopping his face again. He looked as though someone had lifted a weight off his shoulders as he turned to exchange words with Zane Chas.

Aiden glanced over at Martin Hollowell, whose expression was severe, but his old friend was already engrossed in a conversation with Shane Briscoe and Akiva Taft.

Beside Aiden, Kane Fenton huffed a laugh as he pushed back his chair. "Brace yourself. I can already see the headlines."

"No matter what choice we make," Aiden said as he rose to his feet as well, "we were never going to escape a backlash."

The only question now was how severe that backlash would be.

"I just hope this quells some of the rioting." Fenton shook his head. "The majority of our constituents are interested in some sort of peaceful agreement."

Amid, the laughter and relieved conversations eddying through the Chamber, the two men shared a grim look. They both knew the trouble would be the small—but fierce—anti-merger, anti-trade alliance minority.

# Chapter 26

A channel request from Riley Callahan brought Lilia up short the morning after the Triumvirate announced they were officially opening peace negotiations with the Galactic Union. She and Kevin were both in the galley aboard the *Talia*, which was still berthed in Sonela Spaceport. She and Kevin had needed to get away from Ferndale for a little while. Making a face at Kevin, she allowed the channel request. [Mr. Callahan. What can I do for you?]

[The NCDC's figured out what to do with you two,] he said, by way of greeting.

Lilia opened a joint Nancom channel to her brother in time to hear his response. [Oh, really?]

[It's taken them a few days,] Callahan continued, [but they've finally come up with an assignment.]

*Oh, boy.* Lilia felt her heart sink. *This can't be good.*

[They've decided to take the Triumvirate's announcement and your recent actions and family background into account and are assigning you to upcoming events where Ambassador Kedis will be in attendance as an extra layer of security.]

Instead of making her feel better, this sank Lilia's heart all the way to her toes. *Forced attendance at political events?* [How many of them?]

[Probably most of them.] Callahan's Nancom voice sounded wry. [I did remind the Board that you have an off-world shipping business, but they determined you would likely be attending a few of them anyway, thanks to your grandfather.]

[Not if we could avoid it,] Kevin said honestly. [It's not really our—]

[—thing,] Lilia finished. [I figured we'd have to make an appearance or two because of Grandfather and—]

[—our brother Lon,] Kevin said, [but we were hoping to—]

[—avoid the bulk of the social scene.]

[Wishful thinking after this, I'm afraid,] Callahan said. [Frankly, I'm amazed you aren't more involved.]

[Never had a reason to be,] Kevin said.

[Well, now you do.] Callahan paused. [Look at the up side. At least it's not another Uva situation.] He paused again. [Or even dealing with the scientists.]

[I don't know,] Kevin said darkly. [Ever spent much time in high-stratosphere social circles? I think I'd almost rather face the Tarynians.]

[Interesting perspective. Let me know when your first event is.]

[We will,] the twins answered together.

Callahan closed his channel and Lilia slumped against the counter in the galley. "You *do* realize what this means, Kev."

"What, that we're going to be spending a heck of a lot more time around a bunch of people who can't stand us?"

"Besides that."

"You lost me, sis."

"I'm going to have to go shopping." Lilia folded her arms across her chest, scowling. "I don't have enough dresses if we're going to be attending that many social functions."

"Most people wouldn't consider that a hardship. Particularly since you know Grandfather will pay for them."

"That's not the point." Lilia could feel a knot of panic slowly working its way up her throat. The idea of having to spend evening after evening around people like Alan Birch and his girlfriend left her cold. "Clearly, somebody on the Board realized this is the best way to torture us."

"Maybe. Or maybe they just decided to use us again." Kevin paused. "You have to admit, it does kind of make sense. Not a bad thing to have extra undercover security at things like that."

Lilia's scowl deepened. "You're awfully calm about this."

"I know. It's weird, isn't it? Maybe it hasn't—"

"—sunk in yet?" Lilia shook her head. "Let me know when it does."

"Whoa." Erik sauntered into the galley and stopped short when he caught sight of the black scowl gracing Lilia's features. "I'd back away slowly an' leave you alone, but we both know I've never been that smart." He eyed her. "What happened to you?"

"The NCDC figured out how to punish us."

Erik's pale eyebrows rose. "That so?"

"Yeah. They're sending us to upcoming political and social functions with Ambassador Kedis as an 'additional layer of security'." She made air quotes with her fingers.

"Right," Erik said slowly. "Obviously, somethin' from the seventh circle of hell."

Lilia shot him a withering look. "Would *you* like to spend your evenings with that lot?"

He snorted. "Not a chance."

A glint of humor poked through Lilia's ill mood. "I could probably bring you in as my escort."

"No thanks," Erik said promptly. "I'll stay right here an' take care of this old girl." He patted the nearest bulkhead.

"Thought so." Lilia picked up her coffee, though she was almost too out of sorts to drink it, and swept out of the galley. *I'm going to have to talk to Alexis.* Her best friend had a better fashion sense than she did.

As she settled back down on a couch in the living compartment to finish up some bookwork, an unbidden thought crept into her mind. *It might not be all bad. Jasper will have to be at most of those things too.*

Lilia sighed. *Well, at least there's one friendly face.* She debated sending a message to Derek asking for a list of upcoming events their grandfather would be attending, but decided against it. *I think I'd rather explain the NCDC involvement in person.*

That night, after dinner, the twins pulled their brothers aside in the kitchen long enough to outline the situation. "Well," Derek said after they finished, "I'm sure Grandfather will love to have you there."

Lilia and Kevin exchanged glances out of the corner of their eyes.

"But?" Lilia prompted. She was almost positive there was a 'but' coming.

"I think he was hoping to downplay your involvement in all this." Derek looked between them, a slight frown gracing his features. "I don't think he wants you plastered all over the media anymore than you have to be."

"This could be a good thing," Michael said. "If they make appearances, the media will eventually move on because they've lost their anti-social mystique."

"We're not anti-social," Kevin protested. "We just don't want to talk to them."

Derek smiled. "Same thing, as far as they're concerned. But you may be on to something, Mike. They probably *will* lose interest pretty fast."

*One can only hope*, Lilia thought.

Derek pulled out his comlink and held it out for them to see. "This is Grandfather's schedule for the next six weeks. It's always in flux, but here are the things we know for sure he'll be attending." He indicated a solid stretch of social engagements and Kevin's face progressively grew paler.

"That's…a lot of parties," he said weakly. "The Triumvirate only decided to open peace talks *yesterday*."

Lilia glanced sideways at him. "Sinking in now, is it?"

He elbowed her in the side—none too-gently—and she arched away from him. "Maybe."

"Sinking in?" Michael asked quizzically.

Lilia tipped her head toward her twin. "He was way too calm about this earlier. Figured it'd catch up with him eventually."

"I see." Derek tapped his comlink display. "Here. I've sent you the dates of all the events you could be reasonably expected to attend."

Kevin squinted at the comlink again. "The next one's *tomorrow*."

"Yeah." Derek suddenly looked tired. "In addition to all the time they'll be spending at the Four Towers, Kedis will be making the rounds in Sonela's upper circles, too." He nodded to his comlink. "This one is at Representative Manji Zontak's house in Sonela. He's from Sector 2."

Michael's face split with a sudden grin. "All these parties mean that eventually they'll include some sort of gathering thrown by none other than Madame Olga."

Lilia blanched. "Oh, no."

Olga Lieb, who went by Madame Olga, was a menace to society, a well-to-do widow with far too much time on her hands who fancied herself a matchmaker. She'd been chasing Martin Hollowell for years, with little success.

"Oh, yes. Got the invitation today. It's in five weeks."

"Good grief." Lilia rubbed her face. "I guess they're all banking on Kedis sticking around that long."

It was their older brothers' turn to exchange glances. "He's got more than a foot in the door," Derek said soberly. "They'd have to forcibly throw him onto a spaceship and launch it through the shield to dislodge him now."

"What are you going to tell Grandfather about this sudden change of heart?" Michael asked.

"The truth," the twins said together.

Lilia sighed. "There's no point keeping it from him. Especially since it's—"

"—nothing compared to everything else we've been through so far," Kevin finished.

"Good point." Michel nodded. "Scary to think about, but a good point."


As they had expected, Aiden was both delighted his grandchildren would be attending with him, and concerned for them. He took them aside in the foyer a few minutes before they departed the next evening to impart instructions.

"We'll be all right, Grandfather," Kevin assured him. "I'm pretty sure we can keep our mouths shut when we need to."

"It is not that." Aiden waved a hand. "I would simply prefer you not be hounded."

"Unfortunately," Lilia said, adjusting her wrap in the mirror hanging on the wall to their left, "we *did* kind of bring this on ourselves."

"Just be careful." Aiden's wrinkled face was sober. "I would also prefer Ambassador Kedis not use his connection to you for his own ends."

"We'll try," Kevin said.

Lilia took one last look at herself in the mirror before resolutely turning away. She had gone shopping that morning, with Alexis's help, and the two of them had found several last-minute options for her to wear. One of them was a jewel-tone scarlet and gold gown that Alexis insisted she had to wear her first evening out.

Alexis agreed with Michael. "Make a splash on the first night and just get it all over with. Then you can show up in something more demure the next time, and they'll get bored and move on."

Lilia still wasn't completely convinced that was the best tack to take, but she trusted her friend's judgment. It helped that Aiden had approved of the theory when she explained it to him.

The hardest part about shopping for new evening gowns was the fact that she refused to leave her upper arms bare. She wasn't self-conscious about the scar on her left bicep from the failed as-sassination attempt, but she wasn't sure she wanted it as a topic for conversation. And while scar removal was still an option, she hadn't decided about that either. Part of her wanted to keep it as a reminder not to let her guard down—especially in situations where she felt safe.

Alexis had therefore helped Lilia find a red evening gown with snug sleeves that extended almost to her elbows. What resembled a sheer gold sari wrapped around one shoulder and ran diagonally across her body to her waist, where the two ends flowed down her skirt and shimmered when they caught the light. A wide gold band encircled her left wrist, and circular gold earrings peeked out from her chin-length dark hair whenever she turned her head.

"I don't look like myself at all," she had told Alexis in amaze-ment. "This is something I could see *you* wearing."

Alexis had just laughed. "I'd do a few things differently. I think it suits you. They won't know what hit them." Her brown eyes nar-rowed in sly humor. "Particularly a certain lieu—"

"Don't even say it." Lilia held up a finger. "That was all just for show."

"Uh huh." Alexis nodded agreeably, but her expression told Lilia she didn't buy it.

Now, Lilia found herself with butterflies in her stomach—and they weren't all from the fact she had to attend a major social func-tion. Jasper *would* be there…and part of her *was* curious to know what he'd think about her being there.

She promptly scowled. *He better not think I'm doing this for him.*

"Whoa." Michael tapped her on the shoulder, startling her. "I wouldn't wear *that* expression when you walk out the door if I were you."

"Sorry." Lilia schooled her expression into something more pleasant. "I was—thinking."

"Word of advice." Derek came up behind her. "Don't think about whatever it was you were just thinking about tonight. At all." He gave her a semi-stern look, before smiling. "You want to blend in—and *that* is the opposite of blending in."

"Got it." She sketched a salute, a faint blush burning her cheeks.

Departing the penthouse, they took the accelevator down to Ferndale's underground parking level, where Hank Jenson waited with Aiden's skimmer and Kerrigan Bryce waited with the skimmer in which Lilia and Kevin would be riding. Jenson had been Aiden's chauffeur for over four years now. A short man in his thirties with crew-cut black hair, he tended to keep to himself, but his hazel eyes never missed a thing—including the bomb someone had planted in Aiden's skimmer a few weeks before.

Bryce was in his late twenties, and had been part of Aiden's security team for six years. He was tall, with ebony skin, broad shoulders, and wide features, and he kept his head shaved smooth. He preferred not to talk about what he'd done before Will Graves had recruited him, but clearly knew his business.

A glance at the evening sky through the window as both skimmers pulled out of the street did not reveal any media cams lying in wait for them, but that didn't mean one wasn't lurking around. Settling the sheer golden fabric of her wrap more securely around her shoulders, Lilia wondered just how crazy their arrival would be. To Kevin, she said, "I suppose it's too much to hope we can just slide in unnoticed."

He gave her an incredulous look. "We're showing up with Grandfather for one, and second…" He lifted a hand to his hair, but stopped himself from raking his fingers through it just in time. "We haven't been out in public like this since the Gala."

Lilia bit the inside of her lip, dread pooling in the pit of her stomach. It had only been a week, but she knew in the political, high society realm, it might as well have been a month.

Kevin rightly interpreted her dubious expression. "Hey, like we said earlier, we'll just get it over with, and then they'll get bored and move on to somebody more interesting. We can do this. Just ask God to give you the grace to deal with these people. It's what I'm doing." He waited for her to meet his eyes. "Okay?"

"…okay."

"That's the spirit." Kevin flashed her a grin, before gingerly leaning back in his seat. "They won't know what hit 'em."

*I wish I had your confidence,* Lilia told him silently. She bit the inside of her lip again. *Oh, God, please help us get through this.*

All too soon, they left the main city behind, headed for an upper-class suburb. The houses here were not so much houses as they were grand mansions, most of them with high walls and fences to give their owners privacy. Bryce followed Jenson through a decorative—though no less secure—gate separating Representative Zontak's mansion from his neighbors' and, despite herself, Lilia felt like she'd stepped into some sort of fairyland.

Glow posts lined the grand driveway leading up to the three-story mansion's massive front porch, and clusters of tiny, delicate gold lights twinkled between them. The lights seemed to dance in midair, wafting gently up and down with the breeze, but not abandoning their posts. More lights floated along the roof of the porch and adorned the large marble pillars supporting it. Trees dotted the well-manicured front grounds, and each one had been filled with tiny lights that slowly shifted from color to color.

After a second, Lilia realized they were cycling through sapphire blue, emerald green, and gold—representing each of the Coalition's worlds—with scarlet added to the end. She frowned. *Is that for the Galactic Union?* If s o…She smoothed the skirt of her dress. *I might have worn the wrong color tonight.*

It was far too late now. If Kevin noticed the light pattern, he did not mention it. He was peering out the window, trying to gauge what kind of reception greeted guests. Bryce followed Jenson in the line of skimmers wending their way to the front door to deliver their occupants, and within a few moments, he slowed to a halt.

"Looks like the media's here after all." Kevin shook his head slightly. "I wondered if Representative Zontak was going to let them in."

"They've probably got special passes for tonight. This is private property, after all."

"Oh, yeah, we can't miss out on publicity."

The twins shared a wry grin, and then pasted smiles on their faces as Bryce came around and opened the door.

"Thanks," Lilia said softly as she climbed out.

"Have fun," Bryce answered, without moving his lips, his dark eyes twinkling at her.

She suppressed a snort. *That's not how I'd put it.*

It felt more like she was marching to a torture session—one she was expected to act like she enjoyed.

# CHAPTER 27

THE reporters and their cams were still fairly busy with Aiden and his hoverchair, but the ones closest to the skimmer turned their attention to the twins. Lilia smiled at the reporters and cams while Kevin climbed out beside her. He nodded amiably to their media welcome committee and offered his sister his arm.

They followed Aiden's hoverchair and their brothers up the stairs to the wide front porch and then stepped into a wash of golden light issuing from the massive double doors. Several imposing security guards stood here, keeping an eye on the media presence. Derek presented their invitation—they had received an elaborate piece of paper—and the guards nodded respectfully to Aiden.

The five of them crossed the threshold into a massive, three-story room packed with people. A woman standing just inside the door offered them autotranslators, which Lilia and Kevin declined. They had a good handle on the Coalition's main languages plus Tarynian; unless they ran into someone speaking a seldom-used dialect, they would be able to converse with everyone.

The ballroom reminded Lilia of the Mansion's ballroom, except that this room had two sets of staircases—one on either side of the room—leading down from the second and third floors. Also, there were windows; marble archways led off into other parts of the house. Beautiful strains of music floated through the air; one corner of the room had been converted into a dance floor with a live band. She registered all of that in a series of quick impressions, before the crowd of people swelling the room noticed their presence and faces turned toward them.

"Representative Monroe, how good to see you tonight," cooed one older lady, from the arm of an old gentleman whose name Lilia could not recall for the life of her. She was short and plump with a flushed rosy face, a striking contrast to her husband, who was tall, pale, and rail-thin. "You're looking well."

"Thank you, Gladys," Aiden replied courteously.

Lilia knew he would have much preferred to leave his hover-chair at home, but his grandchildren had insisted on it. He wasn't strong enough yet to spend an entire evening on his feet—or even parked in a chair somewhere.

Gladys's gaze traveled over the rest of them, and Lilia knew the moment the woman recognized her and Kevin. Something shifted in her blue eyes, turning them cold. "It's so lovely you've brought your grandchildren."

"Indeed." With a polite smile, Aiden tipped his head toward a large cluster of people at the back of the room. "If you will excuse me, I must speak to our host."

"Certainly," Gladys's husband replied.

Lilia held her head high as they wound their way through the room. She felt eyes on her and it made her skin crawl, but she tried to look unaffected. *We're getting it over with*, she reminded herself. *They'll forget and move on soon enough.*

Not nearly soon enough to suit her, though.

As they neared the cluster of people, Lilia glimpsed Leo Kedis through the shifting mass of guests gathered around them. A second later, she glimpsed Lon. Her heart began to beat faster in her chest; she willed it to remain steady. It didn't listen.

If Lon and Kedis were both here, then…

Recognizing Aiden, men and women stepped aside to let his hoverchair glide past them. Lilia, Kevin, Derek, and Michael fol-lowed in his wake.

Representative Zontak caught sight of them at the same time they finally saw him. "Aiden!" he boomed cheerfully. "So glad you could make it tonight." He was a tall, ruddy man gone slightly to fat, with salt and pepper hair and keen brown eyes.

"Thank you for the invitation, Manji," Aiden replied with a smile.

"And you brought your grandchildren," Zontak continued, turning a sharp eye on them. "Excellent." He offered Lilia and Kevin a sly smile. "I daresay you know this gentleman already. Ambassador?"

Kedis turned away from another conversation and a broad smile lit his face.

Lilia barely had time to realize he was genuinely pleased to see them before Kedis strode forward and clasped both her hands in his. Bowing his head over them, he said in Tarynian, "I am delighted to see you here tonight." Raising his head and letting go of Lilia's hands, he turned to Kevin. "And you, Kevin. Wonderful."

[Yeah,] Kevin muttered to Lilia via Nancom, [a wonderful opportunity for him to do some more politicking.]

[What did you expect?] she shot back, glancing discreetly past Kedis's shoulder. She would never admit it, but she was searching for another blond man. Jasper was, however, nowhere in sight.

Lilia suppressed a wave of disappointment. *He has to be here somewhere. And you have to be careful anyway.* Aloud, she said, "It's good to see you, Ambassador. Have you enjoyed these first few days of negotiations?"

"Oh, immensely."

Lilia thought he actually meant that.

"I believe," Kedis continued, "the Coalition and the Galactic Union have a great deal more in common than any of us dreamed." His dark eyes were alight with determined fire.

"I'm glad to hear it." Lilia couldn't think of anything else to say.

Settling a hand on her shoulder, Kedis set his other hand on Kevin's shoulder and turned them toward their host. "None of this would have been possible without their help."

Lilia's smile froze on her face. *Oh, honestly, there's no need to keep bringing it up.*

"We have gathered that, yes," Zontak said.

Kevin shifted uncomfortably. "It wasn't that much, really." He shrugged. "Our brother Lon is responsible for the bulk of it."

"Ah, but I couldn't have done it without you." Lon appeared beside their host, a broad grin on his face. He opened Nancom channels to both of them. [So glad you made it. I was afraid you wouldn't show.] He paused a beat. [I wouldn't have, if I were you.]

Lilia glanced sideways at Kevin. They hadn't told Lon what the NCDC had done yet. [Yeah, well, it's complicated.]

[We'll tell you the story later,] Kevin promised.

Lon was still smiling. [I'll hold you to that.] He caught Lilia's gaze wandering around the faces gathered together. [Looking for Wright?]

It took a great deal of effort not to let her surprise show. [What? No. I'm just—looking for people I know.]

[He's here,] Lon said, before stepping forward to greet Aiden.

Ruffled, Lilia ignored the look Kevin sent her and tried to act like she had been following Kedis's conversation this entire time. The Ambassador had apparently moved on to another topic, and she thought she could probably direct a polite smile at their host and slip away. Catching Zontak's eye, she offered him a curtsey. "Thank you for inviting us."

"Oh, you're more than welcome." He fluttered a hand at her in a shooing motion. "Go mingle. My grandson and his sister are here, and so are a number of other young people."

With a gracious nod, Lilia turned away and slipped sideways through a knot of people to escape. *Not another potential matchmaker*, she thought with an internal groan. It was bad enough already she'd have to duck Madame Olga. The woman was here—Lilia could have *sworn* she'd heard a snatch of her voice above the chatter and the music.

Waitstaff glided around carrying trays of champagne flutes; Lilia snagged one and made her way toward the edge of the room, where she was not in the general flow of traffic eddying and swirling about the room. She had just raised the flute to her lips when a voice spoke behind her.

"I was hoping you would be here."

Lilia froze. Then, very slowly, she turned her head. Lieutenant Jasper Wright stood beside her, wearing a black G.U. dress uniform with gold lieutenant's bars at the collar.

He smiled at her, his gray eyes warm. "I almost didn't recognize you."

Her heart did *not* flutter. Lilia motioned toward him with her champagne. "I'd have recognized you. I'm afraid you stand out a little."

"So do you." A slight smile curved Jasper's mouth. "I don't think I've ever seen you wear red before."

She shrugged, a touch self-conscious. "It was Alexis's idea. She thought I might as well stand out tonight and then from here on out I can just disappear."

"Interesting idea."

Silence fell between them for a moment, filled with music and the rise and fall of dozens and dozens of conversations. Lilia found she didn't quite know what to say. Intellectually, she knew the Jasper Wright she had come to know at the Mansion and the man standing before her now were one and the same, but her thoughts kept stumbling over his uniform. It was dressier than most of the uniforms she'd ever seen, either on Kyman or in the various places in occupied territory she'd been in a few months earlier, but it was still a G.U. uniform and it still made her uneasy.

"I don't know if anyone's told you this yet or not," Jasper said at last, "but you look beautiful."

"Thank you." Lilia ducked her head a little, one hand smoothing her skirt. Etiquette would demand that she return the compliment—he did look rather handsome—but that uniform…The words stuck in her throat.

She glanced back at him to see him regarding her with a slightly furrowed brow. *Oh, dear.* She took a hasty sip of her champagne. "What?"

"You don't like my uniform." His faint frown abruptly smoothed into something that looked half-teasing.

Caught off-guard by his bluntness, Lilia could only stare at him for a few seconds. "I—"

Jasper lowered his voice. "You can tell me the truth, you know."

Her eyes flicked from him to the rest of the room—no one seemed to be paying them the slightest bit of attention just yet—and back. "No," she said at last. "I don't like it. I mean, it's a nice enough dress uniform, but I still don't like what it stands for."

Jasper nodded. "I thought as much." His expression turned wry. "Easier to think of us as fellow human beings when we're wearing regular clothes, isn't it?"

His words were mild, but they still carried a sting. Lilia gave him a terse nod. "Yes."

"We have had this conversation before—or at least a variation of it."

Though she tried, Lilia found she could not quite restrain a smile. "Yes, we have."

"And we are now friends, are we not?"

She'd been wondering that same thing for days, but standing here looking up into his gray eyes took her back to the last dance they had shared before Kedis's grand entrance at the Gala. "Yes, I think so."

Jasper smiled; it crinkled the corners of his eyes. "In that case…" He extended a hand to her. "Would you dance with me?"

"Don't you have guard duties?" Lilia asked, even as she accepted his outstretched hand.

His smile turned conspiratorial. "The Ambassador made it very clear that we are to mingle as a part of our duties. And given how new my dancing skills are, I am afraid more practice is required."

Lilia found herself smiling back at him. "Oh, well, if that's the case…"

They garnered a few looks as they wended their way to the dance floor arm-in-arm and took up position. Lilia had no doubt the room would soon be buzzing, but at the moment…she couldn't bring herself to care. Being around Jasper again, especially in this situation, was a little awkward, but she had to admit that part of her had missed him. Their sporadic text-only conversations weren't the same…

…and he couldn't look at her that way through a text-only message.

Lilia raised her eyebrows at him. "Do I have something on my face?"

"No." Jasper led her through a waltz. "I was just thinking it's nice to see you." He smiled ruefully. "We have met a large number of people the past few days; it's refreshing to see a familiar face."

"Oh, they'll become familiar eventually." Lilia nodded to the room at large as they glided around.

"No doubt," Jasper agreed, though his eyes told her that was not what he meant and she knew it.

He changed the subject a moment later. "What happened after we parted ways at the Gala?" His fingers tightened on hers just a little. "Other than the fact that you were arrested, you've said very little about it."

"And I suppose Lon didn't say anything?"

Jasper's golden eyebrows quirked. "He's said very little about it too. I almost begin to wonder if it's a family trait."

Lilia shrugged. "There isn't much to say. I was arrested on treason charges, locked up in a conference room for a couple of hours, and then remanded into Grandfather's care until we faced the Triumvirate."

"You weren't…hurt?"

She glanced up into his gray eyes again before dropping them to his collar. Her mind flashed to the impactor, but even if she could have told him, in the grand scheme of things it was hardly worth mentioning. "No."

His Adam's apple bobbed as he swallowed. "I'm glad."

It was Lilia's turn to give him a rueful smile. "I'm fortunate enough to be related to Grandfather. They wouldn't have dared."

"That is good to know."

The song ended, and another began. "What do you think of the Beliana Hotel?"

Jasper shrugged. "It's very nice. Probably the most luxurious place I've ever stayed." He cracked a grin. "Definitely a few steps up from my quarters in—" he caught himself, "—the last place I was stationed."

Lilia appreciated his forbearance; the last thing she wanted to talk about tonight was what had or had not happened in Challa. She nodded, mock-soberly. "Nothing but the best for the Ambassador."

Jasper twirled her away from him in time to the beat before spinning her neatly back into his arms. "Although personally," he said, his voice barely audible, "I much preferred the Mansion." His eyes were bright and soft; the way he was looking at her just now made Lilia think he'd forgotten the entire ballroom existed.

All of the oxygen seemed to have been suddenly sucked out of the room. Lilia couldn't breathe, and she couldn't think. Her mind had gone completely blank. She laughed, a little breathlessly, in an attempt to rally her scattered brain cells. "Well, that's…nice. I'm glad you…liked the Mansion."

She needed to get away from him—he couldn't *look* at her like that—but at the same time, she didn't want to leave. Jasper had been floating around in the back of her mind the past few days; she was amazed at how much part of her had actually missed him.

[Seen anything suspicious yet?]

Kevin's dry Nancom voice broke through the haze turning her brain to mush. Lilia seized the interruption for the accidental lifeline it was and gave Jasper a genuinely apologetic smile. "As much as I've enjoyed this, I'm supposed to be talking to people." She gave an airy shrug. "Letting them know Aiden Monroe's youngest grandchildren haven't lost their minds."

To Kevin, she replied, [Not yet.]

Jasper released her smoothly. "That sounds like fun."

"You have no idea."

They smiled at each other, and then Lilia forced herself to turn away and depart the dance floor. She'd barely taken six steps when she bumped into a tall figure as he turned around. "Oh, excuse me," she said, before she realized who it was. Her eyes narrowed. "Mr. Birch."

"Miss Strong." Alan Birch, who held two champagne glasses, gave her a blink-and-you'll-miss-it once-over. "I was under the impression you would be…mingling…not ensconced on the dance floor."

*He knows about our new assignment.* Lilia straightened her spine. "Not that it's any particular business of yours, but I'm doing exactly what I'm supposed to be doing."

"Is that so?"

"Yes. Now, if you'll excuse me?" She started to sweep around him, but he blocked her path. His green eyes were hard.

"We're watching you."

Lilia lifted her chin. "Of course you are." Tossing her head, she swept past him without another word—and willed her fingers to unclench. It was all she could do to keep a pleasant expression on her face. *That man sets my teeth on edge. As if he doesn't have better things to do.*

She resisted the urge to cast a suspicious glance over her shoulder as she wound her way through the crowd. *Hopefully I'll be able to avoid him the rest of the night.* Catching sight of Parisa Briscoe, Shane Briscoe's lovely wife, Lilia headed in her direction. *I can handle a conversation with her.*

# CHAPTER 28

LILIA wasn't entirely sure how it happened, but somehow she and Jasper seemed to gravitate toward each other's orbit the rest of the evening. This alarmed her a little at first; she couldn't explain it, and part of her was afraid they would draw unnecessary, unwanted attention. *The last thing I want to do is end up in the media because someone thinks something is going on.*

Even she could see the potential for the story—the star-crossed lovers angle. *It's ridiculous, of course, but someone like*—she caught sight of a too-familiar face in the crowd, shuddered, and quickly moved away,—*Madame Olga would totally eat it up.*

As the night wore on, however, she found herself increasingly less inclined to run the opposite direction whenever she glimpsed Jasper through the sea of people. G.U. soldier or not, as far as she was concerned he was infinitely better company that ninety-five percent of the people filling this room.

"If I didn't know better," Jasper said in Tarynian, as he neared her and she did not disappear, "I'd be tempted to say you have been avoiding me."

Lilia met his eyes long enough to give him a one-shouldered shrug before she looked away. "Too many eyeballs."

"I see." He came up to stand beside her. "So I suppose another dance is out of the question."

"I'm afraid so. At least for tonight." Lilia gave him a genuinely regretful smile. "Even though I'd enjoy it more than just about everything else this evening."

She hadn't meant to say that last part aloud, but it slipped out anyway.

Jasper eyed her champagne flute. "Have you been carrying the same glass around all evening?"

She shrugged again, a trifle self-consciously. "Every so often I exchange it for water. This—" she tilted the glass, "—is mostly for show."

"And to ward off the occasional gentleman eager to get you something to drink?" Jasper guessed.

Lilia gave him a wan half-smile, but made no reply. *He's sharp.* To her surprise, more than a few gentlemen had been interested in making conversation with her—the fact that she was Representative Monroe's granddaughter was the only viable reason that came to mind.

The two of them stood in companionable silence for a few minutes, out of the way against a wall by a tall window, watching the party swirl and eddy around them.

"Look at this," Lilia said at last, unable to keep her thoughts to herself any longer. She raised her glass in the room's general direction. "What's the point of all this?"

Jasper considered the glittering crowd. "Is this a trick question?"

His tone was teasing, but Lilia was not in the mood. She felt heavy all of a sudden, as though the molecules of the very air around them carried invisible weights. "I'm serious." She waved her glass again. "What's the *point?*"

Her eyes swept over the crowd, taking in the laughter, the flirtation, the gossip, the business and political maneuvering being conducted between sips of champagne and other beverages, but she was acutely aware of Jasper's thoughtful gaze resting on her.

"Politics," he said softly. "Networking. Climbing the social strata."

"It's meaningless," she said quietly. "All of it." She turned to face him just as he leaned in to catch what she was saying and her eyes widened at how close they were.

"What do you mean?"

Lilia took a measured step backward to put a little space between them. "There's no thought of Christ here. Well," she paused, "maybe in a few people, but the bulk of this crowd?" She swallowed, tasting bitterness. "Everything is glamorous, beautiful, opulent—and completely devoid of any real meaning. It's all transient."

Jasper surveyed her thoughtfully. "This could be your life."

"Never wanted it." She shook her head. "None of us did. Not after we grew up and saw how the galaxy really works." Her mouth flattened into a thin line. "It's hard to swallow all of…this…when I've seen how people on Glo'Stea are suffering."

Jasper just looked at her.

"Don't you see?" Lilia raised her glass again. "Most people would love to be *here*, would love to be part of all *this*. I mean…" She indicated her own evening gown with a sweep of her gloved hand. "Look at this dress. I hate to think about how much Grandfather paid for it—and I tried to find middle ground." She shook her head. "It's ridiculous."

"It's a very pretty dress," Jasper said blandly.

"I know it is, but that's not the point."

"Then what is?"

Somehow, there was less space between them again. Looking up into his face, Lilia bit her lip. "My point is, most of the people in this room are spiritually dead. Can't you feel it?" She shook her head. "And they don't even *know* they're dead. This is their life."

Jasper cupped her elbow with one hand; she felt the warmth of his skin through the thin material of her glove. "Lilia…" His voice was earnest. "Why are you here? I didn't think this—" it was his turn to indicate the room around them, "—was something that interested you."

It took her a few seconds to decide whether or not to answer. Finally, she shrugged and stepped away. "You're right. It's not." She smiled wryly. "Unfortunately, tonight I don't have much of a choice."

Too late, she realized she'd been far too honest. Jasper's forehead wrinkled with a faint frown. "I did not have the impression this was something your grandfather was likely to force you to attend."

*It's not*, she wanted to say, but that would only make things worse. Instead, she gave an airy shrug. "It's a long story."

Jasper scrutinized her over his own glass as he took a sip, his gray eyes measured. "Perhaps one day you will tell me that story."

"Perhaps," Lilia agreed flippantly, before inclining her head in a gracious nod. "If you'll excuse me?"

Without waiting for an answer, she melted into the crowd. She resisted the urge to look back over her shoulder. *It is entirely too easy to talk to that man.*

Lilia shook off thoughts of Jasper as she wended her way around people, searching for her grandfather's hoverchair. She needed to find him; she wanted to escape this place and go home. She took a deep breath tinged by the cloying smell of far too many different kinds of perfume and cologne. *Surely we've been here long enough we can go home now. If someone was going to attack Kedis at this party, they'd have done it by now, right?*

She could only hope so.

# CHAPTER 29

THE next few days passed without incident. The NCDC had required Lilia and Kevin to attend another party on Sunday night, and then they were free to return to their usual business. This had included their weekly run to Redesh.

They had just returned to Sonela, and the twins had decided to keep Erik company and spend the night aboard the *Talia*; neither of them was in the mood to head back to Ferndale this late. The three of them were now sprawled in the *Talia*'s living compartment, though Kevin had spent the better part of fifteen minutes pacing back and forth while Erik watched a recap of the Tri-Global Tournament's highlights and Lilia sorted through their new list of upcoming social events.

Kevin abruptly rounded on Lilia and Erik, his hands locked behind his head. "You *do* realize what this means?"

Lilia exchanged glances with Erik; Kevin had a rather manic gleam in his violet eyes. Clearly, he'd been thinking about something—hard—and was now prepared to share.

"Realize what, exactly?" Erik drawled, looking faintly amused. "That all this pressure you've been under from the media is startin' to make ya go a little crazy?"

Kevin shook his head, completely ignoring the jibe. "If Freedom's Children was behind the attempt on Grandfather's life, then it means they've got transporters, nano-armor, *and* nanoblades."

A chill ran down Lilia's spine; she felt suddenly cold and a little sick to her stomach. "I hadn't put all that together yet." Her nausea increased. "And I should have—I'm the one who fought that assassin."

"That's your big revelation?" Erik raised an eyebrow.

"*Think* about it." Kevin resumed pacing, shaking his head. "They could show up anywhere, at any time, and your standard security detail wouldn't be able to do a thing to stop them. Laser bolts would just bounce off them." He stopped abruptly to shoot Lilia a significant look. "They could show up at—"

"—any of the social functions Kedis is attending." Lilia pressed a hand to her stomach. "As much as I hate to say it, maybe it'll be a good thing the NCDC is making us attend."

Erik glanced back and forth between them. "Need I remind you two that you don't actually *know* any of this? It's all speculation."

"It's not outside the realm of possibility." Lilia shrugged uneasily. "I mean, they managed to restore Glo'Stea's shield. That's a pretty huge accomplishment."

"Doesn't mean Freedom's Children automatically want to bump Kedis off," Erik argued.

The twins shared glances. Kevin's expression turned wry. "I'd be more surprised if they *didn't* want—"

"—to get rid of Kedis," Lilia finished. "From what we saw a few months ago, they're definitely—"

"—anti-Tarynian." Kevin flopped into a chair, frowning. "I wonder how many Guardians the NCDC has got at these things to begin with."

Lilia shook her head. "No idea. And I can't say I've tried searching for any yet, either." She bit the inside of her lip. *I've been too busy bemoaning the fact that we're stuck attending these blasted parties.*

Getting a chance to talk to Jasper was a nice perk, but it didn't completely make up for hours of grueling interaction with people she didn't want to be around.

"Well..." Kevin leaned forward in his seat, rubbing his hands together. The manic gleam was back in his eyes, but it had shifted into something a little happier. "You know what this means?"

Erik just stared at him. "Now what?"

Lilia raised an eyebrow. "I'm afraid to ask."

"We need to spend more time fencing," Kevin said matter-of-factly. "I've been thinking we ought to do that anyway, since I've noticed it's a huge topic of discussion among the younger people we're around, but now we've got a really good reason. If Freedom's Children shows up, we have a duty to defend the people around us." He half-smiled. "Even if they're Tarynians."

Lilia blew out a breath, taking all that in. "You're probably right," she said at last. "I don't think the NCDC ever intended us to actually end up *fighting* with nanoblades—"

"I dunno, I always had the impression we were supposed to test 'em out," Erik said.

"—but at this point we could." She made a face. "I know I need more practice."

"All right. It's settled." Kevin slapped his knees and rose to his feet. "We'll hammer out a practice schedule and head over to Chakin's in the morning." His voice saddened. "It's not like we're exactly drowning in business at the moment."

"It'll pick up," Erik said confidently. "If nothin' else, you two are a curiosity piece." He flashed them a grin. "An' I'm along for the ride."


Sweat trickled down Lilia's cheek inside her protective face mask as she parried a blow from her brother with one blade and lunged forward with the other. Her twin fencing blades whirled around her as she and Kevin danced back and forth across their practice square. She'd had enough practice in the months since she left Kyman to have regained some of her old skill; it was harder for Kevin to beat her now.

They were at the Chakin Lifestyle Center five streets over from Ferndale, inside the arena that occupied half of the four-story building's first two floors. Only fencing matches were allowed in the arena, though a track snaked around the upper level. A handful of white-clad competitors occupied other practice squares, dancing around each other with varying degrees of skill.

Chakin's was a fully-equipped gym, but their primary claim to fame was their long, illustrious history—stretching back at least eight decades—as home to the East Sonela Knights Fencing Club. Across the Coalition, the breakdown remained the same. If you fenced, or if you fenced and had aspirations of making it to the Tri-Global

Tournament, you belonged to a club. If you didn't fence, you supported a club.

Kevin finally scored one last point on Lilia and the match ended. He immediately removed his facemask. His dark hair was plastered to his forehead. "You're definitely giving me a run for my money, sis."

"That's the idea, isn't it?" Lilia asked wryly, tucking both blades under her arm to remove her own facemask. She'd pinned her short hair back to keep it out of the way, but sweat had ensured it wasn't going anywhere. She arched her back and made a face as muscles in her shoulders and back twinged. "I may feel this one tomorrow."

"Shake it off." Kevin grinned at her. "You'll be fine."

"We have a party to go to tonight. It'll be hard to explain why I can't dance."

Kevin looked at her like she had sprouted a second head. "Just tell them you had an intense fencing match today."

"Oh." Lilia hadn't thought of that. She smiled wryly. "Guess I'm a little tired."

"Yeah…" Kevin shook his head in mock-sympathy. "But somehow I think you'll recover." They turned to leave the arena together, skirting other fencers. "Wonder how Lon's holding up? I'll have to ask him if he's had any time to practice."

Lilia raised her eyebrows. "Unless he's sparring with somebody on Kedis's security team, I don't know how he'd have a chance."

"Good point."

The twins parted ways at the locker rooms. When Lilia emerged twenty minutes later, clean and dressed in street clothes, she found Kevin talking to a dark-haired, dark-skinned man who looked vaguely familiar. Her footsteps slowed as she approached; Kevin's body language told her this was not a friendly conversation. His arms were folded across his chest and he looked grim.

It wasn't until she reached them that Lilia recognized the man. They had never met in person, but he had attempted to persuade them to become part of the Hesperia shipping conglomerate a couple of months before via holo-call. *What was his name? James? Jake?*

Kevin's eyes darted to her. "Lilia, you remember Jake Ibaka."

"Yes, I do." Lilia shifted her gear bag a little higher on her shoulder. "I didn't know you lived in Sonela." *Or that you're a member of Chakin's,* she thought darkly.

"I don't," Jake said cheerfully, flashing her a gleaming white smile. "But I'm in town and thought I'd stop by to talk to you two while I'm here."

Lilia stared at him. "How did you know where we were?"

Jake just grinned again. "I have my ways."

She glanced involuntarily at Kevin before narrowing her eyes at Jake. "What do you want?"

"What do you think he wants?" Kevin raised his eyebrows at her. "Take a wild guess."

"Still?" Lilia asked, incredulous.

Jake spread his hands in a *what can you do?* gesture. "You two have got talent, skill, and perseverance—three qualities my employers prize."

"How many times do we have to say it? We're not interested," Kevin said firmly, turning away and striding toward the exit. "Thanks for your time, but no thanks."

"Don't be too hasty." Jake was not to be deterred. He followed after them as Lilia matched Kevin's quick strides. "I know business is down right now. You two get props for not folding in the face of adversity."

They passed the front desk and the chrome reception 'bot—dressed in a red-on-black East Sonela Knights jersey and matching hat—and exited onto the street. Once clear of the door, Kevin stopped on the sidewalk and rounded on Jake. "Look," he said, fighting to keep his voice even, "we're a small, independently-owned shipping business. We're *content* to be a small, independently-owned shipping business."

He glanced at Lilia to confirm this; she nodded.

"And it doesn't matter how many goons Hesperia sends after us to change our minds, we won't budge."

Jake raised his eyebrows in an expression of polite surprise. "I don't—"

"Don't bother denying it." Kevin held up a hand. "Some of your…associates…attacked me and a friend of ours a few weeks ago and said they were sending us a 'message'."

Lilia suppressed a grimace at the memory. Erik had gotten stabbed as a result of that last message, though his injury had partly been a result of his own bullheaded stubbornness, and it had resulted in him finding out the twins were helping Lon and Kedis.

"Well," Kevin continued, "tell your boss he can't scare us into joining. At this point, I'd rather see the *Talia* a pile of scrap metal than work for Hesperia."

Lilia caught her breath at the grim intensity in her brother's voice.

"I'll pass it along," Jake said after a long moment. He looked from Kevin to Lilia, friendly smile gone. "Although I must say that's a serious accusation, claiming that Hesperia sent men after you."

"Don't bother denying it," Kevin said flatly. "Frankly, I'm amazed you'd stoop so low. Now, if you'll excuse us, we've got places to be." He turned away, starting off down the sidewalk without a backward glance, and Lilia fell in step beside him.

"If we *were* in the business of making threats like that," Jake called after them, "you two would be in serious trouble right now."

The twins exchanged darting sidelong glances before stopping and pivoting in unison to face the older man. It was probably pointless, engaging him further, and yet…People streamed around them, most of them unconcerned as to why they were standing in the middle of the sidewalk.

Jake slowly sauntered up to them, his expression still friendly, though his eyes were hard. He spread his hands. "Hypothetically speaking, if my employers had issued a threat that severe and you disregarded it, you'd be in pretty dire straits right now."

"Lucky for us you don't do that, right?" Kevin asked sardonically.

Jake ignored him. "You two have been in the media a lot lately." He grinned. "You've been into all kinds of trouble lately."

[Where is he going with this?] Lilia asked Kevin. He didn't answer.

"If my employers had wanted those men to deliver you a message—which they had nothing do with, of course—they'd want me to tell you that given your current…situation…you've been granted a temporary reprieve." Jake raised one shoulder in a shrug. "Hypothetically speaking, of course."

"Right." Kevin folded his arms across his chest. "Is that it?"

"That's it." Jake started to turn away. "You'll hear from us again when you aren't quite so…busy." He raised a hand in a jaunty farewell as he strode away from them and disappeared into the ever-present stream of pedestrians.

For a second, the twins stared after him in disbelief. Then Kevin laughed shortly, dragging a hand over his face. "Who'd have thought all the media scrutiny we've been under would turn out to be a good thing?"

Lilia shook her head as they set off again. "So, basically, they're backing off because they don't think they'll get away with putting any more pressure on us until we fade back into obscurity."

"Something like that. The nerve of him, showing up *here* after what they did to tell us about our 'temporary reprieve'." Kevin made air quotes with his fingers.

"Lucky us." Lilia snorted. "I still don't understand why Hesperia wants us so badly."

Kevin's mouth flattened into a thin line. "Has to be our connection to Grandfather. Can't think of any other reason."

"This was another message, Kev." She looked up at him, her violet eyes full of concern. "They want us to know that they can find us if they want to."

Kevin made a scoffing sound in the back of his throat. "All they had to do was put a tail on us from either Ferndale or the spaceport. It's not like they really had to work for it. They're just trying to un-nerve us."

"It's partly working," Lilia said dryly. "I don't like this. Not on top of everything else."

"We've got bigger things to worry about." Kevin waved a hand. "Hesperia is minor league compared to Freedom's Children."

"Maybe." She glanced sideways at him. "I hope it doesn't come to that. The *Talia* being a pile of scrap metal, I mean."

"It won't." Kevin's face darkened. "Not if I have anything to say about it."

# Chapter 30

O THER than the announcement that the Triumvirate had agreed to open peace negotiations, it had been a week and a half since Chesnee had heard anything substantial from Leo Kedis, and the silence was starting to wear on him. Oh, the Ambassador had sent the occasional brief communiqué, detailing a point gained in his favor in peace talks here and a well-placed connection at a dinner party there, but none of it was information that pertained to the Blockade Division. Chesnee felt foolish even passing it along to Admiral Tyler, but he did so faithfully.

He was currently seated in his office, awaiting an official report from General Deam. Reports out of Glo'Stea were becoming a little more stable, but things were still chaotic. His comm panel lit up right on schedule—Deam was nothing if not punctual—and Chesnee touched the panel.

Deam's holographic head and shoulders bloomed in front of his desk. "Admiral," Deam began without preamble, snapping his left fist to his right shoulder in a salute, "I have more information on the situation on Glo'Stea for you."

Chesnee had no idea what to expect. He tensed inside, though he let none of it show. "Let's have it."

"The cease-fire has made things damned tricky, sir, if you'll pardon my language." Deam rubbed a frustrated hand over his short hair. "That said, we *have* learned that in addition to contributing to the planetary shield, the majority of the new shield generator sites also possess secondary shield systems to protect them from our ground and air forces. I'm transmitting the data now."

Chesnee looked down at his datapad as it vibrated softly. He scrolled through the data; he would peruse it more carefully later, but for now…He looked up sharply. "Some of these shields cut through inhabited buildings."

Deam nodded grimly. "This group that's claimed responsibility, Freedom's Children, well, they don't seem to care much about collateral damage." He grimaced. "At least not when it comes to the shields."

"It would certainly appear they put a higher premium on maintaining the shields than protecting their people," Chesnee agreed. He skimmed through the rest of the data, his eyes pausing now and then on particularly alarming sentences. He looked back at Deam. "Your ground forces are having difficulty maintaining order?"

"That's an understatement, sir." Deam's expression said he would rather have teeth pulled than admit failure, but it wasn't like he could hide anything. "We've got riots on both sides of the equation—some of our occupied sector's citizens are elated at the shield being up; the other half are terrified of what's going to happen next." He shook his head. "We may have an official cease-fire, but certain quarters are choosing to ignore it."

"I see." Chesnee glanced back down at his datapad. He hesitated to ask this question, under the circumstances, but it couldn't be helped. "Have your people made any attempts to reclaim the shield generators?"

Deam's face twisted further. "No, sir, not officially. We are abiding by the cease-fire."

Chesnee eyed him, before arching a sandy eyebrow. "And off the record?"

"Off the record, sir?" Deam hesitated.

"I need to know, Ira." Chesnee leaned forward in his seat. "Kedis is negotiating with the Triumvirate, but it is our people who pay the price in the meantime."

Deam inhaled, and then blew it all out at once. "Off the record, I can tell you several attempts have been made. We're trying to get Challa back under control, as well as a few other places." He shook his head. "Needless to say, it's not going too well. For starters, we've got media crews crawling up our sixes, and these Freedom's Children people are only too happy to poke their heads out and start shouting that we're violating the cease-fire." His face darkened. "Never mind the fact that there are groups of *them* stirring up trouble all over the place."

Chesnee frowned thoughtfully. "Anything you can prove? We do have an Ambassador relatively handy."

"Unfortunately, no, sir. They're very careful not to outright identify themselves."

"Of course they are."

Deam's face darkened further. "They're picking our men and women off one by one. A sniper shot here, a well-placed bomb there." He shook his head. "Frankly, sir, in all the time I've served in this capacity, it's never been this blatant. Hook our men on drugs as fast as we can detox them, yes. But outright murder?"

Chesnee recognized the pattern at once. "They're escalating."

"Drastically. No witnesses. No traces left behind. Nothing to prove they're violating the cease-fire except for our soldiers' dead bodies. And the occasional civilian—like I said, they don't seem to mind if other people get caught in the crossfire."

Chesnee could hear the pent-up frustration in the other man's voice. "Do the best you can, Ira." He lifted his hands. "My hands, so to speak, are tied. High Command and the Senate have effectively given Kedis the ability to override my decisions."

Deam's jaw clenched. "With all due respect, sir, I still think that's ridiculous."

"Oh, I agree, but there is little I can do about it."

"Is it true about their teleportation device?" Deam's holograph looked him straight in the eye. "Because I'm starting to wonder if this Freedom's Children bunch isn't using it here. Some of the things that have been happening…well, let's just say a teleportation device means they make more sense."

Chesnee frowned at that. "It's true," he said slowly. "But according to Kedis, the Coalition is only in possession of two such devices and the Triumvirate controls both of them."

"Or they're only *admitting* to have two of them." Deam snorted. "You think that's really true?"

"I don't know what to think." Chesnee shook his head again, leaning back in his seat. "At the moment, I'm not sure there's enough data to bear out a supposition that more than two devices exist. I think the Coalition would have found a way to put them to use en masse by now."

"Maybe." Deam didn't look convinced.

Chesnee's frown deepened. "Send me whatever you have on these mysterious happenings and I will see what I can do."

"Thank you, sir."

"Is there anything else, General?"

"No sir. You've got everything."

"Very well. Keep me posted, General."

"Will do, Admiral."

Deam's holograph dissolved, leaving Chesnee alone in his office…his thoughts in an uproar once again. His eyes dropped to the datapad before him and he felt the sudden throb of an oncoming headache. His people were dying—*slaughtered*, by the sound of it—and at the moment there was nothing he could do about it.

Nothing except relay the information to Kedis to add to the Ambassador's arsenal and hope the man pulled off something spectacular.

Chesnee wasn't holding his breath on that front. He sent a message to Kedis anyway, asking the Ambassador to call him at his earliest convenience, and set about studying Deam's data more thoroughly. The more information he could gather, the more clearly Freedom's Children's pattern of behavior would emerge. It looked like they were the enemy to be fought now—and Chesnee intended to keep as many of his people alive as possible.

Cease-fire or no cease-fire, if it came to that.

However, as he'd said to Deam, he *did* have an Ambassador handy. *And I'm not afraid to use him, if it comes to that.*

# Chapter 31

[I don't think things can get any duller than this, Lil. Seriously.]

Lilia glanced around the sumptuous downtown Sonela penthouse, searching the crowds of well-dressed partygoers for her brother. The penthouse belonged to a wealthy Sta'Gloan family with ties to Riley Nessan, the Sta'Gloan Director of Finance. Aiden was in attendance…and so was Leo Kedis. Lilia and Kevin hadn't had the option of refusing to attend.

[What, you aren't having fun?] she asked dryly. She wore a short-sleeved, jade green gown tonight, with a neckline that dipped a little lower than she was comfortable with. If she *did* have to materialize stealth-mode armor, she'd have a tricky time avoiding having it show. [This is only our…what? Seventh party? Shouldn't we be having fun by now?]

[I wish.] A pause, and then Kevin said, [I think I've figured out the NCDC's grand master plan.]

Sidestepping a group of men and women laughing uproariously at a joke someone had just said, Lilia wove her way through the crowded living room. The penthouse was spacious—easily twice the size of their home in Ferndale—but absolutely packed. As much as she would prefer to find a spot up against a wall, or near a window, Lilia had finally learned that if she kept moving, she was less of a target and less likely to get dragged into a conversation she didn't want to have with someone she really didn't know.

[Well, don't leave me in suspense, Kev.]

[It's punishment. Excruciatingly boring punishment, under the guise of providing extra protection.]

[Can't argue with that.] Lilia finally spotted her brother over in a corner of the room, glass in hand, making small talk with a group of older men and several women. Though he covered it well, she could tell he was uncomfortable.

One of the women was Sta'Gloan Representative Helen Urquart, who was on friendly terms with their grandfather. Lilia thought she recognized several of the men, but their names eluded her. They were business men, though, not politicians. She *was* sure of that.

As Lilia approached, Representative Urquart glanced at her. Iron gray hair framed a stern, angular face. "Ah, Miss Strong. We were just talking about the difficulties of running a small business in this economy."

Lilia forced a smile. "It's a challenge some days."

"Kevin was telling us you're in charge of the bookkeeping?"

"Yes."

"And she learned to be my copilot after we lost Lon," Kevin said.

Lilia shrugged modestly. "It was either that or shut the business down; we couldn't afford to hire another pilot."

Urquart nodded. "Sensible choice." She spared a glance for the rest of their small group before addressing the twins again. "It was a very bold move on your part, assisting the Ambassador."

"Yes, well, I might be regretting it now." Kevin offered them a rakish grin. "Now that we've got all these parties to attend." Still smiling, he gestured with his glass. "No offense, ladies and gentlemen, but I'd much rather be flying."

Laughter rippled through the group. One of the men, a portly businessman with dark brown skin, curly gray hair, and brown eyes, clapped Kevin on the back. "I understand completely. I miss the cockpit myself." He shook his head. "The boardroom just isn't the same."

The group splintered shortly thereafter when Urquart moved away, though she beckoned Lilia closer with a crook of a finger. "Walk with me."

Lilia exchanged a darting glance with Kevin before obeying. She fell in step with the Representative as the older woman made her way through the crowd at a leisurely pace. She seemed to glide through the room like a trickle of water streaming over the ground.

"I'm curious, my dear." Urquart tilted her head slightly to one side. "Have you ever considered becoming a diplomatic translator? Or a diplomat, for that matter?"

Caught completely off-guard, Lilia could only stare at the Representative. "I beg your pardon?"

The corners of the older woman's black eyes crinkled with faint amusement, though it did not translate to her mouth. "I've been watching you, you see." She took a sip of her champagne. "I've noticed that you don't wear an autotranslator."

Lilia shrugged uncomfortably, unsure where this was headed. *No one else has ever noticed.*

"I've also noticed that, like your brother Lon, you greet Ambassador Kedis in Tarynian." Urquart's expression grew knowing.

*I do?* Lilia froze, thinking back to her interactions with Kedis. Her violet eyes widened a fraction. *I do.*

"I only speak a little Tarynian myself, but I recognize it when I hear it." Urquart stopped walking and tapped Lilia's breastbone with a bony finger. "You're fluent, aren't you?"

It wasn't a question. The hair on the back of Lilia's neck prickled. "What does that have to do with anything?"

"Simultaneously nothing and everything." Urquart waved a hand. "In a day and age when everyone relies on technology to translate for them, it is a rather unique skill to posses." She pursed her lips. "In fact, I've often wondered if we shouldn't have required more of our people to learn it over the years. Would have been helpful from both a commercial and military aspect. But, I digress." She waved a hand again.

Bewildered, Lilia tried to make sense of that. "I'm sorry, Representative," she said at last. "I don't think I'm following. I understand the need for translators in places like medcenters on the fringes of free Glo'Stea—" a tiny pang of guilt pierced her at this; she had never been able to bring herself to volunteer to be around Tarynians, "—but if you have autotranslators, why would you need someone—"

"—fluent?" Urquart interrupted. She met Lilia's eyes, her expression serious. "Because technology can be disrupted. It's not likely to happen, I grant you, but it *can* be done."

Lilia considered that. "It wouldn't be pretty."

"No, it would not." Urquart lifted one elegant shoulder in a shrug. "And then there are those who prefer to deal with a person's brain instead of a computer filtering language for them." She gave Lilia a wry glance. "I'm sure I don't have to tell you language is often subjective."

"No, I know."

"As for you possibly becoming a diplomat…" Urquart offered her what she clearly intended to be a kind smile. "You handle people well, and you certainly managed to make an impression on Ambassador Kedis. You should hear him sing your praises."

A flush rose from Lilia's neck to her cheeks. "I just tried to be hospitable." She gave another uncomfortable shrug. "Grandmother would never forgive me."

"Ah, yes. I remember your grandmother." Urquart nodded sharply. "Teresa was a lovely woman. She and Aiden complemented each other wonderfully." Her voice dropped to a conspiratorial whisper. "I will confess I was sometimes jealous of how well they seemed to get on with each other. I don't believe my own marriage was ever that smooth."

Not entirely sure what to say to that, Lilia could only nod.

"Well, think about it, young lady." Urquart paused long enough to give her a piercing glance that felt like she could see straight through Lilia's skin and muscle to her bones. "I have a feeling you would do well in a diplomatic environment." She shook her head once. "Frankly, I'm surprised the thought has never occurred to your grandfather."

Lilia started, struck by a sudden thought. "But what about my—"

"Treason conviction?" Urquart asked knowingly. Her eyes traveled beyond Lilia, as though gazing into the future. "You may well find that will not be an issue at all if these peace talks go well. But who knows how these things will turn out?" The Representative looked at Lilia once more, before gliding off, leaving her feeling decidedly off-kilter.

*What was* that *all about?* Lilia inhaled sharply, trying to gather her composure and not let anyone know how startled she was. Glancing around the room, which suddenly felt too small and stuffy, she took a glass of some clear, iced fruit drink off a passing tray carried by a humanoid 'bot dressed in black and white and then her eyes met gray.

*Jasper.*

Without much conscious thought, her feet carried her in the lieutenant's direction. It was the first time she'd set eyes on him all evening; if she hadn't seen Kedis earlier, holding court in the next room over, she would have thought this gathering was Tarynian-free. *Of course,* she thought wryly, *if the gathering had been Tarynian-free, Kevin and I wouldn't be here.*

As she approached, Jasper said in Sta'Gloan, "We have to stop meeting like this."

An unbidden smile formed on Lilia's lips. "Well, hello, Lieutenant. Fancy seeing you here."

Jasper shook his head slightly, the dazzling light from the sparkling chandelier overhead picking up the darker gold glints in his short hair. "Don't tell me you're seriously joining the ranks of the local socialites."

Lilia shot him a wry smile. "Maybe I don't have anything better to do?"

"I don't believe that. If nothing else, you have a business to run."

"True." She inclined her head in an acquiescent nod.

"How is business?"

Lilia sighed. "A little slow, to be honest. We're not sure if it's just slow across the board, or slow because potential clients are leery of us right now."

Jasper nodded in understanding. "Enjoying the party?"

"Well..." Lilia glanced automatically over her shoulder in the direction Urquart had gone, but Representative had already been swallowed up by the crowd. "It's been interesting." She offered Jasper a smile. "How are you?"

"As well as can be expected," he said soberly, though one corner of his mouth twitched. "I find myself wondering if we will be attending multiple parties a week for the duration of the Ambassador's stay here."

Lilia sighed. "We will. I've seen Grandfather's schedule. And I don't think we'll be able to get out of them, either." They shared a commiserating look, and then she motioned to crowd with the delicate glass in her hand. "Speaking of the Ambassador, how goes everything?"

It was Jasper's turn to favor her with a wry smile. "Oh, I would say he's definitely in his element." They stood in companionable silence for a moment, surveying the crowded room, and then he asked, "How is your grandfather? I have not seen him yet tonight."

"He's doing pretty well, although he's still got some healing to do." Lilia tucked a lock of hair behind one ear. Her hair was mostly pinned back tonight, but she had left a few locks loose to frame her face. "He threatens to ditch his hoverchair occasionally, but on the whole he's been a good patient."

"I'm glad."

Lilia glanced sideways at him. Once again, Jasper was dressed in his black G.U. dress uniform. "Is that uniform the only thing Kedis lets you wear to a party?" She offered him a smile, to let him know she was only teasing.

Jasper made a show of straightening his cuffs, but was unable to repress the glint of mischief in his gray eyes. "Miss Strong, need I remind you that I am an officer of the Galactic Union, and as such have the great privilege and honor of wearing this uniform?"

Had he been anyone else making such a statement, Lilia probably would have been ill. As it was, by now she was hard-pressed not to laugh at such an overdramatic statement. "Oh, I see. Well, by all means, carry on."

"You don't have to like it."

"Oh, believe me, I don't."

They shared a laugh—and that, too, was a novel concept, that she could even make jokes about a Tarynian uniform—and then Jasper snagged a couple of tiny hors d'oeuvres from a passing tray carried by a humanoid 'bot dressed in black and white. Just before he popped one into his mouth, he nodded over his shoulder. "What was that all about?"

It took Lilia a second to realize he meant her conversation with Urquart. "You saw that?"

He shrugged. "I know she's a Sta'Gloan Representative, though I admit I can't remember her name."

"She thinks I ought to be a diplomatic translator. Or a diplomat." The words popped out before Lilia could stop them.

"A diplomat?"

"Yeah." Lilia smoothed a hand down her jade green skirt. "She's figured out I speak Tarynian, and she said something about me being good with people." Her eyes flicked up to Jasper again. "And apparently the Ambassador is talking about me?"

Jasper nodded, one corner of his mouth twitching again as though he wanted to laugh. "The Ambassador is still quite impressed with how you, Kevin, and Lon managed things."

"Great." Lilia started to fold her arms across her chest, but remembered her neckline and thought the better of it. "A diplomat," she repeated, half-under her breath. "Of all things…"

"It's not that far beyond the realm of reality."

"What?" She glanced at Jasper sharply.

"Think about it, Lilia. You speak Tarynian, you have political connections, and you're levelheaded." He shrugged. "I can see why the thought would occur to her. She's likely thinking ahead, planning out all the various ways the peace talks can turn out."

Lilia tried to imagine herself as a diplomat traveling to Taryn, exchanging polite conversation with a planetful of people who had spent twenty years oppressing her people, and failed. She shook her head. "I don't think so."

Her throat felt dry; she swallowed convulsively. *I don't think I could travel to Taryn.*

Jasper tactfully changed the subject. "What have you been doing with yourself, since business is slow?" He grinned before taking another bite and swallowing. "Other than attending parties, of course."

*Researching Freedom's Children,* Lilia wanted to tell him, but she didn't. Instead, she shrugged. "Taking care of a few things for Grandfather, brushing up on my fencing…those sorts of things."

"Ah, yes." Jasper nodded. "You mentioned you fenced while we were at the Tournament." He gave her a sharp look. "And if I remember correctly, you promptly changed the subject when I asked if you were any good."

Lilia blushed. It had been a throwaway conversation during a lull in the action the day she and Kevin had taken Jasper with them to Aiden's box seats at the Tri-Global Tournament. At the time, she hadn't really wanted to discuss her own swordsmanship. "Well…" She waved a hand. "We *were* at a Tournament celebrating the very best of the best."

"So we were. And now we're here." He raised his eyebrows. "Are you any good?"

She shrugged, modestly. "Passable."

Jasper laughed. "And by 'passable', you mean 'pretty good'."

"I'm not as good as my brothers," Lilia said honestly. "I need more practice."

"Which you've been getting lately, according to Kevin."

Lilia blinked; she hadn't realized Kevin and Jasper had interacted much lately. "Might as well." She shrugged again. "Like I said, business has been slow." A shadow crossed her face. *Have to be sharp, when Freedom's Children has got their hands on nanoblades.*

"I would like to see the two of you spar sometime. I have watched Lon spar with several men on our security team and it looks like fun."

"It's fun. And it's work." Lilia reached for another passing tray bearing tiny fruit skewers. She offered one to Jasper; when he accepted it, their fingers brushed.

"When did you first start fencing?"

Lilia bit into a green slice of kiwi while she thought about it. "Kevin and I were little. Maybe too little," she grinned up at him, "but we wanted to join in with our brothers and Grandfather indulged us. He said something about us not being too young to start learning the right way."

She shrugged. "Grandmother wasn't so sure, but she agreed, as long as we paid attention and were careful. It was hard, sparring with older brothers who'd had a lot more practice than we had, but it was also a really good learning experience. We had to work to be faster and catch up because they were better than we were."

"I'd like to see that sometime," Jasper said again, his eyes fixed on her.

Under his scrutiny, Lilia found herself flushing once more, and looked away—

—straight at Martin Hollowell, who had come up beside them. Her eyes widened in surprise. "Uncle Martin. Hello. I didn't realize you were here tonight."

Hollowell gave her a slightly indulgent smile. "I would say there are few who are not." He glanced around the crowded living room with the faintest trace of distaste. "In fact, one might argue the fire marshal will make an appearance any moment and scold Pyu Kwan for over-extending his guest list."

Lilia laughed. "It *is* rather crowded in here." Feeling only a little nervous, she motioned to Jasper. "You remember Lieutenant Wright, Uncle Martin."

"Yes." Hollowell's measured gaze said he also remembered the day he'd met Jasper and Lilia had introduced him as her boyfriend, but he made no mention of it.

"We were just discussing fencing, sir," Jasper said.

"Ah, yes." Hollowell's smile warmed as he looked at Lilia. "Have you told him the story of how you ended up with twin blades?"

"No." Lilia fought the urge to fidget. "I hadn't gotten that far."

"Twin blades?" Jasper arched a golden eyebrow at her. "That does sound impressive."

She shrugged. "It's more a matter of my brothers deciding they needed a sparring partner with two blades, and I was small enough—"

"And fast enough, if memory serves," Hollowell said.

"—to learn how to use them." Lilia shrugged again. "And then I decided I liked having two blades." She shot Jasper a wry smile. "Hence the need for more practice lately."

He raised his glass to her. "I definitely have to see this."

The warmth in his gray eyes brought another flush to her cheeks; to cover it, Lilia raised her own glass to her lips and took a healthy sip. *Get a grip!* she scolded herself. *You're being ridiculous.* She darted a glance at Hollowell, and the blush died as quickly as it had risen. For an instant, she thought she saw displeasure flicker through his dark eyes, but it passed, leaving her uncertain.

Jasper glanced over his shoulder. "If you will excuse me, Representative, Miss Strong," he nodded to them both, "I believe it is time I located the Ambassador."

"Certainly," Hollowell said smoothly. He waited until Jasper had melted into the sea of people before pinning Lilia with a stern look. "I know I am not your grandfather, child, but I would caution you to be careful around them. Particularly that one."

Part of Lilia bristled at him calling her a child, but the rest of her let it slide. Hollowell had known her since she was tiny and she knew he meant well. She offered him a confident smile. "Don't worry, Uncle Martin. Everything is fine."

"I am serious. People are talking about the two of you."

That gave Lilia qualms, but she maintained her smile. "It's all right. I knew there would be rumors after I smuggled him into the Gala, but that's all they are—rumors."

"I certainly hope so." Hollowell held her gaze a few seconds more, and then his stern look dissolved. He offered her his arm. "Shall we find your grandfather?"

"Yes." Lilia accepted his arm and allowed him to lead her through the penthouse in search of Aiden, but her thoughts were a tangled, tumbling jumble. Concern about rumors regarding her involvement with Jasper faded to the background as Urquart's words returned.

Lilia swallowed. *I'm pretty sure I'm not cut out to be a diplomat.*

# Chapter 32

KEVIN hadn't seen his sister since they were in the knot of people talking to Representative Urquart. He'd glimpsed his grandfather once or twice through the crowd over the past half hour, but he had otherwise begun wandering the penthouse, casually moving from group to group. He'd come to the conclusion that if anything posed a danger to this crowd, it was the copious quantities of alcohol being consumed.

"Do you fence, Strong?"

Startled, Kevin looked to his left at the speaker, one of the younger aides to one of the Sta'Gloan Representatives—he couldn't remember which one. He had not expected to be addressed; he had stopped on the fringes of a group that had started off discussing the Tri-Global Tournament and had since moved on to fencing clubs. "Yes."

The young man raised black eyebrows, his olive-toned face expectant. He was almost Kevin's height, with brown eyes and black, curly hair. Kevin thought his name was Franco. Guillard Franco. "Well? Where?"

"Chakin's. Here in Sonela."

"Chakin's," said the man standing next to Franco. He was another of the other aides in the group, a whip-thin man with pale, freckled skin and neatly coiffed red hair. "I've heard of it."

He named the club team and Kevin raised his still-half-full glass. "That's the one."

"Are you any good?" Franco asked

"Decent."

"We'll have to fence sometime then," Franco declared. "I'm always on the lookout for a challenge."

*That confident, are you?* Kevin raised his eyes slightly, but did not comment.

Franco held out his comlink. "Give me your comm details." Kevin complied, and Franco slid his comlink back into his pocket. "I'll comm you later, set up a fencing session." His teeth gleamed white as he flashed Kevin a satisfied smile. "Should be fun."

"Should be," Kevin agreed. "I could always use more practice."

Franco smiled again, exchanging glances with the redheaded man beside him. "Oh, you'll get more practice." He clapped Kevin on the shoulder. "And if you're any good, well…that's when the fun really starts."

He strode off, and several of the group trailed after him, including the redhead. Kevin stood there for a moment, one hand in his pocket, staring thoughtfully after them. *What was* that *supposed to mean?*

Kevin heard from Franco the next morning, while he and the rest of the family were in church. The aide sent him the location of his club, Hawthorne, and a list of times that would work best for them to meet up. As soon as they were out of church, Kevin scanned through the list and picked the first one, which just happened to be the following evening.

"I don't know exactly what's going on," he told his sister Monday night as he slung his gear bag over his shoulder in the penthouse foyer, "but I've got a funny feeling about it." He wore loose tan slacks and a pale green button-up shirt.

Lilia leaned up against the doorframe leading into the kitchen, one hand propped on her hip. Her feet were bare, and she wore dark capris and a soft turquoise shirt. "What kind of funny feeling?"

He shook his head. "Not sure. But there's something going on here, something more than just a group of guys getting together to fence. They're way too into it."

"Too into it?" Lilia raised her eyebrows. "Have you heard how you, Mike, Derek, and Lon talk about fencing?"

"This is different." Kevin shook his head again. "I don't know how else to explain it."

"If you say so." Lilia pursed her lips. "Just be careful. I could see those guys ignoring the rules and playing dirty."

Kevin grinned at her. "Oh, that wouldn't surprise me at all. Good thing I have some street fighting experience, eh?" He waggled his dark eyebrows at her. "At least they won't be fighting with nano-blades like those guys on Lanx."

It was Lilia's turn to shake her head. "I mean it. Be careful, Kev. We helped bring Kedis in, and you don't know how these guys feel about that."

"Don't worry." Kevin's grin turned reassuring. "I'm a Guardian—and I'm Aiden Monroe's grandson. It'll be fine." He strode out the door and down the hall to the accelevator, leaving Lilia frowning after him.

Once he emerged from the apartment building, Kevin caught a hoverbus to the edge of the upper-class district on the southern side of Sonela where Hawthorne was located. The club was positioned such that it catered to both upper-class and upper middle-class clientele, and was abuzz with activity in the evenings.

Pushing through the door into a ritzy lobby, Kevin approached the orange-and-gold receptionist 'bot seated at the front desk. "Hello. I'm here to meet Guillard Franco?"

Before the 'bot could respond, Franco rose from one of the burnt orange armchairs clustered in a corner and waved a hand. "He's with me, Giano."

The 'bot's photoreceptors flashed as it consulted its internal computer. "Very good, sir." It extended a metallic hand palm-up toward the doors that led deeper into the club. "Enjoy."

"Thanks." Kevin nodded to the 'bot before shifting his bag higher on his shoulder and turning to Franco.

"Glad you could make it." Franco's dark eyes glittered. "Let's get going."


Franco, Kevin learned a little while later, was good. Very good. He had put in a *lot* of practice.

Hawthorne was larger than Chakin's, but laid out much the same way. Franco marched them both to the men's locker room, where they changed into protective gear, and then they stepped out into the fencing arena. Most of the practice squares marked out on the floor were full, but Franco led the way through the airy room to a free corner. A glance around told Kevin this must be Franco's usual spot—and he must have some sort of arrangement with the club—because there were several spots here no one had taken.

One of the men Kevin remembered from the party, the thin redhead, was there waiting for them, along with two others he didn't recognize. All three also wore protective gear.

"Gentlemen," Franco said grandly, "this is Kevin Strong." He looked at Kevin and pointed to each of his companions in turn. "Renaldo Tieran." Tieran was a tall, broad-shouldered young man with keen brown eyes, deep black skin and a smooth-shaven head. "Ulrich Quilleran, goes by Quill." Quill was half a head shorter than Kevin, with tan skin, hazel eyes, and slicked-back white-blond hair.

Last, Franco motioned to the redhead. "Flynn Sparin." Sparin nodded once to Kevin in recognition.

Introductions finished, Franco indicated Kevin should take up his position. He nodded to the blond. "Quill here will be your partner today."

Quill stepped forward to take his place opposite Kevin. "This," he said with a broad smile, "should be fun." He saluted Kevin with his sword. "First touch."

"First touch," Kevin agreed, returning the salute. *That's an odd choice*, he thought, but he didn't have time to consider it further.

The duel that followed reminded Kevin of the battle he'd fought in that underground arena on Lanx. He'd been facing a young woman wielding a nanoblade then; this was every bit as intense and required every ounce of his skill. He'd been expecting a duel, but this…this was something different.

Quill spent a moment exploring Kevin's defenses with a few light jabs, before he escalated. He was quick on his feet, which reminded Kevin of dueling Lilia—and made him grateful the other man only wielded one sword. They circled each other, searching for openings, and Kevin lunged forward. Quill parried the blow and countered with a sideways strike at Kevin's protected ribs. Kevin blocked it and danced away.

Their blades flashed bright silver beneath the arena's lights as they fought. Kevin's blade was an extension of himself; the world narrowed down until it was just him and Quill. Eventually, Kevin saw his chance—and took it. Batting Quill's blade aside, he breached his defenses to score a point on the other man's shoulder.

"First touch," he said breathlessly, stepping back, blade at the ready.

Quill yanked his protective facemask up. His expression was curious; he wasn't smiling, but neither did he look particularly perturbed to have lost. "First touch. Congratulations, Strong." Strands of his white-blond hair were plastered to his forehead. "You're better than I expected."

Kevin pushed his own facemask up, feeling sweat trickle down his forehead. "You made me work for it."

Quill glanced at his three companions, who had spent this entire time watching them, and cocked a questioning eyebrow. All of them nodded. Looking back at Kevin, he smiled ruefully. "I'll have to step up my game." He turned away toward the locker room, raising his sword in a gesture of farewell. "We're done for the night."

"That's it?" The words slipped out before Kevin could stop them.

Franco stepped forward to clap Kevin on the shoulder. "For tonight." A sudden grin split his olive-skinned face. "We'll set up another duel soon."

Bemused, Kevin watched him cross to the locker room after Quill. Tieran and Sparin followed, both nodding to Kevin in turn. As they disappeared inside, Kevin hefted his sword thoughtfully in his hand. *That…almost felt like an audition.* He glanced around the fencing arena, nodding to several other fencers as he happened to make eye contact. *An audition for what?*

He didn't know…and that only fueled his curiosity. There had to be a purpose behind all this. He smiled grimly to himself. *Guess I'll just have to wait and find out.*

# CHAPTER 33

L ILIA was stretched out on one of the long dark blue couches in
the living room with her datapad when she heard the front door
open. "How was it?" she called out.

"Strange. Very strange." Kevin's voice floated to her from the foyer.

She glanced up at the doorway as he walked through it , his gear
bag slung over his shoulder and a puzzled look on his face. "What
do you mean?"

"I mean it felt like a test of some sort. Or an audition."

"For what?"

"I have no idea."

Abandoning her datapad, Lilia sat up. "Tell me about it."

In a few sentences, Kevin outlined the evening.

"That *is* strange." Lilia stared at him, considering. "Think you'll
fight him again?"

Kevin shrugged. "I don't know *what* to expect."

"If he invites you to another one, are you going?" Kevin just
gave her a look and Lilia raised her hands, laughing. "I know, I know.
Dumb question. Of course you're going."

"Out of curiosity, more than anything else." Frowning, Kevin
glanced toward the wide windows providing an evening view of Sonela. "I'm headed over to the *Talia*. We've got an early morning and

Erik probably shouldn't be left alone too long anyway." He raised an eyebrow. "You coming?"

Lilia shook her head. "I can't leave yet. Grandfather wants to talk to me when he gets home; he said he had something for me to do."

Kevin looked around, as though expecting his grandfather to pop into view. "Did the Triumvirate run late today?"

"No, some Sonela businessman threw a dinner party for Kedis."

"Ah." Kevin frowned. "Well, then I guess I'll stay here. We'll head out together in the morning so nobody has a fit." He nodded in the direction of the security penthouse.

Lilia smiled wryly. "Good point. Sorry to make you wait though."

Kevin waved that aside. "I've got things to do anyway." Turning, he headed down the hall to his room.

Lilia picked up her datapad again, but her attention was not on the news article about Glo'Stea she'd been perusing. She stared blankly at the arm of the couch. *What in the galaxy could Kevin be auditioning for?*

When the front door opened again an hour later to admit her grandfather and eldest two brothers, Lilia looked up from her datapad with a smile. Her smile faltered as she watched Derek guide her grandfather's hoverchair through the doorway into the living room. Aiden's face was pale and his eyes were closed.

"Grandfather?" Lilia scrambled up off the couch. "Are you all right?"

Aiden raised a hand without taking the trouble to open his eyes. "I am merely tired, my dear. It has been a long day."

Biting her lip, Lilia exchanged concerned looks with Derek and Michael. Both of her brothers looked a little grim. Gently, she said, "Looks like you might have overdone it a little today."

"Indeed." Aiden exhaled heavily and opened his eyes, a wry smile curving his mouth. "When one gets to be my age, my dear, one finds that one's mind is perfectly willing, but one's body sometimes refuses to cooperate."

"I'll keep that in mind." She glanced back at her comlink; if her grandfather was home, the Ambassador probably would be soon as well…which meant she'd probably hear back from Jasper soon. Her heart gave a little lurch at the thought. "You'd probably better go straight to bed."

"That's what we said." Derek shook his head, angling Aiden's hoverchair around and directing it toward his master bedroom down the hall.

"Wait." Aiden held up his hand again. "I still need to speak with you, Lilia." His green eyes were tired, but clear. "I know you have a run to Glo'Stea in the morning."

Catching the three siblings exchanging glances above his head, Aiden sighed. "It will not take long."

"If you're sure, Grandfather…"

He mustered another weary smile. "Quite sure."

"Got it." Lilia glanced at Derek, lifting her eyebrows in a silent question. *Any ideas?*

He only shrugged in response.

"Follow me." Aiden craned his neck around to look up at Derek. "I believe I can take it from here."

Derek stepped back from the hoverchair. "Sure thing, Grandfather."

He and Michael, Lilia noted, both looked exhausted as well. As Aiden floated down the hall, she paused to glance back at her brothers. "How was dinner?"

Their answers overlapped. "Long."

"Tedious."

Michael sank down onto the couch and stared up at the ceiling. "It'll be nice when things calm down a little."

"Don't expect that any time soon," Derek advised wryly, turning to follow Lilia as she started down the hall after their grandfather. "You're lucky you missed this one, Lil. Dullest thing I've attended in a long time." He ran a weary hand through his dark hair. "And that's saying something."

Lilia patted him sympathetically on the back before turning into the open doorway leading into Aiden's bedroom. It was larger than her room and those of her brothers, with a walk-in closet, a desk and chair made of warm, golden wood that had been her grandmother's, and an attached hygiene unit. She took a seat on the gold loveseat settled against the wall by the door as Aiden wheeled his hoverchair to face her. "What's up, Grandfather?"

He was silent for a few seconds. Then, slowly, he shook his head. "Before I left this evening, I intended to speak to you about hosting a dinner party at the end of the week." He turned one hand palm up. "The Ambassador is here, after all, and my grandchildren were involved in his arrival. I intended to invite him here, along with a few others." He smiled softly. "Your first real job as my social planner."

Lilia blinked, letting that sink in. *I suppose that makes sense.* She felt a brief flutter of nervous excitement, before she processed the rest of his statement. Her eyebrows knit together in a frown. "Have you changed your mind?"

Aiden nodded, his expression growing faintly troubled. "I have. Dinner tonight…" He glanced away. "It is difficult to explain, but suffice to say that I have come to the decision that it would be…unwise…to invite Kedis here until things are more…settled. It would be more of a hindrance than a help."

"That's understandable," Lilia said with a small smile.

"Also, at the moment, I have no desire to stir up another media storm." Aiden shook his head. "There will be a time and place, but not yet." He held out a hand to her. "I am sorry to delay your debut."

Laughing, Lilia took his hand and squeezed it gently. "That's quite all right, Grandfather." She grinned impishly. "I don't mind having a little more time to mentally prepare before I'm under that kind of scrutiny."

"You will do admirably. I have no doubts."

The fond pride in her grandfather's green eyes filled Lilia with a warm glow. Rising to her feet, she leaned toward Aiden and hugged him gently. His chest was still a little tender. "I love you, Grandfather. Get some rest."

"Thank you, child. I love you too. Good night."

As she stepped out into the hall and tapped the door release to close the door behind her, Lilia felt her comlink vibrate in her pocket. She pulled it out on the way to her own room, and glanced at the display. Her heart gave a funny little lurch. *Jasper.*

*Hope your day has gone well,* his message read. *I see you were able to avoid the party tonight.*

*Yes, I was,* she sent back, entering her own room and hitting the door release. *Kind of a relief, actually.*

You missed nothing. Anything interesting happen today?

Lilia changed into a sleep shirt and soft pants before answering. *Grandfather wanted me to throw a dinner party for him, but then he changed his mind.*

The instant she hit 'send', she almost regretted telling Jasper that, but her initial, panicked knee-jerk reaction passed. Sometimes it was hard to remember the lieutenant served Kedis and he wasn't *just* the fascinating man she was coming to know—until that realization kicked her in the gut. But this…this was harmless.

Wasn't it?

*Oh, really?* Jasper responded a short while later.

*Yeah,* she sent, curling up on her bed. *He hired me as his social event planner a while back, but we haven't had much of a chance to do anything yet.*

A pause, and then, *May I ask why he changed his mind?*

Lilia sighed, frowning down at her comlink. *He decided it wasn't the right time yet.* She almost added that she thought part of the reason might be that he simply didn't have the energy with everything else going on right now, but refrained. They *thought* Jasper's comlink was secure, but that didn't mean it actually *was.*

Not in this game.

She had to wait a moment for Jasper's response. *Ah, I see. Well, I am sure your grandfather knows best.* Another pause. *Would the Ambassador have been invited?*

Lilia snorted softly. *Yes.*

She didn't trust herself to say anything else; she was afraid she'd sound disappointed. It wasn't like she'd have seen much of Jasper anyway—security personnel always stayed in the penthouse across the hall with Aiden's team whenever he did have company to keep an eye on things from there. Of course, *Jasper* didn't know that.

*It's for the best, anyway,* she told herself. *You'd be entirely too distracted otherwise.*

She was honest enough with herself to admit *that.* She and Jasper were becoming good friends—something she'd never had dreamed possible with a G.U. soldier—and when he was around, she wanted to talk to him. *No, it's best that if and when Grandfather does throw a party, he won't be there while you're trying to play hostess.*

Her comlink vibrated against her fingers. *I am sure the right time will present itself eventually.*

*Look at the bright side,* Lilia sent back. *One less social engagement for people to attend.*

His response came quickly. *Somehow, I don't think you'll have any problems enticing people to show up.*

Lilia smiled at that. *Oh, I don't know. Have you seen some of the schedules these higher echelon people keep?*

She could almost hear the smile in Jasper's next words. *Getting an up close and personal look at them. Honestly, I don't see how they do it and keep up with everyday life.*

Lilia considered that for a few seconds. *I don't think they do. At least not in a normal sense. Most of them have staff to take care of the mundane things normal people have to think about.*

A moment later, her comlink vibrated again. *Which is probably what I would have thought of you and your brothers, if I didn't know you're much closer to the rest of us than most of the people I've met at those parties.*

*It's true,* Lilia responded, *we could have turned out the same way.* She bit her lip as she considered her next words. *It's weird though—sometimes I feel like we straddle two worlds and don't really belong to either of them.*

Jasper took a moment to respond. *Well, if it's any consolation, I'm glad you didn't turn out the same way. I doubt we would have ever met otherwise. Your brother would have never ended up crossing paths with the Ambassador.*

*Probably not,* Lilia sent back.

She spared a thought for what that life would have been like. *Actually, it doesn't even have to go back that far,* she thought. *If we'd never joined the Guardians, Jasper and I definitely would have never even met.* She, Kevin, and Lon would have had no reason to leave Glo'Stea, and their interplanetary shipping business would not exist.

She couldn't tell Jasper that, however.

Her comlink vibrated again. *Will you be at the dinner party Director Thane is hosting tomorrow evening?*

Lilia didn't have to glance at her schedule to answer that. *No. We won't make it back from Glo'Stea in time.*

Her mouth flattened into a thin line. The NCDC Board wasn't too happy about them missing an event here and there, but she and Kevin *did* have a business to run. And, barring extreme circumstances, Guardian duties were meant to slot right into a Guardian's ordinary life.

*Erik isn't a pilot; he can't help Kevin fly the* Talia. *That's my job.* Besides, Malik Thane was probably one of the last people she wanted to be forced to spend an evening around.

Her comlink vibrated. *I am sorry to hear that. You will be missed. I have most definitely decided that social events like these are not my forte.*

Lilia's stomach threatened to give a little flip upon reading these words, but she forced her elation away. *Distraction, remember?* she thought. *You can't spend too much time talking to him at these things anyway, or rumors will fly. Again.*

Despite Martin Hollowell's concerns, certain quarters of the news media had begun settling down when they realized nothing was going on between Lilia and Jasper. Just as Derek had predicted.

*Maybe next time,* she sent back at last. *Anyway, I'm off for the night. We fly to Redesh tomorrow.*

Understandable. Good night.

Setting her comlink on the nightstand beside her bed, Lilia slid under her covers and stretched out on her bed, staring up at the ceiling. "Lights, off," she commanded.

The soft glowpanels mounted above her obligingly switched off, filling the room with darkness. Her eyes soon adjusted to the faint light from Sonela's streetlights streaming through her window, but she paid it no mind.

For a moment, she let herself entertain thoughts of what hosting a dinner party with Kedis in attendance would be like. Of having Jasper in their home here in Sonela. Then she firmly thrust those thoughts out of her head.

*This is for the best,* she told herself. *Having Kedis in our home here might be more provocation for whoever has been trying to kill Grandfather.*

They didn't need that. Not with the fate of the Coalition's future on the line. Her grandfather's voice needed to be heard on the Triumvirate.

She contemplated Nancomming Kevin, but decided against it. *Nothing I can't tell him tomorrow.*

# CHAPTER 34

THE first thing Kevin said when Lilia told him the news was a heartfelt, "Thank God Grandfather changed his mind." He gave an exaggerated shudder. "Bad enough to have Kedis poking around Ferndale."

"Was he goin' to invite Kedis?" Erik asked from his flight seat behind Kevin.

"Yep." Lilia scanned her console, making sure everything was in order as the *Talia* sailed through the air far, far above the sparkling blue ocean below. The familiar thrum of the engine and the faintly metallic smell of the air in the freighter was usually a comfort to her, but she'd been agitated since they set foot on board that morning. "He would have been the guest of honor."

"I *am* a little surprised though." Kevin shook his head. "Everybody else on the Triumvirate is hosting dinners and parties, trying to play nice—"

"Whether they mean it or not is another story," Erik interjected.

Glancing over her shoulder at him, Lilia rolled her eyes. "That's beside the point. Nobody cares whether or not they mean it. From what I've seen, half of the people don't seem to like each other much, but that doesn't mean they won't send each other invitations."

"An' we wonder why our system is in the state it's in." The blond Guardian sat back in his seat, making a gagging sound. "Politics."

"My point," Kevin said loudly, shooting them both quelling looks, "is that nobody else seems to be terribly worried about political repercussions."

Lilia shrugged. "They don't have grandchildren involved in this mess, either." She sighed, pinching the bridge of her nose with the tips of her fingers. "He's walking a fine line. This is just a reprieve. If the Triumvirate continues to talk to Kedis, Grandfather will be expected to do something eventually."

Kevin's face scrunched with distaste. "Great."

The three moved on to other topics of conversation after that, each of them happy to let this particular subject drop. It took Lilia a while to shake the unease churning the pit of her stomach, however. She wasn't even entirely sure why she was so agitated.

*It was just supposed to be a small dinner party. Nothing to be so anxious about.* She snorted softly to herself. *Yeah, right. Just an evening with a small group of some of the most powerful people in the Coalition.*

Sobering thought, that.


Business picked up a little after they returned to Sonela, for which Lilia and Kevin were both thankful, and the next week and a half passed without incident. In between cargo runs and the parties they dutifully attended for the NCDC, they spent time at Chakin's. Erik accompanied them most days; he preferred guns to swords, but enjoyed the challenge. And, despite his initial skepticism, he saw the wisdom of making sure they could hold their own against nano-armor-clad opponents armed with nanoblades.

Thursday evening found Lilia at *Sal's* having dinner with Alexis, who was on break. With as crazy as everything had been lately, she hadn't seen her best friend in too long and tonight was the perfect opportunity. Kevin had another fencing appointment with Franco, while Derek, Michael, and their grandfather were having dinner at the Briscoes. Talking JP Cobb into letting her walk the two blocks to the café without an escort had taken a little finagling, but Lilia had managed.

Now she settled back into her seat at one of the booths along the wall with a happy sigh. It felt good to be out doing something normal for a change. She'd even dressed up; she wore a silk turquoise short-sleeved blouse, black capris, and black flats. The café was full, filled with the buzz of muted conversation and the clink of silverware, and a mix of delicious smells wafted through the air.

"So…" Alexis leaned forward, her elbows on the table, a mischievous light dancing in her brown eyes. She pointed her fork at Lilia. "Are you still keeping in touch with your 'boyfriend'?"

Lilia rolled her eyes at her best friend, but shrugged and glanced down at her plate. "Some."

She stabbed a piece of ravioli and Jasper's words from one conversation they'd had at the Mansion weeks earlier floated through her mind. *I've never been a woman's dirty little secret before.* Guilt knotted her insides. Biting her lip, she looked up. "Actually…"

Alexis was looking at her in amusement, as though she'd *known* there was more to the story. She raised her dark eyebrows in a silent gesture for Lilia to continue.

*This is harder than I thought it'd be.* Lilia heaved a deep breath. "We're messaging back and forth," she said in a rush. "Daily. And it's not all about Lon and the Ambassador and how the peace talks are going." She waved her fork in a vague circle. "These days, we talk about…everything."

"I figured as much." Alexis grinned at her, before taking a bite of her own food, a savory eggplant and potato dish. "I've noticed you check your comlink more often than you used to, for one. And second…" She smiled again, her cheeks dimpling impishly. "I've seen holos of the two of you lately. The way he *looks* at you sometimes…and the way you look at *him*…" she trailed off suggestively.

"Alexis…" Lilia groaned, dropping her fork onto the table with a clatter and burying her face in her hands. "Not you too."

"Hey, it's hard to avoid. You keep randomly popping up on the celebrity circuits. Things have quieted down, but people are still speculating whether or not you two are an item."

"We're not," Lilia said through her fingers.

"Uh huh."

"It's *true*. We're friends, that's all."

Alexis reached across the table to pat her hand. "I believe you, sweetie, but I can't vouch for the rest of the Coalition. Besides, he's really cute. For a Tarynian," she added thoughtfully, taking another delicate bite.

"Nebullian," Lilia said before she could help herself. She finally dropped her hands to face her friend. "He's from the Nebullian system."

"Really?"

"Yeah. Grew up on a space station."

Alexis's eyes widened. "Wow. That's cool."

Lilia shrugged. "He says he prefers being on an actual planet."

"Huh." Alexis took another bite and chewed thoughtfully. "I suppose I could see that," she said after she swallowed. "I'd never thought about what it would be like to live on a space station before."

"Yeah, me either."

The two young women ate in silence for a few moments, letting the hustle and bustle of *Sal's* surround them.

"You like him though, don't you?" Alexis asked after a little while. "As a person?" she added teasingly.

Lilia rolled her eyes again, but nodded. "He's a good man, I think." She smiled wryly. "Not something I ever thought I'd say about a G.U. soldier, but he is." She tilted her head to one side, considering Jasper in her head. "He's a Christian—"

"I remember you telling me that," Alexis interjected. "That surprised me."

"It surprised me too." Lilia bit her lip again. "I guess we just don't think about the fact that there can be people on the other side of this who love God too."

"Yeah, it's kinda hard sometimes, what with the whole invasion angle." Alexis waved her fork in the air. "But it's cool that he is and you've been able to get a different perspective."

"It is."

Alexis cast Lilia a sly glance over the top of her water glass. "And I'm sure he enjoys having somebody to talk to, considering the only other people he knows on the planet are probably Lon and the Ambassador."

Unbidden, a blush rose in Lilia's face; she ducked her head to hide it. "I hadn't really thought about that."

"That's what best friends are for." Alexis grinned cheerfully. "To help you think of these things." She glanced at her watch. "I've got five more minutes, and then I need to get back to work."

It was her turn to roll her eyes. "Miguel's been a real stickler for timeliness lately."

Lilia glanced off to the side, where Alexis's older brother was delivering a tray of food to an elderly couple at a table in the center of the café. "You certainly are busy tonight."

"It's a good thing, but not great for my social life." Alexis polished off the last of her salad. "I'm glad you could come tonight."

"Me too." Lilia smiled at her across the table. "I'm sorry it's taken so long. Things have been—"

"—crazy. I know." Alexis matched her smile, sliding out of her seat and standing. "I watch the news." Her smile faded into seriousness. "Just…be careful, okay? You seem to have developed a habit these days of getting mixed up into insane things."

Lilia bit back a laugh. *Oh, Alexis, if you only knew the half of it.* She shook her head. "Don't worry. Grandfather's got enough security restrictions on us to keep anybody safe." She tilted her head toward the door. "I only got a pass to visit tonight without an escort because *Sal's* is so close."

She slid out of her seat as well, and threw her arms around her best friend in a hug. "Have a good rest of the evening, Alexis."

"I will. Be careful going home."

"All two blocks of it," Lilia said with mock solemnity. "I think I'll manage." She waved to Sal, Alexis's father, who had popped out of the kitchen to see how things were going, and headed for the door.

The air outside was hot and humid, with a sluggish breeze. Regardless, a smile rose to Lilia's lips. It could have been absolutely sweltering and as far as she was concerned, it was a beautiful night simply because she had a few moments to herself.

Humming softly under her breath, Lilia set off down the sidewalk in the direction of Ferndale. The streets in this part of Sonela were busy, but not too crowded. It was late enough that the bulk of the dinner crowd had come and gone, but not yet time for the late diners to arrive. *Sal's* had been a popular eatery before the Deleóns' friendship with Lilia and her family had come to the media's attention; now, they never lacked for customers.

*Even if some of those customers are only hoping to get inside information on us*, Lilia thought wryly.

As she neared the end of the block, the hair on the back of her neck prickled. Somebody was watching her. Resisting the urge to shudder, Lilia cast a discreet glance up and down the street. *Nothing.*

She didn't see anything out of the ordinary, but, huffing to herself, she picked up her pace anyway. *You're getting paranoid*, she told herself. *Just because* everybody *has been so interested the past few weeks doesn't mean somebody's watching now.*

Of course…it didn't mean somebody *wasn't* watching either.

Something suddenly struck her in the middle of the back. Though she was wearing stealth armor beneath her clothes, electrifying *pain* blossomed across her muscles and nerve endings. Lilia staggered a step, crying out.

For a second, she didn't know what had happened. Part of her mind registered something *familiar* about the pain, but she couldn't place it. She started to whirl around, her right hand automatically reaching for her pistol in her ISF, but then the air above the sidewalk in front of her *rippled* as a portal sphere swirled into existence.

Her jaw dropped. *I'm not causing that!* She gaped at the portal, temporarily forgetting the pain. "What is—"

That was all the warning she had before a body slammed into her, sending them both tumbling into the portal. It closed as soon as they were through, the only trace of its presence a little rush of displaced air.

The few pedestrians who witnessed their disappearance blinked and shook their heads, unable to believe what they had just seen... and uncertain anyone *else* would believe them.

# CHAPTER 35

Lilia cried out again as she landed on a ridged, dark metal circular platform with a heavy body on top of her. Her attacker attempted to keep the bulk of his weight from crushing her—it was a *he*, it had to be—but did not give her the opportunity to fight him. Seizing her arms, he twisted them behind her back while simultaneously pinning her legs down with his own.

"Hey! Let me go!" Lilia bucked against her captor's hold, but it only resulted in more pain. She wasn't going anywhere. Panic bloomed in her chest, but she beat it back and opened Nancom channels to Erik and every one of her brothers.

Nothing happened.

Fear washed over her, leaving her cold. *We must be off-planet.* Thoroughly frightened now, she bucked harder in a vain attempt to dislodge her captor.

"Hold still," commanded a deep voice in her ear, putting enough pressure on her that she gasped in pain again.

"Who are you?" she demanded, trying to raise her head from the platform. He was speaking Sta'Gloan, but that meant nothing. "What do you want?"

*How in the galaxy did you open a portal?* was the question she really wanted to ask, but the words stuck in her throat. Asking that question would mean revealing she knew what portals were…and even in the midst of her panic she knew that would reveal too much.

"All in good time, Miss Strong."

A chill danced down her spine. *They know who I am. This was definitely on purpose.*

Footsteps rushed toward them. Lilia turned her head to the side—and her breath caught in her throat. They were in a large, empty room with a white stone floor and featureless stone walls…and the figures approaching them all wore dark gray visors and facemasks that suspiciously resembled those of Guardians. Hands reached for her; she was yanked to her feet and her arms restrained behind her back before she could do more than blink.

*Oh, this is not good.* She tried Nancomming her brothers again, but nothing happened. She swallowed, willing herself to keep calm. *This is* so *not good.*

The man who had attacked her and brought her through the portal turned to one of the others. Like the others, he was clad in regular street clothes, and he, too, wore a visor and facemask to obscure his features. "Tell the boss we got her; everything was right on time."

*The boss?* Lilia thought in bewilderment, her eyes darting around, taking everything in. Belatedly, she realized that the circular ridged platform they were standing on looked awfully familiar. She craned her neck to look behind her—and her heart nearly stopped in her chest.

Her kidnapper had brought her through a portal created by an actual transporter. Behind the transporter stood a bank of familiar computer arrays, though they were manned by two masked women she did not recognize.

*Well…* Lilia swallowed the hysterical laugh rising in her throat. *I guess that explains how we got here.*

She knew, with a gut instinct so strong that it nearly made her ill, that this was *not* one of the two transporters the scientists had built for Internal Affairs. *The operators wouldn't all be wearing visors and facemasks.*

Besides, what possible reason would Internal Affairs have for tackling her through a portal? Lilia swallowed. *They'd just talk to the NCDC.*

No, this was something different. This was…

Her violet eyes widened. *This has to be Freedom's Children.*

Lilia didn't know who else it *could* be. *Nobody else has access to a transporter, much less one that the government doesn't know they have.*

One of the faceless figures before her spoke. "Boss says to put her on ice for a while; he'll be here as soon as he can." He had a faint Lanxian accent.

"No problem." Another man, shorter than the others and clearly Glo'Stean, turned to her captors. "Take her to the conference room."

*The conference room?* That seemed an odd choice for a prison, but Lilia wasn't about to complain. If they left her alone…she had a chance of escaping. *I have a nanoblade and a transporter of my own,* she thought darkly. *And I've escaped worse places.*

But as the men holding her arms frog-marched her down the two steps leading up to the platform, across the giant room, and then through a maze of white stone halls, she recalled the electrifying pain she'd experienced right before she'd been tackled into the portal. *What* was *that?*

It felt like she'd been shot. Except…clearly they hadn't been trying to kill her.

A terrifying thought came to mind. *Did they hit me with an impactor?* Her heartbeat picked up as the blood drained from her face; she almost stumbled. How could they know she was a Guardian? Access to the NCDC database was restricted.

*Oh, please, Lord, let that not have been what happened.*

She needed to get out of here—and she couldn't do that if her nanites were frozen.

The men kept her on her feet and roughly propelled her onward. Lilia was too freaked out to say a word. There was only one way to find outher nanites had been immobilized—but at the moment she couldn't take the risk of either dematerializing her stealth armor or materializing something else.

She gulped. *It'll have to wait until I get to the conference room.*

After what felt like an eternity, but was probably only a couple of minutes, they rounded a corner and approached a set of exotic-looking wooden double doors with intricately carved panels. The taller of her captors let go of Lilia long enough to shove one of the doors open—

—and she promptly head-butted his stockier companion in the face. He reeled back in shock, gray-gloved hands automatically flying to his face, and Lilia twisted sideways to kick the taller man in the knee as hard as she could. He went down with a grunt of pain, still propping the door open.

Before she could run, before she could do anything else, the man she'd head-butted roughly seized her by the arms and bodily propelled her through the door into the conference room. "Nice try," he said thickly. "Where'd you think you were gonna go?"

Lilia said nothing. She had the satisfaction of knowing she'd caused some damage, but that was about it. *He has a point.* Even if she'd managed to take both men down, she'd still have to deal with the restraints.

The conference room was massive, large enough to hold a crowd of at least a hundred people. The stone walls were decorated with carved pillars and a raised stone dais at the end of the room held a rectangular table made of teak with ten matching chairs and a podium. The stocky man shoved Lilia toward this dais.

His taller companion hobbled inside, muttering under his breath. "We're supposed to leave her here."

"Alone?"

"They didn't say nothin' about us stayin'."

"Huh." The stocky man marched Lilia up onto the dais and yanked out one of the chairs. "Sit."

She resisted, glaring up at him, and he put a hand on her shoulder, shoving her down onto the chair. She bit back a grimace as her restrained arms scraped against the back of the chair. She heard a rustle and then felt her arms jerked back against the chair as the man threaded a piece of rope through her bound arms and around the back of the chair.

"She's not going anywhere," he told his companion, satisfaction dripping from his voice.

"Good."

Without another word, the two men departed the conference room, leaving Lilia alone at the table.

*Great. Just…great.* She looked around the room, struggling to control her breathing and contain the panic swelling in her chest. *I've been kidnapped, I'm God-knows-where, my nanites are frozen, and I'm tied to a chair.*

It could be worse, she supposed. *At least I'm wearing stealth armor.* It would protect her vitals—but wouldn't shield her from losing an arm, a foot…or her head.

She tested her restraints, but they were solid. *Won't be breaking out of these by myself.* She swallowed, restraining a grimace. *Nothing to do but wait.*

Minutes slipped past, stretching with every heartbeat into an immeasurable, unfathomable amount of time. The air was cool in here, with an underlying scent of plant life. Gradually, she registered pain as her adrenaline dump drained away and the bumps and bruises caused by being tackled through that portal made themselves known. Her hands were skinned from skidding along the transporter's ridged platform when she'd instinctively tried to catch herself, and her ribs ached from her attacker landing on her.

*It could be worse. At least nothing's broken.*

Eventually, Lilia blew out a breath, ruffling the short locks of dark hair framing her face. *Surely they're not going to just leave me here. What would be the point of* that?

They had to have kidnapped her for a reason.

*You don't just tackle people through portals.* Her mouth twisted into a grimace. *I wonder if anybody even noticed.*

It had been a smooth operation, she would give her kidnappers that. First the impactor, and then the impact that sent her through the portal. *Even if anybody* did *notice, they probably blinked and concluded they'd been seeing things. People don't just disappear on sidewalks.*

Not to mention that the average Coalition citizen had absolutely no idea that the newly-announced transporters could do anything other than open portals to each other.

A sudden flicker of light out of the corner of her eye roused Lilia from her thoughts. She glanced up from the table—she'd been absently staring at the grain of the wood—to find a holographic form coalescing in the seat at the head of the table.

She bit back a gasp of surprise. The holograph was male—and faceless. A Guardian's visor and facemask shielded his identity from her. Aside from that, he appeared to be dressed in formal evening wear.

"Good evening, Lilia." He spoke Sta'Gloan, and his voice was synthesized, preventing her from having any idea what he really sounded like.

*Of course he knows who I am.* Raising her chin, Lilia narrowed her eyes at him. "What is the meaning of this?" She nodded to her bound arms without breaking eye contact with the figure. "Who are you? Why am I here?"

"Patience, young one." The man leaned back in his chair, quite at his ease, and considered her. "I do apologize for the necessity of bringing you here the way we did, but I doubted you would be easily persuaded to come of your own accord."

*Damn right I would*, Lilia thought, but she kept it to herself. "Where is *here*, exactly?"

The masked man considered her for a few seconds, before spreading nano-armor gloved hands. "Glo'Stea."

*I am off-world.* Lilia just barely managed to keep her surprise from reflecting on her face. More questions burbled to the tip of her tongue, but she held them back. She had a gut feeling this man would not tell her a thing until he was ready.

"You're not going to ask where on Glo'Stea?" Amusement flooded his synthesized voice.

"Would you tell me if I did?"

"I might."

Silence stretched between them. Lilia's eyes narrowed even further. *He's going to make me ask.* Irritation flared to life inside her chest, but she kept her voice relatively pleasant. "Where exactly on Glo'Stea am I?"

For a heartbeat, she thought the man would refuse to answer, but then he spread his arms in a welcoming gesture. "You, my dear, are sitting in the headquarters of Freedom's Children."

If he expected a reaction, he did not get one. Squaring her jaw, Lilia said flatly, "Freedom's Children. Really."

"Really."

"And you would be…?"

The masked man inclined his head. "I am the head of Freedom's Children. You may call me the Mastermind."

# Chapter 36

A sharp laugh escaped Lilia at this. "The Mastermind? Seriously?" She stared incredulously at the man, her eyebrows sky high. "You do realize that makes you sound like a villain from a cheesy holodrama."

He shrugged. "I find it a necessary requirement. It is not yet time for me to reveal my true identity to the Coalition."

"Right…"

"No need to sound so skeptical, Lilia. I dare say you and your brothers would do the same thing were you in my shoes."

Lilia sniffed, settling back in her seat with feigned ease. "I think we'd come up with better code names."

Maybe it was foolish to talk to this man that way, since she was tied to a chair and he could surely summon minions to deal with her, but she couldn't help herself. Panic had given way to irritation, which was steadily bubbling into anger.

"Perhaps." The Mastermind laced his gloved fingers together, regarding her with a thoughtful air.

She fell silent under his gaze, waiting for his next words. The demand to know what was going on clawed at her throat, but she found herself unwilling to give him the satisfaction.

"You asked why you were here," he said at last.

Lilia inclined her head in a brief nod.

"The answer to that, my dear, is slightly complicated. That is to say," he raised a hand, "it has many parts, only several of which concern you directly."

*Oh, great.* Lilia was hard-pressed to keep from rolling her eyes. *I could be here all night.*

"I understand you and your brothers were instrumental in bringing Ambassador Kedis before the Triumvirate." The faintest trace of contempt underlined his words.

Inside, Lilia stiffened. She had the sudden sense that she needed to tread very, very carefully. "We helped him get into the Gala after we found out he and Lon were on Sta'Gloa, yes."

"Why would you do this? Why betray your people and your world to the Tarynians?"

"We didn't betray our people." She narrowed her eyes at him again. "We were *hoping* to put an end to the bloodshed." She swiveled her head, indicating the room at large with a jerk of her chin. "If you're the head of Freedom's Children, you have to know how many people have died over the years in border skirmishes and attacks by Tarynian forces outside the shields."

"And you think you can accomplish this by making an alliance with our oppressors?" His voice turned to razor-sharp ice.

Lilia arched an eyebrow at him. "That depends on the Triumvirate, now, doesn't it? And I don't see the entire Triumvirate agreeing to throw in our lot with the Galactic Union. I think a peace treaty and maybe a trade agreement the more likely option."

"Oh, you do, do you? Quite the budding politician, aren't you?"

"More like common sense," she snapped, before reeling in her rising temper. "I don't think the Triumvirate could agree to join the G.U. without incurring a huge uprising." She shook her head. "What would it do to commerce, for example? We'd have to change our entire monetary system and that definitely wouldn't happen overnight."

It was the Mastermind's turn to fall silent. He studied her for a long moment, as though she was a fascinating specimen that had somehow transformed from one thing to another before his very eyes.

"You are a curious child," he said at last, and changed the subject entirely with a flick of gray-clad fingers. "I understand you are a Guardian."

Lilia kept her face impassive. "What are you talking about?"

Beneath his facemask, the Mastermind seemed to be smiling. "Ah, no need to play coy, my dear. I apologize for the necessity of hitting you with an impactor bolt, but you understand we must take precautions."

He waved a hand again. "You may wonder how I know you are a Guardian, well, it so happens that I know a great deal about a great many things." He tilted his head. "I know you are a Guardian, and I also know that as punishment for their inability to dismiss you from the NCDC, the Board has seen fit to assign you the rather mundane task of providing addition security for parties and social gatherings at which the…Tarynian Ambassador…is present."

This time, Lilia couldn't hide her surprise.

"I'll take your silence as a 'yes'." A note of satisfaction filled his voice. "One might argue that this is a waste of your considerable talents."

*Considerable talents?* His words pierced the temporary, shocked fog that had just descended on Lilia; confusion filled her instead.

"I will grant you, however, that it is perhaps considerably less dangerous than a few of the other things the NCDC has had you do in the past few months."

Lilia managed to control her expression at these words, but the Mastermind still nodded soberly.

"Oh, yes. I'm aware of your…missions." His synthesized voice grew dark. "And you are surely aware that someone else has been pulling strings, placing rookies on missions far better suited to those with more experience."

*How does he know we know?* Lilia finally stirred. "Yes, we know."

"It is all the more impressive that you escaped unscathed."

"Well…" Lilia allowed herself a short, wry smile. "Uva felt more like we got out by the skin of our teeth."

She wasn't touching their week spent bouncing through portals across the Coalition. That was far too dangerous ground to tread just now. *I don't know exactly how much he knows—and if he does know that we've got transporters, I can't let him know that we know.*

Instead, she leaned back against her chair. Her arms ached from being in one forced position for so long, but she kept her expression neutral. "I take it you weren't behind that, then? We've wondered exactly who was responsible."

"We had nothing to do with Uva."

Lilia noticed he said nothing about their portal bouncing. *Either he doesn't know, or else he knows and he can't explain it without revealing we've got transporters.*

That made her think of Dr. Dover, but there wasn't any way to discreetly inquire about her former NCDC doctor. *That would definitely tip our hand.* She couldn't afford to do that.

Her grandfather's assassination attempt came to mind next, but she wasn't sure she should mention it. *Not yet, anyway.* "Well, that's good to know, Mr. Mastermind." She shook her head. "Still doesn't explain why you had your minions shove me through a portal and bring me here."

The Mastermind regarded her for a few seconds, as though deliberating how much to say. "You are a nano-genetic anomaly."

*He really does have access to everything in the NCDC database.* Lilia adopted a bored look. "So?"

"The NCDC," the Mastermind continued, his synthesized voice softening a degree, "does not take kindly to such aberrations in the system. Anomalies do not…fare well in the long run."

"If they want to leave the NCDC," Lilia pointed out, "which I don't. I became a Guardian to help make a difference in our system." She shrugged her shoulders. "Aside from the fact that the NCDC is irritated with my brother Lon, why would being a genetic anomaly cause me trouble?"

"You think the Board will be satisfied with this punishment for your infractions?"

Lilia wasn't sure about that either, but she shrugged again. "Why wouldn't they?" *Let him think me naive.*

The Mastermind shook his head. "That isn't how they operate, my dear." His next words took her completely by surprise. "Do you remember Azaren Carn?"

A chill skipped down Lilia's spine. Eyes fixed on his facemask, she gave him a slow nod. "I do."

"Do you recall how bitter she was?"

*He talks like he knew her.* How was that possible? "I do. She wanted to leave the NCDC and couldn't. That made her miserable, which resulted in the NCDC sending her out on the Uva mission."

"You have the essence of it, yes." The Mastermind steepled his gloved fingers. "There was a little more to it than that."

Lilia arched an eyebrow again, a surreal feeling overtaking her. "What don't I know?"

"I won't go into Ms. Carn's reasons for wishing to leave the NCDC. Her inability to do so certainly made her unhappy, but she would probably have been fine if the NCDC had simply left her alone."

"Left her alone?"

"She no longer wanted to be a Guardian, yet they continued to assign her tasks." The Mastermind shook his head again. "They provoked her until she reached the point at which they determined the Uva mission was the best way to rid themselves of her. Either she and her team would succeed, or else none of them would return."

Goosebumps formed on Lilia's arms. "Are you saying Ren's whole team—"

"—was made up of nano-genetic anomalies?" The Mastermind nodded. "Yes, my dear. That is exactly what I'm saying."

"But—" Lilia thought of her own team. They hadn't all been anomalies—their team leader Vam Neek and teammate Xian Denel alone had been normal. She shut her mouth. *I can't tell him I know* that, *though.*

The Mastermind guessed the general direction of her thoughts. "Does that mean your team was also comprised of nano-genetic anomalies? For the most part, yes."

Lilia stared at him. "How in the galaxy can you *know?*"

She had the distinct impression that he smiled again beneath his facemask; the air around him shifted. "I make it my business to know these things, my dear."

The world seemed to tilt on its axis as she absorbed this information. She shook her head as though to clear it. "Are you saying that whoever put Kevin and me on the Uva roster also knew we were nano-genetic anomalies?" She didn't have to work hard to inject the right amount of disbelieving skepticism into her voice. "We hadn't even been *tested* yet."

"No." Contempt filled his voice. "The person responsible for *that* certainly had no such knowledge. It was a paltry attempt to distract your grandfather."

Lilia eyed him. "You sound like you know who it is."

"I do."

She waited a moment, but when he said nothing further, she prompted, "Will you tell me?"

"That information is not relevant."

*The heck it's not.* Lilia glared at him. "Then what *is* relevant? You *still* haven't explained why I'm here."

"Part of the way the NCDC maintains control over the individuals who become Guardians is their ability to take the nano-tech away."

Lilia shrugged, though the motion hurt her arms. "That's reasonable. Otherwise you might end up with power-crazy Guardians abusing their position." Her mouth flattened into a thin line. "Although I understand that's also why they developed the impactors. How did *you* get your hands on one?"

The Mastermind waved a hand. "That is not relevant either. The point I am trying to make, my dear, is that without the threat of defusion, the NCDC has no real way to control nano-genetic anomalies."

Lilia felt the threat of an oncoming headache. *Would you just get to the point already?* Aloud, she said, "It's been a long day, ah—" *Mastermind* seemed to stick in her throat; it was a ridiculous moniker, "—*sir.* I'm afraid you're going to have to spell it out for me."

"The only recourse the NCDC has for dealing with such individuals is to keep a very close eye on them and eventually arrange circumstances such as what happened to Azaren Carn."

The pressure behind her eyes continued to mount. "Even if said Guardians have no desire to leave the NCDC and are otherwise perfectly behaved?"

The Mastermind shook his head. "You misunderstand, my dear."

Lilia *really* wished he would stop calling her that. It sounded so strange, coming from a faceless man in an unrecognizable voice.

"The NCDC doesn't know a Guardian is an anomaly until something happens that requires them to be dismissed."

His words washed over her…and Lilia went very still. *That* was a lie. According to Nob and the research he'd done, there was no way whichever NCDC doctor was involved with a Guardian did *not* know. *Why would he tell me otherwise?*

Oblivious to her internal debate, the Mastermind continued, "It has taken a rather longwinded conversation to get to the point of all of this," he motioned to her bound figure, "but I wanted to discuss your possible involvement with Freedom's Children."

Lilia blinked at him. "You *kidnapped* me in order to *recruit* me?"

"Discuss the possibility, yes." He tilted his head. "And not just you, but your brothers as well." A cold note slid into his voice. "Kevin, Derek, and Michael, I mean. Obviously, Lon is not a candidate."

Her hackles instantly raised. "Why? Because he got Kedis onto Sta'Gloa?"

The Mastermind's voice chilled further. "Even you must admit he's gone much farther than that. It is impossible at this time to ascertain where his loyalties lie."

"But you think you know where the rest of us stand?"

It was probably stupid, challenging him like this, but Lilia couldn't help herself. She'd been tied to a chair for at least an hour now, on top of being kidnapped, and his criticism of a situation he couldn't possibly fully understand caused her simmering anger to begin to bubble over.

"I have a good idea, yes. Rest assured we will continue to keep an eye on you."

Oh, didn't *that* just fill her with warm fuzzies? Lilia narrowed her eyes at the masked holograph. "How, exactly, is this supposed to help us if the NCDC decides they want to make us disappear?"

The Mastermind spread his hands. "You'll have somewhere to go, someplace safe, and Freedom's Children can definitely use talented young people like you and your brothers."

"What about our grandfather?"

"Your grandfather will manage just fine without you." The Mastermind made a dismissive sound. "Besides, if I were he, I would prefer my grandchildren alive and elsewhere instead of buried in a graveyard on Sta'Gloa."

Lilia swallowed; that was a dire thought. She took a deep breath, wracking her brain for anything else she ought to ask. Her mind felt like it was on information overload, trying to process everything she'd just heard, but she knew she had to probe deeper. She had to learn *more*.

"What, exactly, would we be doing?"

The Mastermind shook his head. "I can't tell you that just yet. Suffice to say it would be in line with your considerable skills, and I assure you that you would most certainly be making a difference in the Coalition."

*Sure we would.* Lilia nodded, like she was pretending to consider it, and then gave the Mastermind her best curious, innocent look. "What happens if we decline?"

For a moment, the Mastermind said nothing. He simply continued to sit there and study her, as though she had just revealed a facet of her personality previously unknown to him. "That is not a question to be asked lightly, my dear. This is serious business, and my offer to you to become part of Freedom's Children has a limited time-frame. We are dedicated to our cause."

"I can see that." Lilia kept her voice light. "Restoring Glo'Stea's shield was an incredible feat."

"Yes, it was. You could be part of something like that."

"I'll have to talk to my brothers."

"Of course you will."

"And we'll need to know more." She lifted her chin. "Since this definitely isn't the sort of organization one joins lightly, we'll *have* to know more. They'll probably have questions I haven't thought of."

"Undoubtedly."

Lilia gave him a wry look. "And they probably won't be happy you kidnapped me. I suppose just sending a message and setting up a meeting was out of the question?"

"Ah, but this got the point across so much better, don't you think?" The Mastermind almost sounded amused.

Resisting the urge to scowl at him, she asked, "Was the impactor *really* necessary?"

"A necessary precaution, as I said earlier."

"*Right.*"

The Mastermind glanced off to the side, before returning his focus to her. "Speak to your brothers, my dear. We will be in touch."

The interview—or whatever it was supposed to be—had finally come to an end. Instead of feeling relieved, a jolt of panic shot through Lilia. She hadn't had a chance to ask the question that had been burning in the back of her mind. "Wait!"

"Yes?" She had his attention, though there was no telling what he thought she was about to say.

Lilia's mouth had suddenly gone very dry, but she gathered her courage. "Are you trying to kill my grandfather?"

# CHAPTER 37

THE Mastermind sat so motionless that his holographic image seemed to have frozen in place. "Kill your grandfather?"

"Yeah. He didn't publicize it, but somebody wearing nano-armor and carrying a nanoblade broke into our house a few weeks back. He just appeared out of nowhere." Her eyes bored into his, searching his facemask. "Like he came through a portal."

"And you honestly think Freedom's Children is behind this? Why not Internal Affairs and the NCDC, working together?"

"To assassinate a Representative?" Lilia let the full weight of her incredulous stare rest on him. "That does seem a little far-fetched. Especially considering that as far as I can tell, Freedom's Children is against any sort of negotiation with the Tarynians, which I know my grandfather is willing to consider."

"Stranger things have happened, my dear."

"You still haven't answered my question."

The Mastermind shook his head. "It isn't worth answering. We will be in touch."

With that, his holographic form vanished from the chair.

Heart thudding in her chest, Lilia scowled at his empty chair. *That's a great way to escape an unwanted conversation.* She snorted; the sound seemed to echo in the massive room. *Wonder how long he'll leave me sitting here before he sends somebody in to collect me.*

Her heart turned over; she gulped. *And what happens when somebody does come?* Would the Mastermind send her back to Sta'Gloa? Or would she just…disappear because she'd asked too many questions?

*It'd be flat stupid not to ask questions*, she told herself. *You don't get into things without asking questions.*

Maybe…*maybe* she'd jumped the gun in asking whether or not Freedom's Children was involved with the assassination attempts on her grandfather, but it was a logical conclusion, especially with all of the new information she had. *And he didn't exactly answer the question.*

A whisper of noise from the other end of the conference room drew her attention. She whipped her head around to find two burly men in full defense-mode nano-armor striding toward her. As neither of them was limping, she concluded they were not the same men who'd escorted her in here.

Lilia raised her eyebrows at them, despite the frission of fear dancing along her nerve-endings. In Glo'Stean, she asked, "Where to from here, boys?"

"You'll find out if you cooperate," the larger of the two men replied. He mounted the steps to the dais and walked around to the back of her chair to undo the rope binding her to it. He helped her to her feet—firmly, but not as roughly as she'd expected—and the pair of them marched her back across the conference room and out into the hall.

In a matter of moments, they had retraced the path to the giant room that held the transporter and its equipment array. Lilia tried to soak in as many details as she could, commit everything she saw to memory. The more she could remember, the more she would have to tell her brothers, Erik, and Nob.

"Boss wants her sent back now," the larger of her two captors told one of the masked women sitting on swivel chairs behind the equipment array as they crossed the room.

"I know." Her fingers danced over a console. "One moment."

Lilia found herself being marched to the edge of the two steps leading up to the circular platform. The smaller man held her upper arms in an iron grip while his companion removed the restraints. In front of them, a portal sphere blossomed into existence on the platform, ruffling Lilia's bangs.

The man squeezing her arms started to push her up the steps, and Lilia shot him a cold look over her shoulder. "I can walk up there myself, thank you."

His punishing grip on her arms vanished. Breathing a mental sigh of relief, she mounted the steps and prepared to plunge into the portal. Just before she stepped into it, someone shoved her in the middle of the back—hard.

With a small cry of surprise, Lilia tumbled gracelessly headfirst into the portal.

She landed hard on a stretch of ground covered in small pebbles, hands and knees spraying across the rough surface. "Oww!" She picked herself up, casting a dirty look over her shoulder, but of course the portal was gone.

A quick glance at her surroundings told her they'd dumped her in a little park, and wherever she was, it was evening. Beneath the blue-white light cast by several well-placed glowposts, she could see swings, slides, and other children's play equipment backed by trees and neatly trimmed bushes. Hot, muggy air caressed her face, carrying with it the faint scent of skimmer exhaust.

She scowled. *Hopefully I'm back on Sta'Gloa.* It was too much to expect them to have the courtesy to return her to the exact spot where they'd kidnapped her.

Lips pressed into a thin line, Lilia sat back on her heels in the pebbles surrounding the play equipment and examined her stinging hands. Her flesh had been scraped raw in a few places; blood welled around tiny stones and other grit embedded into her palms. *That hurts.*

Her capris didn't seem to be torn, but they were dirty now and her knees throbbed. *Definitely going to have bruises.*

Lilia rose to her feet, wincing, and suppressed a momentary burst of panic at the idea of being stranded alone without any way of communicating with her family. *Don't panic,* she scolded herself. *You don't know where you are yet, and the Mastermind wouldn't have dropped you in the middle of occupied territory on Glo'Stea if he's trying to recruit you.*

Stepping onto a winding sidewalk, she followed it out of the park to the street beyond—and nearly collapsed with relief. Not only was she on Sta'Gloa, but she was back in Sonela. An upscale sushi bar across the street proclaimed it was one of the city's finest restaurants four years running.

*The Iridescent Dragon.* Lilia scrunched her forehead, thinking. She'd heard of it, but she'd never eaten there. *I'm in the uptown district.*

Annoyance surged through her. It would take a hoverbus to get home from here; she was halfway across the city from Ferndale. *They could have at least dropped me a little closer to home.*

She slid her hand into her pocket, trying to access the part of her ISF in which she kept her wallet, but her fingers only scrabbled against fabric. *Right. Impactor.* She looked up at the night sky, covered with the iridescent haze of Sta'Gloa's planetary shield, struggling to contain her frustration.

*No wallet, no comlink, no Nancom, no money—wait!* A small burst of hope ignited inside her. She still had the goldcard she'd used to pay for dinner at *Sal's.* She shoved her hand into her other pocket and her fingers closed around the small plastic card. *Thank you, Jesus.*

There wasn't much on it, but it was something. And in this particular situation, she was grateful for anything that would help. Her mind was still a convoluted jumble; her conversation with the Mastermind spun through her thoughts in disjointed fragments.

She raised bruised fingers to her temple; the faint headache she'd registered earlier had suddenly strengthened. She needed to go home. She needed to talk to Kevin, tell him everything that had just happened. No doubt he was wondering where she'd gone—she was supposed to have come straight back after *Sal's* and his fencing meet with Franco wasn't supposed to have lasted all that long.

*What do I do?* She stared blankly up at one of the holosigns flashing across the street. Skimmers zipped past; well-dressed men and women out for an evening stroll passed up and down the sidewalk around her. A few of them darted sidelong looks at her, but no one stopped to ask if she was all right.

Lilia didn't notice. According to a nearby holosign, it was after ten PM; she'd been gone for several hours. *Grandfather, Michael, and Derek are probably still at that evening party.* It wasn't likely they'd return for at least another hour. *And even if I could borrow somebody's comlink to get a hold of them, I can't explain what happened in front of a stranger.*

Her brain ached; her options were terrible. She couldn't contact her family—or friends, for that matter—and she didn't have enough money to make it back to Ferndale. Plus, without access to her wallet, she couldn't withdraw any more money from an account. The goldcard in her hand was a throwaway.

*What do I do?*

The question pounded over and over in her brain. She was tired, she was confused, she was aggravated, and her body ached. *If the 'Mastermind' wanted to recruit me, he sure picked an odd way to go about it.*

She frowned. *Maybe he's punishing me for not immediately signing up.*

It was possible.

*Okay*, Lilia told herself, *calm down. It's not like you've been stranded in occupied territory. You're in Sonela. Sure, you're still stranded, but you've been in worse situations—and survived. This is nothing.*

She pressed the tips of her fingers to both temples and shut her eyes for a few seconds, praying that her headache would subside. She was still reeling from her interview with the Mastermind, her thoughts still spinning wildly as her mind tried to process all the new information she'd received.

She frowned, biting the inside of her lip, and glanced up and down the street. Spotting an info kiosk halfway down the street, she headed for it. A few taps of her finger displayed her precise location. *Upper edge of the business district.* She zoomed out a little to show a larger map of this section of Sonela. *Do I know anybody here?*

Her eyes drifted along the map. *Uncle Martin lives here, but that's way too far to walk.* Her gaze caught on the Beliana Hotel ten blocks away and she jolted, a faint spark of hope flaring to life inside of her. *That's where Lon's staying with Kedis!*

*Lon.* Her brother's face flashed before her mind's eye, followed by Jasper. Her heart gave that odd little lurch that it always did when she thought of him these days. Unless he was busy guarding the Ambassador at a social function she wasn't attending, they'd usually have exchanged a few messages by now. She wondered if Jasper had messaged and was wondering why she hadn't responded.

Lilia bit the inside of her lip. Under ordinary circumstances, she would have never *dreamed* of going to the hotel where Kedis was staying…but this evening had hardly been ordinary. *Uncle Martin is too far away, and I'd have a terrible time explaining what happened.*

Her lips quirked in a wry smile. *I'll have a terrible time explaining what happened to Lon, too, if I can't use Nancom, but, oh, well.* She needed to go somewhere, and this would have to do. Ten blocks was a bit of a walk in her current state, but Lon would be able to get in touch with Kevin and arrange for her to get back to Ferndale.

Lilia noted the hotel's address and started walking. Her knees ached and her hands stung, but she forced herself to stride along like she was simply out for an evening stroll. Her heart began to beat faster in her chest, both from a combination of trying to figure out what she was going to tell her brother, and the fact that she'd get a chance to see Jasper tonight.

Weaving her way through a stream of well-dressed pedestrians, she took a few random turns and slipped in and out of a few restaurants to throw off any potential tails. It was bad enough she'd been kidnapped once; she didn't need it happening again. *Particularly if the Mastermind objects to me visiting Lon*, she thought irritably.

And Jasper, but she didn't dwell on *that*.

The Beliana Hotel was one of the best in Sonela. Lilia scanned the skyscraper as she approached, noting its sleek design. Her gaze drifted up to the top floors; she'd never asked Lon or Jasper, but she'd bet the *Talia* Kedis had a penthouse suite.

She caught a glimpse of herself in the mirrored surface of one of the wide front doors leading into the lobby just before a liveried doorman opened it for her, and suppressed a sigh. She looked disheveled, like she'd just tumbled out of a windstorm. Her dark hair was wild, her face bore a few streaks of dirt, and her turquoise silk shirt was dirty and ripped in a few places from her ungraceful landing in the gravel.

*Be confident*, she told herself. *No matter what you look like, confidence is key.*

Giving the doorman a smile and a nod—this place probably used 'bots, but for other functions—Lilia swept through the door and marched across the lobby's white-and-pale-blue patterned marble floor, past a three-tiered marble fountain illuminated by a glittering chandelier in the center of the giant room to a gleaming glass-and-metal reception desk.

It took a moment for the well-dressed concierge behind the reception desk to acknowledge her presence. Everything about him was thin, from his nose and his face to his body. Lilia knew he'd seen her, but he had no doubt made a few assumptions based on her disheveled appearance.

When he finally glanced at her, he lifted a graying eyebrow in an expression of polite interest tinged with haughtiness. "Good evening. May I help you?" Something in his tone told her he didn't think he'd be of much use.

"Good evening." Lilia flashed him a polite society smile. "I'd like to speak to my brother, please. His name is Lon Strong and he's staying here with Ambassador Kedis and his staff."

The concierge's face could have been carved from granite. "My apologies, miss, but Mr. Strong is in a conference and asked specifically not to be disturbed."

Lilia's heart sank a little, but she was not to be deterred. She rested an elbow on the reception desk's gleaming surface, doing her best to keep any traces of panic concealed. "I think he'll make an exception for his little sister."

"He gave no instructions to that effect." The concierge raised his eyebrow at her again. "Do you have any identification?"

Lilia started to nod, her fingers automatically reaching into her ISF for her identcard—and then she froze. "I did," she said slowly, "but I was…mugged. That's why I need to see my brother."

The concierge was too well-trained to roll his eyes, but she had the distinct impression he was rolling them on the inside. He flicked his fingers at her dismissively. "I've heard it before. I'll admit your look," he eyed her critically, "is a little more creative than the other reporters who've tried to sneak in, but I'm afraid I'll have to ask you to leave."

*He thinks I'm a reporter?* Lilia's jaw dropped. "Wait a minute." She straightened indignantly. "I'm not a reporter. I really am Lon Strong's sister."

"Prove it." The concierge did not flinch. "But even then, I'm afraid you can't see him."

Her heart plummeted to her ankles. Lilia swallowed hard, tasting bitter disappointment, and started to turn away. She'd been so close. *Of* course *security is going to be tight*, she scolded herself. *And if you don't have any ID…*

She hadn't taken more than a step before she jolted as though struck by lightning. Spinning back around, she flattened a hand on the reception desk. Lon and Kedis might be in a conference, but it was possible Jasper and Renner were not. "May I speak to Lieutenant Jasper Wright, then?"

"Miss…" The concierge sounded exasperated now. "I would rather not have to call sec—"

"Please." Lilia leaned forward, her violet eyes wide. "I really was mugged. The lieutenant is a friend of mine."

Her heart started pounding in her chest. There was one way for sure she could prove to Jasper that the strange woman trying to contact him from the lobby was actually someone he knew.

She bit her lip. "I know I don't have my identcard to prove who I am, but tell Lieutenant Wright that the girl who jumped off the cliff is here to see him. He'll know what that means."

The concierge eyed her dubiously.

"*Please.*" Lilia's voice broke. "If he doesn't want to see me, I'll leave, but I don't think that will be an issue."

The concierge continued to stare at her, apparently weighing the pros and cons. At worst, she was a reporter trying to sneak in to badger high-ranking guests, which the hotel would certainly frown upon. But if she was telling truth…she was related to a high-ranking guest and snubbing her would not go over well.

After a few seconds, the concierge tapped the comlink in his ear. "The girl who jumped off a cliff, you say?" he inquired, as though he was asking something as simple as whether or not she would prefer a room on the third floor or the twentieth.

"Yes. Thank you." Lilia flashed him another smile, but she was too nervous to maintain it. Her heart continued to pound in her chest; she absently flattened a hand over it. *Please answer*, she prayed. *Please be there, and please answer.*

"Good evening, sir, this is Rufus from the front desk. May I speak to Lieutenant Wright, please? Ah, good evening, Lieutenant. I apologize for disturbing you at this hour, sir, but there is a young woman here who insists on seeing you." His brown eyes darted to Lilia. "She said to tell you she is the girl who jumped off the cliff." A pause. "She said you would understand."

Lilia's heart lodged in her throat as she waited.

"Very good, sir. I will tell her." The concierge tapped his comlink again and looked at Lilia. "The lieutenant said to wait here. He's on his way to collect you."

Lilia exhaled in a rush, so relieved that her knees wobbled. "Thank you. Thank you so much."

Now that he had confirmation that she was not intent on harassing the hotel's clientele, Rufus unbent a little. "You are welcome."

# CHAPTER 38

JASPER paced the penthouse suite, restlessly wandering back and forth across the luxurious white carpet. He was at loose ends, unsure what to do with himself, and he hated it. Lon and the Ambassador were sequestered in a meeting in Kedis's staff's penthouse suite down the hall, and Kedis had specifically left both Renner and Jasper himself behind. Apparently, he wasn't too worried about security tonight.

It grated a little to be excluded, but since the meeting was bound to be entirely political in nature, a small part of Jasper didn't mind that he did not have to suffer through it.

The problem, of course, was that now he had no idea what to do with himself.

His hand drifted to his pocket, but his comlink remained silent and still. He'd commed Lilia hours before, and had yet to hear back from her. He frowned ruefully at himself. If she'd answer, he wouldn't be at loose ends anymore. Their evening conversations had quickly become his favorite part of the day.

But tonight? Nothing. Jasper's frown deepened; he couldn't shake the impending sense that something was *wrong*. Lilia had always responded, even if it was to tell him that she was busy and didn't have time to chat.

Complete silence was unlike her at this stage of their burgeoning friendship, and it worried him.

Renner was holed up in his room, watching a Sta'Gloan holodrama he'd discovered and getting some exercise in. He didn't like being at loose ends any more than Jasper did, but tonight he seemed to have found a better way to cope with it.

A soft chiming broke the stillness that lay over the suite. Startled, Jasper turned to see the comm panel mounted discreetly on one wall blinking with an incoming call. He crossed to it, feeling his pulse quicken. *Wonder what this is about.*

Tapping a button, he asked in Sta'Gloan, "Hello?"

The man on the other end identified himself as Rufus, the concierge at the main desk, and asked to speak to Lieutenant Wright.

Bemused, Jasper answered, "Speaking."

"I apologize for disturbing you, sir, but there is a young woman here who insists on seeing you."

Jasper's heart gave an odd little leap, but he ignored it. Of all the women on Sta'Gloa, there was only one he would have liked to see—and there was no reason in the galaxy Lilia Strong would be coming to the hotel to see him at this hour. "Oh, really?"

"She said to tell you she is the girl who jumped off the cliff." Rufus paused. "She said you would understand."

Jasper rocked back on his feet, stunned. *The girl who jumped off the cliff...* He swallowed, his heart starting to race. There was no question. *She is here.* "I know her. Tell her to wait there; I'll be right down."

He ended the call and crossed the suite's living room in a few rapid strides to knock sharply on Renner's door. He did not wait for the corporal to speak when he opened the door, but said, "I'm going downstairs for a moment. Lilia Strong is here."

Renner's dark eyes widened and then narrowed slightly. "Why?"

Jasper shook his head. "I don't know yet, but something's wrong."

"What makes you so sure?"

"Why else would she be here?"

Renner shrugged. "Maybe she wants to see her brother."

"At this time of night?" Jasper raised an eyebrow.

Renner gave him a look, as though stranger things had happened since they'd both been assigned to serve Ambassador Kedis. "Guess we'll find out."

"Guess so. I'll be right back." Jasper headed for the door, his heart still racing. He let himself out of the suite and marched down the hall to the accelevator, dozens of different thoughts and scenarios playing through his head.

*She's probably here to see Lon*, he told himself, as the accelevator took him down to the lobby. *But why wouldn't she just say so? Why would she identify herself to me that way?* It was specific—*he* was the only person who would understand the reference. *And that when she won't even admit that she* was *the girl.*

The muscles in his jaw tightened. No, something was definitely very wrong.

# Chapter 39

AFTER a few moments, though it felt like much, much longer to Lilia, a pair of ornate doors in the accelevator bank opened and Jasper strode out. He was dressed in civilian clothes—a dark green button-up shirt over black slacks—and the sight of him flooded her with another wave of relief…one powerful enough to cause her knees to buckle. Her heart skipped a beat and then resumed beating in double-time. Her breath caught in her throat; she hadn't expected the sight of him to cause such an impact.

She didn't have time to think about what that meant.

Jasper's gray eyes scanned the lobby, finding her immediately, and she raised a trembling hand in a mute gesture of greeting.

"Lilia." He crossed the lobby toward her in a few long strides. His gaze swept over her from head to foot, as though verifying she was in one piece. "Are you all right?"

Lilia started to nod, started to shrug it off as nothing, but realized immediately how ridiculous that would be. Obviously she wasn't all right, or she wouldn't be here. She shook her head.

His golden eyebrows knitting together in a concerned frown, Jasper gently took her by the elbow, steering her to the accelevator bank. "What happened?"

Lilia shook her head again and finally found words. "Not here."

Jasper accepted that without question. As they stepped onto the accelerator, his hand drifted automatically to the small of her back. He tapped the button that would whisk them up to the penthouse level and then glanced sideways at her. "Your brother is in a conference with the Ambassador."

"I know." Lilia gave him a wry look. "The concierge informed me of that." She tried to muster up a smile, but failed; it was too early for her to find the humor in the situation. "He thought I was a reporter trying to sneak in."

"And you couldn't prove who you were?" Jasper kept his voice light, but his gray gaze was full of concern.

Lilia glanced away. "I don't have my identcard on me at the moment."

Technically true; her ISF was completely inaccessible for the next few hours.

Jasper shifted toward her. "Lilia, I—"

He broke off as the accelevator doors opened. Stern-faced, he ushered her out into a wide hall. Several security guards in dark uniforms were stationed up and down its length. Jasper nodded to two of them before swiping a card in a door a few meters away. He motioned for Lilia to precede him into the penthouse suite and the door slid shut behind them.

Lilia glanced around in slight surprise. She'd expected him to lead her to the suite where he and Lon were staying with the Ambassador, not a suite that looked like a swankier version of her grandfather's security team headquarters in Ferndale.

"Lieutenant." A short, stocky man in nondescript clothes rose from a seat at a table covered in computer equipment. His dark eyes assessed Lilia, but his expression gave away nothing of his thoughts on her less-than-put-together appearance.

"Corran, this is Lilia Strong." Jasper indicated her with a wave of one hand; the other was splayed against the small of her back again. "Lon's sister."

"I can see the resemblance." Corran glanced from her to Jasper, awaiting further explanation.

Jasper did not precisely elaborate. "She'll be staying here for a little while. Just wanted to let you know."

"Understood, sir."

"Thank you." Jasper gave Corran a curt nod, before looking at Lilia and motioning to the door. They exited into the hall and he guided her to the next penthouse suite. As he unlocked the door, he said, "This is where your brother, Renner, and I have been staying with the Ambassador." He tipped his head toward another door further down the hall. "Kedis's staff has the next suite over."

Lilia nodded wordlessly, wrapping her arms around herself. It was probably crazy, but she felt suddenly exposed. The feeling evaporated as the door slid aside and Jasper ushered her inside.

"It's just me and Renner at the moment," he explained, glancing sideways at her again. "You'll be safe here."

*Safe.* Lilia let a breath she hadn't realized she'd been holding and dropped her arms. Unconsciously, she curled her hands into fists— and winced as the motion sent fiery darts of pain shooting from her palms to her wrists.

Jasper did not miss her pained expression. "What's wrong?" He reached for her hands and Lilia let him.

She watched him examine the scrapes and abrasions on her hands, watched his forehead crinkle and a frown tug at the corners of his mouth, and the strangest sense of surrealism descended on her. *A few months ago, I'd have laughed at the idea that I could feel safe around a G.U. soldier.* She swallowed. *But I do.*

Jasper's piercing gaze traveled up her arms, searching for any other injuries, and his face abruptly darkened. Gently, he pushed back the sleeve of her shirt to reveal finger-shaped bruises forming on her upper arms. His gray eyes flicked to her face. "Who did this?"

Before Lilia could answer, Renner appeared from one of the bedrooms. "Wright?" he asked in Tarynian. "What's going on?" His expression barely changed as he took in Lilia and Jasper's close proximity. "Miss Strong."

Lilia tried to smile. "Hi, Renner."

"She's been hurt," Jasper informed his comrade, before returning his attention to Lilia. "Were you attacked?" He arched a golden eyebrow, nodding at the bruises he'd revealed. "You *are* going to tell me what happened, aren't you?"

"I was—" Lilia swallowed, unsure whether she should say 'kidnapped', which would lead to more questions, or whether she should just run with the 'attacked' theme. *Technically, I was attacked.* She took a breath and the reality of the situation slammed into her. Again.

"Whoa." Jasper steadied her as she swayed on her feet. He slid an arm around her shoulders to help support her. "You'd better sit down."

He guided her to one end of a tan leather couch. Under normal circumstances, Lilia would have protested that she could manage just fine by herself, but at the moment she was still too shaken—and his touch was both solid and comforting.

Jasper knelt by her feet. "We'll get a medkit and clean your hands up. Are you hurt anywhere else?"

"My knees," Lilia said faintly. "Otherwise I think I'm okay."

"I'll get the medkit," Renner said gruffly. "Be right back." Crossing the suite, he disappeared into the main hygiene unit.

Jasper looked up into her face, his expression stormy. "Lilia, who did this to you?"

Lilia shook her head. "I don't know. I couldn't see their faces."

"What did they want?"

She bit her lip, hesitating. "To scare me, I think."

Renner returned with the medkit, and Jasper gently cleaned out the scrapes and abrasions on her hands before applying a clear liquid bandage. Then he turned his attention to her legs. "Your knees?"

"I think they're just bruised." Lilia blocked his hand before he could push the material of her capris up to reveal her knees—her nano-armor-covered knees. They ached, but hadn't been scraped. "My pants aren't even ripped, see?"

Jasper studied her for a few seconds, his expression inscrutable, before he finally nodded. "Fine." He reached into the medkit and pulled out a medi-scanner. "I'm still checking you for any other injuries."

"Okay." Lilia sat very still while he ran the device over her body. After he examined the results, nodded to himself, and returned the medi-scanner to the medkit, she raised an eyebrow. "Am I going to live?"

Jasper glanced up at her, the faintest of smiles touching his mouth and crinkling the corners of his eyes. "Looks like it."

"You said they wanted to scare you." Renner stood close by, his arms folded across his chest and a forbidding expression on his craggy face. "Why?"

Lilia bit her lip again. She couldn't explain without starting at the beginning.

Renner took pity on her. "Want a cup of coffee first?" he asked gruffly, jerking a thumb over his shoulder in the direction of a small kitchenette cattycorner to a little breakfast nook.

A wave of gratitude washed over her. "Yes, please."

"Decaf, Renner," Jasper said firmly, eying her. He shook his head. "I don't think she needs any more excitement tonight."

"Got it."

Renner headed toward the kitchenette, while Jasper repacked the contents of the medkit. Rising to his feet, he extended a hand to her. "Would you like to get cleaned up?"

Lilia suddenly recalled what she looked like, and a flush of self-conscious color rose in her cheeks. "Yes. Thank you."

She accepted Jasper's hand and allowed her to help her to her feet, suppressing a wince as various aches and pains made themselves known. It took a great deal of effort not to limp across the living room to the hygiene unit.

Once there, she took stock of herself in the mirror—and scowled. Her appearance had not improved. Her scowl deepened when she realized that in stronger light, her dark gray nano-armor could be glimpsed through the rips in her short-sleeved shirt. She plucked at the turquoise silk, dragging a fingertip across her armor. *How am I going to explain this?*

A knock on the door startled her out of her reverie. She opened it to find Jasper standing on the other side.

"Here." He thrust something soft into her hands. "Thought you could use this."

It was a blue-grey, button-down shirt. Lilia glanced at it and then looked back up at Jasper, feeling a lump form in her throat at his thoughtfulness. She swallowed it, however, and offered him a tiny smile. "Thank you."

He inclined his head and stepped back.

Shutting the door again, Lilia stripped off her shirt. She held it up to the light, debating whether or not to keep it, but decided it was too damaged from her encounters with the ground and gravel to be salvaged and stuffed the garment into the trash instead. She then spent a moment examining the bruises on her upper arms, her mouth pressed into a thin line.

She'd formed the stealth nano-armor covering her torso—much thinner and more streamlined than regular defense mode—to be sleeveless in order to conceal it under her sleeves, but now she wondered if the bruises would have been as bad if she'd chosen a different outfit.

*Maybe. At any rate, it could have been worse.* She'd definitely lived through worse.

After wiping the dirt off her face, Lilia eased Jasper's shirt over her shoulders and gingerly began doing up the buttons. The shirt smelled like him; for a second she shut her eyes and breathed in the sharp, clean scent. It was comforting, in a strange way; the next best thing to a hug.

Swallowing yet another lump in her throat, Lilia opened her eyes. *Don't go there,* she warned her reflection. Her reflection stared back, violet eyes stormy with frustration and confusion.

Jasper's shirt hung large on her slim frame, but Lilia didn't care. It was clean, and it wouldn't reveal her nano-armor. *That's all that matters at the moment.* She rolled the sleeves up to her elbows and attempted to tame her hair. That done, she took a deep, bracing breath, and exited the hygiene unit.

When she rounded the corner, she found Renner in a tan chair close to the couch, coffee in hand, while Jasper stood beside the glass-topped end table next to the couch, stirring his own coffee on a tray with a third cup of coffee and a selection of sweeteners, milk, and creamers.

Jasper glanced up at Lilia with a smile. "Feel better?"

"Yes. Thank you," she added, glancing from him to Renner.

Renner raised his cup in a salute. He did not say a word about her change in attire.

Jasper moved aside and Lilia settled gingerly into the corner of the couch and leaned over the armrest to fix her coffee. She attempted to pick up a packet of sugar and had to suppress a wince. Her hands felt better than they had, but flexing her fingers still hurt.

"Let me help you with that."

Startled, she looked up at Jasper. "Oh, I—"

"Need help," he said firmly, nodding to her hands. "Anyone would, in your situation."

Biting the inside of her cheek, Lilia sat back and let him prepare her coffee. He poured in sugar, milk, and creamer as directed and stirred it before handing the cup to her.

"Thank you." The heat was faintly unpleasant against her skin, but she wasn't about to let that stop her. Coffee was normal, safe. She needed that just now. Nothing else about this situation was anywhere near normal.

"You're welcome." Jasper took a seat beside her on the couch, closer than Renner would have, but not close enough to touch her.

Lilia took a sip and let the hot liquid stream down her throat. The bulk of her panic had now faded, leaving her exhausted and brimming with questions she didn't know how to answer. Her hand shook slightly; she set the coffee cup back down on the glass surface of the end table before she spilled anything.

For a few moments, neither of her companions spoke. Finally, Jasper shifted in his seat, angling his body toward her. "Can you tell us what happened?"

*Not really*, Lilia thought, but she exhaled slowly and lifted one shoulder in a minute shrug. Even that small movement hurt. "I had dinner with Alexis at *Sal's* tonight, and on my way home…some people jumped me."

It was true enough—though only one man had tackled her, somebody had been on the other end opening that portal.

Jasper and Renner both tensed.

Lilia dropped her eyes to her lap and bit her lip again, searching for the right words to convey the gist of what else had happened without giving away pertinent details. "They…took me somewhere."

"Do you know where?" Jasper asked.

"No." That, at least, she could answer honestly. She had guesses, but nothing concrete…other than the fact that it had been on Glo'Stea.

"What did they want?" Renner demanded.

Lilia shrugged again. "To talk about the Gala and the Ambassador. They…weren't very happy about what Kevin and I did."

A muscle in Jasper's jaw twitched; he seemed to be struggling with something. "They didn't…hurt you?"

"Surprisingly, no." Lilia tried for a smile; this one survived for a few seconds. "I think they were afraid of incurring Grandfather's wrath."

"Good," Jasper muttered.

"Anyway, after haranguing me for a while, they took me away again and dumped me back on the street." Lilia swallowed, tasting bitterness. "No identcard, no comlink, no money, no way to contact anyone or make it back home." She made a vague, fluttering gesture with one hand. "They could have at least dropped me off where I was, but, no."

Renner stirred. "Where *did* they dump you?"

Lilia tipped her head toward the window. "Ten blocks away."

Realization flooded Jasper's face. "So that's why you came here."

She nodded. "I—I didn't know what else to do." She shrugged again. "Figured Lon would be able to at least get me a hovertaxi home and let our family know I'm all right." She smiled wryly. "And then the concierge didn't believe me when I said I was Lon's sister, so I asked for you."

Lilia met Jasper's eyes, betting that he wouldn't call her on referencing Challa in front of Renner. It was a risk, but she thought her odds were good.

"I'm glad you're all right." Jasper ran a hand over his golden hair, his expression troubled. "That—that could have been…" he trailed off, shaking his head.

Lilia inhaled sharply. He didn't have to elaborate; she knew. Granted, she was in a lot less danger because of the protection her frozen nano-armor afforded her, but still…

Renner leaned forward in his seat, cradling his coffee. "So your family doesn't even know where you've been all evening."

Lilia shook her head. "I was supposed to have come right home." She bit her lip again—it would be bloody at this rate—as another painful truth hit her. *They might not even know I was missing for a while.*

Jasper frowned at her. "I'm surprised they didn't send you out with an escort."

Frustration welled up inside Lilia, but she tamped it down. "I was just going two blocks. We thought it would be fine."

It *should* have been fine.

Renner nodded. "You're lucky it wasn't worse."

"I know." Lilia glanced between him and Jasper. "Thank you."

"You're welcome." Jasper looked like he wanted to say something else, but the tiniest of glances at Renner seemed to still his tongue.

For his part, Renner looked unsure. Finally, he drained the last of his coffee and rose to his feet. "Lon and the Ambassador should be back soon; they've been gone a while now." He looked at Jasper and jerked a thumb over his shoulder in the direction of the bedrooms. "I'll be in there if you need anything."

"Thanks, Renner." Jasper waited until the shorter man disappeared into his room before glancing at Lilia and dropping his voice. "He's discovered a holodrama he really likes. *Errant Venture.*"

An involuntary smile curved Lilia's mouth. "I've seen a few episodes of that. It's full of drama."

"We don't talk about it."

They shared a smile, and then the amusement faded from Jasper's face. "Are you sure you're all right?"

Lilia gave him a perfunctory nod and reached for her coffee, using that as an excuse to look away. "I'm fine."

"Lilia. Look at me."

Reluctantly, she met his gaze.

Jasper quirked his eyebrows, silently repeating the question.

Something about the serious, earnest way he was looking at her prompted her to be honest—far more honest than she would have under other circumstances. "I'm fine, really. Or I will be, all things considered." She gave him a small smile. "I just—that—it shook me."

"I can imagine." His eyes dropped to her upper arms, though the bruises were covered, and his face darkened. It was his turn to look away, a muscle twitching in his jaw. "I knew something was wrong when you never messaged me back."

Lilia's eyes widened. *You did?*

"I didn't imagine it was anything like this."

"Yeah…" She blew out a breath, her pulse uneven again. "It's not exactly how I thought my evening would go."

She took another sip of her now-room temperature coffee. *The guys must be so worried right now.* Guilt gnawed at her insides. She didn't know if her grandfather knew what had happened or not yet. She drank half of her coffee and then set the cup aside again; she couldn't finish the rest. Her hands had stopped shaking, but the exhaustion and guilt remained.

Drawing her knees up to her chest, Lilia let herself sink into the couch. She rested her head against the buttery-soft leather and closed her eyes.

"When did you start wearing body armor?"

Lilia went very still, but did not open her eyes. She knew he'd felt it, and she had prepared for this. "A while back. Thought it might be a good idea, all things considered."

"That was wise."

Silence fell over them again.

"I wish Lon would get back," Lilia said eventually. She *needed* to call home.

Beside her, she felt the couch move as Jasper jolted. "I'm an idiot," he said flatly.

Lilia opened her eyes to stare at him. "What? Why?"

Grimacing, Jasper withdrew his comlink from his pocket and handed it to her. "I should have given this to you the moment you got here so you could call your family." He nodded to her. "Kevin's in there."

Lilia's gaze flicked from the comlink to Jasper and back. Her throat had suddenly gone dry. *Now what am I going to do?* "Thank you," she said faintly, taking the device from him. Her fingers started trembling again as she commed Kevin.

It only took a few seconds for her brother to answer.

# CHAPTER 40

"HELLO? Wright?" Kevin sounded tired, and a little wary.

"Hey, Kev."

Complete silence met her for a second, and then, "…Lilia?"

"Yep, it's me." Lilia glanced at Jasper, who was watching her with concern. "I'm at the Beliana Hotel with Jasper and Corporal Renner right now. I haven't seen Lon yet; he's in a meeting with the Ambassador."

"Why?" Kevin's voice held bewilderment. "I thought you were having dinner with Alexis."

"I did." Lilia swallowed, dropping her gaze to her knees as she realized she'd been right—nobody had noticed she was missing yet. Her stomach gave a peculiar twist. "It's a long story." *A very long story.*

"Give me the short version."

"Well…I was…attacked…on my way home."

"*What?*" Kevin's voice rose sharply. "Are you okay?"

"I'm fine," Lilia hastened to assure him, "but they stranded me in uptown without my comlink or my identcard and I don't have enough money to get home."

"And Lon's in a meeting?"

"Yeah."

"I'll have Bryce come pick you up," Kevin said immediately. "Don't go anywhere."

"I won't."

Kevin ended the call and Lilia handed Jasper his comlink. "Thank you."

"My pleasure. I'm sure they're worried."

"He is now." Lilia dropped her head to the back of the couch again and stared up at the ceiling, tasting bitterness. She felt Jasper's eyes on her, but it didn't faze her. "Nobody even knew I was gone."

"They didn't?" Jasper asked, incredulous.

"Nope." Lilia swallowed. "The people who took me definitely did their homework."

They sat in borderline awkward silence for a few minutes, and then Jasper cleared his throat. "Not to change the subject or anything, but does this mean you are finally admitting you're the girl who jumped off that cliff?" A hint of amusement colored his voice.

Lilia stiffened—of *course* he went there—and made a sound that was half laugh, half exasperated huff. She looked sideways at him. "You've been dying to call me on that, haven't you?"

"Hey," Jasper tried to smother a smile, but didn't quite succeed. "You were the one who said it."

"I only said it because I knew you'd know it was me. I wasn't *admitting* to anything."

"Sure sounded like it."

They stared at each other, and then Lilia rolled her eyes and glanced away. "For the last time, Lieutenant, I'm not your mystery jumper."

"Still looks like it from where I'm sitting." His words were sober, but Jasper was smiling.

Lilia shook her head. "You're never going to let that go, are you?"

His smile widened. "Not until you tell me the truth."

"You mean not until I tell you what you want to hear," Lilia retorted, a pang shooting through her amid her amusement. *I can't tell you the truth. Ever.*

"Don't worry." Jasper leaned back against the couch, folding his arms behind his head, the picture of nonchalance. "I'll get it out of you eventually, Miss Strong."

Lilia rolled her eyes again, but she was smiling too.


Bryce made faster time than Lilia had anticipated. It wasn't long before the suite's comm panel chimed; when Jasper answered, Rufus informed him that a chauffeur had arrived for Miss Strong.

Lilia gingerly unfolded herself from the couch and stood. She couldn't hide a grimace; she would definitely be feeling this in the morning. "Thank you for everything, Jasper. I appreciate it. Tell Renner I said thank you, as well."

He shrugged. "I—we—didn't do much. I'm just sorry you didn't get to see your brother." He frowned. "The Ambassador left very strict instructions about not being disturbed, but this should have qualified as an exception."

"It's all right." It was her turn to shrug. Words rose to the tip of her tongue as she looked up at him, but she hesitated, unsure she should voice them.

There was something strangely intimate about this moment— the dark sky beyond the penthouse suite windows, the warm glow of the living room lights, and the two of them standing here alone. They hadn't been alone in a long time, not since they'd both been at the Mansion.

Jasper's gray eyes softened a little as he looked at her. "What?"

Lilia bit her lip—and took the plunge. "I'm glad I got to see you." The words tumbled out a little faster than she would have liked.

"It was good to see you as well." He inclined his head. "I'm just sorry it was under these circumstances."

"Well…" Lilia glanced away and then looked back at him with a wry smile. "Such is the life of a prominent politician's granddaughter."

"Especially when said granddaughter aids and abets the enemy."

"Exactly."

They shared a conspiratorial grin, and then Lilia's eyes dropped to his throat as Jasper swallowed. "I'll escort you down, but first…" He sounded almost hesitant.

She arched a questioning eyebrow at him.

Jasper held out both hands to her. "May I pray for you?"

Lilia stared at him for a few seconds, taken aback. It shouldn't have surprised her—he was a fellow believer, after all—and yet, she hadn't expected it from him. She nodded, but had to clear her throat before she could speak. "Sure. Thank you."

She placed her hands in his, and Jasper curled his fingers around hers before bowing his head. "Father, we come before You today to thank You for protecting Lilia from harm. Thank You that she was not hurt worse, and thank You that the people who took her let her go. I pray that You would keep her safe tonight, and that You would give her and her family wisdom on what to do about this. I pray that You would give her comfort and peace, and that this would not trouble her."

His words washed over Lilia, his voice warm and comforting. She silently added her own prayers in with his. *Thank you that it wasn't something worse, Lord.*

"I pray that You would forgive us of our sins, and help us to please You in everything that we say and do. I pray that You would help our two governments find a peaceable agreement that benefits all of us."

*That* was an understatement if she'd ever heard one. "Yes, Lord," she said softly.

Jasper's grip on her fingers tightened. "Thank You that we got to meet and become friends."

Lilia bit her lip. She had to admit, she was glad of that too.

"We love You and praise You, Lord. All these things we ask in Jesus' Name, amen."

"Amen," Lilia echoed quietly. She opened her eyes slowly, to find Jasper looking at her. She offered him a shy smile. "Thank you."

"You're welcome." He was still holding her hands, considering her with an earnest, thoughtful air. Abruptly, he said, "Come here."

Letting go of her hands, he wrapped his arms around her in a gentle hug.

For a second, Lilia stood rigid, caught off-guard by the embrace…and then she allowed herself to relax. Jasper meant her no harm—she knew that—and she liked him. They were friends. Tentatively, she slid her arms around his waist and hugged him back, resting her cheek against his chest, warm through his shirt.

"I'm glad you're all right," he murmured into her hair.

"Me too." Her voice emerged as little more than a whisper.

They hadn't been this close since the last time they'd danced—and even then they'd never been *this* close. She could hear the steady thump of his heart. A lump formed in her throat as her eyes fluttered shut. After the evening she'd had, it felt really, really good to be held just now. Jasper smelled good, and she could feel the strength in the arms wrapped loosely around her, arms that had only ever tried to help her.

For a few heartbeats, they stood there together and the galaxy narrowed down to the two of them. Nothing else existed. But then reality came crashing back down over Lilia.

Bryce, waiting for her outside.

Kevin, waiting to hear what had happened to her.

The fact that she probably shouldn't be standing here letting a G.U. officer hug her, no matter how good a friend he was becoming.

She dropped her arms and stepped back, but Jasper did not immediately relinquish his hold. His hands rose to her shoulders as he peered down into her face. "Be careful, Lilia. Please."

Lilia gave him a brave smile. "I will."

Jasper's sober expression did not change. "Somebody's managed to kidnap you once; it could happen again."

"Hopefully not." Her smile turned wry. "I'd hate to have to admit somebody got the drop on me more than once."

His fingers smoothed over the tops of her shoulders. Lilia had the impression that he wanted to say something, but then the moment passed. Dropping his hands, he motioned to the door. "Shall we?"

They departed the suite in silence. Lilia wasn't quite sure what to say; half-formed sentences swirled around in her head, but none of them made enough sense to actually risk speaking them. It was only when they were halfway down to the lobby that words came. "Thanks again for the shirt. I'll get it back to you."

Jasper waved a dismissive hand. "Keep it." He gave her a wry look. "I suspect returning it could be problematic, given the scrutiny we're all under."

Lilia imagined the media headlines that might result from her attempting to return his shirt—no matter how innocent the real circumstances were—and promptly blushed. "Yeah." She glanced away from him; even the back of her neck was hot. *That's exactly the type of situation we were supposed to avoid in the first place.*

As the accelevator halted with an imperceptible jolt and the doors opened, she snapped her fingers. "I could always get it back to you via Lon."

"That's true."

They both scanned the lobby as they stepped out of the accelevator. A familiar figure stood by the reception desk, and Lilia quickened her pace. *Bryce.* Relief surged through her.

Bryce caught sight of them at the same time. "Miss Strong." He nodded to Jasper, recognizing him. "Lieutenant." His gaze slid back to Lilia. "I understand you've had quite the evening. We're here to take you home."

"Thank you." Lilia smiled at him, before turning back to Jasper. "Thank you again. For everything."

Jasper had resumed the formal demeanor befitting a G.U. officer in his situation. "You are welcome." He gave Lilia a short bow. "Have a safe trip home. Good night."

"Thank you. Good night." Lilia allowed Bryce to lead her across the lobby and outside, where one of her grandfather's skimmers awaited. Oppelt was driving. Bryce opened the door for her and she climbed inside. She waited until he was back inside to lean forward and say, "Thank you so much for coming to get me."

"You're welcome." Oppelt glanced at her over his shoulder before he pulled away from the sidewalk.

"Kevin said you were abducted on your way home?" Bryce asked.

"Yes." Lilia swallowed. "They let me go after a while. I think they wanted to scare me more than anything."

"You're fortunate," Oppelt observed soberly.

Lilia swallowed again. "I know."

She did not speak again for the remainder of the ride home.


After Oppelt pulled into the parking garage beneath Ferndale, he and Bryce both escorted Lilia up to the penthouse. Kevin met them at the door; he'd been waiting. And, from the looks of it, he'd just gotten home and he hadn't had a shower yet. He was still dressed in his fencing clothes.

"Are you all right?" he asked without preamble.

"Yeah." Lilia turned to Bryce and Oppelt with a smile. "Thanks, guys. I appreciate it."

Neither of them budged. Bryce folded his arms across his chest. "You're welcome. We want to know what happened too."

Before Lilia could respond, the security penthouse door opened and J.P. Cobb stepped out. "What happened?" He was supposed to be off-duty and at home on Ferndale's fourth floor with his wife and family, but either Bryce or Oppelt must have called him. He was tall and lean as a whip, with dark brown skin and curly black hair he kept short.

Kevin looked from Lilia to the three members of Aiden's security team and then crossed the threshold into the hall, letting the door slide shut behind him. He waved everyone toward the security suite. "Come on. Let's just all go in here."

Lilia shot him a look, which he met with a challenging stare. Clearly, he'd figured out something was wrong with her nanites, but he didn't think it was worth cutting the security team out of the loop.

She had to concede he had a point; the night's events had been too strange for her to brush off as nothing…particularly since no one had even known something was wrong until she called.

Kevin waited until Oppelt shut the door to round on Lilia. "First off, are you okay?"

"More or less." Lilia started to shrug, and then thought the better of it. She started for the nearest chair; Bryce anticipated her and slid it closer for her to seat herself. "Thanks." She shot him a grateful look. "I have a few bruises," she indicated her upper arms without raising the rolled-up sleeves of Jasper's shirt, "but I'm okay."

"All right. Next question." Kevin folded his arms across his chest, his expression dark and serious. "What *happened?* Where have you been?"

Taking a deep breath, Lilia launched into the sanitized version of the story. When she reached the end, Oppelt asked, "Could you describe them to the police?"

She shook her head. "They were masked. I have absolutely no idea who they were." She wrapped her arms around herself, locking her hands around her elbows. "I'm just glad Lieutenant Wright helped me."

"No kidding," Kevin muttered. He ran a hand over the back of his neck. "And we had no idea."

Lilia just shrugged, though the gesture made her body ache.

"Your grandfather is not going to like this," Cobb said darkly.

The twins shot him identical sober looks. In unison, they said, "*We* don't like it."

Shaking his head, Kevin straightened up from the wall he'd been leaning against. "Okay, guys, I'm taking her back over now. Thanks for picking her up."

"Not a problem." Oppelt inclined his head, his expression still troubled. "We're going to have to revamp security again. I don't think it's a coincidence that they grabbed Lilia at a time when nobody would notice she was missing for a while."

Lilia nodded; she'd been able to think of nothing else the whole ride home.

"Yeah," Kevin said tightly. "Night, guys."

He did not speak again until they were safely in the foyer of the penthouse and he had locked the door behind them. Rounding on Lilia, he posted his hands on his hips and fixed her with a flat, serious stare. "Okay, what really happened?" He waved a hand in her general direction. "Are your——"

"Yes." Lilia pulled the collar of her borrowed shirt down far enough to reveal her nano-armor. "Come on." She led the way to her room; this wasn't a conversation she wanted Zoë overhearing. "This might take a while."

Kevin sat speechless for a full minute when she finished telling him the entire story. He opened and closed his mouth twice before he simply shook his head and tipped his head back to stare up the ceiling. He was perched on her desk, while she'd settled gingerly on her bed.

"It's pretty unbelievable, isn't it?" Lilia asked wryly, glancing down at her hands, which still ached.

"No kidding." Kevin blew out a breath. "Heck of a recruitment strategy."

"That's what I said."

"And you believe him?"

"About most of it." Lilia shrugged. "Obviously, he told me a couple of lies."

Kevin shook his head again. "I can't wait to hear Nob's take on this." He grimaced. "Erik's going to flip."

They shared a look, and then Lilia changed the subject. "How was your evening?"

"Strange." Kevin didn't look as pleased as he could have about having spent the evening fencing. "Franco started off by having me duel one of his buddies, Tieran. After I won, he told me to take a break for a few minutes and then he challenged me to a duel." He shook his head. "I lost, just barely."

"Then what happened?"

"That's where it got strange. Franco clapped me on the shoulder and told me that was all right, I hadn't been disqualified as a candidate. When I asked what he meant, he just smiled and said he'd comm me about another meet later."

Lilia's eyes narrowed in confusion. "A candidate?"

"Yeah." Kevin's eyebrows drew together in a frown. "Something else is definitely going on. I have a feeling I'm this close," he pinched two fingers together, "to finding out what it is. If I'd beaten Franco, I might know already."

"What do you think it is?" Lilia gave him a quizzical look. "I *know* you've thought about it."

Kevin chuckled, but he sobered quickly. "I've been thinking maybe some sort of arcane dueling club." He shook his head. "This bunch is crazy and rich enough to have some sort of strange, old-fashioned romantic notions about fencing."

"Or?"

"Or…it's something else. Something worse."

"Worse? Like what?" Lilia leaned forward, her aches, pains, and frozen nanites temporarily forgotten. *What could be worse?*

Grimacing, Kevin locked his hands behind his head and stared out through the flimsy curtains separating the windows in Lilia's room from Sonela's nighttime skyline. "Do you remember me telling you about the underground street fighting in Laconia?"

"Yeah. The ones that had—" Lilia broke off, her violet eyes going wide. "You don't think—"

"That's exactly what I think." Kevin met her gaze, his expression grim. "I think there's a really good chance Franco and his buddies have managed to get their hands on nanoblades."

Lilia sucked in a breath. "What about protective gear?"

Dropping his arms, Kevin just shrugged. "You know as well as I do the only protection against a nanoblade is—"

"—nano-armor."

"Exactly. Unless they've also managed to find a way to get nanite infusions, they're playing with fire."

Lilia thought back to the story Kevin had told her about that fight. One of the combatants had lost an arm. "Just like the people in Laconia."

"Except a lot richer." Kevin shook his head. "And crazier. Those people were half-desperate. Franco and his buddies are just bored."

"What are you going to do?" Lilia bit down on the inside of her lip, staring at her brother.

He didn't answer for a long moment. Finally, he sighed and made a half-helpless gesture with one hand. "Until I know for sure what Franco is trying to get me into, I don't know what to do except play along." His mouth twisted in a wry smile. "I could be wrong."

"But you don't think so."

Kevin gave a minute shake of his head.

Lilia nodded, and the two sat in silence for a moment.

Then Kevin stirred. "I still can't believe Freedom's Children had the nerve to kidnap you through a portal."

"It was gutsy," Lilia agreed. "But you have to give them props for ingenuity and timing—I mean," she spread her hands, "one second I was there, the next I was gone. There wouldn't be anything plausible for any witnesses to tell the police, if they even saw something to begin with."

"I don't like it," Kevin said darkly. "Oppelt is right—they had to have been watching us to find a good time to snag you."

"That's the conclusion I came to." Lilia blew out a breath and slumped forward, feeling even more exhausted. "And now there's no chance of keeping it from Grandfather."

"I don't think we *should* keep it from him." Kevin shook his head. "Not now."

Lilia straightened, pinning him with a sharp, incredulous look. "You think we ought to tell him about the Mastermind? What's he going to do?"

Kevin shrugged. "No idea. But this is big, Lilia. Much, much bigger than anything we imagined." He threw his arms into the air. "They restored Glo'Stea's shield, for crying out loud. He ought to know about this guy." He shot her a significant look. "Particularly since I don't think it's a far-fetched theory that he's behind the assassination attempts."

Lilia chewed on her lip for a long moment. "Okay, fine," she said at last. "But I'm not going through all that again tonight. I'm too tired." She glanced at the time display glowing softly on the wall above the window. "Particularly since my nanites are frozen for another couple of hours."

"Fine." Kevin slid off her desk. "I'll explain things to Grandfather, and I'll tell Erik and Nob." He shot her a look. "Nob's probably going to want to hear all the nitty gritty details from you personally, though."

Lilia waved a hand. "Which I'll be happy to tell him, just not tonight."

Kevin paused in the doorway long enough to look at her over his shoulder. "I'm glad you're okay." A muscle clenched in his jaw as he swallowed. "And I'm sorry I didn't know something was wrong."

"Kev…" Lilia blinked at him, and then shook her head. "It's not your fault." She motioned to the door. "You heard Oppelt. The Mastermind planned this pretty carefully. He didn't *want* you to know I was gone."

"Still." Kevin's mouth had an unhappy slant. "I should have known."

"It's okay." Lilia eased off the bed and crossed the room to give him a hug. "*I'm* okay. Jasper and Renner took care of me and Jasper enabled me to call you." She smiled. "And you got me a ride home."

Her brother didn't look completely convinced, but he nodded. "Get some rest."

"I will."

Long after she had shut the door behind her brother and stretched out on her bed, Lilia lay staring up at the ceiling. She was exhausted, but sleep evaded her. The Mastermind's words kept echoing through her brain. To distract herself, she pulled the collar of Jasper's shirt up to her nose and inhaled. The smell was comforting; her thoughts traveled to him instead, and the unexpected chance she'd gotten to see him.

In the darkness and privacy of her own room and thoughts, Lilia admitted to herself that it had been very nice to see him, but she was still a little taken aback by how safe she'd felt around him. She hadn't expected that; it was slightly unnerving. *Well*, she thought wryly, *if there was any doubt we've become friends, I think that put it to rest.*

She wanted her comlink badly—wanted to see what he'd written her this evening, wanted to let him know she'd made it home just fine—but it was still trapped in her ISF. She thumped a fist on her mattress, wincing as her hand protested. *Stupid impactors.*

# CHAPTER 41

"DINNER was lovely, Parisa, as always." Aiden laid his sapphire cloth napkin on the table beside his plate, smiling at his hostess across the dining room table.

Parisa Briscoe returned his smile. She was a green-eyed, sprite-like redhead, with a laugh that sounded like a handful of tinkling bells. "I'm glad you enjoyed, Representative."

"It was excellent," Derek agreed, leaning back in his seat.

"Yes, thank you for dinner, Parisa," Shane Briscoe told his wife. "It was delicious."

Aiden's eyes traveled to the other end of the table, where Michael and Dawn Briscoe were deep in conversation and had yet to realize everyone else at the table was now regarding them with amusement. An artist who predominantly created holographic wall hangings, Briscoe's younger sister lacked her brother's charisma—she reminded Aiden of a shy, dreamy shadow—but she was animated enough when the topic suited her. She was almost as tall as Michael, with shoulder-length wavy brown hair and hazel eyes.

Pushing back his chair, Briscoe looked at Aiden. "If you'll join me in my study for a moment, Aiden, I have something to show you."

"Gladly." Aiden inclined his head to his host and rose from his seat. He was grateful to have left the hoverchair at home tonight; he felt more like his old self without it.

"Would you like me to bring you coffee?" Parisa asked.

"Yes. Thank you, darling," Briscoe replied, moving toward the doorway leading out into the living room.

As Aiden left the dining room and followed Briscoe, he caught Derek's eye and nodded imperceptibly. He had a good idea as to what the younger Representative wanted to talk about, but he had no idea how long it would take.

Derek nodded once in reply and flicked his eyes toward his older brother and Briscoe's sister; staying here for a while would not be a problem at all.

The Briscoes lived in a three-story brownstone house in one of Sonela's better middle-class neighborhoods. They had chosen it for their children's sake—they had two little girls—and Briscoe did not seem to mind a slightly longer commute to the Four Towers. Dawn lived with them and had a studio on the third floor.

Briscoe's study was down the hall from the living room. He did not speak until he and Aiden were both safely ensconced inside and he had shut the door. His study was surprisingly spare—he did not seem to care for knickknacks and the decor was rather utilitarian in an elegant way—but the dark wood and leather furniture had a comfortable air. His desk sat along one wall with a window to the side, providing him a view outside when he wanted it, and the walls were lined with bookcases.

The two men settled themselves in matching armchairs, and then Briscoe leaned forward, clasping his hands together. "I have more information to share."

"On Grimes?" Aiden asked. Briscoe's predecessor in Sector 5, Timnus Grimes, had died in a mysterious skimmer crash. Briscoe had been investigating his untimely demise.

"And Hesperia." A small, triumphant smile crossed Briscoe's face. "I think I finally found a connection."

"Really?" Aiden straightened in his chair, his interest piqued. He fixed Briscoe with a sharp, assessing look. "You are sure?"

Briscoe nodded, and then hesitated. "Aiden, I'm not sure if you are aware of this or not, but Hesperia...they've been attempting to recruit Kevin and Lilia."

"I am aware." Aiden waved a hand. "The twins told me." He frowned. "Hesperia has put a great deal of pressure on them, but they are not interested."

"Good." Briscoe looked relieved. "I'm glad to hear that."

His expression changed, relief fading to a sober concern that set off alarm bells inside Aiden's head. He said nothing, however, choosing to let Briscoe speak whatever was on his mind when he was ready.

"I don't know how to say this," Briscoe said at last. "If I wasn't absolutely certain of my information, I wouldn't believe it myself, but…" He broke off, shaking his head.

Aiden continued to wait patiently, though inside his mind had already begun whirling through a list of possible reasons for this behavior.

Someone knocked on the study door.

Briscoe straightened, smiling slightly, though his hazel eyes remained conflicted. "That would be my wife with our coffee."

Rising to his feet, he strode over to the study door and opened it for Parisa. She handed him a tray complete with coffee cups, a small carafe, spoons, milk, and various sweeteners, smiled, and was gone. Briscoe returned with the tray and set it on a small, round table between the two armchairs.

Aiden waited until the younger man had made himself a cup of coffee before he asked quietly, "Shane, what did you find?"

Briscoe grimaced into his coffee cup. "Remember I told you I discovered Grimes was investigating Hesperia?"

"Yes." Aiden stirred sugar into his own coffee and laid the spoon aside.

"Well, it turns out he was doing a great deal more than that." Briscoe set his coffee back on the end table, untouched. "I've found concrete evidence that he was doing business with Hesperia—under the table business. At the same time he was investigating them."

For a second, Aiden could only stare at Briscoe. He had heard the words, but he did not understand their meaning. *Timnus Grimes, involved in something shady?* His white eyebrows knit together in a confused frown. "What do you mean, 'under the table'?"

"Exactly that," Briscoe said grimly. "He was receiving regular payments from a Glo'Stean branch of Hesperia. That's how he funded his antique skimmer collection, as it turned out."

Aiden digested this, before setting his own coffee aside. "Timnus Grimes was a frustrated closet idealist. Why in the galaxy would he—"

"—be taking money under the table from a shipping company?" Briscoe's smile was as grim as his voice. "I wondered that too, so I dug a little deeper." He shook his head again. "What I found reminded me of turning over a rock as a child and discovering all manner of things crawling in the muck underneath it."

*That…does not sound inviting.* Aiden waited, feeling as though his chair was about to be yanked from beneath him.

Briscoe abruptly shot to his feet and strode to the window, jamming his hands into his pockets. He stood there for a moment, gathering the rest of the words he needed—or else the courage to say them. At last he turned back to Aiden. "My apologies, sir. I don't mean to keep you. I just—this—" He shook his head. "It's been something of a shock."

"Understandable." Aiden inclined his head. "But by all means, Shane, kindly do not leave me in suspense."

Briscoe took a deep breath. "Grimes was taking bribes to look the other way concerning certain information he'd found."

Aiden's eyes widened. *What?*

"Apparently, he discovered that a certain faction inside Hesperia has been smuggling certain things past Customs on Sta'Gloa and Glo'Stea without paying excise taxes." Briscoe perched on the corner of his desk. "I don't know *what* they were smuggling—haven't been able to locate that information yet—but whatever it was, it was important enough to someone in Hesperia to pay Grimes to keep his mouth shut." He raised one shoulder in a shrug. "And it seems he did, at least for a while."

Aiden's face could have been carved from stone. "How long?" he asked at last.

"At least eighteen months."

"And do you still think he was murdered?"

Briscoe shot him a knowing smile that held no mirth. "Now more than ever, though I doubt anyone would ever be able to prove it in a court of law."

"What changed?" Aiden shook his head. "Clearly, they had no issues paying him for that amount of time. Something had to have changed."

"I have two theories." Briscoe spread his hands. "Either Timnus decided he wanted more for his silence than they were willing to pay, or he else finally listened to his conscience and decided to put an end to it." It was his turn to shake his head. "At one time, I would have said the latter, but now I simply don't know."

"Nor do I." Aiden pursed his lips. "I never would have suspected it of the man."

"Few would, I think."

The two men sat in silence for a moment, and then Aiden finally picked up his coffee again. "What do you intend to do with this information?"

Briscoe snorted. "What *can* I do with it? Nothing much at the moment, I'm afraid." He pushed off from his desk and returned to his armchair. "Right now, exposing Grimes would do little more than create a small scandal that might take a little of the focus off of Kedis and the Triumvirate."

He drummed his fingers on the arm of his chair, frowning. "If Hesperia *is* smuggling certain items in to evade taxes—which I'm inclined to believe they are, based on my own investigation—it will require more resources to figure out what they're doing."

"So Grimes was killed because they wanted to evade taxes?" Aiden's mouth twisted; it seemed such a sordid, petty end to a man he had quite respected.

"I don't think it's just the taxes. I think it has also something to do with whatever items they're smuggling." Briscoe picked up his coffee, took a sip, and shook his head at himself; it was lukewarm. "I've been able to ascertain that they *do* legitimately list items they've brought past the blockade. The problem is that they're either smuggling something specific out of the system—or else bringing something in."

"Such as?"

Briscoe smiled. "High-grade G.U. weaponry immediately comes to mind, but from what little I've been able to glean from Grimes's records, they were also sending something *past* the blockade. Something they weren't supposed to have."

Aiden knew better than to ask how Briscoe had obtained such information, but given what he knew of the younger man's personal ethics, it seemed strange. He spent two heartbeats weighing his options before he spoke. "At the risk of probing into too-delicate matters, may I ask how you acquired this information?"

Briscoe's expression grew troubled again. "I've obtained most of it through completely legitimate means." He paused. "Although, to be honest, the rest might be construed as borderline gray area."

Aiden spent two seconds deciding if he really wanted to know. "Meaning?"

The younger Representative gave him a long, level look. "Meaning I hired a private investigator. He's supposed to be very good at what he does—and very discreet."

"Anything...else?" Aiden asked delicately.

"Nothing of note." Briscoe exhaled slowly. "I never dreamed this would be what my investigations turned up." He shook his head. "I suspected Grimes had been murdered—and I expected to find evidence supporting that theory—but the rest of it?"

Aiden understood. It was both a shock and a disappointment that left a bitter taste in his mouth. "Do you have any definitive proof of who murdered him?"

"Definitive, no. Enough to convince me personally...well, that's another story."

Aiden waited for a moment, but when the younger man did not elaborate, he raised an eyebrow. "Shane..."

"I can't tell you anything else right now, Aiden." Briscoe shook his head. "I don't have enough proof yet. Suffice to say it was several someones involved with that particular Glo'Stean branch of Hesperia. Besides," he waved a hand, "as important as the 'who' is, I'm more interested in the *why*. I've barely scraped the tip of the iceberg; something tells me this is so much larger than I've imagined."

"Well, a corrupt faction inside an interplanetary shipping company is a rather large situation," Aiden said dryly.

"What I really need to find out is what they're smuggling in and out of the system." Briscoe's expression hardened. "When I know that, I'll have them."

"What was that all about, Grandfather?" Derek asked quietly, after they departed the Briscoes' house and were in Aiden's skimmer headed home.

Aiden shook his head; he did not want to get into it. *Not here, and not now.* "He has been researching something and wanted my opinion."

"I see." Derek let the matter drop, though Aiden knew his grandson would not forget. In that they were too much alike.

Tipping his head back against the headrest, Aiden shut his eyes. It was late; the evening had run longer than he had initially anticipated, and he was tired. The news about Grimes seemed to have sapped some of his energy.

Across the seat from him, Michael made a strange, choking sound.

"What's wrong?" Derek asked immediately.

Aiden opened his eyes; in the lights from passing glowposts flickering across the interior of the skimmer, he could see his oldest grandson's face had gone white.

Michael brandished his comlink. "I've just received a message from Oppelt. They didn't say anything earlier because they didn't want to alarm you, Grandfather, but apparently Lilia was abducted this evening on her way home from *Sal's* and then dumped in Sonela's business district a couple of hours later."

Aiden's heart gave an odd spasm; he clutched his chest.

"*What?*" Derek sat bolt upright in his seat, his violet eyes wide with shock. He concentrated for a second, and then shook his head. "I can't reach her. Is she all right?"

"She's fine," Michael said quickly.

Aiden found his voice with an effort. "What did her abductors want with her?"

Michael waved his comlink. "Supposedly they grilled her about her involvement with Lon and Kedis."

Derek blinked. "That's it?"

"That's all Oppelt and the rest of the security team know." Michael glanced at Aiden. "Don't worry, Grandfather, we'll find out more."

Aiden waited while his grandsons opened Nancom channels, presumably to Kevin, since Lilia was unreachable. Anxiety churned in his gut. *Why is she 'unreachable'?* He understood how Nancom worked; that she did not respond was most troubling.

A moment later, Michael leaned toward him. "Still can't reach Lilia; Kevin says he'll tell us what happened as soon as we get home."

Aiden nodded grimly. "I will hold him to that." *I would rather hear this story firsthand anyway.*

Kevin met them in the foyer. "She's okay," he said immediately, holding up his hands. "Honestly. She's got a few bruises, but other than that, she's fine."

"Where is she?" Aiden strode into the living room, expecting Lilia to be curled up in a chair waiting for them, but the living room was empty. He rounded on Kevin, his expression grimmer than anything his grandsons had seen since Lon's death.

"Asleep." Kevin shook his head. "She was exhausted when she got home."

"I want to know everything." Aiden drew his eyebrows together in a foreboding frown. "Start with how she could be abducted and no one noticed."

Kevin nodded. "Sure, Grandfather, as soon as you sit down."

Grandfather and grandson stared at each other, and then Aiden sighed and headed for his armchair. Kevin was right; he did need to sit down. Kevin took a seat on the couch, but Michael and Derek both remained standing.

Aiden had not thought he could be any more shocked than what he had already experienced this evening. He was wrong. By the time Kevin finished speaking, his face had gone gray.

"Grandfather, are you all right?" Derek took a step toward him, his expression concerned.

"I am fine." Aiden held up a hand to stop him. "Just…deeply, deeply disturbed."

"I know." Kevin ran a hand through his dark hair, leaving it sticking up wildly. "They knew exactly when to take her so that nobody would know she was gone."

"And nobody on the street *saw* anything?" Michael asked incredulously.

Kevin shot him a look. "There wouldn't necessarily be much to see if she got tackled through a portal. She'd be gone too quickly."

Derek began to pace the living room floor. "And now we know for a fact that this…Mastermind…and Freedom's Children *definitely* have a transporter."

Michael shook his head. "Not like we can actually *tell* anybody, though. No proof."

"I agree." Aiden exhaled heavily. "Many things now make a good deal more sense, but it is not enough information to take before the Triumvirate or Internal Affairs, and divulging it without proof would only cause a panic at this point."

Kevin spread his hands. "So what do we do?"

His face somber, Aiden shook his head. "I do not know."

# CHAPTER 42

HALF an hour after Lilia departed, Lon and Ambassador Kedis returned to the penthouse suite. Kedis looked thoughtful; Lon looked profoundly relieved to be finished with the conference. The Sta'Gloan knew better than to say anything in front of Kedis, but the look he shot Jasper spoke of how tedious the evening must have been.

For his part, Jasper had settled himself in the corner of the couch Lilia had occupied earlier, and was trying to engross himself in a holodrama on the large holoprojector discreetly mounted into the wall opposite him. Thus far it had not worked; his mind kept wandering back to Lilia. Though the circumstances were deplorable, he was grateful for the opportunity to see her—especially outside of a ballroom filled with dozens of other people.

Now, he faced the prospect of relaying to her brother—and Kedis—what had happened.

Jasper glanced at the Ambassador, who was pouring himself a liberal glass of an expensive cognac from the suite's wet bar. "I trust everything went well, sir?"

"As well as can be expected." Kedis swirled the liquid around in his glass before taking a sip and striding over to stare out the window at Sonela's nightscape.

Lon had disappeared into the kitchenette and was rummaging for something to eat. Jasper waited until he returned, a bag of salty snack food in hand, to say, "Your sister was here this evening."

"What?" Lon turned startled eyes on him. "Lilia? Here?" He looked astonished. "Why?"

Across the room, Kedis turned to regard both of them, his olive-toned face impassive.

Jasper kept his voice even. "She was attacked."

The bag of snack food slipped from Lon's fingers to land on the carpet, scattering its contents. "*What?*"

Briefly, Jasper outlined the situation, though he left out exactly how Lilia had identified herself to him—that story only had meaning to the two of them. He finished with the report that Lilia had been safely picked up by members of Aiden's security team. Lon, meantime, sank into the chair Renner had occupied earlier, his snack completely forgotten. His face resembled a thundercloud, and he seemed to have temporarily lost all of his words.

"It is fortunate you were here, Lieutenant," Kedis observed from his spot by the window. "Had I dragged you into the meeting with us, poor Miss Strong would have been quite out of luck."

"Yes, sir." Jasper agreed wholeheartedly with that statement.

Finally regaining his faculties, Lon ran a hand through his short, sandy hair before he knelt down to salvage his snack. "Yeah, I'm glad you were here, too, Wright." He shook his head, mouth flattening into a thin line. "If something like that ever happens again, I want you to get me. I don't care what I'm in the middle of."

Jasper glanced at Kedis, but the Ambassador was nodding soberly.

"Oh, I quite agree." Kedis took another sip of his cognac. "Our protocol seems too strict to be practical." He stood by the window for another moment or two, before heading to his master bedroom, raising his glass as he went. "Good night, gentlemen."

"Good night, sir," Jasper said.

Lon merely nodded to the Ambassador, his thoughts elsewhere.

After a stretch, Jasper said quietly, "She's all right. A few bumps and bruises, but nothing major."

"Thanks." Lon's green eyes flicked to him. "I'm glad you were here." He clenched his jaw. "The *nerve* of those guys."

Jasper huffed a little in agreement, before remembering something else Lon needed to know. "Oh. You won't be able to reach her via comlink right now—it was stolen."

Lon jerked his head in a nod. "Figured as much. Logical thing to do." He crinkled the bag in his hands; he seemed to have lost his appetite.

"What was the meeting about tonight?" Jasper cast a significant glance in the direction Kedis has gone.

"They're trying to brainstorm how to get the Triumvirate to let your forces in occupied territory exit the planetary shield in free territory." Lon rubbed a hand over his face. "I've told him the Triumvirate is probably not going to go for it any time soon—seeing G.U. ships fly over their heads will seriously freak out most citizens—but he's convinced there has to be a way."

"Well…" Jasper held out a hand. "They can't stay there forever."

"No."

Lon left it at that, but Jasper heard the words he did not speak. *But that doesn't mean they have to leave any time soon.*

Eventually, Lon roused himself. "I'm done for the night. See you in the morning, Wright."

"Good night."

Once the Sta'Gloan had gone, Jasper pulled his comlink from his pocket and stared down at it. He wished he'd thought to ask Lilia to let him know she made it home safely. As it was, he could only guess.

He smoothed a thumb over the device's readout. It was probably a less-than-gentlemanly thing to think, given that someone had tried to hurt her, but he couldn't help recalling how good she looked in his shirt. He hadn't thought about it, he'd only grabbed the first shirt that came to hand, but the color brought out the purple in her eyes.

*She came to me when she couldn't reach her brother.* A warm glow filled the center of his chest. Regardless of her thoughts on G.U. soldiers, she'd trusted him to help her tonight.

Dropping his comlink into his lap, Jasper leaned back in his seat, locked his hands behind his head, and smiled up at the ceiling. *Tonight was definitely progress.*

Just after breakfast the next morning, Kedis summoned Jasper to the room in their penthouse suite he was using as his makeshift office. Jasper stepped inside, unsure what the Ambassador could need this early in the morning. They were due to depart for the Four

Towers and another grueling session with the Triumvirate in less than an hour.

"You wanted to see me, sir?" Jasper asked politely, his eyes darting over the members of Kedis's political staff occupying chairs and sofas and the datapads scattered across the table, some of them displaying holographic readouts in midair, before coming to rest on the Ambassador himself.

Kedis glanced up from the datapad he'd been leaning over on the table with a slim redhead named Sonja Esperson, one of his attachés. "Ah, yes. You're here. Good." He glanced around the room. "Everyone out for a moment. I need a word with the Lieutenant."

Jasper felt the faintest stirrings of foreboding. Now he was *really* wondering what Kedis wanted. He stepped aside to allow Kedis's staff to file out.

"Close the door, please, Lieutenant."

Wordlessly, Jasper palmed the door release.

Once the door slid shut, Kedis hitched a hip on the corner of the table and waved him forward. "Come in, come in."

Jasper neared the table and stood at attention.

Kedis half-smiled. "No need to be so formal, Wright. You can relax." He drummed the fingers of one hand against the tabletop. "I've been meaning to ask you this for some time. What do you think of the Strongs?"

Jasper blinked; he had not been anticipating that particular question. "Sir?"

"What do you think of them?" Kedis repeated.

*Where is he going with this?* Jasper shook his head slightly. "They're good people, I think." He raised one shoulder in a minute shrug. "A little unusual, maybe—they seem to have made some interesting life choices—but I like them. I believe they are sincere in their desire to see peace between the G.U. and the Coalition."

"Yes…" Kedis looked thoughtful. "They're very interesting— and far too normal for politicians' offspring." He shook his head. "As far as I've been able to determine, they aren't involved with the usual things one finds in this particular social circle—drugs, sex, wild living—and yet they were somehow able to gain access to technology the Coalition hadn't even properly unveiled to its own people yet."

Jasper caught himself before he nodded in agreement. He had wondered about that too. There *was* something different about the Strongs—something he couldn't place. It hovered on the edges of his consciousness when he thought about Lilia in particular, always eluding any attempts to pin it down and identify it.

"They *have* to be involved in something," Kedis continued. His gaze, no longer affable, fixed Jasper in place like a butterfly pinned to a board. "I want you to find out what it is."

Though he did not outwardly flinch, the bottom dropped out of Jasper's stomach. "Me, sir?"

"Yes, you." Kedis smiled, showing a flash of too-white teeth. "You and Lilia Strong seem to be getting close these days. And after the events of last night, it seems clear she's decided she can trust you. Use that."

Jasper swallowed tightly, his Adam's apple bobbing, but he said nothing. He didn't know *what* to say.

Kedis, master of body language, did not miss his hesitation. He arched a dark eyebrow at Jasper. "Need I remind you, Lieutenant, that you swore an oath to serve and protect the Galactic Union? Despite her assistance, until we reach an accord with the Coalition Miss Strong stands opposed to everything our Union holds dear."

Personally, Jasper thought that was a bit of a stretch, but he wasn't stupid enough to tell Kedis so. "I understand, sir."

"Whatever she knows, I want to know. Do whatever is necessary to get her to talk. It's obvious she's still leery about Tarynians as a whole, but it's also obvious she's coming around to your corner. I expect you to use that to your full advantage."

"Understood."

"Good." Kedis waved a hand. "Dismissed, Lieutenant."

Stone-faced, Jasper performed a sharp about-face and left the Ambassador's office, passing Kedis's staff clustered outside in the hall. He felt nauseous. He had built a fragile friendship with Lilia and what he had just been ordered to do had the potential to destroy it.

One careless word, one wrong word in the wrong ear, and she'd never speak to him again.

*She'd never* look *at me again. Not as anything other than a uniform she hates.*

Instead of heading back out into the living room, where Lon and Renner were both involved in a card game, Jasper took refuge in his room for a moment. Sinking down on the side of his bed, he leaned forward and rested his head in his hands. *What do I do?*

Lilia's face swam before him; he gritted his teeth and closed his eyes. Ignoring Kedis wasn't an option. For now, he was the Ambassador's to command—and the Ambassador had noticed his interest in Lilia.

Jasper scrubbed a hand over his face. *I can't help that. We've become friends.* He would much rather talk to her than most of the other people attending all the parties Kedis had been attending, and he was genuinely enjoying their text-only conversations.

She was smart, and funny, and he admired the sense of justice that shone through her words and actions. She was willing to put aside her fear and dislike of the G.U. if it meant saving people's lives…

…and part of him couldn't help but hope that someday he would have an answer to the mystery of her resemblance to the girl who had jumped off the roof wall of that officer's club in Challa. He'd told her before he was good with faces, and that was true.

*Her* face was burned into his memory. Jasper doubted he would ever forget the moment he'd watched her plunge to her death. And yet…she wasn't dead.

*The Ambassador's right about one thing,* he thought grimly, opening his eyes and preparing to rise to his feet. *They're definitely involved in something.*

The question was *what?*

# Chapter 43

GILES Chesnee usually considered himself a patient man. Usually. Dealing with Leo Kedis, however, was straining even his reserves. He had sent the man a report detailing what was happening to their troops on Glo'Stea—and continued to send said reports—and all Kedis had said in return was the politely worded equivalent of, "Thanks, I'll get to it when I can."

When his comm panel lit with an incoming high-priority transmission from Sta'Gloa that evening, a wave of mingled relief and exasperation flooded the Admiral. As soon as Kedis's holographic head and shoulders appeared on the other side of his desk, Chesnee fixed him with a grim, flat look. "I've been expecting to speak with you for some time now."

"My apologies, Admiral. Things have been…busy."

"I'm sure." Chesnee's tone was very dry. He had seen some of the media feeds lately; Kedis's social circuit had certainly been busy.

"You have my full and complete attention now." Kedis glanced down at something, presumably a datapad. "I've read your reports, but I need more information." He raised a long finger. "Specifically, I want to know how everyone in G.U.-held territory on Lanx and Glo'Stea is handling the cease-fire, and I want to know more about these…incidents you mention. It appears there are some anomalies."

Astonishment flooded Chesnee; he was hard-pressed to keep his expression under control. *Just when you think you have a man pegged...* Maybe—just maybe—there was more to the Ambassador's delay than met the eye.

He took his time answering, choosing his words with care. "From the reports I've seen, the general populace on both worlds, the Glo'Stean Resistance, and the Lanxian Resistance seem to have accepted the cease-fire. Our troops are also handling it well."

"But there is a malcontent presence." Kedis arched a dark eyebrow, motioning to his datapad again. "This Freedom's Children group, the ones claiming to have restored Glo'Stea's shield."

"Yes."

"And they're causing trouble?"

Chesnee grimaced. "I'd call it more than 'trouble'. They're outright *murdering* our people—and a few of their own unfortunate enough to be caught in the crossfire. Snipers, bombs...all of it done quietly, with no leads to trace back to any definite suspects. They simply seem to...disappear."

"Disappear," Kedis repeated quietly, his holographic head tilting to one side. "That, Admiral, would be the part of the reports I found most intriguing. Disappear as in they're very good at getting away, or disappear as in the kind of vanishing that can only take place with one of the Coalition's new transporters?"

Chesnee hesitated, glad he hadn't had to spell it out for the younger man. "General Deam, my ground commander on Glo'Stea, and a few of his men believe Freedom's Children is somehow utilizing one of those machines. "

"I see." Kedis nodded, his holographic face thoughtful. "That is a serious allegation, considering the Triumvirate has only admitted to two transporters existing and they are denying any involvement with Freedom's Children."

"Would you expect anything else from them?" Chesnee asked dryly.

An amused smile graced the Ambassador's face, but he did not respond to that directly. Instead, he said, "They are operating on Lanx as well?"

"It would seem so. The methods are the same." Chesnee took a deep breath. *You wanted to talk to him,* he reminded himself. *Holding anything back will not help our endangered troops.* "After making a careful study of these reports, I find myself inclined to concur with General Deam and his men—there are a number of incidents that cannot be explained any other way than via a transporter."

Kedis nodded again. "I would like to see those additional reports, Admiral. Tonight, if possible."

"I'll see that you get them." Chesnee inclined his head.

"Thank you." Kedis's lips stretched in a sharp-toothed smile. "This could be the leverage I need against the Triumvirate."

# Chapter 44

LILIA awoke in the wee hours of the morning to discover her nanites had finally unfrozen. After a mad dash to the hygiene unit, she returned to bed and pulled the covers over her head. The next time she awoke, it was close to 9 AM. It was probably selfish of her, but she was glad she'd slept so long; it delayed the inevitable conversation she faced having with her grandfather.

When she finally got dressed and ventured out of her room in search of breakfast, Lilia found Kevin sprawled in a chair in the living room, along with…She stopped short in the doorway. "Erik?"

Erik Holt glanced up from his datapad; he was comfortably installed in another armchair by the window. "Well, look who decided to grace us with her presence this mornin'."

Lilia gaped at him. "What are you doing here?"

"What does it look like?" Erik glanced at Kevin before sweeping a hand in the direction of the coffee cup sitting on an end table by his elbow. "Havin' a cup of coffee while your brother an' I discuss your next shippin' job."

"But—" Lilia looked from Erik to Kevin and back, still completely wrong-footed. "What are you doing *here*?" She jabbed a finger at the white carpet to indicate the penthouse. "You've always refused to visit us here."

"Oh, that." Erik shrugged casually. "That was before you went an' got yourself abducted. Accordin' to your grandfather, you're both—" he nodded to Kevin, "—on lockdown until further notice."

"*What?*" Her voice hit a high note that made both men wince.

"Yeah…" Kevin sat up in his chair, his expression a mixture of concern and sympathy. "Grandfather doesn't want us going anywhere by ourselves for a couple of days. Not even if we're together."

Lilia pinched the bridge of her nose between two fingers; she should have expected this. Dropping her hand, she posted both hands on her hips. "And you're *okay* with that? We've got a business to run."

Kevin shrugged. "I know we do. I just figured we'd humor him for today, since we haven't got anywhere to be until tomorrow."

Lilia took a deep breath and counted to ten. It didn't help. "I need coffee," she announced, turning on her heel and stalking through the foyer to the kitchen doorway. It was closer than taking the long way through the living room and dining room.

She found Zoë putting dishes away. "Mistress Lilia," the 'bot said in her pleasant voice. "Would you like some breakfast?"

Lilia wanted to say no—she was in no frame of mind to eat—but her stomach chose that moment to grumble loudly. "Yes, please." She got a coffee mug out of the cabinet and began filling it. "Waffles with mango sauce."

"It will be ready shortly."

After she fixed her coffee, Lilia returned to the living room. Settling into a corner of the couch, she fixed Erik with a flat stare. "Why are you really here?"

The blond Guardian met her suspicion with a bland innocence that could only mean he was hiding something. "What, you don't think I wanted a chance to get away from the ship for a while?" He glanced at Kevin. "No offense to your ship, but a man can only stand it so long."

Kevin waved his words aside.

"You've never wanted to visit before." Lilia eyed Erik over her coffee mug.

"That was before I found out that this Mastermind is apparently keepin' tabs on us." Erik shrugged again, looking supremely comfortable in his chair. "Between him an' the media, I think I'd rather deal with the media." His expression darkened. "I don't like the sound of this guy."

Lilia snorted. "You and me both." She cradled her coffee mug in her hands, letting it warm her fingers. The scrapes on her hands had healed quickly overnight; they were still sore, but not nearly as bad. Steam curled up from the hot liquid; she relished the fragrant smell. "Did Kevin tell you the story?"

"Yeah." A lopsided smile curved Erik's mouth. "He's got a hell of a recruitment strategy. Impactors, kidnappin', an' then abandonment in the streets of Sonela."

"Definitely somebody I'd want to work with." Kevin somehow managed to keep a straight face.

"Definitely," Erik agreed. "But, seriously, Lilia." His brown eyes traveled over her as though checking for injuries; it reminded her of Jasper's evaluation…except a little more clinical. "Are you sure you're all right?"

"I've got some bruises," she said honestly, pulling up her sleeves to reveal them, "but I'm okay."

"Glad to hear it." A mischievous glint came into his brown eyes. "Good thing Wright was there to patch you up."

A faint flush rose to Lilia's cheeks, but she forced herself to meet Erik's gaze. "Meaning?"

"Nothin'." The other Guardian shrugged innocently. "I'm just glad somebody was there to help you, since Lon couldn't."

Lilia shot him a glare, which Erik ignored, and tossed her head. "Yes, well, never mind that. The real question is what we're going to *do* about this."

"Nob," Kevin and Erik said at once. Erik extricated himself from his chair and rose to his feet. "He needs to know. Maybe he can shed some more light on this."

"Right now?" Lilia made a face; she wanted to at least finish her coffee and eat.

At that moment, Zoë called from the dining room, "Your breakfast is ready, Mistress Lilia."

Kevin looked amused. "After you eat, Lil. He's at work, so we'll just open channels to him."

"Technically," Erik pointed out, "you can…talk…while you eat." He gave Lilia a significant look, which she ignored.

"After breakfast," she said firmly.


Even with that, Lilia still barely tasted her waffles. In the bright sunlight streaming through the penthouse living room windows, the events of the night before had faded into something resembling a bad dream. Without the bruises and lingering aches and pains in her body, she could almost believe she'd imagined the entire evening.

Almost.

Halfway through her breakfast, Lilia jolted with a sudden lightning bolt of realization—and nearly choked on a bite of waffle. She coughed, tears coming to her eyes, and struggled to get her breathing back to normal.

Kevin and Erik both looked askance at her. Kevin raised an eyebrow. "What's the matter with you?"

Lilia shook her head, tears leaking out of the corners of her eyes, and swallowed. When she could speak, she said hoarsely, "I just realized Kedis could be in real danger."

Erik laughed. "Of *course* he's in danger. He's a Tarynian politician on Sta'Gloa."

"That's not what I meant." Lilia coughed again, setting her plate aside on an end table and glaring at Erik. "I mean that since we know for a fact that the Mastermind has got a transporter, they could literally send an assassin to Kedis's penthouse at any time and his security team would have no way of knowing they were coming."

Kevin sucked in a breath. "Just like Grandfather."

"Exactly." Lilia met his eyes. "We've got to warn Lon." She paused. "Did you talk to him last night?"

"Oh, yeah." Kevin half-smiled. "Wright told him about your visit, and then he Nancommed me when he couldn't get a hold of you."

"Did you tell him everything?"

"Yeah."

Lilia exhaled slowly, the band of tension that had formed around her chest, constricting her lungs, easing a fraction. "So this might have already occurred to him."

Kevin shrugged. "Maybe. It didn't occur to me, but I'm not the one who's liaisioning with the Tarynians."

"Okay." Lilia picked up her plate again. "I'll give him a heads up just to make sure." She suited action to words, opening a channel to their brother.

Lon answered immediately. [Are you okay?]

Lilia rolled her eyes. [I'm fine. I was just a little shaken up.]

[That's what Wright said.]

Her heart beat just a bit faster at the mention of Jasper's name. [I'm glad he was there.]

[Yeah, well, I'm sorry I wasn't.] Lon's Nancom voice turned grim. [Rest assured I've changed the emergency protocols. This won't happen again.]

[Let's hope so, on all levels.] Lilia picked up her plate again and poked at her waffles. [Listen, you may have already thought about this, but it just occurred to me that Kedis could be in a lot more danger than anybody realizes.]

[You mean because of Freedom's Children's transporter?]

*He's thought of it.* Lilia shut her eyes in relief. [Yes. Exactly. They could try something like the attempt on Grandfather's life, and Kedis's security team would—]

[—never see it coming. Yeah. That was the first thing that came to mind when Kevin told me how you'd been kidnapped.]

[I don't know how you'd guard against that.]

[Constant vigilance,] Lon said grimly. [Although the possibility of somebody using one of the Coalition's transporters to sneak up on him is on Kedis's mind too—that's one of the things we've been discussing in all these meetings with his staff and security lately.]

[Really?]

[Yeah. I've assured him Internal Affairs has them under lock and key, but he's not completely convinced. He knows how the realm of politics works better than I do.]

Lilia snorted, drawing looks from both Kevin and Erik, which she ignored. [That's a true statement.] Another thought popped into her mind; she hesitated, swallowing. [Lon...did Kevin tell you that the Mastermind doesn't think you're a candidate for recruitment?]

[He did.] Lon's Nancom voice shifted to something halfway between amusement and disgust. [Can't say I'm surprised.]

[You'd better be careful too.] Lilia bit the inside of her cheek. [He didn't sound happy about it.]

[Well, that's tough.]

[Just wanted to make sure you knew.]

[Thanks, Lil. It's okay, really. I'm keeping an eye on everything. In the meantime, you stay out of trouble and try not to get yourself kidnapped again, all right?]

Lilia sighed. [I had a feeling I wasn't going to live that down. I'll be careful.]

[You aren't. Talk to you later.]

Lon closed his channel and Lilia finished the rest of her breakfast, though she didn't have much of an appetite now.

"Well?" Kevin raised both eyebrows across the room at her, looking expectant.

"He's thought of it and he's trying to take precautions."

Erik nodded soberly. "That's the best you can do, under the circumstances."

Nob *was* working, but he took the time to listen to everything Lilia had to tell him. [Don't really have time to go into it now, but we'll talk more later tonight.]

[Not a problem,] Kevin told him. [We just wanted you to know.]

[I can tell you I don't like this,] Nob said grimly. [Not one bit.]

[Join the club,] Lilia said wryly.

Nob went back to work, and the three of them sat in the living room in brooding silence.

"We have to talk to Dr. Jayce," Lilia said at last.

Kevin and Erik both gaped at her. "What?"

"Why?"

Lilia rolled her eyes at them. "I should think that's obvious," she said tartly. "He suspects—just like we did—that Freedom's Children has a transporter. Now I've got proof."

Erik looked faintly amused. "You can't exactly *prove* it."

Lilia tossed a throw pillow from the couch at him; he ducked before it smacked his face. "You know what I mean. It'll be proof enough."

"What good does that do us, though?" Kevin folded his arms across his chest, frowning.

"He may have more information," Lilia said.

Her brother's expression grew skeptical. "He's basically under lock and key. What else could he have found?"

Lilia gave him a very dry look. "He found that information about Banx, didn't he?" She shook her head. "He definitely wasn't supposed to."

Erik absently tossed the throw pillow up into the air and caught it one-handed. "Won't hurt to tell him. If he *has* found anythin' else out, it might incline him to share."

"Exactly." Lilia withdrew her comlink from her pocket and tapped out a quick message. She didn't know how long it would take Dr. Jayce to respond, but it was a start. *Not like we have anything better to do at the moment.*

"I have a question," Kevin said abruptly.

Lilia and Erik both looked at him. Kevin was now glaring at the ceiling, his arms still folded across his chest.

"What's that?" Erik asked.

"What happens if we decide we don't want to be a part of Freedom's Children?"

Lilia bit her lip. "I don't know. The Mastermind wasn't exactly clear on that point."

Kevin unwound one arm long enough to wave a hand. "I know what you told us, Lil. But it's a rational question."

Erik snorted. "Nobody's denyin' that."

Lilia felt a chill that had nothing to do with the temperature in the living room. "I suppose we'll have to ask him when he contacts us again."

It was Erik's turn to frown. Leaning back in his chair, he locked his hands behind his head. "What makes you think he's gonna contact you? Why not the other way around?"

"Because he didn't give me any way of doing that," Lilia reminded him.

Comprehension dawned on the blond man's face. "Oh. Right. Forgot about that." He snorted again. "You'd think, though, that he'd want to get you signed on as soon as possible."

Lilia shook her head. "He's too cautious for that. I think he's willing to wait a reasonable amount of time."

"Great," Kevin muttered, still staring at the ceiling.

Erik let out a little whistle. "What is it about you two? Hesperia wants you, Freedom's Children wants you. Everybody wants you on their side."

Lilia tasted bitterness. "Probably our—"

"—connection to Grandfather," Kevin finished. "It's the only claim—"

"—to fame we've got." Lilia drew her legs up to her chest and locked her arms around them.

"Uh huh." Erik shook his head. "The fact that you've got a ship an' some common sense might have somethin' to do with it too."

"Probably just the ship," the twins said together, and Kevin finally cracked a smile. "At least, I'm pretty sure that's why *Hesperia* wants us."

Lilia tightened her grip on her legs, her fingers digging almost painfully into her skin. "If Dover is working with Freedom's Children—"

"—which she has to be," Kevin said.

"—then the Mastermind has to know we've got transporters embedded in our nanites." Lilia looked at her brother. "Aside from our political and social connections, why else would he want us?"

"You're puttin' the stock before the rifle barrel." Erik abruptly leaned forward in his seat, shaking his head again. "He probably handpicked you two to get those transporters, an' it's only now that he's approachin' you for membership."

The twins considered that, glancing back and forth between Erik and each other. "Good point," Kevin said. "But that would mean that he's—"

"—put a heck of a lot more planning into this than we realized." Lilia took a deep breath; for some reason, she felt like she couldn't get enough oxygen.

"That'd be my guess," Erik said soberly. "A plan that encompassed restorin' Glo'Stea's shield? It's probably been years in the makin'." A sudden grin split his face. "Which explains why he's not thrilled that you two helped Kedis."

Kevin rose from his chair in one fluid motion and began pacing the living room. "Which also could explain the timing. Why would he approach us *now*?"

"It must not have been time earlier," Lilia said. "It probably depended on when they activated the shield generators."

"Which may have been early than he'd planned, since it happened right after Kedis appeared at the Gala." Kevin rounded on Lilia, his violet eyes wide. "Which means somebody at the Gala is part of Freedom's Children and tipped the Mastermind off."

"That's a good theory," Erik said. "He may want you two to join up now, before you get yourselves into any more trouble."

This made Lilia laugh. "What other trouble can we get into at this point?" She spread her hands. "Look at what we've already done."

"Oh, I'm sure there's somethin' you could do." Erik did not sound as amused as he should have, under the circumstances.

Inside her pocket, Lilia's comlink buzzed. She yanked it out, fully expecting it to be Jayce messaging her back, but she had to confess a tiny part of her was hoping it was from Jasper.

It was Jayce. *Can't talk now. Meet me at our spot at 9 PM.*

Lilia relayed this information to the other two. Kevin scrubbed a hand though his hair, looking conflicted. "I don't know, Lil. Grandfather's probably going to want to talk to you tonight, since he didn't get a chance to earlier."

She shrugged. "I'll talk to him and then we can convince him we need to leave. We've got to get back to the *Talia*; we could meet Jayce from there."

"Maybe." Kevin sounded skeptical.

*What is his problem?* Lilia narrowed her eyes at him. "If you're worried about Freedom's Children coming after me again, I don't think you need to. The Mastermind wanted me to talk you, Michael, and Derek into joining me, remember? I think he'd realize that might take a while."

"It's not that, per se."

Erik regarded him with frank curiosity. "Then what is it?"

"I just had a rather disturbing thought." Kevin glanced at them both in turn, his face sober. "What if Freedom's Children and Hesperia are working together?"

Lilia blinked at him, nonplussed. "What do you mean, working together?"

"Look at the lengths Hesperia has gone to, trying to get us to join them." Kevin threw his arms wide. "What if this Mastermind is the brains behind all of it, and this is just another approach?"

Silence reigned in the living room while Lilia and Erik digested this.

"As theories go," Erik drawled at last, "it's not a bad one." He raised platinum blond eyebrows at Kevin. "I think you're reachin' a bit too far, but I guess it's not outside the realm of reality."

Unfolding herself, Lilia rose to her feet as well. "Hesperia wants our ship, Kev," she said flatly. "Freedom's Children wants *us*. There's a difference."

Kevin shrugged. "I'm just saying it's a possibility."

# CHAPTER 45

THINGS were relatively quiet for the next week. Surprisingly, Lilia's conversation with her grandfather was not as grueling as she had anticipated, and he lifted his rather stringent security lockdown. Though everyone remained on high alert, nothing out of the ordinary occurred. Lilia, Kevin, and Erik departed for their usual off-world shipping runs, and returned without incident. Lilia even returned to *Sal's* without incident, though Kevin refused to let her go alone. Lilia hadn't told Alexis about the kidnapping…and she hadn't decided if she would or not.

Thursday evening found them at the spaceport. They'd made a run to Lanx, transporting a load of antique furniture for a Lanxian businessman, and the twins hadn't felt like leaving the *Talia* to return to Ferndale. Kevin was in the galley, fixing himself a snack, Erik was idly watching the news on the holoprojector in the living compartment, and Lilia was sprawled out on the couch across from his chair having her nightly conversation with Jasper.

"Who are you talkin' to?"

Lilia glanced up from her comlink to find Erik watching her. "Friend of mine," she said casually, belying the way her heart had just skipped a beat. "Why?"

The blond Guardian shrugged. "Just curious." He tipped his head toward her. "You've been spendin' an awful lot of time on that thing lately."

"I've had a lot to do." Her comlink vibrated in her fingers with. Jasper's response to her latest message, but Lilia didn't look at it yet. *Please don't ask any more questions*, she begged Erik silently. *Not now.*

*She* wasn't even sure she could categorize the friendship she'd been forming with Jasper, let alone try to explain it to someone else.

It was not to be.

Erik lifted a pale blond eyebrow. "So who is it? Anybody I know?"

Lilia sucked in a breath, considering her options. She could tell him…or she could not. Either way, she'd have to face the consequences. *What would I rather deal with?*

She matched Erik's raised eyebrow with a look of her own. "Why so curious all of a sudden? Are you bored? Do I ask you who *you're* talking to?"

Erik gave her a small nod in acknowledgment of her point, but continued to scrutinize her. "You were smilin' an' lookin' like you're enjoyin' yourself." Shrugging, he leaned back in his seat and locked his hands behind his head. "Just wanted to know who was responsible for it, that's all."

Lilia bit the inside of her lip. She *had* been enjoying the conversation. *Didn't realize it was that obvious.*

"It's Wright, isn't it?"

Her eyes flew up to meet Erik's too-knowing gaze. A smirk tugged at his lips. "I'm right, aren't I?" He didn't wait for her to answer, but nodded to himself. "Figured as much."

Caught off-guard, Lilia struggled to keep her expression neutral. Panic fluttered in her chest, though she wasn't sure why. It wasn't like they were doing anything wrong. "What are you talking about?"

Erik snorted in amusement. "He's the logical choice. Unless you've got close friends I don't know about." He eyed her again, before apparently deciding that couldn't be the case and leaning his head back to stare up at the overhead, holoprojector forgotten. "You'd Nancom your brothers if you needed to talk to them, an' Alexis is still workin' at this time of night."

He was right—but Lilia wasn't about to actually *tell* him that. Her attention, however, snagged on that last part of his statement.

"Alexis is usually still working at this time of night?" It was her turn to raise a questioning eyebrow. "And just how do you know that?"

"Simple observation," Erik replied smoothly, still staring up at the overhead.

Lilia thought she saw a faint flush rise in his cheeks and leaned forward, her curiosity piqued. "How often *are* you at *Sal's*, anyway?"

"Not often." Erik gave a deliberately casual shrug. "I'm on this ship most of time. Usually only when I'm with you or Kevin."

"Uh huh." Lilia arched her eyebrow again. "And you just *happened* to note her work schedule?" She was torn between amusement and concern. Amusement because it was funny to see Erik acting this way…and concern because he wasn't a believer and Alexis *was*.

"Somethin' like that," Erik said airily.

Silence fell over the compartment, but a few moments later Erik broke it. "Be careful."

"Hmm?" Lilia glanced over at him, unsure she'd heard that correctly. Her attention had been elsewhere.

"I said be careful." All traces of levity were gone from his expression. "Doesn't matter how nice he is or how well he kisses—"

"It's not like that!" Lilia protested, a hot flush rising to her cheeks.

"—at the end of the day, he's still a Tarynian."

"He's G.U., not Tarynian." Lilia couldn't help herself; Jasper had made that point crystal clear. Not all G.U. soldiers were actually from Taryn.

"G.U. Whatever." Erik brushed that aside with a flick of his finger. "Point is, he's not Coalition—which will *not* go over well in many quarters, let me tell ya—an' he's a soldier to boot." His brown eyes grew sympathetic, but entirely unapologetic. "Sooner or later, he's goin' to leave. They'll station him somewhere else, maybe even halfway across the galaxy."

"Wow." Lilia blinked at him, hard-pressed to keep from gaping. "You've, uh, really thought this out."

"An' you haven't."

That *stung*, though she couldn't immediately pinpoint *why*. She sat up on the couch, indignant. "Excuse me?"

Erik shrugged prosaically. "You haven't thought it through."

For a moment, words failed Lilia; her astonishment was too great. Finally, she found her voice. "Erik, you're being ridiculous."

"Am I?"

"Jasper and I are *friends*." She stressed the word. "Nothing more."

"Maybe that's all it is in *your* mind, but I can guarantee that ain't the only thing on *his* mind."

Exasperation conquered astonishment, and Lilia rolled her eyes. "We're *friends*, Erik. He still thinks I'm his suicide jumper, but we don't talk about it."

"You talk about everythin' else."

"Well, yeah." Lilia shot him a puzzled look. "That's what friends *do*."

"An' you dance with him at those fancy parties, an' all the tabloids think you're an item."

A hot flush rose in Lilia's cheeks again. "They'd think that regardless," she said flatly, scowling at Erik. "I could have never spoken to him again after the Gala and they'd still think we're having a torrid love affair."

Erik looked torn between amusement and concern. "It's a great story. Star-crossed lovers, an' all that." He waved his hand again. "The Coalition Representative's granddaughter an' the G.U. lieutenant."

"Oh, good grief." Lilia rolled her eyes again. "Give it a rest, Erik."

"Promise me you won't let him break your heart." Erik flexed his fingers. "Because, unfortunately, due to that whole diplomatic immunity thing, your brothers an' I may not be able to break his face if he hurts you."

"Erik." An incredulous laugh bubbled up in Lilia's throat, but she swallowed it and pinned him with an exasperated glare instead. *Only in my life.* "I appreciate your concern, but it's not necessary. Jasper is my friend, nothing more." She shook her head. "And in the… unlikely event that that were to change and he did break my heart, I'm more than capable of handling it myself."

"'Course you are." Erik nodded solemnly. "But you gotta understand, it's a brotherly duty to take care of idiots."

This time, imagining Jasper facing off against all of her brothers plus Erik, Lilia couldn't restrain her laughter. "That's hardly a fair fight."

"Not sure some fights *should* be fair," Erik said darkly. He turned his attention back to the holoprojector. "Just be careful. That's all I'm sayin'."

"I'll take it into consideration." Her comlink began vibrating in her fingers with an incoming call; Lilia glanced down at it and felt a little jolt run through her body. Jasper was *calling* her. Apparently, messaging back and forth wasn't enough.

Feeling heat rise to her cheeks again, Lilia slid off the couch and made her way out of the living compartment, trying to move as nonchalantly as possible. She didn't look at Erik as she raised her comlink to her ear. "Hello?"

"I hope you don't mind that I'm calling," Jasper said. "I thought our conversation might be better if we could actually talk."

"No, that's…that's quite all right." Lilia stepped into her cabin and closed the hatch behind her. "Lights, on, low." She sank down on her bunk, her heart thumping.

"You asked me what the hardest thing about this assignment is."

Lilia nodded, even though he couldn't see her. It had been the last question she asked before Erik interrupted. "I did."

"I would have to say it was leaving my church family in Challa behind," Jasper said thoughtfully.

*His church family in Challa?* Lilia blinked, too surprised to filter her next words. "I wouldn't have thought you'd have found much of a church family in Challa."

"There *are* churches there too, you know."

She flushed at the faint amusement in his voice. That hadn't been what she meant. "Of course, Challa has churches. I—" She stopped herself. Perhaps it was best that she didn't actually *say* what she'd been thinking.

Jasper seemed to understand anyway. "Ah." He was silent for a few seconds. "You meant churches that would accept a G.U. soldier as a brother."

Lilia's flush deepened, heat crawling up her neck. She was profoundly grateful he couldn't see her. "I don't mean the churches. I mean, the medcenter where I last worked on Glo'Stea was one of the few places that would accept wounded G.U. POWs. I just—" Her face continue to flame, but she forged ahead. *In for a grain, in for an ounce.* "I wouldn't have thought a G.U. soldier would have found a church *family* there, that's all."

Not with the bitterness most people held toward the G.U.— even people like her, who called themselves Christians but hadn't quite been able to let go of that bitterness and forgive the invaders for everything they'd done.

Lilia swallowed, staring down at the gray metal deck beneath her feet. *I've come a long way though.*

It had helped to have human faces to assign to those formerly faceless, nameless Tarynian invaders.

She could almost see Jasper shrug. "They got to know me. It took time, of course, but I was always there for church whenever I wasn't on duty. Eventually, they realized I wasn't a monster, and I realized a few things about them too." His voice grew quiet. "Being a follower of Jesus Christ transcends everything else."

Lilia pursed her lips, knowing he was right, and yet…"Maybe it *should* transcend everything else. That doesn't mean that it does. Or that it's easy."

Jasper chuckled warmly. "Of course it's not easy. If it was easy, we wouldn't have scripture verses that talk about the way being narrow."

"True."

"What about you? What is your church family like?"

He'd assumed she *had* one. Lilia bit her lip, uncomfortable and not entirely sure why. The truth was…she didn't exactly have a church family. Not like the interconnected support system of prayer, encouragement, and friendship Jasper had just described.

"My church family…is a lot smaller." She would have preferred to leave it at that, suddenly embarrassed, but she knew by now he wouldn't let it go. Jasper would ask questions and prod—all out of genuine interest—until he got the answers he wanted.

It was a persistent quality she simultaneously admired and disliked about him.

"Grandmother and Grandfather always took us to church growing up, but it was hard to really be involved in anything because we kept moving back and forth between Sta'Gloa and Glo'Stea for Triumvirate sessions." Lilia took a deep breath and exhaled slowly. "I think the closest thing I've had to a church family was my Bible study group on Kyman."

"Do you miss them?"

"Yes." A soft, wistful smile played over her face as she thought back to those months she'd spent on Kyman. "But that phase of my life is over. I'm not supposed to be there anymore."

"That is understandable. What about here in Sonela?"

Uncomfortable again, Lilia hunched her shoulders. "It's different here. We've—I've been gone a long time. Grandfather still attends the same church, but things are different. People are different." The words felt stuck in her throat; it was difficult to get them out. "I don't feel like I belong. Everybody's got their own little groups and their own friends, and I've always gotten the impression they don't have room for anybody else."

It felt strange to say these words aloud; she had never done that before.

Jasper was silent for a moment. Then he said, "So you don't feel very welcomed."

"Not really. It's like being on the outside looking in." It was a bittersweet sensation, being in the midst of a crowd of people gathered in the sanctuary to praise God together, and yet feeling alone.

"What about your friend Alexis?"

Lilia sighed. "Her family goes to a different church. And, yes, before you ask, I've visited a few times, but it feels weird to not go with Grandfather and my brothers."

"And does maintaining your grandfather's image figure into that?"

Lilia reared back at the blunt question. "You don't pull any punches, do you?"

"It…is an obvious question."

"Yeah…I guess it is." Abandoning her bunk, Lilia began pacing the confines of her cabin. "Yes, no…I don't know. Maybe. Grandmother always tried to shield us from the media side of Grandfather's political life, but we've always known we were under a microscope."

She ran a hand through her still too-short hair. "I suppose that was one of the most freeing things about being on Glo'Stea. The blockade had been going on for so long that nobody in the media cared what went on in the fringes anymore. It didn't matter who we were related to as long as we did our jobs."

"And being back on Sta'Gloa?" Jasper asked.

"It's—" *Smothering*, Lilia realized, breaking off. *But that's our own fault. We went and helped a G.U. Ambassador.* "It's different," she finished lamely. "Very different."

"I'd like to visit your church," Jasper said after a moment.

This startled a laugh out of Lilia. "Why?"

"For comparison. To see if your church is really that cold towards newcomers, or if it's something else."

For some reason, that stung. Lilia posted a hand on her hip, narrowing her eyes at the bulkhead without seeing it. "You mean something like me being stand-offish and intimidating?"

"I did not say that." Jasper's tone was mild.

"That's what you meant, though, isn't it?"

"Lilia—"

"I'm always polite. I'm friendly. I smile at people." Words bubbled up out of Lilia as she continued to pace, giving voice to thoughts and emotions she hadn't even realized she'd been harboring. "Most of them smile back." She waved her arms in the air, narrowly missing smacking her hand into the bunk above hers. "But I *still* don't belong."

Another pause, and then Jasper said dryly, "You haven't needed to talk about this at all."

Lilia laughed again, despite herself, and rubbed the back of her neck. "Maybe a little."

"Uh huh." She could hear the smile in his voice.

"I mean it, though. I've always felt like an outsider there."

"Maybe you're not supposed to be there. Churches have personalities too, you know, and sometimes they don't mesh with individuals."

Lilia had never considered that before. "You know," she said slowly, "that explains a lot. I'll have to think about it."

"Do that." A smile carried through his voice. "On a completely unrelated note, will you and you family be attending an event being hosted at the Wycliffe Hotel Saturday evening?"

Lilia snorted softly. "I'll have to be there. There'll be no getting out of it." She made a wry face, though Jasper couldn't see her. "Not where Madame Olga is concerned."

"I remember meeting her at the Gala. She seems a…formidable woman."

"Oh, she is. And not necessarily in a good way."

"And yet everyone attends her parties."

Lilia grimaced. "I suppose it's one of those things that are all about caché. Apparently, she's got enough pull in society that snubbing her is not something most people want to do."

Jasper considered this for a few seconds. "It is fascinating how the upper echelons work."

"Yeah." Lilia rested her back against her hatch, curling her free arm around herself. "We can't avoid it now, because of Grandfather and, well…everything…but I don't think I'd want to spend the rest of my life running in these circles."

"Too high-stratosphere for you?" Jasper asked wryly.

Lilia stared down at her boots; the toes were slightly scuffed. "Something like that."

"You handle it well, I must say." His tone turned teasing. "If I didn't know better, I'd think you were born for that kind of life. Maybe you should seriously consider Representative Urquart's suggestion."

Her cheeks warmed. "Yes, well, that would mean spending a lot more time around these types of people and I'm not sure that's where I'm supposed to be."

"It's just a thought." Jasper tactfully changed the subject, but he did not stray far from it. "Have you ever thought about what you will do with the rest of your life? Do you plan to work with your brother forever?"

Lilia laughed. "Forever is an awfully long time, Lieutenant."

"You know what I mean."

Closing her eyes, Lilia pictured the exasperated look on his face and continued to laugh. After a moment, however, she sobered. "I don't know that I'll do it forever. I mean," she shrugged, "at some point one of us might get married, and that would change things."

"Marriage does tend to do that, from what I understand," Jasper agreed, tongue-in-cheek.

"At any rate," Lilia rolled her eyes, "I suppose the proper answer to your question is that I don't know. Maybe Erik will want to work for us full-time after all of this is said and done, and that will free me up to do something else. Maybe we'll expand." She propped one elbow on her knee and rested her cheek in her hand. "I suppose it really depends on what happens between the G.U. and the Coalition."

On the other end of the comlink, Jasper grew solemn. "I believe you are correct."

He paused, and Lilia had the sudden sense that their chat had come to an end. She bit her lip, realizing she wasn't ready for that yet. *There are still things I haven't gotten the chance to tell him.* Small things, mostly from earlier in the day—things she had found amusing and thought she might share.

"I'm sorry," Jasper said, "I've got to go."

"I understand." Lilia forced a smile into her voice. "Have a good evening."

"You too." His voice deepened. "I enjoyed talking to you."

Her smile softened into something genuine. "Likewise."

Jasper ended the call and Lilia continued to lean up against her door for a moment, a trifle disappointed. *Oh, well,* she told herself, straightening and preparing to rejoin Kevin and Erik in the living compartment. *It's not like you won't see him on Saturday.*

# CHAPTER 46

THOUGH it was sad to say, as far as Aiden was concerned, the day's Triumvirate session had not really begun until Ambassador Kedis's arrival late that afternoon. All they had managed to accomplish was another round of squabbling that led nowhere. Oh, there had been a few good arguments made about the Coalition's future, but with no new leads or information on any of the fronts currently facing them, the day had felt like an impotent waste.

That all changed the moment Kedis stepped into the Chamber and took his place near the Chairman's podium.

Septien Yu, of Sta'Gloa's Sector 7, now presided as Chairman; the Triumvirate had begun a new term and had chosen a new Chairman. A short, slim man with slanted dark eyes, pin-straight hair, and a rather large nose, Yu was known throughout his Sector for being a passionate advocate for causes he supported. Now, he tapped his bell and ran through the Triumvirate's customary formal greeting of the Ambassador.

It was a speech they could now all quote word for word. There were times Aiden wished they could dispense with some of their usual formality and this one was one of them.

Kedis made his customary bow to the Triumvirate, but before he could so much as open his mouth, Representative Nakuruma Minoru, of Glo'Stea's Sector 1, rose to his feet. He was tall and slender, with shrewd almond eyes that were narrowed at Kedis in a challenge. One of the younger members of the Triumvirate, he tended to dress in dark grays and blues that dramatically set off his light skin and wavy black hair.

Tapping his gold bell, Septien Yu recognized the Representative…and Minoru went straight for the jugular.

"Ambassador Kedis, when will the G.U. withdraw their forces currently occupying sections of my homeworld?"

A short, stunned silence greeted these words.

Then, from the Lanxian section, portly Nolan Snyder rumbled, "And mine."

Kedis bowed politely in Nakuruma's direction, before spreading his hands in an apologetic gesture. "I am afraid that it is neither part of the cease-fire nor our peace negotiations. Rather, it falls under the purview of a trade—"

"You removed the ships around the mining stations." Martin Hollowell's voice cracked through the Chamber like a whip.

Kedis's dark eyes flicked to him. "Yes, I did." He spread his hands again. "*That* I could control. An operation of such long-standing as the G.U. bases on Glo'Stea?" He shook his head. "That is far more complicated."

In the Lanxian section, Oded Xerxes—who had been voted in by the people of Sector 2 to replace Katya Vogel as their Representative after Vogel died in the explosion that had rocked the Tri-World Tournament's Opening Gala—rose to his feet. He was a tall man of medium build and a dark olive complexion, with dark, short-cropped curly hair and an impeccably groomed goatee.

Septien Yu tapped his bell. "The Triumvirate recognizes Representative Xerxes."

"Ambassador, the G.U. installations on Lanx are only a few months old. What of them?" Xerxes raised his eyebrows in a polite challenge, straightening the cuff of his white suit jacket. "What stands in the way of *their* removal?"

It seemed to Aiden that the Triumvirate held their collective breath at this. His green eyes darted back and forth between Kedis and the Representative. *How* will *Kedis handle this?*

By way of answering, Kedis held out his hands. "The blockade around the mining stations was a relatively straightforward matter— and its removal was a show of good faith on our part." He lifted his shoulders in a shrug. "I am afraid the removal of troops from Lanx is also a much more complicated matter than a simple cessation of hostilities can address."

*In other words*, Aiden thought shrewdly, *you have no intention of removing any troops until you get what you want.*

Which was, at the very least, a trade agreement.

Xerxes dramatically threw his hands into the air. "If you cannot authorize something that would truly show the Coalition that the Galactic Union is interested in peace, of what use *are* you, Ambassador?"

The hair on the back of Aiden's neck prickled. He could have sworn something like triumph glinted in Kedis's dark eyes, as though he had been waiting for just such an opening.

The G.U. Ambassador took his time answering. He studied Xerxes for a long moment, locking his hands behind his back. When the first stirrings of restless unease began to rustle through the semicircle of men and women facing him, he said softly, "Of what use am I?"

He laughed once, a polite expression of incredulity. "We have a cease-fire, do we not? Coalition lives are being spared while we attempt to find peaceful middle ground."

"In fact," Kedis continued, so smoothly that it took a second for the full weight of his words to penetrate, "G.U. lives are the ones still being lost in this situation, despite the cease-fire."

Silence fell over the Chamber like the swing of an executioner's ax.

Xerxes looked momentarily taken aback, but Aiden, happening to glance at the Lanxian Representative at just the right moment, thought he looked peculiarly as though this knowledge did not surprise him—only that it astonished him that Kedis dared to mention it. Narrowing his eyes, Aiden made a mental note to investigate later. Clearly, something was going on in occupied territory that was not being reported to the Triumvirate at large.

Kedis shifted his gaze between the Glo'Stean section and the Lanxian section. "Isn't it true, ladies and gentlemen, that near-daily attacks are being carried out against G.U. soldiers in occupied territory on both Glo'Stea *and* Lanx, despite the cease-fire?"

When no one gave an immediate response, Kedis tilted a dark eyebrow at Xerxes. "Well?"

"We are aware there have been some…difficulties," Xerxes conceded stiffly. "Small…dustups, here and there."

"Difficulties? *Dustups?*" Kedis's eyebrows climbed higher. "Those are wonderful political designations for it. I assure you Admiral Chesnee would phrase it differently." Withdrawing a datapad from his breast pocket, brandished it. "I have all of the data, should any of you wish to peruse it."

An edge slid into his voice. "Since the cease-fire was implemented, over a hundred G.U. soldiers have lost their lives in attacks from an unknown person or group. They have been picked off by snipers, they have been blown up by hidden bombs. And, thanks to the cease-fire, they *have not retaliated.* In addition, twenty-two Glo'Stean and Lanxian citizens have lost their lives to those same bombs."

Anger curled Kedis's lip. "I believe that shows a good more faith than the Coalition has extended thus far. And you demand to know why our troops have not been removed completely?"

Sick horror pooled in the pit of Aiden's stomach. He was aware there was unrest, but the exact specifics of what was happening in occupied territory had never been disclosed. *And they should have been.* Beneath the lip of the table, his hands tightened into fists. *I cannot be the only one who was unaware of this.*

Just as Xerxes could not have been the only Representative who knew. He was from *Lanx*, for heaven's sake.

Martin Hollowell stirred in his seat, but it was Egan Ashford who spoke. "At the risk of sounding pedantic, Ambassador, your troops would not be dead if they had not been on Glo'Stea or Lanx."

Uneasy murmurs greeted this pronouncement.

Ashford held up a gnarled hand before Kedis could speak. "I am not condoning murder. I merely wish to remind you that over two decades of bad blood exists between our people in various quarters, and revenge is a strong motivator—particularly when it sees an opportunity to express itself."

"It does not change the fact that you should have better control of your people," Kedis shot back.

Aiden refrained from shaking his head. *That was a tactical mistake.*

"Ambassador," Egan Ashford said dryly, a sardonic smile curving his wrinkled face, "the Coalition has not had control of its citizens in occupied territory since the blockade began."

Kedis did look frustrated then—a momentary flash, more with himself than anything else. He inclined his head. "Point granted." He raised his head. "However, that does bring me to another point. Admiral Chesnee has attempted to withdraw troops, and Glo'Stea's Shield Controls have categorically refused to allow them egress through the shield."

"It is not so pleasant to be trapped on a world, now is it?" Dion Pamos drawled from his place a few seats down from Aiden.

A few snickers traveled around the Chamber.

"Also…" Shane Briscoe rose and was recognized. "G. U. troops being allowed ingress and egress through the shield is not part of the cease-fire." He paused. "To use your own words, Ambassador, it is a more…complicated matter than that."

Aiden wanted to laugh at the Ambassador's excuses being used against him, but he swallowed it. He did, however, allow himself to share an amused look with Kane Fenton beside him.

Kedis accepted this with relatively good grace, acknowledging Briscoe's jibe with a bow and a rueful smile. "Touché, Representative." He held out his hands once more. "It would seem we both have pressing concerns. You wish all G. U. troops to be removed from Coalition soil—"

"And space," someone said loudly.

"—and space," Kedis continued without missing a beat, "while the G.U. would like our troops to be able to pass through Glo'Stea's shield. Surely we can come to some sort of arrangement."

"I am sure, Ambassador Kedis," Helen Urquart said tartly, "that Glo'Stea would not object to allowing your troops to depart once they've all packed up for good." She cocked a wry gray eyebrow at him. "But of course, that is not what you have in mind, is it?"

"Sadly, Representative," Kedis offered her a bow, "I cannot extend that offer. Not with the way things presently stand."

"Well," Devlin Vance said unexpectedly, "then they're likely to remain the same, since you have no intentions of conceding anything, Ambassador."

Kedis glanced at the Glo'Stean Chief Minister, apparently caught a little off-guard by his sudden intervention.

Before he could formulate a reply, however, Vance slapped his holographic hands against the table and stood. "Ladies and gentlemen of the Triumvirate, I move that we end things here today." He cast a glance around. "It is past time, and I believe we could all use some time to ponder today's discussion." He gave Kedis a significant look that spoke volumes.

"Seconded." Martin Hollowell raised a hand.

Ambassador Kedis drew himself up to his full height. "I thank you for your consideration." With that, he marched across the Chamber to the wide double doors.

When he had gone, Septien Yu glanced from the Chief Ministers to the rest of the Triumvirate and then tapped his gold bell. "This session of the Triumvirate is now adjourned."

A rush of muted conversation filled the Chamber. Aiden sat for a moment, contemplating the spot where Kedis had stood, and then he glanced sideways at Kane Fenton. "Did you know?"

Fenton grasped his meaning immediately. "About the attacks on G.U. soldiers?" He shook his head, looking grim. "I'd heard rumors that things weren't as peaceable as we had hoped, but no particulars." He suddenly looked very tired. "I'll be speaking to my fellow Directors—that's not information they should have…neglected to pass along."

Aiden nodded, feeling weariness settle over his own shoulders like a heavy mantle. He waved one hand to indicate the Chamber. "Even with this information, the essential foundation of our respective arguments have not changed. We continue to remain at an impasse."

"Yes." Fenton sighed. "And I can't say I'm looking forward to arguing in circles for the next few weeks, or months, or however long Kedis remains with us."

"Neither am I." Slowly, Aiden rose from his chair. "Something will have to change, but I must admit I see no possibility of that at present."

"You're not the only one." Fenton snorted grimly, casting a sober look at their colleagues, who had begun to file out of the Chamber. "Cease-fire or no cease-fire, we can't keep on like this indefinitely."

# CHAPTER 47

S ATURDAY evening arrived with more alacrity than Lilia would have expected. The last party of Madame Olga's that she had attended was the birthday party the older woman had thrown for Martin Hollowell six months earlier. *You'd think him not showing an iota of interest in all this time would deter her,* Lilia thought wryly, as she allowed Jenson to help her out of the skimmer and she stepped forward to take her grandfather's arm.

"I feel like we've done this before," she joked quietly, pasting a polite smile on her face for the cams awaiting them.

"It would seem Olga favors the Wycliffe Hotel," her grandfather agreed, raising a hand in polite greeting to the media crews crowding either side of the cordoned-off walkway leading up to the hotel's grand entrance. He had decided to forego his hoverchair for the evening.

On par with the Beliana, which stood halfway across Sonela's business district, the Wycliffe Hotel was a sleek, forty-story building that boasted a ballroom on the top floor. Lilia focused on not tripping on the hem of her emerald green evening gown as they made their way past the doormen into the hotel lobby and followed a velvet-roped path to an accelevator bank. Her brothers brought up the rear, and the five of them crowded into an accelevator, which whisked them up to the ballroom.

When the doors opened and they stepped out, Lilia cast a critical glance around, taking in the similarities and the differences between this and Hollowell's birthday party. The room was large and square, with high windows. Madame Olga had decorated with Coalition colors—sapphire blue, emerald green, and gold—and threaded the Galactic Union's signature red and black in for good measure.

Black tablecloths covered the round tables scattered around the edges of the room, leaving plenty of space for a dance floor and a string quartet playing on a stage behind it, and the buffet tables were also draped in black. Bright splashes of color in the form of flowers and ribbons kept things from looking somber, and entwined streamers were strung from the ceiling to form an airy canopy through which the ballroom's glittering chandelier cast its refracted light.

The effect was…quite stunning. Lilia leaned close to Aiden. "She's outdone herself as far as the decorations go, I think."

"I believe you are correct," he said in a low voice. "The effect is quite pleasing."

Lilia scanned the knots of people already scattered across the ballroom floor, searching for a familiar face. Disappointment welled in her throat; Jasper wasn't here yet. Neither was Kedis, as far as she could tell. She forced herself to maintain a placid expression. *Calm down. He'll be here soon.*

Kedis probably wanted to make an entrance, since he was the guest of honor.

"Brace yourself," Aiden murmured, just as the clump of people ahead of them split apart and Madame Olga glided forward to greet them.

Their hostess was resplendent in a black gown with gauzy black wrist-length sleeves that sparkled when the light caught them. An airy sash made of gold, sapphire blue, and emerald green material looped over one shoulder and tied at her waist, leaving the ends to trail free. She wore her still-dark hair up, with the front parts folded like wings, but Lilia thought she glimpsed a ruby pin set in the older woman's hair as she descended upon them.

"Aiden! How good to see you up and about again!" Madame Olga held out both hands to him, a smile lighting her rosy cheeks; he dropped Lilia's arm and bent obligingly over her hands.

"Olga. Thank you for your invitation." Aiden gestured to the ballroom. "It would appear you have outdone yourself once again."

Madame Olga simpered like a teenager. "You're too kind, Aiden." She turned her attention to Lilia and her brothers. "I'm glad you could make it as well."

Lilia curtseyed; her brothers bowed. None of them mentioned the fact that they had all recently attended the same party the week before. That wasn't how the game was played.

"Well, I dare say you'll find some familiar faces already here." Madame Olga's dark eyes glittered in Michael's direction. "Representative Briscoe and his family arrived a few moments before you."

Out of the corner of her eye, Lilia saw the tips of Michael's ears turn a little pink, but he bowed gravely to their hostess once more.

"And as for you…" Madame Olga turned her attention to Lilia. "I'm afraid I have some bad news." She dropped her voice a little, leaning toward Lilia. "It would seem you've lost your chance with Alan Birch. I understand he's off the market."

Lilia stared at her, hard-pressed not to laugh. The idea that she and Birch could be compatible in any way, shape, or form existed solely in Madame Olga's head. "I think I'll survive."

"That's the spirit, my dear. Put a brave face on." Madame Olga sighed theatrically, pulling a colorful, ornate fan from a pocket and opening it with a flick of her wrist. Her dark eyes, however, were sharp and still focused on Lilia. "The Ambassador and his escorts have yet to arrive."

For a second, Lilia froze in place, uncertain what the older woman was implying. She felt hot and cold by turns. *Has she* noticed *something? But we're only friends—and we've been discreet.*

Before Lilia could fumble for words, Aiden swiftly intervened. "Madame Olga," he said evenly, "I would prefer it if you would refrain from playing matchmaker with my grandchildren's lives."

"Oh, you." Trilling a laugh, Madame Olga snapped her fan closed and gently tapped Aiden's chest with it. "It's hard watching them grow up and letting go, isn't it?" She flicked the fan back open with a smile. "Enjoy your evening. If you'll excuse me?"

"Certainly." Aiden stepped aside and Madame Olga flowed forward to greet more new arrivals.

Kevin nudged Lilia with his arm. "At least she's given up on Birch now."

Lilia rolled her eyes heavenward. "Thank God." She fell in step with her twin as they followed Aiden farther into the ballroom, pausing now and then to greet people they knew. She switched to Nancom. [Isn't it interesting how we're starting to get to know people here?]

[Yeah. Not just a sea of nameless faces anymore.]

It was the strangest feeling. Lilia could remember the first time she'd attended one of these events—it had been Uncle Martin's birthday party, come to think of it—and how strange and overwhelming the glittering sea of people had been. Now she could list a number of the guests in attendance tonight by name.

Waiters bearing trays of champagne and other assorted drinks, as well as trays of hors d'oeuvres were circulating through the swelling crowd of people. A band on a stage in one corner played well-known pieces of music composed by Lanxians, Glo'Steans, and Sta'Gloans alike. Lilia accepted a long-stemmed glass of sparkling fruit juice and listened to the snatches of music audible over the rise and fall of several hundred conversations.

She glanced sideways at Kevin, an impish smile tugging at the corners of her mouth. [I wonder if Madame Olga has requested any Tarynian music.]

Kevin almost choked on the sip of champagne he'd just taken. [That would be gutsy of her.] He swallowed and coughed. [Don't think it's likely, though.]

[Because of Uncle—]

[Martin? Yeah. She knows where he stands on the spectrum, and I think she likes him too much to—]

[—attempt to curry *that* much favor with Kedis?]

[Pretty much.]

[Makes sense.] Lilia raised her glass to her lips again, her gaze sweeping the ballroom for familiar figures with whom she'd actually want to hold a conversation right now. There weren't many names on that list. She swallowed, already resigning herself to the inevitable fact that she would be talking to a lot of people she didn't want to talk to tonight.

*Thank you, NCDC Board,* she thought grimly.

[Lil...]

She glanced sideways at her brother; he sounded hesitant. It was only then that she realized he'd spoken inside her mind. [What?]

[Why was Madame Olga telling you Kedis isn't here yet?]

[What?] Lilia blinked at him, even as her heart skipped a beat.

Kevin nodded in the general direction of the entrance. [She made a point of telling you that after she mentioned Birch.]

Lilia raised a skeptical eyebrow. [I don't think she's trying to set me up with Kedis, if that's what you're implying.]

Kevin didn't bite. [You don't think she's taken those rumors about you and Wright seriously, do you?]

[Who knows?] Lilia twitched her shoulders in a tiny shrug. [We're friends. That shouldn't be cause for alarm.]

It was Kevin's turn to raise his eyebrows at her. [Friends, huh?]

His Nancom voice was entirely too knowing for her liking. Lilia started to retort that he should know better, but before she could say anything, a sudden hush fell over the ballroom. Conversations abruptly broke off, and a rustling sound swept around the giant room as everyone turned to look at the double doors leading into the ballroom.

Ambassador Kedis had arrived.

Her heels gave her a boost, but Lilia raised herself up onto her tiptoes anyway in a vain attempt to see over the other guests' heads. It was fruitless; there were too many bodies between her and the entrance. Her heart skipped another beat in anticipation—if Kedis was here, then Jasper was here—before settling into calm excitement. She clamped down on the smile threatening to engulf her face.

If Jasper was here, he'd find her.

Because that's what friends did when they were trapped at an event like this.


Half an hour later, Lilia and Jasper had still not crossed paths. She wasn't terribly worried—Madame Olga's guest list was *massive*, and Jasper had to stay close to Kedis as the Ambassador made his rounds. They'd meet eventually; if there was one thing she'd learned over the past few weeks, it was that the two of them tended to gravitate toward each other.

In the meantime, she made small talk with the people around her. Some of it was mind-numbingly boring and she escaped as soon as she possibly could, drifting away to another clump of people, but she also had a fascinating conversation on current events along the fringes of formerly occupied territory with the wife of one of Representative Egan Ashford's staff.

Lilia kept her eyes peeled for anything out of the ordinary, any strange behavior that could indicate someone had infiltrated the party bent on causing trouble, but everything seemed normal. *It's just another boring party.* She snagged a second glass of fruit juice, mentally shaking her head at her own paranoia. *Just because the Mastermind has a transporter and* could *attack Kedis at something like this doesn't mean he will.*

It would mean giving away his secret to the entire galaxy. Call it a gut feeling, but she didn't think he was ready to lose the element of surprise yet.

Sensing movement to her left, Lilia turned in time to find herself face-to-face with Jasper. As usual, he wore his military dress uniform. He greeted her with a dazzling smile that crinkled the corners of his eyes.

"Good evening, Miss Strong." He offered her a bow. "You are a difficult lady to track down tonight."

Lilia couldn't help but return his smile. "Well, there *are* a ton of people here."

"True." Jasper cast a glance around. "I wasn't expecting Madame Olga's guest list to be this large."

She laughed. "I'm not sure anyone was."

Jasper nodded to her, his gray eyes frank and sincere. "You look beautiful."

Her smile softened as she dipped her head in acknowledgment. "Thank you."

"Would you like to dance?" He extended a hand to her.

Lilia peered over his shoulder; she could just glimpse Kedis in deep conversation with several Representatives and a few people she recognized vaguely as prominent businessmen and businesswomen. She cocked an eyebrow at him. "Shouldn't you be keeping an eye on your Ambassador?"

Jasper's smile turned mischievous. "I have a few moments. Long enough for a dance."

"Oh, well, in that case…" Returning his smile, Lilia set her half-empty drink on a passing tray and accepted his outstretched hand. "I'd love to."

Her heart thrummed in her chest; she'd been looking forward to this, hoping she'd get a chance to talk to him in person for a few moments.

They had barely set foot on the dance floor when part of the ceiling caved in above them.

Lilia stifled a scream as a round slab of concrete smashed into the floor at their feet…followed by a silver canister emitting noxious fumes. Jasper reacted instantly. Pushing Lilia sideways, he sent them both tumbling to the floor with his body shielding hers, but the canister did not explode. It merely continued to pour out clouds of smoke as it rolled to a stop.

Around them, screams drowned out the music as more chunks of the ceiling fell to the floor, crushing a few people unfortunate enough to be standing beneath them. Conversation and laughter died a sudden death; the ballroom was filling with panic as fast as it was filling with smoke.

Through the haze, Lilia glimpsed armed figures clad in black body armor dropping from the holes in the ballroom's ceiling. *Oh, my God.* She clutched Jasper's forearm in warning. "We've got incoming."

"I see them." Rising to one knee, Jasper extracted a pistol from within his uniform jacket. He helped Lilia up with one hand, his eyes scanning for threats. "Stay behind me." He coughed—the smoke was burning both their lungs. "I've got to get back to the Ambassador."

Lilia's heart jumped into her throat. Jasper probably didn't realize it, but his G.U. uniform made him a prime target. Materializing her stealth amour beneath her gown—she didn't want to give herself away as a Guardian just yet if she could avoid it—she withdrew her own pistol from her ISF. Jasper would wonder where she got it, and so would others, but at the moment, it didn't matter. He needed backup.

The sounds of laser shots pierced the cacophony of screams and panicked shouts as people stampeded toward the exits.

Jasper worked his way through the smoke and panicked guests to the spot where Kedis had last been standing, aiming his pistol with one hand and tugging Lilia along behind him with the other. Ahead of them, through the haze, the crowd abruptly parted to reveal a masked figure in black body armor aiming a laser carbine straight at Kedis.

Jasper shot him without hesitation. His laser bolts left sizzling impact burns on the attacker's back, but they could have been bubbles, for all the notice the masked man took of them.

"No!" Dropping Lilia's hand, Jasper barreled forward in a desperate attempt to tackle the man before he pulled the trigger.

At that moment, a gray-clad figure surged between Kedis and his attacker. A glint of silver whirled between them…and half of the attacker's carbine clattered to the floor just before Jasper tackled him to the floor.

Lilia choked—and not from the smoke.

A Guardian in full defense-mode armor and wielding a nano-blade stood between the G.U. Ambassador and death.

Keeping one eye on Jasper and the attacker, who was struggling furiously to free himself from Jasper's hold, the Guardian turned to Kedis. "Are you all right, Ambassador?"

It was Lon.

# CHAPTER 48

LON maintained a pleasant expression through sheer dint of will. He stood beside Ambassador Kedis, listening as he and Lanxian Representative Zane Chas discussed rosy future possibilities if the G.U. and the Coalition ever reached any kind of peace agreement. They were deep in the midst of outlining what trade would look like, the avenues of travel and tourism that would be open between their worlds.

*It's a heady thought, I'll grant them that.* Lon sipped his champagne, barely tasting it. The only thing he really registered was its temperature—lukewarm. He'd been holding the same glass the better part of an hour. It gave him something to do—or at least pretend to do—and it was less awkward than standing around with his hands shoved into his pockets.

He suppressed a grimace. *I'm not sure this evening could get any more boring.* He'd had a few moments' excitement when Madame Olga attempted to set him up with one of her high society girls, but even if he hadn't been tasked with keeping a close eye on Kedis, he wouldn't have been interested.

*We've got nothing in common, except that we're both related to somebody with political influence.*

Madame Olga swore they were perfect for each other, and did her best to guilt Lon into at least dancing with the poor girl, who had stood at the older woman's elbow, her perfectly made-up face growing stiffer when it became clear Lon was immune to her charms. Lon had resisted. Silky black hair and wide blue eyes set in a delicate face weren't enough to tempt him tonight.

Now, however, Lon found himself almost wishing he *could* dance with the girl…just for a break from the boring monotony of listening to Kedis's shoptalk.

The novelty of his involvement in getting Kedis here was wearing off; he was fading into the background like Corran. That wasn't a bad thing—Lon found he preferred to be ignored instead of yanked into the spotlight—but at least answering questions had passed the time.

Jasper and Renner were in similar positions. Renner's craggy face was as expressionless as always, his dark eyes constantly scanning the crowd of people in the ballroom for anything out of the ordinary, but Lon fancied he knew the man well enough at this point to detect the subtle signs of impatience.

As for Jasper…well, the Lieutenant had politely fended off several offers from star-struck socialites—several of them old enough to be his mother—to dance, citing his need to stay close to the Ambassador. Now Lon noticed him staring into the crowd, his gazed fixed on someone out of Lon's line of sight. His expression struck Lon as odd—a curious blend of excitement and grim resolve.

A few seconds later, having apparently made up his mind about something, Jasper glanced briefly at Kedis before turning to Lon. "I will be back shortly."

"Okay."

Lon watched him depart, easily threading his way through a group of men and women in glittering evening wear. On the other side, Lon glimpsed a familiar figure in an emerald green dress…and something settled in the pit of his stomach. *Ah. So that's it.*

He wasn't sure whether to laugh or frown.

He wanted to laugh, because a person would have to be blind to miss the rapport Lilia and Jasper had formed since the Mansion, but at the same time…Jasper's expression remained stuck in his mind. 'Grim resolve' was out of character for the lieutenant's interactions with his sister.

Lon took another tiny sip of champagne. *Wonder what that's all about.* He'd have to ask Lilia later, though he already knew what she would tell him—that she and Jasper were friends, and that was all. *I'm inclined to believe that's what she thinks, but I'm not so sure about him.*

At any rate, Jasper would dance with her, and then he would return to his post.

*Then maybe I'll take a break for a few minutes.* The collar of his crisp white shirt beneath his tuxedo jacket felt constricting; Lon itched to unbutton it and loosen his tie.

He glanced back at Kedis as an unusually loud burst of laughter echoed from the knot surrounding the Ambassador. At that moment, chunks of the ceiling caved in across the ballroom. Plumes of noxious smoke began filling the air. The party's atmosphere changed instantly from lighthearted to panicked.

*What the heck?* For an instant, Lon was confused, unsure what had just happened. He tensed, scanning the growing haze for some explanation…and then he glimpsed black-clad figures who were most definitely *not* guests. None of Madame Olga's guests carried weapons—or wore masks.

*Oh, stars.* Lon's mouth went dry. He didn't know who they were, but they had to be here for Kedis. He whirled around in time to see Corran and Renner seize Kedis's elbows and extract him from the knot of politicians. Only two meters separated the four of them; Lon closed that distance in two long strides and took up position in front.

The smoke was rapidly getting thicker, and it burned their throats and eyes. All four of them began to cough. Around them, panicked guests stampeded for the exit. Through the screams, Lon thought he heard laserfire.

"This way," he choked out, motioning to a set of double doors on the left of the ballroom. He didn't know what had happened exactly, but they needed to get the Ambassador out of here before one of those shadowy figures spotted him.

He was sorely tempted to materialize his facemask and visor— the facemask had a built-in filtration system that would enable him to breathe and at least one of Kedis's escorts needed to be able to *see* what was going on.

*Not sure I can risk it*, Lon thought grimly. *Not yet.* There had to be a way to get out of this without flat-out revealing he was a Guardian. *There* has *to be a way.*

"Where is Wright?" Renner growled. "He shouldn't have left."

Kedis said nothing; he was too busy coughing.

At that moment, they found themselves face-to-face with a masked, black-clad figure that had just appeared from the smoke. The figure raised a laser carbine, preparing to fire, and Lon made his choice.

Materializing full defense-mode armor in a couple of heart-beats, he lunged forward, drawing his nanoblade from his ISF in the process. He sliced through the carbine as though it was made of air, and half of it clattered to the floor at the attacker's feet. He arced the blade around, prepared to cleave the attacker himself in two, but at that moment, someone tackled the figure to the floor.

It was Wright.

He and the attacker fought, but Wright had the element of surprise on his side. He slammed the masked figure's head against the floor once, twice, until the man went limp, stunned, and then quickly bound his hands behind his back.

Lon glanced from the subdued figure to the smoke-filled ballroom. The fire alarm system should have kicked on by now…that it hadn't meant something else was seriously wrong. He turned back to Kedis, Renner, and Corran. The first two were both gaping at him through streaming eyes, but Corran only looked grim. "We've got to get you out of here, Ambassador."

"What about him?" Wright indicated the attacker…and then his watering eyes widened as he took in Lon's new look.

"Leave him," Lon and Renner said at the same time.

Someone coughed off to his right. It was only then that Lon realized his sister was standing nearby, peering at him through the smoke with something akin to horror. Feeling faintly relieved that at least he knew where part of his family was, Lon jerked his head toward her. "Come on. We've got to get out of here."

[Something's wrong with the hotel's smoke detectors,] Lilia said via Nancom. [They should have kicked on.]

[I know.] Lon's gaze caught on her pistol. [Put that away.]

She stiffened. [But, Lon—]

Lon gritted his teeth behind his facemask. Yes, it was probably better that she be armed in this particular situation, but… [Look at your clothes, Lil. It's bad enough that they know about me now— they don't need to be wondering about you too.]

Some things, at least, should be kept under wraps longer.

He gritted his teeth again. *I didn't have much of a choice.*

# Chapter 49

Part of Lilia wanted to argue, wanted to protest that she could certainly have been carrying her pistol in a thigh or ankle holster, but the larger part of her agreed with her brother. He'd just revealed the existence of Guardians to a group of Tarynians; the possible repercussions from that were horrifying at best and terrifying at worst. The notion of Kedis, Renner, and Jasper discovering *she* was also a Guardian frightened her. She'd been discreet about it since she joined the NCDC; it was her ace in the hole. The last thing she wanted was for the entire galaxy to know.

Accordingly, she immediately slid her pistol back into its holster inside her ISF beside her right thigh, and pressed close to Jasper, Renner, Kedis, Corran, and her brother. She cast one last glance at the bound figure lying prone on the floor before they moved far enough forward that the smoke swallowed him up. [You think that guy will still be there later?]

[Don't know,] Lon replied grimly, [but we've got bigger things to worry about.]

Jasper put a hand on the small of her back, pushing her ahead of him next to Kedis.

[Lilia!] Kevin's voice sounded in her head, a little panicked. [Where are you?]

[With Lon and Kedis. We're trying to get out of here.]

[So are we. Accelevators are packed; stairs are jammed.] Kevin's Nancom voice grew grim. [And Grandfather can't take the stairs.]

Lilia's lungs burned; she coughed violently. [What are you going to do?]

[We're getting Grandfather out of here. Remember the Ladder?]

The memory came to Lilia in an instant. [You're cutting through the floor?]

[You'd better believe it. They just tried to kill him, Lil.]

Lilia blinked watering eyes at the wavering form of Kedis's tuxedo-clad back. [They tried to kill Kedis too.] She abruptly switched Nancom channels. [Lon, I know how we can get out of here.]

Her brother didn't spare her a glance, but his Nancom voice sharpened. [How?]

[Cut a hole through the floor, take Kedis down to the next level.] She coughed again; the noxious fumes seemed to be getting worse. She thought longingly of her facemask, but of course she couldn't materialize it. Not now. [That's how they're getting Grandfather out.]

[It's worth a shot,] Lon said grimly. [God knows we won't be getting Kedis out any other way right now.] He stopped short, and the three Tarynians looked at him in alarm.

"What are you *doing*?" Renner demanded hoarsely. "We've got to get out of here."

"We will." Lon inserted the tip of his nanoblade into the floor and pressed down. The sword cut through the floor with incredible ease; he proceeded to drag it around in a rough circle. Gravity sent the circle of flooring crashing to the floor beneath.

He turned to Renner and Corran, his facemask revealing nothing of his expression. "I'll go first; you two follow to make sure it's clear."

Both men nodded.

Lon produced his hoverdisc, expanded it, and stepped aboard. He immediately floated over the hole and descended into it. "Come on."

Renner sat down on the edge of the floor and slid off. Lon eased his transition to the floor below; a few seconds later, he called up, "Clear!"

Lon's gloved hand poked up from the hole. "Ambassador."

Kedis's face was chalk-white beneath his olive-toned skin, his eyes red and watering from the fumes in the air, but he copied Renner's actions without a word and disappeared from sight.

Jasper motioned for Lilia to go next. She did so, and Lon eased her down through the floor on his hoverdisc.

The air was mercifully clear down here. Lilia inhaled deep lung-fuls, though they were all—except for Lon—still coughing. Wiping her eyes, she swiftly took in their surroundings. They'd landed in one of the bedrooms of a really nice suite. Having no way of gauging what lay beneath them, Lon hadn't cut them a hole over the bed—which would have made the transition easier—but it didn't matter. The important thing was that they were out of the ballroom.

Lon helped Jasper down beside her, and they immediately traded the bedroom for the living room beyond. Jasper and Renner dragged a heavy sideboard over to block the door. Lon, meantime, dematerialized his helmet, facemask, and visor, but left the rest of his armor intact.

Corran immediately hastened to check the hall outside the suite. "It's clear," he reported back in a low voice. "Everybody's taking the stairs and the accelevator banks."

Renner frowned. "That is a problem," he said hoarsely. "We can't risk the stairs and the accelevators are bound to be jammed full of people. No guarantee there'd be room."

Jasper waved a hand to the suite. "And we obviously can't stay here."

Lilia's eyes flicked to the hole in the bedroom ceiling at the same time Kedis looked up.

"Preferably not," the Ambassador said in Tarynian, before coughing into his hand. When he could speak again, he leveled Lon with a sharp look that held more than a little astonishment. "Where did you get that outfit? And that sword?"

Lon shrugged. "It's a long story, Ambassador. Let's just say I'm not your average liaison and leave it at that."

By the look on Kedis's face, it was clear he had no intentions of leaving anything anywhere, but he said nothing further. Lilia swallowed; there would be hell to pay for this, she just knew it.

Kedis moved on to the next topic with the highest priority. "Who *are* those people?"

"No idea, sorry." Lon looked at Corran. "Where's the rest of the team?"

"Denisk and Lutz are in the parking garage with the skimmer." Corran's craggy face tensed. "Swift is still in the ballroom, and I can't raise Terrence on the comm."

A chill ran down Lilia's spine; that couldn't be good. She bit her lip. It was possible the attackers wouldn't figure out they'd gone through the floor, but…*We can't take that risk. If Kedis dies in the midst of peace talks…*

She promptly shoved that thought out of her mind. Now wasn't the time to consider such dire implications; they had more important things to consider. She Nancommed Kevin. [Where are you now?]

[We got Grandfather down to the lobby on a service accelevator along with Briscoe and Uncle Martin.]

Her knees wobbled with relief. [Oh, thank God.]

[Where are you?]

[One level beneath the ballroom. Lon cut a hole in the floor, but now we've got to figure out where to go from here.]

[Can you get to a service accelevator?]

Lilia glanced in the direction of the door leading into the hall. [Don't know.] She turned to Lon, intending to ask if that was an option, but at that moment, Corran spoke.

"We could always go through the window." He tipped his head toward the wide expanse of plastiglass offering a beautiful view of downtown Sonela.

Lilia stared at him in confusion. *The window?*

She wasn't the only one. Renner squinted at the security team leader as though he suspected smoke inhalation had fried half his brain cells. "What are you *talking* about?"

Corran ignored him in favor of regarding Lon with a flicker of impatience. "It's not like we've got a lot of other options here, Strong. Not to mention…" He gave Lon a significant look.

Lilia bit her lip again. *Not to mention Lon just revealed he's a Guardian.* Her eyes widened with a sudden burst of understanding. *But if Corran's talking about the window, that means—*

She looked at Corran through new eyes. *He's a Guardian too.*

This revelation was confirmed a scant moment later when Corran produced a hoverdisc from what looked like the pocket of his trousers.

"You're right," Lon said at last. "It's our best option." He glanced up at the ceiling. "They won't be expecting that."

"They *can't* be expecting that," Corran said grimly. Expanding his hoverdisc, he stepped aboard. "Strong, cut us an exit and get the Ambassador." He motioned to Renner and Jasper. "One of you is coming with me to stay with the Ambassador once we get him on the ground. The rest of the team will join us there."

Kedis looked from Corran to Lon, and his expression reminded Lilia of someone putting puzzle pieces together.

"Sounds good." Hopping down from his hoverdisc, Lon picked it up and headed over to the window.

"What about Lilia?" Jasper pushed her forward, but Lilia shook her head.

"They don't want me. I can wait."

A muscle in his cheek twitched. "They'll want you if they break in here and the Ambassador has slipped through their fingers."

That was not a pretty picture. If she was anyone else, Lilia would have been frightened. As it was, she could only shrug. Jasper's concern was touching, but unnecessary.

Corran spared Jasper a glance. "This won't take long. We'll have everybody out of here within minutes."

Thrusting his nanoblade into the plastiglass, Lon looked over his shoulder at Corran. "I'm going to have to do it in pieces. Can't risk dropping the glass onto people down there."

"Just get it done. Fast."

Lon cut out chunks of plastiglass, and Corran stepped up beside them to take each one and lay it aside. A cool breeze whipped through the room; the evening was hot and muggy, but the air up this high was colder. After a couple of minutes, Lon had created an opening large enough for two human beings to pass through on a hoverdisc.

Still grasping his nanoblade, Lon mounted his hoverdisc again and beckoned to Kedis. "Come on, Ambassador."

Kedis moved forward automatically and climbed up onto the hoverdisc behind Lon. He glanced at Jasper and Renner. "I'll see you gentlemen on the ground."

Lilia had to give him props; he didn't look as scared as he probably should have been.

Lon disappeared through the window, Kedis in tow, and Corran turned to Renner. "You're with me."

A second later, Renner had climbed up behind him on the hoverdisc and the two of them were flying through the window, leaving Lilia and Jasper alone in the hotel suite living room. Jasper's expression was grim.

Lilia bit the inside of her lip, the wind lashing her hair around her face. It wouldn't take long for either Lon or Corran to return for them. *Hopefully nobody figures out where we went until we're safely out of here.*

"That's some sword your brother has got."

"I'm sorry?" Lilia glanced sharply at Jasper, taken aback. She hadn't expected him to mention the nanoblade. Not yet.

Jasper nodded toward the window. "It cut through that plasti-glass like it was butter."

"I'm glad." Lilia regarded the window as well, praying she'd see Corran's head and shoulders reappear.

They both whipped around as a muffled crash sounded behind the door they'd blocked off with furniture. Lilia's heart jumped into her throat. "Somebody's in there."

Jasper shooed her over to the window, raising his pistol and training it on the blocked door. "You're going next."

Lilia wasn't about to argue with him. She had a feeling she wouldn't win. Instead, she opened a Nancom channel to Lon. [You've got to get back up here—somebody's found the hole.]

The door opened, and a man's voice cursed when he saw the furniture barring his way.

"I'm here."

Heart pounding, Lilia whirled around in time to see Lon floating through the hole in the window.

Jasper nodded toward her. "Get her out of here, Strong."

Lilia did not waste time jumping onto Lon's hoverdisc behind him. Sliding her arms around her brother, she held on for dear life. "What about Jasper?"

"Corran's on his way up."

Lon glided back out of the window—and plunged into an al-most-vertical drop.

Lilia immediately lost her stomach. She held onto Lon for dear life as they plummeted to the street below; hard-pressed to keep from screaming—though whether from terror or exhilaration, she didn't know. The wind whipped the folds of her emerald gown around her legs and lashed stray locks of her hair in her face.

When Lon slowed and eased to a halt above the sidewalk less than twenty seconds later, Lilia's heart was pounding hard enough in her chest that she thought it might just beat straight through her rib-cage. The rush of adrenaline coursing through her made her knees wobbly as she stepped off the hoverdisc.

Lon had obviously aimed for a specific landmark—in this case a pair of decorative trees to one side of the Beliana's entrance. A sea of panicked people, both party guests and guests staying at the hotel, filled the sidewalk and spilled out into the street.

[Act natural,] Lon said via Nancom, before hopping down from his hoverdisc and dematerializing his nano-armor in order to blend in.

Lilia caught a couple of people gaping at their astonishing arrival, but the crowd around them shifted and she knew they'd been swallowed up. *Hopefully no one will remember us that well in all this chaos.*

Lon took her arm and herded her over to the other side of the tree, where Renner stood with Kedis. The Ambassador did not look the slightest bit ruffled by his unorthodox delivery to the sidewalk. A moment later, Corran and Jasper rounded the tree and formed up around Kedis.

"We've got to get you out of here, Ambassador," Corran said grimly. "Denisk and Lutz are bringing the skimmer around, but we may not be able to get to them because of the crowd."

Lilia glanced over her shoulder, searching the crowd for familiar faces. [Kev, we made it outside. Where are you?]

[Parking level. Where are you exactly?]

[Out on the sidewalk in front of the hotel.] She swallowed as someone jostled her. [There are a *lot* of people out here.]

[Figured you coming to us was out of the question. Hold on.]

"...lia. *Lilia.*"

Lilia jerked, startled back to her immediate surroundings by Lon's voice saying her name. She looked at him, only to find all five men staring at her. "What?"

"You're coming with us until we can get you back to Grandfather."

Lilia shook her head, jerking a thumb over her shoulder. "I can wait here. Kevin can pick me up once they get Grandfather to safety."

Beside her, Jasper made a noise of protest that was lost in the swell of the crowd.

To her astonishment, Kedis intervened. "That is ridiculous, Miss Strong. We are well aware how capable you are, but I'm afraid this situation is beyond you. For your own safety, I must insist you come with us."

"But—"

"You heard the Ambassador." Lon shook his head. "No 'but's. You're coming with us."

Lilia clenched her jaw. She couldn't insist on getting her way without explaining *why* she'd be just fine...and obviously that was out of the question.

Kevin's voice flooded her mind. [Stay where you are; Bryce and I are coming to get you in the other skimmer.]

[Change of plans.] She couldn't quite keep the resentment out of her Nancom voice. [Lon and the Ambassador are insisting I come with them.]

To her surprise, Kevin accepted this without question. [Okay. That works too. We can pick you up again once they've gotten Kedis to safety.]

A hand splayed against the small of Lilia's back, keeping her tucked in close to the formation around Kedis. Lilia resisted the urge to shrug Jasper off; it wasn't his fault she was stuck with them for the time being. [There's something else you should know. Lon had to reveal he was a Guardian to Kedis.]

There was a long pause. At last, Kevin said, [Oh, boy.]

[Yeah.]

[Too late to worry about it—]

Lilia didn't comprehend the rest of her brother's words. Ahead of them, a smoke canister dropped out of the sky, striking one of Olga's guests on the shoulder before bouncing off and spewing noxious fumes. The man's agonized screams quickly changed to equally agonized coughs.

Around them, more smoke canisters impacted the crowd, eliciting further screams and a frenzied dash to get away from the renewed assault.

Lilia glanced over her shoulder again, expecting to see more canisters dropping into the crowd behind them, but even through the rapidly gathering cloud of fumes, she could see none. The hair on the back of her neck tingled. *That wasn't random.*

She looked back at Kedis, at the light reflecting off his bald head, and glanced up at the sky. She couldn't see anything…but that didn't mean someone wasn't up there.

[Lon, I think they're targeting Kedis specifically. I think they can *see* him. We've got to get him out of here.]

Another smoke canister dropped into the crowd, this one landing less than three meters away. Lilia suppressed a scream as the woman it landed on crumpled to the pavement, the side of her head caved in from the impact.


His sister's words weren't a revelation; Lon had reached the same conclusion. He gritted his teeth. [We're *trying.*]

He and Corran forced their way through the sea of mingled bodies and smoke, making a path for Wright, Renner, Kedis, and Lilia to follow. They were nearly to the sidewalk; the skimmer should be arriving any moment. This should have filled Lon with relief, but the knot of anxiety and dread in his stomach did not abate. *If they can* see *Kedis...*

They didn't have much time. Lon's feeling that something was very wrong increased. The wind had caught the fumes by now, spreading them further down the sidewalk, making people cough between panicked yells and screams.

*If they can see us...* He caught Corran's eye, switching to Nancom. [We can't put Kedis into that skimmer. Those canisters are coming from above.]

He did not have to explain further. Corran nodded sharply. [We'll stage it.]

[Tell Denisk and Lutz to get ready to tuck and roll.]

A sleek black skimmer bearing holographic diplomatic markings glided up to the sidewalk, crowding people out of the way.

There wasn't time to explain much of the plan. Corran muttered a few things to Wright and Renner, while Lon reached into his ISF near his bellybutton. Withdrawing a soft black cap, he slapped it into Kedis's hand. "Hold this. Put it on when I tell you."

To his credit, the Ambassador did not balk. He palmed the cap, folding his fist around it.


Lilia could see the skimmer pull up ahead of them. Lon and Corran herded Kedis forward, but Jasper and Renner held back. Confused, she looked up at Jasper. He met her eye and gave the tiniest shake of his head.

Lilia frowned. *What is going on?* Clearly, they'd concocted some sort of plan in the past few minutes, but she had no idea what it entailed.

She watched Lon climb into the skimmer, followed by Kedis and Corran. *Are they leaving us here for now?*

It would be understandable—three were easier to get out of this mess than five, but still...

She lost the rest of that thought as Kedis's skimmer exploded in a massive fireball.

# CHAPTER 50

FOR one long stretched-out second, Lilia could not believe her eyes. Then comprehension flooded her and she screamed. She tried to run forward, toward the flames and thick black smoke roiling up out of the skimmer's wreckage, but an arm around her waist held her back.

Jasper.

"Let me go!" she wailed.

*Lon* was in that skimmer. All at once, every memory of every dark moment before, during, and after his funeral slammed into her at once. They couldn't have lost him again.

She bucked frantically against Jasper, but he only held her tighter, drawing her up against his chest. "Let me go! Lon! *Lon!*"

Jasper was speaking, but her ears were ringing and she couldn't hear him.

Lilia drove an elbow into his ribcage; Jasper winced, but maintained his iron grip. His embrace, which she'd found so comforting after being attacked by Freedom's Children, now felt like a stranglehold. "Let me go!"

This wasn't how the evening was supposed to go. She'd *warned* Lon. Tears welled in her eyes. *We can't live through this again.*

Jasper held onto Lilia's writhing body for dear life. She was stronger than she looked—and much faster than even he had given her credit. His ears were ringing; he couldn't hear her cries, but he could read the desperation and grief in her body language.

"Hold still," he told her, tightening his grip on her. "It's all right. It's all right." He couldn't even hear his own voice. *I hope to God that worked, Strong.*

His ribs ached from where Lilia had elbowed him, but he couldn't let her go. Not yet.

*Keep her clear,* Lon had said, right before he climbed into that skimmer.

Lilia was shaking in his arms. Jasper wanted to turn her around so she could read his lips, but he didn't dare release his hold. At this particularly moment, he wouldn't put it past her to knee him in the groin and take off. He pinned her arms against her body, pressing his cheek up against the side of her neck. He caught the faint scent of her perfume as he murmured over and over against her skin, "It's okay. It's okay."

He felt the moment she sagged against him, the fight draining out of her. He didn't trust that, however. The Strong siblings had bonds that ran deeper than most families he'd known; he had a gut feeling she'd bolt the second he eased his grip.

*But…*

Carefully, Jasper shifted his hold on Lilia enough that he could get a look at her face. She cooperated, and it was only then that he saw the tears streaming down her cheeks and the devastated grief filling her violet eyes. "It's okay," he told her firmly, trying to convey as much encouragement with his expression as he could.


Lilia had gone numb inside. Tears obscured her vision as Jasper shifted her around. He was talking to her—she could see his mouth moving—but she didn't comprehend.

How could he look so hopeful? Lon was dead. Again.

Jasper continued mouthing the same words, over and over, and she finally registered them. "It's okay. It's okay."

White-hot anger flared to life inside her. She wanted to shriek. *How can it possibly be okay? Lon is dead!*

*Again.*

The sound of the skimmer exploding in a bright fireball would have been deafening if Lon hadn't materialized his helmet and facemask seconds earlier. The sensors in his helmet automatically protected his ears. Kedis, Denisk, and Lutz weren't so lucky, but that couldn't be helped.

*At least they're alive.*

Raising his head, Lon scanned the smoke-filled street around them before rolling off of Kedis and rising to a knee. As soon as they'd gotten into the skimmer, he'd shoved the Ambassador across the seat and out the other door. They'd slammed into the asphalt coating the street, with Lon bodily shielding the other man, seconds before a canister impacted the skimmer and it exploded.

[That was close,] Corran said via Nancom.

Lon glanced to the right; the other Guardian had succeeded in getting Denisk and Lutz out in time, though both men looked dazed. Blood covered one side of Denisk's bald head. [Too close,] he said grimly. [Way too close.]

Bracing himself for the acrid smell of smoke and burning metal, Lon dematerialized his helmet and facemask—he wanted to avoid showing up on the news in Guardian regalia—and shook Kedis's shoulder. "Ambassador. Are you all right?"

Kedis's only response was a groan.

Behind them, the fire consuming the skimmer continued to roar. Lon squinted at it through eyes that had begun to sting and water from the smoke and proceeded to drag Kedis some distance away, back toward the crowd. It was safer that way—at least in theory—than turning themselves into lone targets in the middle of the street.

In the process, he got a good look at the Ambassador. One side of Kedis's face was scraped and bleeding from where he'd impacted the street and his tuxedo was mussed, but he didn't seem to have any major injuries. *Thank God for that.*

Corran's voice flooded his mind again. [We've got to get him out of here. Is he conscious?]

[Don't know yet.] Lon bent over Kedis and checked his pupils, which seemed normal, before shaking his shoulder. "Ambassador, you've got to get up."

Kedis's eyes fluttered open. For a second he looked puzzled to see Lon, and then the events of the past few moments caught up to him. His eyes widened in dazed horror.

Despite the urgency flooding his system, Lon spoke slowly. Even if Kedis couldn't hear him, he would hopefully be able to read his lips. "We've got to get you out of here. Can you stand?"

Regardless of whether or not Kedis could lip-read, he understood Lon's intent. He allowed Lon to help him up, but as soon as the Ambassador put weight on his left foot, his leg buckled. He would have fallen, if not for Lon's iron grip on him.

Lon bit back a curse. He'd hoped Kedis would emerge unscathed, but clearly he'd been injured. *No time to look at it now.* It would have to wait until they got the Ambassador out of the line of fire.

[Kedis is wounded,] he told Corran. [Left leg.]

[Bad?]

[Not sure.] Out of the corner of his eye, Lon saw Corran half-supporting, half-dragging both Denisk and Lutz. The other Guardian had dematerialized his facemask and helmet as well, though he still wore the armor.

[We'll deal with it. Get Kedis back to Wright and Renner. We need to disappear.]

[That would be good.]

Wrapping one of Kedis's arms around his shoulder, Lon helped the Ambassador limp around the burning, smoking remains of the skimmer. Corran, Denisk, and Lutz joined them, and together they plunged back into the gasping, coughing crowd.

[Where are we taking him?] Lon's eyes darted back and forth as he scanned the hazy crowd for any further signs of danger.

[The other car,] Corran responded. [Terrence is on the way. He's okay.]

[Thank God for that.] Shifting his grip on Kedis, Lon opened a channel to Lilia. [We're taking the other skimmer. It's going to be a tight fit—you might have to sit on me.]

Her response came immediately, edged with a combination of anger and relief. [I thought you were *dead.*]

Lon grimaced; he heard the word his sister had left unspoken. *Again.* He hadn't even considered that. [Sorry. Just wanted whoever the hell is after Kedis to think they got him.]

[Did you succeed?]

[I guess we'll find out.]

Just ahead of them, Lon finally caught sight of Lilia, Wright, and Renner. Something eased inside his chest; at least they were all right. Renner and Wright closed ranks with him, Corran, and Lutz, with Wright pushing Lilia to the center along with Kedis, and they worked their way through the panicked crowd as quickly as they could, given Kedis and Denisk's injuries.

They made it halfway down the block before Terrence arrived with the skimmer. Lon had never been so happy to see a vehicle in his life.

Lilia choked on a sob as Lon's voice flooded her mind. Grief turned to relief before morphing into a wave of anger. She'd been so frightened, so sure they'd have to bury Lon again. She buried the anger as Lon briefly explained the plan, sweeping it into a dark corner of her mind. She would have to deal with it eventually, but she couldn't think about it now.

Not in the midst of a panicked crowd, where one misstep would end in someone being trampled to death.

As though sensing she would no longer fight him, Jasper let go of her long enough to wrap an arm around her shoulders. "This way!" he shouted, using his body to shield her from the mass of people surrounding them, everyone pushing their way forward in an attempt to escape their attackers.

They worked their way through the crowd until Lilia finally saw her brother, supporting Kedis. They then formed a tight group and proceeded down the block with the rest of the crowd spilling out onto the streets.

Lilia experienced a brief crisis of conscience. They needed to keep Kedis alive, which meant getting him out of here before the attackers succeeded in murdering him, and she had the means to do that. She swallowed, her eyes still stinging from the noxious gas. *Can't risk it. Too many people.*

It was too public…and she couldn't risk accidentally transporting someone else—or part of someone else, if the portal closed too soon.

The faint whine of an engine and a rush of wind were their only warnings before a skimmer dropped out of the sky above them. Its gravcoils successfully cleared a spot for it as the driver came to an abrupt halt a meter above the street.

"Go!" Corran bellowed, waving Lon and Kedis forward.

Lon helped Kedis climb into the skimmer and the rest of them followed. It was an official government vehicle, meant to comfortably transport up to six passengers. They were…rather crowded… but an escape vehicle was an escape vehicle, and no one was about to complain.

As Lon was busy trying to determine where and how badly Kedis was injured, Lilia ended up perched on Jasper's lap. She shot him an apologetic look, which he wordlessly waved off.

Renner was barely inside the skimmer before the driver took off, fast enough to send half of them pitching back in their seats and the other half pitching forward. Lilia almost fell off Jasper's lap and onto Kedis, but the blond lieutenant caught her just in time. He anchored her to him with an arm around her waist as they shot up into Sonela's night sky.

Lilia would have straightened to keep some space between Jasper's front and her back, but his arm kept her snug against his chest. A blush darkened her cheeks; she was grateful for the semi-darkness. She was still wearing stealth armor beneath her gown, but still…

*Oh, if the media could only see us now*, she thought wryly. *The things they'd say about this!*

If the streets around the hotel were pandemonium, the interior of the skimmer was not much better. Everyone seemed to be talking at once, trying to determine the extent of both Kedis and Denisk's injuries, and a safe destination.

In the midst of all the noise, Lilia felt a familiar channel request. She bit the inside of her lip, but allowed it. She had to.

Riley Callahan's voice filled her mind, competing with the noise outside her head. [Lilia! Where are you? What's going on?]

Lilia explained in a few terse sentences, ending with, [I'm with the Ambassador and my brother now, on our way to a safe house.]

[Good,] Callahan said grimly. [Stay with him as long as you can without drawing suspicion. I'm sure the Board will agree the more Guardians around him right now, the better.]

His Nancom voice had an odd note to it, but Lilia lacked both the time and the mental energy to figure it out. [Doesn't look like I have much of a choice anyway.]

Callahan ignored that. [Do you have any idea where you're headed?]

Lilia glanced out the window at the brightly lit restaurants and shops flashing past them. [Not yet. We're still in the middle of the business district.]

[Keep me apprised,] Callahan ordered, and then he was gone.

Under normal circumstances, Lilia would have been taken aback by such abrupt behavior from their handler, but as it was, she was too relieved to care. Renner and Corran were arguing about where to take Kedis.

"How do you know this place you have in mind is safe?" Renner demanded. "How do you know they won't attack him there too?"

"It's only an issue if we're being followed," Corran countered, his face as hard as granite in the periodic flashes of light from the glowposts on the streets. "Which we aren't."

"How can you guarantee that?" Jasper asked, his chest rumbling against Lilia's back.

"Because we're trained for this." Corran shook his head. "And we'll be stopping before we get there to make sure we're not being tracked. But right now? The most important thing is getting the Ambassador away from the Wycliffe."

Renner glowered at Corran before addressing Lon. "How is he?"

"*He* is quite well, all things considered," Kedis answered in Tarynian. Another passing light revealed his eyes were open, though he still looked a little dazed.

"Piece of shrapnel hit his leg," Lon said, "but other than that, he appears to be okay." He glanced sideways at Corran. "How long until we reach this safe house of yours?"

"Safe house?" Kedis had apparently missed this part of the discussion. "No." He shook his head, struggling to sit up properly in his seat. "No safe houses. I want to return to my hotel."

"Sir—" Corran began, but Kedis cut him off.

"No. I wish to return to my hotel. I will not be bullied by terrorists."

Lilia sat very still, watching the scene unfold before her. She couldn't read Renner's expression, and she couldn't see Jasper's face, but Lon looked wary and Corran clearly looked frustrated. She understood; on the one hand, Kedis had a point, but on the other… they didn't know yet who had attacked Madame Olga's party or how they'd pulled it off.

*Or if they've got people waiting for Kedis at the Beliana.* The thought sent a fine shudder of horror through her. Jasper, noting her quick intake of breath, gently curled his fingers around her upper arm and gave her a comforting squeeze.

At last, Corran exhaled heavily. "As you wish, Ambassador. But be aware it is against your security team's advice."

"Noted." Kedis waved an imperious hand. "Now, turn us around."

# CHAPTER 51

THE remainder of the trip to Kedis's hotel passed in a blur. Lilia's thoughts were a jumbled stream of babble inside her head, jumping from what had happened to what would happen when Kedis woke up and demanded a real explanation as to how Lon had saved his life. Oddly enough, Jasper's arm around her waist served to tether her to reality. She was trembling; he was not.

Fleetingly, Lilia wished she wasn't wearing stealth armor. If she had to be in this position, she would have liked to feel the warmth of his body against her back, feel the steady, reassuring beat of his heart. *You'd think I'd be used to dealing with crises by now.*

She took a breath. *I probably ought to apologize for hitting him.* Not now, but later, when they had both time and space to breathe.

The skimmer pulled into the Beliana's underground parking garage and Corran and Lon lost no time whisking Kedis up to his suite. The accelevator couldn't move fast enough to suit them. When the doors finally opened on the penthouse floor, Kedis's security team rushed him down the hall and into the relative safety of his suite. They reminded Lilia of a swarm of ants.

She and Jasper trailed behind, bringing up the rear. Once inside, Lilia moved over to the couch she and Jasper had occupied the last time she'd been here. She took a seat in the corner, figuring it would be best if she stayed out of the way. She caught a glimpse of the damage to Kedis's leg as Renner and several of Corran's men carried him through the living area and into his large bedroom; he was bleeding freely, but she'd seen worse on Glo'Stea.

Corran had called a med 'bot; it arrived at the door a moment later. His security team examined it before they allowed it entrance to the suite.

"Where is the patient?" the 'bot inquired in a flat, metallic voice. It stood almost two meters tall and looked humanoid, aside from the fact it had four arms and was shiny silver.

"In here." Jasper motioned for the 'bot to follow him. As he strode toward Kedis's room, he glanced once over his shoulder at Lilia, as though checking to make sure she was all right. His face was streaked with grime, probably from the skimmer explosion.

She gave him a reassuring nod. She would be just fine where she was.

Corran and Lon had remained in the living area; they stood by the full-length windows at the end of the room. Lon had his scanner out, and Lilia suspected he and Corran were holding a Nancom conversation. Corran's face was impassive, but every once in a while, Lon's eyelid twitched as though he disagreed with something.

Belatedly, Lilia realized that she ought to let Alexis know she and the rest of the family were all right. Pulling out her comlink, she sent her friend a brief message. She got a response back almost immediately; Alexis was relieved. The attack was all over the news.

Alexis proceeded to pepper Lilia with questions, which Lilia tried to answer as best she could. She wasn't sure how much to say—and she didn't want to mention the Guardian issue—but she did tell Alexis she'd had to go with Lon and Ambassador Kedis.

She was on the verge of opening a Nancom channel to Lon when Jasper emerged from Kedis's room and approached Lon.


As the med 'bot disappeared into Kedis's bedroom, a knot formed in the pit of Lon's stomach. A small, selfish part of him hoped Kedis would be unable to talk for a while; he didn't want to deal with the Ambassador and attempt to answer the questions he was bound to have after this. *I don't even know what to tell him.*

Lon pulled his scanner from his ISF without thinking about it and began scanning for anything out of the ordinary. It was something to do; he did not honestly expect to find anything. Not after Kedis had deviated from protocol.

Corran came to stand beside him, his expression still grim. Without looking at him, he said via Nancom, [He's going to ask questions.]

Lon snorted under his breath. [Wouldn't expect anything less.] He *didn't* expect anything less—not from Leo Kedis.

[How much are you going to tell him?]

[No idea.]

Lon glanced at Corran in time to see the older man's expression harden further. [You'd better figure it out. Ask the NCDC.]

Lon's eye twitched at the mention of the NCDC, but now wasn't the time to be stubborn. He knew that, even if the idea grated on his nerves. Grudgingly, he nodded once. [Good idea.]

He'd never had a handler at the NCDC up until his return from the dead with a Tarynian Ambassador in tow. And no matter what Kevin and Lilia said, he still wasn't sure what he thought about Riley Callahan.

Callahan answered his Nancom channel request immediately, which shouldn't have surprised Lon, but somehow it still caught him slightly off-guard. [Is the Ambassador alive?]

Lon spared half a brain cell to wonder how Callahan already knew about the attack before he remembered the twins had probably been in contact with him. [He's alive.]

[That's good news.]

Lon took a second to brace himself before he spoke again. [I've been compromised. Had to materialize my armor and use my nano-blade to save Kedis's life tonight.]

A brief pause met his words. [I see.]

[I need some advice. He's going to want answers.]

[And you're wondering how much to tell him?]

[Yes.] Lon gritted his teeth. [I'd prefer to tell him nothing at all, but I'm afraid that's not an option.]

[The Ambassador does strike me as too tenacious to let something like this go,] Callahan agreed. [Give me a moment.]

[Make it fast. Unless the med 'bot has knocked him out, he'll be raking me over the coals as soon as he's patched up.]

Callahan did not answer.

Lon settled in to wait, his brooding stared fixed on the door leading into Kedis's bedroom. It was only a matter of time.

Fifteen minutes later, Wright emerged from Kedis's room. He approached Lon, his expression set. "The Ambassador wishes to speak to you."

Giving him a brisk nod, Lon pushed off from the wall. As he strode past Wright, he addressed Callahan again. [Any time now, Mr. Callahan. Kedis wants to see me.]

He half-expected Callahan to ignore him again, but the response came almost immediately. [You are authorized to tell the Ambassador what the NCDC is and that you are a Guardian belonging to it. Nothing more.]

[That won't satisfy him.]

Callahan's Nancom voice was crisp. [Then he'll have to get his information elsewhere.]

[Okay.] Lon shook his head to himself, pausing on the threshold into Kedis's room. [Thanks.]

Callahan closed his channel, and Lon steeled himself before stepping into the room. Kedis lay stretched out in the bed, propped up on a number of pillows. The lower half of his trousers on his wounded leg had been cut away; Lon could see the quick-heal bandages. "Ambassador. How are you?" He nodded to the med 'bot, which was gathering its things. "All patched up?"

"Yes." Kedis's dark eyes were still bright and alert, but Lon could see the pain medicine the 'bot had given him was doing its job. He was much calmer and more lucid than he had been when they arrived. "Again, I thank you for saving my life."

Lon waved his thanks aside. "It's what I'm supposed to do, Ambassador." He nodded to the older man, hardly daring to hope he could talk his way out of this. "You should probably get your rest."

"Oh, I will." The expression on the Ambassador's olive-toned face did not change, but something shifted in his voice. "After you answer a few questions, Captain Strong."

Lon raised his eyebrows in feigned ignorance.

Kedis shifted in his bed, changing position to make himself a little more comfortable, but his dark gaze did not leave Lon's face. "I am curious as to *how* you saved my life."

*Here it comes.* Lon kept his voice light. "Ambassador?"

"Don't play coy with me." Kedis shook his head. "You know exactly to what I'm referring." He lifted a hand. "Somehow, you produced body armor out of thin air. I saw it." His expression changed to something halfway between hunger and incredulity. "And then you produced a rather remarkable sword."

It was harder to keep a straight face than Lon expected. He said nothing; he merely continued to meet the Ambassador's challenging gaze.

Kedis narrowed his eyes, scrutinizing Lon. "How did you do that? What are you?"

A few seconds passed, and then Lon shrugged. "I'm something called a Guardian. I'm part of a civilian defense group called the Nanotech Coalition Defense Corps."

"Where did that armor come from?" Kedis leaned forward hungrily. "You did not have time to change."

"I'm not authorized to tell you that part." Lon held up his hands, palms out in a conciliatory gesture. "Sorry."

Shock washed over Kedis's face; his dark eyebrows shot up in astonishment. "*I* am not authorized?"

Lon stood his ground, though his heart pounded in his chest. "No, sir, I'm afraid not."

It took Kedis a moment to digest this, and then something cold and calculating flitted over his face before he smoothed his expression into dignified neutrality. "I see. What of the sword, then?"

That was a little trickier. Lon shrugged again. "The Coalition is famous for our love of fencing. People are always innovating, coming up with new blades and other gear."

"A fencing blade that can cut through a floor?" Kedis raised his eyebrows again. "That is quite…remarkable. Where in the galaxy did you *keep* it?"

"Someplace handy."

"Extraordinarily handy." Kedis stared at Lon again, and the younger man held his gaze. Finally, the Ambassador spread his hands. "After everything we've been through, Lon, this is all you will tell me?"

"It's all I *can* tell you," Lon corrected him.

"I see." Kedis pursed his lips, his eyes narrowing again. At last, he flicked his fingers toward the door. "You may leave. Close the door behind you."

"Thank you." Lon inclined his head. "Good night, Ambassador."

He escaped the room, his heart rate slowly returning to normal. *I've escaped, for now, but it's not over.* Kedis wouldn't let something like this drop.


It felt like Lon had been gone for an eternity, but it was only a handful of minutes. As soon as her brother reappeared in the living room, Lilia opened a Nancom channel to him, her violet eyes sharpening with keen interest.

Lon spared her a glance as he returned to Corran, who was still standing by the window. [How did it go?]

[About as well as I expected. He'll be going to other sources for more information.]

[Will they give it to him?]

Lon gave the tiniest of shrugs. [Who knows?]

[What can I do?]

[Hang tight and keep an eye out, I guess. Don't know what else to say. You shouldn't leave yet.]

[I figured as much.] Lilia wrapped an arm around her torso. [Who do you think those guys were? Freedom's Children?]

[That would be my guess,] Lon said grimly. [Although I suppose it's possible there's another anti-Tarynian, anti-peace terrorist group out there.]

Lilia glanced past the two men at the window without seeing it. [How did they get onto the roof without anyone seeing them?] Even as she asked the question, the answer came to her. [The transporter and nanoblades.]

[Probably. Although we won't know for sure for a while.]

[Grandfather will know as soon as anybody.]

[That's true.]

Lilia met her brother's eyes. [Do you think they'll risk attacking Kedis here?]

[Who knows?] For a second, Lon's confident façade slipped and Lilia saw his apprehension. [They tried to kill him tonight, in a public venue with lots of eyeballs and potential casualties. I don't know if they'll try again in private or not.] He hesitated. [I think they're—]

[—trying to make a statement?]

[Exactly.]

They shared a significant look, and then Lon spoke to Corran in low tones.

Sensing movement out of the corner of her eye, Lilia glanced to the side. Jasper was approaching, his expression grave. She could see the fatigue in the faint lines around his eyes. He had stepped out of the suite—either to speak to someone in the security suite or else Kedis's staff—and now he had returned. He had removed his uniform dress jacket; he carried it slung over one arm, revealing a white button-up shirt beneath.

He offered her an apologetic smile. "I'm sorry you got swept into all this." He made a vague gesture toward the living room. "If I hadn't asked you to dance, you would probably be with your family now."

"Technically," Lilia gave him a wry half-smile, "I *am* with family."

Draping his jacket over the back of the closest armchair, Jasper arched an eyebrow at her, his expression lightening only a fraction. "You know what I mean."

"I do."

For a second, Jasper looked like he was about to reach out and touch her, but he shoved his hands into his pockets instead. "Are you all right?"

"I'm fine." Lilia gave him another small smile. "A little bruised, but otherwise all right." She raised her eyebrows at him. "You?"

The blond lieutenant shrugged. "The same."

Belatedly, Lilia realized she probably ought to ask how Kedis was doing.

Jasper saved her the trouble. "The Ambassador will be fine. Couple of little pieces of shrapnel embedded in his leg, nothing major."

"Good. I'm glad to hear it."

"Your brother saved his life."

Lilia glanced over at Lon—and unbidden tears burned her eyes. "I thought he was dead again," she admitted in a shaky voice.

"I know you did."

Blinking back the tears before they could fall, Lilia looked back at Jasper. His face was full of compassion. "I'm sorry I hit you."

To her surprise, Jasper grinned at her. "It's understandable. I would have done the same thing, were I in your position."

His grin was infectious; Lilia found herself smiling back. "Crazy night."

"Very crazy," Jasper agreed, before nodding over his shoulder. "Would you like a cup of coffee? I have a feeling our night is not over yet."

"Thank you." Lilia gave him a soft, grateful smile. "A cup of coffee sounds wonderful."

"It won't be decaf." It was Jasper's turn to smile, albeit wryly.

Lilia's smile widened. "That's perfect."

Jasper turned toward the breakfast nook, and as he did, his gaze fell on Lon and Corran. Lilia felt the atmosphere suddenly shift. Jasper's faint smile disappeared, his mouth flattening into a thin line. His gray eyes filled with hard suspicion, but he continued on to the breakfast nook without a word.

Lilia swallowed, her mouth suddenly bone-dry. Lon's armor and the sword he had wielded had been pushed to the background, but now that Kedis was out of danger, clearly they had just returned to the forefront of Jasper's mind.

Her eyes still on Jasper's broad shoulders, Lilia addressed Lon via Nancom again. [What are you going to tell Jasper and Renner about tonight?]

[The truth,] he said promptly. [Or at least the part of it they're allowed to know.]

A mirthless laugh rose in Lilia's throat; she strangled it. [I can think of a number of people who would argue they're not entitled to know *anything*.]

[Yeah, well, unfortunately that's not an option for me. They know I lied about nanoblades, at least.]

Lilia frowned before she could stop herself. Her gaze flicked to her brother. [What? How?]

Briefly, Lon told her about Lieutenant Armal and the nanoblade Chesnee's forces had reclaimed from the *Sprog*. [It's a mess I would have rather avoided, but…] he trailed off, his Nancom voice bearing a resigned air.

Lilia understood. There wasn't anything else he could have done. Kedis would be dead if he hadn't intervened. [I think the NCDC will take everything into account.]

[Frankly, I don't give a damn what they think. Not now.] Lon's face grew even stonier. [I did exactly what I was supposed to do—which was keep Kedis alive. They can't possibly expect to have kept the Guardians existence a secret forever. Not after a peace treaty.]

Lilia hadn't thought about that aspect of it until just now. She bit the inside of her lip. [What are you going to do?]

[Wait for them to ask.] Lon's lips twisted briefly. [I'm not volunteering anything I don't have to.]

Lilia glanced toward the breakfast nook again, where Renner had just joined Jasper. The two were obviously conferring about something; Renner cast a suspicious look at Lon. [I don't think you're going to have to wait very long.]

Lon did not react. [Might as well get it over with.]

# CHAPTER 52

JASPER returned shortly bearing two cups of coffee. He handed one of them to Lilia. "Here you are."

"Thank you." She accepted it with a soft smile, her gaze meeting his briefly. Suspicion still burned in his gray eyes, though she knew it wasn't directed at her. She took a careful sip—and her smile widened. Jasper had remembered how she liked her coffee.

Lilia glanced up at him through her lashes in time to see him shift to face Lon. *Well, that answers* that *question.* He wouldn't be sitting down just yet.

Renner joined them, also carrying a cup of coffee, though he seemed less than interested in it. He, too, fixed Lon with a hard stare.

Lon could hardly be unaware of such intense scrutiny. He looked at the two Tarynians, raising both eyebrows in an almost amused question. In Tarynian, he asked, "What's on your mind, gentlemen?"

A glance at Corran told Lilia Lon had filled him in on at least part of the story; he did not look as confused as he should have.

"You have some explaining to do." Jasper's grip tightened on his mug. "About tonight."

Lon glanced from Jasper to Renner, his amusement turning sardonic. "Save a man's life and they never let you live it down."

"Oh, we're grateful," Jasper shot back. "Don't misunderstand. But you…" He shook his head.

"You lied to us." Renner's voice was as hard as his expression. "You *have* seen swords like that before—hell, somehow you've got one."

"Technically, I lied to your Lieutenant Armal," Lon corrected him, almost lazily. "You weren't the ones asking me questions about it." He moved away from the window toward the chair nearest the couch where his sister sat; this wasn't a conversation he wanted to have standing up.

Lilia flicked her gaze toward him and then resumed resembling a statue seated in the corner.

Renner exchanged a frustrated look with Jasper before advancing on Lon. "Where did you get that sword? You didn't have it earlier."

"And where did you get that body armor?" Jasper demanded. "How did you make it appear and disappear out of thin air?"

Lon sighed. [The bad thing,] he told Lilia via Nancom, [is that I just had this exact same conversation with Kedis.]

She did not answer, but continued pretending to examine the depths of her coffee mug.

"It's rather difficult to explain, actually." Lon waved a hand toward the other chairs in the room. "You might want to have a seat."

Reluctantly, suspiciously, Jasper and Renner both sat. Renner took a chair opposite him, while Jasper sat down on the couch near Lilia.

Lon eyed him, but he didn't have time to deal with *that* at the moment. Instead, he took a breath and let it out slowly. "I'm something called a Guardian. I belong to the Nanotech Coalition Defense Corps. We're civilians."

Renner stared at him. "A civilian defense corps with armor that appears out of nowhere?"

"And swords sharp enough to cut through a floor?" Jasper asked.

Lon shot them a crooked grin. "Our tech is pretty good."

Jasper shook his head. "Why would you lie to Armal?"

"You're kidding, right?" Lon snorted derisively. "Why would I give him that kind of information?"

"The swords exist," Renner said. "You can't deny that."

The corners of Lon's mouth turned down in a frown. "They weren't supposed to be on the *Sprog*, that's for sure. Only Guardians are supposed to have nanoblades right now."

"Nanoblades?" Jasper pronounced the Sta'Gloan word with great interest. "Is that what they're called?"

Lilia shifted in her seat, a little uncomfortable. [Don't tell them too much, Lon.]

[I've got this.] Lon did not look at her. "Yeah, it is."

"And the armor?" Renner demanded.

Lon shrugged. "Let's just say it's there when I need it."

Jasper and Renner exchanged glances, before they both asked, "*How?*"

"That's not relevant." Lon lifted one shoulder in a shrug. "Sorry." He wasn't, really.

Jasper considered him a moment through narrowed gray eyes. "The Ambassador will not be satisfied with that answer."

Lilia suppressed a snort. *That* was an understatement if she'd ever heard one.

One side of Lon's mouth curled in a cocky smile. "Yeah, well, he'll just have to deal with it. Let's just say I'm probably one of the best candidates he could have had for a liaison and leave it at that."

Both Tarynians looked frustrated with this lack of an answer, but Lon didn't care. Neither did Lilia. *He doesn't owe them an explanation for his abilities…and frankly, they don't* need *to know.*

After a pause, the two officers moved on to other questions. "How long have you been a Guardian?" Renner asked.

"Couple of years." Lon shrugged. "Wanted to make a difference in people's lives."

Jasper started to ask another question, but Lon shook his head. "Nope. That's all you get."

Jasper promptly rounded on Lilia. "Did you know about this?"

Lilia had half-expected this, so Jasper's abrupt inquiry failed to catch her off-guard. She lifted her shoulders in an elegant little shrug. It occurred to her that she could refuse to answer, but what was the point of that? Jasper already knew how close-knit their family was. "I did eventually."

Also true—she hadn't heard about it until after Lon had undergone the procedure and he and Kevin stopped by the medcenter on Coral Island to see her.

A chill skipped from vertebra to vertebra. *Please, God, don't let him ask me if I'm a Guardian too. I don't want to lie, but I can't tell him the truth.*

To her everlasting relief, the thought did not appear to have even crossed Jasper's mind. He only shook his head and looked down into the depths of his coffee mug, his mouth thinning.

Renner folded his arms across his chest, half-glaring at Lon. "How many of these 'Guardians' are there?"

Lon shrugged. "No idea. Never kept tabs on that kind of thing."

Lilia scraped a fingernail against the side of her own mug. *I don't think that's information the NCDC would give us anyway.* She couldn't recall ever hearing a number in anything Dr. Dover or their instructor, Neela Vini, had told them.

She glanced toward the window, momentarily forgetting her surroundings. *I never thought it was all that important.* Now she found herself wondering exactly how many other Guardians were out there, scattered across Lanx, Sta'Gloa, Glo'Stea, and the mining stations.

Unbidden, another thought came to mind. *I wonder if the Mastermind knows.* If anybody outside of the NCDC higher-ups had information like that, the Mastermind probably did. How he'd gotten it was another story, but then, how had he managed most of the things Freedom's Children had done so far?

"...lia?"

A hand passed in front of her face. Lilia blinked, startled, and jerked backward. She glanced sideways as Jasper withdrew his hand, looking faintly amused.

"Sorry." A little embarrassed she'd spaced out, Lilia brushed a lock of hair out of her face. "I was—" She shook her head. "I'm tired."

"Understandable." Jasper checked his wristwatch. "It is very late."

Lilia bit her lip, tilting her coffee mug to look into it. She wanted to go home and crawl into bed. *Wonder how much longer I need to stay here.*

It was unlikely that Freedom's Children would attempt anything else tonight. Not at this point. Setting her mug down on the glass end table at her elbow, Lilia pressed the heels of her hands into her eyes. The resulting darkness was blissful; her eyes felt gritty.

Lon broke the silence that had enveloped the hotel suite. "Lilia, we need to figure out how we're going to get you home safely."

Lilia nodded, scrunching the fingers of one hand in the fabric of her evening gown. She wanted to go home so badly she felt it itching beneath her skin. "That would be nice." She opened a Nancom channel to her brother. [Although Callahan told me to stay here and help protect Kedis.]

[It'll be more suspicious if you stay here when you could have gone home.] A muscle twitched in Lon's cheek. [You don't want to give the media any more fuel for their crazy star-crossed lover thing they think you've got going with Wright, do you?]

[No.] Lilia cast an involuntary glance at Jasper, seated on the other end of the couch. As though feeling her eyes on him, he turned his head toward her. She quickly looked away, her heart giving a funny little jump.

Lon turned to Corran, whose face appeared to have settled into a permanent grimace. "Do you think things have calmed down enough to send her home now?"

"Maybe." Corran nodded to the wide window. "But there are still media cams down there, waiting for the Ambassador, or you, or someone."

Jasper stirred in his seat. "That seems to be a perpetual occurrence."

Corran raised his eyebrows. "Sure, but how's it going to look if Representative Monroe's granddaughter comes strolling out of the Beliana at this hour of the night?"

Heat flared to life in Lilia's cheeks. Oh, she knew *exactly* what they'd think.

"Given what just happened?" Lon protested.

"Want to risk it?" Corran's dark eyebrows rose several more millimeters. "They won't care if earlier footage shows her coming in with all of us."

"No." Lilia cleared her throat. "I'd rather not risk that, thank you." Corran, it was clear, had a good deal of experience dealing with potentially sticky situations.

Corran gave her a brisk, approving nod. "It will be best if you leave in broad daylight." He glanced at Lon. "Probably when Kedis leaves tomorrow—I mean, today."

"Wright." Lon addressed Jasper. "It's Sunday morning. You think Kedis will be up to going anywhere later?"

Lilia suppressed a snort. *That's a dumb question. I don't see him staying put.*

Jasper unknowingly echoed her sentiment. He smiled wryly. "Do you really think he'll stay cooped up here after tonight's events?"

"No." Lon scrubbed his hands through his sandy hair. "No, he'll milk this for all it's worth." He cast a regretful look at his sister. "Sorry, Lil."

"It's all right." Lilia twitched one shoulder in a shrug. "It's been a crazy night."

Lon tipped his head toward the bedrooms. "You can have my room. I'll sleep out here."

"Thank you." Lilia hated to put her brother out, but if she was honest, she'd much rather sleep in a bedroom than out in the open here. She'd feel a lot more comfortable if she had a door between her and everyone else. If it was just Lon, Jasper, and Renner, that might be one thing, but she really didn't know Corran and the men on his security team.

After a few minutes, Lilia got up and went to the hygiene unit. There wasn't much she could do without any luggage, but she could at least wipe a few streaks of grime off her face. When she returned, she found the living room empty save for Jasper.

She must have looked surprised, because he half-smiled at her from his seat on the couch. "Your brother is prepping his room for you, Renner went to bed, and Corran went to the other suite to talk to our security team." He nodded toward the door.

"Ah." Lilia stood frozen in place for a handful of heartbeats, unsure what she should do. She knew what she *wanted* to do—namely sit back down on the couch and talk to Jasper—but she wasn't sure what she *ought* to do. Unconsciously, she straightened her shoulders before marching back over to the couch and resuming her seat.

Jasper cleared his throat, shifting in his seat to angle his body toward her. "You handled everything that happened tonight very well." He met her gaze, his gray eyes filled with a kind of steady admiration. "You didn't fall to pieces and lose your head."

Heat rose to Lilia's cheeks; she ducked her head, tucking a lock of dark hair behind her ear. *Oh, if you only knew the half of it.* "Well, it wasn't my first time dealing with a crisis. I have a little experience."

Amusement now mingled with the admiration glinting in Jasper's eyes. "Just say thank you."

"Thank you."

"You're welcome."

They shared a smile, and then companionable silence fell over them, until Lilia felt words rise to the tip of her tongue. She bit her lip, eyes darting instinctively to the hallway through which her brother was due to emerge at any moment, and swallowed. "Thank you for trying to protect me when they came through the ceiling."

She would have been fine, thanks to her nano-armor, but Jasper hadn't known that. His actions had been both sweet—and instinctive. Looking back to those hazy, crazy few minutes, Lilia could recall that he hadn't hesitated.

"'Trying'?" Jasper pretended to look affronted, before his expression relaxed into a smile. He dipped his head in a courteous nod. "You're welcome." A beat, and then, quietly, "I did not want anything to happen to you."

His voice—low and sincere—sent the blood rushing to Lilia's cheeks again. Her breath caught in her throat as the hotel suite seemed to fade around them until the two of them were all that remained. The air seemed charged; the same magnetic force that kept them in each other's orbit drawing them closer together.

"Thank you." The words emerged sounding breathless; her heart had sped up in unconscious anticipation.

Jasper leaned toward her, lifting a hand to breach the remaining distance between them and touch her cheek. His gray eyes dropped briefly to her lips.

Just then, Lon emerged from the hall, shattering the spell that had fallen over them. He carried a pillow and folded blanket under one arm. "Lilia, you're all set."

Lilia and Jasper sprang apart as though they had both received an electric shock. Lilia's heart was still pounding, though now for a completely different reason. She swallowed, unable to look at Jasper—she hadn't realized how close they had gotten until that moment.

"Thanks, Lon." She sounded more composed than she felt.

Lon nodded, waving aside her thanks. "Second door on the left. Light's on."

Lilia took that as her cue to depart. Rising from the couch, she smoothed out the folds of her gown. When she turned to Jasper, her cheeks were back to their normal color. "Good night."

"Good night." Jasper rose from his seat as well. "I hope you sleep without bad dreams."

Touched by his thoughtfulness, Lilia smiled softly at him. "Thank you." She turned to her brother and gave him a tight hug. "Night, Lon."

"Night, sis."

As Lilia moved toward the hall, Lon dropped his armful of bedding onto the couch they had just vacated. Jasper exchanged a few words with him before following Lilia out.

Warm light spilled out into the dark hall from Lon's room. Lilia paused on the threshold, taking it in at a glance. Aside from the rich, expensive look to everything, it wasn't that different from any other upscale hotel room she'd ever seen. A large bed, a large holoprojector taking up one wall, a desk and chair, and metal-and-glass nightstands. A wardrobe stood against one wall, with mirrored doors. Striped silver, turquoise, pale blue, and lavender curtains fell to the floor over the windows, matching the bedspread.

Lilia blinked, and then laughed once. It didn't look like Lon at all.

"He drew the short straw," Jasper said from behind her.

Still smiling, Lilia glanced over her shoulder at him. "It's not very…manly."

"That would be why we drew straws."

"I don't blame you."

They grinned at each other, and then Lilia quickly jerked a thumb toward Lon's room before things could get awkward. She was too exhausted to deal with anything else tonight. "Good night. Again."

Jasper just smiled and continued down the hall, but as he passed her, he grazed his fingertips along her shoulders in a wordless goodbye.

Sparks erupted along her skin in his wake, giving her a delightful shiver. Unable to suppress a pleased little smile, Lilia stepped into her brother's room and hit the door release. It slid shut behind her with barely a sound and she made her way over to the wardrobe. Snagging a clean shirt of Lon's, she extricated herself from her gown and draped it over the back of the chair. She wore a half-slip beneath it; she pulled Lon's shirt on to cover her torso, climbed into the bed, and turned out the lights.

Despite the fact that she was exhausted, the moment Lilia closed her eyes, her mind flashed back to the seconds before Lon had returned to the living room. A fresh blush heated her cheeks in the darkness; she wiggled her toes beneath the sheets and covers.

*Jasper was going to kiss me!*

Or if he wasn't, he'd been thinking about it. Her cheeks heated further. That moment had been too electrically charged to be anything else.

Lilia rolled over, half-burying herself in the pillows, and finally allowed herself to admit the truth she'd been unconsciously avoiding for weeks now. *He* likes *me.*

It was obvious in the way he looked at her, the way he talked to her, the way he treated her.

Her brothers had noticed; Alexis had seen it in *media coverage* for crying out loud.

Lilia had just never allowed herself to see it, because…well…because it would have required admitting she'd *noticed*, first, and also…

*He's never outright* said *anything.*

This…*thing*…growing between them was easier to pass off as simple friendship if she only went by what had been spoken aloud.

Her blush faded as the facts about their situation flood her mind. Jasper was a lieutenant in the Galactic Union StarFleet. He stood for a system she'd been opposed to her entire life. She pressed her face harder into the pillows. Where was his interest in her going to go? Where *could* it go?

It was getting harder to breathe. Lilia finally flopped back over onto her back and grimaced up at the ceiling. She liked him back. She really did.

*And I shouldn't.*

It would be much easier for everyone if she squashed those feelings, buried them so far down they would never, ever see the light of day.

Her grimace grew pained. Except…if she was honest with herself, it was probably too late.

*How in the galaxy did* that *happen?*

# CHAPTER 53

ADMIRAL Chesnee woke to the sound of an incoming high-priority comm alarm. He rubbed the sleep out of his eyes, wondering if middle-of-the-night interruptions were to be his fate now that Kedis was on Sta'Gloa. *What's happened now, I wonder?* He had specifically requested that incoming comms from any of the Coalition's worlds be immediately routed to him.

Padding out of his quarters and into his office, he tapped the comm panel mounted in the corner of his desk. "Admiral Chesnee."

Instead of the Ambassador, Lieutenant Wright's head and shoulders appeared in front of his desk. The younger man looked tired and disheveled, his face faintly streaked with grime. "My apologies for disturbing you, Admiral, but I thought you should know the Ambassador just survived an attack tonight."

"What kind of attack?" Chesnee leaned forward, his hands planted on the surface of his desk. "Who is responsible?"

"We're not yet sure who is behind it, sir." Wright went on to describe the evening, concluding with, "The Ambassador is resting now. He'll make a full recovery."

"Thank heaven for that," Chesnee said dryly. *I'd hate to have even more politicians descend on me.* Kedis's death would be a disaster, for all sorts of reasons. "I am glad Captain Strong was able to save his life."

"Yes."

Chesnee squinted slightly at the Lieutenant. Was it his imagination, or did the younger officer look vaguely uncomfortable, like he was conflicted about something? "What's on your mind, Lieutenant?"

For a few seconds, Wright did not answer. He only continued to look conflicted.

Chesnee's gut instinct told him this was probably important. "Lieutenant Wright?" He put a hint of stern command into his voice.

Wright instinctively straightened. "Sir, what I'm about to tell you may sound crazy."

Chesnee almost smiled. "When it comes to the Coalition, son, I have a feeling I've heard crazier."

"Well…" Wright took a breath, obviously trying to put his thoughts into order. "Have you ever heard scuttlebutt about a group of people called Guardians?"

"Guardians?" Something crystallized inside Chesnee. His voice sharpened. "Yes. What about them?"

Wright took another breath. "Well, sir, it would seem Captain Strong is one of them, and that's how he was able to save the Ambassador's life tonight."


When Chesnee finally dismissed Lieutenant Wright, advising him to get some rest before he cut the connection, he sank back down into his chair on legs that were just a little unsteady. He hardly knew what to think. *They* do *exist.* All the years of scuttlebutt, all the odd reports that had been made in the past few years…*They're real.*

Somehow, the Coalition had created technology that allowed people to produce armor out of thin air. And, apparently, they were armed with more of those swords Lieutenant Armal had found so intriguing. Chesnee massaged his temples. *I suppose that's not much of a stretch, considering they've also created transporters.*

That Captain Strong was one of them was also a shock. Chesnee stared out the wide viewport lining his office at Lanx's surface and the star-studded expanse of space beyond, recalling his various interactions with the young Sta'Gloan. *I never would have guessed.*

Strong had seemed…well…relatively normal. Not much different from any other young freighter captain Chesnee had ever encountered, even if he *was* related to a high-ranking politician. And over the course of his time aboard the *Winds of Change*, Strong had done nothing to draw attention to himself, nothing that would have indicated he possessed advanced technology.

Chesnee snorted softly to himself. *Well, on that front at least, it seems he had some common sense.* Even if Strong had attempted to use his advanced tech to escape, where would he go? He could have used an escape pod or perhaps a Piranha, if he'd gotten really lucky, to leave the *Change* behind, but thanks to Lanx's planetary shield, he would have been well and truly stuck.

The more he thought about it, however, the more the notion of these Guardians and of Lon Strong being one of them made Chesnee uneasy. Part of him thought it wasn't much different than having a concealed weapon, but the rest of him thought it an extremely unfair advantage. He found himself wondering how many of the people around Kedis were Guardians without the Ambassador having the slightest idea.

Kedis prided himself on being so in tune with everything going on around him that the idea of him being oblivious to the presence of more than one Guardian almost made Chesnee laugh.

Too quickly, he sobered. *Transporters, nanoblades, and advanced armor tech.* The military implications of nano-armor were stunning— and that was without even considering either of the other two. *Kedis would be a fool not to make some sort of play for technology like that.*

Chesnee drummed his fingers against the surface of his desk. He wasn't sleepy any more; his brain had hummed to life. The Coalition would no doubt be reluctant to yield these secrets to the Galactic Union, but they had a long way to go before peace negotiations were over.

*And with Leo Kedis involved,* he thought wryly, *he'll get* something *out of them.*

The real question now was what he, Chesnee, was supposed to *do* with this information. Should he pass it along to High Command now, or wait for Kedis to inform him and then tell his superiors? Chesnee's eyes slid again to the portion of Lanx visible through his viewport. The world's night side glittered with pinpricks of light—a sight he had yet to tire of seeing.

In the end, Chesnee decided to keep everything to himself for the time being. *Admiral Tyler can do nothing except pass it along to High Command, who will in turn inform the Senate. And the only thing they can do is put pressure on me to do…something, who knows what, exactly…instead of Kedis.*

He was under no illusions about *that*; for the moment, Kedis was untouchable.

Chesnee smiled grimly. *We'll see how long that lasts.* Even if the Coalition cooperated with the Ambassador, Chesnee doubted they would fully integrate into the G.U.—and that would have a profound impact on the trading of technology like transporters, special armor, and swords that could cut through metal bulkheads.

*The Senate's golden boy might emerge from this a little tarnished after all.*

# CHAPTER 54

AFTER occasions like the night before, Jasper always found himself profoundly grateful for caffeine. Too much excitement and not nearly enough sleep combined with an early wakeup made for the start of a very, very long day. On top of that, he hadn't slept well; his mind too restless and conflicted to allow him to relax. The attack, Lon's strange revelation and all the ramifications it produced, and Lilia revolved around and around in his head.

He had just sat down at the table in the breakfast nook with his first cup of coffee when his comlink beeped softly. He glanced down at the display, where an imperious command awaited.

*COME HERE.*

Kedis. Jasper rubbed a hand over his face, suppressing a sigh. *Shouldn't he still be asleep?* Nevertheless, he rose from the table and headed for the Ambassador's room—taking his coffee with him. He had a feeling as soon as Kedis got going, today was going to be non-stop action. *Strike while the shield's down.*

As he passed the closed door to Lon's room, Jasper's stride slowed just a fraction. He swallowed. He'd almost kissed Lilia last night. If Lon hadn't interrupted them, he probably would have. If he was honest with himself, he'd wanted to do that for a while now.

His face softened. Even exhausted, she'd looked so pretty sitting there, smiling at him with an openness it had taken time for him to earn.

He'd never expected his assignment to the Blockade Division to result in meeting someone like her.

*Can't think about that now.* His hopes for the future would have to wait; he had a duty to perform.

Jasper reached Kedis's door and squared his shoulders before entering. He didn't know yet what the Ambassador wanted, but he was sure Kedis would have something to say about Lon.

"There you are." Kedis was still in bed, his bandaged leg stretched out in front of him and a breakfast tray with dirty dishes sitting beside him.

Jasper came to attention and saluted. "Good morning, Ambassador. How are you?"

"I'll be fine." Kedis waved the inquiry aside to focus on more important things. "At ease, Lieutenant. Were you aware Lon Strong is one of these mysterious Guardian people?"

*Knew it*, Jasper thought. "He informed us of that a few hours ago, sir. After he spoke to you."

"I see." Kedis fixed his gaze on him, his dark eyes sharp and unreadable. "Thoughts, Lieutenant?"

*Like I've had much time to think about it.* Jasper glanced down at the caramel brown surface of his coffee. "It was a surprise, sir. I wasn't expecting it."

"But?" Kedis arched an eyebrow, clearly expecting more.

"Well…" Jasper shrugged. "It does make sense of a few things about him."

"Oh? In what way?"

Jasper hesitated. "It's difficult to put it into words, Ambassador."

Kedis gave him a dry look. "Try."

Jasper let his eyes wander around the room while he thought about it, trying to break Lon down into categories. "I think it explains some of his confidence in certain situations."

"Ah, yes." Kedis drummed his fingers on the bed, glancing down at his datapad. "If I had body armor that mysteriously appeared on demand, I believe I'd be a little more arrogant when faced with my enemies as well."

He frowned at his datapad, but it was more a thoughtful expression than angry. "I wonder if any of his siblings also belong to this Nanotech Coalition Defense Corps."

That thought had occurred to Jasper too. "I don't know, sir."

"Find out." Kedis's gaze snapped back to Jasper, pinning him in place. "My previous orders still stand. Lon is a piece of the puzzle, but there is more to this situation. I can feel it."

Jasper's gut clenched. "Yes, sir."

Kedis flicked his fingers at him in a dismissive wave. "You may go."

Jasper remained where he was. "If I may ask, Ambassador, what are your plans for today?"

"It depends." Kedis's smile had a feral edge.

*Depends on what?* Jasper wanted to ask, but he knew that was all the answer he was going to get for now. Inclining his head in a polite nod, he marched out of the room.

Returning to the breakfast nook, he resumed his seat, resisting the urge to slump in his chair. It was too much to expect Kedis to let him off the hook as far as investigating the Strongs was concerned. *If anything, this will pique his interest even more.*

And, really, when it came down to it, Jasper found he couldn't blame the Ambassador. Lon, at least, was mixed up with something fantastic—something Jasper had never dreamed could actually be real. *All those years, scuttlebutt was right.*

He grimaced into his coffee, his mind's eye painting a terrible picture. *Magic armor and swords that can cut through bulkheads. How do you defend against those?*

# Chapter 55

LON woke his sister what felt like far too early the next morning. It was nine A.M., but after the night they'd had, Lilia could have slept another five or six hours. Groggily, she rolled over in bed and slung an arm across her eyes as Lon tapped a button on the wall, making the curtains parted to flood the room with dim light, and commanded the lights to come on.

"How much coffee have you had?" she demanded.

"Not nearly enough."

Lilia dropped her arm to squint at her brother and Lon shot her a bleary grin. "I'd let you sleep all morning, but Kedis is raring to go."

"Of course he is." Lilia shut her eyes again, but the room's lights were still bright against the backs of her eyelids. "How much coffee has *he* had this morning? He got blown up last night."

This prompted another smile from her brother, but all Lon said was, "See you shortly. I'll leave you some coffee."

"You better."

"Oh, by the way. What do you want for breakfast? They have really good crepes here."

"Sounds good." Lilia waved an arm in the air. "Pick something."

"Ooh." It sounded like Lon was rubbing his hands together. "You're giving me free reign over your breakfast?"

"Don't make me regret it."

Lon just laughed and closed the door behind him on his way out.

When he was gone, Lilia heaved a sigh. *I don't want to get up.* Actually, she didn't want to deal with anything from last night's events. With the adrenaline rush gone, all she felt was deep exhaustion.

Problem was, she couldn't stay here. She needed to go home.

Rubbing her eyes, Lilia forced herself to sit up and swing her legs over the side of the bed. Through the windows, she could see the sky outside was dark and heavy with storm clouds. *What would we do without caffeine?*

When Lilia entered the living room, dressed again in her emerald green evening gown, she found everyone but Kedis scattered around eating breakfast. Renner gave her a courteous tip of the head, Jasper smiled at her over his coffee. The sight sent a giddy rush through her, which she ruthlessly tried to squash. She was not entirely successful.

Lon nodded to a covered tray sitting on the table in the breakfast nook. "I think you'll like it."

"Thanks, Lon." Lilia fixed herself a cup of coffee before sitting down at the little table and lifting the lid off her tray. Three crepes filled with peaches and cream greeted her, along with several slices of bacon. Her mouth watered. "This looks really good."

"I'm glad." Lon looked pleased. "Eat up."

It did not take Lilia long to clean her plate. Once she took the first bite, she realized how hungry she was—and the crepes were delicious. By the time she was finished, Kedis had emerged from his room. He walked with a slight limp, but otherwise seemed fine. He acknowledged her presence with a brisk nod, before moving over to the windows to confer with Jasper, Renner, and Lon.

Lilia watched them out of the corner of her eye while she poured herself another cup of coffee. When Kedis finally turned away, pulling his comlink from a pocket, Lilia opened a Nancom channel to Lon. [What do you want me to do?]

Lon glanced at her from his spot by the window. [I don't know what to tell you. Other than the fact that he's in an all-fired hurry, Kedis hasn't made his mind up yet. He's thinking of holding a press conference before he does anything else.]

[I can leave before he does that, right?]

[There may not be time.]

[Great.] Suppressing a sigh, Lilia moved over to the couch and tucked herself into the corner. Over the top of her coffee cup, she watched Kedis limp back and forth across the living room. Clearly, he was feeling much better. [Pain meds probably didn't hurt,] she thought shrewdly.

Three minutes later, a pleasant chime filled the air. Renner moved to answer the door, and several people Lilia assumed must be among Kedis's chief staff members entered the suite. They all glanced at her, but seemed to dismiss her entirely afterwards.

That was fine with Lilia; she didn't want their attention. *The less attention I draw, the better.* Impatience began thrumming in her veins; she wanted to get out of here. Even Jasper's presence wasn't enough to assuage her burning desire to go home.

"Did you get any sleep?"

*Speaking of Jasper…*Lilia looked up as he approached her. She offered him a slight smile. "I did, thanks."

He smiled back. "I imagine you're ready to go home."

Her smile grew rueful. "You have no idea."

"Oh, I can guess." Jasper took a seat at the other end of the couch, casting a thoughtful look toward the door through which Kedis had exited. "We should be able to get you home soon."

"That would be nice."

"I must admit I've enjoyed seeing you."

"You too." It wasn't hard to look pleasant; after all, hadn't she found herself smiling more readily around him? Regardless of anything else, he had become her friend—and she really did enjoy his company.

A warm, mischievous glint entered his gray eyes. "Although I confess that as much as I enjoy our nightly conversations, I prefer having them in person."

"What, you don't like doing everything through a comlink?" Lilia relaxed, giving him an impish smile in return. "The technological advances humans have made in the galaxy, and you prefer to actually be in the same room." She shook her head in mock-sadness. "I don't know what we'll do with you."

"When you put it that way…" Jasper pretended to look solemn. "I do seem to have a problem. What remedy would you suggest I try?"

He looked so sober and serious that a snort of laughter escaped Lilia before she could help herself. She clapped a hand over her mouth to hide her grin and focused on her coffee cup, lest they draw Lon, Renner, and Corran's attention. When she thought she could speak without laughing, she dropped her hand and contemplated him with pursed lips. "I don't know, Lieutenant. Perhaps you'd better immerse yourself in technology and attempt to embrace it?"

Jasper's eyes were dancing, but before he could respond, Lilia's comlink began to vibrate with an incoming voice-only call. She held up a finger. "Hold that thought." Picking it up out of her lap, she glanced at the display—and froze.

It was Jayce.

Her heart skipped a beat in sheer consternation; she couldn't take the call with Jasper sitting right there. It was far too risky. Mouth dry, she stared at the display. *What do I do? Why is he calling now?*

In the span of a few seconds, she weighed her options. She *could* ignore Jayce for the moment and get back to him later…but she couldn't take the risk that he was calling about something truly important.

There was only one way to find out.

Flashing Jasper a smile she hoped was innocent, Lilia set her nearly empty coffee cup down on the glass end table at her elbow. "I need to take this. I'll be right back." She tried to keep a normal pace as she strode toward the relative privacy of Lon's room.

Jayce started talking as soon as she answered. "You have to help me! They're after me!" His words—low and panicked—tumbled over each other.

"What? Slow down."

"There isn't *time!*" Jayce hissed, still in low tones, as though he was trying not to be overheard. "They're here for me. I need you to get me out of here!"

Lilia blinked, startled by the desperation in his voice. "Who's after you?" She kept herself from saying his name at the last second… just in case Kedis—or someone else—had bugged the hotel suite.

"I don't know, but they look like Guardians. Get me out of here, Miss Strong. *Please.*" He rattled off a set of coordinates. "This is my location."

*Guardians?* Lilia felt as though somebody had just dumped freezing water over her head, temporarily shortcutting her brain. *What is going on?*

Panic made her head feel like it had been stuffed full of cotton—she couldn't *think.* Her thoughts spun and whirled in her head, tumbling over themselves in a chaotic jumble. *What do I do?*

She couldn't let Jayce be kidnapped, but what in the galaxy was she supposed to *do* with him once she got him here?

*"Miss Strong!"*

Lilia snapped back to herself, a semblance of a plan coalescing her mind. "Okay. Get ready." She bit her lip. "I can't guarantee how far off the ground it'll open."

"I'll chance it. *Hurry.*"

Heart palpitating in her chest, Lilia fixed the coordinates in her mind as she materialized her gloves and held out her hands toward the middle of the room. She concentrated, and a portal sphere blossomed in the empty air before her.

It was barely big enough for a person when a wild-eyed Jayce scrambled through. "Close it, close it, close it!" he chanted breathlessly, nearly tripping over his feet and falling flat on his face in his haste to get away from the portal and the possiblity of someone coming through after him.

Lilia hushed him, casting a nervous look at the door, even as she collapsed the portal. It disappeared with a little pop and she rounded on him. "Are you all right?"

"I—I think so." Jayce straightened, smoothing his hands down the front of his lab coat. He was breathing hard. "Thank you."

"Don't thank me yet." Lilia took a deep breath, realizing her own heart was pounding. She cast another glance at the door. "It probably won't be long before the Ambassador's security team realizes another body has showed up here."

Jayce's eyes widened. "Ambassador?" He finally looked around, taking in his surroundings. "Where are we, exactly?"

Lilia shot him a wry look. "Ambassador Kedis's hotel suite." His eyes widened further and she sighed. "It's a long story. The important thing is that we get you out of here."

She opened a Nancom channel to Kevin. [Where are you?]

[Well, good morning to you too. Who spit in your coff—]

[*Kev.*] Lilia cut him off. [I just brought Dr. Jayce through a portal.] Silence greeted these words. [He was being attacked—probably Freedom's Children.]

[Wow.] All amused annoyance faded from his Nancom voice. [Are you still—]

[Yes. I need you to open a portal here and get him out. Fast.]

[I can do that. Give me your coordinates.]

Scooping her comlink up from the bed, Lilia used it to determine their location and read the coordinates off to her brother.

[Hold on.]

Ten seconds later, a portal sphere appeared to one side of the bed—four feet off the carpeted floor. Ordinarily, that wouldn't have been a problem…except that Lilia's fingers grazed the spot where her hoverdisc lay in her ISF without being able to access it. She bit back a frustrated exclamation; if there was ever a time they could have used a cooperative portal, it would have been now.

She looked at Jayce. "My nanites are frozen—I can't get to my hoverdisc."

He canted his head to one side, scrutinizing the portal. "Not a problem. I think I can jump."

Alarm flooded Lilia. "Jump?"

"It'll be fine." Waving a hand, Jayce clambered up on to the bed. He offered her a shaky smile. "Thanks for rescuing me."

Kevin's mental voice—tense and strained—came through their Nancom channel. [Tell him to get his butt through the portal *now*.]

Lilia made a shooing gesture with her hands. "Go now. He can't keep it open much longer."

With a nod, Jayce turned and leaped from the bed into the portal. The fluttering tail of his lab coat had just barely disappeared when the portal collapsed.

Lilia felt like collapsing along with it. She leaned against the bed on knees that had suddenly turned to jelly and flattened a hand against her thundering heart. *That was close.*

It was only then that she realized she was still wearing her gloves—and she wouldn't be able to dematerialize them for an hour.

She stared down at her hands in dismay. How was she going to hide her gloves? Or explain them without giving everything away?

Someone banged a heavy fist against the door.

Lilia nearly jumped out of her skin. She stared at the door in horror. *What do I do?*

# CHAPTER 56

"MISS Strong?" Corran's deep voice called out. "Open the door." The banging continued.

Lilia's eyes fell on the shirt she'd slept in, lying discarded on the bed, and a crazy idea occurred to her. Bounding over to the wardrobe, she opened it and grabbed another of Lon's shirts. Whirling the jade green material about her shoulders, she shoved her arms into the sleeves to hide her gloved hands and hurried over to the door.

Slapping the door release, she arranged her features into an expression of confusion. "Is something wrong?"

Corran stood in the hall outside her door, along with Jasper, Renner, Lon, and another member of the security team named Terrence. Corran's expression was hard. "Are you alone in here?"

"Alone?" Lilia lifted her eyebrows in polite incredulity. "Of course I'm alone." She nodded to the room behind her, clutching the shirt. "See for yourself."

She stepped aside to allow Corran entrance. He pushed past her and immediately dropped to the floor to stare under the bed. "Nothing there."

"I'm telling you, sir," Terrence said, "there was another person on the scanner." He was a brawny man with coal black skin.

Lilia looked at Lon and then Jasper. "What is going on?"

Lon ignored her question. "Is that my shirt?"

"Yes." Lilia lifted her chin. "I had to take a call, and then I decided to concoct a plan to slip out of here without the media recognizing me." She opened a Nancom channel to him. [It's a long story, but I had to open a portal and I can't dematerialize my gloves for an hour.]

A slight frown was Lon's only answer.

After making a thorough examination of the room, Corran turned to Terrence. "There's nobody here." His gaze slid to Lilia. "You didn't see anything suspicious?" She shook her head and his attention returned to his man. "Scanner must have been wrong, Terrence. Better run a diagnostic."

"Yes, sir." Terrence was too professional to openly deflate, but an undercurrent of frustration tinged his words.

The two security men filed out, followed by Renner. Lon shook his head at his sister. "Good luck with your escape plan. I don't think my pants are going to fit you."

"Oh, don't worry." Lilia shrugged airily. "I'll figure something out."

Via Nancom, Lon said, [That was close. What in the galaxy were you *thinking*?]

[It was an emergency. I'll fill you in later.]

[You better.]

Lon returned to the living room, leaving Jasper standing in the doorway. He leaned against the doorjamb, looking amused. "What are you going to do with your dress?"

Tightening her fingers in the shirtsleeves instinctively to hide them, Lilia lifted one shoulder in a shrug. "I'll have Lon send it to me, I guess." She wrinkled her nose. "I really do need to go home. Has the Ambassador decided what he's going to do yet?"

Jasper did not move. "Press conference." He tipped his head toward the window. "Here."

Lilia nodded, already calculating how she could best use that to her advantage.

"You should be able to slip out without anyone taking much notice." A teasing grin curved Jasper's lips. "As long as you don't venture out in that particular getup."

Eyebrow raised, Lilia looked down at herself, noting the way Lon's jade green shirt clashed against the emerald material of her gown. "What, you don't think I'm the picture of high society?"

Chuckling, Jasper shook his head.

Lilia smiled back, but inside she felt the faint stirrings of panic. *This would be so much simpler if I could get away with pulling clothes from my ISF.*

"We missed church this morning."

Her eyes snapped to Jasper, who looked a little sad. "Yes, we did."

He shrugged one shoulder, still leaning up against the door-jamb. "I was planning on attending a church down the street. One of Corran's men was going to go with me."

"I'm sorry." Lilia started to reach out to him, but remembered her gloves at the last second. She curled her fingers into fists inside the too-long sleeves of her brother's shirt. *Idiot. You'll give everything away if you're not careful.*

"Of course, nobody could have seen *this* coming."

"No, they couldn't."

Neither of them spoke for a moment. Snippets of conversations from the living room filtered down the hall to them. Lilia glanced at Jasper, fiddling with the cuffs of Lon's shirt, but Jasper's gaze had dropped to the carpet.

At last, he roused himself. "The Ambassador seems to think the Triumvirate will call an emergency session today."

"It's likely." Lilia offered him a wry smile. "They don't usually work on Sundays, but there have been a few of those emergency sessions since Admiral Chesnee took command of the blockade."

Jasper grinned. "The Admiral *has* been disrupting things, hasn't he?"

Despite herself, Lilia couldn't help but smile back. "He does seem to be rather good at his job."

"Why, Miss Strong." Jasper pretended to be shocked. "Complimenting the enemy. What will Sonela society say?"

Lilia rolled her eyes. "Nothing more than what they've already said, I'm sure."

"You really don't like it, do you?" Jasper looked at her, his gray eyes clear and steady. "Attending all the parties."

Grimacing, Lilia shook her head. "It's a different world. Sure, it was interesting at first, but I look around and see all the fancy dresses, and the fancy food, and I think about the people in places on Glo'Stea who are barely getting by. I still wonder what the point is."

"Understandable." Jasper nodded soberly, but then smiled. "For the record, I'm glad you are attending some of these parties." His voice grew low. "Dancing with you makes them a little more bearable."

A warm flush flooded Lilia; butterflies erupted in her stomach. Her eyes locked with Jasper's, giving her the courage to voice the words that sprang to the tip of her tongue—words she would have ordinarily held back. Words she probably *should* hold back. "Just the dancing?"

His smile warmed as the look in his eyes intensified. "Not just the dancing. Seeing you. Talking to you."

"That's my favorite part too," Lilia admitted softly.

Jasper still stood in the doorway, separated from her by over a meter of carpet, but the air between them electrified. Her heart was hammering in her chest. All the reasons why it wasn't a good idea to be his friend, to flirt with him the way they were flirting, to *like* him fell away.

For a moment, they were just two unlikely friends, a man and a woman on opposite sides of a conflict who had found they had more in common than either of them could have ever dreamed.

"Is that why you come to the parties, even though you don't like them?" The words were teasing, but his expression remained intense and serious.

"I—" Lilia opened her mouth to respond, but the words wouldn't come. How could she tell him that his presence was a much-needed boon, but she would have had to be there anyway?

Footsteps down the hall snapped them both back to reality. "Wright," Renner's voice said, "the Ambassador wants to hold his press conference now."

Jasper glanced over his shoulder at the corporal. "Understood. I'll be there in a moment."

Renner's footsteps receded, and Jasper returned his attention to Lilia. "We can finish this conversation later." He smiled ruefully, pushing away from the doorjamb to stand up straight. "Unfortunately, duty calls."

Lilia nodded, a wash of conflicting emotions engulfing her— disappointment mixed with a huge swell of relief. Suddenly feeling shy, she dropped her eyes. "I…probably won't be here when you get back. I need to go—"

"—home. I know." Jasper hesitated a fraction of a second and then stepped into Lon's room. Two quick strides brought them face-to-face. He brought a hand up to the side of her face, delicately brushing a stray lock of dark brown hair back behind her ear. "Just—be watchful."

She quirked a smile at him. "You too."

They looked at each other, and then Jasper leaned in and pressed a quick kiss to her temple. "I will call you tonight."

"I'd like that." Her words emerged sounding breathless; her heart rate had tripled at his touch. Sparks shot along her nerve-endings. He was so close, so very close; she could feel the warmth radiating from his body. Her mind flashed back to the night before and, almost of their own accord, her arms came up to embrace him in a hug.

Jasper hugged her back, his face resting in the curve of her neck for a few seconds before he released her. Staring down at her upturned face, he looked like he wanted to say something else, but once again it passed. With a small smile and one last intense look, he turned and strode out of the room.

Lilia's knees wobbled; she pressed a hand against her chest, un-mindful of her gloves, and tried to *breathe*. The way he'd just looked at her…He was *definitely* interested. Her skin tingled with phantom memories of where he had touched her; her heart still thudded in her chest.

Her nascent plan for escaping the hotel temporarily forgotten, Lilia stumbled over to the edge of the bed and collapsed on it. Her face flushed; she fanned herself with a jade-green sleeve. *I am in so much trouble.*

# CHAPTER 57

DARK storm clouds stretched over Sonela, threatening imminent rain. The living room was dim, but Kevin didn't bother turning a light on as he paced back and forth across the white carpet. He'd been roving the penthouse since he woke up that morning, too restless to settle down. He heaved an impatient breath. Lilia was stuck at the Beliana with the Tarynians and he was stuck here at Ferndale.

Granted, it was of his own volition, but still…Stuck was stuck. He rubbed bleary eyes as he approached the doorway leading into the dining room, turned, and headed back across the living room. As badly as he itched to open a portal and join Erik in the *Talia*, he couldn't shake a nagging sensation of impending doom.

It had been bothering him ever since he and his brothers returned home with their grandfather in the wee hours of the morning, the feeling that the fight wasn't over, that the attack at the hotel was only the beginning. For that reason, he hadn't wanted to risk opening a portal and rendering part of his nano-armor useless for an hour.

That was why when Lilia Nancommed him to ask him to open a portal for Dr. Jayce, he wasn't surprised. He'd been expecting *something* to happen. The fact that *Jayce* was the one they were rescuing was a surprise, but not the fact that Freedom's Children had struck again.

Jayce shot out of the portal, his momentum carrying him straight into the navy blue couch along the wall opposite the windows. He landed with a thud. "Oof!"

Kevin lost no time collapsing the portal. His brain had begun screaming at him, reminding him that he couldn't keep the portal open forever or bad things would happen. It disappeared and he strode across the living room to haul Jayce to his feet. "Are you all right?"

Jayce blinked at him, wild-eyed. "They kidnapped Phillip!"

Kevin had wondered why Jayce hadn't said anything about his older colleague. "What happened?"

"They came out of nowhere. Must have used a transporter." Jayce ran his hands through his red hair, still looking wild, and began to pace. Unknowingly, he took the same track Kevin had been walking a moment earlier. "We're building another transporter, you know."

"I remember you mentioning it," Kevin said dryly. "How did you escape?"

Jayce didn't seem to have heard him. "They were Guardians." He rounded on Kevin. "Why would *Guardians* try to kidnap us?"

*Because they weren't Guardians*, Kevin thought, but all he said was, "How do you know they were Guardians?"

Jayce passed a shaking hand over his face. "Recognized their facemasks and helmets."

"That's it? They weren't wearing full nano-armor?"

"No." Jayce shook his head a second time. "Just headgear."

"And you're sure it was nano-armor?" Kevin asked sharply.

"Of course I'm sure." Testiness bled into Jayce's tone. "I know what nano-armor looks like, remember?"

Kevin brushed that aside. "How do you know they used a portal?"

Jayce stopped pacing long enough to round on Kevin. "How else would they have gotten into the lab? There's only one entrance."

Suspicion flickered to life in Kevin's mind. Something about this didn't seem right. Folding his arms across his chest, he narrowed his eyes at Jayce. "It's Sunday. Were you working?"

"Didn't have anything else to do."

"How did you get away without them seeing you and capturing you too?"

"I was lucky." Jayce swayed a little on his feet, his adrenaline rush of the past ten minutes fading, but instead of sitting down on the couch, he continued to pace. "They didn't see me." His steps paused. "At least, I don't *think* they saw me."

"You'd better tell me *exactly* what happened," Kevin said tightly.

His tone pierced the haze enveloping the scientist. Jayce stopped pacing altogether and turned to face Kevin, his eyes wide. "You don't believe me. Why don't you believe me?"

Kevin did not even blink. "I don't know what to believe. You haven't told me the story yet." His eyebrows drew together in a frown. "I *do* know that if they were Guardians, you wouldn't have had an easy time escaping them."

Jayce stared at him for a long moment, before he exhaled heavily. All of his remaining energy seemed to leak out of him with that breath. He staggered over to the couch and sat down, leaning forward to prop his elbows on his knees and rest his face in his hands. "I told you," his voice was muffled, "I was lucky."

He audibly swallowed. "They weren't Guardians, either, were they?" He gave a short, hollow laugh. "I wasn't thinking straight. They were Freedom's Children operatives. Of course."

That was Kevin's guess. "Probably." He took a seat in the armchair across from Jayce. "Please, Dr. Jayce, tell me what happened."

Jayce nodded, before dropping his hands from his face and sitting up. "Phillip and I were both in the lab working. Had to urinate, so I went to the hygiene unit at the other end of our floor." He grimaced. "I needed the walk—I needed to get out of the lab for a few minutes before I strangled Phillip with his own lab coat." He shook his head. "He's been a bear to work with lately—too much pressure from Director Fenton and the rest to work faster. It's been a nightmare." His hands twitched convulsively.

Kevin nodded, waiting for the rest of the story.

"Anyway, I was on my way back when I heard laserfire." Jayce swallowed, his brown eyes haunted, and one hand rose to touch the place where he'd been shot when they rescued him from the Tarynians in Uva months earlier. "I poked my head out to see what was going on and I saw a Guardian—or whoever he was—standing there over the body of one of our guards outside the lab."

He shuddered. "I ducked back into the hygiene unit before he saw me. That was when I called your sister."

"I'm curious. Why Lilia?"

Jayce shrugged again. "She was the last person I'd commed."

Kevin nodded again, but now he was frowning. "But how do you *know* they used a portal to kidnap Cait?"

Jayce gave him a look, as though he was completely missing the glaringly obvious. "That building has security on par with the Four

Towers, remember? The only way anybody could get in without setting off all the alarms is via a portal."

"I see." It made sense, but Kevin still felt a little uneasy. "And you're *sure* they didn't see you?"

Jayce started to shake his head, but paused, listing his head to one side as he considered the question more carefully. "I don't think so," he said at last.

"But it's possible."

"I suppose so." Jayce gave another little shrug. "Can't conclusively rule it out." he looked askance at Kevin. "Does it matter?"

It was Kevin's turn to shrug. "I guess not. They didn't follow, and they'd have no way of knowing where you were going." His eyebrows drew together. "For all they know, Dr. Lang opened a portal to you."

Jayce jumped as though he had just been shot. "Jun!" He rounded on Kevin, desperation filling his face. "If they came after Phillip and me, they might have gone after Jun too!"

Kevin was regarding him with raised eyebrows, but his surprise gave way to compassion. "If they did, Dr. Jayce, I'm afraid they've probably got her." He held up his hands. "Even if I had her coordinates, it'll be an hour before I can open another portal."

Jayce's face fell. "Right." He bit his lip, visibly pulling himself together. "I'll comm her in a while, see if she's all right."

Alarm flooded Kevin; he took an involuntary half-step forward. "You can't."

"What?" Jayce looked startled.

Kevin made an impatient noise in the back of his throat. "Dr. Jayce, you can't call anybody yet. Not until we figure out a way to explain how you avoided being captured without giving away the fact that my sister and I have transporters embedded in our nano-armor."

"Oh. Right," Jayce said in chagrin. "Forgot about that for a second." He scrubbed a hand across his face again. "I'm afraid I'm still a bit shaken."

"That's understandable." Kevin would have said more, but at that moment Erik sent him a Nancom channel request. He allowed it, and the other man's voice flooded his head.

[Are you watchin' the news?]

[No.] Kevin scrunched his brow. [Why?]

[Turn it on.] Erik's Nancom voice sounded grim. [Somebody just blew up the buildin' where the IA Department has been keepin' the scientists.]

Kevin immediately turned on the living room holoprojector and he and Jayce both gaped at the coverage being shown.

The redheaded scientist sank to the couch again, wide-eyed, as though his legs could no longer bear his weight. "What in the—?"

[Are you watchin'?] Erik asked.

[Yes,] Kevin replied numbly, his eyes fixed on the holoprojector and the plumes of black smoke rolling up into the sky from the industrial complex.

[That was a massive explosion. Looks like Jayce an' Cait are gone.]

Kevin shook his head, even though Erik was aboard the *Talia* at the Sonela Spaceport and couldn't possibly see him. [No, they're not.]

A pause, and then, [Kevin, there's no way they lived through that. Trust me.]

[Oh, I'd believe you if they were there when the bomb went off, but they weren't.] Before Erik could demand an explanation for that puzzling statement, Kevin filled him in on everything that had just happened. He finished with, [I'm planning on bringing Jayce to you as soon as my nanites unfreeze. I don't want to keep him here at Ferndale.]

[Makes sense. Until we have a better idea of who's behind this, it's probably better that your grandfather doesn't know a thing about him. He'd probably be duty-bound to report Jayce an' Cait are still alive.]

[Yeah. Probably.] Kevin wasn't sure about that—he didn't know how his grandfather would react to something like this—but it was clear *somebody* wanted the scientists...

...and whoever it was wanted the rest of the Coalition to think the two men were dead.

He bit his lip. *Wish we could find out if Dr. Lang was abducted too.* Short of Jayce attempting to get in touch with her, which was a bad idea on a number of levels at the moment, he didn't know how to go about that. He glanced back at Jayce, who couldn't take his eyes off the holoprojector. *Maybe Nob can do something.*

To that end, he opened a Nancom channel to the older Guardian. [Hey, Nob. Something's come up.]

[I'll say. Somebody just blew up Jayce and Cait.]

Kevin glanced at Jayce. [Not exactly...]

Nob insisted that Kevin bring Jayce to him as soon as possible. Kevin agreed, but insisted that Erik accompany them. That delayed them another hour; Kevin took Jayce to the *Talia* via a portal and then they had to wait for his nanites to unfreeze again.

When the three men finally emerged in the small living room of Nob's apartment, the older Guardian greeted them with terse nods before fixing his attention on Jayce. He was a stocky man in his early thirties, with wavy black hair and dark eyes. "Dr. Jayce, I'm sorry to have to tell you this, but it looks like Dr. Lang has been kidnapped as well."

All the color drained from Jayce's already pale face. "How do you know?"

Nob tilted his head toward his office, one of the apartment's two bedrooms. "I've been monitoring certain…feeds. It didn't make more than the local news, but a building in a city on Lanx was also blown up shortly after the attack here in Sonela."

If possible, Jayce paled even further.

Kevin and Erik exchanged grim glances. "And you think that's where she was?" Kevin asked.

"I'd bet my nano-armor on it."

Jayce took a half-step toward Nob. "And you're sure she's not dead?"

"Why would they kill her? Especially when they just got done kidnapping Dr. Cait and attempting to kidnap you?" Nob shook his head. "No, the explosion was probably to cover up her disappearance."

Erik scowled at the muted news coverage playing on the holoprojector. "You've heard the official line about the explosion in Sonela, right?"

"Yes." Nob folded his arms across his chest. "They're attributing it to more anti-peace talk violence without being specific as to why the building was targeted."

Kevin dropped into an armchair and locked his hands behind his head. "Well, it's not like they're going to come out and admit the people behind the transporter have vanished. Not so soon after announcing the transporters exist."

"Or worse, that they're dead." Nob looked at Jayce again. "Until they comb through the wreckage, Dr. Jayce, it's highly likely the Internal Affairs Department thinks you and Dr. Cait are both dead."

"An' Dr. Lang," Erik reminded them. "Unless they've got security footage of them bein' kidnapped."

Nob dismissed that with a shrug. "Even if they did, I doubt they'll actually release that information to the public."

"It'd cause too much chaos," Kevin agreed. "I mean, somebody mysteriously using a transporter to kidnap people? Not the kind of thing that inspires trust."

Jayce still stood in the middle of Nob's tiny living room, looking awkward and out of place in his white lab coat. It suddenly struck Kevin that for the time being, the scientist was homeless. Jayce was wearing the only things he possessed. He frowned again, this time out of compassion. "Dr. Jayce, you know you can't go home, right?"

"Home?" Jayce shrugged, shoving his hands into his pockets. "Don't exactly have one. The lab's been my home since we arrived on Sta'Gloa."

"Well, if you did happen to have someplace else to go," Erik said, "you can't risk actually goin' there. Not until we get this figured out."

Jayce raised both eyebrows in an expression of fatalistic curiosity. "What's to figure out? My colleagues have been kidnapped by the entity that subverted Dr. Banx, and now we're all presumed dead."

*That hasn't occurred to him yet, though*, Kevin thought shrewdly. Jayce's thoughts and attention were very much elsewhere.

"Why would they take her?" Wringing his hands, the scientist began to pace small circles in the limited floor space. "Why do they want any of us?"

Kevin glanced from Erik to Nob and back. *That* much should have been obvious.

Erik eyed Jayce with a healthy dose of skepticism. "All those brains an' you can't figure it out?" he drawled. "They want you to build 'em another transporter."

"But that's just it!" Jayce rounded on him, brown eyes suddenly ablaze. "They—or Freedom's Children, or whoever 'they' are—have already *got* one!" He flung his hands into the air. "If Dr. Banx was working with them, they should have everything they need to duplicate the process. They shouldn't *need* us!"

It certainly *sounded* reasonable. Kevin started to nod, started to frown at the thought that they'd have to find a new theory…when a memory floated to the forefront of his mind. He started. "Dr. Jayce, that may not be the case."

By the look on Nob's face, the older Guardian realized it too. "Dr. Banx might have been working with Freedom's Children, but I have a feeling he didn't just hand them the proverbial keys to the kingdom."

Erik snapped his fingers. "Good point." He focused on Jayce. "Think about it. If they already had everythin' they needed, why would they break into your lab after you came to Sta'Gloa an' steal all Banx's data?"

Taken aback, Jayce stared at him. "I've been under the impression it was because they removed everything that could incriminate him and link him to them."

"Oh, they probably did." Erik sprawled out in his chair, stretching his legs in front of him. "But that doesn't mean they didn't have another purpose for all that data."

Jayce scrunched his forehead. "That makes no sense. If they can't rebuild the transporter by themselves, why wouldn't they take *everything*?" His frown deepened. "Mind you, they'd still have to crack our encryption, but…" He turned both hands palm up.

"They might well have copied everything," Nob said, "but they had no reason to attempt to wipe your system clean. Entirely too suspicious, for one."

"An' it doesn't look like they wanted to cripple the Coalition's chance of havin' transporters," Erik added.

Kevin snorted. "Well, they don't seem too concerned about crippling the Coalition right now. They just blew up two of the Coalition's three transporters, didn't they?"

Jayce groaned, his pacing ceasing as the reality of what had just happened hit him. "All that work. Everything we went through trying to get the transporter to Sta'Gloa." His expression turned haunted. "Gone."

Silence fell over Nob's apartment as the four men considered the implications of this. After a moment, Kevin leaned forward. "If I didn't know better, I'd think Hesperia or some other shipping conglomerate is behind this. Talk about an industry in for big change."

He shook his head. "I don't know what'll happen to Three Cords Shipping if and when a large-scale transporter system is put into place. Think about what the rest of the industry is considering right now."

Nob dismissed that with a wave of his fingers. "It makes a good cover story. And without any other information, Internal Affairs may well believe that's what happened. But that's not the real reason." He glanced at Jayce. "Internal Affairs has all your data backed up, don't they, Dr. Jayce?"

"Yes." Jayce collapsed on the sofa and buried his head in his hands. "Director Fenton insisted on it. Top-level security, from what I understand, but still…" He groaned. "It'll take weeks to rebuild."

Erik's eyebrows rose. "Is that all it takes to build a transporter? A couple of weeks?"

Jayce gave a despondent shrug. "If we have everything we need. There's a delay, naturally, if we're missing components."

Erik's next question gave the scientist pause. "How fast can the Department of Internal Affairs build one without any of you?"

Jayce sucked in a breath and let it all out in a whoosh. "I don't know. Probably something similar. Maybe a little longer. We did design the machines, after all."

Erik nodded, as though he'd expected this, and turned his attention back to Kevin and Nob. "Okay, so Freedom's Children hasn't *completely* derailed the whole transporter thing. Delayed it, definitely, but not destroyed it."

"This Mastermind must want them to build him more transporters on a faster timetable," Nob said.

"That…does not bode well," Kevin said slowly. "Look at what they did with just *one* transporter."

Jayce's head popped up, his brown eyes bright with a sudden flare of hope. "Could you stage a rescue? Like you did on Lanx?"

Silence fell over the apartment again as the three Guardians looked at each other. Nob considered Jayce for a few seconds. "Dr. Jayce, we don't know for sure where they're holding Dr. Cait and Dr. Lang."

*Yes, we do.* A muscle twitched in Kevin's jaw. "Oh, yeah, we do, Nob. They're probably somewhere inside that fortress I found on Meloran."

Nob considered his words for a full five seconds before he shook his head. "Unlikely."

"Why?" Kevin leaned forward. "It's secluded and they wouldn't have to worry about anybody finding the scientists there, much less looking for them."

"I agree with Nob." Erik folded his arms behind his head, his keen gaze flicking back and forth between Kevin and the older Guardian. "Why would they build it on Meloran when they've probably already got a transporter there?"

"Oh." Kevin deflated. "I didn't think about that." He raised a hand to the back of his neck, frowning. "But still, there's got to be something going on there."

"There probably is," Nob agreed. "But we have no way of determining that." He looked at Jayce. "I'm sorry, Dr. Jayce, but without knowing where your colleagues have been taken, we have no way of staging a rescue."

Disappointment flooded Jayce's face; he lowered his gaze to the floor and swallowed before he could speak. "I understand." A moment later, he gave a funny little jolt. "I just realized—I'm homeless, aren't I?" He blinked a couple of times. "And if Internal Affairs thinks I'm dead, I can't access any of my accounts, can I?"

Kevin, Erik, and Nob exchanged glances. "'Fraid not," Erik said. "Sorry."

"Well, damn." Jayce sat down heavily on Nob's couch, staring blankly at the opposite wall. "Now what am I going to do?"

[What's that old sayin'?] Erik asked wryly via Nancom. [Save a man's life an' you're responsible for him forever?]

[Something like that.] Kevin waved a hand, drawing Jayce's attention. "Don't worry, Dr. Jayce. You'll be all right."

"He can stay with me for the time being," Nob said brusquely. "Your freighter isn't the best choice, Kevin. You and your sister are under far too much scrutiny for now."

"Tell me about it." Kevin shook his head. "You're the safer bet anyway. Nobody knows we've been in contact with you, so you shouldn't come to mind."

Erik fixed the redheaded scientist with a steely look. "That means no communicatin' with anyone. Your friends, family—they all have to think you're dead for this to work."

"But what if Jun—"

"*Nobody*," Erik said firmly. "Not even Dr. Lang." He glanced at Nob. "An' *that's* highly unlikely because I doubt they're goin' to let her have comm access."

"Unless they're trying to draw Dr. Jayce out," Nob said grimly. "They have to know he disappeared from the building—it's likely they'll realize he used a portal as well." He nodded to Jayce. "Though they can't know *how* you managed it."

They discussed theories and threw around ideas of what Freedom's Children intended to do next until Kevin's nanites unfroze. When he realized he was free to leave, he slapped his hands against his knees and stood. "Dr. Jayce, I'll leave you here. I've got to drop Erik back aboard the *Talia* and head home."

"Not a word of this to your grandfather," Nob warned him. "Even he can't know Jayce is actually alive."

Kevin started to argue, started to protest that he was trying to do a better job of avoiding telling his grandfather lies and half-truths, but he shut his mouth before a word escaped. Someone in the Internal Affairs Department was a traitor working with Freedom's Children and they couldn't risk that person finding out where Jayce was.

*It's for the best,* he thought, a heavy weight settling on his shoulders. At least this way his grandfather's surprise, shock, and dismay over these major setbacks to the transporter program would be genuine.

With a terse nod, Kevin stepped into the middle of the floor and opened a portal. Seconds later, he and Erik were gone.

# CHAPTER 58

AIDEN stared blankly out through the plastiglass side of the accelevator at the side of the Internal Affairs Tower facing them as they rose to the top of Triumvirate Tower. His thoughts were unusually snarled; his mood matched the dark storm clouds stretching over Sonela. Lightning flickered in the distance, but he paid no attention. A scant few hours' sleep had not been enough to dispel the ominous weight he felt hanging over the Triumvirate.

He felt old today, felt brittle and withered by the events of the past few months. *I need strength, Lord.* He swallowed. *Strength and wisdom to deal with all of this.*

Michael and Derek stood silently to one side. The three of them were not the accelevator cab's only occupants; Representative Urquart and her aides had joined them. Other than a handful of terse "Good morning"s, no one spoke.

It was not until they had nearly reached the Hall that Urquart seemed to draw herself together. She, too, seemed paler and sharper than usual, though that could have been because of the icy blue suit she wore, setting off her iron gray hair. She turned to Aiden, her mouth puckering in a wry, pessimistic frown. "I expect Malik Thane will drone on about security again. He's got the perfect opening."

"Indeed." It took effort on Aiden's part to speak. "I believe the only thing that could have made last night's events worse is if the Ambassador had been killed."

Urquart huffed a laugh, even as her face tightened. "I must confess I am glad we're not mopping up *that* particular disaster." She shook her head. "Regardless, we're in for another security lecture."

Aiden only nodded. No doubt the young Sta'Gloan Director of Security would take great delight in having a captive audience.

The accelevator doors opened and Urquart strode out into the Hall, but paused to wait for Aiden. He joined her and they began to walk side by side down the hall toward the Chamber entrance. "Frankly," she continued, "the whole thing is unsettling. There'd best be an explanation for last night."

Despite her calm tone, Aiden heard the faint undercurrent of fear. He understood it too well. They were all in more danger than usual. The bomb that had exploded at the Tri-Global Tournament's Opening Ceremonies Gala, killing two Representatives and several other staff members along with causing numerous injuries, had opened their eyes to *that* reality.

He resisted the urge to press a hand to his chest, where he bore faint scars from shrapnel injuries. He could not bring himself to admit it to anyone, least of all his grandchildren, but that brush with his mortality had left him shaken. It was a different kind of shaken than the fear he had experienced when his would-be assassin nearly killed Lilia instead; it was instead a reminder that life was as fleeting as a wisp of morning mist in the sunlight.

Sooner rather than later, his time on this world would end…and he found himself wondering if he had accomplished the tasks the Lord had intended him to perform during this life.

"…all right?"

A light touch on his arm snapped Aiden back to his surroundings. He realized Representative Urquart had stopped, her usually severe expression filled with concern as she looked at him. Michael and Derek did not speak, but he felt their gazes heavy on his back.

Aiden forced a smile. "My apologies, Helena. My mind went… elsewhere." They began walking again, and he shook his head. "I suppose it might be lack of sleep talking, but this whole business has brought up a great many heavy issues."

"I understand." Urquart gave him a faint, sympathetic smile that quickly turned acerbic. "If one listens to our dear friends in the media, turbulent times such as these are precisely what we politicians live for. Something to validate our existence."

Despite the weight he felt pressing down on him, Aiden chuckled. "If only they knew."

His sharp gaze traveled the length of the Hall as they neared the Chamber, searching for Ambassador Kedis, but the Tarynian politician was nowhere to be seen. "It would appear Ambassador Kedis has yet to make an appearance."

"Oh, he will," said a new voice. Aiden and Urquart both glanced to the side as Martin Hollowell fell into step beside then, his expression dour. "He won't miss a chance to milk last night for all it's worth."

"Oh, come now, Representative." Dion Pamos now joined them. "Would any of us?" He gave Hollowell a knowing look, but strode briskly ahead of them without waiting for an answer.

Aiden considered the shorter Sta'Gloan Representative's retreating form with a measure of concealed surprise. *That is perhaps the most honest thing I have ever heard him say.*

The four of them merged into the stream of men and women flowing into the Chamber and crossed the celadon marble floor to their respective seats. Aiden nodded to Kane Fenton as he sat down. "I am glad to see you escaped last night unscathed."

"In a matter of speaking." Fenton tried to smile, but it emerged as more of a grimace. The Sta'Gloan Director of Internal Affairs had the air of a man who had traded sleep for caffeine. "You as well, Representative."

"Thank you." Aiden scanned the Chamber, searching for a head of red hair. "Is Malik Thane not here yet?"

Fenton snorted. "Last I heard, he was supposed to be briefing the Chief Minister before this morning's emergency session."

"Oh?" Aiden lifted his eyebrows, a sudden spike of adrenaline shooting through him. His mind flashed back to everything his grandsons had told him once they had returned to Ferndale, and cold certainty settled over him. Malik Thane had discovered the truth about the attack.

Over the next few minutes, the milling crowd of Representatives and their most trusted aides dispersed to their seats along the semi-circle facing the Chief Ministers' table, and the holographic forms of those on Lanx and Glo'Stea appeared. Septien Yu, took his place at the Chairman's stand, but seemed reluctant to call the session to order. His eyes kept darting to the double doors at the back of the Chamber, clearly expecting Chief Minister Koen to appear at any moment.

At last, when he could apparently no longer ignore the discontented rumbles sweeping through the Chamber, the Chairman tapped his gold bell. "This session of the Triumvirate will now come to order."

Whispers and mutters continued unabated.

"Order! We will come to order!" Septien Yu struck his gold bell several times in succession.

Reluctant silence fell over the Chamber. Yu took a deep breath. "This is an emergency session," he said, his words biting. "I am sure I am not the only one who would like to resolve things today and have a chance to spend a few hours at home with my family before we meet again tomorrow."

When no one spoke, Yu nodded sharply. "The first order of business on today's agenda is the attack at the Wycliffe Hotel last night, but as Director Thane is not present, I move that we—"

The double doors swung open and Chief Minister Koen strode in with Chief Minister Gammick, followed by Malik Thane and several advisers. Aiden's eyebrows rose a fraction; the Lanxian Chief Minister clearly enjoyed using the transporter to attend Triumvirate sessions in person.

"Our apologies for the delay," Koen said briskly, raising a hand as he strode to his seat at the north corner of the triangular Chamber. "Please, continue."

Yu glanced at Malik Thane, who had almost reached his seat in the Sta'Gloan section. "Director Thane, our first order of business is last night's attack."

Thane remained standing. From his own seat, Aiden could see that the young Director looked harried and exhausted. His pale features were sharper than usual, his demeanor not as well-groomed.

"Yes. Last night's attack." Thane took a breath and glanced down at the datapad he had set on the desk before him as though buying a moment to gather his thoughts. Looking up, he swept his gaze around the Chamber. "After reviewing all available security footage we could gather from the buildings around the Wycliffe Hotel, my Department and I have come to the conclusion that the attackers used a transporter to open portals onto the roof."

Shocked gasps greeted this pronouncement. Beside him, Aiden noticed Fenton stiffen imperceptibly.

Thane tapped his datapad, and a holo of the compiled security footage sprang to life in the center of the floor. The entire Triumvirate watched a group of black-clad individuals appear out of nowhere on the roof. Thane stood a little straighter. "As you can see, and as, no doubt, some of you witnessed last night, the attackers then proceeded to cut holes through the roof and dropped smoke bombs to disorient everyone before beginning their killing spree."

For a second, dead silence hung in the air. Then, in the Lanxian section, Cy Bali rose to his feet. "A *transporter?* Director Fenton, how is this possible?" He shook his head, his dark face disbelieving. "Are not the transporters under your protection and supervision?"

Septien Yu was too stunned by this turn of events to remember to ring the bell.

Fenton stood, tension radiating from every centimeter of his frame. "The transporters *are* under my purview, and security is very tight around them." He nodded to Thane. "As soon as Director Thane informed me of his findings, I immediately began an investigation. I can categorically and emphatically state that these attackers did *not* use either of our machines."

The Chamber filled with noise as everyone broke out into disbelieving speech at once. Yu had to strike the bell several times to restore order.

Dion Pamos rose to his feet and was recognized. He glanced between Thane and Fenton, who were both still standing. "Do you mean to tell us, Director Fenton, that there is a *third* transporter out there somewhere?"

He waved a hand vaguely, raising his voice to be heard over the low murmurs flooding the Chamber again. "Because if neither of your machines was used, that is the conclusion we must draw, yes?"

Fenton's expression could have been carved from stone. He took his time answering. "It's *possible* a third transporter exists, yes. Before we moved Dr. Cait and his colleagues to a more secure location, there was a break-in at their lab here in Sonela and data was stolen."

Dion Pamos nodded, as though he had expected this. "So it's possible, then, that these thieves, whoever they are, could have built themselves a transporter?"

"Yes," Fenton conceded, though Aiden had the impression it cost him dearly to admit it. "It's possible."

In the Glo'Stean section, Martin Hollowell had risen to his feet.

"The Triumvirate recognizes Representative Hollowell." Yu tapped his bell.

Aiden glanced at his colleague as Hollowell drummed his fingers absently against the surface of the table before him. "Have you discovered any information as to the identity of these thieves?"

Fenton's face soured further. "No. Unfortunately they were well-versed in espionage. I've had people looking into it ever since, but we've turned up no new information."

"Perhaps," Hollowell turned his gaze toward Malik Thane, "this might be a good time to bring the Sta'Gloan Department of Security in to help."

Aiden suppressed a wince at the no-so-subtle chastisement.

To his credit, Fenton did not react. "Already done, Representative. I had no wish for further incident."

Hollowell inclined his head. "I am glad to hear it." With that, he re-seated himself.

Hugh Koen rose ponderously to his feet, and Yu lost no time in striking the bell. "The Triumvirate recognizes Chief Minister Koen."

The murmurs sweeping through the Chamber quieted—but only a little. Aiden's eyes darted left and right along the semi-circle facing the Chief Minister, observing the faint little tics his colleagues displayed denoting apprehension. No one liked the idea of an unknown party having possession of a transporter.

The memory of Lilia, bleeding, after the assassination attempt, came to mind, but Aiden locked it away. More than anyone else here, perhaps, he had reason to be wary of the damage that could be caused.

Koen drew himself up to his full height. "Director Fenton, Director Thane, this needs to be handled immediately." He pinned both men with his gaze before encompassing the rest of the Triumvirate in a piercing look. "The idea that an unknown entity has access to secure facilities," he waved a hand to indicate Triumvirate Tower, "or, worse, our homes?"

He paused to let the full weight of that sink in. "It is untenable. We are looking at the potential for assassination attempts on a massive scale."

"Potentially *successful* assassination attempts," Pryce Gammick said from beside him.

"Yes." Koen spared him a glance. "These people could go anywhere, be anywhere, and then simply disappear without a trace." He shook his head. "A more immediate problem, however, is that this now places Ambassador Kedis and his entourage in incredible danger."

"We are working on handling the situation, sir." Malik Thane shot Fenton a look that could only be described as malicious. "The NCDC is assisting us by providing Guardians for additional security."

*Wait for it*, Aiden thought.

"Frankly, Chief Minister," Thane continued, "this might be the time to rethink the Triumvirate's stance on the NCDC and Guardians. As my predecessors have argued in the past, the Department of Security's lack of access to the Guardians' nanotechnology has put us at a clear and distinct disadvantage when it comes to situations such as this."

Mutters swept through the Chamber again.

Koen fixed Fenton with a stern, disapproving look. "Perhaps you can explain how your Department let this theft occur in the first place."

Fenton remained standing ramrod straight, his dark face now impassive. "Given that Dr. Cait and Dr. Jayce had to rebuild the transporter after a team of Guardians successful rescued them from occupied territory on Lanx, I thought it prudent that their lab be located on the edge of the city in case something went wrong. I did not want to risk lives unnecessarily."

*You cannot fault him for that*, Aiden thought.

"That's all well and good," Helena Urquart interrupted sharply. She ignored the irritated look Yu shot her. "But what about the lab's security?"

"They had an excellent security system," Fenton answered. "The only reason I didn't post an armed guard was because of their location. I thought it best to avoid drawing unwanted scrutiny by having too much activity going on."

"Clearly, Director," Cy Bali said, "you were wrong."

"Perhaps." Fenton lifted one shoulder in a shrug. "I do not, however, believe an armed guard would have made much difference. The break-in was an inside job."

It took a few seconds for his words to register—

—and then chaos broke out.

# Chapter 59

AIDEN rocked back in his chair as several more pieces of the puzzle fell into place. *An inside job. That would explain a few things.*

"Order! Order!" Septien Yu had to shout to be heard over the noise, striking his gold bell so hard Aiden was surprised it did not crack in two.

*We need a gong,* a stray corner of his mind observed, with a twinge of something that under completely different circumstances could have passed as amusement. *Or a pair of cymbols. Something louder than that bell.*

When the Chamber had halfway quieted, albeit reluctantly, Yu took a deep breath. "This is an emergency session," he said, his words biting. "I am sure I am not the only one who would like to resolve things today and have a chance to spend a few hours at home with my family before we meet again tomorrow."

When no one spoke, the Chairman nodded sharply. "Very well." He motioned for Fenton to continue.

"It had to be an inside job. The thieves knew exactly which security protocols were in place and were able to easily bypass them." Fenton allowed himself a grim smile. "It was only when the thieves attempted to break into Dr. Jayce's data that they tripped additional security measure he had implemented and sounded an alarm."

"Have you found the thieves and arrested them?" someone called out.

"Yes." Fenton looked grim again. "Only a few people had access to that information. After careful investigation, we discovered one of my department heads had been given a substantial bribe for the scientists' location and pertinent information. The trail, unfortunately, ended there. She did not know who the buyer was; they met in carefully chosen locations to exchange goldcards and datachips."

"Excuse me, Director Fenton." In the Glo'Stea section, Shane Briscoe raised his hand.

"The Triumvirate recognizes Representative Briscoe," Yu intoned.

"Did the thieves steal, ah," Briscoe glanced down at his datapad. "Dr. Jayce and Dr. Cait's data as well?"

Fenton shook his head. "Not as far as we can tell."

"I see." Briscoe nodded, as though he had expected this answer. "Then did Dr. Banx's stolen data contain everything these thieves needed to build themselves a transporter?"

A sick feeling pooled in the pit of Aiden's stomach. *Of course.* He alone knew the real reason the thieves had attempted to steal the rest of the data. It was a ruse. An intrusion meant to keep everyone from realizing they were covering up Banx's involvement with Freedom's Children. *They already* have *a transporter.*

The knowledge churned in his stomach. Knowledge he could not share with the Triumvirate. Not until he could determine how to reveal it without endangering his grandchildren.

The problem, however, was that Shane Briscoe had spotted the one flaw in the story.

How had the thieves managed to build a transporter out of only Banx's data?

The answer to that was simple. *They could not.*

Darting a glance along the semi-circle, Aiden saw comprehension being to dawn on more than one face.

How the rest of this session would unfold was—

"Chief Minister Koen," Malik Thane interrupted abruptly. "May I have a moment to confer with Director Fenton?"

*That is unusual.* Aiden glanced over at Thane…and his eyes narrowed. The young Director seemed to have gone pale, his fingers curled around the edge of his datapad, which he had just picked up from the table. *What has happened now?*

To everyone's surprise, it was the Glo'Stean Chief Minister who answered. "What has happened?" His holographic form leaned forward in his seat, as though to get a closer view. "What is wrong?"

Malik Thane darted a look at Kane Fenton that almost bordered on the helpless before he gathered his frayed composure and gestured to his datapad. "I've just received word that someone has set off a bomb in the complex where we've been keeping Dr. Cait and Dr. Jayce. The entire section has been wiped out. So far there are no signs of survivors."

Thane visibly swallowed. "It would also appear the transporter they just finished constructing has been destroyed."

Horrified gasps filled the Chamber, before tumultuous cries of, "How could this have happened?" and "Who is responsible?" began to ring out.

Aiden was almost too stunned to notice when the holographic form of Oren Holden, the Lanxian Director of Internal Affairs, reluctantly rose to his feet. He was a stocky, middle-aged man with tawny skin and short black hair that was graying at the temples.

It took a moment before Septien Yu could silence the members of the Triumvirate enough for Holden to be heard. In sepulcher tones, he said, "I'm afraid it's worse than that." Holden took a breath, as though bracing himself for a blow. "I've just been notified of an explosion at the lab where we're keeping Dr. Lang and the second original transporter. The building was a total loss. No survivors."

"*How?*" demanded a slew of voices at once.

Holden shook his head. "That's all I have at the moment. It literally just happened."

"Has anyone claimed responsibility?" the Glo'Stean Chief Minister demanded, glancing from Holden to Kane Fenton and then to Malik Thane.

"Not yet," Holden responded.

Fenton and Thane both shook their heads. Fenton glanced at Holden before looking around the Chamber. "Ladies and gentlemen of the Triumvirate, it would appear that we have a larger issue." He held out a hand. "Dr. Cait and Dr. Jayce have been under heavy guard since they were relocated, and their location was classified."

"The same with Dr. Lang," Holden interjected.

"I do not say this lightly, but," Fenton braced himself, "it would appear indicative of a larger problem. We have a leak in the upper levels of the Triumvirate."

"Speak for yourself," Thane grumbled, nettled.

Fenton barely spared him a glance. "At this point, it is undeniable fact." He shook his head. "The theft could be explained as a coincidence, or a lucky guess, or a one-off. But this? Both locations destroyed simultaneously on two planets?"

Aiden nodded in silent agreement. The odds were astronomical.

Hugh Koen directed his attention to Malik Thane. "Director Thane, is the transporter here in Triumvirate Tower safe?"

"As safe as we could make it." Thane's mouth twisted. "I've had no reports to the contrary."

"The transporter program has been delayed, "Oren Holden said, "and perhaps crippled, but not destroyed. We have the scientists' data; we can rebuild." He shrugged. "It will just take a few weeks or months longer."

In the Lanxian section, Representative Neva Rehmel, from Sector 6, rose to her feet and was recognized. "This will be a nightmare to explain to the general public. To announce the transporters' existence and then turn around and admit two of them have been destroyed?" She shook her head. "Has anyone claimed responsibility yet?

"I've received nothing yet," Fenton said, before glancing at Malik Thane, who shook his head. Oren Holden and Wade Talon, the Lanxian Director of Security, also shook their heads.

Shane Briscoe raised a hand. "I would say Freedom's Children is a strong possibility."

"Yes," Malik Thane agreed. "Another strong possibility is one of the major shipping conglomerates."

*Every once in a while*, Aiden thought, *Malik Thane says something that explains how he landed his position.* If he, Aiden, did not already know Freedom's Children was most likely behind these explosions, he would have been inclined to agree with the Sta'Gloan Director of Security.

Uneasiness rippled around the Chamber.

"A shipping conglomerate?" Representative Nolan Snyder asked, before guffawing loudly. "What possible reason would they have for these acts of terrorism?"

Aiden was hard-pressed to keep the exasperation he felt at this inane question out of his face. *Really, it does not take a genius to understand this angle.*

Thane remained cool and unruffled. "The very best reason, Representative. Not to mention a motivation that extends back through history." He locked his hands behind his back. "The transporter program is a threat to the shipping companies' bottom line.

Import, export, and passenger travel will all be affected by this in the future to some degree."

Murmurs of agreement met this.

"In addition, it would have to be a group with access to considerable funds. As the lab theft has already proved, a great deal of money paves the way for them to gain otherwise classified information." Thane gave a completely unapologetic shrug. "I am fully aware this will be an unpopular opinion in certain quarters of the Triumvirate, but it is *my* job to consider every possibility."

Up until now, Aiden had considered Thane's ambition the kind easily swayed by the right political influence. *I did not take into account the man's pride.*

Thane's brown eyes hardened. "Be it Freedom's Children or someone else, I intend to find these perpetrators and bring them to justice."

"Hear, hear," several people called out.

Yu motioned for Fenton and Kane to resume their seats, and Aiden glanced left and right along the semi-circle, waiting for someone to ask the next obvious question. No one did. Holding back a sigh, he pushed back his chair and stood.

Yu tapped his bell. "The Triumvirate recognizes Representative Monroe."

"How do we explain this matter to Ambassador Kedis?" Aiden paused. "*Do* we explain it?" He held out a hand. "The Ambassador may not yet know how last night's attack came about, but it is likely that he will learn a transporter was involved. In addition, though he has not yet added the transporters into his bargaining, he will."

Aiden swept his gaze around the Chamber. "Make no mistake, the Galactic Union will want this technology. Do we admit that we have suffered a major security breach, or do we keep quiet in the hopes that the situation will be resolved before it comes up for discussion?"

Martin Hollowell raised a hand. "I don't believe we owe Ambassador Kedis an explanation for a damn thing. Let him wonder what happened. He only knows about the one transporter, anyway, and we still have that."

Murmurs of agreement met this.

Shane Briscoe rose to his feet and was recognized, while Aiden sat back down. "I agree with Representative Hollowell in as far as it comes to us not owing the Ambassador an *immediate* explanation."

He nodded to Hollowell, before addressing the entire Triumvirate. "As long as we do not experience any other security breaches, I think we could successfully suppress this tragic turn of affairs for quite some time. The problem is that eventually, we will have to tell Kedis *something* about the transporter program."

He shook his head gravely. "We will need a reason as to why it is not advancing as fast as it should at this stage."

In the Lanxian section, Zane Chas scoffed loudly. "How is Kedis to know how fast the program should be advancing?" He scowled at Briscoe. "This is brand-new technology—it's not like anybody has a measurable timetable."

Briscoe inclined his head. "That is a good point. However, if the scientists who engineered the transporters did in fact die this morning, we *will* experience a setback."

"That," Malik Thane interjected abruptly, "sounds a good deal like you expect the Triumvirate to come to some sort of agreement with Kedis very soon."

"Of *course* we'll have to come to some sort of agreement." Exasperated, Briscoe threw his hands into the air. "Our only other choice is to *refuse* any kind of trade alliance or agreement and kick Kedis off of Sta'Gloa."

He looked around the Chamber. "And while I think a few of you would enjoy that, I think you will also agree that it is hardly the best thing for the Coalition right now." He shook his head. "No, ladies and gentlemen, I'm afraid we're stuck with the Ambassador—and the Galactic Union. It comes now to what price we place on our freedom."

The Chamber erupted at this.

Briscoe sat back down, not looking the least bit apologetic. His jaw was set in a way that indicated he had spoken his mind and intended to stick to it, regardless of the consequences.

*I do not know why they all act so taken aback.* Aiden surveyed the chaos. *We all knew this is what Kedis's arrival would come down to.*

Briscoe had just forced them to face the truth a little sooner.

*How much do we value our freedom?*

"Order!" Septien Yu shouted again.

When he could be heard, Hugh Koen addressed Malik Thane. "What about security footage from last night?"

The Sta'Gloan Director of Security bowed his head. "Our people are working on it."

From the way Thane hesitated slightly before answering, Aiden surmised the younger man had been hoping to have a chance to review said footage before sharing it with the Triumvirate at large.

Helen Urquart leaned forward in her seat, her sharp eyes alight with interest. "You have footage even though the building was destroyed?"

"Of course." Thane straightened. "And not all of the complex was destroyed. Just the section that contained the lab." He paused. "Although the building did sustain heavy damage as a result."

In the Lanxian section, Cy Bali also leaned forward. "How soon can you get it, Director? This will have a profound impact on how we handle Ambassador Kedis."

Thane glanced down the Sta'Gloan section at Kane Fenton, who gave a little shrug. "I should be able to pull it up momentarily." His fingers danced over his datapad.

"While we are waiting…" Dion Pamos rose to his feet. He waited for the Chairman to recognize him before continuing, "There is one more small matter concerning Ambassador Kedis it would be wise to consider."

"And just what would that be?" Martin Hollowell asked dryly, echoing Aiden's thoughts.

Pamos locked his hands behind his back, looking grave, and Aiden instinctively braced himself. Whatever the other Representative had to say, he already knew he would not like it.

"I have reason to believe that after last night's attack, Ambassador Kedis is aware Guardians exist."

Pamos paused dramatically, but this apparently did not cause as much of a stir as he had expected, because his dark eyes narrowed a fraction.

Aiden, on the other hand, went cold. *I do not like where this is headed.*

"What of it?" Kane Fenton asked brusquely. "We partnered with the NCDC to appoint several individuals already working for us as additional Guardian protection."

"Well…" Pamos drew the word out. "One of them revealed his Guardian status to Kedis last night."

Fenton cleared his throat. "You should amend that to 'was forced' to reveal his status, Representative, in order to save Kedis's life."

"Is there footage of this?" Zane Chas demanded.

"Yes," Fenton and Pamos said together. Fenton cleared his throat again. "Also, the Guardian in question informed the NCDC of this, and they in turn contacted me."

"Who is this Guardian?" Nolan Snyder demanded.

A wave of icy cold washed over Aiden. He knew Kedis had several Guardians assigned to him, but he only knew one of them. *Lon.*

Dion Pamos glanced sideways at Aiden, and even before he said the words, Aiden *knew.*

"I believe he is Representative Monroe's grandson, Lon Strong."

No sooner did these words sink in, then the Triumvirate dissolved into chaos again. Some were outraged that Lon was still a Guardian after his betrayal, or that he had ever been a Guardian in the first place. Other lamented the necessity of Lon revealing the Guardian technology to Kedis.

When Septien Yu finally regained control, he lifted his eyebrows at Aiden. "Representative Monroe, do you have anything to add?"

Aiden almost declined…and then thought the better of it. He rose to his feet. "My only comment is this: my grandson is a grown man who makes his own decisions. Several of these decisions have resulted in the first cease-fire we have experienced in two decades, among other things. And if he had not saved Ambassador Kedis's life last night, today's emergency session would be vastly different. At least we are not at risk of open war with the Galactic Union."

"At the moment," Hollowell said loudly.

Aiden cast his old friend a sharp look, but inclined his head. "At the moment."

"Thank you, Representative Monroe." Yu prepared to strike the bell, but glanced around long enough to ask, "Does anyone else have anything more to say on this subject before we move on?"

Shane Briscoe raised a hand, his face filled with genuine curiosity. "What *will* we tell the Ambassador when he no doubt demands an explanation of Guardians?"

It was Kane Fenton who answered. "That the Guardians belong to a civilian defense corps and he can't have it."

More than one chuckle greeted this calm pronouncement.

"I doubt," Pamos said thinly, "that the Ambassador will be satisfied with that."

"He'll have to be," Fenton said bluntly.

"If the joint Departments of Security can't touch the NCDC nanotechnology," Malik Thane said coldly, "a damn Tarynian is sure as hell not getting *his* hands on it."

Aiden found he could not disagree. But, looking at Malik Thane's mutinous expression, yet another ominous feeling settled over him. *Last night's even may well have set in motion a way for Thane to gain access to Guardian tech after all.*

# Chapter 60

CHESNEE'S comlink buzzed beside him, interrupting the smooth, mellow jazz filling his quarters. The Admiral pursed his lips. It was Sunday morning—not that it meant anything to whoever was comming him—and he was stretched out on the couch catching up on game scores. His homeworld, Veridia, was playing Taryn today in the G.U. interplanetary football tournament.

It had been a long night. He had tried to go back to bed after hearing from Lieutenant Wright, but his expectation that Ambassador Kedis would be contacting him with some sort of instruction—wounded or not—was so strong that sleep had evaded him. Well, that and the fact that his brain was still spinning from everything the young lieutenant had told him.

*Guardians.* He'd have to tell Armal. His aide had been convinced scuttlebutt was true for the entire time Chesnee had been in command of the Blockade Division—nearly a year now.

Chesnee picked up the comlink. He was supposed to be taking a break for a couple of hours this morning, but clearly fate had other plans. "Yes, Armal?"

"Admiral, you have an incoming transmission from Sta'Gloa. Ambassador Kedis's frequency."

Chesnee blinked, caught slightly off-guard. "Well, I suppose that is not entirely unexpected." He wondered if the Ambassador was calling to tell him about Guardians. "I'll take it, Lieutenant. Patch it through to my office."

"Aye, aye, sir."

Sitting up, Chesnee swung his legs over the edge of the couch and stood. Still frowning, he made his way into his office and took a seat behind his desk. Armal had done as requested; a silver comm light blinked in one corner of his desk.

For a second, Chesnee considered donning his uniform jacket, but dismissed it as unnecessary. Even Admirals occasionally had a few moments of downtime. It was Sunday morning; his dress shirt would suffice. He tapped a button on the comm panel.

Kedis began talking as soon as his holograph appeared. "Admiral. Good morning."

Chesnee inclined his head. "Ambassador, I am relieved to see you are still in one piece. How are you feeling?"

"Oh, that?" Kedis waved a hand, as though nearly being blown up was a regular—and minor—occurrence. "I'm fine. In fact, I think it's turned out to be a blessing in disguise."

"Is that so?" Chesnee raised his eyebrows, realizing for the first time that Leo Kedis was not quite his usual…smooth, dapper self. His obligatory suit jacket was missing, and he had a manic look in his eyes that made Chesnee wonder exactly what he was up to. He seemed not to care how Chesnee had learned of the attack.

"Yes, it is." Satisfaction rolled off Kedis in waves. "I think I've figured out how to bring the Coalition and the Galactic Union together."

Chesnee couldn't help himself; he huffed a laugh. "Oh, really?"

Kedis nodded, and then his tone became brusque. "Admiral, the Blockade Division is still keeping all communications from any of the Coalition's worlds from leaving the system, correct?"

"Yes."

"In that case, I need you to patch me through to Taryn." Kedis leaned forward a little. "I need to speak to members of the Senate, and leaving Sta'Gloa to return to the *Winds of Change* is not an option at the moment."

Chesnee studied the younger man for a moment. "I'll be happy to assist you, Ambassador, but you *do* realize it's Sunday, don't you?"

A broad smile stretched Kedis's olive-skinned face. "Oh, they won't mind. Not when they hear what I have to tell them."

"Very well. I'll transfer you to Lieutenant Armal, and he will help you from there."

"Thank you, Admiral."

Chesnee reached for his comm panel, but Kedis said abruptly, "There isn't time to tell you the whole story at the moment, Admiral, but your fabled Guardians are real. Lon Strong is one of them."

Feigning surprise, Chesnee sat back in his chair. "I look forward to hearing this story, Ambassador."

Putting Kedis on hold, he commed Armal and gave him instructions to assist Kedis in any way he could. That done, Chesnee left his desk and went to stand by the wide viewport that provided him a stunning view of Lanx. *What in the galaxy is Kedis up to?*

How was this latest revelation of the Coalition's technology supposed to make them change their minds?

It was almost enough to make him want to be down on Sta'Gloa to witness the plan Kedis was feverishly setting in motion.

Almost.

He wasn't *that* far gone.

# CHAPTER 61

LON opened a Nancom channel to Lilia on his way down to the press conference. [Have you decided what you're going to do?]

[Looks like I'm going to have to stay here until everything unfreezes.] She wrapped her arms around her torso, leaning against the bedroom wall to look out the window at the street far, far below. [I don't know what else to do. I don't know how to explain where I got clothes if I just pull something from my ISF.]

[Call the penthouse in twenty minutes or so and have them send somebody to pick you up. By the time they get here, you should be able to walk out like normal.]

Some of the anxiety cording Lilia's muscles dissipated. She let out a long, slow breath. [That's a good idea.]

[I know. Gotta go.]

The minutes until her nanites unfroze ticked by with a glacial, agonizing speed. When her internal counter told her it was time, she called Michael. Nancom would have sufficed for this, but she felt she needed to keep making actual comm calls to justify still being shut up in Lon's room.

Michael promised to send somebody to get her and Lilia settled down to wait again.

A few minutes later, Lon announced via Nancom, [We're back. How much longer?]

[Fifteen minutes.] She was still wearing his shirt, in case anybody barged in on her.

[Not bad. Could be worse—at least you're not dealing with an impactor.]

Lilia suppressed a snort. [No kidding.]

A knock sounded on the door; she jumped. "It's me," Lon said in a muffled voice, before he entered the room.

Lilia eyed him. "How'd it go?" She was surprised the press conference had been so short; she'd expected Kedis to take longer.

Lon shrugged, shoving his hands into his pockets as he leaned against the desk. "Fine. There were only so many questions they could ask."

"Did he...?" Lilia trailed off, giving her brother a half-expectant, half-hesitant look.

"Out me?" Lon shook his head. "Nah, I think he's keeping that one close to the vest for now."

"Well, it would make sense."

Lon nodded, and then changed the subject. "When the skimmer gets here, I'm walking you down." He shot her a warning look. "I know you'd probably rather have Wright do it, but we don't need any more fuel on that particular media fire right now."

Lilia gave him her best I-don't-know-what-you're-talking-about look. "That's fine."

"Good." Lon jerked a thumb over his shoulder. "Come out and join us as soon as you can."

The instant her nanites unfroze, Lilia wasted no time in shedding Lon's shirt and dematerializing her gloves. Comlink in hand, she swept out of Lon's room. Kedis was nowhere to be seen, but Jasper and Renner were both with Lon in the living area. Jasper was sitting down on the couch, while Renner paced.

Lilia flashed Jasper an apologetic smile. "Sorry. I had more calls to make than I realized."

A moment later, Lon's comlink vibrated. "Yes?" He listened for a second. "Okay, thanks." He looked over at Lilia. "Your ride's here. Let's go."

"That's great." Lilia glanced from Renner to Jasper, her gaze lingering on the latter. "Gentlemen. Tell the Ambassador I appreciate his hospitality, if you would."

Renner nodded curtly; Jasper met her gaze. "Certainly." He looked like he wanted to say more, but after another darting glance at Lon he seemed to think the better of it.

Lilia understood the feeling.

Lon chivvied her out the door before she could say anything else—not that words had readily come to mind. The memory of her conversation with Jasper before the press conference returned to her and she was hard-pressed to keep from blushing.

*It's fine*, she told herself. *You'll hear from him later anyway.*

As the accelevator whisked them down to the lobby, Lilia smoothed her gown—slightly singed from last night's events—and held her head high. If she wanted to make it out without drawing too much unwanted attention to the fact that her dress looked like it had been through a war, attitude was everything.

*Act confident, like you belong—and nobody gives you a second thought.*

Just before the door opened, Lon glanced at her. "Ready?"

She nodded.

Together, they stepped out into the lobby, which was full of people—guests, 'bots and human valets, and one or two media crews no doubt stationed there to keep an eye on Kedis. Lilia was acutely aware of the grime and soot staining her dress, but she tried not to let it bother her. Even if people noticed, she'd be out of the building in less than three minutes.

Through the glass doors, she saw Oppelt standing beside the skimmer. Turning to Lon, she offered him a smile and a quick hug. "Thanks."

"You're welcome." He shot her a look. "Keep your head down for a little while, okay?"

"I'll try," she said, before stepping into the revolving door that would take her outside. *No promises though. If Freedom's Children is starting terrorist attacks, all bets are probably off.*


Save for Zoë, the penthouse was empty. Lilia took a quick shower, changed clothes, and made herself a sandwich before settling down on the couch in the living room. She wasn't entirely sure what to do with herself. She was tired, but not enough to take a nap. Part of her wanted to see her grandfather, but she also wanted to join Kevin and Erik at the spaceport.

She dragged a hand down her face. She'd have to use a portal if she wanted to leave the penthouse without a security detail. Oppelt had made it very clear when he picked her up that her grandfather had left strict instructions. She almost smiled; if she didn't know better, she'd have thought her grandfather had forgotten about the transporters.

*It makes sense, though.* With everything going on—with Freedom's Children openly attacking now—there were no guarantees they wouldn't start targeting politicians' families.

A glance at her comlink showed no message from Jasper. She suppressed a pang of disappointment. *He's busy*, she told herself. *Besides, you'll talk to him tonight.*

The longer Lilia sat in the living room, the more oppressive the silence became. Zoë was in stand-by mode, having apparently finished all of her chores for the moment, and the penthouse was so quiet Lilia could have sworn she heard her own pulse in her ears. She wanted to do something, *needed* to do something…but she had absolutely no idea what that should be.

When her comlink buzzed a little while later with an incoming holo-call, she immediately snatched it up. It was Alexis. "Hey! You have no idea how glad I am to hear from you." She laughed ruefully. "I'm back at Ferndale and I've been sitting here going crazy."

"I suppose it's better than being blown up again."

"…that's a good point. What's up?"

"Did you know you're on the news again?"

Lilia blinked. "What, from the attack footage from last night?"

"Not exactly." Alexis blew out a breath. "One of the cams caught you leaving the Beliana and now there's all sorts of speculation going on as to why you were there."

"You've got to be kidding me." Lilia rolled her eyes. "Did that cam also happen to catch Lon walking me out?"

"Yeah. You can see him. But they're still making all kinds of suggestive comments."

Grimacing, Lilia slumped down on the couch. "Great. Just what I need." She waved a hand in the air. "Never mind the fact that several prominent people *died* in that attack last night, let's focus on why Representative Monroe's daughter is at the Tarynian Ambassador's hotel *with her brother*." Frustration laced every syllable. "What do I need to do, release a statement that I had to evacuate with my brother and the Tarynians?"

"Maybe." Alexis bit her lip. "Of course, there's also that old saying about never believing anything until it's been officially denied."

Lilia exhaled heavily, shading her eyes with one hand. "Great."

Both of them were silent for a moment. Then Alexis flicked a black curl out of her face. "If I were you, I wouldn't worry about it. The only reason I called you is so you wouldn't be caught off-guard."

"Thanks, Alexis." Lilia dropped her hand. "I do appreciate it."

"Well…" An entirely impish smile spread across Alexis's face; her dark eyes began to sparkle. "You can repay me by telling me the latest with you and Lieutenant Tall, Blond, and Handsome."

Lilia couldn't restrain the blush that suffused her face. "There's not a lot to tell." Even to her own ears, the words sounded flimsy.

"Oh, really?" Alexis raised a skeptical eyebrow.

Lilia's mind flashed back to the night before, and her shoulders slumped in defeat. There would be no getting around this conversation. Not with Alexis. *Maybe it'll do me some good to talk about it.* She took a breath and let it out slowly. "I think he almost kissed me last night."

Alexis squealed, clapping her hands together and nearly dropping her comlink in the process. Her holographic image wobbled alarmingly. "I knew it! I knew he liked you!" She leaned closer to her comlink. "Tell me everything."

By the end of the story, Lilia was pacing the confines of her bedroom and waving her hands in the air. She had long since transferred Alexis's call to a holoscreen on her wall; she couldn't have this conversation standing still. "I like him, Alexis, but there's no future with a Tarynian soldier. I must be crazy."

"Love does that to—" Alexis began, but Lilia rounded on her.

"I am *not* in love with him!" She swallowed. "I like him a lot, but that doesn't mean—"

"You're in denial, Lil," Alexis interrupted. "Big-time. *Listen* to yourself. You've spent the past fifteen minutes telling me all about this guy, all the things you like about him, and yet you're not even a little bit in love with him?" She gave Lilia a stern look reminiscent of her mother, Raven.

Lilia could only meet her all-too-knowing gaze for a few seconds before she had to look away. "It's crazy Alexis. *I'm* crazy."

"Nah." Her best friend waved a hand. "I'd think you were crazy if it was Ambassador Kedis—"

Lilia shot her a horrified look.

"—but since it's Jasper Wright…" Alexis waggled her eyebrows.

"There's no future in it," Lilia repeated stubbornly. She held onto that thought with both hands; she had a terrible suspicion she would sink like a rock tossed into the ocean if she didn't.

"Maybe not one that *you* see." Alexis tapped her chin thoughtfully. "I mean, honestly, you could have never imagined the way you'd meet him.

*A stone wall, waves crashing against sharp rocks below. A hand, outstretched toward her.* Lilia blinked the memories away. "No.

"And he's a Christian."

"True."

Alexis gave a pragmatic shrug. "Who knows where God will take you both?"

Lilia sighed. "Alexis…"

"No, no, hear me out." Her best friend held up a hand. "Why can't you at least explore the idea? You won't know if you never give it a shot."

"He's G.U."

"So?" Alexis shrugged again. "From the sound of it, we could end up having some kind of agreement with the Tarynians."

Panic clawed at Lilia's throat. That was true, but…She stared reproachfully at her friend. "Aren't you supposed to be talking me *out* of this?"

Grinning, Alexis shook her head. "I'm supposed to help you be honest with yourself." She pointed a finger at Lilia. "And the honest truth is that you like this guy." She paused. "Even if you think you shouldn't."

Lilia's stomach proceeded to tie itself into knots; she dropped her gaze to the carpeted floor. It took her a moment to reply. "Can you *see* the media headlines?"

When Alexis failed to respond, she turned to look at the holo-screen and found her friend staring at her like she'd sprouted a second head. The back of her neck prickled uncomfortably. "What?"

"Are you *listening* to yourself?" Alexis demanded. "Since when do you care what people think about you? You've been dealing with being half-Tarynian as long as I've known you, and you've never acted like this before." She peered suspiciously at Lilia. "It's almost like you're *ashamed* you like Jasper. Does that mean——"

Lilia had a split-second to realize where Alexis was headed.

"——you're ashamed of your dad too?"

"No!" The denial emerged with more force than Lilia would have preferred. She blew out a breath, ran her fingers through her short hair, before continuing in a calmer voice, "I could never be ashamed of my dad."

She had *never* been ashamed of him.

Even though he'd died when she was too young to remember him. Even though people had tried to make her ashamed of her heritage.

Alexis nodded, as though she'd expected this. "Are you ashamed of being half-Tarynian?"

"No." Lilia snorted. "It's just frustrating dealing with people's prejudice sometimes."

"Then why are you ashamed of Jasper?" Alexis looked genuinely puzzled. "Why do you care what the media will say?"

Lilia just pressed her lips together and mutely shook her head. She wanted to protest, wanted to tell Alexis she was wrong, but the words wouldn't come. Like it or not, Alexis had illuminated a dirty little place inside her, a place where she'd stuffed all those odd, lingering feelings of guilt and prayed they'd just go away.

Alexis opened her mouth and shut it, apparently debating the wisdom of speaking her next words. She swallowed decisively and went for it. "Is it because of what happened on Coral Island?"

Lilia inhaled sharply, but shook her head. "No," she said at last. "I made peace with that after the whole Kedis thing."

"Then what is it?" When she didn't respond, Alexis prodded, "Lilia?"

"I don't know!" Lilia threw her hands up in the air. "I can't explain it! I just—" She shook her head in frustration, unable to put her jumbled thoughts into words.

"I think I can." Alexis rested her chin on her hand.

"Oh, really?"

"Yeah. You've changed a little, Lilia." It was Alexis's turn to shake her head. "I think it started after you came back to Sonela. You haven't been yourself since you started going to all those fancy, high-society parties."

Lilia stared at her for a few seconds, before she laughed incredulously. "You're kidding me. *That's* what we're going with? Peer pressure?"

Alexis's solemn expression did not alter. "You've told me how much pressure you feel like you're under, how much scrutiny. It's a reasonable explanation."

"Alexis—"

"The Lilia I know," she interrupted, "the Lilia I've been friends with most of my life, wouldn't decide she doesn't like or love someone just because of where they're from."

Her words found their mark. Lilia winced, stung, and her defenses flared. "Alexis, he's a soldier of a government that thinks it's okay to *kill* us if we don't cooperate with them!"

"Yeah, that's definitely an issue." Alexis did not budge. "But like I said, it looks like that's about to change. Then what will you do?"

Lilia just stared at her, struggling to find words—the right words, words that adequately explained the maelstrom whirling inside her at the moment.

Alexis looked nervous, as though she couldn't believe she'd just said all that, but she raised her chin. "You're my best friend, Lilia, and somebody had to tell you." She bit her lip. "Don't change who you are to fit into your grandfather's society. He wouldn't want you to do that." She hesitated, before adding, "Your grandmother wouldn't want you to do that."

At the mention of Teresa Monroe, Lilia felt like she'd just been sucker-punched—the more so because Alexis was absolutely right. Her grandmother would *hate* that. The thought scorched her insides.

She reached for her comlink. "I've got to go."

"Lilia—"

She managed a small smile. "Thank you for the heads up about the media coverage. I'll talk to you later, okay?" She ended the holocall before Alexis could finish, her stomach churning and tears burning her eyes.

Her best friend's words ricocheted inside her head; she shut her eyes to keep the tears from escaping and pinched the bridge of her nose. *I am not ashamed of Jasper. And I haven't changed. I've just had to pay more attention to how I represent myself, because it reflects on Grandfather.*

She, Kevin, and Lon hadn't really had to worry about that while they were on Glo'Stea.

For a moment, as she stood in the center of her room, she wished they could go back in time, back to before she and Kevin had joined the NCDC, before Chesnee had attacked Lanx. It was selfish, she knew, since the number of people dying as a result of the blockade was less now that Kedis and the Triumvirate were negotiating, but still…

Things had been less complicated then. The distinction between black and white had been clearer. She swallowed, hugging her arms around her torso. *Right now it feels like we're all swimming through gray water.*

And lately, the shadows in that gray water had started growing deeper than she was comfortable with.

Lilia made her way over to her bed on unsteady legs and sank down on the side. Clenching her hands in the bedspread, she stared down at the carpet. *A lot has happened since we came back to Sta'Gloa.*

A lump formed in her throat. *I—I killed a man on a crazy rescue mission, I got bounced all over the Coalition and nearly got—* she swallowed hard, *—nearly got raped, and then somebody blew up the Opening Ceremonies Gala.*

Alexis knew about some of what had happened, but not all of it. *And I don't know how to tell her the rest.* She pressed her lips together. Her best friend would be so hurt that she had kept becoming a Guardian from her, but Lilia still didn't think it was a good idea to tell her.

Her thoughts turned to Jasper and her heart wrenched. *I don't know how to tell him either.* Thanks to Lon, he knew what Guardians were now, but...as much as she liked him, she didn't know if she could tell him. *That would inevitably lead back to Challa.*

Her guts twisted. *I'm not ready to talk about that with him.*

She wasn't sure she'd *ever* be ready to talk about that with him.

# CHAPTER 62

AIDEN retired early that evening, citing fatigue and the need for an early start the next morning. This surprised the twins, who had fully expected him to tell them Jayce and Cait were dead and ask questions, searching for any nugget of information he might have missed before.

Afterward, Kevin pulled Lilia aside in the dining room and opened a Nancom channel to her. [Do you think he's decided we don't know anything?]

She shrugged helplessly. They'd both spent the remainder of the day on pins and needles. [I don't know.]

Kevin cast a frown in the direction of their grandfather's master bedroom. [At least it takes some of the pressure off of us for not saying anything.]

"What are you two doing?"

At the sound of Derek's voice, both siblings jumped. Neither of them had noticed his approach from the kitchen.

Lilia flattened a hand over her heart. "You scared me."

"I can see that." Derek lifted a dark eyebrow at them. "What are you doing whispering in corners like you're nine again?"

Exchanging slightly panicked glances, the twins chimed together, "Nothing."

"Right."

Derek eyed them suspiciously, and Lilia had to squelch a sudden nervous laugh. In that instant, it felt like all three of them had regressed about fifteen years.

[I don't know what to do,] Kevin said.

[Me either.]

Kevin abruptly pulled his comlink out and brandished it toward Derek. "I have another match tomorrow night."

"With Franco?" Derek frowned, his eyebrows knitting together in concern.

"Yeah."

"I still think you ought to take me with you," Lilia called over her shoulder as she headed back into the living room. "If they can bring their buddies, you should—" The rest of her sentence died unspoken as she stopped short, staring in shock at the sight of a portal collapsing in on itself in the center of the living room.

Noting the way she had frozen, her brothers both rushed up behind her, demanding in unison, "What is it?"

Raising a trembling hand, Lilia pointed to the spot where the portal had been. "There was a portal." Her voice was shaky. "Right there."

"A portal?" Derek asked in disbelief. He glanced between them before staring into the living room as though he expected a visible trace of it to remain.

"What's that?" Kevin's sharp voice sliced through Lilia's shock. Sliding around her, he strode into the living room and bent to pick something up off the white carpet.

Derek and Lilia crowded around him and together the three of them peered at the object in Kevin's hand.

It was a datachip reader.

Kevin frowned at it. "This isn't mine." He glanced up at Lilia and then at Derek. "Is it yours?"

Both of them shook their heads.

They all looked up at the sound of muffled footsteps rushing toward them; Michael skidded around the corner from the hall three seconds later. He looked alarmed. "What happened?"

Part of Lilia's mind acknowledged that Derek must have Nancommed their oldest brother, but the rest of her was still in shock. She reached out to touch the datachip reader. "They must have sent it through the portal."

"*Portal?*" Michael's voice hit a high note. Completely bewildered, he stared at his siblings. "Does someone want to—"

"Somebody opened a portal into our living room and dropped this off." Lilia swallowed, fear growing inside her like a tangle of thorny vines. She looked at Kevin. "Who could have done that? They'd need—"

"—pretty exact coordinates," he said grimly, turning the datachip reader this way and that. "Looks like it's got a chip."

Michael started. "Wait! It could be a—"

Kevin turned the device on and the holographic head and shoulders of a masked man clad in nano-armor appeared.

"—bomb," Michael finished faintly.

"Oh." Kevin gulped. "Didn't think about that."

"Who *is* this?" Derek demanded incredulously, without taking his eyes off the figure.

Lilia's heart stuttered in her chest. She knew *exactly* who that was. *The Mastermind.* She exhaled shakily. *He could have chucked a bomb into the penthouse and we'd never even have known what hit us.*

She had to swallow twice before she could force words out. "It's the Mastermind."

As though he had been waiting for them to finish, the recording began to speak. "Pardon the rather unorthodox method by which this message has been delivered, but time is running short."

A chill skipped down Lilia's spine at the distorted voice and its vaguely familiar cadence.

"Kevin and Lilia Strong, you have had ample time to consider my offer." The Mastermind paused. "I now require an answer."

Lilia and Kevin exchanged infinitesimal looks before returning their attention to the recording.

"Join us in fighting for the liberty of the Coalition—or face the same fate as those who abandon their world and system to the Tarynian vermin."

"He's not biased at all," Derek commented wryly.

"If you will join us, come to the Reclata Park at eight P.M. Thursday evening." The Mastermind paused. "If you do not make an appearance, we will assume you have declined."

He paused again, more ominously, his holograph staring straight at them. "Believe me, this is not something you want to decline. You *will* regret your choice, before the end."

Shaking his masked head, the Mastermind continued, "Do not make the mistake of assuming you can be neutral parties. In our present situation, 'neutral' does not exist. You are either with us—or against us."

The recording ended; his holograph disappeared.

Michael blew out a breath in silence filling the living room. "Well, that's cheery." His tone was light, belying the darkness in his violet eyes. "You either join the terrorist group, or you get terrorized along with everyone else in the Coalition."

"Or worse," Derek said quietly.

Lilia's gut clenched. She wrapped her arms around her torso, locking her hands onto her elbows. "I knew we'd have to give him an answer sooner or later; I just—" she shook her head mutely.

"—thought we'd have a little more time than this," Kevin finished quietly, staring down at the datachip reader.

Michael and Derek exchanged grim looks. "I still don't understand why he wants you two so badly." Derek shook his head. "And you specifically."

Lilia shrugged. "He knows we're nanogenetic anomalies. I got the impression he's been collecting them."

"Yeah, but why not me?" Michael dragged a weary hand down his face, his fingers rasping against the stubble that had accumulated over the course of the day. He tipped his head toward Derek. "Why not you? Obviously, Lon is out, but you two helped him. Why does this Mastermind want you and not us?"

He realized how that sounded as soon as the words left his mouth; a sheepish grin curved his mouth. "Not that I'm jealous you've been recruited by a terrorist group or anything, but…" He shrugged his shoulders.

"He's got a point," Derek said thoughtfully. "What's their criteria? It doesn't make any sense that he'd single you two out when—"

"Sure it does," Kevin interrupted. "You and Mike both work for Grandfather. Anybody with any sense—or a connection to the Com-Net—knows where Grandfather stands." It was his turn to shake his head. "No offense, guys, but he probably assumed you agree with him. Grandfather, I mean," he added for clarification. "Not the Mastermind."

Derek was frowning. "And yet he's willing to overlook your involvement with getting Kedis in to see the Triumvirate?"

Lilia tucked a short lock of hair behind her ear. "I know. It's peculiar." She caught her lower lip between her teeth. "Is it just me, or does he seem *familiar* somehow?" She looked hopefully at her brothers. "Something about the way he talks, even with the voice distorter."

"I know what you mean." Michael's eyebrows knit together. "Can't quite put my finger on it though."

"What about you, Kev?" Lilia looked at her twin, curious to know what he'd heard. What she found sent ice curling through her veins. "Kevin?"

Kevin was staring out the wide windows framing the living room on one side, his mind obviously a parsec away and working furiously. He turned back to them abruptly, an odd fire alight in his eyes—

—and Lilia's gut clenched again. She knew that look too well. That was her twin's patented I'm-about-to-do-something-crazy look. A wary note slid into her tone. "Kevin?"

"What if we *did* join?" he asked in a rush, snapping his attention back to them at last. "What if we infiltrated Freedom's Children and worked to bring them down from the inside?"

Lilia did not hesitate. "No." She stepped towards him, throwing her hands into the air. "Infiltrate a *terrorist* group? Are you *crazy*?"

"It could be done." Kevin's face took on a stubborn slant. "Think about it. We could find out what they're planning on doing with the transporters. We could—"

"Promptly get yourselves killed," Derek said flatly. "You're too high profile. *We*—" he swept a hand through the air in a motion that encompassed all four of them, "are way too high profile to get away with something like that. We're under too much scrutiny from the media."

His green eyes narrowed, sharp with worry. "And if you think for one second this Mastermind is going to just blithely trust you…" He made a frustrated sound in the back of his throat. "You're crazy."

"They're essentially a terrorist group," Michael said. "They're responsible for dozens of deaths. More, if you count the chaos they unleashed on Glo'Stea when they turned on those shield genera-tors." He spread his hands. "What will they ask you to do to prove yourself?"

Blowing out a frustrated breath, Kevin turned away, fiercely scrubbing his hands through his dark hair. "I know. I *know*. I just—" His fingers tightened in his hair. "What if we could find Lang and Cait and rescue them?"

Both of them missed the sharp looks their older brothers ex-changed.

"We wouldn't get the chance for a long time," Lilia said flatly. "I'll bet you anything the first thing they'll do if we were to meet with them is hit us with an impactor. They'll do that precisely to keep us from potentially pulling any stunts."

Her fingers tightened their own grip on her elbows until her knuckles turned white. "Even if we joined, I think it would be a while before the Mastermind trusted us with anything important."

"Because of Lon and Kedis." Kevin tipped his head back to frown up at the ceiling, as though it was responsible for this mess.

"Pretty much." Lilia swallowed hard. "It won't be worth it, Kev." She waited until he glanced at her to finish. "Whatever price we have to pay to prove we're trustworthy won't be worth infiltrating Freedom's Children." She swallowed again. "He'll ask us to murder people."

Her words fell like stones in the middle of the room, their edges hard and unyielding.

"And even if by some miracle he *doesn't* ask us directly, he'll want information or access to something that will result in someone's murder." Lilia felt it in her gut; a twisting, roiling certainty that their admission would come with bloodshed—both as punishment for perceived sympathies and crimes and to ensure they made a break with their past loyalties.

They'd be in—but there would be no coming back.

*And how can we stand before God on Judgment Day and confess to that?*

Helpless frustration coiled Kevin's muscles; he gritted his teeth. "I *know!*" he burst out. "I just wish there was something else we could *do!*"

"I know." Unwinding her arms and letting them fall to her sides, Lilia stepped over to him and put a hand on his shoulder. "Believe me, I know." She tilted her head toward the datachip reader. "That isn't it." Scorn dripped from her words. "Whatever he had Banx and Dr. Dover do to us, we won't be his puppets."

Kevin did not answer. He only stared grimly at the datachip reader for a long moment…and then his shoulders suddenly slumped. In the face of such brutally honest truth, what could he say? "You're right."

The fist that had clamped a merciless fist around Lilia's heart eased.

Tossing the datachip reader to Derek, Kevin locked his hands behind his head and began to pace the length of the living room.

Michael, meantime, folded his arms across his chest and stared at the twins through narrowed violet eyes. "What do you mean, 'find

Cait and Lang and rescue them'? They were killed this morning." His voice deepened with authority. "Weren't they?"

The twins both winced. Kevin stopped pacing, and a hot flush of shame crept up Lilia's neck. *This is exactly what I was afraid would happen.* They'd blown it.

"Kevin? Lilia?" An edge slid into Derek's voice. "Do you know something the rest of us *don't?*" He paused. "I thought we were done with keeping secrets."

Violet met violet as the twins stared at each other, the same panicked thoughts tumbling through both their brains.

Finally, Kevin turned to their brothers and lifted his chin. "They're not dead. Freedom's Children has Cait and Lang, but we helped Dr. Jayce escape this morning."


"You've got to stop hiding things from us," Michael said in frustration, when they finished their story.

Kevin scowled. "Well, it's not exactly like we had a lot of time today to tell you."

"You've got Nancom, remember?" Derek tapped the side of his head.

Lilia had curled up on the couch. "Yeah, well, if we'd told you right when it happened, your reactions would have been off if anybody was paying attention to you."

Derek frowned. "Because of you two?" He received twin nods.

Michael sighed heavily, resting his forehead against the cool glass of one of the wide windows. "I understand why you did it. I just wish you'd *trust* us."

"We do," Kevin said immediately, and both Derek and Michael shot him strained, disbelieving looks. "We *do*," he protested. "We just needed some time to think about the best way to go about this."

"And we couldn't have helped you with that?" Derek asked pointedly.

"You'd been gone all day," Lilia said from the couch. "It's not like we had a lot of time anyway. And the news—"

"—showed the building had been blown up." Kevin dropped his arms. "It's got to be an inside job. *Somebody* gave Freedom's Children exact coordinates to the scientists' locations."

Michael and Derek looked at each other again. "That's what the Triumvirate has concluded," Derek said. "They're launching an investigation."

Lilia spread her hands in a helpless gesture. "And that's why we aren't telling anybody about Jayce. Not even—"

"—Grandfather," Kevin said grimly.

Derek shook his head. "I still think that's a mistake."

Lilia glanced at the center of the living room and realization washed over her like someone had dumped a bucket of frigid water on her head. The hair on the back of her neck stood on end. "We're missing the most important thing about all this."

"What?" All three of her brothers looked at her.

"The Mastermind opened a portal into our *living room.*" She waved a hand toward the middle of the room. "How in the galaxy did he get those coordinates?"

Her brothers all blanched, silence gripping them. At last, Michael shook his head. "I don't know."

"There are only two possibilities." Derek held up a finger, his lean features grim and cold. "One, the Mastermind got them from someone working for Freedom's Children who could have visited Grandfather here at Ferndale—"

"Or someone on Grandfather's security team is working for him." Kevin shifted his eyes toward Michael. "Sorry, but it had to be said."

Michael brushed his words aside. "We'll deal with that in a minute." He addressed Derek. "What's the second possibility?"

"That the Mastermind is actually someone we know—someone who's been here and could have gotten the coordinates himself." Derek dropped his hand to tug at the collar of his shirt with a finger, loosening it.

Lilia blinked at this. "The Mastermind could be someone we *know?*"

Derek shrugged, his face twisting unhappily. "It's a possibility."

"Who?" Lilia and Kevin demanded at the same time.

"You're asking me?" Derek arched an eyebrow at them. "I just said it's possible."

"It's probably someone working for him." Michael glanced out the window at Sonela's night skyline. "That's more likely. The Mastermind himself is probably holed up in their headquarters on Glo'Stea, orchestrating everything."

That was entirely likely, but...Lilia bit her lip. "He *does* have access to a transporter." It was her turn to shake her head. "He's not limited to any one world. Or city, for that matter."

Kevin blew out a breath. "That's still—" he performed a few mental calculations, "—a *lot* of potential suspects."

"Yes, it is." Derek's grim, unhappy expression did not fade. "And I don't know how we'd go about narrowing them down without enlisting help."

The twins exchanged glances. "Maybe Nob could help," Kevin said.

"Maybe." Michael lifted one shoulder in a shrug. "I'm not sure it matters at the moment though." He nodded to the datachip reader in Derek's hand. "That could have been a bomb. We could all be dead right now."

"Hey, look at the bright side." Kevin tried for a smile. "The Mastermind doesn't want us all dead."

"Yet," Lilia couldn't help muttering.

"My point is," Michael continued, shaking his head. "We already know somebody's got coordinates that get them into the Mansion. And now they've got coordinates into the penthouse?"

"Not to mention we have no idea what the Mastermind will do when you don't show up," Derek said. "For all we know, they could have coordinates to the *Talia* too."

Lilia buried her fingers in her hair and tugged, but she barely felt the resulting pain. "What do we do? Go into hiding? We can't join him."

"The first thing we do," Michael said firmly, holding out a hand to Kevin and another to Lilia, "is pray. We'll deal with everything else as it comes."

# CHAPTER 63

THE morning's Triumvirate session had barely begun when Septien Yu broke off in the middle of the customary opening statement to glance down at the comlink that lay before him on the Chairman's podium. After an eyeblink, he shifted to address the three Chief Ministers. "It would appear Ambassador Kedis has arrived and is requesting an audience."

"Not unexpected," Kane Fenton murmured from his seat beside Aiden.

Aiden gave him an imperceptible nod. "I believe a coma is the only thing that could have kept him away."

His thoughts were in turmoil. Derek and Michael had informed him about the Mastermind's ultimatum to the twins during their ride to Triumvirate Tower and he had no idea what they were going to do about that yet. Nor was this the time to consider it.

Fenton suppressed a snort. "Quite. I was expecting him to show up at our emergency session yesterday."

"No doubt he was recuperating—and plotting."

The Sta'Gloan Director of Internal Affairs suppressed another snort.

Hugh Koen, Pryce Gammick, and Devlin Vance exchanged glances, and then Vance raised a holographic hand. "I move that we grant the Ambassador an audience." His lips pursed. "We might as well get it over with."

"Seconded," Koen rumbled.

Yu looked back out at the rest of the Triumvirate. "All in favor?"

Along the semi-circle, green bars lit up as almost the entire Triumvirate voted yes. Aiden spotted several red bars in the Glo'Stean and Lanxian sections, but he suspected it was more as a form of protest against Kedis's presence than anything else.

"The motion has passed." Striking the bell, Yu reached for his comlink. Everyone else reached for their autotranslators, if they were not already wearing them.

A moment later, the Chamber's double doors swung open to admit the Ambassador. Kedis strode briskly through the semi-circle of tables and chairs and across the marble floor to stand near Yu, where he could address the entire Triumvirate. A slight limp was the only evidence of his injuries.

"The Triumvirate recognizes Ambassador Kedis."

Kedis offered them a short bow. He was, as usual, impeccably dressed in a navy blue bespoke suit. "Good morning," he said in Tarynian.

"Ambassador." Koen leaned forward slightly in his chair. "We are glad to see you were not badly injured in last night's incident."

Kedis smiled, motioning to his leg. "Ah, the marvel of modern medicine. I thank you for your concern, Chief Minister." He glanced out at the rest of the Triumvirate. "I understand several of you were also injured last night—I am glad it was not more serious."

"So are we," Zane Chas said loudly from the Lanxian section, drawing a few darting glances.

"Has there been any progress in determining who was responsible?" Kedis asked.

Kane Fenton cleared his throat and stood. When he was recognized, he said, "Our investigation is ongoing, Ambassador. We are still sifting through evidence and security footage."

Kedis held out a hand. "I quite understand." His dark eyes glittered as he bowed his head. "Do keep me informed as to your findings."

Fenton's gaze darted across the Sta'Gloan section to Malik Thane before he nodded. "Certainly."

"Ambassador Kedis," Yu leaned forward over his podium, "in the interest of expediting matters, may we inquire as to what exactly you wish to speak to the Triumvirate about this morning?"

*Probably a pointless question*, Aiden thought. There could only be two topics—and they were both intertwined.

"Certainly, Chairman." Nodding solemnly, Kedis spread his hands. "Your investigation into last night's dreadful attack may still be ongoing, but it is clear to me, especially in light of incidents since my arrival here on Sta'Gloa, that an active anti-peace terrorist group is behind everything."

The Chamber was so quiet Aiden almost imagined he could hear their collective heartbeats.

"At the moment, the specifics don't matter. What counts is the fact that they have escalated their acts of violence." Kedis's dark-eyed gaze traveled around the Chamber. "Now, I ask myself, why would they do that? Simply because I continue to be here?"

He shrugged. "Perhaps. However, I think it more likely that they have seen what I have seen."

He paused dramatically, and Aiden felt a flicker of annoyance. *Get on with it*, he thought. *You already know we are all listening.*

"And what might that be, you ask?" Kedis raised his arms. "Peace. Peace between our two governments."

A wave of exasperation rippled around the Chamber. Aiden was not immune to it. He stared at Kedis with narrowed eyes. *Is that not what we have been discussing for* weeks *now?*

"I know what you are thinking." Kedis smiled broadly. "We've been debating the intricate ins and outs of  trade alliances and the Coalition's inclusion in the Galactic Union since my arrival." He lowered his arms. "But last night—my brush with death gave me, if you will, an epiphany."

*Oh, this should be good.* Aiden glanced at Fenton before looking toward the Glo'Stean section at Shane Briscoe and Martin Hollowell. Briscoe looked cautiously intrigued, while Hollowell's face was set in a neutral expression that gave nothing away.

"And what, might you ask, was my epiphany?" Kedis continued to smile. "It was this. We have been looking at these peace talks from the wrong angle." He waved a hand in the air. "The Coalition's inclusion in the Galactic Union is a matter for another day. What we need is a simple trade agreement. Everything else stems from that."

"And so," he raised his voice above a sudden swell of whispers, "I propose that the Coalition and the Triumvirate implement such a trade agreement." Before anyone could react to this, he said, "The terms are simple. I propose the blockade be lifted and both trade and travel be allowed to resume between our two governments."

It took a moment for the full weight of his words to sink in. When they did, the air in the Chamber electrified. For his part, Aiden was so stunned that he could only stare unblinking at Kedis. *Did he really just propose to* lift *the blockade?* Without *a long string of caveats?* He had not expected that.

*No one* had expected that.

In the Glo'Stean section, Egan Ashford rose to his feet and was recognized. "Ambassador Kedis, you do realize what you've just said."

Kedis turned both hands palm up. "Certainly."

Ashford gave him a hard stare. "What is the catch?" He shook his head, eyes narrowed in suspicion. "I can't be the only one who thinks that this sounds too good to be true. What does the G.U. get from this?"

"Aside from the Blockade Division being freed up to be posted elsewhere in the Galactic Union?" Kedis raised his eyebrows. "We get the benefit of being able to exchange goods and commodities, and for people to travel."

He shrugged. "And the ability to then negotiate further down the line. Given the resulting import and export tariffs on both sides, and the exchange rate of our respective monetary systems, you, the illustrious members of the Triumvirate, may well decide it is in the Coalition's best interest to join the G.U. later."

Aiden exhaled slowly. *It does sound too good to be true. And so suddenly.*

Dion Pamos rose to his feet. "Ambassador, while we appreciate such a…generous offer, I'm sure we're all wondering the same thing." He cocked his head to one side. "This *is* an offer you are authorized to make by the G.U. Senate, correct?"

"That is correct." A smile stretched across Kedis's face; he looked quite pleased with himself. "It comes through the proper channels, I assure you. I spent most of yesterday negotiating this."

The three Chief Ministers exchanged darting glances. "That decision seems to have been made rather quickly," Pryce Gammick said, eying Kedis. "It is our experience that few things in the political realm happen quickly."

Kedis's smiled widened, though he attempted to look modest. "Ah, well, Chief Minister, when one looks at the past twenty years, it tends to put things into perspective. The Senate wishes to see this matter resolved in the most expeditious manner, and they agree with me that this would seem to be our best option."

Murmurs rippled around the Chamber, equal parts excited and skeptical.

Glancing around at the rest of the Triumvirate, Kedis withdrew a datapad from his pocket and deposited it on Septien Yu's podium with a flourish. "Here is our written proposal of a trade agreement." He flashed another smile, his teeth white against his olive skin. "You will find it is as simple as I just mentioned."

"It will require discussion," Hugh Koen said sternly.

"Of course." Kedis drew himself up and then gave them a courteous bow. "I shall leave you to it. Thank you for your consideration."

Septien Yu tapped his bell. "Ambassador Kedis, you are dismissed."

With another smile, Kedis swept out of the Chamber.

When he had gone, Yu held up his hands for silence before anyone could speak. "The Ambassador's proposal will be transmitted to all of you for review." He glanced at the Chief Ministers. "The Triumvirate will officially consider it after we have all had the opportunity to do our due diligence. In the meantime, we will proceed to our next scheduled order of business." He tapped his bell and carried on.

It was, Aiden conceded, a sensible plan, but he doubted anyone would be paying much attention the rest of the day.

Beside him, Kane Fenton leaned a little closer. "What would have prompted him to make such an offer all of a sudden?" he asked quietly. "What has changed since the attack?"

Aiden gave a tiny shake of his head. "I do not know." He hesitated. "Is it possible his discovery about Guardians could have had such an impact?"

It was Fenton's turn to shake his head in mute bewilderment.

*Something* had changed, however…and Aiden doubted it was Kedis's brush with death. Whatever it was, it tempered the excitement he would have otherwise felt about their chances of finally reaching a trade agreement. *Kedis has gained some kind of leverage—or else* thinks *he has gained some kind of leverage.*

Aiden could only wonder how long it would be before Kedis revealed his hand…and what the consequences would be.

# CHAPTER 64

AIDEN called a family meeting in his study as soon as he arrived home that evening. Lilia darted a glance at her older brothers, both of whom looked grim, before returning her attention to their grandfather.

"Your brothers informed me of what happened last night," Aiden said without preamble. Behind his neat white beard, his expression was severe. "The audacity of this so-called 'Mastermind'." He shook his head. "First he kidnaps you, Lilia, and now this?"

Lilia and Kevin exchanged sidelong glances. "We're sorry to have—"

"—put you and everyone—"

"—else in Ferndale in—"

"—danger."

Aiden brushed their apology aside with an impatient flick of his fingers. "It is not your fault. If Freedom's Children has a transporter of their own, no one is safe." His wrinkled face darkened further. "As if we do not have enough on our plates, now a terrorist group is attempting to recruit my grandchildren and issuing threatening ultimatums by opening portals into my home in the process."

The twins exchanged glances again; Lilia bit the inside of her lip. "What are we going to do?"

"We could temporarily relocate," Michael said. "It'd be a hassle, but we could rent a random series of hotel suites or condos for the next few weeks."

Aiden considered his eldest grandson's words for a moment, before dismissing them with a shake of his head. "That would be too much of a hassle on top of everything else right now." His mouth thinned. "And I refuse to be chased out of my own home. Portals or no portals."

"If we stay," Derek said quietly, "we'll have to have JP and the security team scan Ferndale for the sudden appearance of additional bodies. Or anything else, as best as they can determine."

The twins traded tiny dismayed glances out of the corners of their eyes. They had known it was inevitable, after this, but still…

Lilia looked back at their grandfather to find him watching them. His sharp green eyes softened with a hint of compassion as he said, "I am aware that you have been departing and arriving from Ferndale via your…you know." He waved a hand in the general direction of their wrists.

"While I appreciate the security and discretion of such a means of travel, unfortunately, that must now come to an end." Aiden tilted his head. "Unless of course you would prefer that JP and the rest of my security team knew about—"

"No," Kevin said quickly. "That's not necessary, Grandfather." His eyes flicked to Michael and Derek before returning to Aiden. "We understand." He tried to smile. "We knew it couldn't last forever."

"Good." Aiden exhaled heavily. "I trust my security team, but I believe it would be best for everyone if you continued to keep that information under wraps."

Lilia studied him for a few seconds. Instead of seeming relieved by their agreement, he continued to seem torn, shoulders bowing under a heavy, invisible load. "What happened today, Grandfather?"

A wry smile curled Aiden's lips. "Ambassador Kedis used his recovery time yesterday to get the G.U. Senate to authorize a no-strings-attached trade agreement and the lifting of the blockade."

The twins exchanged startled looks. "He's been proposing something like that from—"

"—the beginning, though, hasn't he?"

"Not as final as this." Aiden leaned back in his chair, pressing the tips of his fingers together in a steeple. "It seems the Triumvirate will be voting on it in a few days."

Goosebumps erupted across Lilia's skin, though whether from excitement or trepidation, she did not know. "They're actually going to lift the blockade and give us unimpeded access to the rest of the galaxy?"

Aiden dipped his head in a slow nod. "That is what the document states."

"What's the catch?" Kevin asked warily, folding his arms across his chest. He glanced at his older brothers. "It sounds too good to be true. And so fast? There has to be a catch."

"That's what I'd like to know," Derek said grimly.

"I do not know." Aiden spread his hands. "Something about the attack or its aftermath spurred Kedis to action. I believe he thinks he possesses some kind of leverage he did not have until now."

Heart sinking in her chest, Lilia looked sideways at Kevin. She saw the same thought reflected in his violet eyes. *Lon.*

Kevin cleared his throat. "Kedis, ah, knows about Guardians now, knows they're real. Lon had to—"

"—materialize his armor in order to save Kedis's life," Lilia finished. "Maybe that's what changed. Maybe he thinks—"

"—a trade agreement is a springboard for potentially getting his—"

"—hands on NCDC tech down the road."

"The Triumvirate is aware of this and I have considered it." Eyes narrowed in contemplation, Aiden leaned back in his seat. "Kedis has no assurance of such a thing, of course."

"He doesn't need it." Michael shook his head. "Not now. If he gets his foot in the door, he can finagle that later." He shot Aiden a wry look. "Him and Malik Thane both."

Lilia twisted her fingers together. "What will the Triumvirate *do*, Grandfather? Do you think they'll—"

"—accept Kedis's proposal?" Kevin furrowed his brow. "Being able to safely travel interplanetary and interstellar will definitely shake the shipping industry up." He snorted. "And that's not even counting the transporters."

Aiden drummed his fingers on the surface of his desk for a long moment, before finally shaking his head. "What I think at this point is irrelevant. I may turn out to be completely wrong."

Not satisfied with this answer, Kevin pressed, "But you think the Triumvirate will accept it." He shrugged one shoulder. "Enough to pass it, at any rate."

"I think it is likely," Aiden said at last. "We are all weary of the blockade." The wrinkled lines in his face settled into sad lines. "Unfortunately, it will open up an entirely new set of problems."

"And there's still a segment of the Coalition that will oppose any kind of peaceful agreement with the G.U.," Michael added.

Lilia bit her lip. "It would be worth it though. Not being blockaded." She looked around the office at her family. "Wouldn't it?"

"In the long run, yes." Aiden sighed, rubbing his chin. "The trouble will be ensuring everyone in the Coalition understands that fact."


"And we're back to a daily commute." Kevin shook his head as he and Lilia left Ferndale early the next morning, headed for Sonela Spaceport and the *Talia*. "We definitely got spoiled, sis."

"Yes, we did." Lilia glanced up at the blue sky visible above the buildings around them, relishing the hot sunlight soaking into her skin. "Although it's nice to be outside for a little while."

As they passed *Sal's*, Kevin jerked a thumb toward the door. "Want to stop in and get something for the road?"

Lilia did not even glance at the café. "Nope."

"No?" Kevin arched a dark eyebrow at her. "What's wrong with you and Alexis now?"

She just shook her head and kept walking.

"Lilia."

"Leave it alone, Kev." She flung up a hand. "Just—please. I don't want to talk about it."

"Fine. Be that way."

They took a hoverbus to the spaceport, and hurried down the line of smaller commercial ships until they reached their freighter. Erik was waiting for them at the top of the landing ramp, coffee mug in hand.

"You two are cuttin' it close," he observed from his spot leaning up against the side of the hatch.

"Yeah, well," Kevin cut a sideways glance at his sister as he followed her up the ramp, "I forgot how much travel time to factor in."

Erik nodded sagely as he stepped aside to allow them entrance. "You've gotten spoiled."

Kevin snorted. "Tell me about it."

"What's on the agenda for today?" Erik asked as Lilia raised the landing ramp and the three of them turned their steps to the living compartment.

# CHAPTER 65

IT took the Triumvirate three days to reach a decision—an inevitable decision, as far as Aiden was concerned. Whatever the Coalition might do in the future, for now they wanted the freedom of being able to trade with the rest of the galaxy without fear of reprisal.

*We would be fools not to take this chance.*

That was not to say the decision was unanimous. Kedis's proposal was hotly contested in some quarters, with passionate complaints that the Triumvirate was overcorrecting and moving much too fast, and fresh riots had sprung up again all over the Coalition. Some of the Representatives' constituents saw the trade agreement as an answer to prayer or the only logical solution to the Tarynian problem. Others remained convinced that the Triumvirate was selling them to the devil.

The chaos and the emotion behind this decision took Aiden back over twenty years, back to the Coalition's refusal to join the newly-formed Galactic Union and the subsequent bloody start to the blockade. In all his years of serving as a Representative, he had never experienced anything quite like those tumultuous days...until now.

Chesnee's breach of Lanx's shield had rocked the Coalition, and Ambassador Kedis's arrival had rocked them again...but not like this.

Aiden exhaled heavily. *There will be blood in the streets today.*

He knew what the Triumvirate had to do. They *all* knew, whether they wanted to acknowledge it or not. For the greater good, for the freedom and safety of citizens throughout the Coalition, he and his fellow Representatives had only one logical choice. Kedis would get his trade agreement.

*And Freedom's Children will make us pay for it.*

His thoughts turned briefly to the Mastermind and the ultimatum hanging over his youngest grandchildren's heads, but he swiftly redirected them. Now was not the time.

A grim undertone tempered the excitement flooding the Chamber. This was a historic moment—a day that would go down in the annals of Coalition history—and yet they all felt the specter of unseen assassins, ready to make their displeasure known at a moment's notice. More than one person cast the occasional uneasy glance around, searching for anything out of the ordinary.

Malik Thane had tightened security as much as possible, but even he couldn't protect them against a bomb chucked into their midst through a portal.

Representatives and Directors alike settled into their seats with more decorum than usual—and glancing up and down the semi-circle of tables and chairs, Aiden saw forbidding expressions on more than one face. His eyes lingered on Martin Hollowell.

His colleague's face was expressionless, but his dark eyes blazed. Hollowell believed the Triumvirate was moving too quickly. He had argued that something of this magnitude could not be decided just a few days; they needed to spend more time exploring it.

Aiden felt sorry for him. *It will be interesting to see which way he votes. His personal preference—or that of his constituents.* For a man who hated the Tarynians as much as Martin Hollowell, he was in the uncomfortable position of having the majority of his constituents decide they were in favor of a trade agreement.

The three Chief Ministers took their seats, and the last few stragglers' holographs appeared. Septien Yu struck his gold bell; the sound echoed ominously in the hush that had fallen over the massive room. "This session of the Triumvirate will now come to order."

Yu cleared his throat. "The Triumvirate's first order of business is Ambassador Kedis's trade agreement." He swept his gaze around the Chamber. "We have heard all the arguments, all the pros and cons. Now it comes time to put it to a vote. Do I have a motion?"

Nolan Snyder raised a fleshy hand. "I make a motion that we vote on it."

Yu nodded solemnly. "Do we have a second?"

"Seconded." Four voices rang out. Helen Urquart in the Sta'Gloan section, Shane Briscoe and Egan Ashford in the Glo'Stean section, and Zane Chas, in the Lanxian section.

"Very well." Yu tapped his bell again. "The Triumvirate will now put it to a vote."

This was it. Aiden paused a few seconds to say a silent prayer… and then he pressed a button on the table. A green bar lit up in front of him. A weight seemed to lift off his shoulders, though he did not relax his rigid posture.

*It is done.* Whatever happened next, he knew he could stand before God and say that he had faithfully discharged the duties entrusted to him by his constituents to the best of his ability.

Four measured breaths later, Aiden allowed his eyes to dart right and left. Several of the Representatives had yet to make up their minds, but of the ones who had voted…Relief swelled in his chest. A few red bars were sprinkled along the semi-circle, but they were vastly outnumbered. And, one by one, the last few blank bars flared green.

Including Martin Hollowell's.

Septien Yu glanced from the semi-circle to his datapad on the podium before him. He paused a few seconds, letting the weight of the moment sink in, and then looked back out at the rest of the Triumvirate. "The final vote stands at twenty-two in favor of the trade agreement, and five against."

He allowed himself to break into a smile. "Ladies and gentlemen of the Triumvirate, the blockade is over." He tapped the bell, but its now-bright peal was lost in a flurry of cheers.

*It is finally over.* Aiden held up his hands, bowing his head and closing his eyes. *Thank you, Jesus. Thank you, Father God. The blockade is finally over.*

They would have details to work out, the fine minutia of such an arrangement and the signing of the actual trade agreement itself, but after more than two decades of oppression, the Sta'Gloan system was finally free.

It took a moment before Septien Yu could regain control of the Chamber. "We are bringing Ambassador Kedis in to tell him the news."

Aiden was certain the Ambassador would be thrilled—and not the least bit surprised. He exhaled a small laugh. *But then, I suppose that does not matter. The blockade is over.*

# CHAPTER 66

THURSDAY morning, the day of both the Triumvirate's vote on the trade agreement and the Mastermind's ultimatum, Guillard Franco commed Kevin. He was in the penthouse kitchen, fixing himself some breakfast. Lilia was in the living room, going over Three Cords Shipping's books. With the fate of the trade agreement hanging over everyone's heads, neither of them had wanted to be far from Ferndale today.

"Tonight is your final test," Franco said without preamble. "Meet us at Tieran's penthouse tonight. Amethyst Towers. Nine PM sharp. Understood?"

He barely waited for Kevin to respond before he ended the call.

Bemused, Kevin blinked at his comlink. "Strange man," he said to no one in particular. It hadn't taken long for the cloak-and-dagger routine Franco and his friends delighted in using to wear thin, but Kevin knew he was almost in. He was so close to finding out what they were really up to he could almost taste it.

His gut still said they'd gotten their hands on nanoblades.

He grimaced to himself, thinking of the underground street fighting in occupied Glo'Stea he'd been forced to take a role in during that insane week he and Lilia had been bounced all over the Coalition. *They've definitely got the money to pay for access to nanoblades. Can't get anything more top of the line than those.*

His grimace deepened. *Except they won't be able to protect themselves.* It was a dangerous, dangerous game—which was exactly why it appealed to this crowd. The adrenaline rush from using one's skill and speed to dance on the razor blade edge between life and death.

*Are you ready for this, Strong?* he asked himself. *Are you ready to play this game?*

He'd win tonight. Kevin had no doubt of it.


Renaldo Tieran lived in a penthouse that could have housed Ferndale's entire top floor and still had plenty of room to spare. It was located on the top floor of Amethyst Tower, a giant apartment complex on the inner edge of Sonela's business district, which was prized for its closeness to the Four Towers. Lower-ranking politicians, many of them from Lanx and Glo'Stea, had apartments here, as did a multitude of wealthy businessmen and women from all over the Coalition.

Tieran's father owned one of the largest, most productive mining operations on Lanx. He split most of his time between Lanx and related business concerns on Sta'Gloa, but his only son preferred the atmosphere in Sonela to anything else.

"I enjoyed Quinton," Tieran was saying laconically, as he ushered Kevin through the penthouse on a brief tour. "But of course, nobody's been back since those blasted Tarynians took it over."

"Careful," Franco said with a sly smile. "Thanks to the Triumvirate, those 'blasted Tarynians' are now our allies."

Tieran gave a haughty sniff. "I don't care if they are. Good friend of mine and his family are still stuck there." His expression darkened. "My mother would have been trapped there too, but she left for Sta'Gloa a day earlier than she'd planned and missed the whole thing."

"Good timing," Kevin commented, one hand casually holding the strap of his fencing bag still slung over his shoulder. The penthouse was decorated in an elegant, minimalist style; Kevin was willing to bet practically every single piece of furniture and ornamentation was worth more than what he and Lilia made on a cargo run.

It was the sort of place he could envision Leo Kedis living in, after everything was settled.

*At least until the Tarynians build an embassy.*

When Kevin had arrived at Amethyst Tower, he was not terribly surprised to find himself facing a security checkpoint manned by discreet armed guards in crisp black uniforms. They eyed both him and his fencing bag with cool suspicion, but as soon as he gave them his name, they let him pass into the elegant lobby without a word. Tieran had apparently put him on a whitelist.

Kevin had strolled across a purple marble floor flecked with darker speckles to an executive accelevator, as instructed, and rode it up to the penthouse level. There were four penthouse apartments up here; Tieran's father owned #2. A sober-looking black and silver house 'bot had greeted him at the door and ushered him into a massive living room, where Tieran, Franco, Quill, and Sparin were waiting, dressed in expensive exercise clothes. Tieran had offered him a drink, but Kevin had declined, stating that he never drank and fenced. The other young men had laughed, and Tieran set off on his tour.

"Here we are," Tieran said at last, as they strode down a long hall lined with closed doors. He touched the door panel and motioned for Kevin to precede him into the room beyond with a little flourish. "Our exercise room."

Kevin stepped past him…and was hard-pressed to keep his mouth from dropping open. The room was massive, reminding him more of a large ballroom than something used only for exercise. The floor was covered with a special high-grade matting material, but his gaze skipped over that and the variety of exercise equipment dotting the room to the wall on his right, which was nothing but plastiglass. It provided a stunning view of the city.

"Wow," Kevin said at last, finally remembering he wasn't the only person in the room. He nodded to the transparent wall. "That's pretty spectacular."

"Privacy shielded, of course," Tieran said proudly. "What's the point of having such a magnificent view if you can't keep people from being nosy?"

"Although it's not like you're in much danger of neighbors spying on you up here," Flynn said dryly. The redhead held a whiskey glass in one hand; Kevin had a feeling he wouldn't be one of his sparring partners tonight, despite his outfit.

Tieran only shrugged and turned to Franco, who was decked out in a formfitting hunter green shirt and black pants. "Are we ready?"

"Oh, I think so." Franco clapped Kevin on the shoulder. "After tonight, be prepared to have your mind blown. If you succeed, that is."

Kevin unslung his bag from his shoulder and hefted it in one hand. The air in here was cooler than the rest of the penthouse, with a light scent in the air that was probably supposed to neutralize the smell of sweat and body odor. "And what happens if I lose?"

The four men exchanged secretive grins. "Then I suppose you'll spend the rest of your life wondering 'what if'." Franco's grin widened. "But something tells me you won't have to worry about that."

"I appreciate your confidence." It seemed the appropriate thing to say. Kevin glanced around the massive room. "Changing room?"

He didn't miss the glances the four men exchanged.

"Won't be necessary tonight," Tieran said smoothly, running a hand over his smooth-shaven dark head. "We're doing things a little differently."

Kevin raised an eyebrow. "Oh, really?"

"It's more fun this way," Franco said. "More of a…challenge."

*And more dangerous*, Kevin thought, but he kept it to himself. He could understand the appeal of fencing without all the protective equipment. He and Lon had done it before. It was fun. Dangerous, but fun. "All right." He jerked his chin toward Tieran. "Where are we setting up?"

Tieran waved a dark hand to the center of the floor. "Right here."

That was simple enough.

"Okay." Kevin withdrew his sword from his bag and dropped the bag to the floor. Unsheathing the blade, he dropped the sheath on top of his bag. He was grateful he'd worn comfortable, loose-fitting clothes. He hadn't quite expected this lot to forego protective gear, but he'd wanted to be prepared for anything. "Rules?"

Franco and Tieran exchanged glances again, as though having a silent conversation. It reminded Kevin sharply of how it looked when he and his siblings used Nancom, but he was reasonably sure neither of these two were Guardians. "First blood," Franco announced.

Kevin looked at him sharply. "Really?"

"No pain, no gain." Franco spread his hands in a gesture that said, 'what are you going to do?' He shot Kevin a sly smile, his dark eyes sparkling with mischief. "You don't have to play the game, of course." He nodded to the door through which they had entered. "You're welcome to leave."

A small part of Kevin—a voice that reminded him oddly of his sister—was clamoring for him to take the out. Whatever game Franco and his buddies were playing, it was getting progressively more dangerous. *And if they really do have nanoblades and this is just a* *precursor to see if I'm any good before we get there…*Well, that would be even more dangerous.

He couldn't quit now, though. Not when he was so close to finding out for sure what they were doing. His curiosity was too strong. Kevin shrugged. "I'm still in."

Franco's smile did not waver. "Good."

"Who's my opponent?"

"Me." Franco was still smiling, but there was now a cool, calculating gleam in his eyes.

Kevin studied him for the span of two heartbeats before he pasted a confident smile on his face and waved a hand to the empty arena before them. "Let's do this."

Franco jerked his chin to Quill, who immediately handed him the fencing bag slung over his shoulder. Franco withdrew his sword and unceremoniously dropped the bag onto the floor. Unsheathing his blade, he rested the flat on his shoulder and gave Kevin a challenging look. "First blood, Strong. Unless you impress me."

Of course there was another caveat. Still smiling, Kevin shot back, "What if I get first blood and I *don't* impress you?"

Franco, Quill, and Sparin all laughed. Tieran raised his glass in amusement. "Somehow I don't think you'll have to worry about that."

Franco strode to the center of the massive room with long, easy strides and pivoted to face Kevin. He waited until Kevin had taken up position in front of him to raise his blade in a salute. "This is going to be fun."

Kevin saluted him back, his pulse just this side of steady. This was the first time he'd dueled Franco—and he hadn't seen him duel anyone else before. He was going into this fight completely blind as to his opponent's style.

*That's reality, though,* he reminded himself as he dropped into a ready stance. *When do you ever go into a real fight and automatically know how your opponent is going to react?*

Tieran held up an arm. "On my mark. One, two, three…" He dropped his arm. "Fight!"

For a moment, Franco and Kevin circled each other, with the occasional jab to test each other's defenses. It was a dance that could go on indefinitely—would go on indefinitely—until one of them grew tired or impatient. Kevin was half-tempted to wait for Franco to make the first move, see how long the other man would be content to circle. He didn't think it would be very long.

He had a feeling, however, that this too was part of the test. They wanted to see how badly he wanted into their little club.

Well, the answer to that was not as badly as they wanted him to want it, but enough that he'd go ahead and make the first attack.

Kevin launched into a series of quick jabs and thrusts designed to keep Franco on the defensive without giving him time to counter-attack. Franco blocked him, but retaliated by sliding away and directing a whirling slash to Kevin's unguarded left side. Kevin parried and countered with a similar move.

Tieran, Flynn, and Quill and backed up as the duel became more intense. Kevin and Franco ranged all over the center of the floor, their blades glints of silver flashing furiously beneath the glow panels in the high ceiling. The ring of metal on metal echoed through the room.

Narrowly blocking a slash that would have opened up his bicep, Kevin grinned tightly at Franco. "You're pretty good. I've been wondering."

"We like to save the best for last." Franco's smirk was as sharp as his sword blade. "If you're successful," he jabbed at Kevin's midsection; Kevin pivoted sideways and batted the blade away with his own, "you'll find there are a number of us in the top tier."

*Top tier.* Just how big *was* this secret club, anyway?

Sweat dripped down the side of Kevin's face; he didn't bother wiping it away. Franco was easily one of the best swordsmen he'd encountered in the past few years. Kevin's thoughts briefly flashed to that illegal nanoblade street fighting match in Laconia and the girl named Jade he'd fought. *She'd give Franco a run for his money.*

Now wasn't the time to be thinking about things like that, however. Franco came within three millimeters of nicking his cheek; Kevin barely blocked the blow in time.

"Almost had you," Franco said, his voice sing-song and border-line taunting. "Come on, Strong, you can do better than this."

Grimacing at his own foolishness, Kevin flexed his fingers on the hilt of his sword. "This club of yours. Are you gentlemen, or do you use street rules?"

Franco guffawed, though he never took his eyes off Kevin. "We're gentlemen." One corner of his mouth turned up in a wicked grin. "Mostly, anyway."

In other words, they weren't above fighting dirty if it made for a good show.

That was all Kevin needed to know. He and Franco circled each other again, their blades flashing in and out as they both fought to get past the other's defenses, and then Kevin stepped in close, locking his blade against Franco's. At the same time, he brought a knee up into the other man's gut.

It was a dirty move, something that would never, ever be allowed in a formal match.

It served its purpose, though.

Franco doubled over and Kevin shoved him away, slashing downward with his sword as he did. Franco stumbled backward, heaving for breath, a thin line of crimson blooming on his left green sleeve.

A triumphant thrill shot through Kevin as he settled into a loose, ready stance, waiting. He had drawn first blood. By unorthodox means, sure, but still…

First blood.

His violet eyes narrowed. *Now to see how they respond.*

# Chapter 67

TIERAN, Quill, and Sparin let out startled, borderline angry cries and stepped forward, but Franco held up a hand. Straightening up, he glanced down at his left bicep. He looked almost angry. "That was a dirty, rotten move, Strong."

Kevin only shrugged, remaining where he was. "You said you were only *mostly* gentlemen." He glanced at Tieran and the others before leveling a challenging stare at Franco. "If you'd rather not count it, we can keep going."

He didn't think he'd miscalculated, but if he had…well, he'd keep dueling. That was fine. He'd come prepared for an ordeal tonight anyway.

Tieran, Quill, and Sparin exchanged wary glances, before they also fixed their attention on Franco.

"Well, I must say I didn't expect you to fight dirty." Franco raised his blade in a salute, indicating the duel was over. "Is it the Tarynian in you or just your time on Glo'Stea?"

Quill stirred, rattling the melting ice cubes in his glass. "Franco…" His voice held an edge.

"I meant no offense, Quill." Franco waved the fingers of his injured arm. "Fringes of Glo'Stea, I should have said."

Quill subsided, though he still looked slightly irritated. Clearly, he was Glo'Stean, and this wasn't the first time someone had made derogatory comments about Glo'Stea's inferiority to Sta'Gloa.

Kevin didn't let the crack about his Tarynians blood rile him. "Call it spending some time in the real world," he said, saluting Franco in return. "Not everybody plays by the rules."

The giant exercise room fell silent as the five men studied each other. Blood continued to drip down Franco's arm, forming a little puddle on the matted floor; he ignored it. Kevin stood motionless, his posture easy and relaxed. His focus remained on Franco, but he kept the other three in his peripheral vision.

Tieran finally guffawed loudly, slapping a hand against one leg. "I think he'll fit in just fine, Franco. Nothing like the potential for a little danger to better our odds. It'll keep things interesting."

*Odds?* Kevin narrowed his eyes at that, but kept his mouth shut. *There'll be time for questions later.*

"Yes," Franco said at last. "It'll definitely keep things interesting." He looked from Tieran to Quill, to Sparin, and received two nods and a shrug. Franco then proceeded to hand his sword to Tieran and roll up his bloody sleeve to inspect the gash on his arm. As he did, he shot Sparin a look from beneath his eyelashes. "Ambivalent, are we?"

"Technically, he cheated." Sparin shrugged again. "Can we really call that a victory?"

*Purist,* Kevin decided, glancing briefly at Sparin. Clearly, he was someone who followed all the rules when it came to fencing...which made him a somewhat strange fit for Franco and Tieran's little upper-class gang. *He must really love fencing.*

"What's your reasoning?" Franco raised his eyebrows at Tieran and Quill.

"He showed initiative." Tieran folded his arms across his broad chest. "Clearly, Strong's got the skill, he just..." he grinned, showing white teeth, "...expedited matters a little."

"And demonstrated he can operate outside the box when necessary." Quill rubbed the faint pale stubble on his chin. "As my discerning, upstanding comrade mentioned a moment ago, it'll better our odds."

Sparin made a semi-disgusted sound in the back of his throat. "Odds?" His voice dripped derision. "Have your standards dropped so low?"

Kevin couldn't let that one slide. "I've beaten you once already, Sparin." He tipped his head toward the glass in the redheaded man's hand. "If you hadn't been drinking, I'd take you on again right now."

Sparin's dark eyes flashed; for an instant it looked as though he was seriously considering snatching Franco's sword from Quill and taking Kevin on. But it passed, and he only smiled coldly at Kevin instead.

When Franco continued to stare at Sparin, the thin man finally shrugged. "He's in, all right?" His tone, however, said, *But he'd better watch his back.*

The back of Kevin's neck prickled faintly with unease. *Barely in the club and I've already made an enemy.* His gaze slid from Sparin to Franco and back. Maybe 'enemy' was too strong a word, but…he had the distinct impression it would be a while before Sparin let his little stunt go.

*Ah, well, I'll deal with that later.* Besides, it wasn't like he hadn't behaved perfectly up until now. Sparin couldn't complain about anything else.

"Well, then." Franco turned to Kevin, a broad smile lighting his olive-toned face. "Looks like it's official." He stopped fussing with his injured arm long enough to extend his hand. "Welcome to our little fencing club."

"Thank you." Kevin switched his sword to his left hand and stepped forward to meet Franco. They solemnly shook, and then Kevin glanced around at the four of them. "Does this club of yours have a name?"

Franco and Tieran exchanged amused looks. "Of a sort," Tieran said. "We thought about calling it the Gentlemen's Fencing Club when we first began, but we ran into a few ladies with extraordinary fencing skills, so that was out." He gave a prosaic little shrug.

"We've found it's best to keep things simple." Franco waved an impatient hand at Quill. "Toss me a bandage out of my bag, will you?"

"You need to have a med 'bot look at that," Quill rejoined, but he complied, rummaging through Franco's fencing bag until he found a small medkit. Extracting a bandage, he handed it to Franco, who immediately slapped it over his gash.

Kevin's gaze dropped briefly to the medkit. That was interesting; he hadn't quite expected Franco to be practical enough to carry something like that with him. *But they might if they're using something as dangerous as nanoblades,* a little voice whispered inside him.

Picking up his sheath, he returned his blade to its home and replaced it in his fencing bag. "So..." He spread his hands. "Is that your big secret? You don't really have a name?"

Sparin chuckled coldly. "Hardly. Have a little patience."

"I think I've been fairly patient." Kevin slid his thumbs through his belt loops. "I've put up with weeks' worth of cryptic little comments and teases as to what'll happen if I managed to make the grade. You've taken great pains to pique my interest; well, now, it's time to follow through."

This, too, was a gamble. They might be expecting him to be so gratified to get in that he was overeager to please and almost subservient. There was no way in the galaxy Kevin would act that way; they might as well get used to it.

"He *has* been more patient than most, I'll agree." Quill drained the last of his bourbon and glanced at Franco. "You'll do the honors, I suppose?"

To Kevin's surprise, Franco shook his head. "Tieran will. We are, after all, enjoying his hospitality."

Tieran seemed to stand a little taller at this. "Well, in that case..." He waved a hand in the direction of the doors. "I suggest we retire to the lounge. This calls for a celebration. " He eyed Franco. "After I call the med 'bot, of course."

"Appreciated," Franco said wryly.


Once Tieran summoned a med 'bot from a closet—his family apparently kept one on staff, though Kevin wasn't sure it was because of Tieran's extracurricular fencing activity or just because they thought it was a good idea—and the 'bot expertly patched Franco's arm, they made their way back to the lounge. Kevin still felt sweaty, but the penthouse was cool enough that he dried quickly along the way.

Franco took a massive black leather armchair along the back wall, while Sparin, and Quill arranged themselves in chairs on either side, leaving the armchair next to Franco empty for Tieran.

Kevin sat down in a corner of a matching black leather couch, dropping his fencing bag to the rich, white carpet by his feet. He accepted a glass of whiskey from Tieran, who spent a moment playing bartender, but other than an initial sip while his host was watching, didn't drink any more.

Tieran settled himself in his chair and took a contemplative sip of his drink before he tapped the rim of his glass with a manicured fingernail, as though considering how far back the story should begin. "We started the Fencing Club a couple of years ago," he said at last. "We wanted more of a challenge than we were finding at our local fencing clubs."

He flashed a smile. "Finding recruits was easy. There are quite a few of us in the upper social circles who've been given rather extensive training and just don't have enough opportunity to employ it. Our duels are much as you experienced tonight—we don't use fencing gear."

"That makes the duels more dangerous," Kevin pointed out.

Beside Tieran, Quill smiled sharply. "But so much more fun." He leaned forward in his seat. "Admit it, Strong, wasn't it thrilling to face Franco without a safety net? Your skill and speed pitted against his skill and speed?"

"Oh, I agree it's definitely more exciting." Kevin could see the appeal. He'd felt that thrill before, when he and Lon had fenced without safety gear before. It was a heady feeling; it was easy to feel invincible.

*At least until somebody gets hurt.* He'd found the glamour faded pretty quickly after that.

"Also," Franco waved his uninjured hand, "it gives us the occasional opportunity to make a few bets. If we feel like it."

*Of course.* Kevin knew there had to some kind of gambling going on—high-risk duels between people with more money than sense and nobody tried to make a profit?

"That too," Tieran agreed. "We meet regularly, as schedules allow, at each other's homes and…other places."

The slight hesitation before those words told Kevin those 'other places' probably weren't in the ritzy part of Sonela.

"But…after a while, all of it became quite blasé. There wasn't anything new and exciting about it anymore."

Kevin arched a dark eyebrow. "Are you telling me your club members are so good that you all got bored of dueling each other?"

"Why not?" Sparin challenged. "Several of them were in the Tri-Global Tournament, in fact."

*That* caught Kevin off-guard. He shot a startled look at Sparin. "Seriously?"

The other man nodded, his lip curling in a faint sneer.

Tieran frowned at Sparin before continuing, "Eventually, we realized we needed to somehow step up our game. And then one of our members came up with the solution." He reached down into the shadows beside his armchair and withdrew a long, narrow, ornate wooden box. Presumably, it had been waiting there for precisely this moment.

Kevin's breath caught in his throat. *Nanoblades. It has to be.*

Tieran held the long box balanced on both outstretched palms. "This would be the reason we've become even more selective in inducting candidates to our club."

"May I?" Kevin stood and crossed the floor to Tieran, reaching out his own hands for the box. His heart had begun to pound. *I'm right. I know I'm right.*

Tieran allowed him to take the box back to his seat, and Kevin set it on his lap. Undoing a fancy gold clasp, he opened the lid to reveal a beautiful, gleaming sword nestled in a bed of crimson velvet. Triumph flooded him, but he managed to tamp it down. Glancing up at Tieran, he feigned ignorance. "I'm confused. It's a sword."

The other man shook his head. "Not just any sword." He jerked his chin toward the box. "That sword is something called a nanoblade. It is so sharp that it can cut through just about anything."

Quill grinned, holding up his glass in a salute. "And believe me, we've tested it out."

Kevin wanted badly to say he knew, he'd *used* one before, but he held the words back. Unless he wanted to tell them he was a Guardian, he couldn't let on he knew what they were. Instead, he lifted the sword out of the box. "This I have to see."

Franco nodded to Tieran, who produced a length of metal pipe from the same shadows that had hidden the nanoblade. Rising to his feet, he brandished it like a sword, his grip tight but his posture relaxed.

Kevin had to hand it to Tieran; he didn't think he'd be quite that calm in the face of someone who—as far as any of these four knew—had never used a nanoblade before. A second later, he found out why.

"Hand it over, Strong, if you please." Franco flapped his fingers at Kevin. "We'll demonstrate."

Kevin raised an eyebrow, even as he reluctantly complied. "What, you don't trust me not to cut his arm off?"

All four men chuckled. "Not quite." Franco smiled that sharp smile of his again. "But we'll get to that."

Rising to his own feet, Franco whirled the nanoblade in a fancy arc before swinging it through the air. None of them heard the sound of the blade cutting through the pipe; they only watched as the top half of Tieran's makeshift weapon tipped over and clattered to the carpeted floor with a thud.

Kevin exhaled slowly. No matter how many times he witnessed such an event, it still left him amazed at how far technology had come. "Impressive," he said at last, realizing he was supposed to speak now. "Where did you get it?"

Tieran and Franco exchanged glances and Tieran said, "One of our members has certain…contacts that've come in handy."

"Technically," Franco drawled, handing the nanoblade back to Kevin before he dropped back into his seat again, "these beauties aren't on the market yet. At least not for civilian or military purposes." His face darkened. "Apparently, Guardians—I'm sure you've heard of them, some sort of secret defense group—are allowed to carry them, but the manufacturers won't sell them to anyone else."

"So if you get caught with one of these," Kevin began, but Sparin interrupted him.

"We won't," he said curtly. "And so far, we haven't."

Kevin carefully replaced the nanoblade in the protective velvet inside its box and touched a finger to the flat of the blade. "And you duel with these?"

"We duel with them," Franco said proudly.

"Has anybody ever lost a limb?" The question popped out before Kevin could stop himself. He glanced up in time to see Tieran and Quill exchange darting looks.

"There have been a few injuries," Franco said smoothly, "but nothing we couldn't handle."

Kevin nodded shrewdly; he knew exactly what that meant. With enough money, they could keep even a nanoblade injury from warranting further investigation. Slowly, he closed the lid and passed the box back over to Tieran. "Do all of your members have one?"

He was a little disconcerted when the four men glanced at each other and chuckled under their breath.

"Hardly." Sparin waved a hand. "For one thing, they're expensive. For another…" He shrugged. "A member has to be thoroughly vetted before we'll risk procuring one for them."

"Thoroughly vetted?" Kevin snorted, leaning back in his chair. "I take it all this," he waved a hand to indicate the penthouse at large, "was just window dressing, then?"

"Oh, no." Franco shook his head. "It definitely served a purpose."

"I see." Kevin raised a challenging eyebrow. "So let me get this straight. I'm in the club, so to speak, but not really."

"You won't get a nanoblade anytime soon, if that's what you're asking," Sparin said coolly. "We have several for communal purposes."

Franco shot Sparin a hard look. "What my friend here *meant* to say is that having a nanoblade of your own is a mark of distinction. It means you've been with us for a while, and won a number of duels."

*And that you can be trusted not to rat them out to the police or anyone else,* Kevin thought, but he kept it to himself. "I see."

Tieran smiled. "I'm sure you'll get one soon enough. You've made it through our selection process; your chances from here on out are excellent."

"That's good to know." Kevin paused before asking his next question. "Has anyone in the Fencing Club ever been caught with a nanoblade?" He didn't miss the way his four new comrades exchanged glances out of the corners of their eyes.

"Not as such," Sparin said at last. He tipped the rest of his drink down his throat, before closing his eyes and shaking his head as he swallowed. "We had a close call a couple of months ago, but nothing we couldn't handle."

He did not, apparently, intend to elaborate any further, but Franco, catching Kevin's confused look, clarified, "Our friend got caught with a substantial amount of drugs in his possession." He gave that sharp smile again. "It never occurred to the police that his fencing gear could be anything out of the ordinary."

"Lucky for him," Kevin commented.

"Indeed." Tieran shook his head. "Stupid on his part."

"His family took care of it, of course," Franco waved his hand, "and since then we've made it quite clear that we will not tolerate our members carrying both drugs and nanoblades." He smiled again; it didn't reach his eyes. "It's one or the other."

"Sensible." Kevin kept his voice light, but inside he felt a little sick. *This is reality,* he reminded himself. *You know this kind of stuff goes on in Grandfather's social circles.* He just couldn't say he wanted to be this closely connected with it.

*You wanted to find out what was going on,* a voice inside his head that sounded suspiciously like Michael reminded him. *You* had *to know.*

"So…" Kevin set his relatively untouched glass aside on a beautiful end table made of dark wood carved with intricate detail. "What now?"

"You go home." Franco motioned for Tieran to top his glass off. "We'll let you know when the next event takes place."

Kevin nodded. "What happens if I can't make it? I do have a business to run, you know."

It was Sparin who answered, shrugging carelessly. "Then you can't make it. Your loss. Hardly the end of the galaxy."

"Good to know." Kevin looked around the lounge, before rising to his feet and collecting his fencing bag from the rich carpet by his feet. "Well, then, gentlemen, I'm afraid I must be going. Early morning tomorrow."

"One thing before you leave…" Franco held up a finger. "You don't speak of our little club to anyone. It's nobody's business but ours."

Kevin shot him an easy smile. "I thought that went without saying."

Tieran half-rose from his seat, as though to walk him to the door, but Kevin held up a hand. "I can show myself out." He offered the other man a short bow. "Thank you."

As he strode through the penthouse back to the front door, Kevin let out a long, shaky breath. He'd made it—and he'd been *right* about the nanoblades—but he had the sudden sinking feeling that this Fencing Club deal might prove to be more trouble than it was worth.

It wasn't until he had excited Amethyst Towers into Sonela's muggy evening air that he felt like he could breathe. His initial giddiness was fading, to be replaced with trepidation. *Grandfather won't be happy about this.* Neither would Derek and Michael. Intrigued, yes, but not comfortable with the idea.

Kevin snorted softly to himself. *Guess it's a good thing I'm not telling them everything.* He flagged a hovertaxi, hauling his fencing bag higher onto his shoulder. *The only downside is that I'm not supposed to tell Lilia.*

He snorted again. *Not like they'd actually know I told her, but still…*

His sister knew everything else; she was almost as curious as he was at this point to find out what was really going on. And, if they were honest, Franco was unlikely to recruit her. Her fencing skills had improved greatly since their return to Sta'Gloa, but she wasn't quite in the Fencing Club's league.

*Especially not if they're dueling with nanoblades and no nano-armor.* His mouth settled into a grim line. She didn't need to be anywhere *near* that. He wasn't even sure *he* wanted to be part of this, now that he knew the truth, but…

He had the distinct feeling this Fencing Club fell into the category of things easier to get into than out of…and there had to be a reason this particular door had opened for him.

Lilia sent him a channel request just then and his gut clenched in sudden realization. The time the Mastermind had set in his ultimatum had come and gone. His heart jumped into his throat. [What's wrong?]

Across Sonela, Lilia stood frozen in the middle of the penthouse living room, holding another datachip reader in her hands. An image of the Mastermind's masked face hovered above it. She had been talking to Alexis about the trade agreement, the two of them speculating as to what the future would hold for the Coalition.

[We just got another message from the Mastermind.]

[What *kind* of message?] Kevin's Nancom voice sounded strained and borderline panicked.

A chill skipped down Lilia's spine. [He just said, "You were warned."]

[That's it?]

[That's it. Nothing else.]

Kevin was silent a moment. [Well, that can't be good.]

[My thoughts exactly.] Lilia forced herself to breathe. [How'd your duel—]

[I won,] Kevin said brusquely. [I'll be home soon—tell you the story then.]

[Okay.] Lilia stumbled over to the couch and sank down onto it, still holding the datachip reader. Tendrils of dread and fear crept through her; she swallowed and shut her eyes. *Oh, God, please help us. What do we do now?*

The Mastermind's grim, distorted voice still echoed in her head. *You were warned.*

# Chapter 68

IT was just after dinner and Admiral Chesnee had retired to his quarters to take care of some of his never-ending paperwork. His datapad carried a file full of reports that needed to be read, and he had other sundry tasks to accomplish. He was knee-deep in an operations report from General Deam detailing the latest happenings in G.U.-held territory on Glo'Stea when a silver comm light began blinking in one corner of his desk

Chesnee suppressed a sigh. *What now?* Dropping his datapad onto the surface of his desk, he reached for his steaming coffee cup with one hand and tapped a button on the comm panel with the other. "Yes?"

"Admiral, you have an incoming transmission from Veridia."

*Veridia?* Chesnee frowned. Why was someone calling him from his homeworld? "Oh, really?"

"Yes, sir." Armal sounded just the slightest bit hesitant. "It's your wife, sir."

*My wife…* Chesnee inhaled slowly, his coffee cup frozen halfway to his lips. "I see."

He sat motionless for a handful of seconds, a hundred different thoughts and emotions bombarding him. How long had it been since they'd spoken via anything other than perfunctory vmails? Three months? Five? She'd told him she was moving back to Veridia, but that was it.

His brow creased with a frown. *Why is she contacting me now?* "Admiral?"

Chesnee shook off those thoughts. "I'll take it. Thank you."

A silver light began blinking in the comm panel again. Chesnee considered it for a beat, his mind sifting through all the possible reasons Sylvia could have for breaking the stiff, frozen silence between them.

His lips twitched. *Knowing her, it will be something entirely different.* Schooling his features into impassivity and hoping his fatigue didn't show on his face, Chesnee tapped the panel.

His wife's holographic head and shoulders bloomed into existence on the other side of his desk and Chesnee's breath caught in his throat. Whatever her other faults and failings, there was no denying Sylvia Chesnee was the sort of woman who aged like good wine.

Only a few lines graced the corners of her dark eyes, and her glossy black curls were pinned up in an elaborate twist. She wore a gold blouse he had always thought set off her sun-kissed brown skin to perfection; noting this, a small corner of his mind put up his guard. They hadn't seen each other in months and she was wearing something she knew he liked?

They looked at each other, and then Chesnee inclined his head. "Sylvia."

"Giles." Her lips upturned in a small smile, and he was surprised to see that the expression actually reached her eyes. "How are you?"

Chesnee shrugged. "Busy."

"I've heard that." Her eyes roamed over his head and shoulders—all she could see on her end of the holo-call—and that small smile graced her face again. "You look well. A little tired, perhaps, but commanding the Blockade Division seems to agree with you."

He kept his face neutral. "What do you want, Sylvia?"

"I wanted to say congratulations on helping the G.U. move towards peace with the Coalition, Giles."

"You're a little late for that—the cease-fire happened over six weeks ago."

She flinched at his curt tone, but kept going. "You've accomplished a great deal since you left."

"Not that you had any faith in me." Despite his best efforts, bitterness tinged his voice.

"And we're back to this." Sylvia threw her holographic hands into the air. "What was I supposed to think, Giles? They assigned you a career graveyard!"

She was right—he'd thought the same thing at the time—but the fact that even his wife had believed he was done for still rankled. He gritted his teeth, but she dropped her hands and spoke before he could get a word out.

"Believe it or not, I didn't call you to argue."

"Oh, really?" He raised an eyebrow at her, leaning back in his seat to give himself some semblance of being in control of the situation.

"No." Sylvia bit her full bottom lip. "I called because I—because I miss you."

Chesnee actually laughed at that. "And it's taken you all these months to realize it?"

"No!" She tensed, as though she was gripping the arms of a chair he couldn't see. Her voice softened. "Believe it or not, Giles, I really have missed you. It just—took me a while to get up the courage to call."

Her words fell like soft rain on parched earth, but Chesnee refused to let it show. He indicated with one hand, a sardonic glint in his eyes. "Clearly."

Dark eyes flashed at him, a response he used to enjoy provoking. "Well, it's not like you call either! And when you left on your reassignment, you called me an ungrateful social climber and strongly insinuated it wouldn't be long before I climbed into someone else's bed!"

Chesnee winced. He'd forgotten the exact particulars of his parting words. He recalled only that they had been ugly, the sting of her lack of faith burning in his soul. "And did you?"

The question escaped him before he could stop it; he knew immediately he had made a giant tactical error. Had this been a military maneuver, he'd have lost.

Badly.

He caught a flash of deep hurt before anger twisted Sylvia's beautiful features. She tossed her head. "Well, I can see you don't miss me at all. I don't know why I bothered."

Her lips twisted into something that was probably supposed to be a smile. "No wonder you forgot my birthday. You have much more important matters to worry about. Well, I won't take up any more of your precious time, *Admiral.*"

She ended the transmission before Chesnee could speak—the virtual equivalent to storming out of the room in high dudgeon.

He was left staring at the space where her face had been. "That," he said to his empty office, "could have gone better."

He dragged a hand down his face and reached for his coffee, regret already seeping in along the edges of his mind. He hadn't intended to antagonize her. Again.

His coffee tasted like ashes; he set it aside, glancing at the calendar floating to one side of his desk. It hadn't fully sunk in yet, in the midst of dealing with Kedis and everything else, but he had been commanding the Blockade Division for almost a year now. How was it possible that time had flown by that quickly?

A sudden—and profound—wave of sadness engulfed him. How was it possible he had gone nearly a year without being in the same room as his wife? How had this…chasm…opened up between them?

Sinking back in his chair, Chesnee filtered back through the events of the past year. *We parted in anger.* His lips pressed into a grim line. They had fought before he left and he had just assumed Sylvia would get over it—her temper tended to flare up and then fizzle out. He was a patient man; he could wait a few weeks for her to come around.

But after the first three months, all of his plans and patience had finally paid off. He'd successfully breached Lanx's shield, setting in motion a chain of events the likes of which even he couldn't have fully planned for. He'd changed the course of history as far as the Blockade Division was concerned, and now the G.U. and the Coalition were considering a trade agreement.

*But in the process, I forgot Sylvia's birthday.*

Chesnee dragged his hand down his face again. It would have been right after he captured Uva and Quinton. *No wonder she's still angry. After what I said to her, then I neglect to remember her birthday?*

In some respects, it was a wonder they'd had any communication at all.

A thought occurred to him; he sighed. *She never got around to telling me exactly what she wanted.*

His hand hovered over his comm panel, and then he shook his head. If it was important, she'd call back. That was their usual pattern after an argument. Sylvia regularly stormed off in a huff, but she always came back once she'd calmed down.

*Granted*, he thought wryly, *it's never taken us this long to work through an argument before.*

Maybe it would be better if he called her now. Before he could make up his mind, his comm panel lit with an incoming transmission. His pulse quickened. *That was fast.*

Sylvia, back for round two.

He tapped a button. "Yes?"

It was Armal. "Admiral, Ambassador Kedis would like to speak to you."

A jolt of electricity flooded Chesnee, adrenaline overriding his fatigue more effectively than a cup of coffee could ever hope to achieve. He straightened instinctively in his chair. This was the call he'd been waiting for. "Patch him through."

"Good evening, Admiral," Kedis said with a bow of his head, as soon as his holographic form coalesced on the other side of Chesnee's desk. "I come bearing news."

"I've been waiting for your call."

"Yes, well, it took the Triumvirate a few days to chew everything over." Kedis allowed his face to split in a wide, satisfied grin. "I'm happy to report, however, that they voted in favor of our trade agreement today."

Though he had known it was a possibility, Chesnee still felt astonished. He sat back in his chair, shaking his head in amazement. "Congratulations, Ambassador. I can't believe they actually agreed to it." He held up a hand. "They would be fools to refuse, I know, but still…"

A small voice in the back of his mind remarked that perhaps some of his astonishment stemmed from the fact that *Kedis* was delighted about this—a trade agreement was so much less than the G.U. had been fighting for all these years.

"It is a banner day," Kedis agreed, still grinning. "You're the first person I've informed, Admiral. I thought you should have the honor, after all of your service to the G.U. in this area."

A small spark of surprise flared to life inside Chesnee's chest, but he only dipped his head in acknowledgment.

"My next order of business is to inform the Senate." Kedis rubbed his hands together gleefully. "I must confess I'm quite looking forward to that call."

"We will patch you through to Taryn."

"Excellent. Also, Admiral, this new development means that a few more civilians will be arriving in-system as soon as I can arrange it. No doubt the Senate will send a few people of their own, and I require a few more of my staff members and several others. They'll need to stay aboard the *Winds of Change* with you until I can arrange transport for them down to Sta'Gloa."

That was to be expected. "We will accommodate them."

"Excellent," Kedis said again, a peculiar smile hovering around the corners of his mouth—the kind of smile that said he knew something Chesnee didn't and was quite pleased about it.

Something about that smile set Chesnee's teeth on edge, but he didn't let himself dwell on it. Kedis's battlefield was the realm of words, tones, and body language. In situations like these, sometimes it was best not to even engage.

He glanced to the side, noting the time. "If that's all, Ambassador, I—"

"Actually, Admiral, I have one more request. I would like you to move the *Winds of Change* to orbit outside of Sta'Gloa."

*Orbit Sta'Gloa?* Chesnee eyed the younger man sharply, raising an eyebrow. "Won't the Triumvirate see that as an act of aggression?"

"Leave the Triumvirate to me." Kedis waved an airy hand. "Keep a friendly distance. You'll be making an appearance planetside soon enough. It makes sense that you would move your flagship." It was his turn to arch an eyebrow. "You *do* realize your presence will be required at the signing of the trade agreement?"

"The thought has crossed my mind," Chesnee answered coolly. He considered Kedis's request for only a moment before shrugging. "As you wish, Ambassador. I could stand a new view from my office anyway."

"That's the spirit." Kedis smiled broadly. "I'll be in touch, Admiral."

The Ambassador ended the call, leaving Chesnee struggling to compartmentalize his thoughts enough to return to work. He exhaled slowly. *Two monumental occasions in one day.*

Sylvia and the Coalition.

And now Kedis wanted him to move the *Change*.

*First order of business in the morning,* Chesnee decided abruptly. They'd do it properly. No need to show up unexpectedly in the middle of the night. His battleship would arrive in state, in full view of the Sta'Gloans.

He had no doubts, however, that Kedis would have his hands full smoothing things over with the Triumvirate.

# Chapter 69

AT precisely 8 AM Sonela time, Admiral Chesnee's flagship, the *Winds of Change* dropped out of hyperspace into real space outside of Sta'Gloa.

Exactly six minutes later, Sta'Gloan Director of Security Malik Thane sent out a special alert to every member of the Triumvirate. Aiden read the short missive while sitting at the penthouse's dining room table drinking his last cup of mint tea and honey before he, Michael, and Derek departed for Triumvirate Tower for the day. Despite the gravity of the situation, he almost had to smile.

*This has Kedis written all over it.*

Only the young Tarynian ambassador would have the guts to move the Blockade Division commander's flagship like this after just having secured an unprecedented trade agreement.

Aiden drained the last of his tea, relishing the combination of cool mint and soothing honey as it slid down his throat. He settled his jade green china teacup back on its saucer with the faintest of clinks and pushed his chair back from the table. If nothing else, today's session would be far from boring.

He could imagine the consternation the Triumvirate would be facing only too well.

A moment later, Derek skidded through the doorway separating the dining room from the living room. He held his comlink in one hand, and he looked a little frazzled. "Grandfather, have you seen this? Admiral Chesnee's flagship just dropped into real space outside our shield."

"I heard." Aiden nodded to Zoë as the 'bot trundled forward to collect his dishes. "Malik Thane just informed the Triumvirate."

Michael appeared behind Derek, his violet eyes full of concern. "What is he doing?"

Aiden slid his own comlink into his pocket. "Oh, I doubt very much this was the Admiral's doing. I am sure Ambassador Kedis will tell us all about it later today."

Michael and Derek exchanged dubious looks. "But—"

"—why?"

"Oh, no doubt this is all part of Kedis's master plan." Aiden turned one hand palm up as he rounded the table and approached the doorway. His grandsons both stepped back to let him pass into the living room.

Derek held up his comlink. "You should see the news. They're already in an uproar over this—speculation is running wild and rampant."

"I guarantee there will be protests before lunch." Michael shook his head. "I hope the Ambassador knows what he's doing. It doesn't seem like a smart move to me."

"On the face of it, perhaps not." Aiden checked his pockets to make sure he had everything—comlink, datapad, the glucose tablets he carried everywhere these days—and motioned to the door to indicate he was ready to leave. "I am sure, however, that the media on Lanx is now singing a much happier tune."

Out of the corner of his eye, he saw his eldest two grandsons exchange looks again. Then Michael nodded. "That's a good point. From their perspective, this is the best day since Admiral Chesnee showed up in our system."

Aiden inclined his head. "Precisely."


Protesters were already gathering in the streets around the Four Towers. Aiden watched them flash past his skimmer's window, catching glimpses of frightened and angry faces. He understood why they were upset, truly.

The difference was that he had a slightly better grasp on the bigger picture.

All at once, he felt very old. All seventy-seven of his years seemed to press down on his shoulders with an almost unbearable weight.

This was nothing new. He had seen it all before.

The protesters, the inevitable riots, the breakdown of the public's trust in their government…this had all happened before. It was almost a never-ending cycle in Coalition history—a cycle of which he had grown profoundly sick. Maybe it was a fool's hope to believe that a trade agreement would actually change anything.

*No. You can't allow yourself to think that way.* Aiden shook his head once, putting a firm and abrupt end to that line of thought. *This is not for nothing. We have made the right decision.*

He had to hold firmly to that belief—or else a relentless wave of doubt would pull him under and crush him against the pitiless shores of uncertainty.

*All hope is not lost—and it* does *matter what course we choose.*

Now, more than ever.

Aiden took a deep breath, banishing those thoughts and the heaviness weighing him down. He was not yet too old to fulfill the duties and tasks the Lord had set before him.

*There is a reason I am still alive.*

The Triumvirate still needed his conscience, his mind, and his voice.

The people of Sector 4 still needed him to represent them.

*Let us not become weary in doing good,* a verse from Galatians 6 floated through his mind, *for at the proper time we will reap a harvest if we do not give up.*

Letting his eyes slide shut for a moment, Aiden slowly exhaled. *I am ready, Lord Jesus. Use me however you see fit.*


The too-familiar trek from the secure parking garage into Triumvirate Tower and up to the Hall and Chamber passed by without Aiden remembering any of it. The second he walked through the great double doors into the Chamber, he felt the tension crackling in the air. It raised the hairs on the back of his neck, sending unease creeping along his skin.

He had the strong impression that this moment teetered on the edge of a razorblade, and the slightest imbalance would cause catastrophe.

Golden sunlight slanted through the Chamber's floor-to-ceiling windows, but it seemed strangely muted, unable to pierce the pall hanging over the Triumvirate. His fellow Representatives, too, seemed oddly muted, for all their drawn faces and frenetic exchanges in hushed voices. Malik Thane looked grim and harried.

If he had not been so concerned, Aiden would have almost been amused by the effect a single flagship had on the ruling body of an entire star system.

As he settled into his seat, Aiden exchanged nods with a few of his colleagues, including Director Kane Fenton who occupied the seat beside him. The Chief Ministers had not yet arrived, but everyone else was there—either via transporter or holograph.

Looking around again, Aiden reflected that the morning's one saving grace was the fact that Ambassador Kedis would have to make an appearance. *No one will be able to focus on anything else.*

The man could demur all he wanted—though Aiden doubted it would actually come to that—but he would not be able to wiggle out of explaining himself.

Not when they had just voted on a trade agreement.

Chief Minister Koen swept in and took his seat at north point of the triangular room, and Chief Ministers Vance and Gammick's holographs materialized in their seats next to him.

The second they were settled, Chairman Septien Yu struck his gold bell. The usually pleasant sound seemed to jangle in the air as his voice rang out across the Chamber. "This session of the Triumvirate will now come to order."

Yu glanced at the Chief Ministers. "In light of this morning's event, our first order of business today is an interview with Ambassador Kedis."

A satisfied rumble swept around the semi-circle of chairs and tables; more than one head nodded emphatically.

Chief Minister Koen raised a skeptical eyebrow. "Do you mean to say that the Ambassador is actually here and ready to come before us?"

"That is correct, Chief Minister."

Satisfied murmurs echoed through the massive triangular room; the unease washing over all of them seemed to abate a fraction.

Koen waved a hand. "Then, by all means, Chairman, send him in."

Seconds later, the double doors swung open and Kedis breezed into the Chamber with his usual easy grace, affable expression firmly in place. If he noticed the tension suddenly electrifying the Triumvirate, he betrayed no sign of it.

Taking his place off to one side of Yu's podium, he bowed once to the Chief Ministers and then again to the rest of the Triumvirate. "Good morning."

His magnified voice sounded entirely too cheerful.

Aiden expected a brief, slightly undignified scramble as multiple people vied to be the first to question the Ambassador, but to his surprise, only two people immediately rose to their feet: Representative Helen Urquart and Director Malik Thane. The redheaded Director of Security cast Urquart a sharp glance before silently resuming his seat.

Aiden blinked. *Interesting.* That was an unexpected move on Thane's part.

"The Triumvirate recognizes Representative Urquart." Yu tapped his bell.

Urquart pinned Kedis with a flat look. She wore an icy white pantsuit today that set off the iron-gray of her hair. "I think we would all like to know, Ambassador," she began briskly, "why Admiral Chesnee's flagship is now orbiting Sta'Gloa."

A murmur of agreement followed from the Sta'Gloan section.

"I don't see why it's a problem," Representative Chas said sotto voce from his seat in the Lanxian section. "No one's had a problem with him being parked outside of Lanx for all these months."

Urquart did not even deign to spare him a glance. It was a petty, irrelevant comment, and everyone knew it.

Kedis spread his hands in a conciliatory gesture, offering her a smile. "It is not meant to be threatening, Representative. Given everything that has happened, it makes sense for the Admiral to be close to Sta'Gloa. He will be joining us for the signing of the trade agreement, for one thing, and for another, I expect him to also make several appearances between now and then so that you, esteemed members of the Triumvirate, can meet him."

"I don't imagine the people of Taryn would take kindly to a massive battlecruiser parking itself outside their atmosphere," Urquart retorted tartly.

Kedis's amiable expression did not slip. "It is only temporary. And, as Representative Chas has pointed out," he nodded to the Lanxian man, "the Admiral's flagship has been orbiting Lanx for months now. Moving to Sta'Gloa will help facilitate the remainder of our arrangements for the implementation of the trade agreement, and then Admiral Chesnee and the Blockade Division will be departing the Sta'Gloan system."

For the span of three heartbeats, dead silence filled the Chamber as everyone digested this. Aiden tapped his knee thoughtfully beneath the lip of the table before him. On the one hand, it was gratifying to hear yet another reassurance that the Blockade Division would soon be packing up and leaving.

On the other hand…a massive battlecruiser suddenly parked outside a planetary shield was still a frightening thing.

"That…*is* what you want, is it not?" Kedis looked around at the members of the Triumvirate, his expression a curious blend of feigned confusion and ignorance. "Admiral Chesnee's ultimate departure?"

Waving an irritated hand, Urquart pinched the bridge of her nose as though she had suddenly developed an acute headache. Her stern demeanor cracked, shifting into something that reminded Aiden of an exasperated elderly aunt. "Ambassador, surely it occurred to you that the people of Sta'Gloa might consider this an act of aggression? We are already dealing with riots and other violence, as you are well aware."

Kedis took his cue from her and allowed a hint of bashfulness to seep into his demeanor, like a schoolboy called to task by a stern teacher. "Yes, Representative, it did."

He rocked back on his heels, clasping his hands behind his back. "But I thought the fact that the people of Lanx would consider it an act of peace might offset that."

"Oh, there is great rejoicing on Lanx right now, that is for certain," Zane Chas said loudly. Around him, his fellow Representatives murmured in agreement.

Septien Yu sent the entire Lanxian section a sharp look of reprimand, rapping his bell for order.

Dropping the schoolboy act, Kedis took a step forward and spread his hands. "Ladies and gentlemen of the Triumvirate, please. Consider the facts. We are preparing to sign an unprecedented trade agreement. In addition to Admiral Chesnee's attendance, I will require some of my staff join me here on Sta'Gloa."

He shook his head. "This is the most expedient way to get everyone here in a timely fashion."

*And yet…*Aiden thought, *we still need to calm people's fears and quell any new riots.*

Drawing in a deep breath, he rose to his feet. At the same time, Shane Briscoe stood in the Glo'Stea section. Aiden motioned for Briscoe to go ahead, but the younger man shook his head and resumed his seat.

Representative Urquart sat down as Septien Yu tapped his bell and recognized Aiden.

Aiden cleared his throat. "Ambassador, what our people need right now is assurance that this is not the beginning of a new age of terror. Would you consider speaking to the Coalition and assuring everyone of what you have just assured us?"

Holding Kedis's gaze, Aiden fancied he could almost see through those dark eyes to the Ambassador's brain whipping through various calculations.

Kedis reached a decision within seconds. "It would be my honor, Representative Monroe." He inclined his head toward Aiden before casting a searching glance around the Chamber. "In fact, if you would care to call a press conference, I would be delighted to give a statement right now."

More than one person blinked in shock, but Aiden just allowed himself a tiny smile and sank back down into his seat.

From his seat at the north point of the room, Chief Minister Hugh Koen leaned forward over the table before him. "Ambassador, I think that is an excellent idea." He motioned to the Chamber. "We will hold it here."

Surprise washed over the Triumvirate, but it was quickly followed by nods of approval. The Coalition needed to know that their ruling body was still in control of the situation.

Aiden leaned back in his seat as their morning's session was put on hold to prepare for a press conference. He glanced at Kane Fenton beside him. "I hope this calms things down."

Fenton was still watching Kedis. "It should. We don't need any more violence."

*No*, Aiden thought, *we most certainly do not.*

He had a feeling, however, that even this might not be enough to stem the oncoming tide.

# CHAPTER 70

WITH all of the general craziness that engulfed Sta'Gloa, and Sonela in particular, in the days following the Triumvirate's monumental decision, the *Talia* felt like an oasis in the midst of a chaotic political storm. Lilia sat at the table in the galley, poring over her datapad, a roast beef sandwich on a plate at her elbow. It was peaceful here, seemingly removed from the rest of Sonela and everything else. She could almost pretend they were surrounded by nothing but stars and the black vacuum of space.

Almost.

It had been nearly a week since the Mastermind delivered his ominous warning—six days of jumping at shadows and wondering when he would strike. She and Kevin had shared the warning with their brothers and Michael had increased security, but there was only so much they could do. Lilia hated feeling like they were walking around with a nanoblade dangling above their heads. She was having nightmares again, memories from the past few months combined with new shadowy figures with distorted voices.

Neither of them wanted to discuss it, but the dark smudges under Kevin's eyes told Lilia he was having trouble sleeping too.

One of her comlinks chimed with an incoming call; the distinctive tone informed her it was her work comlink. Lilia's gaze flicked to it, even as her mouth pulled into a dubious frown. It could be someone with a legitimate job…or it could be more of the same thing they'd been dealing with for weeks.

Pushy reporters and gossip columnist wanting interviews.

Angry, hateful, harassing calls from complete strangers.

*Except*…Her frown eased. It was a holo-call. The knot of tension inside her stomach loosened. Most of their harassers didn't have the guts to show their real faces.

Reaching for the comlink, Lilia accepted the call. As the holographic head and shoulders of a middle-aged woman with milky brown skin, almond-shaped eyes, and silver streaks in her long, black hair appeared, she said in Sta'Gloan, "Three Cords Shipping, this is Lilia. How may I help you?"

The woman blinked and then swallowed. The skin around her dark, liquid eyes was puffy, as though she had been crying recently, and an air of grief hung around her. "Hello. I was wondering if you would be able to help me." Her Sta'Gloan was hesitant and heavily accented, as though she hadn't used it in a long time.

Wondering why the woman hadn't just depended on the comm's autotranslator to help her, Lilia switched to Glo'Stean. "We'll do our best. What do you need?"

The woman's face brightened with relief. "Oh." Switching languages herself, she dipped her head in an almost apologetic nod. "You speak Glo'Stean. My Sta'Gloan is…rusty."

A shiver danced down Lilia's spine. Something about the woman's Glo'Stean accent was familiar, but she couldn't quite place it. "That's all right." She gave the woman a gentle smile. "How can we help?"

"My name is Usagi Hito." The woman fixed her eyes on Lilia through the holo-call. "I need transport to Yumiko, Sta'Gloa for myself, my two children, and some of our belongings."

"You're on Glo'Stea?"

"Y-yes."

"Well, your belongings won't be an issue, but we don't normally carry passengers." Lilia furrowed her brow. "Are you sure you wouldn't rather travel on a—"

"They will not take us." Mrs. Hito held up her hands and then set them down again, presumably in her lap, as though she didn't quite know what else to do with them. She wore a wedding ring. "And we cannot get to them."

The crease in Lilia's forehead deepened. "That is…very odd." She leaned forward, studying the older woman. "Where *are* you?"

Mrs. Hito seemed to brace herself. "We are in…Sector 2. Occupied territory." She hesitated, and then reluctantly added, "Challa."

The word crashed into Lilia like an unexpected ocean wave; for an instant, she couldn't breathe. *Challa.* Her heart began to thud; she felt cold all over. *Why did it have to be Challa?*

Realizing Mrs. Hito was waiting for a response, she cleared her throat and tried to sound like she hadn't just had a nasty shock. "Ah. I see."

"Please—" The older woman blinked very fast, as though trying to ward off a sudden onslaught of tears. "My family is from Sta'Gloa. I haven't seen them since before the blockade. I was visiting friends at the time and, well…"

She raised her hands in another half-weary, half-helpless gesture. "I was stranded. Eventually, I made a life for myself and married." She took a deep breath, as though bracing herself. "My—my husband was killed in a bombing two weeks ago."

Empathy flooded Lilia, thawing some of the ice that had encased her insides. "Oh, I'm so sorry."

Mrs. Hito inclined her head in acknowledgment; her lips pressed firmly together in an effort to maintain her composure. After a few seconds, she swallowed again. "He was—he was a G.U. officer." She lifted her chin and met Lilia's eyes, as though daring her to comment.

Somehow, the information didn't surprise Lilia. What *did* surprise her was the unexpected sympathy she felt welling up inside her. She was ashamed to realize that just a few months earlier, she wouldn't have had any sympathy for this newly-made widow.

She blew out a breath. "That's why you haven't been able to hire anyone yet. Your husband and the fact that no one wants to risk flying into G.U. headquarters."

"It's mostly because we're in Challa." Mrs. Hito shrugged and hesitated again before saying quietly, "I have not made much mention of my husband, other than the fact that he is—that he is dead." Her voice cracked on the last word.

Lilia's eyebrows rose, but before she could ask the older woman why she'd decided to share that tidbit with *her*, Mrs. Hito continued.

"I saw you on the news after the Ambassador came, and when I realized that your family runs a shipping company, I thought you might be willing to help me."

The two women stared at each other for a moment. "Well," Lilia said at last, "we've never actually flown into occupied territory before." *Dropped into it via portals, yes, but flown a ship?* She managed a small smile. "I'll have to talk to my brother, but there's a first time for everything. Might as well go big, eh?"

Relief flooded Mrs. Hito's face. "Thank you."

"You're welcome. I'll give you a call back in a few minutes."

"I'll be here."

Lilia started to end the transmission, but paused, struck by a sudden thought. "Not to be intrusive or anything, Mrs. Hito, but you do realize that by coming back to Sta'Gloa you're probably going to face some backlash from people—most of them complete strangers who ought to mind their own business—about having married a Tarynian? And the fact that your children are half-Tarynian?"

She flattened a hand on her chest. "I mean, my father emigrated here from Taryn, a long time before the blockade, and my brothers and I have dealt with that kind of bigoted nonsense our entire lives. I know you're still grieving, and I'm so sorry, but are you and your children prepared for this?"

Mrs. Hito smiled slightly. "It is nothing new. Those whispers circulate in Challa as well. People accepted the G.U. because they had no other choice, but it does not mean they were ever happy about it." Tears pooled in her dark eyes. "I never intended to fall in love with my husband, but I did." Her breath hitched. "He was a good man."

Unbidden, Lilia's mind flashed to Jasper—a vision of him smiling at her, the dark gray of his G.U. uniform reflected in his gray eyes. She bit her lip. The uniform still made her skin crawl, but she could separate it from the man underneath. Not so long ago, she couldn't have imagined how anyone could look at a Tarynian soldier and see someone worth getting to know, but over the past few months the Lord had changed both her attitude and her heart. "I can understand that."

"Thank you."

"Oh." Lilia started and flashed Mrs. Hito a rueful smile. "I almost forgot. When did you want to depart?"

"As soon as possible. I'm not moving back to Sta'Gloa yet—at least I don't think so—but I want my family to meet my children."

"Okay. You'll hear from us shortly."

For a moment after Mrs. Hito ended the transmission, Lilia remained seated at the table, thinking it over. *We've got a cease-fire*, she told herself at last, standing up. *We're getting ready to sign a trade agreement. It shouldn't be that dangerous.*

'Shouldn't be' being the key words. She thought of Mrs. Hito's husband dying because someone in Challa couldn't accept that they were finally reaching peace. *If nothing else, it'll be interesting finding out from her what's really been going on in occupied territory lately.*

She swallowed. *Even if it means going back to Challa.*

Lilia found her brother and Erik in the engine room. Kevin had opened a panel and currently had his head stuck in it while he fiddled with whatever lay inside. "Hey," she said, with more confidence than she felt. "You two up for an adventure?"

Kevin withdrew his head long enough to shoot her a half-curious, half-wary look. "What kind of adventure?"

She filled them in, and he let out an astonished chuckle. "You're kidding. Challa? As in G.U.-headquarters-of-occupied-territory Challa?"

Lilia nodded, not looking at Erik. It didn't matter; she could feel his speculative brown eyes on her. She willed him to keep his mouth shut.

Erik complied—so to speak. Folding his arms across his chest, he opened a Nancom channel to her instead. [You still haven't told Kevin what happened in Challa.]

She shook her head slightly, still not meeting his eyes.

[Why not?]

Lilia resisted the urge to shrug, a hot flush beginning to rise up her neck. [Haven't gotten to it yet.]

[Uh huh. You sure you're up for this?]

She did look at him then, violet clashing with brown as they stared at each other. Erik was the only other person who knew the truth about Challa—and she'd only told him because he'd figured out something had happened to her and called her out on it. The funny thing was that it had been while she was patching him up at the Mansion in Marina and trying to talk him into getting counseling for nearly committing suicide by proxy after Hesperia sent that last 'message'.

[I can do it.]

His gaze sharpened. [If you say so, kid.]

"Well," Kevin said, unaware of their conversation, "We haven't done this yet." He looked at Lilia, a cautious smile curling one corner of his mouth. "Flown a *ship* into occupied territory, I mean."

She snorted a laugh. "No kidding."

"I know this ain't my ship," Erik drawled, "but I'm game." His gaze slid past the twins to the bulkhead, as though seeing through the thick metal to some vista beyond the confines of Sonela Spaceport. "Occupied territory." He held up both hands, framing an invisible holo with his fingers. "The final frontier…"

"At least," Kevin said wryly, "as far as the Sta'Gloan system is concerned."

Lilia tilted a dark eyebrow at him. "Think it's safe enough to try?"

Her brother sucked in a breath and exhaled slowly while he pulled up a holographic map of Glo'Stea on his comlink. "Believe it or not," he said at last, "I'm more concerned about flying *out* of Sector 2 than flying into it."

Erik nodded in agreement, jabbing a finger at Sector 2. "Listenin' to all the chatter comin' out of occupied territory now, it sounds like the Tarynians are on their best behavior."

"Exactly. They're not going to do anything to jeopardize Kedis's trade agreement." Kevin shrugged. "So as long as everybody in the Glo'Stean Resistance behaves, we should be fine. Then it'll just be up to Customs to decide if they're allowed to leave Glo'Stea."

A troubled look flitted across his face, the memory of his last active encounter with the Glo'Stean Resistance coming to mind. He had used his nanoblade to cut open a G.U. submarine that had bypassed the shield protecting free Glo'Stea and one of the Resistance ships had opened fire on the survivors after the G.U. submarine commander surrendered. Kevin had stopped the slaughter, but many of the new prisoners of war had been murdered.

"All right, then. I'll call Mrs. Hito back and tell her we're in." Lilia propped her hands on her hips, her mind already started to work through the logistics of such a trip. "When do we tell her we'll be there and what are we going to charge her?"

Kevin glanced at Erik before looking at her again. "Good question. We've never carried passengers before." He made a face. "I'm sorry she's lost her husband, but I don't think we ought to take a haircut on this. Not if we're flying into *Challa*."

"I don't think she expects us to." Lilia listed her head to one side, considering her brother thoughtfully. "Especially not when she can't get anybody else to take them."

"Okay. How about this? We charge her normal fare for transport between Sta'Gloa and Glo'Stea, and add a small cargo fee. Maybe a couple of hundred more." Kevin shrugged. "You can negotiate down a little if absolutely necessary."

"Okay."

"As for when we leave…" He glanced down at the holograph of Glo'Stea again. "It's too long of a flight from Redesh to Challa to attempt to swing by and pick them up. We'll be late getting Sulamon's cargo back to Sonela." He shrugged prosaically. "Besides, I don't want to risk her cargo in case something goes wrong."

"That's a lot of money to lose," Erik agreed.

"Yeah." Lilia drummed her fingers on her hip. "Particularly when we have no idea what getting in and out of Challa is going to be like."

"Exactly." Kevin made a face. "We could be there for hours."

"Okay. I'll tell Mrs. Hito to expect us sometime Wednesday."

"Remind her about the time difference," Kevin added, indicating Glo'Stea's holographic globe. He performed a quick calculation. "Challa is thirteen hours ahead of Sonela."

That sounded about right. "Got it." Lilia nodded to the open panel behind her brother. "Everything good?"

"Oh, yeah, it's fine." Kevin waved a grease-stained hand. "Just needed to tighten a few things and clean a filter." He paused. "If Mrs. Hito balks at having to wait, tell her we've got a prior client on Redesh who takes precedence."

Sketching an airy salute that belied the nervous flutters in her stomach, Lilia returned to the galley.

Mrs. Hito, she learned a few moments later, was so delighted to hear her family would have passage to Sta'Gloa that the prospect of waiting an extra day barely fazed her. The older woman didn't blink an eye at the price, either. She was too busy being grateful Three Cords Shipping would risk flying into occupied territory to come get them.

When the transmission ended, Lilia set her comlink back down on the table and exhaled shakily. *We're really doing this. We're really flying to Challa.* Her stomach knotted; she flattened a trembling hand over it. *It's not the same,* she reminded herself. *You never saw the spaceport… before. It's not the same at all. Everything will be fine.*

She buried her face in her hands, ignoring the little voice that whispered that they had all lost their minds. *Everything will be fine.*

# Chapter 71

MONA Shield Control let their convoy to Glo'Stea depart at 8:25 AM.

"Finally," Kevin muttered, deftly easing the *Talia* out of their berth and up into the early morning sunshine. The cockpit viewshield darkened protectively to compensate for the brilliant light. The *Talia* fell in with the rest of their convoy, a string of glittering ships against a beautiful blue sky, and they shot up through the atmosphere. Sta'Gloa's shield loomed ahead, sparkling with iridescent hints of blue-green in the sunshine.

A gap swirled open in the expanse of the shield and the convoy punched through it to open space beyond. Once they were clear of Sta'Gloa's gravitational field, they made the jump to hyperspace. Scant minutes later, they dropped back into real space outside of Glo'Stea's night side and waited for Shield Control to let them in. Once through the shield, Kevin dropped their freighter into an airlane that would take them toward Kyman and the edge of formerly occupied territory.

The flight took over ten hours. Kevin set the autopilot, but he and Lilia still spent most of their time in the cockpit, taking turns monitoring things. Erik drifted back and forth between the cockpit, the galley, and the living compartment.

"It's funny," he said at one point, looking over at Lilia as he leaned back in the copilot's seat and locked his hands behind his head. "Takes longer to cross from one side of a world to the other than it does to travel to a different one."

Lilia smiled. "You're right. Doesn't make much sense, does it?" She cast a perfunctory glance at the controls, but everything was humming along just fine. Kevin was taking a nap; he wanted to handle the final leg of their flight himself.

She had just taken a sip of water when Erik said slyly, "You mentioned you're goin' back to Challa to Wright?"

Lilia choked, nearly spraying water all over the console—an effect the former police officer seemed to have been going for. When she could breathe again without coughing, she leveled him with a glare. "What?"

"You heard me." Erik sounded entirely unconcerned.

She had heard him—that was the problem. Pressing her lips into a thin line, she shook her head.

"Why not?"

"All sorts of reasons. It's none of his business, for one."

"Uh huh." Erik was still looking at her, his gaze sharp and thoughtful.

Heat flared in her cheeks. "Well, it isn't."

"If you say so." Erik faced forward, but he continued to watch her out of the corner of his eye.

Lilia could feel the heat rising, though she didn't know why she was getting upset. "What's your point, Holt?"

"My point, *Strong*, is that I think that would've been an interestin' conversation." He shrugged far too innocently to actually be innocent. "That's all."

Lilia stared at him with narrowed eyes. "I *might* tell him about Challa after we get back. Maybe. But I don't want him—"

"—goin' on about you bein' his mystery jumper again," Erik finished, nodding as though he'd heard it all before.

"Exactly." Suspicion flooded her voice. "Seriously, Erik, what are you driving at?"

The blond Guardian was silent for a moment, as though choosing his words carefully. At last, he lifted one shoulder in a shrug. "Other than Wright an' me, nobody else knows what happened to you in Challa, do they?"

Alarmed, Lilia shot a look over her shoulder in the direction of the hatch to make sure Kevin wasn't there. When she turned back around, she found Erik regarding her with a knowing half-smile. Irritation flared inside her, but she gritted her teeth and choked it down. "No."

Erik's smile faded. "Will you be all right?"

"I'll be fine." Lilia waved his concern away. "Honestly, I will." It was her turn to shake her head. "We won't be on the G.U. base."

Erik's expression told her he didn't quite buy it, but he let it slide.

"How about you?" Lilia raised both eyebrows at him questioningly. "How are you doing?"

He grinned, but it didn't quite meet his eyes. "Haven't taken any more knives, have I?"

"That's a good thing."

"Yeah, that's what they say."

Lilia watched as he settled a little deeper into his flight seat and closed his eyes. "Do me a favor," she said at last. "Don't do anything to tick off some Tarynian soldier and get yourself shot, okay?"

This time, Erik's grin was genuine. Without opening his eyes, he said, "Only if you tell Kevin about Challa."

His words were teasing, but they brought Lilia up short just the same. She exhaled shakily, considering that option, and then slowly nodded to herself. "I—I think I can do that."

"What?" Erik's eyes popped open. "Lilia, I was—"

"—kidding?" She gave him a wry smile. "Yeah. I figured. But—" she blew out another shaky breath. "But…I think I can do it. Not now," she amended. "After we get back from Challa." She snorted. "I'm not going to tell him something like that right before we fly in."

"It'd make the whole experience a lot more entertainin'." Erik chuckled at the dry, nonplussed look on her face and closed his eyes again.

Lilia cast another unconscious look over her shoulder, but her brother was still asleep in his cabin. She bit her lip, feeling jittery and nervous—but not sick to her stomach with dread. She nodded to herself. *You can do this.*

It was time.


As the *Talia* neared the invisible line between Sector 1 and Sector 2 that had formerly divided the expanse of deep blue ocean into occupied territory and free territory, Lilia half-expected someone to hail them and demand to know where they were going. She could tell Kevin was thinking the same thing; every so often his eyes would flick from the radar to the silent comm panel. No one bothered them.

It wasn't until they were two hours from Challa that the comm crackled with an incoming transmission from a G.U. cruiser patrolling the ocean below. "Unknown ship," said a brusque voice in accented Glo'Stean, "this is Captain Muerto, of the *Daggerpoint*. Where are you headed and what is your purpose?"

The twins shared a "here goes" look and Kevin leaned forward to toggle a switch on the comm panel. "*Daggerpoint*, this is Captain Strong, of the *Talia*, out of Sta'Gloa. We have been hired to transport a Sta'Gloan citizen and her two children from Challa to Sta'Gloa." He paused, glancing at Lilia again, and added, "The lady's husband was a G.U. officer who was recently killed in a bombing, I believe."

Lilia lifted her shoulders in a tiny shrug. It couldn't hurt to mention that detail.

"I see," Captain Muerto said at last. "Your client's name?"

Erik leaned forward in his flight seat. "I don't really see what business that is of his."

Kevin and Lilia exchanged glances again. "I don't know if we'll be able to get through without it," Kevin said.

Lilia nodded. "We really don't know what their protocol is."

"An' Mrs. Hito didn't mention whether or not she had to report she was leavin'?" Erik asked.

"Nope." Lilia shook her head. "Didn't say a word."

"All right then." Kevin toggled the switch. "Our client is a Mrs. Hito, from Challa."

"One moment. Cut your speed."

"Understood." Kevin settled back in his pilot's seat, but he remained tense and alert. He slowed the *Talia* to a crawl while they waited to hear back from the *Daggerpoint*.

A moment later, the comm panel crackled to life. "Captain Strong, you are cleared to approach Challa. Give Spaceport Control this authorization code when prompted." Captain Muerto transmitted a string of numbers and letters to the freighter.

"I guess she did notify them," Lilia said under her breath.

Kevin just grimaced at the thought. "Thank you, Captain."

The comm panel fell silent again, and all three of them breathed a sigh of relief. "First hurdle down." Kevin rolled his neck from side to side, and sent the *Talia* streaking through the air at her former speed again.

Lilia's stomach began to squirm as they neared Challa and caught the first glimpses of the city's skyline gleaming in the distance. She pressed a hand to it absently, her attention riveted on the tops of tall buildings just visible through the viewshield, but growing closer with every passing second. *Challa. Who would have ever thought I'd come back here?*

She wondered if she would see the Museum or anything else she remembered from their approach to the spaceport, but it must have been on the other side of the city. Nothing tickled her memory. The tension knotting her shoulders began to relax. *I can do this.*

"I'd better call the Hitos." She reached into her pocket for her comlink. "Let them know we'll be landing soon."

"By the grace of God." Kevin blew out a breath. "Provided we don't have any issues."

"It'll be fine." Erik waved a hand. "They aren't goin' to risk anythin'. Not now."

Kevin shot him a sober glance over his shoulder. "Let's hope so."

Everything went smoothly. Thanks to Captain Muerta's authorization code, Challa Spaceport Control gave them no trouble when the freighter approached for a landing. Kevin settled the *Talia* into their assigned berth as directed and he and Erik went to pay the berthing fee.

This was Erik's doing; he refused to let Kevin go alone. "Not in the heart of the Tarynian headquarters on Glo'Stea," he said grimly, shrugging into his brown leather jacket.

"I thought you said they weren't going to try anything?" Kevin asked, half-amused, half-irritated.

"Not when it comes to ships." Erik's grim expression did not change. "People are another matter." He jerked his chin toward Lilia. "You'll be fine right here." He raised a pale blond eyebrow at her. "Right?"

"Right." She held up her comlink. "Besides, I need to tell the Hitos where to find us."

The commercial section of Challa Spaceport itself resembled any other commercial section in any other spaceport Lilia had ever seen…aside from the fact that every once in a while a group of G.U. soldiers in uniform passed by. What they were doing here, Lilia didn't know, but she did notice that while no one seemed to pay them much overt attention, everyone kept an eye on them just the same.

The Hitos were already at the spaceport; it took Mrs. Hito and her children only a few moments to locate the *Talia*. Lilia lowered the freighter's landing ramp for them, wishing Kevin and Erik were back already. There was either a line or else the process of paying the berthing fee had hit some sort of snag.

Mrs. Hito and her two teenagers waited for the ramp to touch down, a pile of luggage at their feet. All three of them were dressed in black. As Lilia strode down the ramp to greet them, she took in the stony expressions of the two teenagers, who both resembled their mother a great deal. There was grief there, as well as anger—though whether it was from the loss of their father or the fact that they were leaving Challa and Glo'Stea, Lilia wasn't sure.

"Mrs. Hito," she called out in Glo'Stean.

The older woman's face brightened. "Miss Strong." She stepped forward to offer Lilia a bow. "I can't tell you how grateful I am that you have arrived." She glanced behind Lilia at the freighter, looking slightly anxious. "Did you have any trouble?"

Lilia shook her head. "Everything went pretty well."

"Good." Mrs. Hito indicated her children. "This is Mai, my oldest, and this is Ruis."

Ruis was taller than his sister, with spiked dark brown hair and the gangly look of a boy growing into a man. Lilia guessed he was probably around fourteen. Mai was petite and slender like her mother, but her black hair was cut as short as Lilia's own. Neither of them looked particularly impressed to be standing here this morning, but Lilia thought she saw a spark of interest in Ruis's dark eyes as he looked up at the *Talia*.

Lilia bowed to them both. "It is a pleasure to meet you. I am very sorry about your father."

Ruis clenched his jaw and looked away, scuffing the toe of one shoe against the concrete floor. Mai's eyes filled with tears, but she lifted her chin, her expression hardening.

*They're still processing.* Lilia understood, she really did. She'd felt the same way after they thought Lon had died. "Please, come aboard." She waved a hand to the landing ramp. "Let me help you with your luggage. My brother and our associate will be back momentarily. They had to pay the berthing fee," she added, when Mrs. Hito's brow creased with sudden worry.

"Oh. Oh, yes, of course. The berthing fee," the older woman murmured, unable to quite hide her anxiety. She fluttered her hands at her children, directing them to pick up their travel bags. They obeyed, albeit reluctantly, and moved ahead of Lilia and their mother to the ramp.

Halfway up the ramp, Mai balked. "Do we *have* to leave?" She glared balefully at her mother. "I don't want to go."

Mrs. Hito's expression hardened; she looked just like her daughter had a moment before. "We have been over this, Mai. We're going to visit your grandparents." She pointed up the ramp. "March. Now."

Mother and daughter stared at each other, and then Mai suddenly capitulated, as though she had realized this was a battle she couldn't win. Her shoulders slumping, she stomped the rest of the way up the ramp.

Ruis slouched his way after his sister, but he couldn't hide his interest in the freighter. Grief-stricken or not, Lilia had a feeling he would have plenty of questions for them later.

Kevin and Erik arrived just as Lilia was starting up the ramp after Mrs. Hito. Lilia introduced them, and then asked, still in Glo'Stean, "What took you so long?"

Erik snorted. "They didn't want to take our money at first." His Glo'Stean was not quite as fluid as the twins', but passable.

"Really?" Lilia looked askance at Kevin. "Because we had a goldcard instead of G.U. credits?" She had wondered how that was going to work.

"Exactly." Her brother waved a hand. "We got it all sorted out though." He offered Mrs. Hito a kind smile as she looked at him over her shoulder. "We'll be on our way shortly."

"Thank you, Captain."

When their client turned around, Kevin waggled his eyebrows at Lilia. [She calls me Captain. I could get used to this.] He tipped his head toward Erik. [You could both start.]

Glancing over her shoulder, Lilia rolled her eyes at him. [You sound like Lon again.]

[Maybe he was on to something.]

[I'll tell him you said so.]

Behind her, Kevin made a face. [Don't you dare. His head's big enough already.]

Lilia just shot him a grin.

The twins took a few minutes to deposit their clients' luggage in the cabin they would be sharing and give them a tour of the freighter before they started preparations to depart. Mrs. Hito was pleased with everything, Ruis looked around with concealed interest, and Mai folded her arms across her chest and made it clear she would in no way, shape, or form enjoy anything to do with this trip.

Lilia left Erik in the main living compartment to give their clients instructions on strapping themselves in and returned to the cockpit to help Kevin. They ran through the pre-flight checklist and then Kevin contacted Challa Spaceport Control. Once they had the all-clear, he engaged the *Talia*'s gravcoils and the freighter rose gracefully off the concrete floor and floated up into the bright morning sky.

Once he had settled the freighter into an airlane headed toward Kyman, Kevin blew out a sigh of relief. "Well, we're half-done, at least." He shook his head. "I'll say this, I wasn't expecting getting in and out of Challa to be that easy. Kedis must have somebody's you-know-what's in a vice."

Lilia nodded, feeling a writhing knot of nerves form in the pit of her stomach as Challa receded behind them. She wet her lips, debating fiercely with herself. *Do I tell him now or wait until we're back in Sonela?* They *did* have a pretty lengthy flight ahead of them before they would reach a safe zone city that would allow them through the shield. *Maybe I'd better just get it over with.*

Heart hammering in her chest, she opened her mouth, but at that moment, Erik breezed through the hatch and dropped into his usual flight seat behind her. "This is goin' to be a *long* flight," he said grimly.

Kevin tossed him a glance over his shoulder. "You don't think the kids will settle in?"

"The younger one maybe, but his sister?" Erik shook his head. "It's pretty chilly back there."

Accepting the temporary reprieve she had been given, Lilia leaned back in her copilot's seat. "Things have probably been pretty rough for them. Losing their dad and all."

"Yeah," Erik said, but he didn't quite sound convinced. He wasn't as understanding of Mrs. Hito marrying a G.U. officer as Lilia had been.

Lilia could feel his eyes on the back of her head, but he said nothing else. She was grateful for this; she didn't need him pushing her to tell Kevin any sooner. Nor did she need an audience. The conversation was going to be hard enough without Kevin finding out immediately that he hadn't been the first person she'd talked to.

Their course would take them past a series of small, uninhabited islands beyond Kyman; they were a half-hour away when the comm crackled to life. Lilia experienced a flash of déjà vu as a voice demanded to know who they were and where they were going. This time, however, they had been hailed by Captain Argos, of the Glo'Stean Resistance cruiser, the *Patriot's Blood*.

"Captain Strong, what were you doing in occupied territory?"

Lilia narrowed her eyes. "*Formerly* occupied territory," she muttered, but Kevin just shook his head at her before he touched the comm panel again. "Captain Argos, we were hired to transport a widow and her two children from Challa to Yumiko, on Sta'Gloa."

A very long, suspicious pause greeted these words. Finally, the comm crackled. "Captain Strong, do you mean to tell me you are taking people from *Challa* through the planetary shield? To *Sta'Gloa*?"

Behind Lilia, Erik rolled his eyes heavenward. "Is he deaf?"

His lips twisting wryly, Kevin shot Erik a quelling look over his shoulder. "That is correct."

Another suspicious pause. "Captain Strong, you are hereby ordered to divert to the Resistance base on Epico Island and land. Prepare for boarding."

# Chapter 72

LILIA'S jaw dropped. She turned sideways in her seat, her expression a picture in disbelief. "Are they *serious?*"

Kevin's face hardened as he toggled the comm. "Under whose authority, Captain Argos?" he asked calmly, though a muscle in his jaw had begun to twitch. "It sounds like you are attempting to illegally detain a Sta'Gloan citizen who has been forced to live on Glo'Stea as a result of the blockade."

"Are her children Sta'Gloan citizens?" the *Patriot's Blood*'s captain shot back. "They could all be spies."

"That's for Customs to sort out, isn't it? They have paperwork. Besides, my crew and I are Sta'Gloan citizens too."

"Captain Strong, you are ordered to divert to Epico Island and—"

"No," Kevin said firmly. "I will continue on course to Antar, where my passengers will talk to the proper authorities at Customs."

Captain Argos began to splutter dangerously.

"May I remind you, Captain, that we have a cease-fire and that the Triumvirate and the G.U. just signed a trade agreement?" Kevin's voice was still calm, but tight.

Beside him, Lilia sat motionless, hardly daring to breathe. *Oh, God,* she thought, *we weren't thinking about this.* She'd expected the hassle to come from the Tarynian side of things; she hadn't expected trouble from the Glo'Stean Resistance.

"Captain Strong, this is your last warning. If you refuse to divert , I will have no choice but to consider you a hostile threat to Glo'Stean safety and open fire upon you."

"Try it, *Captain*," Kevin retorted, his hands tightening on the steering yoke, "and I *guarantee* you will regret it. I have the greatest respect for the Glo'Stean Resistance, but I am not about to let my passengers be subjected to illegal detainment just because they happened to live in Challa. I will deliver them to Customs at Antar Spaceport and we'll proceed from there."

Another long pause met this statement. At last, Captain Argos growled, "I'm sending a message to Antar. If your passengers *don't* go through Customs, you'll never fly again. Do you hear me?"

"Good evening to you too," Kevin said blandly, ending the transmission. He glanced sideways at Lilia. "Keep an eye on the radar. I don't trust him to not send something after us."

"Got it."

None of them relaxed until they had left the cruiser—and its proximity to that Resistance base—far, far behind.


Seven hours later, they reached Antar Spaceport and Kevin settled the *Talia* into their assigned berth. Erik wasted no time in unfastening his safety harness and rising to his feet. "I'll pay the berthin' fee." He gestured with his thumb over his shoulder. "You two take 'em to Customs."

"That's a good idea." Lilia stood as well, stretching her muscles. It had been a while since they had spent this long on the freighter. "Who knows how long that will take?"

Kevin snorted. "It could take all day, depending on what kind of trouble Captain Argos stirred up." He turned off the ship's engine. "On the bright side, we won't be able to leave Antar until tonight, so it's not like we don't have time."

Mrs. Hito and her children had been good passengers. Mai had kept to herself, stiff and unyielding, while Ruis had eventually thawed enough to be curious about the freighter. Their mother had relaxed once they had left Challa behind, but the closer they came to Antar, the more nervous she became.

"We're here," Lilia announced unnecessarily, as she stepped into the living compartment. She nodded to Mrs. Hito. "Kevin and I are going to go ahead and take you all to Customs." She smiled kindly. "Might as well get it all sorted out now."

Her face paling a little further, Mrs. Hito unsnapped her safety harness and stood on wobbly legs. She smoothed down the fabric of her black skirt with trembling hands.

Lilia approached her and touch a hand to her shoulder. "It's going to be okay." She offered the older woman a reassuring smile. "You've got your paperwork. It'll be all right."

They hadn't told Mrs. Hito about Captain Argos's threat—neither Kevin nor Lilia had seen the point in upsetting her further.

"What about our luggage?" Mrs. Hito glanced from Lilia to her children and back.

"You'd better bring it with you. They'll want to inspect it." Lilia started for the hatch that led to the corridor with the cabins. "I'll help you."

"Mai, Ruis." Mrs. Hito motioned for the two to follow Lilia.

A few minutes later, luggage in tow, Lilia and Kevin led the Hitos down the *Talia*'s landing ramp and through the commercial section of the spaceport to the Customs main office. The air was already warm, promising a hot, humid day, and filled with the scent of engine grease, oil, and a hundred other things.

By contrast, the Customs office was almost unnaturally cool. It was a large, sterile-looking room divided into a number of cubicles, with a reception desk to handle walk-ins. There were several people already in line at the reception desk; one by one they were directed to cubicles and waiting Customs officials. An indistinct hum filled the room; over a dozen voices blending together.

At last, it was their turn. Kevin stepped up to the desk first and flashed a smile at the middle-aged woman with mocha skin seated behind it. Her wiry black hair, liberally streaked with gray, was pulled back in a tight ponytail that poufed out behind her. A holographic name plate read: LaToya Renfrew.

Renfrew returned Kevin's smile with a perfunctory one of her own. "Good morning, welcome to Customs." She had a deeper voice than they had expected.

"Good morning. My sister and I—" Kevin gestured toward Lilia, "—run a small shipping business and we just landed with some passengers we picked up in Challa. They—" he nodded to Mrs. Hito and her children, "—need you to inspect their paperwork so they can return to family on Sta'Gloa."

"Did you say Challa?" Renfrew looked past Kevin and Lilia to drill Mrs. Hito with a keen, almost suspicious look. "As in—"

"Galactic Union headquarters, yes." Kevin nodded. "Mrs. Hito can tell you all about it." He paused. "You, ah, might have heard we were coming. A few hours ago, from a Captain Argos, of the *Patriot's Blood*."

Renfrew's gaze swung back to encompass both him and Lilia. "I do recall that, yes. You said you run a shipping business?" She raised both eyebrows. "Are you licensed to carry passengers?"

Lilia froze, feeling the faint stirrings of panic come to life in her chest. She swallowed them down. "I wasn't aware we needed a specific license in order to carry the occasional passenger."

"They were my last resort," Mrs. Hito piped up unexpectedly. "I have spent *days* trying to charter a flight out of Challa, but no one would take us."

"I see." Renfrew looked around again, before motioning Mrs. Hito to hand over her information. Mrs. Hito passed her several identcards and a couple of datachips, and Renfrew spent a moment perusing them. Finally, she looked up and cleared her throat. "I think we'll be able to sort this out." She pointed a stylus at Lilia and Kevin and waved toward a cushioned bench along the wall to her right. "You sit over there. You—" she indicated the Hitos, "—head to Cubicle 5." She pointed off to the left.

Mrs. Hito bowed. "Thank you." Mai and Ruis in tow, she marched off toward the indicated cubicle with the air of someone who was not entirely sure she wasn't marching to an untimely demise.

Lilia and Kevin took seats on the bench and waited. Lilia tried not to wring her hands in her lap. [You don't think we're going to actually end up in some kind of trouble over this, do you?]

Kevin darted a sideways glance at her before giving his head a microscopic shake. [I doubt it. We can't be the first ship to bring people in from occupied territory. And even if we are, Customs is still going to have to figure out how to handle it. The Hitos won't be the last.]

Renfrew dealt with two more people who had come in behind the twins and the Hitos before beckoning the twins back over to her. She scrutinized them for a moment before leaning in a little and dropping her voice. "You're the ones who helped that Tarynian Ambassador."

Lilia and Kevin both blinked. That…was not what they had expected her to say. Kevin cleared his throat. "We are."

"Thought you looked familiar." Renfrew nodded, seeming pleased with herself, and then tipped her head in the direction of Cubicle 5. "Is that why you were willing to risk flying into Challa?"

The twins exchanged glances. "Well," Kevin began, "that wasn't why we—"

"—went. Mrs. Hito called, you see. She was desperate." Lilia turned one hand palm up. "She needed help, so we—"

"—helped." Kevin shrugged. "We don't usually take passengers."

Renfrew shook her head slightly, looking as though she couldn't believe they were still in one piece. "And you didn't have any trouble? They just let you fly in?"

"Pretty much." Kevin allowed himself a wry smile. "I think Ambassador Kedis has the Tarynians on a tight leash. They seem to be on their best behavior. The only trouble we had—"

"—came from Captain Argos," Lilia said, "and we weren't about to hand the Hitos over to him when—"

"—they needed to be here talking to Customs. If they're spies—"

"Which we don't think they are," Lilia put in.

"—we figured Customs would be able to sort everything out." Kevin rested an elbow on the desk. "Have you dealt with many people from occupied territory yet?"

Renfrew's dark eyes slid past them as she considered this, one hand absently rising to pat her poufy ponytail. "A few. Like your Mrs. Hito, they're having trouble getting transport."

"It'll be a business opportunity for somebody," Kevin said sagely. "Besides us, I mean." He smiled at Renfrew, and she smiled back, though her expression was tinged with resignation.

"It's going to mean a lot of paperwork."

The door opened again to admit several well-dressed businessmen, and the twins stepped aside to let Renfrew deal with them. Returning to the bench, they resumed their seats and pulled out their comlinks to pass the time while they waited for the Hitos. Every so often though, one of them would glance over in the direction of Cubicle 5.

After a good half an hour had passed, Erik opened a joint Nancom channel to them. [How's it goin'?]

[No idea,] Kevin said. [We're—]

[—still waiting. The receptionist—]

[—recognized us, though. That was kind of—]

[—surreal,] Lilia and Kevin finished together.

Erik took it in stride. [Well, give me a heads up when you're on your way.]

Over three hours later, Mrs. Hito, Mai, and Ruis finally emerged from the den of cubicles. Mrs. Hito looked a little pale, but a good deal more cheerful than when she had walked into the Customs office. Mai and Ruis were both trying to look cool and unaffected, as though this place hadn't intimidated them, but Lilia could see relief bleeding through both of their expressions as well as they caught sight of her and Kevin. The twins both rose to greet their passengers.

"We will be allowed to leave." Mrs. Hito was clutching several datachips in her hand, which she waved at the twins. "They do not believe we are spies."

"Glad to hear it." Kevin offered her an encouraging smile, before turning to nod to Renfrew. "Have a good day, Ms. Renfrew."

The receptionist peeked around her latest customer to nod back. "Same to you."

As they departed the chilly Customs office and stepped back into the hot, sticky, morning air, Mrs. Hito explained what had happened. "We were interviewed by two Customs agents, and they both asked a great many questions about our life in Challa. They were able to find me in their database, but not Mai and Ruis." She tipped her head toward her children.

"Right." Lilia was nodding. "Because they were born well after the blockade and you were stuck in Challa."

"Yes." Mrs. Hito tightened her grip on the datachips in her hands. "The Customs agents accepted my old Sta'Gloan identcard and my G.U.-issued Glo'Stean identcard, and, based on Mai and Ruis's G.U. identcards, were willing to issue temporary passes for us to depart Glo'Stea. We will need to report to Customs when we land on Sta'Gloa and explain the situation again, but…"

She shrugged, and it seemed a weight rolled off her shoulders. "We are being allowed to leave the planet!"

"That's excellent news," Kevin said enthusiastically. He glanced up at the sky. "We're going to be here a while, though. Shield Control won't let the next Sta'Gloa-bound convoy out until nightfall."

At these words, Mai perked up. "Mom, would we have time to leave the spaceport then and see the city?" She cast a hopeful look at her mother. "Maybe do some shopping?"

"Shopping?" Ruis made a face.

His sister rounded on him. "Yes. *Shopping.*" Mai waved a hand in the air. "We've never been outside of G.U. territory before. You aren't the slightest bit curious to see what it's *like?*"

Ruis gave a matter-of-fact shrug, making a face. "Shopping is shopping."

Mai looked from her mother to Lilia and back. "Please? Can we, Mom? *Please?*"

"I—I don't know," Mrs. Hito hedged. "It depends, Mai."

"On what?" she demanded. "If you're going to drag us off-world, we might as well get to see things along the way, right?"

Glancing from the Hitos to her brother, Lilia was about to suggest that she could take the ladies out and around Antar if Ruis wanted to stay with Kevin when the back of her neck began to prickle. Someone was watching them intently. She almost missed a step, but kept going.

[Don't look now,] Kevin said abruptly via Nancom, [but I think someone's—]

[—following us?] Lilia restrained an exasperated sigh. [Yeah, I got that feeling too.]

They strode on through the line of open-air berths in this part of the spaceport's commercial section, back to the waiting *Talia.* A moment later, under the guise of stepping away from the group long enough to seemingly admire a sleek, new *Honeybee*-class freighter they were about to pass, Kevin said, [There are three of them. Keeping a good distance away, but they're definitely tailing us.]

[Us, or the Hitos, or both?]

[No idea. Don't think it's a good idea for any of us to leave the ship once we're aboard. Not now, anyway.]

[I agree.] Lilia caught his eye as he rejoined them, cutting her eyes significantly in their passengers' direction. [Do we—]

[—tell them?] Kevin gave a tiny shake of his head. [Not outright. No need to scare them before we're sure of anything.]

Lilia cleared her throat, breaking into Mai and Mrs. Hito's ongoing dialogue. "Under ordinary circumstances, I think it would be a great idea to go explore Antar while we're waiting here, but considering we just brought you from Challa—"

"—it's probably better that you stay with us for right now," Kevin finished smoothly. "We don't want anything getting in the way of your family making it off-world tonight." He shot Mai an apologetic smile. "Trust me, there will be plenty to see on Sta'Gloa when you get there." He circled a hand in the air. "And much better shops. Due to everything that's happened, Glo'Stea hasn't had as much access to stuff as Sta'Gloa or Lanx."

Mai's face crumpled with disappointment, which she hastily tried to hide. "Whatever," she muttered, tossing her head as though she couldn't care less.

The back of Lilia's neck continued to prickle; she was glad they were nearly to their berth. Up ahead, she could see the *Talia*'s gray lines.

Kevin subtly picked up the pace, and the Hitos matched it. [They're still following us, Lil.]

[I can feel it.]

As soon as they were close enough, Kevin hit a button on a tiny remote he pulled from his ISF by his left wrist and the freighter's landing ramp lowered to meet them. Once all five of them were aboard, he wasted no time raising it, and he and Lilia both breathed silent sighs of relief.

Lilia discreetly peeked out through a viewport and saw three men converge some distance away. They appeared to be deep in conversation; every so often one of them cast a glance in the *Talia*'s direction. She glanced down the corridor to make sure the Hitos had vanished into the living compartment, and looked at her brother, who stood beside her. "Think they're friends of Captain Argos's?"

"Maybe." Kevin crossed his arms over his chest, his expression grim. "I don't know why else somebody would be tailing us today."

"Me neither." Lilia chewed on the inside of her lip before shrugging. "I'm going to go figure out lunch. You—"

"—fill Erik in." Kevin jerked his chin in a tight nod, but he remained standing in the corridor, staring out the viewport.


The faces changed every few hours, but someone remained posted outside the *Talia* the remainder of the day. Lilia, Kevin, and Erik took turns checking both the spaceport outside and their scanners periodically, and their sense of foreboding continued to deepen. The three of them concluded the men were either a rogue faction of the Glo'Stean Resistance—or else they were Freedom's Children. If that was the case, they were either here for the twins, or they were waiting for an opportunity to deal with the Hitos because they considered them traitors.

None of those scenarios were good.

When evening finally stole over Antar, casting the city in twilight and shadows, the tension in the *Talia* began to mount. Mrs. Hito and her children were nervous, anticipating actually leaving Glo'Stea behind, but were clueless to the real danger.

As Kevin and Lilia ran through the pre-flight checklist and prepared the *Talia* for takeoff, Erik said tightly, "You don't think they'd actually try somethin' to keep us from gettin' out of here, do you?"

"It won't be a bomb." Kevin's fingers danced over the console, flipping switches and pressing buttons. "We haven't seen anyone bring anything close enough to us for that."

"You don't know that." Erik's voice was dark and grim, sending a shudder down Lilia's spine. She glanced over her shoulder at him as he continued, "If they don't care how much collateral damage they cause, it could be anywhere." He waved an arm to encompass the spaceport.

"Good grief." Kevin shook his head. "Surely we're not worth that kind of trouble."

Erik just snorted. "With these kind of crazies?"

Lilia swallowed; the cockpit suddenly felt colder.

Antar Shield Control contacted them a few minutes later, giving them coordinates and instructions for joining their convoy. When the all-clear came, Kevin navigated the freighter up out of their berth and into Antar's muggy evening air. He fell in with the rest of their convoy, forming a line of dark masses soaring up through the night sky, the ships made visible only by their running lights.

The convoy punched through wisps of atmosphere as they neared the shield, where Shield Control was opening a gap for them. Lilia kept a wary eye on both the *Talia*'s scanner and the radar, but when everything remained normal, she started to relax. *We're just another convoy in a long list of convoys that has exited the shield this week.*

The last ship in the convoy—a small *Ladybug*-class yacht—cleared the gap and Shield Control immediately closed it, rendering the faintly iridescent planetary shield as smooth and impenetrable as usual. The *Talia* and the other ships proceeded to clear Glo'Stea's gravitational field and build up enough velocity in order to make their microjumps to hyperspace.

The convoy's lead ships—a *Bumblebee*-class freighter, a couple of *Cicada*-class freighters, and a large *Grasshopper*-class yacht—began to disappear one by one.

"Almost there." Kevin shot a sideways glance at his sister. "Ready to jump to hyperspace on my mark. One, two—"

At that moment, an assorted bevy of corvettes, frigates, and the odd freighter dropped out of hyperspace in front of them and opened fire on their convoy.

# CHAPTER 73

"WHAT the—" Kevin immediately yanked on the steering yoke, banking the *Talia* hard to the port side and away from the hail of laserfire. Unfortunately, this put him on a collision course with a large *Cricket*-class freighter from their own convoy; he promptly rolled the *Talia* to the starboard and squeaked by the other ship with meters to spare.

Lilia's heart jumped into her throat as the ships and streaks of laserfire visible through the viewshield spun round in circles. Thanks to the *Talia*'s gravity field, Lilia's stomach couldn't feel the move, but her mind protested.

Behind her, Erik swore loudly.

Regaining a measure of control, Lilia hit the ship's intercom. "Sorry, guys, we've encountered some interference." She winced as a lean *Fireant*-class frigate strafed their freighter, laserfire splattering against the shield protecting the *Talia*'s nose and starboard side. "Stay strapped in and hang tight."

"Something tells me these aren't Tarynians," Kevin said through gritted teeth, as he struggled to clear the melee and get far enough away to make the microjump to hyperspace.

"You mean besides the fact that none of them are *registering* as G.U.?" Lilia scrambled for the comm panel. "Antar Shield Control, this is the *Talia*. We are under attack from unknown forces! Repeat, we are under attack from unknown forces!"

Only static greeted these words.

Erik leaned forward in his seat. "Either they're jammin' us, or there's too much comm traffic an' we can't get through."

That went without saying—and Lilia didn't have time to say it anyway. A starburst of flame blossomed to their starboard. Her eyes dropped to the scanner before darting back to the viewshield in horror. "That was one of the yachts from our convoy!"

"We've got to get out of here." Kevin juked starboard again, sending the *Talia* through a series of evasive maneuvers the freighter had probably never been through before. "We just have to get clear long enough to—"

A high-pitched alarm began to wail.

"What's that?" Erik demanded, trying to peer around Lilia to see the console. "Never heard th—"

Lilia cut him off. "Somebody's got a missile lock on us!"

"Oh, great. They've got missiles now?" Kevin turned the freighter on its side and banked—hard—in an attempt to lose the missile chasing them.

It didn't work.

Inside her fingerless gloves, Lilia's palms began to sweat. Her heart was racing. "Kev—it's getting closer!"

Her brother did not respond, but only set his jaw in grim defiance. As the missile closed in on them, he abruptly dove toward two of the attacking ships—a slender *Dragonfly*-class corvette and a larger *Hornet*-class frigate—and flipped the *Talia* on her side again. He arced close to the frigate—close enough that Erik actually yelped and covered his face with his hands.

Lilia's eyes grew wide. "Kevin—"

"I know what I'm doing."

The *Talia*'s hull shields sparked and flared as they scraped along the frigate's shield. The missile—unconcerned by small details like another object getting between it and its original target—zoomed along until its proximity sensor determined it was close enough. It detonated just as Kevin cleared the frigate's engine and started to peel away in the opposite direction.

The resulting concussion took out a section of the frigate's shield—and also slammed into the *Talia*'s rear end. The freighter gave a tremendous shudder, jolting all of them forward into their safety harnesses.

They were clear though—at least for a few seconds. Kevin opened the throttle and their ship shot forward into space, away from the melee and away from Glo'Stea's gravitational field. Someone else fired a missile at them, but by then it was too late.

"Punch it!" Kevin commanded.

Lilia hit the hyperspace button and the stars elongated into streaks of light around them. They were free.

A moment later, they dropped back into real space outside of Sta'Gloa. A few ships from their convoy were already there, several of them obviously damaged. As Lilia anxiously watched the scanner, four more ships dropped out of hyperspace around them.

Several warnings were chiming noisily, their details flashing on the console panel before her. None of them were life-threatening; Lilia silenced them with a flick of her fingers. Her hands were still trembling. "Who *were* they?" she demanded of the cockpit at large.

No one answered. Instead, Kevin leaned over to touch the comm panel. "Thera Shield Control, this is the *Talia*." He gave their verification code.

"Roger that, *Talia*."

"Shield Control, we were attacked by unknown ships. I do not believe they were Tarynians. Repeat, I do *not* believe they were Tarynians."

Lilia nodded in approval as Kevin stressed this, biting the inside of her lip almost hard enough to draw blood. If it wasn't the Tarynians—and she had a gut feeling they weren't responsible— the best thing was to make that clear before everybody went crazy.

A brief pause, and then, "Stand by, *Talia*."

Kevin slowed the engine to an idle and they floated in space just outside Sta'Gloa's gravitational field. The rest of their convoy waited with them. Exhaling loudly, he reached for the ship's intercom. "Sorry about that rough patch, Mrs. Hito. We should be through it now; just sit tight."

A chill skipped down Lilia's spine. "I hope they let us in soon." She ran her fingers through her hair, anxiety churning her insides. "If whoever attacks us has these coordinates and follows us, we're—"

"—sitting ducks," Kevin said grimly. "I know." They all knew Thera Shield Control would keep them stranded out here if there was an ongoing firefight. His hands tightened on the steering yoke, before he consciously made himself loosen his grip. "Just like the convoy Lon was part of, back when we thought he'd died."

Lilia's stomach roiled again; she pressed a hand against it in a vain effort to calm it. "Yeah." She stared at their homeworld through the viewshield, her oceans and land masses visible below the glistening iridescent shield. They were so close to home—and yet they might as well have still been on Glo'Stea for all the good it would do them.

They weren't the only ones thinking about being stranded out here. When several more precious minutes had slipped past, during which the tension in the cockpit continued to rise, the comm crackled with an incoming transmission from the *Night's Breeze*, a *Cicada*-class freighter.

"*Talia*, this is Captain Fiyero. You heard anything from Shield Control yet?"

"Captain Fiyero, this is Captain Strong." Kevin glanced at Lilia, tilting his eyebrows questioningly; she only shrugged in response. "They haven't told us anything other than to stand by."

"Same here." A pause, and then, "What'd you tell them?"

"That we were attacked by unknown ships, but that I don't believe they're Tarynian."

Another pause, this one longer. "That's what I told 'em too."

At this, Lilia straightened in her seat. "Oh, good. We won't be the only ones talking crazy."

"Take any damage?" Captain Fiyero continued.

Kevin shrugged, even though the other ship's captain couldn't see him. "A little. You?"

"Half my shields are down. Took a couple of concussion missiles before we could escape." Captain Fiyero did *not* sound happy about this. "If those mucks come back and Shield Control doesn't let us in, we've got problems."

"Agreed." Kevin toggled the comm button and looked over at Lilia. "It's a good thing we've got a cease-fire and we just signed a trade agreement, because I'm pretty sure we're setting a record for sitting out here in unprotected space so long."

She nodded in response. Her mouth was dry; swallowing didn't help.

"It's gotta be connected to those guys at the spaceport." Erik leaned forward in his seat, his brown eyes too-bright and his leg jiggling fiercely. "They targeted our convoy on *purpose*."

Lilia glanced over her shoulder at him. "You don't think it's random?" Even to her ears, the question seemed weak.

"Don't tell me you do." Erik raised an eyebrow, his lips twisting into a hard, cynical smile. "It's gotta be Freedom's Children. Think about it. If nothin' else, they know our convoy contains people from occupied territory."

The bottom dropped out of Lilia's stomach; she felt cold all over. "So this is all our fault. They targeted the convoy because of us."

The people who had just been killed, the damage to the surviving ships in the convoy. *All our fault.*

Still smiling that terrible smile that didn't reach his eyes, Erik jerked a thumb over his shoulder in the direction of their passengers. "We've contributed, but I think technically it's *their* fault."

"It's nobody's fault but Freedom's Children, if they're the ones who attacked us." Kevin twisted around in his pilot's seat to stare at the blond Guardian. "It's not the Hitos's fault any more than it is ours."

Erik shrugged. "It could be random. We could just have really bad timin'. But my gut says no. An' I'm sure as far as Freedom's Children is concerned, every person aboard this ship has collaborated with the Tarynians."

Lilia pressed her lips into a thin line. "Captain Argos probably called a friend when we didn't cooperate. That's how they knew."

"An' then the Hitos didn't get detained at Customs…" Erik spread his hands.

"So they attacked our entire convoy." Lilia curled her fingers around the edge of the control panel in front of her.

Heavy silence fell over the cockpit for a moment. The *Talia* continued to drift just outside Sta'Gloa's gravitational field along with the rest of the survivors from their convoy. The comm panel remained quiet.

*Thud!*

Lilia jumped as Kevin smacked the flat of his hand against the steering yoke. He was still half-twisted in his seat. "It doesn't make any sense!" Shaking his head, he made a broad gesture toward the expanse of space behind them. "Where did they get those ships?"

"What?" Lilia glanced from him to Erik and back. "What do you mean?"

"Those definitely weren't Resistance ships." Kevin was still shaking his head. "The Resistance has never had much of a fleet anyway, and those didn't have Resistance markings."

"Freedom's Children could have painted 'em an' done that pondswappin' thing on the transponders," Erik said. "Not that big of a deal, Strong."

Awareness dawned on Lilia like the flash of sunlight on a knife's blade. "But they got through the shield in occupied territory."

"Exactly." Kevin shot her a grim look. "So how did Resistance ships get past the Tarynians to even be able to exit the shield there?"

"Wait a minute." Erik unstrapped his safety harness to lean forward more comfortably. "Are you sayin' a Freedom's Children cell somehow already got those ships into occupied territory past the Tarynians' noses?"

"Yep. And I'll bet they used a transporter to do it."

"Whoa." Lilia blinked and held up a hand. "A *transporter*, Kev?"

"Sure. Think about it. The only limit to a portal's size is the transporter itself." Kevin mimed a portal blossoming open. "If they've built a big enough frame…"

Lilia and Erik both digested this, and then Erik said flatly, "That's crazy."

Kevin only shook his head again. "Then how did they do it?"

No one answered.

After a long pause, Lilia said. "We don't even know for sure it *was* Freedom's Children. Until they actually announce something…" She bit her lip. "It's just conjecture."

"Oh, they'll say somethin'." Erik folded his arms across his chest, still looking grim. "Just you wait. That was Freedom's Children."

Just then the comm panel lit with an incoming transmission. Kevin lunged for it.

"*Talia*," came a harried voice, "this is Thera Shield Control. Your convoy has been cleared for entry through the shield."

"Praise God!" Lilia breathed.

Kevin flashed her a relieved smile. "Thanks, Shield Control. That's the best news I've heard all day."

"Stand by for entry coordinates."

"Standing by." Kevin toggled the comm panel and then reached for the ship's intercom. "Mrs. Hito, Mai, Ruis, we're about to make our approach through Sta'Gloa's shield."

A moment later, feet pounded up the corridor to the cockpit and Ruis almost skidded through the open hatch. His face was alight with excitement. "Can I sit here and watch?"

Kevin glanced at Lilia, who shrugged, before nodding. "Sure. So long as you strap yourself in and keep quiet for the time being."

Via Nancom, he told Lilia and Erik, [I'd rather not have to explain things just yet.]

Grinning from ear to ear, Ruis immediately dropped into the flight seat behind Kevin and fumbled for his safety harness.

As their convoy began their approach vector to Sta'Gloa, Lilia kept one eye on the scanner and the other on the gap slowly swirling open in the planetary shield. She hardly dared to breathe until Kevin had piloted their freighter into their homeworld's protected upper atmosphere.

As soon as the last ship in their convoy had safely passed through, Thera Shield Control closed the gap.

Lilia breathed a long, shaky sigh of relief. *We're home free. Even with having to explain things to Customs, we shouldn't have any more trouble from here on.*

She didn't know it yet, but she was dead wrong.

# Chapter 74

THEY landed at Thera Spaceport without any trouble. Once again, Erik stayed behind to keep an eye on the ship, while the twins escorted the Hito family to Customs.

Thera lay on the southwestern side of a large continent in Sector 4, and the air here was warm and muggy as well. After the cold of space, it was both a relief and an adjustment.

Lilia was just happy to have firm ground under her feet again.

"It's only an eleven hour flight from here to Yumiko," Kevin was telling Mrs. Hito. "Once we're through here, it won't be long before you can ask your family to meet you."

Mrs. Hito nodded stiffly, clutching the handle of her travel bag with both hands. She looked weary and pinched around the edges. Mai and Ruis were in slightly better shape, but they all looked like they would be happy to be done with all of this.

Lilia could understand that. *I'm ready to go home too.* She smiled wryly to herself. *Or at least have an uneventful flight back to Sonela.*

As they neared the Customs office, Lilia caught sight of a large crowd of people gathered around it. She unconsciously slowed her steps, glancing sideways at Kevin. "What is that all about?" she asked in Sta'Gloan.

"I don't know." He'd slowed as well, holding a hand out for Mrs. Hito and her children to match his pace. Squinting at the group,

Kevin tipped his head toward them—and the occasional silver flash of something hovering in the air above their heads. "Are those media cams?"

Lilia groaned. "Oh, great."

"Media cams?" Mai caught those Sta'Gloan words and her dark eyes widened. She stepped closer to her mother. In Glo'Stean, she asked, "Why are there media cams here?"

"Media cams?" The faint lines around Mrs. Hit's eyes tightened with alarm. She cast a half-panicked, half-helpless look at Kevin. "What—" she swallowed. "Why—why are they here?"

Kevin raised a hand to the back of his head. "Probably because of the attack on the convoy. But it's possible they've heard about you," he admitted.

"Particularly if whoever attacked the convoy issued a statement," Lilia added.

The Hito family continued to look bewildered—and frightened.

"It'll be okay." Kevin patted Mrs. Hito awkwardly on the shoulder. "We'll get you through this." He glanced from her to Mai and Ruis and received shaky nods. "All right. Onward."

Kevin took the lead again, motioning for the Hitos to stay behind him and for Lilia to bring up the rear. They shepherded their passengers up to the Customs office, where the crowd—a mix of reporters clearly waiting for someone in particular and citizens holding signs that threatened consequences for collusion with the Tarynians and also a few 'welcome home' signs.

Lilia's stomach sank. She opened a Nancom channel to Kevin. [So much for a non-hostile return. Somebody—]

[—tipped them off,] he agreed grimly.

The reporters took one look at the group headed their way and immediately perked up. Cams darted forward to record what they clearly hoped would be an impromptu interview.

"Excuse me." A young man dressed in a gray business suit stepped forward to address them. He had dark skin and a smooth-shaven head. His eyes skipped past Kevin to focus on Mrs. Hito and her children as he inclined a tiny mic in their direction. "Were you aboard the convoy that was attacked outside of Glo'Stea just a little while ago?"

Mrs. Hito glanced helplessly at Kevin, who shifted protectively in front of them. "Yes, we were part of it. We were fortunate enough to make it back to Sta'Gloa." He cast a stern look at the reporter, before turning his head to encompass the rest of the crowd. "Would you mind letting us through? It's been a long day."

The reporter wasn't finished. "Is it true that you are Usagi Hito and up until today you've been living in Challa, in the heart of G.U.-occupied Glo'Stea?"

"Let us through, please." Kevin started to shoulder the reporter aside, but he refused to budge.

"Mrs. Hito," called out another reporter, this one a tall, thin woman with angular features and platinum blonde hair. "Freedom's Children has announced that they only attacked the convoy because they consider you and your children traitors and spies and were attempting to keep you from landing on Sta'Gloa. What do you think about this?"

"Traitors!" shouted several voices from the crowd. "You're not welcome on Sta'Gloa!"

Shock flooded Lilia, promptly followed by cold disgust. She put her arms around Mai and Ruis's shoulders, keeping them close to her. [This is ridiculous.]

"Don't answer that," Kevin told Mrs. Hito. He raised his voice. "Can we get some Security over here, please?"

The first reporter jabbed his tiny mic in Kevin's face again. "You're Kevin Strong. You and your sister—" his gaze cut to Lilia, "—are responsible for Ambassador Kedis being on Sta'Gloa."

"Not completely." Kevin narrowed his eyes at the reporter, but before he could ask what that had to do with anything, the reporter indicated the Hito family behind him.

"And now you're aiding and abetting—"

"—a Sta'Gloan citizen," Kevin said loudly, "who was trapped on Glo'Stea after the blockade began over two decades ago, just lost her husband to current violence, and is now trying to get her children home to her family. She's innocent of any allegations of wrongdoing until proven guilty. Now, if you'll excuse us, we need to talk to Customs."

A couple of spaceport security guards arrived just then and cleared a path for them to reach the door to the Customs office. They beckoned for Kevin, Lilia, and the Hitos to enter quickly. A cacophony of shouts and questions followed them into the building, until the door closed and merciful silence fell.

Kevin extended a hand to one of the security guards. "Thanks."

The man, tall and dark-skinned, gave his hand a perfunctory shake. "Let's get this sorted out. This way."

Lilia was beginning to suspect that Spaceport Customs offices had all been built with the same set of blueprints. Were it not for the fact that she knew they were on Sta'Gloa, she could have sworn they were back in the Customs office in Antar. The security guards took their statements, and then directed the Hito family to a Customs official to begin the process of proving they could legally depart the spaceport.

Kevin cast a baleful look in the direction of the door and the crowd that was no doubt still gathered beyond it. "That was an ambush. Freedom's Children did that on purpose."

Lilia nodded, already reaching for her comlink. "Since they didn't succeed in blowing us up." She grimaced. "We're going to be—"

"—on the news again." Kevin matched her expression, before dropping his head into his hands. "I just want this trip to be over."

"You and me both." Lilia tried to smile, but didn't quite make it. "Guess Erik was right."

Kevin just snorted, not bothering to lift his head. "I'll fill him in. We could be here a while."

Two hours later, they were still waiting for Mrs. Hito and her children to re-emerge from the labyrinth of white cubicles. Lilia was stretched out flat on a bench with her knees bent and her eyes closed when she felt her comlink vibrate in her pocket. She fished it out and her heart gave a odd little gallop. *Jasper.*

His message read: *When you told me you were taking a job to pick up passengers on Glo'Stea, you didn't mention you were going to Challa.* She could almost *hear* his wry tone.

She winced. She'd done that on purpose, of course. She pressed her lips into a thin line, trying to quell the irritation she felt with the media crowd outside. *Of course they're broadcasting this everywhere.* Jasper must be watching the news.

If she was honest with herself, however, Lilia couldn't blame the reporters—they were doing their jobs. An attack on a convoy after the Coalition and the G.U. had just agreed to sign a trade agreement *was* big news. *I just wish we weren't in the middle of it.*

Sighing, she sent back, *That's because I knew you'd start up about your mystery jumper again.*

*Very funny. Are you all right?*

For one, heart-stopping second, Lilia thought he was asking about her mental state after being in Challa again. His next message cleared that up.

*Did your ship take much damage in the attack?*

Her muscles relaxed. *A little, but I don't think it's too bad.* She glanced towards the cubicles again. *What is the media saying about our passengers?*

A pause, and then, *Well, they're confused as to this family's exact legal status. They can't decide if it's a heartwarming tale of a lost daughter returning home or a perfidious traitor attempting to worm her way onto Sta'Gloa.*

Lilia rolled her eyes. *No surprise there.* She gave Jasper a brief explanation, ending with, *I don't think most people know how bad things have been in occupied territory since the cease-fire. I didn't know, up until I started talking to Mrs. Hito.*

*I've heard bits and pieces.*

Lilia frowned. From Kedis, no doubt.

Her comlink vibrated again. *This Freedom's Children group seems to be doing everything they can to derail things.*

She snorted softly to herself. *They can try.*

"Who are you talking to?" Beside her, Kevin tilted a curious eyebrow.

"Jasper." Lilia did not look up. "He's watching this—" she waved a hand to indicate their general situation, "—on the news."

Kevin blanched. "Oh, great. That's just what we need. Coalition-wide media coverage." He let his head thump back against the wall. "Should have seen that coming."

Registering soft footsteps padding toward them on the carpeted floor, Lilia glanced sideways to see a tall, rather gangly man in a business suit approaching them, followed by Mrs. Hito, Mai, Ruis, and three burly spaceport security guards. The man in front had pale skin, almond-shaped eyes, and a shock of black hair he had carefully slicked back. His hair was so glossy it glistened beneath the too-bright industrial lighting of the glowpanels in the ceiling.

Leaving her last message unfinished, Lilia immediately sat up and swung her feet to the floor. Beside her, Kevin straightened. All three members of the Hito family looked rather pale and anxious, but they didn't look crushed. The twins exchange minute sideways glances. Things must have gone fairly well.

"Captain Strong, I presume?" The Customs official held out a hand to Kevin as he neared them. A cloud of rather expensive cologne followed in his wake.

Lilia tried not to blink. *Something tells me he's not a lower-tier bureaucrat.*

"That is correct." Kevin motioned to Lilia. "My first mate, Lilia Strong."

The man nodded, as though he already knew this. "Jun Pyu Wau, head of the Customs officer here at Thera Spaceport."

Lilia's gaze flicked from Mr. Wau to Mrs. Hito and back, wondering exactly why this man needed to see *them*.

Kevin was wondering the same thing. "Can we help you with something, Mr. Wau?"

"Oh, not really." Mr. Wau shook his head, smiling benignly. "I simply wished to meet you."

"To meet *us*?" the twins asked at the same time. "Why?"

Mr. Wau only shook his head, rocking back and forth a little on the balls of his feet. "Call it curiosity." He studied them both, before lifting one black suit-clad shoulder in a shrug. "I remember seeing you on the news, of course. And now you're here," he waved to the Hitos, "and you've just survived an attack on your convoy."

"Well…" Kevin raised a hand to rub the back of his neck. "It's been a long day so far." He nodded to Mrs. Hito. "Were you able to get everything straightened out?"

Mrs. Hito nodded, but before she could speak, the Customs official intervened. "Oh, I think so. We've issued visas for her children, until we can get the matter of their legal immigration sorted out."

"That's good," Lilia said.

"In the meantime," Mr. Wau continued, "we have notified the Department of Security and they will be monitoring the Hitos." He shrugged, smiling slightly. "You understand. We think it is unlikely that they are threats, but they *did* come from formerly occupied territory."

Lilia nodded tightly, her eyes flicking to Kevin's. Neither of them liked it, but they understood. Lilia tipped her head toward the door. "Are we free to leave?"

"Certainly." Mr. Wau spread his hands. "As I said, I merely wished to meet you." He offered Mrs. Hito an ingratiating smile. "We will escort you out. Just in case there are any more reporters hanging around."

Understanding broke over Lilia like the sun peeking through a break in cloud cover. *Ah. That's it.* She traded knowing looks with Kevin. Clearly, Mr. Wau sensed an opportunity for publicity.

Several different media crews were indeed still loitering outside, no doubt waiting for the results of the Hitos' visit. Mr. Wau did not wait for one of them to address him, but immediately strode forward to greet them. He raised his arms. "We here at the Customs Office in Thera Spaceport are happy to report that we have welcomed one of Sta'Gloa's own citizens home after more than two decades spent trapped off-world." He waved Mrs. Hito forward; she obeyed reluctantly.

A dozen different questions zinged through the air at him, but Mr. Wau only waved his hands. "We will not be answering questions at this time. If you like, our office will release a formal statement later this afternoon. Thank you, that will be all."

He turned away, even though several of the reporters were still calling out questions, and motioned to the security guards. "Please escort these folks back to their freighter. The *Talia*, is it?" He glanced at Kevin, who nodded.

And that was that.

Once they were safely aboard the *Talia* again, Lilia pulled Mrs. Hito aside. "You may want to call your family and warn them that there could be media crews waiting for you when we get to Yumiko."

The older woman's face grew a little pinched around the edges again, but she gave a decisive nod. "That thought occurred to me as well." She managed a small, rueful smile. "Although it almost seems presumptuous to think the Sta'Gloan media would have any interest in us."

"They will for now, I think." Lilia patted her on the shoulder. "At least until the novelty of people arriving from formerly occupied territory wears off." She tipped her head down the corridor toward the cabins. "Try to get some rest. We've got a long flight ahead of us. You might as well take advantage of it."

"Thank you." With a polite bow, Mrs. Hito moved off in the direction of the living compartment to collect her children, while Lilia turned her steps toward the cockpit.

She blew out a steadying breath, briefly shutting her eyes. *I'm ready for this trip to be over.* She opened her eyes. *One last hurdle to go.* A frown wrinkled her forehead. *Maybe two hurdles, if there's a media crew waiting for us when we get back to Sonela.*

Lilia hoped there wasn't, but given the circumstances she knew it was probably a futile hope.

She was right.

# Chapter 75

THE Hitos had indeed been swamped by reporters and cams as soon as they arrived in Yumiko Spaceport, all of whom had captured the touching, if slightly awkward reunion between Mrs. Hito and her father and younger brother. Lilia and Kevin had lingered long enough to ensure their passengers would make it out of the spaceport in one piece before they escaped back to the *Talia* and set course for home.

Neither they nor Erik quite knew what to expect when they returned to Sonela…but they weren't surprised when they finally emerged through Customs to find several small media crews milling around the spaceport waiting for them.

Erik took one look at the reporters and hovering cams charging toward them and swore softly under his breath. "That's it," he said flatly, starting to turn around. "I'm goin' back to the ship."

Lilia shot him a sideways glance, even as her heart dropped like a stone in her chest. "What, you don't want to face the firing squad with us?"

"Nope."

"It's too late, anyway." Kevin patted him bracingly on the back. "They've spotted us and your name is already floating around the Coalition because somebody figured out you're part of our crew now."

To his credit, Erik managed to wrangle his black scowl into a less forbidding frown as the reporters and their cams descended on the trio.

The back of Lilia's neck prickled uncomfortably as her peripheral vision caught the many glances and stares they were now drawing from other people in the spaceport, but she didn't have time to dwell on it. They were well and truly caught now.

"Captain Strong!" called out a petite woman with caramel skin and luscious dark curls. She was dressed in a crimson pantsuit, with an identbadge proclaiming her to be from Sonela's biggest media station. "Meridia Vaughn, from Capital Media. Welcome back to Sta'Gloa. How does it feel to be one of the survivors of an attack the Department of Security is calling the worst since the attack on the convoy that nearly killed your brother?"

Lilia barely suppressed a wince. *They're not pulling any punches.*

Kevin flashed her an awkward smile. "We're, ah, happy to be alive, of course." He shook his head. "We were among the lucky ones."

A brash young man with bright blond hair and copper skin angled slightly in front of Vaughn and extended a small mic toward them. He wore an expensive dark blue suit. "Captain Strong, Elij Kaas. Sonela Entertainment. Are you aware that Freedom's Children is claiming—"

"Wait a minute." Kevin held up a hand, cutting him off. He glanced from Vaughn to Kaas to the two other reporters bunched around them. "We'll be happy to give you an interview, but could we possibly do it someplace a little more private?" He gestured to the spaceport around them and the crowd of gawkers they had drawn. "It's been a long trip and we're tired."

Lilia nodded emphatically; Erik just folded his arms across his chest and continued to frown, clearly none-too-happy.

The three reporters exchanged uneasy glances, as if they didn't quite trust each other, before Meridia Vaughn claimed the forefront again and appointed herself spokeswoman for the group. "Certainly," she said with a bright smile. "We'd love an in-depth interview." She didn't wait for a consensus from her fellow reporters, but nodded across the spaceport commons. "There's a waiting area over there that is mostly empty."

"That will work. Thank you." Kevin made sure to meet each reporter's eye as he nodded. [Sorry,] he told Lilia and Erik via Nancom as they walked across the spaceport to the waiting area Vaughn had indicated. [I didn't think there was any way we were getting out of this.]

[There wasn't.] Lilia did her best to maintain a pleasant expression. [We might as well get it over with now.]

[Speak for yourselves,] Erik said grumpily.

Lilia and Kevin exchanged tiny glances out of the corners of their eyes. Neither one of them bothered to point out to their friend that this was a risk he took when he started working for them. They knew he knew.

Lilia flicked her gaze to the reporters, who all looked quite keen and alert now. She swallowed uneasily, biting down on the inside of her lip. *No doubt they're coming up with all kinds of other questions to ask us.* Her stomach began to writhe anxiously. There was such a wide scope for questions, too. [I just hope we don't regret this,] she told Erik and her brother.

Neither of them responded.

Vaughn continued to take the lead. As soon as they reached the waiting area, she clapped her hands together and began to issue brisk instructions, directing the proceedings as efficiently as a drill sergeant. This surprised Lilia a little—the woman looked like she was all curves and soft edges, the sort of reporter who covered high-society parties and the goings and comings of Sonela's social elite—but then, she couldn't have made it as one of Capital Media's news reporters if she didn't have a little gumption. Clearly, Vaughn had higher aspirations.

"You three sit in a row over here." Vaughn pointed a well-manicured finger to three chairs in a row along the wall at a spot that provided a partial backdrop of the words "Welcome to Sonela Spaceport".

Lilia and Kevin obeyed, but Erik did not move. He continued to stand in the center of the waiting area, feet planted on the carpeted floor, arms folded across his chest. "I'd prefer to stay out of this."

"No can do," Kaas said flippantly, carrying a chair over and setting it across from the twins. "You're part of the story."

Vaughn, however, considered him through dark, narrowed eyes. She cocked a hip and propped her hand on it. "Why?"

Erik just shrugged. "Ain't necessary."

"Why?" Vaughn continued to assess him. "Because you're a former Sonela police officer?"

"That has nothin' to do with it." Erik uncrossed his arms long enough to make a sharp, dismissive gesture. "I just don't want my face plastered all over the Coalition."

Vaughn glanced from him to the twins and then cast a quick look at her fellow reporters. "Well, I can't speak for my associates," she said at last, looking back at Erik, "but I think I can keep you out of my interview if you would prefer."

"I would," Erik said grimly.

"On one condition." Vaughn held up a perfectly manicured finger.

Lilia and Kevin both tensed, but Erik just raised a blond eyebrow as though he had expected this. "An' what would that be?"

"You let me quote you as an anonymous 'crewmember.'"

"Done," Erik said immediately. He addressed Kaas and the other reporter. "I'll give you the same deal."

After only a second's worth of hesitation, both of them nodded.

"Great. Glad we could work that out." Erik promptly sat down a few seats away, folding his arms across his chest again as he leaned back in his chair.

Lilia looked at the third reporter, who had yet to identify herself. "And you would be?"

"Yuuki Soijiro." The woman flicked straight black bangs out of her dark eyes. "Glo'Stea Coalition News." She was tiny, but she carried herself as though she was much taller. "I'm on assignment to Sonela at the moment to cover the Triumvirate's dealings with Ambassador Kedis." She wore a jade green blouse over a black skirt with minimal jewelry, the picture of an administrative assistant at the Four Towers.

Kevin blinked. "How'd you end up here?"

Soijiro favored him with an oddly indulgent smile. "Let's just say I got a tip from a friend on Glo'Stea and thought I'd follow a hunch."

Beside her, Kaas snorted. "Follow a hunch?" He gave her a thin smile. "More like you got a whiff of how big the potential for this story could be and though you'd get your claws into it."

"Just like you and me," Vaughn cut in. Her pleasant tone held an edge. "Face reality, Kaas, we're all here because we're following the story." She turned back to Lilia and the two men. "Let's get going." She squinted at Kevin. "I'd tell you to comb your hair, but you've just escaped an attack on your convoy. This tousled look you've got going is probably more realistic."

Startled, Kevin traded a minute look with Lilia. His hand rose a few centimeters, as though he was self-consciously contemplating flattening his hair, but then it dropped back to his lap.

For her part, Lilia thought about her own attire and the fact that she hadn't bothered with makeup since they left Sonela and swallowed grimly. [You've been working,] she reminded herself. [This whole thing has been a long process. You're not going to look like you just arrived at one of Madame Olga's parties.]

It didn't matter. People who saw this interview would probably relate better to them anyway if they didn't look cam-ready.

"Before we start, a few ground rules," Kaas said. His flat stare included Soijiro, but was primarily directed at Vaughn. "All three cams are positioned to get a good view, and all three of us will ask questions."

"We'll take turns," Soijiro interjected. "Agreed?"

Vaughn flipped a black curl over her shoulder. "Agreed."

A moment later, all three sets of reporters and cams in position, the interview began. Lilia had been afraid they'd come up with more questions; she wasn't wrong.

Not surprisingly, Meridia Vaughn launched the first volley. "Captain Strong, let's start with a little background information. I understand you and your sister run an interstellar shipping business. Do you often take passengers?"

"No," Kevin shook his head, "not—"

"—usually," Lilia finished.

The twins explained how everything had come about and the interview moved on quickly from there. It didn't take long to reach Freedom's Children and the attack on the convoy.

Kaas leaned forward. "Were you aware that Freedom's Children is claiming you and the Hitos are responsible for the attack on the convoy? They've issued a statement claiming that they were only attempting to keep what they've termed 'traitors' and 'spies' from breaching Sta'Gloan space."

Kevin's expression hardened. "Customs on both Glo'Stea and Sta'Gloa cleared the Hitos. We didn't know Freedom's Children had anything to do with the attack until after we reached Sta'Gloa."

He shook his head. "They can blame us all they like," he said flatly, "but it doesn't change the fact that they're still the ones who opened fire on our convoy. They're responsible for the lives lost on the ships they destroyed."

"I don't know if you're aware of this or not," this from Soijiro, "but it's circulating the Coalition that you and your family are G.U. sympathizers."

Lilia glanced sideways at Kevin, before smiling tightly at the reporter. "Do you have any context for that?"

Soijiro blinked in surprise, but recovered smoothly. "I'm not sure I know what you mean."

"Oh, you know." Lilia waved a hand. "We helped Ambassador Kedis, so we *must* be G.U. sympathizers." She shook her head. "Never mind the fact that the cease-fire and now trade agreement he's reached with the Triumvirate have helped save Coalition lives."

She raised an eyebrow at the dark-haired reporter. "Or is this just because our father happened to be a Tarynian expatriate who left his homeworld years before the blockade ever happened?"

All three reporters looked slightly taken aback—as though they hadn't *actually* expected the twins to *admit* they were half-Tarynian in a live interview.

"Not that it should matter," Kevin said. "We're Sta'Gloan citizens. And the only reason we helped the Ambassador was, as my sister just said, because we knew the cost of life that could be saved by reaching some sort of peace agreement." He glanced from Vaughn to Kaas to Soijiro. "I don't know if any of you have ever actually been in the war zone on Glo'Stea, but it's—"

"—not a pretty sight. I worked on a couple of medcenters along there." Lilia's throat tightened as words rose to the tip of her tongue; she swallowed and forced herself to continue. "In fact, I was one of the few survivors of the attack on Coral Island over a year ago. We've—" she motioned between her and Kevin, "—seen firsthand the kind of—"

"—damage this conflict has inflicted. Can you blame us for—"

"—wanting to keep more people from getting wounded or killed?"

"I think we can certainly see how you might make that argument," Kaas said smoothly. He glanced back and forth between the twins, his expression one of polite concern. "You mentioned you are half-Tarynian. What kind of impact has that had on your lives?"

Off to the side, Erik snorted. Kaas's gaze flicked to him, but then returned to the twins. Via Nancom, Erik asked, [What kind of a stupid question is that?]

The twins ignored him.

"Depends." Lilia raised one shoulder in a shrug. "We run into people who can't see past bloodlines." Her mind flashed to Alan Birch and his girlfriend. "But it's not like it's written on our foreheads." She cracked a smile. "Honestly, none of us have any idea how many people on Sta'Gloa, Lanx, or Glo'Stea have family on other worlds. The last two decades of being trapped in our own system have really—"

"—narrowed our view of the galaxy." Kevin spread his hands, indicating the spaceport around them. "I mean, think about it. Before the blockade, hundreds and thousands of ships from all over the galaxy visited Sonela Spaceport. Now our interstellar traffic is pretty much limited to our system alone."

Meridia Vaughn raised an eyebrow. "And you think the trade agreement will change that?"

"It has the potential to change everything." Kevin shrugged. "We might like some of that change and we—"

"—might not." Lilia mirrored Kevin's shrug. "That's just the way the galaxy—"

"—works. But we can't keep living under this blockade. It's not—"

"—helping anyone, Glo'Stea and Lanx especially."

Kaas nodded slowly, shooting the cams a sober look. "Whatever your opinions of the Galactic Union, I think we can all agree on that."

They covered a few more topics before Vaughn nodded briskly. "Well, I think that about wraps it up."

"I have one more question." Soijiro leaned forward, a sudden glint in her dark eyes. "This one is for you, Miss Strong."

*Uh oh.* That didn't sound good. Bracing herself, Lilia met the other woman's gaze and tried to look politely interested. "Yes?"

"Half of Sonela is dying to know…Just what exactly is going on between you and a certain Galactic Union Lieutenant?"

The bottom dropped out of Lilia's stomach. "Excuse me?"

"We've all heard the official story." Soijiro waved a manicured hand. "But it's been months since Ambassador Kedis arrived in Sonela, and you and Lieutenant Wright still seem to be quite close."

[You don't have to answer this,] Kevin's voice echoed grimly through her head.

Lilia's heart was pounding. Of course she didn't, but what was that old saying? *Never believe anything until it's been officially denied?* She forced a smile, trying to look as though the question *hadn't* just encased her insides in ice while simultaneously sending her heart into overdrive. "Lieutenant Wright and I still keep in touch." Her smile turned a touch more genuine. "It's nice to run into someone you know at some of these big social events."

"Particularly someone as handsome as the Lieutenant?" Soijiro suggested, with a suddenly wicked smile. "Even if he is G.U.?"

"When you get down to it," Lilia said with another shrug, "people are people. It's just easier for us when bad things happen to look at uniforms and forget there are real human beings wearing them." Her mouth flattened into a thin line. "There's been a lot of bloodshed on both sides of this conflict, and someday we'll all have to answer for it."

A couple of fast blinks were the only indication Soijiro gave at this abrupt segue from her chosen line of questioning; she rallied quickly. "So there's nothing going on between you and the Lieutenant?"

"Is this really necessary?" Kevin cut in, a flicker of annoyance in his voice.

Meridia Vaughn gave a tinkling laugh. "Now, really, Captain Strong, I'm sure you can see why people would be curious. A Sta'Gloan Representative's granddaughter and a Galactic Union officer?" She gave him a knowing look. "That has quite the potential to be a charming love story."

"Lieutenant Wright and I are friends." Lilia wanted to twist her fingers together in her lap, but she made herself sit very still. She offered the three reporters a coy smile. "That's as far as it goes, I'm afraid."

And, as far as words spoken aloud were concerned, it was. Unspoken subtext was none of their business.

"If you say so." Soijiro tipped her head in a gracious nod. "Thank you." She looked at the others. "That's all I've got."

"One more thing." Vaughn held up a finger. "Your brother Michael's sweet little romance with Glo'Stean Representative Shane Briscoe's sister is melting hearts all over the Coalition."

*It is?* Lilia thought in shock. She was hard-pressed to keep her expression from betraying her surprise; she couldn't remember hearing much of anything about them lately.

"They've done a good job of staying under the radar," Vaughn continued, "but I've heard from reputable sources that things are heating up." She shot the twins a dazzling smile. "Now that we've got the opportunity to ask, any word on when we might expect to hear wedding bells for Michael and Dawn?"

*…and we've definitely moved on to gossip.* Irritated, Lilia shook her head. "No idea."

Vaughn leaned forward. "But a proposal *is* coming?"

The twins exchanged darting glances. [Can you believe this?] Kevin asked.

Lilia flashed the reporter a polite smile. "We really can't say. If there is, we—"

"—haven't heard anything." Kevin's voice held a tone of finality. He cast a glance around. "Are we finished?" He rose to his feet before anyone could answer. "We've got places to be."

"Thank you for your time," Vaughn said smoothly, dismissing her cam with a flick of her fingers. She stood up and extended a hand to Kevin and Lilia in turn. "You can expect to see this on the news tonight."

"That's great." Kevin just barely managed to keep the sarcasm from his voice.

Lilia shot him a warning look as she left her chair. [Remember, they still have to edit this thing. They can hack everything we said to pieces.]

[Then why in the galaxy did we tell them anything?]

She just pursed her lips and gave a tiny shake of her head.

Erik unfolded himself from his chair and stood with his arms crossed, looking like he couldn't wait to leave.

"It's been illuminating." Kaas nodded to them both, before summoning his cam and striding off across the waiting room, leaving a cloud of expensive cologne in his wake. He disappeared into the crowd of people in the spaceport's main concourse.

"Yes." Soijiro offered them a polite bow. "Most illuminating." Reaching into a pocket, she pulled out a datachip and extended it to Lilia between two fingers. "Should you have anything else you wish to share…"

*We won't,* Lilia thought, but she bowed politely in return and took the datachip. "Thank you."

As soon as Soijiro and Vaughn were out of earshot, Erik turned to the twins. "Can we blow this joint yet?"

"Can't wait," Kevin said wearily. He jerked a thumb toward Lilia. "We've got to go home."

"You're welcome to come with us," Lilia said.

Erik snorted. "And face whatever's waitin' for you at Ferndale? No thanks. I've gotta stop by my apartment an' then I'll come back here."

"Thanks a lot, Erik." Kevin screwed his face into an expression that was half-amusement, half-grimace. "Hadn't thought about *that* yet."

"You need to." Erik turned to leave, raising a hand in farewell. "Later."

# Chapter 76

THE only downside to the cease-fire and pending trade agreement was that it made commanding the Blockade Division a good deal less interesting. Admiral Chesnee knew he wasn't alone; his crew felt it too. He suspected it was probably harder for the men and women under his command—they had finally been allowed to put their training to use after years of being curtailed by corrupt commanders, only to have their purpose for being here all but stripped away.

Peace.

Chesnee liked the concept; he considered himself to have spent his military career fighting to gain it. Unfortunately, he couldn't shake the feeling that the way this peace had come about left something lacking.

*If I didn't know better*, he thought wryly, tapping the arm of his chair in his Flag Tactical Command Center while his crew bustled about him, *I'd almost say we were cheated out of a victory that should have been ours.*

They'd certainly worked hard enough for it.

Oh, he knew in the eyes of anyone else this outcome would be considered a victory—and one with a good deal less bloodshed and property destruction than there could have been—but it still felt a little…hollow.

He and his command had done the hard work of breaking the Coalition—

—and Leo Kedis had swept in to mop things up and claim the glory.

The thought tasted bitter; Chesnee brushed it away. *Let it go*, he told himself. *You can go anywhere after this.*

*That* was the victory he would claim. He had taken a career graveyard and done the impossible. *And once things are settled with the Coalition, the Blockade Division will be reassigned.*

There were plenty of other stray corners throughout the Galactic Union that could use a few extra military ships to quell a little local unrest.

Chesnee didn't know how much longer they would be staying in the Coalition system, but he doubted it would be for more than a couple more months. *Not once they sign that trade agreement.*

He suppressed a sigh. When he first announced the *Winds of Change* would be making a micro-jump to Sta'Gloa, an undercurrent of excitement had run through the corridors and decks of the battlecruiser. They had orbited Lanx for nearly a year now, and the entire crew was excited to be moving on. Particularly when it meant getting a look at Sta'Gloa.

Chesnee himself had been excited…though if he was honest, a small part of him remained disappointed he wasn't here because they were conquering Sta'Gloa. It was a selfish desire, one he had squashed ruthlessly. Conquest might be more satisfying, but the overarching goal was to bring the Coalition into alliance with the G.U.—one way or another.

That the Sta'Gloans were nervous about the *Change*'s presence beyond their planetary shield was obvious in the sudden and dramatic reduction of incoming and outgoing convoys on that side of the world. Chesnee could only imagine the havoc this was wrecking. *That's Kedis's problem, not mine.*

The Ambassador had smoothed things over with the Triumvirate, but it required the *Change* to be on a rather tight leash. Chesnee hadn't minded acquiescing too much—thanks to the cease-fire, half of the demands the Triumvirate made were things he was already unable to do.

The only thing that really stuck in his craw was his inability to send out the occasional Piranha scout to gather information on the other side of Sta'Gloa. The Triumvirate had flat-out refused to even consider it—as far as they were concerned, there was nothing 'friendly' about such an action—and Kedis did not press the point.

If he'd been able to gather intel properly, Chesnee would have known about Freedom's Children's attack on the convoy as soon as it happened—and he might have even been able to help the beleaguered ships. As it was, he did not hear about it until Lieutenant Wright sent a brief communiqué detailing the attack at Kedis's request.

*That group is a problem*, Chesnee sent back. *Be wary.*

Half an hour later, he received a call from the bridge. "Sir," Captain Sanford began briskly, "a transport and its escort just dropped out of hyperspace outside the Blockade and hailed the *Requiem*. They have diplomatic transponder codes. They are requesting permission through the Blockade to jump to Sta'Gloa and dock aboard the *Change*."

"Ambassador Kedis's reinforcements." Chesnee kept his tone even. "Grant them permission."

"Aye, Admiral."

Chesnee glanced at Lieutenant Armal, who stood at his post nearby. "Find Lieutenant Macy and have him make sure everything is ready for them." Macy was the officer he had assigned to be Kedis's liaison. The lieutenant had not been transferred to Sta'Gloa with the majority of the Ambassador's staff, but had remained aboard the *Change* to facilitate things from here.

"Yes, sir." Armal saluted and exited the TAC command center, leaving Chesnee to contemplate what further demands Kedis would make on him now that his political pieces were falling into place.

It took Armal over twenty minutes to return. Ordinarily, Chesnee would have thought nothing of that, but the odd look on his aide's face gave him pause for concern. He set his datapad aside, eyes narrowing slightly. "Lieutenant?"

"Admiral, Lieutenant Macy has a slight, ah, situation."

"What *kind* of situation?"

"Well, sir…" Armal hesitated, looking as though he would rather have been anywhere else aboard the *Change*. "There's a woman in the hangar bay who says she's your wife."

"What?" Chesnee froze, as if his entire body had just been turned to ice. He couldn't have heard that right. "My *wife*?"

Around him, several of his crew shot him covert glances.

"Ah, yes, sir." Armal was far too experienced to give in to the desire to shift uncomfortably on his feet, but the tension cording his shoulders gave away his unease. "One Sylvia Chesnee, according to her identchip. She arrived with the rest of the Ambassador's people."

Chesnee blinked, still reeling, and the memory of Kedis's peculiar smile flashed across his mind. He gritted his teeth; the command center suddenly felt hot and stifling. *So* that's *what that was all about.*

"Admiral?"

With an effort, Chesnee pulled himself together. Neither Armal nor Macy would recognize his wife—none of his crew had ever met her and he had been too bitter to display holos of her in his quarters. He did not doubt her identity, however; the mere fact that she had arrived aboard a diplomatic transport meant she was really here.

"Tell Lieutenant Macy I'm on my way."

"Aye, sir." Armal sounded relieved.


It took far too little time for Chesnee to make his way from his command center to Hangar Bay 4A. Every footstep felt like it took him closer to the edge of a precipice; his gut churned. The smell of engine fuel and hydraulic fluid combined with the ever-present faintly metallic scent in the ship's air greeted him as he strode toward the wide hangar bay doors. It was a familiar smell, but for some reason now it made him even queasier.

His heart pounded in his chest. Sylvia, here in the Sta'Gloan system, aboard his flagship.

*What is Kedis playing at?*

But even as the thought crossed his mind, the answer followed it—and Chesnee almost kicked himself for being an idiot. The Ambassador was obviously preparing for all of the various social functions that would be part and parcel of peace with the Coalition…and he *clearly* expected Chesnee to make an appearance at some of them with his wife on his arm.

Chesnee forced himself to maintain a calm expression. Far too many of his crew bustled about these corridors; it wouldn't do to start scuttlebutt. *She's your wife,* a wry voice said inside his head. *A man shouldn't feel sick at the thought of seeing his wife in person after all this time.*

To be honest, the Admiral wasn't sure *what* he felt. He entered the hangar bay and his gaze immediately narrowed in on the familiar tall, curvy figure of his wife standing by a sleek shuttle. For an instant, the hangar bay was empty save for the two of them.

Sylvia was dressed in a stylish pale brown faux fur coat over black slacks and a turquoise blouse, and her dark hair was pinned up. Her traveling style, a corner of his mind noted. She was talking to Lieutenant Macy, animatedly waving her hands, but feeling his gaze on her, she turned her head. Their eyes met.

In that instant, Chesnee saw her face light up at the sight of him…and then a reserved mask fell into place like heavy emergency doors sealing off a damaged section of the ship hemorrhaging oxygen into space. He suppressed a sigh, his feet automatically taking him toward her. Sylvia was happy to see him, which was good to know, but she hadn't forgiven him yet.

*I suppose I can't blame her for that.*

Beyond his wife, the Admiral finally noticed the rest of Kedis's people milling around the shuttle, trying not to look impatient at this delay. None of them ranked high enough for the Blockade Commander himself to greet them personally; Macy should have already begun to escort them to their quarters. Sylvia's arrival had altered protocol.

As he drew near, Sylvia did not hesitate. Her crimson lips curved into a beautiful smile as she stretched out her hands to him. "Giles. It is so good to see you."

"Sylvia. This is a surprise." Taking her hands, Chesnee leaned in to kiss her. He'd meant for it to be perfunctory, but the caress lingered a little longer than intended. He *had* missed her.

A faint cloud of perfume wafted around him as Sylvia pulled back, and Chesnee resisted the urge to inhale. He'd always loved that particular fragrance. He doubted she had selected it by accident.

"Ambassador Kedis arranged it." Sylvia's dark eyes were bright with a faint sheen of something that could be tears, though her expression was light and airy. "He told me he wanted to surprise you and that I shouldn't contact you ahead of time." She held her head high, daring her husband to comment.

In truth, Chesnee didn't know what to say. Part of him clamored that Kedis should have *warned* him, should have given him advance notice of something like this. The other part of him though it was probably better this way—he didn't have time to stew about it.

Or build up defenses.

"Well, my dear, welcome to the *Winds of Change*." Chesnee waved a hand to the hangar bay around them. "This is my flagship."

He glanced at Macy. "See to the rest of our guests and then have my wife's luggage brought to my quarters."

Sylvia would have to stay with him; he didn't know where else to put her that wouldn't look suspicious. *Particularly with Kedis's people roaming around.*

Lieutenant Macy saluted briskly and trotted off to carry out his orders.

Looking at his wife, Chesnee found himself at a sudden loss for words. His entire day—indeed, his foreseeable future—had just been completely turned upside down in ways he had not expected. *Now what do I do?*

Giving him a strange smile, Sylvia slipped her arm through the crook of his elbow. "Ask me about my trip, Giles."

He took it for the lifeline it was. "How was your trip?"

"Long, but not as long as I expected." Sylvia tipped her dark head toward the force field separating the inside of the hangar bay from the crushing vacuum of black space beyond. "I don't think many people in the G.U. realize how close the Sta'Gloan system is to the Core. I know I didn't."

Chesnee was inclined to agree with her.

"Have you been down to Sta'Gloa or any of the other worlds yet?"

"Not yet." Despite himself, Chesnee smiled ruefully. "I expect that will change now that you're here. Ambassador Kedis seems to have plans for us."

"Yes." Sylvia gave a little hum. Her shoes made sharp clicking sounds against the deck. "He did mention something about making sure I had evening gowns for various parties."

They left the hangar bay behind and Chesnee shot her a cool sideways glance. "Is that the only reason you came? The promise of parties?"

"Oh, yes." She smiled archly, waving her free hand. "It had nothing to do with seeing my husband for the first time in forever. I'd have forgotten what you look like, if it weren't for holos and our last conversation."

Though her tone was light, almost teasing, Chesnee felt a stab regardless. Almost a year hadn't been long enough for him to forget what she looked like. It had, however, been long enough to build a plastiglass wall between them. He wasn't sure how to surmount that wall…or if either of them even wanted to.

"Are you giving me the tour?"

"What?" Startled, Chesnee looked down at her. "A tour?"

"Yes." Sylvia regarded him as though this should have been self-evident. "This is your flagship, is it not? I would like to see where my husband has spent his time." When he did not immediately answer, she stopped dead in the middle of the corridor and untangled her arm from his in order to face him. "Surely you're not too busy today to give you wife a tour of your pride and joy?"

They stared at each other for a handful of heartbeats, and then Chesnee smoothly stepped forward and tucked her back into his side. If she wanted to see *Winds of Change*, he would show her. Perhaps it could be the first crack in that wall between them.

"Certainly not." He offered her a dry smile, his heart both constricting and jumping at the pleased surprise that flashed across her face before she schooled her expression into cool politeness. "Haven't you heard there's an impending trade agreement? My entire Blockade Division has suddenly found themselves with too much time on their hands."


All things considered, Chesnee enjoyed the day more than he thought he would have. Sylvia seemed genuinely interested in the workings of his command, and Chesnee found himself warming to his subject—and his wife—as they traversed the ship. His irritation with Kedis and his unwanted machinations did not diminish, but for a few hours it was easier to put it out of his mind.

An hour before dinner, Chesnee finally directed their steps to his quarters. "We can finish the tour later," he promised. "For now, you might like the chance to freshen up before we eat."

"Thank you, Giles. I'd like that."

Chesnee keyed in the door code and, once the door slid aside, waited for his wife to enter. He debated saying something about the decor in his office, but decided against it. It would be more amusing to see Sylvia's expression.

His wife did not disappoint.

Her dark eyes widened as she took in the heavy tapestries and dark paneling. Stopping in the center of the carpeted deck, she made a full circle in silence before raising an eyebrow at her husband. "This is..." She gestured with one hand, apparently at a loss for words.

"Appalling?" he suggested, following her inside. "Depressing?" He nodded toward the corner. "I think that one has eyes."

"Eyes?" Sylvia followed his gaze and shuddered. "I take it this place *came* like this? And you've just *lived* with it?"

She knew him too well. Chesnee shrugged. "I've been busy."

"Apparently." Sylvia shook her head. "I don't think I could stand looking at this all the time."

"You get used to it."

Chesnee strode across the office and opened the door to his quarters. The first thing he saw was a pile of luggage. Had his wife brought her *entire* wardrobe aboard his ship? Maybe she was better off with her own quarters after all.

He sucked in a breath, but let it out quickly. *Kedis probably didn't tell her how long she'd be here, so she came prepared.* He turned back toward Sylvia. "My cabin and hygiene unit are through here. Macy's already brought your things."

"Thank you."

For a few seconds, they stood there, staring at each other. Chesnee's only consolation was that Sylvia seemed to feel the awkwardness as keenly as he did. Finally, Sylvia cleared her throat, breaking the uncomfortable silence. "I won't be long."

"Take all the time you need."

That earned him a smile. "I know how you are about punctuality, Giles. I won't be late for dinner."

Chesnee only inclined his head. He watched Sylvia approach her luggage and then forced himself to pivot and march back out into his office. It was best that she was occupied for a little while.

He had a call to make.


"Admiral." Kedis answered immediately, as though he'd been expecting Chesnee to contact him. His voice was cheerful. "To what do I owe the honor?"

Behind his desk, Chesnee drew himself up stiffly in his chair. "I think you already know the answer to that question, Leo."

Kedis gracefully inclined his head. "Indeed, I do. I take it your wife has arrived safely, then?"

"You had no right to involve her in this."

Kedis's holographic eyes considered him for a long moment. At last, he brought a teacup to his lips and sipped. Once he had set the cup aside, he said, "On that point, Giles, I'm afraid you are quite mistaken. You, dear Admiral, have well and truly entered the realm of politics now, whether you like it or not. Our impending trade agreement means that you will be required to make a few appearances here on Sta'Gloa—and what better way to do that than with your lovely wife on your arm?"

It galled Chesnee to tell Kedis anything personal, but there was the possibility, however slight, that on this front Kedis had failed to do his due diligence. Perhaps he didn't know. "My wife and I," the words tasted bitter in his mouth, "have not exactly been on speaking terms lately."

"I know. And I do sympathize with your domestic troubles, but our current situation must take precedence." One side of Kedis's mouth turned up in a sly smile. "Perhaps you will find that now is the best time to mend fences, as they say."

Chesnee bristled. "Have you been interrogating my wife, Kedis?"

"Oh, no. There was no need for that. It's common knowledge among your wife's friends that you had a sharp disagreement right before you assumed command of the Blockade Division." Kedis gave an insouciant shrug. "After that, all that needed to be done was make a few discreet inquiries into the state of her comm logs, and the rest of the story revealed itself."

"You have no right to meddle in our affairs."

Kedis waved a hand. "Oxygen out the airlock, Admiral. I told you, there are much more important things at stake now. It's important that we present a unified front, and this is exactly the type of situation where a man like you would be expected to showcase his lovely wife." His dark eyes glittered. "It eases people's minds, you see, when a military commander such as yourself brings civilians into a situation like this."

"Just because I can see the logic behind this doesn't mean I like it," Chesnee said grimly.

"Consider it a gift." Kedis smiled again. "You'll be moving on from here, Admiral. Wouldn't it be nice to take your wife of twenty-six years with you?" He glanced off to the side. "One of my aides will send you the list of upcoming social events you will be expected to attend." He held up a hand before Chesnee could speak. "It will not be extensive—I am well aware you have a Blockade Division to command."

He'd taken the words right out of Chesnee's mouth. The Admiral settled for a cold glare instead.

Kedis smiled at him. "Trust me, Admiral. This is a good thing. You'll see." With that, he cut the comm connection.

Chesnee sat for a moment in his chair, fuming and staring at the blank spot the Ambassador's holographic form had just occupied.

He then exhaled loudly and tried to push his anger aside before he interacted with his wife again. *It's not Sylvia's fault Leo Kedis is a manipulative bastard.*

Taking his frustration out on her would only result in an even more unpleasant situation…and he had no desire for his marital issues to end up a topic of discussion on his flagship. And it would—thanks to Kedis his crew had nothing better to do than talk.

That first dinner was one of the most awkward evenings of Chesnee's life. Oh, in some respects it was easy to play the role of a magnanimous host, introducing Sylvia to Captain Sanford and everyone else who usually dined with him. The hard part was bridging the chasm that now existed between him and his wife. They knew each other, but they both changed in the past year—and some of those changes lurked beneath the surface like water mines waiting to explode and maim the unwary.

After inadvertently bumping into one of those mines at the start of the meal—when he had unthinkingly commented on Sylvia's job as a real estate agent without knowing she had given that up since moving back to Veridia—Chesnee realized he needed to change tactics. He needed treat conversation with her like Kedis was involved, as though every word was a potential weapon that could be turned against him. Things had proceeded more smoothly after that, though he could still feel the plastic, superficial awkwardness of it all.

That hadn't changed by the time they retired for the evening. It was at that moment Chesnee had to ask himself if his pride was *really* worth the awkwardness of standing in the same cabin as the wife he hadn't seen in almost a year and realizing they would be sharing the same bed. Sylvia just looked at him, her chin lifted, her dark eyes flashing a kind of challenge…and he realized it was.

The darkness of his cabin, once they both undressed and crawled into bed, had—oddly— helped to chip away at the barrier between them.

After ten or fifteen minutes of stilted, awkward silence, Sylvia said quietly, "I know you probably don't believe me, but there hasn't been anyone but you. Not," she added as an afterthought, "that I didn't have the opportunity."

Regret stabbed at him. Chesnee swallowed, closing his eyes against the darkness. "I know." If there was one thing anyone could say about his wife, she was loyal. Intensely, fiercely loyal. "Sylvia, I—" He broke off, the words clogging in his throat.

*You're an Admiral, blast it,* he scolded himself. *Be an Admiral. Be a man.*

He swallowed again. "I should not have said what I did before I left. I was…angry…and I was trying to—"

"—hurt me," Sylvia finished softly. "The way I hurt you."

They both lay still and silent in the bunk, not touching; a good twenty centimeters separated them.

"It did hurt," Chesnee found himself saying. "That even you thought I was done for." He held up a hand, though neither of them could see it in the darkness. "I understand why you thought it, I just…"

"You expected me to have more faith in you."

"Yes. You, of all people."

It was her turn to be silent. He could hear her inhale and then she said conversationally, "I didn't like living on Taryn without you."

That surprised Chesnee, though he supposed it shouldn't have; she had after all moved back to Veridia. He had wondered why, but at the time she hadn't given him a reason.

"With you gone and us not speaking, it made some of my usual social engagements rather pointless." The covers rustled as she rolled over onto her side to face him. "I decided I'd much rather be around our family and friends on Veridia." A wry note entered her voice. "Not to mention the cost of living is a little cheaper."

That startled a laugh out of Chesnee. "I never thought you paid the slightest bit of attention to our finances."

"Oh, I do." He heard the smile in her voice. "I pretended not to, but I always keep an eye on things."

Bemused, Chesnee shook his head. "Do you mean to say we could have avoided all of those arguments over your new wardrobe, or the apartment remodel you wanted, or—"

"—that boat you were eying?" Sylvia asked slyly.

"'Eying' was all I was doing."

"Of course. That was why you were watching eight different listings for it."

"If the price had ever dropped into something I thought we could afford…" Chesnee shrugged. It was oxygen out the airlock now.

"I only spent what I thought we could afford. Besides," Sylvia's hand suddenly brushed his. "I always enjoyed the aftermath of our arguments."

This prompted another short chuckle. "You certainly did."

Her fingers brushed his again before retreating. "So did you."

It was true, though admitting that to her at the moment touched all the raw places inside him. Instead, he shifted subjects. "I hope you know what Kedis has gotten you into. We'll be rubbing shoulders with the crème de la crème of Coalition political society." His tone made it clear what he thought about *that*.

Sylvia made a humming sound in the back of her throat. "It's not like we don't have any experience dealing with those people."

That might be true…but it didn't mean Chesnee *liked* it.

# Chapter 77

A few cams and reporters lingered around Ferndale, but the twins managed to avoid them. They could not, however, avoid the aftermath of the interview. As they discovered that evening, the interview ran on each of the reporter's networks almost in its entirety.

That wasn't so bad in and of itself; their grandfather even commented that they'd done a good job. The real trouble lay with the sources that picked it up afterward—and cherry-picked sound bytes designed to maximize the salacious and outrageous. It didn't take long for Lilia to grow heartily sick of seeing their faces whenever she happened to turn on the holoprojector.

The only saving grace was that the furor died out less than two days later, eclipsed by a newer, much bigger scoop.

Galactic Union Blockade Division commander Admiral Chesnee himself and his wife would be setting foot on Sta'Gloan soil to attend an event held by Dion Pamos that evening.

Lilia didn't know how the woman had gotten her hands on the information, but Meridia Vaughn broke the story to the Coalition a whole half-hour before Riley Callahan opened a joint Nancom channel to her and Kevin.

[For your sake,] their NCDC handler said without preamble, [I hope Representative Pamos's dinner tonight isn't one of those evenings you were counting on skipping out of your bodyguard duties.

If you have business, you'll have to tell your clients there's been an unavoidable delay. You two need to be there.]

Lilia snorted aloud, though of course Callahan couldn't hear her. The sound echoed faintly in her changing stall; she and Kevin had just arrived at Chakin's for a sparring session. [Good morning to you too, Mr. Callahan.]

Callahan ignored the faint sarcasm in her Nancom voice. [It is imperative that you two be there tonight. I've just received word that Ambassador Kedis made a last minute addition to Pamos's guest list.]

[If you mean that he's bringing Admiral Chesnee and his wife,] Kevin said from the men's locker room, [we've heard already.]

Stunned silence greeted this pronouncement, but Callahan rallied quickly. [Let me guess—Lon or one of your other brothers?]

[Actually, it's all over the media. One of the reporters who—] Kevin began.

[—interviewed us just broke the story,] Lilia finished.

Another stretch of silence as Callahan digested this. [How did *she* know?] He brushed his own words aside. [Never mind that. Point is, Pamos's party is now an extremely high-priority event and the NCDC wants you two there.]

Lilia pulled on her white gloves before settling her facemask on her head and picking up her fencing blades. [We were going to be there anyway.]

Dion Pamos had sent out invitations for this dinner the day after the Triumvirate voted in favor of the trade agreement and had specifically included them on his invitation to their grandfather. She saw no point in telling Callahan that, however.

[Good.]

[And for the record, Mr. Callahan,] Kevin said dryly, [we've been pretty good about attending everything the Board wants us to attend.]

[They can't complain too much,] Callahan agreed. [Tonight is important, though. With Admiral Chesnee and the Ambassador both in attendance, Freedom's Children or some other group of nutcases could decide tonight is a prime opportunity for another attack. Stay as close as you can without raising suspicion. I'll be in touch.]

With that, he closed his Nancom channel.

Rolling her eyes at their handler's abrupt dismissal, Lilia exited the locker room and stepped out into the fencing arena. Kevin had just emerged from the men's locker room; they met in an empty fencing square and saluted each other.

"Well," Kevin said, raising his blade and settling into an aggressive stance. "Tonight should be even more interesting."

Lilia just shook her head, her lips pressed into a thin line behind her facemask. She hadn't been thrilled about attending Pamos's dinner party in the first place; this was icing on the cake. *Good thing we're sparring this morning,* she thought wryly. Maybe she could work some of her irritation out before tonight.


She put a holo-call through Alexis that afternoon. Voice-only would have been easier, but it felt like too much of a cop-out. "Hey." She managed a small smile, settling down at her desk in her bedroom. The penthouse was quiet; Kevin was busy and everyone else was at Triumvirate Tower. "I don't know if you've seen it or not, but we took your advice."

"I've seen it." Alexis pursed her lips, her expression, uncertain, before she offered, "I think it's good that you did an interview finally. Now maybe they'll leave you alone."

"Maybe."

Awkward silence fell between them, and frustration tightened Lilia's throat muscles. *This is terrible.* she thought, glancing down. *All these years we've been friends and we can't even talk to each other.*

The worst part was that it was mostly her fault. Again.

"You got shot at again."

Lilia's eyes snapped to Alexis's. "Yeah." She grimaced. "That wasn't fun at all."

"But you were able to help that lady and her children?"

"Yeah. They needed it." Lilia shook her head, a brisk motion that sent her short hair flying. "They shouldn't have had to stay trapped in occupied territory any longer. Not now."

Alexis nodded in agreement, but after a couple more awkward seconds stretched between them, she said, "It would probably have been different if her husband was still alive. Wouldn't it?"

"Probably." Lilia sighed. "I think a lot of things would have been different for her if her husband was still alive." She shifted uncomfortably in her desk chair, an apology bubbling up inside her. "Look, Alexis—"

Her best friend beat her to the punch. "I'm sorry I pushed you to talk about you-know-who," she said in a rush, her dark eyes regretful. "I was so excited thinking about the possibilities of it all I didn't stop to think how scary it probably is for you."

Lilia opened her mouth, closed it, and then opened it again, but no words came. She blew out a surprised breath, flicking her gaze up to the ceiling. "And I shouldn't have snapped at you, Alexis." She dropped her gaze to her best friend's face. "Forgive me for that, please."`

Alexis nodded again, looking relieved. "Forgive *me* for pushing you." She tucked another wayward black curl behind one ear. "I just…" She stopped abruptly, looking as if she knew she was about to veer into sensitive territory again.

"Just spit it out," Lilia said wryly. "Like you said before, you're my best friend. If you don't tell me these things, who will?"

Laughing a little, Alexis leaned in. Her face took on an impish cast Lilia knew well. "I was going to say it's just that I can see the effect Jasper has had on you. He's a good influence; he makes you think."

Lilia rolled her eyes, a faint flush rising to her cheeks. "Oh, he makes me think all right. Sometimes about things I'd rather not."

"Like seeing the human beings behind the Tarynian uniforms."

A few months before, those quiet words would have made Lilia flinch. Now, she only nodded slowly. "Yeah." She hesitated, and then took a deep breath. "Is it really that obvious that he likes me? From the media coverage, that is?"

Alexis just giggled. "Why do you think that reporter asked you?" She grinned slyly. "It's a little harder to tell you're interested back, but for somebody who knows you?"

Lilia's blush deepened. "Great."

"It's not that bad," Alexis said consolingly, but she ruined it by giggling again. "You're too cute."

"It would never work," Lilia found herself blurting out. "I mean, how could it?" She shook her head. "Even with a trade agreement in place, he's *still* a G.U. lieutenant." Her chest ached all of a sudden. *This is reality—and the reality is that when it's all said and done, we're still on opposite sides.*

"Well," Alexis said after a very long pause, "there's no telling how things will shake out in the next few months. If you're supposed to be together, the Lord will show you how."

Lilia shook her head again. "Alexis, I don't know if we are or not."

Her best friend just bestowed a gentle smile on her. "But wouldn't you like the chance to find out?"

Lilia found herself nodding before she could think too hard about it.

"Well," Alexis waved a hand, "instead of denying that you like him, why don't you give him a chance? Why don't you give *yourself* a chance? Find out if the door is even open before you decide to shut it."

Another long paused ensued, before Lilia exhaled, a trifle shakily. "Okay. Okay, I will."

"Good." Alexis's impish look returned. "And then you can tell me all about it."

They move on to a rundown of the latest happenings at the café, and Lilia forgot about Jasper for a while. She was too busy holding her sides and laughing as Alexis described an encounter they'd had a few days before with a customer who was convinced Ambassador Kedis had planted bugs all over Sonela…including one at the bottom of his soup bowl.

Several hours later, Lilia and Kevin stood in the vast expanse of Dion Pamos's living room scanning the crowd of guests who had already arrived. Faint strains of elegant music could be heard above the chatter of dozens of conversations, though the source was not immediately visible. Floor-to-ceiling windows draped with a dark gold valance framed one side of the room; the other walls were pale gold. Arranged tastefully around the room were assorted couches, chairs, and end tables in various shades of brown, dark red, and gold. The floor was covered in a richly patterned carpet that tied everything else together.

Lilia leaned toward her brother. "Clearly, Representative Pamos and I have different definitions of the term 'dinner party'."

The evening was a formal affair, and far larger than either of them had expected. Dion Pamos and his wife, as it turned out, occupied another of the penthouse suites in the Amethyst Towers. This had surprised the twins when they arrived—Kevin having previously mentioned to Lilia that one of Franco's buddies lived here as well.

"I must admit, I was expecting something a tad smaller." Kevin glanced around, pulling the collar of his white shirt away from his neck with two fingers. He stopped as he caught the pointed look his sister threw him and just grimaced. "I think I've spent more time in this tuxedo lately than I have anything else."

"At least it looks good on you." Lilia nudged him with her elbow, nodding to the other side of the living room. She wore a sleek black dress with a halter neckline and sleeves that capped her shoulders. The fabric glittered with subtle pinpricks beneath the penthouse's soft, warm lights. "I think I see Parisa. Let's head that way."

Along the way, the pair of them nodded greetings to other various guests. A few months before Lilia would have never thought it possible that she would actually start to know some of the people in her grandfather's social circle, but at this point it was inevitable. The hardest part, however, was still being polite to the snobs and bigots who turned up their noses at her family.

*Hopefully Birch isn't here tonight*, she thought, raising a hand in greeting as she caught Parisa Briscoe's eye.

The sprite-like redheaded Glo'Stean woman finished her conversation with an older woman with black hair pinned up in hundred little braids and came forward to meet the twins with a broad, genuine smile. She wore a strapless gown of sea-blue that floated down from her hips.

"Lilia, Kevin!" Parisa took Lilia's hands. "I am glad you could make it tonight." Dropping her voice, she added, "And thank you for providing me an excuse to get away—Mrs. Efar was telling me *all* about her daughter's upcoming wedding." She shook her head slightly. "I don't think I needed to know they were considering matching the groomsmen's undergarments to their boutonnieres."

The twins both laughed, and then Lilia smiled impishly. "Is Dawn here tonight?"

"Oh, yes." Parisa matched her expression. "I think under different circumstances she would have preferred to stay home tonight, but since your brother was going to be here…" She held out one hand palm up as if to say, *what do you expect?*

Kevin craned his neck to see over the heads of other guests. "Is Admiral Chesnee here yet?"

"I don't think so." Parisa took two champagne glasses from a tray held by a passing server 'bot and handed one to Lilia. "Shane and I have been here for a good twenty minutes and I don't think we'd have missed the kind of stir *his* arrival will cause."

"Definitely not," Lilia agreed, accepting the glass. "Even with this crowd." She wanted to ask if Parisa had seen Ambassador Kedis yet, but refrained. Both Parisa and Kevin would see through that to what she really wanted to know, and she would rather avoid that. Her heart, however, was already racing with anticipation.

*Calm down*, she scolded herself. *It's not like it's been that long since you saw each other last.*

It felt like much longer, though. Lilia didn't let herself dwell on what that meant.

"Mrs. Briscoe, Miss Strong, Mr. Strong—I mean, Captain Strong," someone said from behind them. "Delighted you could join us tonight."

The three of them turned to find their host standing less than a meter away, a small, slight woman with black hair, and oval face, and proud, dark eyes on his arm. Dion Pamos wore a black tuxedo, while his wife was clad in a clinging gown of silky crimson.

The twins exchanged imperceptible darting glances—they were both sure Pamos's slip had been on purpose—before stepping forward to greet their hosts. The Pamoses had been busy with other guests when they arrived with Aiden and their older brothers.

"I must confess," Parisa said with a smile, "I am quite interested in meeting Admiral Chesnee." She shook her head in slight amazement. "Of all the soirees happening in Sonela these days, however did you manage to convince him to come here?"

*Yes*, Lilia thought, her violet eyes narrowing slightly, *how* did *you manage that?*

Pamos only waved a hand, smiling broadly. "My dear Mrs. Briscoe, let me state that fortune favors the bold and leave it at that." He glanced at his wrist. "Speaking of which, the Admiral should be arriving any moment. Ambassador Kedis wished to make an appearance after most of our guests had already joined us."

It was probably her imagination, but Lilia fancied his dark, beady eyes flicked in her direction for just a second. She kept her expression politely neutral.

One corner of Kevin's mouth turned up in a shrewd smile. "Makes for a more dramatic entrance."

Parisa laughed, and Mrs. Pamos tittered. "That does seem to be the Ambassador's style," she said, in a deeper, huskier voice than either of the twins expected.

"Well, if you'll excuse us…?" Pamos waved a hand again. "Enjoy yourselves."

After the Pamoses had disappeared into the crowd, Parisa looked at the twins. "I really ought to find Shane. I promised I'd rescue him." Her forehead crinkled with something halfway between amusement and concern. "Some of these older ladies find him quite…dashing… and they're surprisingly forward."

The twins both nodded in understanding. As Parisa turned away, Kevin shook his head. "She's never mentioned that before, but it doesn't surprise me. I've noticed Shane tends to get surrounded when he's talking." He lifted his eyebrows in wry amusement. "I suppose that's the downside to being as charismatic as he is."

Lilia started to agree, but at that moment an excited murmur rippled through the crowd in the living room, followed by a hush. Her heart skipped a beat and then resumed pounding in double-time. Chesnee was here, which meant Kedis was here, which meant *Jasper* was finally here.

She took a deep breath and exhaled slowly, willing herself to look normal, while she, Kevin, and everyone else in the room turned to face the wide doorway leading from the living room to the foyer.

Kedis stood in the doorway, impeccably dressed as always, standing next to a tall man in a resplendent gray G.U. uniform so crisp it could probably draw blood if someone accidentally brushed up against him. Even an untrained eye could tell this man held a high rank—the front left of his uniform jacket glittered with a multitude of colorful bars and medals. He had a craggy face and graying sandy hair.

The woman on his arm formed a stunning counterpoint. She was dressed in a strapless ruby-red sheath that flared out at her knees, setting off her golden skin, with dark, luscious curls piled atop her head. Behind the pair stood Lon, Jasper, and Renner. Lon wore a tuxedo, the other two, as always, wore dress uniforms.

Dion Pamos materialized in front of them, having slipped through his guests with practiced ease. "Ambassador Kedis, welcome to our humble abode."

Lilia let *that* outrageous statement pass without blinking an eye; just like everyone else she was too engrossed in the scene unfolding before them.

"Representative Pamos," Kedis said smoothly, gesturing to the side, "may I present Admiral Chesnee and his lovely wife, Sylvia?"

The Admiral and his wife both bowed stiffly, amidst a wave of hushed whispers. Pamos and his wife returned the bow, and then Pamos held his arms wide in an expansive gesture. "We are delighted to have you with us tonight. Please, join us."

Lilia lost sight of the Chesnees as the men and women around them surged forward to meet the Tarynians. She turned back to find her grandfather; she had a feeling it would be a while before Jasper was free to talk to her. Besides, given Lon's connection to Kedis and Chesnee, it was entirely likely that her brother would bring the Admiral to meet their grandfather.

As she did, she heard a woman remark to another, "What are the odds that the Admiral's wife would show up wearing the same color as Ana Pamos?" The conversation devolved into catty comments about who wore what best and Lilia quickly left them behind.

Halls led off to either side of the living room; after a moment of searching, she found her grandfather in Pamos's study. Instead of the dark, heavy furniture and decor Lilia had expected from Pamos, the study was surprisingly airy. The desk to one side of the room and the end tables scattered about were made of glass and silvery metal, while the chairs were modern-looking white and silver contraptions that were probably more comfortable than they appeared. The bookcases were black wood; the carpet was a pristine white plush. Lilia's heels sank into it slightly as she stepped into the room.

Her grandfather stood with Helen Urquart and Egan Ashford by the window on the far end of the room, looking out at the impressive view of Sonela's evening skyline. Aiden glanced toward the door as Lilia entered and his face softened with a small smile. The other two followed his gaze and Lilia nodded politely to each of the Representatives in turn.

"I don't mean to interrupt," she said as she approached, "but I thought you might like to know that Admiral Chesnee and his wife are here."

Ashford and Urquart exchanged glances. "Fashionably late, I see," Urquart observed, her lips pursing slightly.

"Come now, Helena." Ashford smiled, though it held no real warmth. "This has the Ambassador written all over it. Military men are more punctual than that."

"True." Drawing herself up to her full height, Urquart swept across the study to the door. "I confess I *am* curious to meet the man."

"I think we all are," Aiden said as he brought up the rear, moving a touch more slowly than his companions.

Lilia waited until her grandfather reached her and looped her arm through his. She almost asked if he was all right, but stopped herself at the last second, her eyes darting suspiciously around the room. *I wouldn't put it past Pamos to have bugged his penthouse in case anybody says anything interesting.*

# CHAPTER 78

W HEN Lilia, Aiden, and the two Representatives rejoined the rest of the party in the massive living room, they spotted Chesnee easily. He and his wife stood with Kedis in the center of the room, surrounded by people. Lilia was just wondering what their best course of action was when Lon sent her a channel request.

[Hey, Lil, where are you? And where's Grandfather?] Through the crowd, Lilia saw her brother glancing around the room. Their eyes met and he smiled crookedly. [Never mind, I see you. Bring Grandfather and come meet Admiral Chesnee.]

Lilia leaned in close to Aiden. "Grandfather, Lon wants you to come meet the Admiral."

Aiden gave her a look of mild curiosity, though his green eyes sharpened. "Oh, does he?"

"That's what he said." Lilia glanced over her shoulder, searching for her other brothers, and found Kevin, Derek, and Michael converging on them. Lon had apparently Nancommed them as well.

With Aiden leading the way, the five of them worked their way through the clumps of other guests to Kedis, the Admiral, and his wife. Lon joined them as soon as they arrived. A greeting line of sorts had formed, but he bypassed this without a care and deftly cut in front of a Lanxian businessman and his wife.

They both shot Lon dark looks. Lilia bit the inside of her lip, resisting the urge to apologize to the pair. When her gaze turned to the three Tarynians, she noticed that the Admiral's expression remained stoic, but Kedis and Mrs. Chesnee both looked mildly amused by this breach of decorum.

"Admiral Chesnee," Lon said without preamble, motioning to his grandfather and siblings. "May I introduce my grandfather, Representative Aiden Monroe, my brothers, Michael, Derek, and Kevin, and my sister, Lilia?" He then indicated the Chesnees. "This is Admiral Chesnee and his wife, Sylvia."

"Representative Monroe," Chesnee said in Tarynian, "it is a pleasure to meet you." He took a step forward, his hand outstretched.

Aiden, who wore an autotranslator, shook his hand gravely. "I would congratulate you, Admiral, on your military success if it had not resulted in hardship for our system." He smiled slightly. "But, that is behind us now."

"So it would seem." Chesnee shook each of the Strong siblings' hands, as did his wife. The Admiral then looked Lilia and her brothers over, before turning back to Lon. "I can certainly see the family resemblance."

His gaze flicked to Lilia and Kevin. "I understand you two were the ones who assisted the Ambassador in procuring an audience with the Triumvirate."

The twins exchanged infinitesimal glances, before Kevin nodded. "We were," he replied in Tarynian.

Mrs. Chesnee looked a trifle surprised at this, but Chesnee's expression did not change as he inclined his head. "That was brave of you."

Feeling uncomfortable again, Lilia raised one shoulder in a shrug, before answering in Tarynian, "Lon convinced us it was necessary." She swallowed, her thoughts flashing to the fringes of free Glo'Stea. "There may be a few pockets of resistance, Admiral, but I know that the majority of our people throughout the Coalition are very grateful for the cease-fire and this opportunity for peace."

Chesnee met her gaze, and she had the sudden impression that he was studying her, correlating what he saw in her standing before him with what he no doubt knew about her.

After a few seconds, the Admiral nodded. "Speaking of those pockets of resistance, Miss Strong, I believe you and your brother," he tipped his head toward Kevin, "were also involved in the attack on that convoy a few days ago by Freedom's Children?"

Kevin grimaced. "We were. Can't say it was a pleasant experience, but we survived." He smiled wryly. "I'm sure you've heard the justification they cite for the attack."

"I have." Chesnee's craggy face settled into grave lines. "I hope Mrs. Hito and her children are doing well."

Lilia blinked, but otherwise kept a straight face. *I shouldn't be surprised he knows her name.* Mrs. Hito's husband had, after all, been a G.U. officer. "They're grieving, Admiral, but other than that I believe they are fine."

Chesnee nodded again, and his wife took the opportunity to raise a fingertip to indicate the autotranslator in her ear and ask, "Do many people in the Coalition speak Tarynian?"

Kevin flashed her a smile. "Not many, Mrs. Chesnee."

"Although I am sure that will change now," Aiden interjected, before nodding to Kedis. "Ambassador."

Kedis returned the nod. "Representative."

Looking at their little group, Lilia suddenly felt dizzy, overcome by the surrealism of the moment. *We're standing in the same room as the commander of the Blockade Division, carrying on polite conversation. Who would have ever dreamed that possible?*

Behind Kedis, she glimpsed Jasper watching them and a tiny jolt of electricity shot through her.

Aiden nodded to the Admiral and his wife. "Enjoy your stay on Sta'Gloa, Admiral." His eyes glinted with a touch of humor. "It must be quite a different view from the ground."

Chesnee cracked a smile. "Indeed, Representative. Quite different."

They stepped away to allow the rest of the guests to meet the Chesnees, but Lilia couldn't help glancing over her shoulder in Jasper's direction. Their eyes met; he smiled at her and cast a significant glance at the other side of the living room. His implication was clear; he would meet her there when he got the chance.

Lilia gave him a tiny nod in return and followed her family through the Pamoses' penthouse.


"So that was Aiden Monroe," Chesnee said in a low voice to Kedis, watching the elderly Representative and his grandchildren weave their way across the crowded living room.

"An interesting individual," Kedis replied, before stepping forward to introduce Chesnee and his wife to the next few people waiting to meet them.

Chesnee suppressed a sigh. The Ambassador had prepped them for this, giving them a crash course in the most notable faces of Coalition high society—political and otherwise. The problem was that he found events like this tedious and time-consuming. A glance at his wife told him that she was beginning to enjoy herself, despite the awkwardness of being surrounded by complete strangers, but Chesnee himself couldn't wait for the night to end.

Only a few of the faces on Kedis's list bore any real interest to him...and he'd just met five of them. He'd been curious about Lon Strong's grandfather and siblings for months; it was gratifying to finally meet them.

One corner of Chesnee's mouth lifted in a rueful smile. *I'd have preferred to have the chance to actually* talk *to them longer, but long conversations are clearly not on the Ambassador's agenda for tonight.*

In fact, as the evening wore on, even Sylvia picked up on this. Looping her arm through her husband's as the Pamoses finally directed everyone to the dining room for dinner, she leaned in close enough to whisper, "Is the Ambassador purposefully keeping us from talking to anyone more than two minutes?"

"You've noticed that too?" Chesnee replied, barely moving his lips.

"Oh, yes." Sylvia maintained a pleasant smile, but her eyes darted around the room. "It's almost like he doesn't quite trust us to manage on our own."

At that, a genuine chuckle rumbled in Chesnee's chest. "You may be right, my dear. Although," he bent his head toward hers, "I imagine it is more on my account than yours. He probably thinks I've spent too much time on my battlecruiser away from the rest of society and is afraid I don't remember how to behave."

To his delight, Sylvia laughed. The tinkling sound brought back a slew of memories; Chesnee found himself wondering again how they could have possibly spent so much time apart.

Sylvia patted his arm. "He doesn't know you very well at all, Giles." Her dark eyes twinkled. "You only misbehave on purpose."


The rest of the evening dragged on. Dinner was delicious—some sort of beef dish Lilia had never heard of served over fat noodles, with a salad or steamed vegetables on the side—but she found it increasingly hard to sit still.

The dining room, also decorated in rich browns, golds, and reds, was large enough to hold a dozen round tables. The Pamoses had broken their family up, seating Aiden, Michael, and Derek at one table, and the twins at another a few meters away. Lilia and Kevin knew the other guests at their table only in passing. They were a couple of lower-tier aides and their wives.

Glancing around, Lilia noticed that Shane Briscoe and his wife were seated at the table in the center of the large room with the Chesnees, Kedis, and the Pamoses, along with Representative Zane Chas, who was alone. His wife had apparently been unable to attend. She did not immediately see Lon, Jasper, or Renner. While slightly disappointing, that didn't surprise her. Pamos and his wife were no doubt attempting to place their most interesting guests where they thought they would have the most impact.

Toward the end of the meal, Lilia excused herself to go in search of a hygiene unit. The closest one down the hall was occupied; one of the server 'bots gave her directions to another off of Mrs. Pamos's sunroom, but cautioned there was a line. Her heels made no sound on the plush carpet as she made her way in that direction.

The sunroom was dimly lit; the only illumination came from a few tiny golden globes scattered around the edges of the room. It was full of windows, giving it an airy feel, with white walls and striped ice blue and purple cushions on the wicker furniture that matched the curtains tied back at the corners of the room. Lilia reached the doorway in time to catch a glimpse of the hem of Sylvia Chesnee's red gown swishing into the hygiene unit.

Just before Lilia stepped across the threshold, something *moved* from a shadowy corner of the room.

She froze instinctively and watched in shock as the unmistakable figure of a woman clad in dark gray nano-armor materialized out of thin air. The figure glided across the white carpet to the hygiene unit, drawing a nanoblade as she went. Intent on her target, she didn't notice Lilia in the doorway.

One corner of Lilia's brain noted that the woman must have been using stealth mode, but the larger part of her reacted with horror. *She's going to kill Sylvia Chesnee!*

For a split-second, Lilia remained rooted to the spot, racked with indecision. Her options were limited—and terrible. If she screamed, she'd momentarily draw the assassin's attention…but she'd have to reveal herself as a Guardian to survive the inevitable attack. If she drew her nanoblades and went on the offensive, she'd *still* reveal she was a Guardian.

That wasn't something she'd planned to do tonight. Not here.

*Get over it*, she scolded herself. *The whole point of joining the NCDC was to save people's lives.* Sucking in a deep breath, she proceeded to scream at the top of her lungs, "Help! Assassin!"

At the same time, she blasted through her brothers' open Nancom channels, [Someone's trying to kill Mrs. Chesnee in the sunroom!]

Startled, the would-be assassin spun around a meter from the hygiene unit door. Her masked features reflected the room, giving no inkling as to her expression, but Lilia had the distinct impression she was seriously ticked off.

The woman growled low in her throat, obviously assessing her options. She could attack Lilia and shut her up before she dispatched the Admiral's wife, or she could kill her primary target and worry about Lilia after the fact.

If she were the assassin, Lilia knew which option she'd pick. *Have to distract her!*

Switching to Tarynian, she shouted, "Mrs. Chesnee, don't open the door!"

The wooden door would offer laughable protection from a nanoblade, but the Admiral's wife didn't need to make the assassin's job any easier by doing something stupid like poking her head out to see what all the commotion was about.

With another growl, the assassin made her choice. She lunged for the hygiene unit, nanoblade flashing in the dim, golden light from the floor globes—and so did Lilia, drawing both of her own nanoblades and materializing her armor from shoulder to fingertips in the process.

Hurling herself between the assassin and the hygiene unit, Lilia caught the blow meant for the door on one of her blades and deflected it to the side. Moving was awkward in her gown, but she'd never been more thankful that she always picked dresses that didn't confine her legs.

Shouts echoed in the distance; heavy footsteps thudded through the penthouse toward them.

The assassin lunged forward again, counting on her nano-armor to protect her as she held her blade out in front of her in a straight line intended to bypass Lilia's defenses and impale her.

Lilia batted the blade away again and sidestepped, but the force behind the blow was a little too much for her. The tip of the nanoblade caught her armor just above her right elbow and punched through. Lilia didn't feel it, however, not with the adrenaline pumping through her veins and the way her heart was pounding.

Settling into a defensive stance with both blades in front of the door, she leveled the assassin with a defiant glare and hissed in a low voice, "I *dare* you to come any closer."

She wouldn't last long attempting to fight in her gown—not without destroying it, they both knew that—but time was not on the assassin's side. Reinforcements were almost upon them.

If body language could kill, Lilia would have been a smoldering pile of ash. Cursing fluidly in Glo'Stean, the woman abruptly backed away and thrust her nanoblade into her ISF. The air between the two of them suddenly rippled as a portal sphere appeared in the space between the wicker coffee table and Lilia. The woman wasted no time in plunging through it headfirst.

Lilia wasn't surprised; she'd half-expected an escape route of this sort. She sheathed both of her own nanoblades and dematerialized her armor just as the portal disappeared with a rush of air and a group of men burst into the sunroom.

Lon was first, followed by two of Pamos's security guards, and, to Lilia's surprise, both Admiral Chesnee and Dion Pamos. Lilia flattened a hand against her chest, allowing herself to sag back against the hygiene unit door for a brief second. Her knees had decided to go a little wobbly, though not from her encounter with the assassin. *That was close.*

Pamos might know she and Kevin were Guardians, but it certainly wasn't something she wanted *Admiral Chesnee* knowing.

"Lights," Lon commanded, before demanding, "Was that a portal?" He had drawn his nanoblade; the two guards had drawn their pistols. The golden globes brightened to fully illuminate the room, but of course it was empty now save for Lilia.

"Looked like it," Lilia replied with a nod in the portal's direction. "She just disappeared."

Dion Pamos rounded on his two security guards. "How did she get in here in the first place without tripping my security alarms?" Instead of the frantic tones Lilia had expected, his voice was low and cold.

The two guards exchanged glances before shaking their heads in tandem. "We don't know, sir, but we'll find out."

Admiral Chesnee did not stop, but headed straight for Lilia and the hygiene unit. His sharp blue eyes scanned her from head to foot. In Tarynian, he said, "You're bleeding, Miss Strong."

*Forgot about that.* Lilia glanced down at her right arm; her forearm was red and slick. Swallowing, she forced a smile and moved away, covering the wound with her left hand. "I'm all right." She tipped her head toward the door. "Your wife is in there."

Chesnee rapped sharply on the door. "Sylvia? It's me. Are you all right?"

The door opened so suddenly it startled all of them and Sylvia Chesnee flew out, practically throwing herself into her husband's arms. Her face had lost its color. "What happened? All I heard was shouting."

She buried her face in the Admiral's chest for a moment before lifting her head to peer around. Her dark eyes found Lilia, widening when they took in the blood seeping between her fingers.

Pulling a small bandage from his ISF, Lon stepped up to his sister and gently examined her wound. "We've got to get this cleaned up." Via Nancom he asked, [What happened?]

Lilia's violet eyes flicked to his face. [She had a nanoblade and nano-armor, and I'm pretty sure she was using stealth mode to hide in here.]

Lon pressed his lips into a thin line. [That explains this.] He nodded to her arm as he pressed the bandage against the wound. [I'm guessing you were wearing armor?]

Lilia nodded and then winced as he applied pressure, but didn't protest.

"Miss Strong, are you all right?" Dion Pamos approached them, with the Chesnees right behind him. His face was the picture of concern, but cold fury lurked in his dark eyes.

"I'll be fine, Representative." Lilia managed another smile. "I don't think it's that bad."

Pamos glanced at Chesnee before looking back at her. "Can you tell us what happened?"

Briefly, Lilia gave them a slightly altered version of what had happened—the version that left out her holding the assassin off with her own nanoblades. Sylvia Chesnee's face lost even more color as she realized how close to death she had come; her eyes filled with tears. Lilia noticed that Admiral Chesnee's arm tightened instinctively around her shoulders.

When she finished, the Admiral gave her a keen look. "That was very brave of you, Miss Strong."

"Not really." Lilia shrugged uncomfortably. "I suppose I've spent too much time around my brothers. I couldn't just stand there." She motioned to the bottom of her gown with her left hand. "I forgot how hard these can be to move in, though."

Pamos looked at Mrs. Chesnee. "Do you need to lie down?" He waved a hand toward the doorway. "We have rooms if you—"

"No." Mrs. Chesnee shook her head. "I thank you, Representative, but I would prefer to remain with my husband."

The Admiral gave her an odd look. "I'll stay with you if you want to lie down, Sylvia," he said gruffly.

A tremulous smile curled her lips. "Thank you, Giles, but I'd rather finish dessert. Mrs. Pamos assured me it is the best chocolate mousse on Sta'Gloa, and so far I'm inclined to agree."

A flicker of amusement broke through Admiral Chesnee's stony expression. "Well, galaxies forbid you miss out on chocolate." He looked at Pamos. "We will be returning to the dining room."

Pamos only offered a silent bow in reply. Once the Chesnees had left the room, he sent his security guards after them with a series of instructions murmured in a low voice and turned back to Lilia. "I've sent for a med 'bot. We'll have you patched up in no time."

"Thank you, Representative." Lilia inclined her head. "It really isn't that bad."

She wanted to get out of here, to escape scrutiny and return to the dining room as well. Lon was hovering; while she appreciated his concern and support, she just wanted to sit down and pretend none of this had happened.

"Door, close," Pamos said unexpectedly. Lilia and her brother both stared at him as he drew in a deep breath and exhaled it in a rush. He then leveled an intense look at Lilia. "Tell me what really happened, if you please, Miss Strong."

Lilia blinked at him. "I beg your—"

"No." Pamos held up a hand. "I think it is time we all drop the pretense, Miss Strong. I know you are a Guardian."

# CHAPTER 79

SURPRISED, Lilia lifted her chin. She hadn't expected Pamos to actually come right out and *admit* that. Beside her, Lon stood very still.

A slight smile tilted one corner of the Representative's mouth. "I also know that if your grandfather has half the brains I suspect he does, you are aware that I know."

Lon folded his arms across his chest. "What's your point?"

"I'm not an idiot." Pamos shot him a scornful glance before turning back to Lilia. "You spun a good story, Miss Strong, but in the face of an armed assassin, both you and Mrs. Chesnee should probably be dead. How did you hold her off?" He motioned to her arm. "And why didn't you materialize your armor? Or did you?"

When she hesitated, he snapped, "Come now, we haven't got all night."

Lilia hesitated again, narrowing her eyes in distaste. She wasn't sure she should give this kind of information to Dion Pamos, of all people, but... "Whoever that woman was, Representative, she had a nanoblade. I had to draw mine to keep her from cutting through the door."

Pamos nodded, as though he had expected this. "And presumably you..." he waved his fingers in a circle, "...made it disappear just before we arrived?"

"Yes."

"Anything else?"

*Do I tell him?* She wasn't used to thinking of Pamos as anything but an opportunistic politician who was not above manipulating people to achieve his own goals. There were so many things she and her brothers couldn't tell anyone, things they knew or suspected about Freedom's Children, but…

A sense of certainty gelled inside her. *They've gone too far now.* Lilia wet her lips. "I think she had nano-armor too. And I think she was using stealth-mode to hide in your penthouse."

She nodded to the room around them. "She could have been hiding here for hours, which ensured your security didn't pick up on any sudden arrivals tonight."

She could tell she had surprised Pamos; he froze for a few seconds as he digested her words. He then arched a black eyebrow at her. "You left that out of your original story. Why would you tell me now?" He cocked his head to one side. "No concern for the impact this could have on your dear NCDC?"

*Tell me he didn't just say that.* Restraining the urge to roll her eyes, Lilia gave him a thin smile instead. "You and I both know that some of the people inside the NCDC can be manipulated, Representative."

The only acknowledgment Pamos made of the oblique jab was a tiny smile, as though she had just impressed him. Lilia wasn't sure that was a good thing.

A knock sounded on the door. "That would be the med 'bot." Pamos turned away. "Door, open." He glanced back over his shoulder. "You have my most sincere thanks for averting disaster tonight, Miss Strong. Sylvia Chesnee's death would have been a catastrophic blow to everything we have worked so hard to achieve. Please rejoin us as soon as you feel up to it."

He waited for a silver med 'bot to glide into the room before departing.

"He's not wrong," Lon said quietly, as the med 'bot approached and requested that Lilia sit down on a chair before it began running diagnostics on her.

Just then Jasper strode through the door into the sunroom, sparing her from answering. His face was tense, but his shoulders relaxed a fraction when he spotted her. "Are you all right?"

"I'm fine." Lilia managed a small smile, even as the med 'bot hummed at the sudden spike in her pulse. "It's nothing."

Lon briefly rested a hand on his sister's shoulder. "We'll talk later. I've got to get back to Kedis." Nodding to Jasper, he exited the room, leaving them alone with the med 'bot.

Jasper crossed the white carpet to her, his mouth thinning as he took in the bloodstains on her skin. The med 'bot was fast; it had already dealt with the puncture wound itself and was applying a bandage. "That's a lot of blood for 'nothing'."

"I'm fine," Lilia repeated. She took a handful of sterile wipes from the 'bot and waved it aside as she briskly cleaned her arm and rose to her feet. "I can handle this, thank you."

She cast a wry glance down at her gown. The black fabric was forgiving; unless one looked closely, it was hard to tell it bore bloodstains. "I suppose it's a good thing I wore black tonight, don't you—"

Jasper moved so quickly it almost took her breath away. One second he was a meter from her, the next he was enveloping her in an embrace so tight it was borderline crushing. Lilia could feel his heart pound against her chest.

"Jasper—"

He pulled back long enough to look her in the eye. His expression was tense, his gray eyes stormy. And then his hands came up to frame her face and he leaned in and kissed her.

Lilia froze…and then her nerve endings exploded beneath his touch. The pressure of his lips against hers was gentle—but left her in no confusion regarding the depth of his mingled concern and relief. Warmth spread throughout her body, electricity flooding her limbs.

Her eyes fluttered shut, but before she could respond, Jasper pulled back, gently catching her bottom lip along the way. The sensation was incredible.

She opened her eyes and they stared at each other; her, breathless and wide-eyed, him, expression still stormy but colored now with nervousness.

When she didn't immediately pull away, some of the tension drained from Jasper. He traced a thumb over her cheekbone; the gesture sent another frisson of electricity through her. "Are you sure you're all right?"

Lilia nodded; she didn't trust herself to speak.

Slowly, almost reluctantly, Jasper let his hands fall to her shoulders. His Adam's apple bobbed in his throat as he swallowed and then gave her a sheepish grin. "I was going to wait until after the trade agreement has been signed."

Lilia's eyes dropped to his lips; she dragged them back up to meet his gaze with an effort and cleared her throat. "To kiss me?"

Jasper wet his lips, his gray eyes still dark. "Yes."

Lilia's body tingled again; she unconsciously curled her toes in her delicate heels. *He's been planning to kiss me?* The very thought sent another thrill coursing through her.

She brought her hands up to rest them on his uniformed chest. His lieutenant's bars bit into the palm of her hand, but she didn't notice. Her heart was thumping so hard a stray corner of her mind was surprised it hadn't beat its way out of her chest yet.

The fact that she was still standing so close to him seemed to embolden Jasper. Skimming his fingers down her arms, barely brushing the bandage on her right arm, he brought his hands up to cover hers on his chest. His fingertips were cool. "Lilia, I—"

"Excuse me, Miss," said a calm, melodic voice. "You need your wound care instructions before I leave."

Lilia's heart leaped into her throat. She and Jasper turned to see the med 'bot standing patiently to one side, regarding them with its expressionless metallic face. They'd both forgotten about it.

"Of course." Releasing her hands, Jasper took a step back to put a respectable amount of distance between them.

Lilia barely had time to mourn the loss before Kevin's voice sounded in her head. [Lilia? Are you all right? What's taking so long?]

She glanced from Jasper to the med 'bot. [I'm almost done. The med 'bot is giving me instructions.]

This seemed to satisfy her brother; he said nothing further. Lilia then offered a polite smile to the med 'bot. Odds were she already knew what she was supposed to do, but it wouldn't hurt to listen. "I'm ready, thank you."

The med 'bot rattled off a list of instructions and Lilia nodded dutifully. "Thank you. I think I can remember that."

"Glad to hear it, Miss." The med 'bot trundled out of the room and Lilia turned back to Jasper. The moment had been broken; she didn't know what to do now.

Neither did he, apparently. Some of the emotion in his eyes had quieted; he'd locked it down. He looked away from her to the door. "We'd best be getting you back. I'm sure your grandfather will want to see for himself you're in one piece."

That prompted a smile. "True."

Their eyes met again and Lilia felt her face warm. Hard to believe he'd actually kissed her just a moment ago. *In Dion Pamos's pent-*

*house, no less!* She looked away, hoping he couldn't see her blush, and moved toward the door. Her limbs felt unsteady and awkward; she'd have blamed it on the assassination attempt and her injury, except that deep down she knew that wasn't true.

She started down the hall back in the direction of the dining room and Jasper followed. Three paces from the doorway, he increased his stride long enough to overtake her. His fingertips grazed the side of her hip as he leaned in close and murmured, "I'm glad you're all right."

Turning her head to the side, Lilia caught his eye. "Thank you." She entered the dining room; he fell back to wait a moment before rejoining everyone.

All eyes turned to her when she strode through the doorway. It felt like everyone could take one look at her and know she'd just been kissed, but Lilia knew it was probably all in her head. Everyone's attention was on the bandage wrapped around her arm. Instinctively, she pressed her arm against her side in an attempt to downplay the injury.

Mrs. Pamos hurried over to her. Save for the faint creases of tension around her dark eyes, she was the picture of gracious composure. "My dear Miss Strong. Are you all right?"

"I'm fine." Lilia shrugged, giving her a polite smile. "It's just a scratch, really." She glanced around the room, which had quieted as everyone stared between her and Mrs. Chesnee, who was back at the central table with the Admiral. "I'm glad reinforcements arrived when they did."

"You must be quite overcome," the older woman said firmly, guiding Lilia back over to her chair. "Have a seat." She beckoned to a server 'bot, which brought a plate of chocolate mousse, decorated with two raspberries, a mint leaf, and an artful swirl of whipped cream. "Dessert will be just the thing to perk you back up."

Lilia wanted to laugh and tell Mrs. Pamos that she was quite perked up enough, thank you, but she held her tongue. The dessert *did* look scrumptious, and the less attention she drew to herself after this, the better. "Thank you, Mrs. Pamos," she said meekly. "I'm sure it will help."

Sensing movement beside her a few seconds later, she looked up. Her grandfather stood beside her chair, looking down at her with concern. "Are you well, my dear?"

Lilia offered him a smile. "Yes, Grandfather." Out of the corner of her eye, she caught a glimpse of Jasper winding his way through the tables to his seat. Her face warmed; she made sure not to look his direction again.

Aiden gently squeezed her shoulder and returned to his table without another word.

"We can't take you anywhere, can we?"

Lilia glanced sideways to find Kevin shaking his head as he regarded her with a mix of concern and wry amusement. She sent a glance around the table at their dining companions before lifting one shoulder in a shrug and returning her attention to her dessert. "I'm just glad I'm not dead."

She didn't really want to talk to anyone right now; her head was too full of Jasper and that kiss. That wonderful, unexpected, glorious, and completely confusing kiss.

When Lilia looked up again, feeling eyes on her once more, it was to find Mrs. Chesnee scrutinizing her from across the room. The older woman held a wine glass in one hand; she raised it to Lilia in a tiny salute.

In response, Lilia dipped her head in a nod. She couldn't help it; she was relieved that her Guardian status was still under wraps. She took another bite of chocolate mousse. *If Freedom's Children keeps this up, though, it's only a matter of time.*

Three bites later, Kevin's voice sounded in her head. [You going to report to Callahan now or later?]

Barely managing to restrain a grimace, Lilia darted a wry sideways glance at her brother. [Obviously not now. The evening isn't over. Not to mention there's no telling how long he'll—]

[—want to talk.] Kevin quirked an understanding eyebrow. [I got it. Just patch me in when you do talk to him, okay? Just to be on the safe side.]

Lilia gave him an imperceptible nod.


It was late when the family finally returned to Ferndale—late enough that Lilia considered reporting to Callahan in the morning. Slipping inside her bedroom, she closed the door and leaned up against it for a moment. After all the noise of the Pamoses' dinner party, her room was blissfully quiet. Only trouble was, her mind still buzzed with a hive of activity.

Meeting Admiral Chesnee in person.

The assassin.

Jasper.

The fact that Jasper had *kissed* her…and he'd apparently been considering it for a while.

The fact that she and Dion Pamos were now on the same page regarding a few things.

At that, Lilia grimaced. She brought a hand up to massage her forehead. *Haven't had a chance to tell Kevin about* that *little conversation yet.*

She shut her eyes, her thoughts jumping back to Jasper. She'd swear she could still smell his cologne. Lowering her hand, she pressed her fingertips to her lips.

He didn't know it yet, but she'd never been kissed before. Not like that. A brief memory of Challa flashed to the forefront of her mind; Lilia forced it away. The way Gillen had attacked her didn't count.

She'd never really had the chance to develop a relationship with anyone when she was younger. *Not with how often we moved because of Grandfather*, she thought absently, her gaze fixed on the window opposite her bedroom door without really seeing it. And then, after she, Kevin, and Lon traded Sta'Gloa for Glo'Stea, she hadn't been interested in anyone on Coral Island.

Even on Kyman…well, who knew how things might have turned out with Greg Bhar if Pamos hadn't manipulated someone in the NCDC to send her and Kevin to Lanx? She hadn't been attracted to Greg the way she was to Jasper, that was for sure.

Lilia blew out a breath. *Of all the men in the galaxy you could like, you had to go and pick a G.U. soldier.* She laughed softly to herself, letting her head thump back against the door. Reflexively, she checked her comlink, but she didn't have any new messages.

*It's probably for the best*, she told herself. *Gives us both time to think.*

In the meantime, she had better deal with Riley Callahan. Steeling herself, she opened a joint channel to both him and Kevin.

Callahan responded faster than she would have expected, given the late hour. His Nancom voice sounded a touch groggy at first, but it quickly turned alert. [Status report.]

*Clearly, he was anticipating some sort of trouble tonight.* Lilia took a deep breath, though it wasn't necessary for Nancom, and gave him a brief rundown of the evening's events. She included her conversation with Dion Pamos. After all, Callahan had been the one to warn them that someone had manipulated the NCDC to put them in danger.

For the most part, Callahan listened quietly, only asking a question here and there to clarify something. At the end, he said, [Well done, Miss Strong. The NCDC would have understood if you had been forced to reveal yourself to the Tarynians as a Guardian tonight in order to save the Admiral's wife, but for discretionary purposes, I am glad it did not come to that.]

[You and me both,] Lilia replied.

[Just for the record, you are *positive* the assassin was in possession of Guardian tech?]

[I'm positive. She had nano-armor, an ISF, and a nanoblade.] Lilia smiled wryly, though her handler couldn't see it. [Would you like me to send you a holo of the hole she left in my arm?]

To her surprise, Callahan took her seriously. [Yes, actually, I would. In this situation I think it will be best to have everything documented.] He paused, thinking, and then asked, [Can you remember anything else about the assassin? Did she have a Guardian insignia on her armor?]

Lilia shut her eyes, picturing the scene in her mind again. A glint of gold against dark gray nano-armor stood out to her. [I think she's from Lanx. I remember seeing a gold insignia.]

[Lanx?] Callahan sounded startled.

[I know,] Kevin said wryly. [You'd think it should be somebody local, but as we're finding out, Mr. Callahan, Freedom's Children has Coalition-wide ties.]

[So it would seem. Anything else, Miss Strong?]

Lilia shook her head, even though their handler couldn't see her. [I don't think so.]

[I will pass this along to the Board. It will be best if you file an official report for this incident tomorrow morning.] He paused. [This will need to be handled…diplomatically. I'm sure you can see why.]

[Yeah,] Kevin said dryly, [a Guardian running around trying to kill people will not go over well.]

[No, it will not.] Callahan sounded grim. [It is unfortunate that you are the only eyewitness, Miss Strong, but that can't be helped.]

[I'll write it as soon as we get back from church,] Lilia promised. They hadn't often had to submit written reports; Callahan usually debriefed them and that was it. The practice had always struck her as odd.

[For now,] Callahan continued, [stay as close to Sylvia Chesnee as you can. If she's been targeted once, it is likely she will be targeted again, even though the assassins must know security measures will be increased.]

[They can open portals,] Kevin said darkly. [Something tells me they're not too concerned about increased security.]

[Remember, Mr. Callahan, my contact with her will be limited to social engagements,] Lilia said. [I don't have a good reason to be anywhere else she might be.]

[I understand. Although,] Callahan's Nancom voice turned musing. [it may not be a difficult task. Admiral Chesnee will undoubtedly shy from placing her in further danger after this.]

[I can't blame him for that.] Lilia snorted, though the sound was heard only in her room. [I'd be leery of Coalition parties after this too.]

[Thank you for the prompt update,] Callahan said briskly. [Keep me apprised of any further developments. If the Board has any instructions for you tomorrow, I'll pass them along.]

[Understood,] the twins said in unison. [Good night.]

Callahan closed his channel and Lilia leaned back against her door again, feeling drained. Her head still buzzed, but it had quieted to a dull roar—one she thought she could ignore.

[You think they'll try again?] Kevin asked through his still-open channel.

[Why wouldn't they?] Straightening, Lilia reached up into her dark hair and started to pluck out diamond hairpins one by one. [What have they got to lose?]

[Besides the element of surprise?]

Lilia digested that as she shook out her hair and crossed the room to deposit the hairpins on her dresser. She was too tired to take a shower tonight, but she'd have to wipe her makeup off. She hated sleeping with it still on her skin. [I don't think that matters at this point. Not when they've got a transporter.]

[How long have we got until they sign the trade agreement? Two weeks from yesterday?]

[Yeah.]

[Can't come soon enough.] Kevin's Nancom voice held a grim note. [We need to just get it over with. Before anything—]

[—else happens. I know.]

Silence fell between them. At last, her brother said, [I'm going to bed. Gotta rest up for tomorrow—who knows how crazy it'll be?]

Lilia chuckled. [No kidding. Night, Kev.]

Kevin closed his channel and Lilia ventured out to the hygiene unit to clean her face and take a holo of her wound before returning to her room to finish getting ready for bed. A glance at her comlink told her she had one new message. She pounced on it eagerly, her heart racing.

As she'd hoped, it was from Jasper. *I'm glad you weren't hurt worse tonight. Get some rest. Good night.*

Lilia blinked at the words, feeling a little piqued. It took her a second to pinpoint why. Her fingers drifted up to press against her lips again. *I guess I expected him to say something about that kiss.*

Surely he wasn't regretting it, was he? She bit the inside of her lip, considering, before shaking her head to herself. No, it was more likely that he didn't want to address it via a text-only message…especially when there was still the chance that his communications were being monitored.

Staring down at her comlink, she debated whether or not to reply. It took her longer than it should have to make a decision. Blowing out an exasperated breath, Lilia tapped out a quick response and tossed her comlink onto the end table beside her bed.

It shouldn't have felt like the galaxy had tipped on its axis after tonight, changing things between the two of them, but it did.

*Go to sleep before you drive yourself any crazier thinking about this,* she scolded herself as she climbed into bed and buried her face in her pillow. *There's enough going on in the Coalition right now without you losing your mind over a man.*

A small voice in the back of her mind whispered, *Good luck with that.*

Lilia ignored it.

# Chapter 80

IF Giles Chesnee had harbored any lingering doubt as to whether or not his emotional attachment to his estranged wife remained, Dion Pamos's dinner party put it firmly to rest. That Sylvia was severely shaken was obvious, though he realized he was the only person present who knew her well enough to see the full extent of it. She stayed close to him the rest of the evening, practically gluing herself to his side. The old Sylvia liked to stay close to remind other women he was taken, but she'd never had a problem roaming the room for a few minutes now and then.

Chesnee maintained his composure until they reached the Beliana Hotel where Kedis was staying, locking down the anger boiling beneath the surface. He and Sylvia were given a suite on the same floor as the Ambassador; he waited until Sylvia was settled in the master bedroom before he stepped outside into the living room.

Sylvia was recovered enough by then to crack a few jokes, laughing off the assassination attempt, but when Chesnee moved to the bedroom door, her fingers tightened on the covers. She was sitting up in bed wearing a turquoise nightgown with delicate straps that showed off her shoulders, her dark, curly hair tumbling over them. She looked twenty again in that moment, staring at him with wide eyes.

"I'll be right back," he said in a comforting rumble. "I need to speak to the Ambassador for a moment." He tipped his head toward the living room. "Out here."

Sylvia nodded and forced a smile, before deliberately snuggling into the covers. "I'll be here."

Chesnee paused before he crossed the threshold. "You're safe here, Sylvia. I promise you."

This time, though small, her smile was genuine. "I know, Giles. I trust you."

When Chesnee stepped out into the living room, he found Kedis standing by the window, peering thoughtfully out at Sonela. He started to speak, but the younger man beat him to it. Kedis was not as unaware of his presence as he seemed.

"You both did quite well tonight." Kedis turned away from the widow and crossed to one of the luxurious leather chairs. "I was impressed with how well your wife handled the situation and I have no doubts others were as well."

"How well she 'handled the situation'?" Chesnee asked, his voice very cold.

"Have a seat, Admiral." Waving to another chair, Kedis smiled at Chesnee, though it never reached his dark eyes. "In some ways, tonight was a test."

Chesnee remained standing. "A *test?*"

"Well," Kedis amended, "it would have been a different sort of test had the assassin succeeded, but, yes. Consider it a test." He commanded Chesnee's gaze. "Will you continue to show your face on Sta'Gloa, or will you run back to the safety of your big, bad battlecruiser?"

Words rose to the tip of Chesnee's tongue, but he held them back. He knew exactly what he *wanted* to do…but he also knew what his duty was. As much as part of him screamed inside that he couldn't put Sylvia in danger again, he knew the answer Kedis wanted. "You already know the answer to this, *Ambassador.*"

Kedis shrugged his shoulders in a rueful little 'what-can-you-do?' sort of way, before leaning forward. "Tell me what happened."

There wasn't much to say. Chesnee relayed the story Lilia Strong had given, and watched as Kedis's eyes narrowed.

"It is interesting," Kedis said slowly, "how entangled Captain Strong's family is in all of this."

"It is fortunate Miss Strong was there to raise an alarm."

"Indeed. Most…fortunate."

Chesnee's eyes narrowed further. "What exactly are you suggesting, Kedis?"

"I'm not suggesting anything." Kedis waved a lackadaisical hand, settling back comfortably in his chair. "I merely note that it is an interesting set of coincidences." He eyed Chesnee. "Won't you sit down, Admiral?"

For a handful of heartbeats, Chesnee considered refusing and continuing to stand. He gave it up as a pointless gesture; Kedis wouldn't pay the slightest bit of attention. He sat down in an armchair. "It seems this terrorist group is getting bolder."

"Oh, yes."

It was Chesnee's turn to eye the younger man. "If I didn't know better, Ambassador, I'd say you are impressed with them."

Kedis smiled. "One does have to admire their bravado. Attacking a high-ranking guest in a Representative's own home?" He shook his head. "And to have pinpointed your wife as a weak point?"

Part of Chesnee bristled at this, but the cooler, strategic part of him understood. Attacking Sylvia meant distracting *him*…and possibly disrupting everything. "They'll try again, won't they?"

It wasn't a question.

"Oh, I wouldn't be surprised." Kedis waved a hand again. "Killing you or myself damages the impending trade agreement substantially, but killing your wife?" He shook his head again, but he was smiling. "Whoever is behind Freedom's Children is using their brain."

Chesnee cast a glance toward the master bedroom door. Resolution settled over him like a mantle; words rose to the tip of his tongue again. He drew breath to speak.

"I know what you're thinking, Admiral. It's not an option."

Chesnee's eyes snapped back to Kedis. The younger man was watching him, a faint smile on his lips, but all hints of levity gone.

"Believe me, I wish I could give you what you're about to demand, but I can't." Kedis slowly shook his head from side to side, his gaze traveling past Chesnee as though fixing on something he saw in the distance. "We're too close to the finish line to surrender ground now."

Chesnee raised his chin. "What, exactly, was I about to say, Ambassador?"

Kedis's smile thinned, edged with ice. "You were about to tell me that you refuse to place your wife in any further danger and that you will be keeping her safely aboard the *Winds of Change* until the day we sign the trade agreement. You were going to tell me, in a way only an Admiral can state it, no doubt, that I can take my political machinations and shove them somewhere dark and unpleasant."

*That's…not a bad assessment.* Chesnee consciously forced himself to lean back in his seat. "Was I?"

"No one would blame you, I assure you, Giles. Our present circumstances, however, call for bravery." Kedis gave a little shrug. "And perhaps sacrifice, though I do hope it doesn't come to that."

A chill ran down Chesnee's spine, but he remained silent.

"I would then, of course, be forced to remind you that High Command, not to mention the Senate, will side with me on this matter, and your reticence, while understandable, would reflect poorly on you after the fact." Kedis's dark eyes glinted. "Not that I think you give a damn for that at this point, Admiral, but you stand to emerge from this with considerable clout. Surely you and your wife can make just a few more appearances here on Sta'Gloa between now and the twenty-fifth."

*All the clout in the world will mean nothing if I've lost Sylvia.* The realization hit him with all the force of a solid right hook. That was the part Kedis seemed unable—or perhaps unwilling—to grasp. Chesnee exhaled slowly, feeling his defiance leak out of him, to be replaced with stony resignation. "I understand you, Ambassador."

"Good." The icy edge to Kedis's voice melted away, to be replaced by cheerful geniality. "I'm glad we understand each other. We're nearly there, Admiral." He snapped his fingers. "We're so close I can almost taste it."

"It will be a bitter victory if Freedom's Children interferes much more," Chesnee said quietly.

"Well, the Coalition will have to ensure that they don't." Kedis uncoiled from his seat in one lithe motion. "Tell your wife I admire her bravery. My staff will send you the details of the next event you are to attend. I assure you, there won't be many between now and the signing." He shot Chesnee a condescending smile. He'd won; he could afford to be magnanimous.

"Ambassador." Chesnee inclined his head, but did not rise from his seat. Kedis could show himself out.

He sat for a long moment after the door slid shut behind the younger man, trying to compose himself. He hadn't expected Sylvia to be in any real danger, but he'd half-anticipated Kedis's reaction to such an incident. *Our lives are nothing but tools for him to use in the political game he's playing.*

# CHAPTER 81

A S far as Aiden could tell in the days immediately following Dion
Pamos's dinner party, plans for the official signing of the trade
agreement and the giant celebration to follow went remarkably well.
Too well, perhaps, for the liking of a few of the pessimists in the
Triumvirate. He had to admit, they had a point. It all seemed too
easy. Too good to be true.

It did not last.

A week before the big day, they hit a major snag—one that
sharply divided the Triumvirate and prompted another spate of bick-
ering. Oddly enough, in the midst of the chaos, Aiden felt almost…
relieved. It cemented events in reality. Peace with the Galactic Union
was truly within their grasp.

The trouble was determining where and when to actually sign
the trade agreement.

Glo'Stea having borne the brunt of the G.U.'s oppression over
the decades, the entire Triumvirate deemed it only right that the signing and celebration take place at the Pearl, the globe-like structure
that housed the seat of Glo'Stea's government in Jamal. Prior to the
revelation that Freedom's Children had access to a transporter, none
of them would have blinked an eye at Kedis and the three Chief
Ministers signing the agreement in front of a host of witnesses in

the Pearl's main conference room. It would have been the practiced, accepted thing to do.

It would have been a bold, public statement that This Day would go down in history as the day the galaxy shifted in the Coalition's favor.

That idea had not accounted for terrorists who could open a portal in their midst long enough to drop a bomb capable of wiping out the Coalition's entire ruling body—and all of their security personnel—in one fell swoop.

It changed things.

The result was a week's worth of arguments over safety vs. statement, when they all had better uses they could have made of their time. Aiden himself did not mind taking a calculated risk, but given the joint Directors of Security and Internal Affairs were still searching for the source of the leak inside the Triumvirate, even he deemed the danger too great.

In the end, the Triumvirate voted to hold the official signing ceremony in secret—the location to be revealed only to Ambassador Kedis, Admiral Chesnee, their bodyguards, and the members of the Triumvirate themselves at the last minute.

*This way,* Aiden thought grimly after Chairman Yu announced the results of the vote, *should something happen we will be better able to trace the leak back to its source.* He chuckled grimly to himself. *Provided we are not all dead, of course.*

# Chapter 82

L ILIA worried her bottom lip as she stared out the skimmer window at the crowds of people lining Jamal's streets. Glo'Stea's capital city was packed; she wouldn't be surprised to learn there were more people here than had flooded Atalia for the Tri-Global Tournament. Ambassador Kedis and the Coalition's three Chief Ministers were set to sign the trade agreement at half-past four that afternoon and Chief Minister Devlin Vance would then host a huge celebration at the Pearl.

The last time Lilia had been in Jamal was the day Admiral Chesnee had breached Lanx's shield. She and Kevin had just finished the process of becoming Guardians at the NCDC headquarters in Glo'Stea's capital city. It had also been pouring down rain.

Today, the skies were clear, but a hot, humid wind blew across the city, funneling between the skyscrapers growing out of the heart of Jamal's business district. It was August, after all, and this part of Glo'Stea reminded Lilia of Marina. Sonela was hot and muggy as well this time of year, but being farther north made a difference in temperature.

Heat waves shimmered in the air above the long, long line of skimmers snaking their way through Jamal's streets, all of them headed for a single destination: the Pearl. The rounded top of the building was not yet visible from street-level, but Lilia expected they'd be able to see it soon. She and her brothers had never been there before; they'd only seen holos.

Their grandfather rode in the skimmer ahead of them, along with Michael, Derek, Felix and Elena Mouta, and several members of his security team. He and the rest of the Triumvirate had all been given a special police escort to see them safely through the city to the Pearl, but traffic was still slow. Lilia wondered what Ambassador Kedis thought of the delay. He and Admiral Chesnee had been given a police escort as well; they were somewhere in the high-priority line of skimmers.

Her thoughts lingered on the Tarynians for a moment. Admiral Chesnee and his wife had made four appearances since Dion Pamos's dinner party. Sylvia Chesnee had stayed close to her husband's side, and on the occasions they were parted, she had two discreet guards—one G.U. and the other provided by Kedis's security team. He was a Guardian, though Lilia was sure the Chesnees were clueless to that fact.

It was a clever balance between taking necessary precautions and maintaining a confident front in the face of imminent danger.

Tension throughout the Coalition had remained at peak intensity over the past two weeks, but a general air of excitement, triumph, and anticipation now pervaded Jamal. Coalition banners hung everywhere, interspersed with Glo'Stean, Sta'Gloan, and Lanxian flags. People were laughing, cheering, and generally appeared to be in high spirits.

On the surface, everything looked perfect, but an ugly undercurrent poked through in places. Lilia glimpsed it in the knots of angry protesters mixed in with the rest of the crowds lining the streets. Flashing hand-held signs denounced the trade agreement—and the Triumvirate for agreeing to it. She also glimpsed police officers moving through the crowd keeping a wary eye on things.

Nobody wanted another riot, especially not today...and it wouldn't take much to spark one.

Lilia understood the sentiment behind the dissenters' vehement disapproval. She really did. *But we can't keep going on like this forever.* All that would result from prolonging the conflict was more death— more losses on both sides to embitter people further.

She reflexively smoothed a hand over the satiny sapphire-blue folds of her evening gown. She had chosen blue in honor of all the Glo'Steans who had given their lives during the course of the blockade—whether as part of the Glo'Stean Resistance, or the friends and colleagues she'd lost on Coral Island. The underlying significance would be lost on practically everyone, but that didn't bother her.

The Coalition's social elite didn't need to know. It was enough that *she* knew.

"You look like you've got the weight of the galaxy on your shoulders."

Kevin's voice broke the solemn silence filling the skimmer, and Lilia jumped, startled. She cast a wry sideways glance at him. "I was just thinking about everything."

He raised his eyebrows at her in a silent question. He was dressed in a black tuxedo with a green cummerbund, his dark brown hair neatly combed.

"You know." Lilia shrugged. "The fact that today means we're no longer at war with the Galactic Union." She turned back to the window. "We'll be able to travel freely from world to world now. We'll even be able to leave the Coalition if we want to. Everything changes."

"That's a good thing."

"I know." Lilia flattened a hand against window; the plastiglass was cool against her skin. "We're living in the end of an era right now." Her mouth crimped. "We *shouldn't* have to worry any more about getting blown up trying to leave the planet."

Kevin exhaled slowly. "Are you thinking about—"

"—Freedom's Children? I can't help it." She shook her head. "We've got the chance for peace and they just can't let it go." She slashed her free hand through the air. "How many more people are *they* going to kill in the name of their idea of 'peace'?"

"Lilia—"

"The Tarynians stopped blowing us up and they took over the job."

Across the seat from her, Erik Holt snorted. "I'm sure in their minds they're doin' the right thing for the Coalition."

As part of their plan to provide additional Guardian security, the NCDC had used Erik's friendship with Lilia and Kevin to their advantage and had politely commanded that Lilia take him as her escort for the evening. Erik therefore found himself all dressed up in a black tuxedo and headed to the biggest event of the century. He wasn't particularly thrilled about it.

"This is supposed to be a happy day." Lilia did not look at either man, but continued staring out the window. "It's a *monumental* day— and I can't shake the feeling that something bad is going to happen."

Kevin considered this in silence for a moment. "You're probably not wrong. We already know the Mastermind isn't happy about this decision. It's entirely possible Freedom's Children will try to pull some stunt." He shot her a grim, but determined look. "The best we can do is to keep our eyes peeled and intervene if we get the chance."

It was Lilia's turn to exhale slowly. "I know." It was why they were all wearing as much of their stealth armor beneath their clothes as they could manage. Just in case.

She leaned back against her seat, feeling the weight of the past two months in the muscles of her shoulders. The weight she and Kevin had been carrying since Lon smuggled Kedis onto Sta'Gloa. *It's almost over*, she told herself. *They'll sign the trade agreement and we'll all find a new normal.*

Three Cords Shipping would continue, and without the constant threat of the G.U. blockade looming over the Sta'Gloan system, she hoped their business would thrive.

Lilia took the opportunity to tilt her head and touch a diamond hairpin, ensuring it was firmly in place. She had put her hair up with her grandmother's hairpins again, leaving a few wispy strands to artfully frame her face, but even after the past several months she still wasn't entirely used to wearing them.

"This is ridiculous," Erik complained after a moment.

The twins both looked at him as he flexed his arms, frowning as the fabric of his black tuxedo jacket strained against his shoulders. He then tugged impatiently at his collar, pulling it away from his neck. "I can't believe this monkey suit is normal for some people."

"But, Erik," Lilia pretended to fan herself, "who knew you'd clean up so nicely?"

"Yeah, yeah, yeah," he grumbled, his jaw set with grim irritation.

Lilia just grinned at him. Her comlink buzzed in her lap and her pulse quickened, nervous anticipation itching just beneath her skin. *Jasper.*

He had *kissed* her less than two weeks ago—and they'd hardly seen each other since. And though they'd communicated almost daily, they hadn't talked about it.

At this point, she was half-tempted to think it was a figment of her imagination…except she knew it wasn't.

Lilia pressed her lips together, her eyes going distant at the memory. Butterflies erupted in her stomach; she flattened a hand against it to quell them and glanced at Jasper's message.

*Are you ready for tonight?*

*I THINK SO,* she sent back. *IT STILL FEELS SURREAL—LIKE ANY MOMENT I'M GOING TO WAKE UP AND FIND OUT IT'S ALL BEEN A DREAM.*

A pause. *I CAN UNDERSTAND THAT.* Another pause. *IT'S NOT A DREAM.*

She knew that, and yet…seeing the words was oddly reassuring. *I KNOW…*

*I'LL SEE YOU SHORTLY. SAVE ME A DANCE.*

Lilia bit the inside of her cheek to keep from smiling. *I SUPPOSE I CAN DO THAT.*

After sending the message, she slid her comlink into her clutch—a delicate little silver piece she would probably end up shoving into her ISF long before the night was through—and straightened her shoulders. Regardless of the reasons they were attending, it was still an honor to actually be here in Jamal for the official ending of the blockade. The more she thought about it, the more excitement began to trickle through her veins.

"The end of the blockade and the invasion," she murmured to herself. "I like the sound of that."

When the Pearl finally came into view some time later, Erik shook his head. "I'd say a giant bubble is a strange design for a government buildin', but…" His blond eyebrows scrunched in a frown. "The closer we get, the better it looks."

"You're right." Lilia leaned her head closer to the window to get a better look as well.

A massive globe, Pearl rose majestically out of the city around it as though a giant hand had plucked it from an equally giant oyster and carefully set it down in the middle of Jamal's business district. Its pearlescent surface glistened softly in the afternoon sunlight. It did not appear to have windows, but Lilia knew from the security blueprints Michael had showed them that it did; they were probably opaque on the outside.

"Do you think the outer office *walls* are curved?" Erik asked with interest.

"No idea," Kevin said. "Guess we'll find out."

"Grandfather said it was designed to be pretty airy inside." Lilia sat back against her seat, smoothing her skirt again. "At least from what he remembers, anyway. If they haven't changed things."

Kevin snorted. "Oh, I'm sure they haven't changed too much. They haven't had a Triumvirate session here since the blockade, remember?"

As their skimmer neared the gates guarding the Pearl, the cheering crowds thickened and the knots of protesters seemed larger. Heightened security became obvious. Armed Glo'Stean Resistance fighters in sea-blue uniforms—the closest thing Glo'Stea had to a proper military—lined the gleaming white fence encircling the Pearl, and armed guards in navy-blue uniforms waited at the checkpoint allowing vehicles access. Invitations and credentials were scanned and matched before anyone was granted passage through the gate.

It slowed the caravan of guests down to a crawl, but after everything, Lilia couldn't blame them for being cautious.

Erik, on the other hand, just leaned back in his seat shaking his head. "They can be as careful as they like, but it ain't gonna matter if Freedom's Children opens a portal into the middle of the Pearl."

"They'd have to have coordinates," Kevin pointed out.

"You think they won't have already figured that out, if that's their plan?" Erik snorted, folding his arms over his chest. "The Triumvirate's got a leak high enough I don't think they'll stand a chance if that's the direction the Mastermind takes things." He shot the twins a significant look. "An' he might, considerin' this is his last shot to keep the trade agreement from bein' signed."

Lilia pursed her lips. "I wouldn't be surprised if he's got a backup plan." She waved a hand to the Pearl looming gracefully above them. "Look at all the prominent people who'll be here today."

"That's why *we're* here." Kevin's grin held more confidence than Lilia felt just now. "To protect everybody if they do pull a stunt like that."

Erik shook his head. "It'd be sour grapes if he did. Impotent fury." His expression turned sharp and knowing. "If they turn up in that conference room though, there'll be a way to trace it back to whoever spilled the beans."

"I know." Lilia blew out a breath. "Still doesn't make me feel better, though."

"Relax." Kevin clapped her on the shoulder. "Your job tonight is to look pretty—and carry a hidden pistol and nanoblade." His eyes danced. "If something does happen, they won't know what hit them."

"That's the spirit," Erik said as the skimmer came to a halt and it was their turn to provide credentials.

Lilia couldn't help but notice he looked a little pale. She nudged him with her elbow. "You'll be fine."

"'Course I will." Erik shot her a smile that did not reach his brown eyes. "I'll blend right in."

# CHAPTER 83

IDEN felt a thrill of excitement as his skimmer glided through the security checkpoint at the Pearl's main gates. He had not been in Jamal since before the blockade began. Jenson took the skimmer along a wide promenade curving around an exquisite garden that stood in front of the Pearl, filled with a collection of Glo'Stea's most beautiful flowers and shrubs. A giant fountain rose from the center of the garden, a cluster of three frolicking dolphins. Water poured from their laughing mouths into a wide, shallow basin; from there it spilled over into a series of small canals that streamed through the garden, lining the smooth stone paths.

A faint pang of old grief mixed with nostalgia pierced Aiden's chest. The last time he had been here, he had walked that garden with his beloved wife after a Triumvirate session. *So many, many things have changed since then.*

A gleaming white columned portico stood guard at the Pearl's main entrance, each end of the roof sweeping upward like a graceful curved wing. A large set of double doors that seemed to have been made entirely of a fragile, lacy network of gold and plastiglass led into the building. Those ornate doors were for show; Aiden knew for a fact that a set of high-security reinforced doors could be slammed shut at the slightest hint of danger.

An honor guard of Glo'Stean Resistance fighters a solemn, sea-blue corridor leading from the edge of the pristine white stone walkway that began at the curb and extended all the way to those massive double doors. Both doors were open at the moment, providing a glimpse of the busy security checkpoint just inside.

A small crowd of reporters and cams, kept at bay by the honor guard, awaited new arrivals. Aiden was pleasantly surprised; he had braced himself for an onslaught from the media. *Interesting. Either the Directors of Security have put their collective foot down in an unprecedented way, or else the media has decided a better story awaits them indoors.*

Derek, peering out the window, echoed his thoughts. "I was expecting a bigger welcome committee."

"As was I." Aiden smiled wryly. "Though I have no doubts we will encounter them inside."

The guests in the skimmer ahead of them disembarked at the walkway—Aiden thought he saw Lanxian Representative Oded Xerxes among them—and the skimmer pulled forward to travel around the garden and find a home in the high-security underground parking garage discreetly located nearby. Jenson eased up to take their place, and Imlay immediately hopped out of the front seat to open the door.

A blast of sweltering air greeted them. Aiden exited the skimmer, followed by his Chief of Staff and his wife, Michael, and Derek. They waited by the curb for the rest of their group.

Jenson drove away, and Oppelt took his slot. Lilia, Kevin, and Erik Holt piled out of the skimmer and joined them, though Holt looked a little awkward. Aiden addressed him. "You do not mind if I steal my granddaughter away for a moment?"

Holt looked momentarily startled, before he shook his head. "Not at all, sir."

Aiden extended the crook of his arm to Lilia and she tucked her hand through it. He then proceeded up the walkway. Smiling down at his granddaughter, he said softly, "You remind me more and more of your mother the older you grow, child. You look beautiful tonight."

"Thank you, Grandfather." Lilia tilted her head back to stare up at the Pearl as they approached the main entrance. "This is incredible."

"I concur."

Though Aiden did not allow his expression to show it, he felt a sense of almost child-like wonder as he set foot in the Pearl for the first time in over twenty years. The massive building had aged—he could relate to that—but it was obvious the Glo'Stean government had funneled precious resources into its upkeep.

The security checkpoint formed a small, circular area just beyond the massive doors, bounded by a gleaming plastiglass and metal railing. A three-meter wide break in the center of the railing, which held a scanning matrix, provided access into the rest of the lobby. Set into the railing along the left was a security control center. Six grim-faced, straight-backed men dressed in the Pearl's navy-blue security uniform manned this checkpoint.

They passed through with no issue. As they moved into the lobby, Aiden took a deep breath. The air smelled of exotic flowers and a hint of an ocean breeze—an expensive air freshener. He liked it; it was just enough to scent the air, but not so cloying that it made one nauseous.

As for the lobby itself, it had the same airy feel he recalled. The front wall curved up and around with the outside shape of the building a distance of three stories, containing several large windows on either side of the main entrance draped with delicate swaths of glittering aquamarine fabric shot through with gold. The windows were opaque from the outside. The walls were pale sea blue, and the floor made of aquamarine marble. Glo'Stea's seal had been etched into the center of the floor, beneath a massive chandelier made of hundreds of glass teardrops.

A long, curved welcome desk made of dark, exotic wood stood to the right of the seal in the floor, and beyond it halls led off in three different directions. The halls to the left and right were cordoned off with sapphire blue velvet ropes; the hall in the center was guarded by four more men in navy-blue uniforms. Several impeccably dressed receptionists sat behind the welcome desk, waiting for guests to ask for assistance, but Aiden doubted it would be necessary.

Guy Caradoc, Director of Glo'Stean Security, had grimly promised the Triumvirate that every guest would know exactly where to go.

Their footsteps echoed on the marble floor as they crossed the lobby to the hall, and Aiden nodded to the security guards. The hall was painted the same pale sea blue, and decorated with holos of past Chief Ministers. Beams of golden light shown down from clusters of vibrant greenery mounted at intervals along the wall near the ceiling, giving the hall a sunlit outdoorsy feel.

Lilia glanced up at the lights with interest. "Are those solar pipes?"

"Yes," Aiden replied. "The Pearl has always predominately used solar pipes instead of glowpanels." He smiled. "I have always thought they make the place feel less like an office and more like a resort."

Behind them, Kevin said, "No kidding."

Ahead of them stood an accelevator bank; the hall instead branched off to the right and left. A cluster of Pearl Security personnel in the same navy-blue uniforms as the guards outside gathered here, sorting guests. Two men escorted Representative Xerxes and his small group of aides and security detail down the hall to the left, while the rest of his party was directed into an accelevator.

Slowing his steps to a halt, Aiden patted Lilia's hand and let her go. "Here is where I leave you." He turned to regard both her and Kevin, offering them a slight smile. "We will see you at the celebration after the signing."

Lilia smiled back at him, her violet eyes reflecting the same mix of excitement and concern swirling in his own mind, and leaned in to give him a quick hug. "Yes, we will."

Kevin bowed. "Go make history, Grandfather."

Aiden only gave him that same slight smile again and turned away. Michael, Derek, Felix Mouta, Imlay, and Booth gathered around him; they would be allowed to accompany him up to a certain point. Elena Mouta would go with the twins and Holt.

*Make history*, Aiden thought. This was only one of many steps. *There is still much to be done.* He and the rest of the Triumvirate could look forward to many more weeks and months of back-and-forth negotiations as the Coalition and the Galactic Union worked out just how they would coexist.

*I suppose, however,* he conceded, as they reached the group of security personnel, *that one could say the hard part is done.* The Coalition had a cease-fire, they were about to have a trade agreement, and the bloodshed—at least as far as the G.U. military and the Resistance were concerned—was over.

He suppressed a frown. It remained to be seen whether Freedom's Children would accept that.

A sober-faced woman in navy-blue stepped forward, holding a datapad in one hand. She gave him a respectful nod. "Representative Monroe, this way if you please." She motioned to the hall to the left, before indicating to two of her teammates, both of whom looked like they could wrestle a sea-monster barehanded and come out on top.

The two men split off from the group and bowed to Aiden. They were both dark-skinned and had short, military-style haircuts, but one of them had an odd scar on his left cheek. This man addressed Aiden. "If you'll follow us, sir?"

"Thank you," Aiden replied in Glo'Stean, and they promptly set off down the hall. Behind them, Aiden heard the woman direct his youngest grandchildren, Elena Mouta, and Holt into an accelevator.

They walked for several minutes, wending their way deeper into the Pearl's main level. Along the way, they passed three sets of security personnel on their way back to escort more guests. Finally, they came to a halt at an accelevator bank, and their guides took them down two levels into the bedrock upon which the Pearl had been built.

"This is where we leave you," the man with the scar said as the accelevator doors opened. He motioned down the hall ahead of them. "You will be part of that group."

Following the direction of his finger, Aiden spotted a group of Triumvirate members and their aides milling around the end of the hall. Oded Xerxes was there, but also Egan Ashford, Zane Chas, and Martin Hollowell. Two security personnel stood with them.

Aiden turned to their guides. "Thank you."

"Good luck, sir." Both men bowed again.

Aiden led the way out of the accelevator, which departed as soon as they had all exited. He picked up his pace, anticipation coursing through him, though walking that fast winded him. He found that more than a little frustrating; he had come so far since surviving the explosion at the Gala, and yet he was not completely back to normal.

*Still, you are alive*, he reminded himself. At the moment, that was better than the alternative—and he had come so close to death.

He had not spoken of it to his grandchildren, but there had been times over the past few weeks when Aiden wished that the Lord would call him home and he could simply lay the burdens of this life down. He loved his grandchildren, and he knew his work on the Triumvirate was important, but… He found himself longing to see Jesus.

And his wife.

And his daughter and son-in-law, and a host of others who had gone on before him.

*But, that time is not now*, Aiden reminded himself, as he drew nearer to his colleagues.

Egan Ashford noticed him first. The Glo'Stean Representative nodded, but did not speak. None of them did. They proceeded down the hall in tense, somber silence.

At the next accelevator bank, their security escort announced that their staff and bodyguards were required to stay behind at this point. Aiden could tell this sent a faint ripple of unease through his colleagues, but they had all agreed to this beforehand. *We all know what is at stake.* He nodded solemnly to his grandsons and Mouta before joining his colleagues in the accelevator.

Their escort took them down another four floors, where they were met by Guy Caradoc himself. The Glo'Stean Director of Security led the group down several twisting corridors into an underground conference room. Half of the Triumvirate was already there.

"Here we are," Caradoc announced without preamble, before departing to retrieve the next set of incoming Representatives.

Aiden blinked, slightly taken aback. They had all talked about how tight security needed to be, but he saw now he had not realized the full impact of what that would mean. The conference room itself was as luxurious as any in the Pearl above, with aquamarine walls and a rich, sea-blue carpeted floor, but it lacked the ornamentation he would have expected for such an occasion.

*No PR department to do the decorating. Or,* he thought, glancing around the room, *a media crew to film this occasion.*

The latter, he was sure, would be rectified shortly; this entire plan hinged on safely broadcasting the signing of the trade agreement across the Coalition.

Holo frames depicting former Chief Ministers and notable places on Glo'Stea graced the walls, and a number of chairs in straight rows faced a large, ornate desk made of sleek, dark brown native wood. Five chairs sat behind the desk, three on one side and two on the other.

As Aiden watched, Yvonne Friest, the Glo'Stean Director of Internal Affairs, arrived with several men in navy-blue Pearl Security uniforms. Under her supervision, they made quick work of rearranging the chairs into a large semi-circle ringing the desk. Friest then stepped up to the desk with an armful of glossy, colorful fabric, which proved to be the Coalition's banner and that of the Galactic Union.

Acacia Hale, the Lanxian Director of Internal Affairs, draped a crisp white tablecloth over the desk and helped Friest arrange both banners to display prominently against it. Hale was a plump middle-aged woman with light brown skin, startling blue eyes, and a surprisingly reedy voice.

Guy Caradoc arrived a moment later, with three hooded men and another small group of his security personnel carrying bundles of equipment in tow. Caradoc removed the hoods from the men and they immediately took stock of the room and began setting up cams and mics.

Having finished with the desk, Yvonne Friest turned back to her colleagues and raised her arms. "If you would all take a seat behind the desk, please." She motioned to the semi-circle of chairs. "The same planetary order as we use for the Triumvirate, but in order of Sectors."

Surprised murmurs greeted this, but Aiden and everyone else complied. They all found their seats and settled in to wait. Aiden found his heart beating a little faster in his chest. *It will not be long now.*

# CHAPTER 84

LILIA, Kevin, Erik, and Mrs. Mouta advanced down the hall as directed and encountered more navy-blue-clad security personnel lining their path, who politely directed them to keep walking. Two intersections later, they were shunted to the left down another hall and found themselves heading toward a set of open double doors guarded by yet more security personnel. They glimpsed members of Representative Xerxes's group just disappearing through the doors.

[If I didn't know better,] Lilia remarked to Kevin via Nancom, [I'd say Alan Birch had a hand in arranging all this. It's borderline paranoid.]

Kevin suppressed a smile. [I remember Grandfather saying something about Director Caradoc being extremely thorough in all his preparations.]

As they approached the doors, Lilia glanced sideways at Mrs. Mouta. The older woman looked composed, but her dark eyes were dancing with excitement.

Feeling Lilia's eyes on her, she met her gaze and smiled. "This is very exciting. I'm glad we get to be a part of it."

Lilia smiled back. "Me too."

"I still can't quite wrap my mind around it," Mrs. Mouta continued, as they streamed into a massive auditorium. "After all these years, we'll finally be able to function like a normal system."

"It will reopen a lot of avenues for us, that's for sure," Kevin agreed, before glancing around. "Where would you like to sit?"

Several hundred sapphire blue chairs were arranged long rows facing a stage holding a giant holoprojector, which currently displayed a countdown. Less than a quarter of the chairs were filled, the members of the Triumvirate having been given first priority in terms of arrival. Lilia had no doubt the auditorium would be absolutely packed before signing took place. A number of media crews were already in place, running final checks on their equipment. They wouldn't be able to capture the actual signing, but they would record the crowd's reaction.

Before Lilia could reply that she thought they ought to perhaps sit toward the back, Mrs. Mouta indicated the front ten rows of chairs, which were all marked with glowing holographic 'reserved' signs. "As Representative Monroe's family, your seats are up here." She proceeded to lead the way down the center aisle to the second row.

Lilia suppressed a rueful sigh. Via Nancom, she told Kevin and Erik, [I was thinking we ought to stay towards the back, in case something happened, but—]

[—that's out of the question now,] Kevin agreed.

The expression on Erik's face clearly stated he wished he could stay at the very back, where Pearl security personnel and other members of various security details had taken up discreet position at the edge of the auditorium, but he grimly marched along with the twins as they hurried forward to catch up with Mrs. Mouta.

As she settled into a seat eleven chairs in from the end on the left, Lilia took the opportunity to scan the conference room, noting both familiar and unfamiliar faces. Part of her automatically began searching for a tall, golden-haired figure, even though she knew Jasper wouldn't be here. *You'll see him soon enough*, she told herself. *Settle down.*

An air of excitement and anticipation began to mount as the minutes ticked down to the appointed time. The rise and fall of dozens of conversations in multiple languages became louder. Beneath the excitement, however, tension mounted as well.

If she focused, Lilia could feel a number of other Guardians were scattered throughout the auditorium. To her right, she caught Kevin's eye. [I think there are a lot of Guardians here.]

[That doesn't surprise me.] He tugged at his collar, but stopped when she shot him a quelling look. [Some of them have to be guests like us—they can't *all* be Security personnel.]

[That's what I thought. The NCDC would—]

[—probably not allow the Pearl to have that many.]

Lilia bit her lip. [Guess we'd better introduce ourselves.] Part of her craved her anonymity, in case something bad *did* happen, but the dutiful part of her knew she had a responsibility in this situation to network.

Several of the other incognito Guardians beat her to the punch. On the verge of sending her first channel request, Lilia received several. She and the other Guardians performed quick introductions, along with an idea as to where each was actually located in the auditorium, and they moved on. Kevin did the same, as did Erik.

*Besides*, she told herself, twisting her fingers absently together in her lap. Her clutch lay beneath her hands; she hadn't had a chance to discreetly dispose of it in her ISF yet. *Some of these other Guardians would probably prefer to remain low-key as well.*

Such as Kalif Thé—a short, slender man with pale golden skin, a shaved head, and dark, slanted eyes. He was a high-ranking member of Glo'Stean Representative Akiva Taft's staff. He sat eight seats to Lilia's right and four rows back, dressed in black slacks and a cerulean blue jacket with a high collar. He had given the three of them tiny nods after they introduced themselves via Nancom, and then had not looked at them again. His attention, however, encompassed the entire auditorium.

"Five minutes left," Erik muttered from his seat to Lilia's left. "Feels like this is takin' an eternity."

"I know." She watched the seconds tick by.

Erik started to slouch down in his seat, but remembered himself and straightened as though someone had just rammed a steel rod down his spine. "I think we'll all be relieved when they get that thing signed."

Lilia nodded. On Erik's other side, Mrs. Mouta nodded as well. Her face was still composed, but Lilia thought she glimpsed a trace of anxiety. She reached over Erik to pat the older woman's hand, giving her a reassuring smile. "They'll be fine. The Triumvirate has been so careful, I don't think they'll run into any trouble now."

Mrs. Mouta tried to smile. "I'm sure you're right, my dear."

Lilia cast a glance over her shoulder. The massive room was now completely full, and more people were still streaming in. When she turned back, her eyes met Erik's.

[Lot of money in here,] he said via Nancom, tipping his head to indicate the auditorium. [Lot of influence an' prestige. Can't help thinkin' that a well-placed bomb would take out the whole lot of 'em.]

[That's a cheery thought.]

Erik did not move. [Call 'em like I see 'em.] His expression grew sterner. [All they'd have to do is open a portal an' chuck it in.]

Despite the warmth of the crowded auditorium, a shudder worked its way down Lilia's spine. She swallowed, her stomach sinking, and turned back around to face the countdown. Three minutes, fourteen seconds. [How are we supposed to guard against something like that?]

[No idea. But since the Triumvirate isn't here, I think we're safe.] He paused. [For now.]

The crowd gradually quieted as the countdown hit the two-minute mark. By the thirty-second mark, it was so quiet that a cough on one side of the room could be heard loudly on the other side. Lilia watched the seconds count down, her heart thundering in her chest, before sweeping glance around her. They were about to witness history unfold—and she prayed Freedom's Children would make no attempt to hinder it.


The three Chief Ministers swept into the ornate conference room with Ambassador Kedis just as the media crew finished the last of their preparations. Admiral Chesnee, and to everyone's surprise, Mrs. Chesnee followed closely behind. Hugh Koen held up a hand in greeting to the semi-circle of assembled Representatives and Directors, before settling into the center of the three chairs on one side of the table. He set two datapads before him. Pryce Gammick and Devlin Vance took chairs on either side of him.

Ambassador Kedis offered a short bow to the members of the Triumvirate before regally taking his seat at the table. He wore a charcoal bespoke suit today that set off his olive-toned skin admirably and, as usual, he had an air of belonging about him, as though he was always supposed to have been here. He smiled affably at no one in particular, the picture of grace and trustworthiness.

To Aiden's right, Sean Caspian, Representative for Sector 3, muttered under his breath, "He made sure he looked good for the cams." He was a middle-aged man of medium height, with pale eyes, graying red hair, and a matching goatee.

"Indeed," Aiden replied softly.

Admiral Chesnee offered the Triumvirate a much stiffer bow. He wore his full dress uniform, while his wife was resplendent in an elegantly-cut black evening gown that showed off her shoulders to advantage and swept the floor in delicate silky folds. Clearly she had come dressed for the ball. When her husband took the last seat at the table, instead of moving up to stand at his elbow, she glided over to stand out of the way of the cams' view near Lon, Lieutenant Wright, and Corporal Renner.

Aiden found himself a trifle surprised; he would have expected her to claim a little more of the limelight today. He caught his middle grandson's eye, however, and gave him a minuscule nod of greeting. He was glad at least one Guardian was present for this. He suspected there were probably others, but he had no idea who they might be.

Despite the need for secrecy, even a few naysayers had been forced to admit that locking two high-ranking Tarynians and the entire ruling body of the Coalition inside a room without any security personnel when a terrorist group could literally drop a bomb in their midst was not the wisest course of action. They needed protection, and Aiden was not surprised Lon had made the cut. After all, he was a Guardian in the unique position of being related to a Sta'Gloan Representative and liaison to the G.U. Ambassador.

A corner of Aiden's mouth twitched. *One could say he has a vested interest in helping keep everybody alive.*

The media crew, therefore, had been carefully instructed not to include the security personnel lining the back wall of the conference room when they panned over the Triumvirate witnessing the signing of the trade agreement.

Hugh Koen looked to the media crew, who gave him the go-ahead. The Chief Minister nodded to them, cleared his throat, and addressed the cams in a strong voice. "It is time to begin."

Watching the Chief Ministers, the Ambassador, and the Admiral, Aiden felt the heavy, portentous weight of the moment begin to sink in. After more than twenty years of hostility, it was actually happening. He glanced around, and in that instant, also felt the wrongness of their entire situation.

*We should not be hiding away in here by ourselves—cam crew or no cam crew.* This was a momentous day—a day that would go down in the pages of history. There should be hundreds of people crowded in this room with them, bearing witness to this moment.

Instead, thanks to a very real threat of death, they were seated here alone. For the span of three heartbeats, Aiden heartily wished that Freedom's Children had never existed. This moment would be viewed by billions across the Coalition and the Galactic Union…but he and the rest of the Triumvirate were its only physical witnesses.

"This," Hugh Koen announced gravely in Sta'Gloan, unknowingly echoing Aiden's thoughts, "is a monumental day for the Coalition. It is a day future generations will celebrate as the day we rejoined the rest of the galaxy."

Aiden noticed the Chief Minister made no mention of the fact that they were signing this trade agreement in an undisclosed location inside the Pearl because of the danger posed by Freedom's Children. As far as Aiden knew, the general population throughout the Coalition remained unaware of the full extent of the terrorist group's capabilities…and he also knew the Triumvirate intended to keep it that way as long as possible.

Koen passed one of the datapads to Vance, who sat on his left, and the Glo'Stean Chief Minister slid it down the table to Kedis.

On Koen's other side, Gammick produced a stylus, which he proffered to the Tarynian. "For you, Ambassador," he said in Lanxian.

Kedis accepted it with a nod and a smile of thanks. Beside him, Chesnee remained silent, his expression impassive.

The Ambassador scanned through the document on the datapad as though seriously studying its contents before he gravely signed his name. He passed the datapad to Chesnee, who also studied it briefly, before affixing his own name and pushing the datapad back across the table to the three Chief Ministers, who were taking turns scribbling their names on the other datapad. That done, they swapped datapads in silence, while the members of the Triumvirate looked on.

Aiden wondered if the respectful, anticipatory silence carried through on the footage, which was streaming to the Pearl's media room. He knew a newscaster had been selected to provide solemn voice-over commentary for the ceremony. He made a mental note to review the ceremony later.

As soon as Kedis and Gammick set the styluses down, someone in the Glo'Stean section began clapping. It was quickly picked up by others and spread along the semi-circle of seats. Aiden joined in, a swell of unexpected emotion rising to clog his throat. This was not the justice he had always hoped his daughter, son-in-law, and the rest of the Coalition's dead would receive. That, he had come to realize, would have to stay in the Lord Almighty's hands. But it was an end to the death—

—at least as far as the G.U. and the Coalition were concerned. *Freedom's Children*, he thought grimly, *is another matter entirely.*

A rush of sound enveloped the massive conference room as soon as Admiral Chesnee and Chief Minister Gammick finished signing the treaty. All around Lilia, Kevin and Erik, men and women surged to their feet, clapping, cheering, and stamping their feet. The three of them stood as well, Lilia blinking back sudden tears.

She felt a hundred times lighter, almost light enough to float up to the ceiling without a hoverdisc. It was like she'd been wearing weighted boots all this time, and carrying a heavy load. Both had vanished. She turned to Kevin, an unspoken look of excited joy passing between them.

"We're free," they said at the same time. Their words disappeared in the happy bedlam surrounding them.

Turning to her other side, Lilia beamed at Erik. He shot her a wry smile, before going back to watching the joyous crowd around them. Lilia then leaned past him again to clasp hands with Mrs. Mouta, who was smiling broadly, her dark eyes also sparkling with joyful tears. "It's over."

Mrs. Mouta couldn't hear her, but she read her lips and nodded happily.

Lilia dabbed at the corners of her eyes. *Thank you, Lord.*

The blockade was over. No more separation between the worlds in their system. No more need of medcenters to care for wounded combatants.

*Thank you, Lord.*

Admiral Chesnee looked on in faint bemusement as almost the entire Triumvirate erupted to its feet. He noted a few stragglers, probably Representatives who had been reluctant to support the trade agreement, but even they eventually joined their colleagues in clapping.

Kedis, a broad smile painting his face, rose to his feet and turned to the three Chief Ministers to offer them a deep bow. Chesnee took this as his cue to stand, as did the Chief Ministers. They stepped forward to shake the Ambassador's hand, before moving on to Chesnee himself. The rest of the Triumvirate left their chairs and streamed forward to engulf the table, some of them still clapping.

The moment had a slightly surreal cast. Chesnee knew he couldn't be the only one who felt it. He automatically sought out his wife's face; Sylvia was beaming and clasping her hands together in front of her in delight. She met his gaze and her smile warmed with pride.

*We did it,* he told her silently. Together, he and Kedis had achieved what more than twenty years' worth of time and effort by his predecessors had failed to accomplish. It wasn't the total submission the Senate had wanted all those years ago, but it was a giant leap forward in assimilating the Coalition into the Galactic Union.

As he shook hands with various Representatives and Directors and posed for holos, Chesnee couldn't help wondering when the other boot would drop. The Coalition's little terrorist group wasn't finished. Something was brewing; he felt it like a deep itch beneath his skin.

He wasn't the only one.


Throughout the ceremony, Lon stood with Jasper, Renner, and Mrs. Chesnee at the back of the room as instructed. He wore a tuxedo; the two soldiers wore their dress uniforms. Lon kept one eye discreetly on his scanner, though he shielded the device from the three Tarynians' view. They might know he was a Guardian, but that didn't mean he was at liberty to reveal any more Guardian tech.

Nothing happened, but he couldn't shake the feeling that it wasn't over. At the end, when the Triumvirate began to celebrate, he leaned toward Jasper and Renner. "Am I the only one who thinks this was too easy?"

Jasper shook his head, his gray eyes darting around the room.

"Either that," Renner said, his voice barely audible above the cheers and clapping, "or we're all entirely too damn jumpy."

Lon considered this, before lifting one shoulder in the tiniest of shrugs. It was a distinct possibility. *Still…*

He sighed. *Trade agreement or no trade agreement, something tells me it's going to be a long night.*

# Chapter 85

THE general air of excitement and relief pervading the conference room showed no signs of waning, though now that the immediate danger had passed, Aiden's colleagues began to depart in small clumps. There were interviews to be given and speeches to be made before the Celebration Ball began.

Aiden found Martin Hollowell in the crowd of Representatives. The other man's somber expression was out of place amid the rejoicing; he had remained one of the few to actively object to the trade agreement to the bitter end.

Aiden clasped his shoulder. "How are you holding up, old friend?"

Hollowell shrugged. "I supposed as well as can be expected." He looked around, shaking his head. "It's over, Aiden. You and I—we witnessed the end of the Coalition today."

This dour pronouncement almost startled a laugh from Aiden, but he restrained it in time. Instead, he raised a bushy white eyebrow. "Now, Martin, I know you are disappointed, but is that not just a touch dramatic?" It was his turn to shake his head. "The end of the Coalition? Really?"

"Just watch," Hollowell said grimly. "They won't be satisfied with a mere trade agreement for long. We moved too quickly—and I fear we will come to regret it."

He looked back over his shoulder at Kedis, Admiral Chesnee, and Mrs. Chesnee, who stood chatting with the Chief Ministers, the Sta'Gloan Director of Finance, Dion Pamos, and several others. If looks could kill, the ice in Hollowell's eyes would have frozen the Ambassador, the Admiral, and his wife solid in less than a heartbeat.

That malevolent animosity sent tendrils of unease curling through the pit of Aiden's stomach. "Well…" He gripped Hollowell's bony shoulder again. "Should it come to that, old friend, you and I will fight them for it."

Hollowell regarded him for a long moment, his gaze going oddly distant, as though visions of the future were playing out before his eyes. At last, he inclined his head. "Yes. Yes, we will."

"In the meantime…" Aiden smiled. "Let us at least celebrate the beginning of peace."

"Now there, old friend, I believe you're mistaken." Hollowell mirrored his smile, though he did not match its warmth. "We might have a trade agreement in place, but I suspect it will be a cold day in hell before we truly have peace."

His calm words sent a chill down Aiden's spine, as though invisible frozen fingers had just trailed across his skin. He looked at Hollowell, really looked at him, and glimpsed for the first time that the other man's bitterness and hatred ran much, much deeper than he, Aiden, had ever realized. He motioned to the conference room at large. "It is too late for Freedom's Children to do anything to stop this. They missed their opportunity."

"Yes, they did." Hollowell gave him a knowing look. "But you know as well as I do that that doesn't mean they can't wreak mayhem anyway and make their displeasure known."

"I hope it does not come to that."

Hollowell flicked his fingers in a dismissive gesture. "We shall see." He moved toward the door. "Enjoy the party, old friend."

Aiden stood for a moment looking after the Glo'Stean, deeply disturbed. A voice calling his name snapped him back to his surroundings. Kane Fenton strode up to him, a broad smile on his dark face, though his eyes followed Hollowell.

Fenton nodded in the Representative's direction. "He isn't pleased."

"Not at all."

"What did he truly expect to happen?" Fenton shook his head. "At some point, you have to let the past go." He swept a hand toward the Tarynians and the three Chief Ministers, who were just now making their way out of the room. "This is what is best for the people of the Coalition." He gave Aiden a confident look. "Martin will come around eventually."

*Of course he will,* Aiden thought, but part of him could not shake the memory of that look in his old friend's eyes. It cast a pall over the relief and thankfulness welling up inside him.

He did not have time to dwell on it. The trade agreement was signed and now he had speeches to make to his constituents.


When the cheers and clapping died down at last, leaving behind an air of general excitement in the auditorium, Lilia looked past Erik at Mrs. Mouta. "What do we do now?" A glance behind them told her a few people were making their way toward the exit.

"I don't know." Mrs. Mouta shook her head. "Dinner isn't until six."

At that moment, a tall woman dressed in a sleek, plum-colored sheath with a silver rose pinned to the single strap over her left shoulder took the stage. She had dark brown skin, keen eyes set in a round face, and a riot of tight black curls springing from her head in every direction. Silver swirls hung from her ears, glinting every time she moved her head.

"Ladies and gentlemen," she said in a magnified voice. "My name is Delena Tepiko and I am head of the Pearl's PR Department. If you will be so kind as to take your seats, we will show the Chief Ministers and Ambassador Kedis's first speech to the Coalition."

She indicated the holoprojector screen behind her with one well-manicured hand, and on cue it switched on to show the view from the Pearl's main press conference room, where several empty podiums awaited Kedis and the Chief Ministers.

[That's smart,] Erik remarked to the twins via Nancom. [Keep everybody entertained in here while Kedis an' the Chief Ministers do their press thing.]

Lilia nodded absently. [There are going to be a lot more speeches than just this, though. Grandfather will have to make one for his constituents, and—]

[—so will all the other Representatives,] Kevin finished, frowning slightly. [We could be here a while if they show all of them.]

[They won't,] Lilia said confidently.

"Should you wish to exit the auditorium and take your seats in the Dome," Tepiko continued, "you are welcome to do that as well. The Celebration Dinner will begin at six. Thank you." She bowed and exited the stage.

Two-thirds of the guests in the auditorium left their seats and began streaming toward the exits. The other third stayed for the speech. Kevin looked from Lilia, to Erik, to Mrs. Mouta. "If it's all the same to you, I'd just as soon leave too."

Erik half-waved. "Hear, hear."

Lilia nodded enthusiastically, and Mrs. Mouta smiled. "I've been looking forward to seeing the Dome," she said in her soft voice. "I've heard a great deal about it."

They joined the stream of people flowing out of the auditorium. Security personnel directed traffic toward a massive accelevator bank four halls away, along the outer edge of the Pearl, and they waited in line to ride up to the Dome.

When it was their turn, they found that the inside of the accelevators was reflective silver, except for its outer wall, which was made of curved plastiglass to provide a glimpse of Jamal's cityscape beyond while it skimmed up the outer edge of the Pearl. They were packed in too tightly for Lilia to get much of a look at it.

Though she, Kevin, Erik, and Mrs. Mouta were silent on the trip up to the Dome, their fellow occupants carried on low conversations in Sta'Gloan, Glo'Stean, and Lanxian. They broke off as the accelevator eased to a stop and the doors opened, allowing them all to filter out into a hall that looped the Dome. Soft gold light spilled from sconces on the walls.

A wide doorway stood in front of them; Lilia caught her breath as they passed through into the Dome. It was a circular atrium occupying the top five floors of the Pearl. Overhead, the curved ceiling was a latticework of giant plastiglass windows, allowing shafts of late afternoon sunlight to pierce the room. More light came from delicately-wrought shells covering solar pipes inset along the top of the walls around the dome, which would grow stronger as the sun set and darkness fell over Jamal. The walls were a pearly white; the floor looked like it was made from mother-of-pearl, though Lilia didn't know how they'd managed that.

Recalling the security blueprints they'd studied with Michael, Lilia glanced up. Supposedly, an observation walkway ran around the upper portion of the atrium. The only signs of it were short sections of railing that appeared spaced every dozen or so meters, breaking the smoothness of the walls. The railing sections looked like they actually merged into the Dome's plastiglass ceiling, but she knew it had to be an optical illusion.

Making a mental note to investigate further if she got the chance, Lilia turned her attention to the rest of the atrium. Opposite the accelevator bank stood a raised dais with a podium; to its left stood another stage where a small orchestra made up of musicians in black evening gowns and tuxedos played a variety of music from across the Coalition.

Dozens and dozens of round tables swirled around the curved outside edge of the massive atrium, covered in crisp white table-cloths and set with sparkling glassware and silverware. Elaborate centerpieces of crimson, sapphire blue, gold, and emerald green adorned each table.

Lilia could see the events of tonight unfolding in her mind's eye. Dinner would be served first, and then the true celebration would begin. Dancing and more speeches, wine and conversation flowing freely. Members of the Galactic Union and people of the Coalition mingling and mixing, old enmities and prejudices temporarily set aside.

*And, Lord willing*, she thought, *nothing will interfere with that.*

Like Erik had said, it was only sour grapes if Freedom's Children attacked now, wasn't it?

"It's beautiful," Mrs. Mouta sighed, looking around with excited eyes.

"Yes, it is," Lilia agreed, before glancing to her right, where a wet bar manned by four silver 'bots had been set up. A crowd had already gathered around it, though she could see more 'bots circulating the Dome with trays of drinks.

Beside her, Erik snorted. "Half these people will be sloshed before we even get to dinner."

*That…sounds about right. Unfortunately.* Lilia eyed him, placing a hand on his arm. "Will you be all right?"

The blond former police officer shot her a wry look. He had started drinking heavily after his partner was killed in a bomb explosion, but he had done better lately. "I'll be fine." He shook his head. "Never did like champagne anyway."

"Probably for the best," Kevin said, craning his neck to look up at the sky visible through the Dome's plastiglass ceiling.

A copper waitstaff 'bot approached them, dressed in black trousers and a crisp white shirt. It bowed briefly and asked in a metallic tenor, "Your names, if you please?"

Kevin gave them, and the 'bot inclined its head. "Follow me." It led them across the Dome's iridescent floor to one of the tables along the eastern side, set with an emerald green centerpiece. "Mrs. Mouta, here is your table."

The twins exchanged startled glances. It hadn't occurred to either of them that they might be at different tables.

"What can we get you to drink?"

"Water, for now," Mrs. Mouta requested. "Thank you."

The 'bot bowed and then turned to Lilia, Kevin, and Erik. "If you will continue to follow me?" It proceeded around the Dome until it reached a table along the southern wall, this one set with a crimson centerpiece. "Here you are."

For a second, staring at the immaculately set table, the deep, rich color of the centerpiece reminded her of spilled blood. Lilia blinked and it passed, though she found herself wondering if there was any significance attached to them being seated at this particular table. "Thank you."

The 'bot bowed again and took their drink requests before moving away to assist another clump of guests.

"Well," Kevin said breezily, "that was—"

"—unexpected?" Lilia frowned slightly. "Does this mean we won't be sitting with Grandfather?"

Kevin shrugged. "Possibly."

Erik stood beside the table, his hands shoved into his pockets, looking around with keen interest. "Lot of 'bots here," he remarked. "I was expectin' more live help."

"Maybe on Sta'Gloa," Kevin said with another shrug, "but 'bots are harder to come by on Glo'Stea. People tend to want to show them off when they have them."

"Interestin'." Turning back to the table, Erik raised an eyebrow at Lilia. "Suppose I better do my duty, eh? Wouldn't want the NCDC on my back for not bein' a convincin' escort."

He pulled out a chair for her and she smiled at him. "Thank you."

Once seated, Lilia set her clutch on the tablecloth beside her plate and glanced around the Dome. About a third of the tables were filled, and more people filed in with every passing moment. As Kevin and Erik settled into chairs on either side of her, she said, "I wonder how they decided where they're putting everyone. The 'bots clearly have a seating chart."

"Might get a clue based on who else ends up at this table." Leaning back in his chair, Erik proceeded to survey the glittering crowd. "Know anythin' else about security measures for tonight?"

Kevin shook his head. "Not much more than what the NCDC told us this morning. Michael said Director Caradoc has armed response teams on stand-by a floor or two below, and they're monitoring the Dome for any unexpected arrivals. And——"

"——supposedly there are a *lot* of Guardians here tonight," Lilia said, her gaze still roaming around the room.

Erik nodded. "Sounds like they're tryin' to play it close to the vest, since they haven't found the leak yet." He paused. "They *haven't* found it yet, right?"

The twins exchanged sober glances. "Not as far as——"

"——we know."

A moment later, a gold waitstaff 'bot dropped off their drinks—water for Lilia and soda for the men. On its heels, another 'bot arrived with two well-dressed couples in tow, one younger and the other middle-aged. Lilia's first thought was, *Well, we definitely won't be sitting with Grandfather. Not enough room.*

Motioning to the table with a silver hand, the 'bot said in Tarynian, "Here is your table, ladies and gentlemen."

Lilia sat very still, several things slotting neatly into place inside her mind. She darted a glance at her brother. [*This* is why we're at this table instead of Grandfather.]

Kevin gave her an imperceptible nod.

Lilia then glanced at Erik, who was still leaning comfortably back in his chair, though his brown eyes had narrowed a fraction and his face had gone expressionless. [Good thing you've got an autotranslator.]

[Yeah,] he said grimly. [Good thing.]

Once the 'bot had taken the new arrivals' drink orders and departed, the seven of them looked at each other. Kevin moved first, breaking what could have been an otherwise extremely awkward start to the night. Rising from his seat, he offered the newcomers a short bow. "Good evening," he said in Tarynian. "I am Kevin Strong. This is my sister, Lilia, and our friend Erik Holt." He indicated them both in turn.

Faint surprise washed over the newcomers' faces at being addressed in Tarynian, and then the older gentleman returned his bow, albeit a little stiffly, as though he did not have much practice at this sort of things. He was of medium height, with a pale brown, oval face adorned with a graying goatee, sharp dark eyes, a mop of graying black curls, and a stomach gone slightly to fat. He wore a black tuxedo with a brilliant red cummerbund.

His wife, after a second's hesitation, dropped an old-fashioned curtsey. She was a head shorter, with glossy black hair pinned up in an elaborate chignon, large, expressive dark eyes set in a round face, and skin a shade darker than her husband's. She wore a flowing gown of burnt orange with wide off-the-shoulder straps.

"I am Zelus Ortiz," the older gentleman said, before waving to his wife. "This is my wife, Sabrina. We are from Taryn."

"But it is not our first visit to Glo'Stea," Mrs. Ortiz said with a smile. "We came here many years ago for our tenth wedding anniversary."

"We loved it so much," her husband said, "that we jumped at the chance to be here tonight." Ortiz gave a modest shrug. "We own a technology company, you see, and we are very much interested in the chance to partner with Glo'Stea's businesses to rebuild this world's infrastructure." He made a small gesture that encompassed the room.

"Glo'Stea could use help in that respect," Kevin agreed, before turning to the younger couple.

Instead of bowing, the man stepped forward to shake Kevin's hand. Tall and lanky, with blue eyes and a receding hairline, he wore a white tuxedo trimmed in black. His companion, a tall, curvy woman with short, glossy black curls and ebony skin, wore a shimmering gold sheath slit almost to her hips on either side.

"Micah Caliban," the man said in rapid-fire Tarynian. "This is my associate Riva Taraji. Also from Taryn. We represent Adamek. We build ships."

Kevin was already nodding. "I've heard of you. Your shipyard is off of Westrom, in the Favri system?"

Caliban smiled as he pulled out a chair for Taraji. "One of them."

[Well,] Lilia told Kevin and Erik via Nancom, [I think we can safely guess why they put us all at the same table.]

[Politics,] Erik said in faint disgust, though he did an admirable job of maintaining a pleasant expression.

Once they were all seated, Caliban turned those sharp eyes on the twins and Erik. "And what, if I may ask, brings you to the celebration tonight?"

"Wait…" Mrs. Ortiz said slowly. "Strong…" She listed her head to one side. "Would you be the same Strongs who helped Ambassador Kedis?"

The twins and Erik exchanged glances. "Yes, we are," Kevin said. "Although our older brother did most of the work."

Comprehension dawned on the four Tarynians' faces.

'Bots arrived just then with several bottles of wine, which they poured for the newcomers. As they departed, Caliban leaned forward. "I am correct in stating that you are related to Representative Aiden Monroe? Of Sta'Gloa?"

Lilia suppressed a sigh. *Here we go.* She offered the man a polite smile. "That is correct."

"I must say," Taraji put in, "how delighted we are to hear someone speaking Tarynian. We did not expect that, you see." She smiled, showing brilliant white teeth, and when she tilted her head, her large gold hoop earrings glinted in the light.

"It's rare," Lilia said with a shrug. "My brothers and I learned years ago because we thought it would be…interesting."

"Are you in politics?" Ortiz inquired, taking a sip of his merlot.

"Oh, no." Kevin smiled. "That would be Grandfather's arena."

"Then what do you do?" Taraji motioned to the three of them with her own wine glass. She and Caliban were both drinking white wine.

[I hate this already,] Erik announced via Nancom. [Can I leave yet?]

Kevin ignored him. "We run a small interplanetary shipping business."

"Ah." Taraji's dark eyes lit with interest.

*Probably thinking about all the spacers we know who might be in the market for a ship upgrade,* Lilia thought wryly, reaching for her water glass. She let her gaze flit around the Dome. The atrium was at least three-quarters full now; the Ambassador and the Chief Ministers should be arriving any moment.

Through the thinning crowd, Lilia caught sight of an unwelcome figure following along behind another copper waitstaff 'bot. Distaste flooded her. *Alan Birch.* Why did they need the head of Triumvirate Security here at the *Pearl?*

The answer slapped her in the face a split-second later. *He's a Guardian and he's got sufficient security clearance. Of* course *he's here.* Hard-pressed to restrain a grimace, she snapped her eyes away from him and prayed that his table would be a good distance from theirs.

It was not to be.

# Chapter 86

THE copper waitstaff 'bot led Birch straight up to their table. "Here you are, sir," it said in a pleasant voice. "May I take your drink order?"

Birch stopped short when he realized who else occupied the table, his green eyes narrowing, but he recovered quickly. "Water."

Despite the horror and shock coiling through her, Lilia noted that at least he had the presence of mind to avoid alcohol at an event like tonight, with the possibility of an attack by Freedom's Children still looming over their heads.

Stiffly, Birch took the empty chair, which happened to be between Erik and Mrs. Ortiz. Seating himself, he nodded curtly to the table at large. "Alan Birch. Triumvirate Security."

"Oh, my." Taraji smiled at him over her wine glass, her auto-translator having done its job. "It is good to know we have security around."

A faint tightening in Birch's jaw was the only indication that being addressed in Tarynian bothered him. He inclined his head in another nod. "I was a last-minute addition to this table, I believe. My date for this evening was in a skimmer accident yesterday."

His girlfriend was the daughter of Chief Minister Koen's chief of staff. Lilia disliked Valencia Covara intensely, but she wished the other woman no ill will. Eyebrows raised in surprise, she asked, "Is she all right?"

Birch waved a hand. "Broken leg. She'll be fine, but it put her out of the running for tonight."

*I'm sure she was thrilled about that.* Lilia tactfully refrained from saying as much, however, as another more pressing thought took hold of her mind. *There are four Guardians right here.* She glanced from Birch to Kevin and Erik, asking via Nancom, [Why would the NCDC put *four* of us at this table?]

[God only knows,] Erik said wearily, [an' it doesn't look like He'll be talkin' any time soon.]

Looking at Birch—it was hard not to, given he was across the table from her—Lilia almost jolted with realization. [Birch has got an impactor.]

Kevin caught her eye, even as he smiled politely at something Mr. Ortiz had just said. [He can't be the only one. *That's* got to be part of their security measures.]

['An obviously they don't trust *us* with 'em,] Erik said sourly, meeting Birch's disdainful gaze with a level look that betrayed nothing.

The four Tarynians, clueless to the mental conversation being carried on around the table, continued to chat. Lilia pulled her attention back in time to catch Caliban's question about what kind of ship they had. Kevin answered, but before he could elaborate, a voice projected through the Dome.

"Ladies and gentlemen, may I have your attention, please?"

All eyes turned to the dais, where a stout man now stood with both arms raised. "Will you all join me in rising for Chief Minister Vance, Chief Minister Koen, Chief Minister Gammick, Ambassador Kedis, and Admiral Chesnee?"

Across the Dome, chair legs scraped against the iridescent floor as everyone stood. The Chief Ministers, Kedis, and the Chesnees strolled through the doors, flanked by the rest of the Triumvirate, and a rousing cheer broke out. Lilia, Kevin, and Erik clapped politely along with the rest of their table, though Lilia noticed Birch's applause was weak at best.

He caught her eye, simultaneously sending her a channel request. She accepted it against her better judgment.

[You shouldn't even be here.]

His icy voice in her head was a sharp contrast to the tumult filling the Dome. Lilia shot him a sharp smile. [You mean as a Guardian?] She shook her head slightly. [You're a bitter, angry man, Mr. Birch, you know that?]

[And you and your brothers are traitors.]

She rolled her eyes at that, pointedly turning away from him. [Not according to the Triumvirate or the trade agreement they just signed.]

Birch started to respond, but she slammed his channel closed before he got more than the first syllable out.

The announcer finally regained control of the room. "If you will all be seated," he said, motioning with his arms, "the Celebration Dinner will begin."

Lilia's stomach rumbled at the mention of dinner. She was hungry; the thought of food filled her with anticipation. It was bound to be good food too. That was one thing, at least, she had really come to appreciate about high society events. The food was usually *fantastic*.

The Chief Ministers, Kedis, the Chesnees, and the Triumvirate fanned out across the Dome to take their seats. Lilia thought she glimpsed her brother Lon and Jasper trailing in Kedis's wake; her heartbeat picked up. *Be patient*, she told herself, settling back down in her own seat. *Just be patient.*


For the record, the food *was* delicious. Lilia enjoyed each course, but her enjoyment was lessened by the nagging pressure she felt to keep an eye on everything, mixed with the need to keep up a running conversation with their Tarynian guests. This, at least, was relatively easy. With a little prompting from her, Kevin, Erik, and occasionally even Birch, the two couples were more than happy to talk about themselves, their businesses, and drop sly hints as to their hopes for the future. Their table made it all the way to dessert—a luscious lemon soufflé—without incident.

[Don't let your guard down,] Erik drawled from his seat, though he appeared to be listening intently to Taraji describe a new line of supply freighters she thought would particularly suit the Coalition. [After dinner is a good time for an attack—everyone's too full to pay much attention.]

[Or even later in the evening, when people have had too much to drink.] Kevin scraped the last of his torte from his plate. [Although they'd have to know they couldn't catch security personnel off-guard like that.]

[Yeah, but think about how much mayhem they could cause with half-drunk guests runnin' around in a panic,] Erik pointed out.

A shudder worked its way down Lilia's spine, despite the warmth of the giant atrium. [Let's pray it doesn't come to that.]

As people finished their dessert, the band began playing music suitable for dancing, but no one was much inclined for that yet. Guests instead began leaving their tables and mingling freely about the Dome, laughing, chatting, and networking.

Taraji leaned forward to rest her arms on the edge of the table, providing a tantalizing glimpse of her cleavage as she smiled across at Kevin. "Is it true that one of your brothers is likely to marry Representative Briscoe's sister?"

A faint widening of Kevin's eyes over the rim of his water glass was the only indication her question had surprised him. "It's a possibility. Why?"

Taraji's smile deepened. "I was wondering if you could possibly introduce me to Representative Briscoe. I've heard quite a lot about him."

*You've done your homework,* Lilia thought tartly, eying the other woman.

Kevin's gaze darted to Lilia in a silent, not-quite-panicked-but-almost question; she gave him an imperceptible shrug.

"Sure." Kevin matched the Tarynian woman's smile with a polite smile of his own. "Follow me." He rose from the table, pausing long enough to say, "It just might take us a second to find him."

"Thank you." Taraji came around the table to clasp his arm, casting a borderline triumphant smile over her shoulder at Caliban.

Directing a thin smile at Caliban, Birch echoed Lilia's earlier thoughts. "You seem to be well-versed in Coalition politics."

The other man waved an airy hand. "Cost of business." He raised his wineglass to the Ortizes. "One must always be prepared to take advantage of any potential opportunities that might fall one's way."

"True," Ortiz agreed with a gracious nod.

His wife offered Birch a smile, which made no impact. "It is an exciting time. There is so much we can offer your worlds."

"And gain in return, obviously," Birch said coolly, pushing his dessert plate aside. He'd only eaten half of his torte; apparently mango was not his favorite. "You smell a profit, or you wouldn't be here."

The atmosphere at the table, which had up to this point been rather pleasant, if a touch superficial, grew uncomfortable.

To Lilia's surprise, Erik, who had been unusually quiet throughout dinner, broke it. Leaning back in his chair with deliberate ease, he leveled an amused look at Birch. "I know you've been workin' in Triumvirate Tower for a while, Birch, but that *is* how business works." He wiggled a hand. "Both parties tend to work out a mutual give an' take."

The other Guardian's expression hardened, but the tension at the table dissipated. Erik tipped his water glass to the Ortizes. "'Course the Coalition has a market for certain things. We've been blockaded for twenty years." He grinned. "But our system has a few things worth tradin' for too."

Ortiz raised his wineglass in acknowledgment. "Very well stated, Mr. Holt."

Sensing an untapped well of conversation, Mrs. Ortiz asked, "Have you worked in the shipping industry long?"

Erik shook his head. "Not really."

"Oh?" Mrs. Ortiz tilted her head. "What did you do before?"

"I was a Sonela police officer. Worked the bomb squad."

"Oh, my." Mrs. Ortiz's dark eyes widened. "That sounds fascinating."

Lilia hid a grin. [Who knew you'd find a captive audience tonight?]

Erik darted a glance in her direction, but did not reply. Caliban had just asked how long he'd worked in that profession—and why he'd left.

Part of Lilia wanted to stay and help Erik navigate any uncomfortable aspects of this conversation, but the larger part of her wanted to find a hygiene unit. *And perhaps spot Jasper,* whispered a little voice inside her head. She squashed that voice, but she couldn't make it completely disappear. Nor could she keep her heart from beating faster.

The trade agreement had been signed…and that changed everything now, didn't it?

She rose from the table, prompting both Caliban and Ortiz to half-rise from their seats as well, Erik belatedly following suit. "If you'll excuse me a moment?" she said with a bright smile, before moving away from their table and slipping into the crowd mingling in the center of the Dome.

Lilia wound her way around clumps of guests until she reached one of the doorways that led into the hall looping around the bottom of the Dome. Much to her relief, she found a hygiene unit that didn't have too much of a line, and was soon emerging back into the Dome. She paused on the edge of the circular room to take in the full effect.

To her left, she could see the Chief Ministers, Kedis, and an assortment of other high-ranking individuals seated at a bevy of tables along the northern rim of the atrium. She thought she glimpsed the shimmering gold fabric of Taraji's dress a little further down. Her gaze skimmed over the rest of the crowded room, noting all the of the different people and groups laughing and planning the business future of the Coalition over a never-ending supply of alcohol and other beverages.

*This is our future, I suppose.* Oh, she knew most of the decisions would be finalized in boardrooms, but the groundwork was being laid here tonight.

In the subdued golden light coming from the shell-covered solar pipes, that fact hardly seemed real. This was a celebration. Lilia snorted softly to herself. *A celebration attended by people with agendas.*

Everyone here tonight had an agenda—even Kevin, Erik, and herself. *Although*, she thought with some amusement, *I suppose ours is a little more altruistic than most.*

Her thoughts turned back to Jasper; she bit her lip. *I still don't see him.* That surprised her, given that strange magnetism that always seemed to draw them together whenever they happened to be in the same place at the same time. She tried to swallow her disappointment. *Oh, well. I'm sure we'll cross paths eventually.*

A 'bot approached her with a tray of drinks; she waved it off with a smile and started back toward her table. *Can't stand here all night, even if I'd rather not spend any more time around Birch than necessary.* Maybe the other Guardian had gotten bored while she was gone and had taken himself off somewhere else. The thought brightened her spirits.

A third of the way across the Dome's iridescent floor, something prompted Lilia to glance to the left…just in time to see Jasper emerge from a clump of laughing guests. Their gazes collided. Her heartbeat sped up as a smile lit his face and he smoothly shifted course to stride in her direction.

Jasper was, as usual, wearing his dress uniform, but for once Lilia didn't even register it. Her attention caught—and lingered—on the broad set of his shoulders, the way the Dome's muted sunlight glinted off his golden hair…and that smile as he approached her.

It was a warm, dazzling smile that melted her insides and set her nerves tingling. At the same time, the sight of him made something else within her relax with relief. Strange dichotomy, that, but she didn't have time to analyze it. She was too busy drinking in the sight of him.

The rest of the Dome around them faded away; for that moment, it was just the two of them.

Jasper came to a halt in front of her. "Good evening, Miss Strong." His smile and the warmth in his gray eyes belied the gravity of his tone.

"Lieutenant Wright." Lilia held out her hand to him; he bowed over it. "I trust you are enjoying yourself now that everything is settled?"

Straightening, Jasper gave a short chuckle. "Immensely." He had yet to release her hand. "You look beautiful, by the way." He nodded to her gown. "Blue suits you."

The way he said it, low and sincere, brought a rush of color to her cheeks. Lilia dipped her head in a nod and murmured, "Thank you," before giving him a sudden, impish smile. "I'd comment on your choice of attire for the evening, except that it's the same thing you always wear."

Jasper laughed ruefully. "Yes, well, it was the Ambassador's idea. He said, and I quote, that tonight of all nights we ought to wear our dress uniforms to show that the Galactic Union is no longer something the Coalition need fear."

"That sounds like something Kedis would say."

"Oh, he did, I assure you. But, I suppose he has a point tonight."

Lilia shrugged airily, a strange blend of giddiness and contentment flooding her at being near him again. "I suppose."

Jasper was still holding her hand. Out of the corner of her eye, she was aware they were garnering a few looks from certain quarters, but not nearly as many as they would have weeks earlier. And while she couldn't help an uncomfortable little twitch, she found that the larger part of her simply didn't care. Not tonight.

They had trade agreement. Everything had changed.

"I was hoping to see you tonight," Jasper said softly, tightening his grip on her fingers. He paused. "I've missed you."

A stray corner of Lilia's mind noted that his Sta'Gloan had improved drastically during his time on Sta'Gloa. The rest of her thrilled at hearing that he had missed her. He'd never said that before. Implied it, perhaps, but never outright stated it.

She took a breath. "I've missed you too."

The words were easier to say than she'd thought they would be.

Something in Jasper's expression softened. He glanced left and right, as though suddenly realizing they'd been standing in the middle of the Dome for an inordinately long amount of time, before focusing on her again. "Would you take a walk with me? I have something I'd like to show you."

Bemused, Lilia tilted a dark eyebrow at him. "Here?" She indicated the Dome with her free hand.

"No, back in Sonela."

His deadpan tone made her laugh, which sparked another of Jasper's charming grins. It was the most relaxed Lilia thought she'd ever seen him. On the verge of saying yes, she hesitated, glancing past his shoulder at the tables scattered along the rim of the Dome. Technically, she was on duty and shouldn't exactly go gallivanting off—

"It won't take long, I promise." Jasper's grip tightened on her fingers. "No one will miss us for a few minutes."

Meeting his eyes again, Lilia was struck by the tense hopefulness she saw there. That decided her; she breathed out a laugh. "You're right. Lead on, Lieutenant."

Some of the tension bled from his frame; his dazzling smile returned, sending a tingle all the way to the tips of her toes. Drawing her hand through his arm, Jasper nodded to the western edge of the Dome. "This way."

Lilia could feel the muscles in his arm beneath the smooth material of his sleeve as she allowed him to lead her across the Dome. They nodded in passing to several people along the way, including a middle-aged Lanxian businesswoman. Lilia took in the way the woman's swathe of still-dark hair glistened against the gold of her sari and felt an unexpected pang of loss.

It had been weeks since she thought about her hair, missed the length and weight of the braid she'd always favored, but at this moment, it hit her hard. Her throat clogged for a few seconds in remembered grief; she unconsciously raised her free hand to touch the wispy strands of her own hair she'd left free to frame her face. *It'll take forever to grow that long again.*

Jasper sensed her change in mood, though he had no idea what had happened. "What's wrong?"

Lilia started to shrug it off, started to half-smile and say it was nothing, but she made the mistake of meeting his eyes. The genuine concern she found there proved to be her undoing. She might not be able to tell him anything relating to the fact that she was a Guardian, but she couldn't lie to him about this.

Not after all the other pieces of their lives they'd shared over the past few months.

*Besides, he already knows the truth about what happened to my hair—or at least* most *of the truth.*

She took a deep breath. "That woman we just passed—her hair reminded me of how long mine used to be. I'm mostly over losing it, but…" She shrugged. "I guess it just hit me all of a sudden."

"That's understandable," Jasper said softly. He paused. "The important thing, though, is that you lived."

Lilia braved a look at him in time to catch his eyes drift to the scar tissue hidden beneath the filmy sleeve covering her left bicep.

One corner of her mouth curved in a wry smile. "I did live."

"Your hair will grow back," he assured her. "Although personally," he ran his gaze over her before meeting her eyes and smiling again, "I think you look lovely just as you are."

Heat flared in Lilia's cheeks; she glanced away to hide it. "Thank you."

"You're welcome."

They reached the edge of the atrium and passed through a doorway into the softly-lit outer hall. It was quite busy here, since they were near the kitchens, but it soon emptied out. They walked another twenty meters and then Jasper halted in front of a single accelevator.

"Here we are." He motioned for Lilia to precede him inside. "This one is not connected to the rest of the Pearl. It only goes up a couple of floors."

Excitement stirred to life. "We're going up to the observation walkway?"

In the soft light provided by the sconce mounted on the wall beside the accelevator, Jasper looked crestfallen. "You've seen it already?"

"No, I haven't," Lilia hastened to assure him. "I just know it's up there." She offered him a pleased smile. "I was hoping to get a chance to see it tonight."

He brightened, and she stepped into the accelevator ahead of him, glancing with interest at the view of Jamal's western night skyline visible through the curved plastiglass outer wall. If she wasn't a

Guardian—and if Jasper had been anyone else—she might have felt more nervous about being alone in an accelevator with him. As it was, she barely gave it a thought.

"Well," Jasper said as he followed her inside, his expression regaining its blend of excitement and anticipation. "I think you'll like this."

# CHAPTER 87

THE ride was short; when the accelevator doors opened, Lilia's breath caught in her throat for the second time that night. "Wow."

Three meters wide, the observation walkway ran the circumference of the Pearl's atrium. The curved outer wall was one-way transparent plastiglass so clear it might not have even been there. The walkway's inner wall matched the rest of the Dome's pearly walls, and was broken periodically by open spaces guarded by the railings she'd seen from below, which were waist-high.

Opaque, pearly light from shell-covered solar pipes embedded along the edge of the marble floor provided faint illumination; the observation walkway was otherwise lit only by the glowing lights of Jamal's cityscape beyond its plastiglass wall. The rush of sound from the atrium below was audible, but downgraded to a dull roar.

An armed security guard stood two meters away with his back to the pearly inner wall, looking out at Jamal. He gave Lilia and Jasper a cursory glance as they strolled past, but otherwise remained motionless. In the distance ahead of them, Lilia saw another security guard stationed at the next section of wall.

"This is about as private as it is going to get, I'm afraid," Jasper said in a low voice, as he led her to a spot hopefully out of hearing range of the guards.

It was understandable. The guards were there in case Freedom's Children had coordinates to this walkway. One corner of Lilia's mouth tilted up. "Privacy is an illusion anyway—they have to have cams monitoring things up here too."

"True. Although cams won't be able to hear us."

Lilia nodded, conceding the point, and stepped up to the plastiglass wall. A silvery handrail had been installed along its length—no doubt to keep people from unconsciously touching and smudging the plastiglass. Her fingers automatically found the handrail—its metal was cool to the touch—and curled around it.

"This is beautiful," she breathed, looking up at Jasper with something akin to awe as he came up to stand beside her. "How did you know this was here?"

He gave a modest shrug. "I saw blueprints too. We had a rather...intense security briefing before we brought the Ambassador here this afternoon."

"That makes sense."

Jasper looked pleased with himself. "I thought you would appreciate it."

"I do." Smiling at him, her heart thumping delightfully in her chest, Lilia turned back to the plastiglass wall to study Jamal. Despite the day's heat, it was a relatively clear night. "I've never seen this city at night before." Her fingers tightened around the handrail. "The last time I was here, it was daytime and pouring rain."

She didn't—*couldn't*—tell him why she had been here. Thankfully, he didn't ask.

They stood in companionable silence for a long moment, soaking in the view and the relative stillness of the observation walkway compared to the celebration taking place below. Lilia was extremely aware of Jasper's tall form beside her; she smelled the strangely comforting scent of his cologne whenever she inhaled. When either of them moved slightly, their arms brushed.

The faint glow of the floor lights combined with the glow from the city beyond to create an atmosphere in the walkway that had a decidedly...romantic feel to it. Her cheeks flushed at the thought; she was glad the light was dim. She was also glad they were some distance from the guards.

The silence between them stretched on, eventually shifting from comfortable to borderline awkward. Something had shifted between them since the night he kissed her, but Lilia didn't know how to categorize it. Biting the inside of her lip, she stole a glance at Jasper's profile. Despite how happy she was to see him again, now that they were both standing here, she found herself at a sudden, terrible loss for words.

It was like her entire vocabulary—in *four* languages, no less—had inexplicably dribbled out her ears, leaving her with nothing.

She would have laughed at herself, if it hadn't been so frustrating. She could *feel* time slipping away from them. That nagging little voice returned, reminding her that she had a job to do—that *both* of them had jobs—and she had no business being up here with Jasper staring out at Jamal's skyline if neither of them was going to talk.

Lilia swallowed, bitter regret and disappointment clogging her throat. She was aware—so very aware—of Jasper's solid presence beside her, but she couldn't stay up here. No matter how much she wanted to.

*He said he had something to show you, and now you've seen it.* It was time to return to the party. *He never said anything about wanting to talk.*

Forcing herself to turn away from the plastiglass wall and the stunning view of Jamal, Lilia gathered her courage and somehow managed to dredge up words. "Jasper, I—"

"Don't."

She froze, the rest of her sentence dying on her lips, more surprised at the quiet intensity of his tone than the fact that he had interrupted her.

Jasper shifted to face her, bracing himself against the handrail with his hip. "Don't go. Please. Not yet." His mouth quirked in a wry smile. "I was hoping to get a chance to talk to you tonight, I just—"

He shook his head, his eyes soft and a little bashful. "Sometimes when I'm around you, I don't quite know what to say."

A rush of warm relief flooded Lilia; she gave him a shaky smile. "I can relate."

Jasper reached out a hand to her, but changed his mind and dropped it to his side. "They won't miss either of us for a few more minutes. Stay here with me." He swallowed. "Just—just for a little while longer."

Meeting his eyes, something in those gray depths made Lilia stay her feet, made her quiet the voice inside her head that was insisting she needed to get back to the celebration. It wasn't like she *wanted* to leave, anyway. Slowly, she ducked her head in an acquiescent nod. "All right."

After a couple of seconds, Jasper smiled ruefully. "I've spent the past few days trying to figure out what I wanted to say to you."

Lilia's heart beat in her chest like a mad, caged thing, but she remained silent, waiting for him to continue.

He glanced out at Jamal's nightscape again. "The trade agreement changes everything, you know."

This seemed to warrant a response, though it wasn't exactly what Lilia had been hoping he'd want to talk about. "I know."

Jasper's Adam's apple bobbed as he swallowed, and then he gave her his full attention. His expression was earnest and serious, tinged with a hint of hopefulness. "We haven't really had the chance to talk about the other night at Representative Pamos's dinner party."

*That* was an understatement if Lilia had ever heard one, but her pulse was hammering too loudly in her ears for her to react. Her mouth was dry; she had to swallow twice before she could speak. "You mean when you kissed me?"

Jasper went a little pink around the edges, but nodded. "Yes." That bashful smile returned. "And then the med 'bot interrupted us."

"Terrible timing, for a machine," Lilia agreed, her words emerging sounding breathy.

In that instant, standing there looking at a man she'd come to regard as highly as one of her brothers, Lilia realized something. That kiss had shifted things between them, altering them forever, but it wasn't too late to back out.

If she wanted to back out.

They stood on the edge of a precipice looming over a dark, deep chasm. She could jump, trusting that Jasper would jump with her and they'd land on the other side together…or she could just walk away. She could gloss things over, pretend they'd never happened.

Tracing the contours of Jasper's now-so-familiar face with her gaze, his strong jaw line and nose, his cheeks, his steady eyes with those eyelashes, Lilia finally admitted to herself it was too late to run now. Had probably been too late for a while.

That private admission sparked a surge of boldness. She had a good idea where he stood—that kiss had been an excellent indicator. Lifting her chin, she let her mouth curve in a small, almost saucy smile. "What were you going to say that night?"

Jasper's smile vanished, to be replaced with a serious, almost nervous expression. He studied her for several heartbeats, before he lifted his shoulders in the barest of shrugs as though he couldn't quite help himself. "I was going to tell you I'm in love with you."

For an instant, all of the oxygen in the observation walkway, the entire Dome itself, seemed to have been sucked right out. Lilia couldn't breathe. *He said it. He actually* said *it.*

Air flooded her lungs again as her body forced itself to inhale. With that breath came a host of emotions—joy, surprise, giddiness, happiness—making her knees wobble and tremble. Instinctively, she stretched a hand out for the railing to steady herself.

Just as instinctively, Jasper reached out to help steady her. His fingers—a little cool; he was nervous—closed around her bare elbow. "Are you all right?" He sounded torn between amusement and alarm, but his eyes glittered with a storm of emotion. "Lilia?"

She finally forced her vocal chords to produce coherent sounds, though she continued to stare at him with wide violet eyes. "You— you're in love with me?"

It came out sounding like a bewildered question instead of the cool, calm statement she'd been aiming for.

Amusement won out over alarm, making his gray eyes twinkle, but Jasper said soberly, "I believe that is what I just said." His forehead suddenly creased with concern. "You had to have known."

*I suspected*, Lilia thought. But for weeks she'd suppressed that line of thought. She wet her lips. "I—tried not to think about it for a while." She smiled apologetically. "Because of—"

"—everything." Jasper nodded. "I know." Releasing her elbow, he skimmed his hand down her forearm to tangle their fingers together. "I didn't want to push you. I was planning on waiting until tonight to talk to you."

His eyes went distant. "But when I saw you that night, covered in blood—"

"I wasn't exactly *covered* in blood."

"You didn't see it from my perspective."

Lilia bit her lip, conceding the point with a sideways tip of her head.

"I never dreamed I'd meet someone like you." The corners of Jasper's smile softened. "Not while assigned to the Blockade Division."

Lilia hardly dared to blink, half-expecting him to say something about Challa, but he didn't.

"That night, when you arrived at the Mansion..." Jasper shook his head, his thumb skimming over the backs of her knuckles. "I think we all thought you'd turn us over to the authorities. Except for your brother, of course. But you didn't."

His gaze was intense; Lilia fought the urge to shift on her feet beneath it. She gave an embarrassed shrug. "Well, at the time, most of our family had just been blown up, and then I found out my dead brother wasn't dead after all. I wasn't exactly thinking straight and I knew it."

"You gave us the chance to make all of this happen." Jasper indicated the Pearl with a sweep of his hand. "You didn't let prejudice and hate keep you from doing the right thing."

"That was the Holy Spirit's influence." Lilia smiled wryly. "There were certainly times I wondered if we'd all lost our minds."

Jasper moved another step closer to her. "Your compassion is one of the things that struck me about you. And your faith in God. We might be from different star systems, but we believe in the same Savior. I've watched you do the right thing even when it wasn't exactly what you wanted to do."

A flush rising in her cheeks, Lilia gave another little shrug. Her heart pounded in her chest; she didn't know what to say. Never in her wildest dreams had she imagined how this conversation might play out—or that it would unfold the way it was right now.

He was still holding her hand.

"I love talking to you at night." Jasper took a breath. "I think I can safely say it is my favorite part of the day."

"It's mine too." Lilia found herself nodding, a sweet smile breaking over her face. She'd never told him just how much she looked forward to hearing from him. She bit her lip. "The day doesn't seem quite right if I haven't talked to you."

His fingers tightened on hers. "I am glad to hear that."

They could have been the only people in the Pearl, for all either of them cared at that moment. Standing there looking up in Jasper's face, Lilia wet her lips again—she didn't miss the way his eyes darted down to her mouth—and gathered her courage once more. "You're the first man who's ever kissed me—and meant it."

She didn't elaborate—or give him time to question her—but continued, "I...haven't exactly dated a lot." She shrugged, a quick, awkward gesture. "Grandfather moved back and forth between Sta'Gloa and Lanx every three months when we were growing up, and then Kevin, Lon, and I went to Glo'Stea."

She shrugged again, her eyes darting past him to the window at the memory of Greg. "I suppose I could have then, but..." She trailed off into silence, biting her lip again.

Jasper remained quiet.

"I don't have much experience at this kind of thing," Lilia found herself saying bluntly—and far more calmly than she could have ever imagined herself admitting. "I'm not really sure what to do." She gave another little awkward shrug. "Or say, really."

Jasper just smiled at her, the tenderness in his expression further melting her insides. "You are doing just fine." He lifted his eyebrows in faint surprise. "Really, you've never been interested in anyone?"

Lilia started to shake her head, but stopped as a memory flitting through her mind—a memory of a summer she hadn't thought about in five years. "Well, there *was* a guy named Riker the summer after Kevin and I turned sixteen." She shook her head. "Wow, I haven't thought about him in forever."

When Jasper just continued to look at her, she realized he was waiting for an explanation. She shrugged again. "Not much to tell, really. He was the son of somebody on one of the Lanxian Representative's staffs, and Kevin and I hung out with him a lot while we were there for that Triumvirate session."

Her eyes went distant; she'd just remembered *why* she didn't think about those three months. "I thought he really liked me—and I think he did, for the most part—but he wanted more than I was comfortable with, and we had more supervision than *he* was comfortable with."

Lilia shrugged again. "Toward the end of the session, he found somebody he liked better. Somebody more fun and not quite so sheltered." She smiled wryly. "Kid stuff, you know?"

It felt like a lifetime ago, instead of only five years. "In hindsight," Lilia continued softly, "I'm glad we were as supervised as we were." She darted a glance up at Jasper. "I think I'd have been tempted to make…mistakes…I'd have ended up regretting."

"Being sheltered isn't a bad thing," Jasper said, equally softly. "I think I probably could have done with a little more sheltering." He paused. His expression was still tender, but held a hint of resolve—like he was steeling himself for something. "Lilia, you are an amazing woman. I've really enjoyed getting to know you. You're smart and kind, levelheaded…a woman of God."

His eyes traced her face. "And you're beautiful. So beautiful. And, like I said, I've fallen in love with you."

His words fell like rain onto parched ground; Lilia hadn't known she'd needed to hear them until he said them. She held her breath, however; she could feel a 'but' coming.

She wasn't wrong.

"But…" Jasper took a deep breath. "I understand if you don't feel the same way. Or—or if you can't get past the fact that I'm G.U.." He smiled wryly. "Obviously I *hope* you can, but…" It was his turn to shrug awkwardly. "Not much I can do about it if you can't accept that."

Lilia finally acknowledged her need for oxygen. She dragged in a deep breath while she considered his words—really considered them. "I…really like you, Jasper. I *really* like you." She wasn't sure she could call it 'love' yet, wasn't sure enough of herself yet.

She let out a breathy laugh. "I didn't mean to—I never dreamed I'd be interested in a G.U. soldier, of all people." She held up an apologetic hand to take the sting out of her words, but the corners of Jasper's eyes crinkled with a smile; he understood. "But…I couldn't help myself once I got to know you."

"It's nice to know you think I'm irresistible."

She shot him a dry look, but Jasper merely grinned at her and motioned for her to continue. She studied him briefly before shrugging. "You love the Lord. That's one of the first things I noticed about you. And, I'll be honest, it took me a while to understand how you could be a Christian and serve in the Galactic Union military at the same time."

Jasper laughed ruefully, bringing his free hand up to run it through his golden hair. "I know. I could see that struggle in you." He gave her an understanding look. "But if I'd been raised in your shoes, spending my entire life cut off from the rest of the galaxy, I'd probably feel the same way."

Lilia looked down at their clasped hands before meeting his eyes. "I don't know how this is going to work, or where exactly we go from here, but…" she licked her lips, "I think I'd like to find out."

Jasper searched her face for a few seconds, as though to confirm she was serious, before a slow smile grew on his face. "I'm glad to hear that." He brought their entwined hands up to rest on his chest above his heart. "Although, just for the record, are you *sure* you're not in love with me yet?"

His teasing tone made Lilia purse her lips. "I don't know," she said honestly. "I know that I really like you, and I know that I love hearing from you, and I miss you when I haven't seen you for a while. And—" she hesitated, then bravely continued, "—I love the way you look at me. As though I'm special and I'm the only woman you can see."

"You *are* special, and as far as I'm concerned, there aren't any other women."

Jasper's voice rumbled in his chest; Lilia felt it vibrating her fingers. Looking up through her eyelashes at him, she allowed herself a teasing smirk. "You do realize, in addition to going through my grandfather, you'll probably have to contend with my four real brothers and one adopted brother?"

"Holt?" At her nod, Jasper just shrugged. "I think I can handle them." He grinned crookedly down at her. "As long as you've got my back."

Lilia laughed, feeling giddy. "I think I can manage that."

"Good."

They smiled at each other, and then Jasper gathered up her other hand in his and raised both to his lips. He pressed a series of feather-light kisses to her knuckles and a delicious shiver ran down Lilia's spine.

*Kiss me.* The thought flitted unbidden through her mind, but it took hold in an instant and grew deep roots. *Kiss me.*

She didn't care that there were guards only meters away, no doubt watching, since they had nothing better to do at the moment. She didn't care that there were security cams along the observation walkway, with people monitoring them. She didn't care about anything except the man standing so close to her she could feel the warmth emanating from his body, smell the crisp, comforting scent of his cologne.

Her thoughts must have been reflected in her eyes, because Jasper's gaze flicked to her lips again. He looked at her, as though gauging her reaction, and then bent his head, leaned in, and pressed his lips to hers.

The sensation was just as incredible this time as it had been the night of Pamos's dinner party. Tingles shot through Lilia's nerves. Her eyes fluttered shut; she kissed him back as best she could. She'd need more practice, noted a corner of her mind, practice she'd probably be sure to get now.

After entirely too short a time, Jasper pulled back far enough to rest his forehead against hers. His gray eyes were dark with desire and emotion. "I would stay here all night with you," he said huskily, "but we probably ought to—"

"—head back to the party," Lilia sighed. "You're right."

Jasper still held her hands against his chest; reluctantly, he released her. Lilia motioned to the walkway. "I'm glad you brought me up here."

His smile was blinding. "I'm glad you came." He cocked an eyebrow. "Dance with me later?"

"Why, Lieutenant," Lilia playfully batted her eyelashes at him, "I thought you'd never ask."

Jasper just continued to grin, and together they walked back to the accelevator. They nodded to the guard again, who ignored them, his expression cold and stern. Lilia didn't care; she was too blissfully happy to let a note of possible disapproval ruin her evening.

# Chapter 88

O N the short ride back down the Dome's main floor, Jasper leaned over and stole a kiss, his lips soft and his eyes full of tenderness. But by the time the doors opened seconds later, he was a respectable distance from her.

Lilia tried to contain her giddiness as they retraced their steps through the hall and into the Dome. *Wouldn't do to go waltzing around smiling like a loon,* she thought with a silent laugh. People might talk—though most of them would probably chalk it up to her over-imbibing like a good number of the other guests here tonight.

With one last lingering look, Jasper left her at the edge of the Dome to find Kedis. Lilia took a second to survey the atrium, but her attention was only half-focused on who was standing where. *Get it together,* she scolded herself. *No matter how happy you are right now, you still have to pay attention to what's going on.*

Her best bet at the moment was to head back to her table and check on their Tarynian guests. Unable to repress a pleased smile, she drifted through the clumps of people dotting the edges of what had become a dance floor, where a medium-sized group of couples were swaying and swirling around in time to a lively traditional Glo'Stean folk song. As the table came into sight, her steps slowed.

Alan Birch was the only person remaining.

Lilia's smile slipped, her high spirits taking a significant hit. The last thing she wanted tonight was to be stuck at a table with a snobby bully. She started to turn away, in the hopes of locating Kevin, Erik, or one of other her brothers, but it was too late. Birch had seen her.

"I was wondering where you'd run off to," he drawled, raising his water glass to her with a sardonic look.

Reluctantly, Lilia slipped into her chair. The dirty dishes had been cleared away, leaving nothing but the centerpiece, various beverage glasses, and after-dinner candies in brightly-colored wrappers scattered on the white tablecloth. She opened one; the pleasant scent of chocolate and mint immediately hit her. Just before she popped the chocolate into her mouth, she pinned Birch with a flat look. "Why would you care?"

He twitched one shoulder in a shrug. "Supposed to be keeping an eye on things." His green eyes were mocking; he didn't have to speak for her to hear the rest of his sentence. *That includes traitors like you.*

Lilia just rolled her eyes and sat back in her chair to survey the Dome again, letting the mint chocolate melt on her tongue. Through the shifting masses of people, she occasionally glimpsed familiar figures. Shane Briscoe. Dion Pamos. Admiral Chesnee and his wife. Michael, dancing with Dawn. That sight made her smile.

Without taking her attention off the crowd, she addressed Birch. "I suppose our Tarynian friends are still off networking?"

"No doubt." Distaste dripped from every syllable. "The older couple left shortly after you did and they haven't been back since."

"I'm not surprised."

She didn't elaborate, and Birch didn't make further inquiries. *As long as he's civil,* Lilia decided, *I can probably stand to sit here for a few minutes.*

Her gaze drifted up to the all-but-invisible observation walkway at the top of the Dome, and a small, unbidden smile curved her lips again. *G.U. or not, Jasper really is amazing.*

A glint of light beyond the railing on the eastern side of the atrium caught her eye. Lilia almost wrote it off as nothing, just other guests exploring the walkway, but then it happened again. She blinked—and frowned. *If I didn't know better, I'd say that almost looks like light reflecting off—*

Her eyes widened. *Is somebody* dueling *up there?*

Uncertain what to do, she turned her attention back to the table—only to find Birch staring straight at her. The hair on the back of her neck prickled uncomfortably. "What?"

"What was that face for?" Birch didn't drop his gaze, his fingers toying with the stem of his water glass.

Lilia considered telling him it was none of his business, but… Her eyes strayed back to the railing on the other side of the Dome. She'd *seen* something—she was sure of it—and tendrils of unease curled through her stomach. *Probably a bad idea to tell* him *that though.*

Even so…could she afford to take the chance? Just in case something *was* wrong? *We're still on the same side, even if we dislike ach other.*

Biting the inside of her lip, she met Birch's cold green stare. "I thought I saw something up there." She surreptitiously tipped her head toward the observation walkway. "Behind the railing, like somebody's dueling up there."

"Dueling?" Birch sneered, his icy green gaze sliding to the railing. "On the observation walkway?"

*So he* does *know it's there*, Lilia thought, even as the sarcasm in his tone made her bristle. She had to press her lips together tightly to keep a scathing reply from slipping out. *You're a Christian*, she reminded herself. *Act like it.*

When she thought she had control of her tongue, she leaned forward and dropped her voice. "I know Freedom's Children has a transporter. I also know that this transporter doesn't have a directional stabilizer to make portal opens on the ground—or floor, in this case."

She shrugged, a trifle self-consciously. "Hopefully it's nothing. I just—something doesn't feel right, and given the situation…" She gestured to the Dome around them.

"They have security cams up there."

"Yeah, and if the Mastermind can open portals to the walkway, who's to say he can't take out the cams too?"

Birch remained oddly silent, still fiddling with his water glass.

Lilia raised a challenging eyebrow at him. "Do you know if any of the guards up there are Guardians?"

To her surprise, a sneer curled his lips. "One or two."

"Can you Nancom them?" It seemed a logical question, given his background in—and one could almost call it an obsession with—security.

"No."

His answer stunned her. Lilia sat back in her chair, hard-pressed to keep from gaping at him.

"Security won't take you seriously, either," Birch continued. "You'll waste time trying to convince them of anything."

*That* was probably debatable, but he was right in that she didn't have time to argue. Not if something really was wrong. Lilia made her decision in that instant. *I'll just have to investigate myself.*

If somebody *was* up there, an incognito Guardian 'accidentally' wandering by was less suspicious than the arrival of security personnel.

Rising from her seat in one fluid motion, Lilia started across the Dome toward the nearest hall entrance.

Birch's cold voice came from behind her. "What do you think you're doing?"

She shot him a dry look over her shoulder. "Investigating, of course. It's probably nothing, but I can't risk being wrong. If you won't take me seriously…"

Birch made no reply, but shoved back his own chair and followed after her, his expression automatically smoothing into something more neutral and less alarming.

*Great*, Lilia thought, rolling her eyes again. Part of her protested that Birch *couldn't* follow her up there—it might give people the wrong idea if anyone saw them disappear together—but the more practical side of her knew she shouldn't go up there alone. *Still…Birch?*

Lilia took the nearest doorway into the outer hall and strode along at a brisk pace, searching for another accelevator up to the walkway. There were several, both because of how large the Dome was and also because the Pearl's architects loved symmetry.

As soon as they were in the hall, Birch matched her pace, his longer legs easily catching up with her. He sent her a channel request, which she reluctantly accepted.

[It's not that I'm not taking you seriously,] he ground out. [Security won't take me seriously either.] It sounded like the admission cost him dearly. [Director Caradoc and I had a…disagreement over the inclusion of Guardians in tonight's events.]

Startled, Lilia glanced sideways at him, trying to imagine him facing off against the Glo'Stean Director of Security.

[I *told* him the upper guard needed to be comprised of all Guardians, but he wanted to assign most of the Guardians on his staff elsewhere.] Birch's jaw clenched in remembered anger.

Lilia resisted the urge to shake her head. [Didn't see that coming.]

Glimpsing an accelevator leading up to the observation walkway some distance down the hall, she increased her stride. At the same time, she opened a joint Nancom channel to Kevin and Erik.

[Thought I saw something suspicious up on the walkway. Headed up there now with Birch to check it out.]

[Birch?] they both sputtered in unison.

She didn't have time for a long, drawn-out explanation. Briefly, Lilia laid out where they were going, finishing with, [Birch thinks security won't listen to me—and he apparently ticked off Director Caradoc, so they won't listen to *him* either.]

[I'd loved to have heard *that* conversation,] Erik remarked.

[We'll head up to the western side,] Kevin assured her.

[You better believe it,] Erik added. [Anythin' to get out of here for a while.]

[Thanks.] That made Lilia feel marginally better.

She and Birch reached the accelevator and he mashed the button with an impatient finger. The doors immediately slid open; they rushed inside. On the way up, she glanced at the tall man. "Kevin and Erik are checking out the other side of the walkway."

Birch's only response was a curt nod. His hands were already in his ISF—Lilia took it as a point in her favor. He might believe her a traitor to her system, but at least he didn't think she was crazy.

*Unless, of course, he's actually up here because he thinks you're the threat.*

Lilia shoved *that* cheerful little thought aside for later.

Reaching over her shoulder, she sank her own hands into her ISF and curled her fingers around the hilts of her nanoblades. The ridged metal was cold to the touch. She drew both blades—a somewhat tricky feat in the confines of the accelevator with Birch right beside her—and dropped her arms to her sides, concealing the shining blades in the folds of her gown.

Her heart hammered in her chest. Best to be prepared if there *was* anybody up here.

As soon as the accelevator doors opened and they emerged onto the walkway, Lilia knew they were in trouble.

By the faint illumination of the shell-covered solar pipes running along the edge of the pearlescent floor, she saw two bodies. Both of the guards who had been stationed at the walls on either side of the railing directly in front of the accelevator lay in pools of their own scarlet blood. Her stomach roiled in horror, but she didn't have time to think about it.

The murderers were still here.

A broad-shouldered figure knelt at on the pearlescent floor at each of the first three railings to their right, aiming sniper rifles down into the crowd on the Dome's floor. Lilia couldn't see any further than that because of the way the walls curved. What she *could* see sent cold fingers of terror dancing across her skin.

The figures wore dark gray nano-armor. Full defense mode, including helmets and facemasks. The Mastermind's Guardians.

Warned by the whisper of the accelevator doors opening, the nearest two armor-clad figures spun around.

[I *told* them they should have put Guardians up here,] Birch growled via Nancom, drawing his nanoblade from his left side, while his other hand withdrew his impactor from the area around his right breast.

Lilia didn't answer. She watched as, illuminated as they were by the light flooding across this section of the walkway from the main part of the Dome, the masked figures took one look at Birch and changed weapons. Letting their rifles hang by the straps around their torsos, they smoothly transitioned to pistols—small silver pistols.

*No*, she realized a split-second later. *Not pistols.*

They had *impactors*.

# CHAPTER 89

TARAJI kept up a lilting conversation about Adamek and the benefits the shipping company could bring to the Coalition as Kevin led her around the Dome to Shane Briscoe's table. She paused now and then to offer passing smiles to various guests along the way, some of them a little entranced by the way her skirt shifted when she walked, but she continued her efforts to tease information about the Safe Zone method out of Kevin. He sidestepped as politely as he could, but he was vastly relieved when they reached the table and he could introduce her to Briscoe.

The dark-haired Tarynian greeted the Glo'Stean Representative with a charming smile—much to his wife's amusement—and effortlessly slid into a pitch for Adamek.

Kevin excused himself and left her to it without a backwards glance. *He can handle her,* he thought with a mental shake of his head. He hadn't made it more than a few steps before he found himself confronted by Madame Olga—who had a rather regal-looking young woman by the elbow.

He stopped short, a feeling of foreboding stealing over him. Madame Olga had a militant look in her eye that promised there would be no escape for him this time.

"Madame Olga." Kevin tried not to look as wary as he felt. "How are—"

The older woman did not wait for him to finish. "This is Erudita Prous." She tugged on the young woman's elbow and she reluctantly stepped forward. "Erudita, this is Kevin Strong. Representative Monroe's grandson."

"I know who he is," Erudita said in a heavy Lanxian accent. About the same height as Lilia, she wore a dark purple sleeveless gown that showcased the golden-brown hue of her skin and hugged her curves before flaring out at her hips. She had wavy black hair pinned up in a loose chignon, plump lips, and deep brown eyes set in an oval face.

Those brown eyes were currently regarding Kevin with cool suspicion.

"Well, then my work is half done." Madame Olga tugged Erudita forward again. "Kevin, Erudita loves to dance. This next number would be perfect." Releasing the young woman's arm, she fluttered her hands at them like a mother encouraging her children to try something new. "Well, go on."

Kevin glanced at Erudita, who looked resigned, and held out a hand. "Shall we?" In this particular instance, their best avenue of escape might be temporary compliance.

Erudita pursed her lips, but placed her hand in his. Her fingers were cool; the warmth of the Dome was clearly not affecting her. *Either that or she's nervous.* Kevin immediately dismissed the thought; if she *was* nervous, this woman hid it very, very well.

They stepped out onto the dance floor and began to sway in time to the music—a slow ballad. Kevin tipped his chin toward Madame Olga. "As soon as we're out of her eyesight, we can make a break for it."

He'd hoped this would prompt something of a smile, since his dance partner was *clearly* just as thrilled to be here as he was, but Erudita's stiff expression did not change. "That would be preferable."

Kevin blinked at her; warning bells going off inside his head. Either this girl had issues, or for some reason she really didn't like him. *And considering we've never met before…*He loosened his grip on her hand. "You're welcome to leave right now."

For a second, he thought she'd take him up on the offer. Then Erudita pursed her lips. "Not where *she* can see us."

Kevin gave her a one-shouldered shrug, but it wasn't like he was going to disagree with her. He steered them around the dance floor, weaving around other couples, until they had put enough space between them that Madame Olga couldn't monitor them. "You've had some experience with Madame Olga's matchmaking attempts."

"Once or twice."

"The woman's a menace."

Erudita sniffed. "That's one word for it." Her eyes flicked up and down, scanning him, and then she said abruptly, "You're not comfortable at these sorts of things, are you?"

Kevin's eyebrows shot up in surprise. "That's a rather pointed thing to say to a complete stranger."

"I saw your interview. You look more at home in spacer's clothes than you do a tuxedo."

Well. She had a point there. Kevin shrugged again. "What's wrong with that?"

"Nothing. It's merely an observation."

"Uh huh." He waited for her to elaborate, but when she did not, he stopped on the edge of the dance floor and released her hand. "Here we are. Enjoy the rest of your evening."

Instead of walking away, Erudita continued to stand there, regarding him with that cool, inscrutable gaze. "I still don't understand."

*This is probably the oddest conversation I've ever had at one of these shindigs.* Confused, Kevin met her eyes. "Understand what?"

"Why you helped Kedis." It was her turn to shrug, the deep purple fabric of her gown glittering in the light as she moved. "I mean, I heard what you said in your interview, but it just doesn't seem *enough*. Not after everything the Tarynians have done to us."

Kevin cast a quick glance around, but no one was paying them much attention. He shook his head. "The cycle has to end somewhere. Enough people have died."

Erudita tilted her head to one side. "You don't think we'll face the same situation again in the future when trade negotiations don't go the way they want?"

Despite the warmth of the atrium, a sudden chill made the hair on the back of Kevin's neck stand on end. He'd considered that thought once or twice in the middle of the night the past couple of months. He took a breath. "I think we've made the best choice for the Coalition under the circumstances."

"You didn't answer my question."

"I think they'd be idiots to try it. They've got too much to lose at this point."

"I see." Erudita studied him for another moment, dark eyes narrowed. Then she tipped her head toward a passing silver 'bot with a drink tray full of champagne. "Get me a drink and we can debate this further."

*Strange girl.* Shooting her a bemused smile, Kevin took a drink from the 'bot and handed it to her. She accepted it from him, her cool fingers brushing his in the process, and proceeded to gulp half of it down.

Kevin's bemusement increased. "You don't like these things either."

"Not particularly."

"Then why come?"

Erudita's smile was brittle. "Much for the same reason you're here, I imagine."

*You don't have a clue,* Kevin thought, but he only inclined his head in agreement.

His sister's voice abruptly flooded his mind, and her words left him cold. He barely managed to keep his shock off his face. She was going up to investigate something on the observation walkway alone with *Birch?*

*This has disaster written all over it.*

He and Erik both promised to help and Kevin looked back at Erudita to find her studying him again. "I'm sorry, but I just remembered that there's someone I need to find. If you'll excuse me?"

She raised her champagne flute in a tiny toast. "Certainly."

Kevin hurried away through the crowd, glad to be leaving, despite the circumstances. *Strange girl,* he thought again. Why Madame Olga had thought they might be suited to one another was a mystery to him.

He promptly forgot about Erudita as his mind latched onto the possibility that Freedom's Children was about to make their move. His heart began to beat faster, adrenaline coursing through him. *If that's true, we might have a chance to stop them before they hurt anyone.*

He scanned the Dome for Erik's whereabouts on his way to the closest hall entrance, but didn't see him. [Where are you?] he asked via Nancom.

[Already in the hall,] Erik answered. [Meet ya up there.]

[Got it.]

Kevin ducked into the softly-lit hall, which was thankfully empty, and walked as fast as he dared. Part of him, the part thrumming with urgency, wanted to break into a run, but he didn't want to draw too much attention. *At least not until we know what's going on.*

He hadn't gone very far before he felt the hair on the back of his neck prickle. Someone was following him.

Listening to his instincts, he abruptly halted and whirled to the right in one fluid motion, hoping to catch whoever it was off-guard. In that, at least, he succeeded.

Erudita Prous stood frozen in the hall behind him, her eyes wide and one hand clasped to her chest.

Bewilderment mixed with a hefty dose of annoyance flooded Kevin. "What are you doing?"

"I'm bored." She lowered her hands.

*Well, go be bored someplace else*, Kevin wanted to tell her, but he bit the words back. "You need to go back to the Dome."

"Why?"

He didn't have time for this. "Please, Ms. Prous, return to the Dome. I need to check something out." He infused his voice with command authority, hoping it would be enough to sway her, and turned away.

[Where are you?] Erik demanded via Nancom. [I'm on the walkway.]

Kevin's sense of urgency increased. [Hit a delay,] he said tightly. [Be right there.]

He hadn't taken more than three steps before something smacked into the middle of his back. A starburst of pain flared out from the impact spot—a *familiar* starburst of pain. *Oh, no, no, no, no.*

Kevin whirled around again, groaning, to find Erudita still standing in the middle of the hallway, aiming a silver impactor at him.

He gaped at her. She was a Guardian. Of course. But that didn't explain…

"What do you think you're *doing?*" he gasped. "I'm a Guardian too!"

"Oh, I know." Erudita tucked the impactor back into the thin air around her right wrist, a cool, smug smile curling the corners of her mouth as she surveyed him with obvious satisfaction.

Anger and panic joined bewilderment in the gamut of emotions roiling inside him. Kevin clenched his fists, suppressing an intense desire to scream in frustration. Nancom was gone, meaning he had no way of knowing what was happening up on the walkway, he couldn't access his ISF, and he couldn't materialize any more of his armor than what he already wore.

"Why?" The word ripped out of his throat as he took a step toward Erudita, violet eyes blazing.

She merely lifted her chin. "Disabling you wasn't actually my assignment tonight, but you're obviously getting ready to meddle. We can't have that." Her left hand disappeared into her ISF beside her right hip and she drew a shining nanoblade. "The Mastermind will understand."

Her words shouldn't have shocked Kevin, but they did. In the wake of that shock, his mission parameters shifted. *Sorry, guys,* he thought, his gaze flicking from Erudita to the nanoblade she now wielded. *You're going to have to handle whatever's happening up there without me.*

# CHAPTER 90

THE realization that somehow the Mastermind had gotten his hands on *impactors* left Lilia cold. Beside her, Birch immediately opened fire, hitting the first two figures with crackling globs of energy in quick succession, but before she could cry a warning about what she'd seen, the closest man fired his impactor in return.

The crackling impactor bolt struck Birch square in the chest. He seemed to barely register it. Instead, he charged forward, thin lips drawn back in a snarl, brandishing his nanoblade in one hand and his own impactor in the other. His unmasked face was a wild contrast to their opponents' featureless masks

The closest masked man then fired at Lilia, but his aim was off. Birch's mad charge forward held the bulk of his attention. The sizzling energy just barely missed Lilia; she felt the hair on her left arm raise as it passed. Instinctively, she materialized her gloves and coated her arms in dark gray nano-armor from shoulder to wrist.

Gulping, she then brought both of her nanoblades up and settled into a defensive stance, but the nearest two men weren't interested in her anymore. Birch had taken them both on singlehandedly and was weaving around them, parrying blows and doing his best to penetrate their defenses and stab them.

This left the third man, the only one Birch hadn't managed to hit with his impactor. For a handful of heartbeats, he looked torn between his assignment and the unexpected assault up here—Lilia could see it in the indecision tensing his broad nano-armor-clad shoulders, the way his helmeted, masked head tracked back and forth between the walkway and the mass of targets below.

She saw the second he made up his mind.

Ramming his sniper rifle into the invisible storage field around his body, the man started toward her. He was the tallest of the three, but not as broad as the shorter man. He casually sidestepped Birch and his companions' whirling blades and charged her, one gloved hand plunging into his ISF, and emerging with a nanoblade. Its long blade flashed as he moved.

Lilia barely had time to sidestep and bat his blade away, preventing him from bowling her over.

Her opponent recovered with all the speed and grace of a seasoned duelist. Skidding to a halt, he swung around to engage her again.

[We've got hostiles up here!] Lilia sent to Kevin and Erik. That was all she had time for before the man was upon her again.

Their blades met in a flash of silver, and then she dodged right, sliding away from the force of his blow. She almost tripped over the hem of her skirt—she wasn't dressed properly for this. Her gown hampered her movements, slowing her down and decreasing her agility.

As much practice as she'd put in since the NCDC recalled them from Glo'Stea, Lilia could tell she wasn't quite on this guy's level—and it seemed he knew it too.

He pressed forward again with a flurry of lightning-quick blows she barely managed to parry. Gritting her teeth, she whirled and dodged, dancing in and out of her opponent's range. His nanoblade might be longer than hers, but she had two blades—and she used them to her full advantage.

The air up here felt oppressive and hot, like someone had cut a section out of the observation walkway's transparent outer wall to let the muggy evening air rush in.

Sweat beaded on Lilia's forehead, a few droplets stinging her eyes. Panic clogged her throat; she ruthlessly forced it down. She couldn't afford to panic.

Keeping her head was all that would save her from losing her head.

Literally.

Her opponent was too good—she wasn't sure she could risk the second it would take to materialize her defense-mode helmet and facemask.

Below them, the party continued to roll on, everyone in the Dome oblivious to the danger they faced from above.

Over her opponent's shoulder, Lilia saw Birch slam the hilt of his nanoblade into the shorter of his opponents' facemask. The blow slowed the man long enough for Birch to deflect a strike from his taller opponent and reverse his blade, plunging it into the stunned man's facemask. The force of the blow drove the tip of the nano-blade clear through the man's skull and out through his helmet on the other side.

He collapsed to the floor, dead.

Snarling again, this time in satisfaction, Birch turned his focus on his remaining opponent. He took advantage of the taller man's surprise at the death of his comrade to attempt to ram his nanoblade through his midsection.

It didn't work.

The man deflected the blow with a gloved hand and, shouting something incoherent, tackled Birch around the waist. They both hit the floor and rolled in a tangle of nanoblades and limbs.

It all happened so quickly Lilia barely had time to process it before she had to fend off a strike intended to decapitate her. The edges of her vision darkened as tunnel vision kicked in, narrowing the observation walkway down around her until all Lilia could see was the man intent on harming her—and everyone else here.

He finally spoke. "Step aside," he growled in Glo'Stean. His deep voice held a scratchy note, like someone had once hit him in the throat and his vocal chords had never recovered. To her disgust, he didn't even sound winded. "You're on the wrong side."

He lunged forward; she danced away again. "Not to mention you're not dressed for this."

*That* was an understatement. Lilia gritted her teeth. "Tell me something I don't know."

"Drop your weapons and walk away." The man gestured to the railing to their left with a careless sweep of his nanoblade. "They aren't worth it."

Lilia glared at him, tightening her grip on her blades. "I took an oath to protect and defend the citizens of the Coalition from people like you."

The man shrugged. "Have it your way." He flicked his wrist, swinging his nanoblade in a loose figure-eight, and then snapped into a high-ready stance and charged forward.

Lilia darted sideways, but he anticipated that and abruptly changed direction to meet her halfway. She raised her twin blades in a defensive cross and caught his blade on them before he sliced her head in two like a watermelon—

—just as he body-slammed her into the railing.

Pain exploded across her back, bright dancing stars clouding her vision. Lilia lost her grip on her nanoblades and they clattered to the pearlescent floor. Beyond the stars dancing before her eyes, she dimly registered that the world was tipping upside down.

Her vision cleared in time for her to realize that was because *she* was going over backwards—the momentum of his blow was carrying her over the railing.

As she fell, Lilia scrabbled frantically for the railing. She glimpsed the atrium floor far below just as the fingers of her flailing left hand caught on the spaces between the balusters where they met the floor, halting her precipitous plunge and wrenching her shoulder painfully in the process. She dangled there, holding on for dear life while she struggled to grab the railing with her right hand as well.

She succeeded after two tries. Adrenaline coursed through her, but even adrenaline wouldn't be enough to save her if she fell. Three stories was too short a distance to allow her time to expand her hoverdisc and hop onto it, but it was high enough that she'd risk breaking a limb—or worse.

Instinctively, she materialized her gloves. They helped her grip the railing better, but she was still faced with the reality that she was dangling three stories above a very hard floor.

She thought she heard screaming from below, but she didn't know if it was because of her or something else. She had to force herself to breathe. *Don't panic.*

[Guys,] she said via her joint Nancom channel to Kevin and Erik, [I'm in trouble.]

Neither of them answered.

# CHAPTER 91

JASPER made his way back through the laughing, chattering press of guests to Kedis's table with his head held high, feeling as light and buoyant as he had in low-gravity training at the Academy. He'd told Lilia how he felt and she hadn't shot him down. She might not be in love with him yet, but she liked him well enough…and part of him suspected she was half-way there.

It was the way she'd looked at him, the tentative way she'd kissed him…the trust she'd placed in him.

The fact that she saw him as a man first and a G.U. soldier second spoke volumes.

*No, I don't have any idea how things will play out from here*, he thought as he approached the table, where Kedis was holding court with a crowd of people surrounding him, including Dion Pamos and his wife, *but I know it will work out.*

It was a gut feeling—strong and unshakable. He'd learned to trust his gut over the years.

That same gut feeling whispered that Lilia and that girl from Challa were connected, but Jasper was starting to come to the realization that girl might be a mystery he never solved.

As of tonight, he thought he might be able to live with that.

On the other side of the table, Lon sat holding a conversation with an older Glo'Stean businessman, but Jasper noticed his eyes were constantly scanning the atrium for potential threats. Renner hovered nearby, doing the same thing. Setting aside happy thoughts of Lilia, though he didn't bother squelching the warm glow suffusing him from head to foot, Jasper joined them.

He didn't see anything out of the ordinary. Nothing about the crowd around them triggered any sort of alarm, except when a woman in a crimson sheath dress bumped into Mrs. Pamos and almost sent a glass of champagne into Kedis's lap. Jasper tensed along with Renner and Lon, but the woman apologized with a tipsy titter and moved on.

Jasper suppressed a sigh. That was probably as exciting as things would get.

He was wrong.

A few minutes later, a woman's scream pierced through the gay cacophony. Another followed. Heart leaping into his throat, Jasper whirled to find the source of the commotion, which turned out to be a couple of women pointing up at the Dome's ceiling.

*No*, he realized in horror. *Not the ceiling.*

A woman in an all-too-familiar sapphire-blue dress was dangling from one of the hidden observation walkway railings.

His heart nearly stopped in his chest.

*Lilia.*

Jasper reacted before he'd consciously considered it and took off for the nearest hallway exit at a dead run. He didn't care who saw him, didn't care what anybody thought. The woman he loved was in danger and he had to save her before it was too late.

A mental image of her lying crumpled on the Dome's floor flashed through his mind; Jasper gritted his teeth and pushed it away. *That won't happen.*

He wouldn't let her fall.

*Not again.*

# CHAPTER 92

HIS eyes burning, Kevin tipped his head toward one of the security cams discreetly mounted in the hall's ceiling. "Aren't you afraid somebody's going to see you?"

Erudita's cold smile widened. "That's the beauty of it." She turned her free hand palm up. "We're in control."

"What do you think you're doing?" Kevin shook his head, unclenching his fists and forcing himself to maintain neutral, non-threatening body language. "Are you planning on killing all the Tarynians here?"

"Oh, our plans are so much bigger than that." Dark eyes glittering, Erudita began stalking down the hall toward him, the folds of her purple gown swishing around her legs like a poisonous mist. Her nanoblade flashed silver each time she passed one of the hall's sconce lights.

Resisting the urge to back up, Kevin raised his eyebrows at her and stood his ground. "I'm pretty sure you're not supposed to kill me. Your Mastermind still has high hopes I'll join your little crusade."

That was possibly a stretch, but considering the Mastermind hadn't just chucked a bomb through a portal to blow them all to kingdom come, he was willing to take the risk.

"He'll forgive me." Erudita raised her blade as she continued to advance.

Kevin's eyes darted from Erudita to the hall beyond her. It was still empty; apparently no one else had left the Dome to wander around. His mouth went dry, but his heart began to race with renewed anticipation. *Up side to this little tête-à-tête? Nobody else gets hurt.*

A thought occurred to him as he focused on Erudita again. She was now less than three meters away. "You conned Madame Olga into setting us up, didn't you?"

"It wasn't hard." She made a scoffing sound in the back of her throat. "The old biddy thinks she's so brilliant at pairing people up. All I had to do was make her think it was her idea."

"Why?"

"You needed looking after tonight."

She would be in lunging range with that blade any second now.

Kevin forced himself to go cool and calm. He knew the stealth-mode armor coating his skin beneath his tuxedo would protect him from most of her blows, but his head, hands, and feet were unprotected. *Not to mention the trouble I'll be in if she stabs me.*

His violet eyes narrowed a fraction. *Have to put her off-balance.* He lifted his chin. "You call me a traitor, but from where I'm standing, you're nothing but a terrorist with a grudge."

Just as he'd hoped, the shot made Erudita bristle. "We're *freedom fighters*. There's a big difference."

"Not when you're killing unarmed civilians."

She shrugged, the movement lifting her arms and causing the flat of her nanoblade to glint again. "Unfortunately, fighting for freedom means there will be a few casualties along the way."

"More than just a few casualties. You *murdered* innocent people."

Erudita's dark eyes flashed. "*We* aren't the ones who—"

Kevin lunged for her.

The rest of her sentence was lost in an incoherent cry of rage. She brought her blade down in a heavy arc intended to split Kevin's head open like a melon, but it was too late. Kevin blocked her blow with a raised forearm—the blade cutting through both his shirt and jacket sleeves like they were made of air and stopping violently against his nano-armor—and tackled her backwards.

They hit the pearlescent floor in a tangle of arms, legs, and masses of purple material. The back of Erudita's head bounced off the floor with a sickening thud, leaving her temporarily dazed. Kevin took full advantage of those precious few seconds to pin her legs with his own.

Stretching out over her, he grabbed her left hand with his right and held it fast while he beat her other hand against the floor until he knocked the nanoblade from her fingers. The deadly weapon skidded over to the wall out of either of their reach.

Erudita regained control of her faculties before Kevin could figure out what to do with her now. Finding herself restrained, she bucked against him, her face twisting with hate. "Get off me! Get. Off. Me. Now!"

Kevin gritted his teeth. "Not a chance."

He hated fighting women, but sometimes there just wasn't any other way around it. Particularly when one was hell bent on doing him bodily harm.

Ignoring Erudita's angry growls and pained whimpers at the force of his weight restraining her, Kevin kept her legs pinned firmly to the floor while he brought her arms together over her head. He needed to flip her over so he could restrain her more easily and fish his comlink from his pocket before she called for backup.

*And so it looks more like I'm arresting her instead of something…else…* he thought uncomfortably.

The same thought passed through Erudita's mind, because she suddenly started shrieking for help.

Kevin winced at the earsplitting sound, but he didn't relax his grip. If anything, he tightened it. Grimly, he heaved Erudita onto her side and shoved her face-down. She elbowed him in the ribcage in the process and did her best to kick her feet free, but he was stronger and unhampered by meters of fabric.

"Help!" Erudita continued to scream. "He's going to rape me! Someone help me!"

Pinning her arms behind her back with one hand, Kevin pulled out his comlink.

Michael answered immediately. "What's wrong?"

"I've got one of the Mastermind's Guardians out in the hall. She hit me with an impactor and then tried to kill me." As he spoke, Kevin kept a sharp eye on both ends of the hall. He fully expected some of Erudita's terrorist friends to appear at any moment to bail her out.

"Name's Erudita Prous. Tell Security, will you?" Kevin grimaced. "I'd do it myself, but…"

"Understood. Bring her out here."

"Got it."

Kevin hauled Erudita up onto her feet, but at that moment they heard distant screams from the atrium. His blood ran cold. A dozen different scenarios raced through his mind, all of them terrible. "What have you done?"

Erudita just started to laugh, abandoning her attempts to scream for help.

"Answer me!" He shook her roughly. "What have you done?"

"You can't stop us!" she gasped through her laughter. "Nothing can stop us now!"

# CHAPTER 93

CLINGING to the bottom of the railing, Lilia tried to find purchase on the wall with her feet in order to leverage herself back up and over the railing to safety, but her heels kept slipping against its smooth surface and the filmy skirt of her gown kept getting in the way. Grimacing, she kicked her heels off and let them fall away before materializing her nanoboots.

They didn't help much.

She made an incoherent sound in the back of her throat, halfway between a growl and a sob. Even with her gloves, she couldn't hang here forever. Her fingers were already growing tired; if she couldn't climb up, it was only a matter of time before she lost her grip.

She tried to scrabble up the side of the wall with her booted toes again, with little success.

She couldn't see what was happening on the walkway; she could only hear fragments of it through the noise from the Dome below. Desperate, she tried Nancom again. [Kev! Erik! I need help! Please!]

Kevin still didn't answer, but this time Erik did.

His Nancom voice was grim and tight as he said, [Hang on, Lilia.]

Lilia swallowed, sweat trickling down the back of her neck. [Hurry. Please.]

A flicker of movement above her caught her eye; she looked up in time to watch a booted foot crash down on the fingers of her gloved right hand. She cried out at the explosion of pain. Not content to merely shove her over the railing, her opponent intended to make *sure* she fell.

The man raised his foot, preparing to stomp her fingers again, and Lilia braced herself, unable to do anything but take it. Tears of pain blurring her vision, she stared defiantly up at him.

The blow never came.

A shout from the walkway behind them sent her attacker's head snapping in that direction—and then someone slammed into him, sending *him* tumbling headlong over the railing beside Lilia as easily as he'd sent her to her doom. He wasn't as lucky as she was. He plummeted to the floor, screaming hoarsely.

Lilia couldn't hear the sickening thud he made as his body impacted the floor, but she could imagine it. Nausea churned her stomach, almost enough to distract her from the throbbing pain in her fingers. That would be her in a few seconds if whoever had just—

Her left hand—the hand that had borne her weight the longest—slipped.

The force of it sent the fingers of her aching right hand sliding farther away from safety. Dangling one-handed, Lilia had a heartbeat to fully comprehend the fact that she was going to fall before she lost what little remained of her tenuous grip on the walkway.

Stomach lurching, she fell.

A hand shot down from over the railing above, latching onto her wrist with an iron grip and arresting her fall. The impact wrenched her shoulder further, but that was the least of her worries. Swaying, the folds of her sapphire blue gown fluttering around her armored legs, Lilia looked up into the face of her savior—

—and found Jasper staring down at her, his gray eyes fierce and his expression set in lines of grim determination. For a second, she almost thought he was looking *through* her at something only he could see, but then he blinked.

"What *is* it with you and heights?" he demanded breathlessly, leaning over the railing and extending his other hand toward her.

Her stomach lurched again, this time for a completely different reason. Half-sobbing his name, Lilia strained her free hand up toward him. Their fingers brushed and then hands locked onto wrists and Jasper easily hauled her up over the railing.

When both of her feet were planted firmly on the firm pearlescent floor of the walkway, he wrapped his arms around her, crushing her to his chest as though he'd half-expected her to vanish before his eyes.

Lilia let him. Trembling with combined fear and relief, she allowed herself a moment to sag against him and be grateful for his timely rescue. That had been close. Way too close.

Shutting her eyes, she slid her arms around his waist and returned the embrace. She rested her cheek against his chest and breathed in the clean smell of his uniform, the heady scent of his cologne. All the things that combined together to create the smell of him. She could hear his heart thundering beneath her ear.

"Thank you," she murmured, sounding just as breathless as he had. "How did you even—"

"Saw you from below." Jasper tightened his grip, as though assuring himself she was still in one piece. "Ran up here as fast as I could. Are you all right?"

Opening her eyes, Lilia tipped her head back to look up at him and managed a tremulous smile. "I'm fine."

In the dim light, his gray eyes looked like storm clouds. He released his grip enough to take her by the shoulders. "What are you doing up here? When I saw you—" he broke off, the muscles in his jaw tightening as he pressed his lips into a thin line.

Sudden alarm spiked through Lilia as she remembered what had been happening up here prior to Jasper's arrival. A quick glance around told her they were alone, save for the two dead guards and both of Birch's opponents. Birch himself was nowhere in sight, but he'd obviously been the victor.

Her nanoblades lay where she'd dropped them when the sniper overpowered her.

"Lilia." Jasper tightened his grip on her shoulders, dragging her attention back to him. "What are you doing up here?"

She shook her head, sudden frustration welling up inside her. *Where do I even begin?*

Instead of attempting to explain, she cupped his face in both gloved hands and kissed him fiercely, trying to convey the depths of her gratitude and affection.

Before Jasper could respond to the kiss, she wriggled out of his arms and ran to scoop up her nanoblades. Her right hand still ached terribly. She resisted the urge to peer over the railing. She already knew what she'd find, and besides, they didn't have time for this.

"Lilia?" Jasper sounded slightly dazed. "What are you—"

The rest of his question died unspoken as screams erupted from the Dome below. The two of them traded aghast glances.

Realization slammed into Lilia like a torpedo from a battlecruiser. *They must have had another sniper team.*

Either that or Erik, Kevin, and presumably Birch had failed and were all—*No.* Ruthlessly, she chopped that thought off at the knees. *Don't think like that.*

She Nancommed Kevin and Erik, but, again, only Erik responded. [Little busy here.]

[Where's Kevin?]

[Don't know.] Erik's Nancom voice sounded strained. [Never made it up here.]

Lilia hissed in a breath. Worry mixed with fear trailed cold fingers across her skin, but she tamped it all down. That could mean any number of things, and she simply didn't have time to think about any of it.

[Birch is here now,] Erik continued tersely. [We're kinda busy. You still need help?]

[Not anymore.]

The screams continued.

Lilia turned to Jasper, her gown swishing around her legs with the abrupt movement. "You've got to get back to Kedis."

He was staring at her twin nanoblades. "What are you doing? Whose are those?"

She took a deep breath. Now was the moment of truth. "They're mine."

"Yours?" Jasper looked dumbfounded as he glanced from her to the blades in her hands and back.

"I have to help. That's why I'm here."

People were dying down there, and more would lose their lives until Security could get up here and deal with the snipers.

Standing frozen in front of the glass wall, the city's nightscape a backdrop behind them, Lilia saw the instant Jasper finally put the pieces together. His eyes flicked from her nanoblades to the armor covering her arms and terrible realization mixed with betrayal flooded his eyes.

Something deep within her broke.

The bond that had formed between them, their fragile new relationship…everything had changed. Nothing would be the same now.

"You're a Guardian too." His voice was hoarse.

She nodded mutely; it felt like her chest was filled with jagged shards.

Part of her wanted to explain, to try to make him understand why she hadn't told him. Why she *couldn't* tell him. Another part of her, the defensive part, wanted to argue that she had every right to keep the information to herself. He was a military officer, after all, and he knew full well that in conflict some things were supposed to be kept secret from the other side.

Not to mention he probably had a responsibility to report something like this to Kedis.

The betrayal in his eyes stole her voice.

In this moment, he wasn't a soldier, he was just a man.

More screams sounded, piercing the bubble that seemed to have formed around them, and a different kind of guilt mixed with horror twisted her insides. They couldn't deal with this now. People were *dying*.

That horror and guilt turned into anger, which solidified into a cold, clear clarity. Lilia knew exactly what she had to do—and fast, before she encountered somebody with an impactor. She spun away, preparing to dash up the walkway until she found the snipers, but she hadn't taken more than step when she caught movement out of the corner of her eye.

To their left, the air *rippled* as a portal sphere swirled into existence several meters above the floor.

Lilia's eyes widened in horror. *Oh, no.*

# CHAPTER 94

UP until someone opened fire into their midst, Aiden thought the evening had been going quite well. He had even been cautiously optimistic enough to begin considering the day a success. The soft music filling the Dome, the golden light filtered down from the sea-shell sconces, the laughter and chatter of dozens of different conversations…it all combined to turn the Dome into something even an old man like himself could consider slightly magical.

The night had brought with it the occasional reminder of his wife. The last time he had eaten a meal in the Dome, it had been with Teresa. Looking around at the mix of faces filling the atrium, Aiden thought she would have been happy they had finally reached an accord with the Galactic Union. Forgiveness had always been one of her stronger suits.

Pushing the plate containing a half-eaten piece of lemon soufflé aside, Aiden removed his napkin from his lap and set it to one side on the table. He had enjoyed his dinner, though his appetite was not what it once was, and the company at his table had been tolerable. It helped that Michael, Felix Mouta, and Elena Mouta were also seated with him. Derek had been placed at another table, as had the twins. Lon, of course, he could see at Ambassador Kedis's table.

Now that the meal was over, the real business of politicking began. Guests left their tables and moved to others to hold conversations—a steady stream of motion and color swirling around the Dome. Aiden spoke to several G.U. businessmen, minor politicians in their own right on their various worlds, before abruptly deciding he would seek out Admiral Chesnee.

Excusing himself from the table with a dignified nod, Aiden paused long enough to quietly inform Michael where he was headed before he made his way over to the Admiral's table. He had left the hoverchair home tonight; his steps were slow, but sure.

As he drew near, he had to restrain a wry smile. The Admiral was deep in conversation with both Malik Thane and Guy Caradoc, Glo'Stea's Director of Security. Even from a distance, Aiden could see the stiffness in the Tarynian's uniformed shoulders.

*The Admiral is not accustomed to rubbing elbows with politicians.*

Maybe that was why Aiden found himself liking the man so much.

He knew most people would consider him crazy for thinking such a thing—Aiden could imagine perfectly the look on Martin Hollowell's face if he were to make such a statement—but it was true. For the time being, Chesnee lacked political guile, and that made for quite a refreshing change.

Chesnee stood close to his wife, who remained seated at the table. Sylvia Chesnee maintained a polite smile, but Aiden saw how her eyes darted to the dance floor every so often. She wanted an escape, that much was clear, though whether or not it was because she loved dancing remained to be seen.

"Good evening." Aiden bent his old frame in a courteous bow as he approached the table. "I was hoping to speak with your husband, Mrs. Chesnee, but since he is otherwise occupied at the moment, I wonder if you would be kind enough to grant this old man the pleasure of a dance?"

Mrs. Chesnee's dark eyes lit, though she flashed a questioning glance up at her husband. Chesnee—who noticed Aiden's approach immediately, though he did not break stride in his conversation— glanced from Aiden to his wife and nodded encouragingly. They had obviously had an extensive conversation about security.

Aiden could not blame them for that. Not after an assassination attempt in Dion Pamos's apartment, of all places. Anyone would be a little skittish after something like that. *He* was still unhappy Lilia had been hurt in the process, though he knew it had been for a good cause.

Rising from her seat, Mrs. Chesnee took the hand Aiden extended to her and allowed him to lead her onto the dance floor.

Aiden had to smile; he could not have timed his request any better. The orchestra had just begun a slower ballad more suitable to an old man like himself.

A short distance away, a young couple excused themselves from their table and joined the dance floor as well, keeping close to Aiden and Mrs. Chesnee. They were both Guardians; Michael had pointed out a few of the Guardians in attendance tonight in case of emergency.

As he and Mrs. Chesnee began to sway and whirl with the music, Aiden offered her a kind smile. "Are you enjoying the evening, Mrs. Chesnee?"

"I am now." She smiled in response, her dark eyes dancing along with them. "I would much rather be out here than stuck at a table."

"I am sure the Admiral would prefer to be out here with you."

"You think so?" Mrs. Chesnee cast an involuntary glance over her shoulder in her husband's direction.

"I do." Aiden deftly spun her around. His body might move slower than it used to, but his feet remembered all the steps. "I know that when my wife was alive, my favorite part of evenings such as these was when we danced together."

Mrs. Chesnee regarded him with an arched eyebrow, her expression halfway between amusement and disbelief. "That," she said at last, "would put you in quite a rare category, Representative." She took her hand off his shoulder long enough to wave it at their surroundings. "I do believe you might be the only politician here who would rather dance with his wife than network."

Aiden smiled wryly. "I suppose it would, my dear. And I cannot claim to have always put my wife first. But you see, I am an old man now, and I have learned age tends to give one a certain perspective on life."

"In fact, when this dance is over, I believe we should go over there and interrupt his conversation." His green eyes twinkled down at her. "Tonight is a celebration, after all. There will be plenty of time later for all the details my colleagues will want to pry out of him."

Thane and Caradoc would not thank him for his interference, but Admiral Chesnee was another matter. *I cannot fault the man for a job well done.*

Mrs. Chesnee hesitated only a second before her face lit with a genuine smile. "Yes." She nodded decisively. "It *is* a celebration."

The song ended with a little flourish, and Aiden spun Mrs. Chesnee around again. When they were facing each other again, she lifted her chin. "Thank you for the dance, Representative Monroe." She dropped him a saucy wink. "And the idea."

Aiden inclined his head in a gracious nod. He escorted Mrs. Chesnee back to her husband and she did not hesitate but glided up to him, hands outstretched.

"Giles, you must dance with me."

A keen-eyed observer such as Aiden usually considered himself could have seen glimpsed undercurrents of something heavier in that momentary tableau. Anyone else would have only seen that they made a pretty picture—Mrs. Chesnee in her glittering black gown, with her dark hair, a golden hue to her bare arms outstretched to her husband, and Admiral Chesnee, strong and sober, in his dark gray uniform, his breast glittering with bars and medals.

The Admiral nodded curtly to Malik Thane and Guy Caradoc. "If you will excuse me? I believe I will dance with my wife." He did not wait for a response, but took his wife's hands and raised them to his lips before settling a palm against the small of her back and escorting her to the dance floor.

Permitting himself a small, satisfied smile, Aiden turned to his colleagues. "Gentlemen."

"There goes that opportunity," Malik Thane observed coolly. He held a drink in his hand and he took a sip, his eyes following the Chesnees into the crowd until they vanished. He did not look as sour as he usually did, though Aiden had long suspected the younger man *always* looked sour, regardless of circumstance. "Just when we had a shot at getting something interesting."

Guy Caradoc guffawed once and slapped the younger man on the shoulder with his free hand. He, too, held an after-dinner drink. "I daresay we weren't going to get much. That man is entirely too cagey. Surprising, for a military man."

"I suspect," Aiden said mildly, "some of his reticence might stem from his recent association with Ambassador Kedis."

Thane snorted. "I suppose."

The redheaded man started to turn away, but Aiden stayed him with a gesture. "Wait." He stepped closer to the two Directors, who both regarded him with veiled curiosity, and dropped his voice. "I have been hoping for the chance to speak privately with you."

Thane's eyebrows shot up at this, though he mastered the expression instantly and only allowed his mouth to curve in a little sneer, as if to ask, *You consider* this *private?*

Caradoc remained relaxed, though his eyes had gone wary. They all had secretaries; Aiden could have simply attempted to make an appointment that coincided with both of their schedules.

A small pocket of space existed around them for the moment, and Aiden intended to make full use of it. Under the cover of the music and conversation swirling through the air, he glanced from Director to Director. "Have there been any developments regarding the explosion and the transporter?"

Thane's sneer deepened. "You don't want to ask your friend Fenton?"

Caradoc shot his younger colleague a faintly reproachful look, which Thane ignored as thoroughly as if the other man had not been present.

"I have." Aiden did not let Thane rile him. He was too old and they did not have time for childish games. "I would like to hear your angle. I know you have been investigating this thoroughly—and from what I hear, very discreetly."

This seemed be the right thing to say. Thane relaxed a little, mollified, his shoulders straightening under the praise.

"There's definitely a leak high up." Caradoc maintained a pleasant smile, as though they were discussing happier news.

"Freedom's Children seems to be cropping up all over the Coalition," Thane said, his characteristic drawl a little clipped, "but the bulk of it appears to stem from Glo'Stea."

Aiden nodded; that fit with everything the twins had told him. The two Directors did not know much more than that. They had located several more people in Triumvirate Tower who had received money from that unknown figure Aiden now suspected was the Mastermind, but nothing beyond that.

Caradoc's smile hardened. "We've found ourselves on the edge of an abyss, that's for sure, Monroe. The more we poke at this—"

"The bigger it gets," Thane finished, before downing the last of his drink. Ice clinked in the glass as he lowered it.

"So it would seem." Aiden took a deep breath, as though he was about to step off the edge of the abyss into nothingness himself. He had thought long and hard about what he was about to say, and he felt a sense of urgency pressing down on him.

*The time has come,* a little voice whispered inside his head. *They need to know.*

Cutting his eyes to the right and left to ensure no one was yet close enough to overhear—though their window of opportunity was closing fast—and pasted a smile on his face and leaned in toward the two younger men as though he intended to relay a private joke.

"On that front," he said quietly, "I believe I have gotten a hold of some information that will significantly narrow your search for Freedom's Children."

Both Directors had far too much experience to show their surprise, but Aiden could feel the air around them begin to crackle with intensity.

"Investigate the island of Meloran, in Glo'Stea's Section 3. I have it on good authority that something odd is happening there."

"Who—" Thane began, but Aiden raised a hand.

"At present, my source remains confidential."

"You're absolutely certain about your intel?" Caradoc's eyes narrowed.

Aiden held his gaze. "Yes."

Caradoc smiled and raised his nearly-empty glass aloft as though Aiden had said something truly entertaining, but the intensity in his eyes did not change. "Very well. I'll—"

He never finished his sentence.

A laser bolt seared a hole through his head and the Director crumpled to the floor. His glass shattered, sending liquid and half-melted ice cubes spraying out around him.

For a heartbeat, Aiden and Thane both gaped at the spot in shock. Then reality kicked back in. As screams rose around them, Thane seized Aiden's shoulder and forced him down to his knees beside the table. He tapped the comlink in his ear, his brown eyes darting around the upper portion of the atrium.

Aiden's gaze fell to Guy Caradoc's corpse, the ruined face half-turned toward him, and felt nausea roil in the pit of his stomach. His vision grew black around the edges, tunneling in on the Director's corpse, and the screams filling the Dome around them cut out.

He remembered another grand event, another celebration that had been marred by tragedy. One hand crept up to flatten itself against his sternum. *It is happening again.*

"…father. Grandfather." A hand grasped his shoulder, shaking him. Blinking, Aiden looked up to see Michael crouched beside him, clad in full defense-mode nano-armor, helmet and all.

Reality—terrible as it was—crashed around him like an ocean wave overtaking an unprepared surfer. A cacophony of sound flooded his ears. The room was too warm and smelled of blood, fear, and the acrid tang of laserfire.

Michael had appeared seemingly from nowhere, though the rational part of Aiden's mind would realize later that his grandson had been doing his job and kept very close to him.

On Aiden's other side, Thane was swearing, beads of sweat having broken out on his forehead. He looked at Aiden and Michael, his brown eyes wide. "Somebody's jamming our comms."

Michael was already nodding. No doubt he was already in contact with other Guardians here tonight.

Guardians like the rest of his grandchildren.

Aiden's heart rate spiked again. His green eyes frantically roved the screaming, rushing crowd, searching terrified faces for Derek, Lon, and the twins. He didn't see any of them.

All at once, Michael's armored body jerked. He uttered a small, surprised grunt that was lost amid the noise, and whirled around, still crouching.

Aiden craned his neck over his shoulder in time to see a flash of silver as a young man with blond hair and dark brown skin lowered something to his side before giving them a curious smile and a salute before disappearing into the crowd. Aiden thought he recognized the man—one of Ashford's staff, wasn't he?—but he did not understand what had happened until Michael bellowed in his ear.

"He just froze my nanites!"

At those words, stark horror flooded Aiden's veins with ice water. Amid the tumult, his brain took the scattered pieces he had been handed over the course of the past few minutes and assembled them into a complete holo. He knelt on the floor, uncaring of the pain that radiated up from his knees, the Dome around him fading away as his mind's eye turned inward to view that holo.

Freedom's Children had bypassed the Pearl's security to attack tonight—and they had come prepared to handle Guardians.

*What do they want? Some of us dead, or all of us?* Cold, logical curiosity stirred. *Am I marked for death? Again?* Since the assassins had hitherto been unsuccessful?

Aiden blinked and returned to his surroundings once more as Michael shook his shoulder again. He could not hear his grandson, but he comprehended the meaning in the way Michael gestured to the next table over. They were moving.

For all the good it would do them.

# CHAPTER 95

ADMIRAL Giles Chesnee led his wife to the center of the dance floor, feeling a profound sense of gratitude to Aiden Monroe. It was a relief to trade polite, if pointed, conversation with a couple of Coalition politicians for a dance with his Sylvia. Romantic strains of music swirled around them as the orchestra began to play a smooth waltz. For a few seconds Chesnee could pretend that the rest of the Dome had faded away, the world shrinking to a little bubble around the two of them.

Sylvia smiled up at him, her dark eyes glowing with happiness in the dim light. "Thank you."

Chesnee allowed himself to return the smile. He had never been one for dancing, but Sylvia had always loved it and waltzes were one of the few dances he knew well. "Remind me to thank Representative Monroe for giving me an out."

Sylvia tipped her glossy dark head back in a laugh, light playing on her slim throat, casting the hollow of her throat in shadow. "I think I like him best of all the politicians we've met so far." Her smile turned saucy. "Except perhaps Representative Briscoe."

Chesnee just huffed softly. Then, unable to help himself, he ducked his head to briefly nuzzle the side of her neck. He caught the fleeting scent of her perfume—one he'd given her a long time ago. It brought a rush of memories back to him, of better times.

That she had brought that particular perfume with her spoke volumes.

"And his lovely wife?" he murmured in her ear.

Sylvia's saucy smile widened. "She is lovely, isn't she? Very elegant, and not stuck up at all." She shook her head. "It's funny, isn't it, how people are people even if they come from completely different parts of the galaxy?"

She tipped her chin toward the room at large. "Most of the women here are exactly the same as the ones I left on Veridia and Taryn. They just have a different fashion sense and speak a different language."

"Will you be glad when all of this fuss and pomp is over?" Chesnee found himself asking. He almost frowned, but caught himself in time. That wasn't what he had meant to say at all.

"Perhaps." His wife lifted one smooth shoulder in a little shrug. The light from the sconces along the wall glinted off the tiny pinpricks of silver in the fabric of her black evening gown. "I won't miss feeling like someone is constantly breathing down the back of my neck."

"Agreed." Despite the gaiety of the evening, Chesnee felt a chill settle over him, like someone had just draped him with a gauzy wet blanket.

Sylvia abruptly dropped his hand and stepped closer to drape her arms around his neck, eschewing tradition. "Are you going to send me back after tonight?"

"What?" Chesnee had to blink; it took him a few seconds to reorient his brain. It had been a long time since they had danced like this. "Send you back?"

"Yes." Sylvia nodded, biting her bottom lip. Her earlier happiness drained away, to be replaced with a solemn hesitance as she looked up at him. "We both know why the Ambassador brought me out here. Now that the trade agreement has been signed…" she trailed off with another little shrug.

Chesnee regarded her for a moment, while the music swirled around them and other couples swayed and twirled at the edges of their little bubble. A storm of emotion and thought erupted inside him. *If anyone had asked me a few months back what I would think of my wife being here…*

At long last, he cleared his throat. "Where do you want to go, Sylvia?" He inhaled deeply, realizing at that moment that most of the galaxy was open to her—them. "After what we have achieved, you could return to Taryn if you wish."

Her eyes widened a little at his use of 'we', but she sidestepped his question as nimbly as she did everything else. "Where will High Command send you now?"

Chesnee let out a slow, slightly breathless laugh. "I have no idea."

It was true.

After tonight, the Galactic Union no longer required a Blockade Division to be stationed in the Sta'Gloan system—or an Admiral to command it.

"I—" he began, but at that instant, sharp screams pierced the cocoon enveloping the two of them. They both whirled to find the source.

The instant he glimpsed that feminine figure dangling from the observation walkway railing, Chesnee knew their reprieve from reality had come to an end.


Like everyone else in the Dome, Lon had whirled to find the source of the screams. Horror engulfed him at the sight of his little sister hanging three stories above them. His feet automatically started taking him toward the nearest exit to go rescue her, but a flash of black and gold stopped him.

Wright was already rushing that direction, forging his way through the shocked crowd with single-minded purpose.

*Kedis*, a voice whispered inside his head. *You can't leave him.*

Lon looked back at the Ambassador's table. Kedis had half-risen from his seat and was staring up at Lilia, as were the people clustered around him.

Lon cast a sharp look around the Dome. Everyone in the immediate vicinity was glued to Lilia's dangling form, including Martin Hollowell, who stood two meters away with a group that included Dion Pamos. As though feeling Lon's gaze on him, Hollowell glanced at him.

Lon nodded to the older man, but Hollowell only gave him a cool look and turned back to regard Lilia. Lon restrained a grimace. *Uncle Martin is obviously still not thrilled about everything.*

Renner appeared at his elbow, having slipped around the table with rather astonishing speed. "I don't see anything out of the ordinary, but something's wrong. We need to get the Ambassador out of here."

"Agreed." Lon nodded curtly. Lilia wasn't up there by accident.

He and the corporal stepped over to Kedis's chair and Lon took him by the arm. In hushed, stern tones, he said, "Ambassador, we need to get you out of here."

"Nonsense." Kedis glanced between the two men before brushing Lon's hand off like it was a piece of lint clinging to the rich black fabric of his tuxedo jacket. His dark eyes flashed with a combination of annoyance and pride. "We've just signed a trade agreement. How will it look if I leave at the slightest hint of danger?"

Lon exchanged a grim look with Renner. This was not the time for the Ambassador to be stubborn. Lon felt it in his gut; the twisting certainty they were on the brink of some kind of disaster.

The Pearl was supposed to be one of the three most secure locations in the entire Coalition—but the Triumvirate had a leak and the Mastermind had a transporter.

*And now we've got the most important people in the Coalition trapped in an upside-down fishbowl.*

Catching Renner's eye again, Lon jerked his chin toward Kedis. They'd have to bodily escort him out. *Better alive and furious than dead.*

They both reached for the Ambassador's arms just as a laser bolt from above drilled Kedis in the face.


An acute sense of danger set off all Chesnee's internal alarms, sending his senses into overdrive. He was acutely aware of the warmth emanating from his wife beside him, smelled the scent of her perfume and beneath it caught the scent of a hundred others. He heard strains of the lovely ballad they'd been waltzing to, but they were quickly lost beneath a rush of sound from the crowd of guests filling the Dome as they gasped and pointed up at that swaying, dangling figure above them, asking each other what was happening.

"What in the galaxy?" Sylvia breathed.

*We need to get out of here.*

Chesnee knew it with an urgent certainty that thrummed in his bones and itched beneath his skin. He looped a protective arm around his wife, who was still staring wide-eyed up at the woman in peril. *I never should have left the* Change. *I never should have let Kedis talk me into bringing her down here.*

He'd allowed Kedis to put her at risk for the sake of appearances because the Ambassador had convinced him it was his duty.

Again.

*You'd think I would have learned something from that first failed assassination attempt.*

Prior to his successful breaching of Lanx's planetary shield, he had spent months absorbing everything he could about the way the Coalition operated, which included the Glo'Stean Resistance's ground forces. This had taught him the people of the Coalition possessed an element of gritty blockheadedness that prevented them from simply accepting facts other worlds and systems throughout the galaxy had already accepted.

That gritty blockheadedness was particularly strong in the Freedom's Children terrorist group.

Chesnee tightened his jaw as it struck him again that all the good intentions in the world, all his achievements since being put in command of the Blockade Division, wouldn't mean a thing if they cost him his wife.

He cast a quick, urgent look around for their security detail. The six men—a mix of both his own crew and Coalition liaisons—had been hovering unobtrusively all evening. They now swooped forward, unapologetically elbowing their way through a cluster of men and women standing frozen on the dance floor staring upward.

*Kedis and his plans,* he thought grimly.

Speaking of Kedis…Chesnee glanced around again in search of the Ambassador.

Across the ballroom, he glimpsed Kedis still holding court at his table, but in between the shifting crowd, he saw Lon Strong and Corporal Renner converge on the Ambassador. A fraction of the sudden weight pressing down on his shoulders lifted. *Excellent.*

They'd spotted the potential danger too.

Chesnee nudged his wife forward. "We're leaving, Sylvia."

She glanced up at him, understanding flooding her face even as a little of the color left it. She didn't speak, didn't ask questions, she merely nodded and allowed him to usher her off the dance floor.

The Admiral leaned toward Lichen Taft, chief of his Coalition security liaisons, a golden-skinned man of medium height with a buzz cut. Taft wore the same standard black tuxedo as every other security guard here. "What is the fastest way out of here?"

"Straight down the executive accelevator, sir." Taft's dark gaze scanned back and forth along their path as they cut through the crowd to the hall encircling the Dome. "That's where we're head—"

The rest of his sentence was lost in a wave of screams as laser bolts burned through the air.

For Lon, time froze.

He saw it all with alien clarity. The faint surprise visible in Kedis's profile. The charred edges of what had once been his left eye.

Their high hopes for a brighter future for the Coalition burning to ash.

Time reset itself.

Kedis's half-full champagne flute slipped from his nerveless fingers as he collapsed. Lon and Renner caught him before he hit the floor, but the champagne flute shattered beside them, spraying cool liquid and shards of glass. Neither man noticed.

Shouts and piercing screams erupted around them. Some of their fellow guests dropped to the floor and covered their heads as though that would somehow protect them from being targeted, while others attempted to make a run for the exits.

Too many bodies, not nearly enough space. Lon gulped; his mouth was as dry as a Lanxian canyon. *We won't be getting out that way.*

Lon met Renner's shocked gaze and indicated the table with a frantic jerk of his head. "Get him under there!"

Something hit him in the back, but with the adrenaline coursing through his veins, he barely felt it. Whatever it was didn't matter anyway, protected as he was by his stealth armor.

Lowering the Ambassador's limp form to the floor, he and Renner shoved him beneath the trailing folds of the white tablecloth, displacing chairs in order to shield his body. They both crawled in after him. Their world narrowed down to a dim, tiny cave, but the screams and shouts from outside remained as loud as ever.

"Oh, God," Renner groaned, hunching over Kedis's body. His face was grim and bloodless. "That was a sniper rifle."

Bile rose in Lon's throat, burning it. Kedis had been wearing body armor—the Ambassador wasn't *that* foolhardy—but body armor couldn't protect him from a laser bolt to the *head*. Gritting his teeth together, Lon hastily inspected the wound.

Kedis's left eye was gone, no doubt about it. The burn from the laser bolt extended from the corner of his eye down to his ear, which was also mostly gone.

Lon doubted he'd find a pulse, but he checked anyway, pressing two fingers against Kedis's neck. To his shock, he found one. Weak and thready, yes, but...

He looked up at Renner, a wisp of hope igniting inside him. "He's still alive."

The corporal just stared at him, his dark eyes full of furious frustration.

Lon slid a hand beneath the Ambassador's head, bracing himself to encounter a charred, bloody mess of an exit wound, but his questing fingers only found hair. He relaxed—if only for a second. "The shot hit him at an angle. He's really fortunate." He looked at Renner again. "We've got to get him out of here."

Kedis might still be breathing, but there was no telling what kind of brain damage he'd sustained losing that eye. Lon started to Nancom Corran—he didn't know where the other man was in the midst of this sudden chaos—but nothing happened.

Lon blinked and tried again. Still, nothing.

A terrible suspicion flooded him. He tried to reach into his ISF for his medkit, but his fingers only scraped the smooth fabric of his trousers by his knee.

His nanites were frozen.

*How did this happen?* Panic fluttered around the edges of his mind like a caged, wild thing, but Lon took a deep breath and squashed the voice clamoring he was useless as a bodyguard without access to his ISF. At the moment, he wasn't sure it mattered how this had happened. The point was that his nanites were frozen for the next six hours and there was nothing he could do about it.

*Have to do things the old-fashioned way.*

The Dome still thundered with screams and shouts and the thud of hundreds of footsteps as people stampeded to the exits, trying to escape. The sharp smell of fear mixed with the scent of a hundred different colognes and perfumes. Lon thought heard renewed laser-fire, but he couldn't be sure.

He touched his ear, triggering the tiny comlink he wore there. He might not be able to Nancom Corran, but their team could still communicate.

Nothing but static greeted him.

A bead of sweat trickled down Lon's neck. *This is* really *not good.*

Before he could share this latest blow with Renner, the corporal burst out, "Somebody's jamming comms." An undercurrent of fear lay beneath Renner's fury. He waved the hand not holding a pistol in the general direction of Lon's head. "Can you—"

His implication was obvious. Lon gritted his teeth; it galled him to admit nano-armor had a weakness. "My nanites aren't working. Not sure what happened."

He'd been hit with an impactor, obviously, but *how* that had happened remained a mystery for now.

Renner's jaw dropped in astonishment—he'd clearly been laboring under the impression that nanotech was practically infallible—but he mastered himself almost immediately. His lips curled into a feral, mirthless smile. "Have to get you a weapon the old-fashioned way."

Lon took a deep breath. "Stay here with Kedis. I'll be right back." Of the two of them, he had the best chances of surviving ducking back into the fray. His stealth armor would keep him alive a little longer.

Rolling out from beneath the table, Lon found himself face-to-face with the business end of a laser pistol.

# CHAPTER 96

CHESNEE tightened his arm around his wife's shoulders as their little group reached one of the doorways leading into the hall. He couldn't say he was surprised everything had gone sideways. Part of him had expected it from the beginning.

His government had blockaded this system for over twenty years, after all. *You can't expect everyone to put aside all that anger in just a few months.*

"Go!" Taft shouted, above the roar of the panicked crowd stampeding for the hall exits behind them.

The urgent thrumming in Chesnee's bones increased. *Have to get Sylvia out of here.*

An eyeblink.

*Kedis.*

He almost groaned. Ultimately, he had a responsibility to get the Ambassador out of here too, didn't he? High Command and the Senate probably thought so, even if he was sorely tempted to leave the man to his fate.

Grimacing, Chesnee risked a glance over his shoulder, but all he could see was a mass of terrified people in elegant evening attire surging toward them. Kedis, Renner, and Strong were lost somewhere beyond them. More laserfire strafed the Dome, though it could barely be heard above the screams and rushing crowd.

Captain Archer Diaz, senior of the three men he'd brought from the *Winds of Change*, seized his shoulder. "Go, sir!"

Chesnee pushed Sylvia through the doorway ahead of him. The instant they set foot in the hall, manic, high-pitched laughter met their ears.

The sound of it raised the hairs on the back of Chesnee's neck. *There's someone already here*, he realized, a sick feeling pooling in the pit of his stomach.

Taft and Diaz both raised their weapons, aiming them up the hall at two solitary figures approaching them at an odd, ungainly pace. Diaz's two subordinates did the same, while Taft's two men covered their rear.

Chesnee focused his attention on the figures, adrenaline pumping through him, though he did his best to keep it under the same cool, calm control he used when he stood in his Command Center. In the soft light of the sconces, the two figures resolved themselves into a young man in a tuxedo and a young woman. The woman was nearly doubled over from a fit of maniacal laughter, and the man had a hold of both her wrists.

Chesnee squinted past Taft's shoulder; the young man looked familiar. Recognition struck. *That's one of Lon Strong's brothers!*


Kevin gritted his teeth as he tried to keep Erudita upright and moving. She was still shrieking with peals of laughter, her voice reverberating in the hall around them, but he fully expected her to resume fighting him again at any moment. He could barely hear the screams from the Dome over her laughter; his stomach clenched again. *What's happening in there?*

Judging by Erudita's reaction, it could only be something horrible.

Ahead of them, a cluster of people emerged into the hall. Kevin started to call out to them, but Erudita chose that moment to buck wildly in his grip, still laughing. It took all his strength to keep her restrained.

*I could really use a pair of cuffs about now*, he thought grimly.

Too bad they were trapped in his frozen ISF.

Erudita stopped cackling—and fighting—long enough to stare down the hall. Kevin couldn't see his captive's expression, but from the sudden tension in her shoulders, he had a feeling it wasn't welcoming.

Unnerved, he risked a look at the newcomers himself…and promptly restrained a groan. Four of the tuxedo-clad figures were aiming weapons in their direction—a laser carbine and a pistol. Security detail, obviously. And behind them…

"Admiral Chesnee?" He couldn't keep a note of sharp incredulity out of his voice. "What's—"

The Admiral cut him off in Tarynian. "The Pearl is under attack." He raised a hand to stop the man with the carbine as he stepped forward threateningly. "Taft, this is—"

"I know who he is," Taft said grimly. "Admiral, we need to get you out of here."

Kevin clamped his jaw shut long enough to hold back the words he wanted to say, his gaze sliding past the Admiral to the doors to the Dome down the hall. Then he shook Erudita's shoulders roughly. "She's part of it."

More screams came from the Dome.

Erudita threw her head back, still cackling wildly. Before Kevin could move, before he could even take a breath, Taft raised his carbine and fired a single shot into the center of her forehead. Blood and charred brain matter sprayed out from the back of her head; she slumped lifeless in Kevin's grasp.

"Not anymore," Taft said simply.

Kevin gaped at him, eyes wide with shock. "She was restrained! You can't just—"

"We haven't got time for this, boy." Taft lowered the carbine. "Be happy I waited for a clear shot."

*He doesn't know I'm a Guardian.* The thought flitted across Kevin's mind, but it was gone almost as soon as he'd considered it, swallowed up by the horror of what he'd just witnessed. He looked down at Erudita's corpse, dimly registering the blood and bits of brain coating the outside of his right sleeve, and then gently lowered her body to the floor.

Ignoring Taft, Kevin straightened and looked straight at Chesnee. "Admiral, I'm a Guardian like Lon, although she," he nodded to Erudita, "temporarily froze my nanites."

"Then what good are you?" Diaz growled in Tarynian.

Kevin ignored him too, a plan already formulating in his head. "I can help you get out of here."

It took Chesnee less than a second to decide. He gave Kevin a sharp nod.

"Okay. Head for the kitchen." Kevin pointed to the kitchen entrance. "I've got to get something." He dashed back up the hall to where Erudita's nanoblade lay discarded, scooped it up and ran to the kitchen door.

Chesnee, his wife, and his six-man security team had entered at a run. One of the men, a tall dark-skinned man with a military buzz cut, held the door open for Kevin, though his eyes widened at the sight of the nanoblade. He let the door swing shut as soon as Kevin was through and beckoned for another man to help him block the door with a moving cart that still held uneaten plates of dessert.

Taft pinned Kevin—and the nanoblade—with an unhappy expression. "What are we doing in here, kid? They're bound to be watching the service accelevators too."

"Oh, I'm sure they are," Kevin said over his shoulder, yanking his comlink out of his tuxedo jacket pocket with his free hand and pulling up the barebones security schematics of the Pearl Michael had given them. "That's why we're going to take the stairs."

He hefted the nanoblade in his hand. "Four floors down."

Taft, Diaz, and the other men looked taken aback, but Chesnee was already nodding. "Just like your brother helped Kedis escape the last time."

"Yes, sir."

"Do it." Chesnee glanced at Taft and Diaz in turn. "I don't see any other viable options."

Taft pressed his lips into a thin line, but reluctantly nodded in agreement. Diaz saluted crisply, though his dark eyes remained suspicious.

"All right, then." Kevin plunged his borrowed nanoblade into the floor. "Get ready to jump."

He started to cut an angled circle in the floor, then paused as a thought occurred to him. He looked up at the Admiral. "First, sir, you'd better trade me jackets."

# Chapter 97

As the portal rapidly blossomed from a tiny sphere into something big enough for a human being to pass through, Lilia's gaze flicked to Jasper. He had been staring after her and was now gaping at the portal—and at the four gray-armored figures tumbling through it onto the observation walkway.

Armored figures carrying nanoblades.

Lilia acted on instinct, whirling back toward Jasper to put herself between him and the oncoming attackers. Trained soldier or not, Jasper couldn't defend himself against four nano-armor-clad opponents wielding nanoblades.

They'd kill him.

He would fight bravely, of that she had no doubt, but they'd kill him. Especially since he was wearing that blasted G.U. uniform.

In that instant, one fact crystallized in Lilia's mind. It would kill *her* to watch him die.

Her fingers tightened on the hilts of her nanoblades. She couldn't—*wouldn't*—let that happen.

A plan sprang to life inside her head; she seized it. *Doesn't matter how crazy it is.* They had to get out of here.

Whipping around, Lilia shouted to Jasper, "Run!" She suited action to words, setting off at a dead run up the walkway.

Jasper hesitated only a fraction of a second before taking off after her.

By the time the four figures finished tumbling out of the portal and realized Lilia and Jasper were even there, the two of them were almost out of sight beyond the curve of the walkway.

The thuds their booted feet made on the floor blended into the screams and shouts rushing up from the Dome's floor beneath them. Lilia's armor automatically adjusted its internal temperature to compensate for her exertion, keeping her from breaking a sweat.

As soon as they were out of sight of the terrorists, if only for a brief moment, she skidded to a halt. "Stop!" she panted. "Stop here." She didn't want to risk running into anyone else.

Jasper halted as well, his gray eyes flicking from her to the walkway around them and back.

Before he could say anything, Lilia shoved both of her nano-blades at him. "Here. Take these." She didn't dare sheath them in her ISF—not with Freedom Children terrorists running around with impactors. If one of them hit her, she wouldn't be able to draw her blades again until it was too late.

Jasper took the blades without question, his expression stony.

Clenching her jaw, Lilia then took a few precious seconds to de-materialize her stealth-mode armor. The dark gray nanites retreated back into the pores of her skin and then almost instantaneously re-appeared as she formed defense-mode armor instead. There would be no saving this dress; it was a sacrifice she'd have to make.

She couldn't fight in this getup. It wasn't even a choice. Her biggest mistake tonight had been thinking she could.

Well, that and the fact that she thought there hadn't been *time* to change.

The skirt of her gown was too bulky to survive the transformation; her nanites sliced through the material around her waist as easily as they had once sliced through her hair. The shimmering sapphire material fluttered to the floor to pool at her feet; she stepped out of it. Lastly, she materialized her helmet, facemask, and visor. If she was going to use defense-mode, she might as well go big and use all of it.

Jasper watched her wordlessly. When Lilia chanced a quick glance at him, she saw he'd shuttered the bulk of his hurt and be-trayal, but traces of it lingered. The jagged shards inside her chest cut a little deeper.

Pushing the pain aside, Lilia reached into her ISF and withdrew her laser carbine and her spare energy packs. "These are for you." She slung the carbine around Jasper's neck—he needed more than a pistol to fight—and tucked the energy packs into his uniform jacket's pockets. She then plunged her hand into her ISF by her ribs for her hoverdisc.

Expanding the smooth metal disc, Lilia dropped it to float just above the floor and hopped aboard. She materialized her magnetic boot soles to stabilize herself and turned to Jasper, holding out her hands for her nanoblades. "Come on."

He remained standing there, staring at her. His grip on the hilts of her blades was so tight his knuckles were white. "You *are* the girl from Challa, aren't you?"

It wasn't a question.

Behind her facemask, Lilia bit her lip. She couldn't lie to him anymore. He deserved the truth now. "Yes."

Jasper gave a sharp nod and passed her blades back to her. After arranging the carbine's sling around his neck with the smooth speed of long practice so that he could easily manipulate the weapon, he climbed onto the hoverdisc behind her. As soon as he slid an arm around her waist, securing him to her, Lilia took off.

Rising sharply into the air, she shot forward along the observation walkway. The transparent plastiglass wall on one side of them and the smooth pearly wall on the other side formed something her firing practice teacher used to call a fatal funnel. *We have to get out of here.*

As soon Lilia reached the first break in the wall, she zipped over the railing and soared out into the Dome.

The worst part about having someone point a laser pistol at him tonight was that his nanites were frozen and he couldn't protect his face. Lon blinked, heart rate spiking and muscles tensing…and then he realized the person holding the weapon was a Guardian in full defense-mode armor, crouched beside Kedis's table with… "Grandfather!"

Aiden knelt beside the Guardian, his eyes unfocused and his wrinkled face oddly blank.

The Guardian immediately lowered his weapon. "Lon!" It was Michael. "Where's Kedis?"

"Under there." Lon jerked his head toward the table. "He's hurt pretty bad." He swallowed. "I'd Nancom you, but somebody hit me with an impactor."

A cold chill skipped down his spine as his older brother nodded. "Me too," Michael said grimly. "Somebody from Ashford's staff."

"They're jamming comms too."

"Great." Michael's helmeted head turned as he scanned their surroundings—including the stretches of railing belonging to the observation walkway above them. "We've got to get out of here. They're disabling Guardians on purpose."

"Tell me about it." Lon looked around, his eyes searching beyond his brother for signs of danger. He felt naked and exposed without Nancom or access to his ISF. "They don't want us cutting our way out of here."

"They learned from the last time."

The Dome was emptying out by now as everyone fled, cramming themselves into the outside hall in a desperate bid to use the accelevator banks to escape. Screams and shouts echoed in the distance. Crumpled figures littered the pearlescent floor around tables and across the dance floor—the dead and badly wounded. A few survivors had taken refuge beneath tables just as they had; white tablecloths flickered as frightened faces peeked out.

A laser bolt splashed against Michael's back. He grunted and shifted to face the threat, shielding Aiden as best he could.

*We're sitting ducks,* Lon realized. *Prime targets, as soon as we try to move.*

An exit to the hall stood ten meters to their left, but they'd be exposed to sniper fire the entire time.

Michael must have reached the same conclusion. "Is there room under there for Grandfather?"

"It'll be tight, but sure."

"Get—" Michael began, but at that moment, someone on a hoverdisc shot over the railing of the observation walkway across the Dome and arced through the air. Laser bolts followed the person.

*No,* Lon thought. *People. There are* two *people on that thing.*

A gray-clad Guardian…and a familiar golden-haired man in a black uniform.

# Chapter 98

EVEN wearing her nano-armor, Lilia could feel Jasper's lean, sturdy frame enveloping her from behind. His arm pressed against her midsection, keeping them locked together, his broad chest pressed against her armored back. They'd never been quite this close before.

If she didn't know better, she'd swear it felt like he was holding her because he wanted to instead of holding on for dear life.

She almost wished she wasn't wearing armor so she could appreciate it more. It would never happen again, of that much she was sure. The memory of that awful betrayed look in his eyes made her eyes sting and the back of her throat threaten to close up.

She pushed both memory and impending tears away. *Later. It all has to wait until later.*

Under different circumstances, she would have enjoyed taking him for a spin on her hoverdisc. She'd thought about it once in the past few weeks, what it would be like if Jasper knew she was a Guardian. The thought had been too fragile and unsubstantial to hold for long; she'd tiptoed around it in her mind before shelving it in the category of Things Too Scary To Think About Now.

Laser bolts had never entered into that equation.

They soared out high above the Dome floor, only a handful of meters beneath the latticed domed ceiling, and Lilia took a second to assess their situation. Beyond the latticed ceiling above them, dark stars glittered in the night sky. Below them, the golden illumination provided by the seashell sconces encircling the Dome revealed a mostly empty atrium. Some of the tables and chairs ringing the room had been overturned; their tablecloths lay strewn about surrounded by shattered glassware and broken centerpieces.

Across the Dome, dark splotches marred the pearlescent floor in places, though it was unclear if they were from spilled drinks or blood, and crumpled bodies littered the floor. Some of them had been shot, but others…even from above, Lilia could see that the crowd's panicked dash to safety had trampled a few unfortunate victims in its path.

Shouts echoed behind them, louder now, and then a hail of laserfire sprayed toward them. Pressing her booted toes down on her hoverdisc's forward controls, Lilia dove down in a crazy sideways spiraling arc, holding tight to her nanoblades. The laser bolts missed. They impacted the Dome's walls instead, leaving ugly black scorch marks on the pearly surface.

Her facemask filtered the air she breathed and kept out most smells, but Lilia's brain supplied the acrid tang of laserfire from memory anyway.

"There!" Jasper brought his free arm up to point at a cluster of tables. "There's Kedis's table. Somebody's there!"

Her helmet automatically adjusted the volume of his voice to keep Lilia from feeling like he was shouting in her ear. "I see them too!"

Several figures crouched beside the white-draped table. Lilia spotted a familiar sandy head, and beside her brother, a figure clad in dark gray nano-armor. She felt a flash of relief. *Another Guardian.* One of the good guys, though she hadn't a clue as to who he might be.

She tried hailing all of her brothers via Nancom again, but she *still* couldn't raise any of them. *Something is seriously wrong.*

Jasper's arm tightened around her waist. "That's Lon."

"I see him."

Arcing around again, Lilia dropped into a steep glide headed straight for that table. As she did, she spotted a solitary figure kneeling beside a table ten meters from Lon and the other Guardian. *That looks like Uncle Martin.*

An uneven staccato spray of laser bolts followed, but she and Jasper were moving too fast for any of them to connect.

Lon and the other Guardian saw them coming. Even if he didn't recognize her armor-clad figure, Lon recognized Jasper. So did the Guardian beside him, apparently. He started to raise the laser carbine in his hands, but then lowered it, turning his focus back instead to the observation walkway railings.

Seconds later, Lilia slid to a halt beside the table. She winced; the landing was rougher than she would have liked. She hadn't had enough practice lately hauling another person with her.

"Where's Kedis?" Jasper asked without preamble, letting go of her immediately and jumping off the hoverdisc.

Lon jerked his chin toward the table. "Under there. He's been hurt. Got to get him out of here."

A pair of feet clad in expensive black shoes poked out from beneath the white tablecloth. Jasper immediately dropped to one knee and lifted the tablecloth to investigate.

Lon's gaze turned to Lilia, his green eyes sharp and questioning. "Who—"

"It's me, Lon."

"Lilia?" Lon's expression sharpened further as he glanced from her to Jasper and back. For a second Lilia thought he was going to say something, but whatever it was he decided against it.

She swallowed, clutching her nanoblades as she dropped into a crouch on her hoverdisc. *Probably for the best.* Anything he could say would undoubtedly be painful, and she couldn't think about any of it right now or they might end up dead.

A fresh flurry of laser bolts sprayed down in their direction, but most of them fell short, scoring the floor instead.

Lilia peeked around the side of the tablecloth draping down to the floor, trusting her armor to protect her. She shifted her grip on her nanoblades, but their tips still scored microscopic lines in the floor. She glimpsed movement along one of the observation walkway railings. "Huh. They must not have hoverdiscs."

"Thank God for that," the other Guardian said in a familiar voice.

Lilia drew back immediately, twisting to stare at him. "Mike?"

"Yeah."

"Where's Grandfather?"

Michael jerked a gray-gloved thumb toward the table. "Under there with Kedis."

"Is he okay?"

"He's fine."

Relief flooding her, Lilia looked around again. "Where's Derek?"

"Took off to help with the sniper situation." Michael tipped his helmet toward the observation walkway above them.

Jasper withdrew his head from beneath the table, his expression grim and cold. "They have multiple sniper teams."

"Yeah." Lilia swallowed. "Birch, Jasper, and I took care of one of them. Kevin and Erik were supposed to take care of another one, but Kevin didn't make it there and I can't reach him via Nancom."

"He had a run-in with one of the Mastermind's Guardians in the hall," Michael said grimly. "She fried his nanites with an impactor bolt just like they did with the rest of us. He was supposed to bring her out here, but he must have gotten stuck."

Lilia's breath caught in her throat. "Your nanites are fried?"

"Oh, yeah." Lon indicated his tuxedo with an impatient flick of his hand. "Wouldn't still be wearing this if I could materialize my armor." He gave her a mirthless, lopsided smile. "Freedom's Children made the guest list and they've got names of Guardians, apparently. Made sure to disable us first."

"Including Derek," Michael added, before nodding to her. "Glad you were able to materialize defense-mode first."

Inside her armor, Lilia felt cold. That explained why she hadn't been able to reach anyone via Nancom. Freedom's Children hadn't just crashed the party, they'd been *included* in it from the start.

Her brother's last statement finally registered; she shook her head. "I haven't been disabled. My nanites are still functional. One of the snipers hit Birch with an impactor bolt, but he missed me."

Beside her, Lon sucked in a sharp breath. "Really?" He exhaled in a rush. "Finally, some good news."

Renner abruptly thrust his head out from under the tablecloth. "What's taking so long?" he growled in Tarynian. "Wright, we need to—"

Jasper silenced him with a look. "I know. We're working on it."

The corporal clamped his jaw shut, though his dark eyes flashed as he glanced around at the three of them. He scowled and withdrew back beneath the table as suddenly as he had emerged.

Jasper leaned toward Lilia and her brothers, still kneeling. His arm brushed Lilia's armor; he immediately shifted so they weren't touching. "What are we going to do?"

Lilia's breath caught in her throat at the instinctive change in his body language; she felt the loss keenly.

"We've got at least one option," Lon said grimly. He looked at Lilia, his eyes dropping to her nanoblades. "We should be able to escape like we did last time. Unless..." he trailed off, his gaze flicking up to meet hers through her visor.

Something cold shifted in the pit of her stomach. "Unless?"

Lon darted a brief look at Jasper before fixing on her again. "Unless you get us out of here another way."

Michael's helmeted head twisted to regard them both. He suddenly seemed to radiate purpose. "That could work!"

"What are you talking about?" Jasper shot a sharp look at Lon, his forehead creasing with confusion. When Lon didn't answer, he shifted his gaze to Lilia. "What way?"

Beneath her facemask, Lilia bit her lip hard enough to draw blood. *He wants me to open a portal.* Her heart began to pound faster—if that was even possible after everything that had happened in the past five minutes.

She swallowed. "If I do this, they'll know I know."

There was no telling what would happen as a result of that.

"We can't let them kill him." Lon made an impatient gesture to Kedis's still form beneath the table. "Not after everything we've been through already."

"Lon's right." Michael glanced over his shoulder at her as well. "You can save him and save Grandfather. We'll worry about the consequences later."

Jasper was still staring at her; Lilia let herself meet his gaze, even though he couldn't see her eyes through her visor. She could see the confusion in those gray depths, but…well, she really didn't have a choice, did she?

*You swore an oath to protect people.*

She took one quick breath and let it out. "Okay. I'll do it. But we've got to get Uncle Martin first." She nodded to the left, in the direction of the table she'd seen him crouched beside. "He's over there—we can't leave him here."

Michael and Lon exchanged quick glances, though Lon couldn't see his brother's expression through his facemask. "Uncle Martin is still here?"

Lilia nodded and raised one of the blades in her hands to point with the hilt. "Couple of tables over."

More laser bolts scored the floor in front of them, this time from a different angle.

Lilia swallowed again. *We're running out of time.*

Michael leaned back, glancing left to right to check the rear side of their tables and the two meter-wide path between the tables and the Dome's curving wall. "I'll get him." He nodded to Lilia. "Get ready to go."

"Got it," she said as Michael left the relative shelter of their table in a half-crouching run and disappeared behind the white tablecloth of the table beside them.

Jasper glanced between them, his jaw tight. "Uncle Martin. Isn't that—?"

"Representative Hollowell." Lon flipped the edge of the tablecloth up. "Renner, we'll be moving in a minute. Get Kedis's shoulders."

Lilia forced herself to breathe, her fingers tightening on the hilts of her nanoblades again. Her stomach churned uneasily. She didn't want Uncle Martin knowing about the transporter either, come to think of it. She didn't want *any* of them knowing about it.

But, again…she really didn't have a choice.

She turned to Jasper, extending her nanoblades to him hilt-first again "Here. I need you to take these again. Just for a minute."

Jasper looked at Lon, who held up a hand. "Don't worry. Renner and I can get Kedis."

"Fine." Jasper let the laser carbine Lilia had given him hang from its sling and brusquely accepted the nanoblades. "What are you going to do?"

Lilia just shook her head. *You wouldn't believe me if I told you.* "You'll see."

"That's not very reassuring," he muttered, his mouth flattening into a thin line.

She ignored him, curling and uncurling her hands into fists in unconscious preparation. *Where do we go?* Given how badly Kedis was injured, it needed to be close to a—

*Of course!* Lilia almost smacked herself in the forehead. She already *had* coordinates to a hospital. Atalia Hospital West, the same place her grandfather had been taken after the explosion at the Tri-World Tournament's Opening Ball.

She nodded to herself, some of her anxiety morphing into resolve. They'd iron out all the diplomatic issues later—with Freedom's Children focused on the Pearl, the safest thing for Kedis right now was to get him out of Glo'Stea's capital city.

The laserfire from above suddenly stopped, leaving a ringing silence in its wake. In that moment the atrium was quiet enough that they could hear faint groans and moans from the crumpled figures scattered across the floor who were still breathing—and beyond that screams and shouts from the crowd still trapped in the hallway beyond. Lilia didn't know what was happening out there, but it sounded terrible.

Lilia scanned what she could see of the observation walkway railings, fresh unease curling through her. *Why did they stop shooting at us?*

Beside her, Jasper echoed her thoughts. "They can't have given up already," he said grimly.

*No.* Lilia shook her head. *Not with the Tarynian ambassador still possibly breathing.*

Lon, who had scooted back to watch for Michael and Hollowell, just scowled. "Probably trying to find a better angle to—here they come!"

Lilia looked over her shoulder in time to see Michael reappear, one arm wrapped around Martin Hollowell's bony shoulders. He helped the old Representative into a kneeling position on the floor. Hollowell's dark, wrinkled face was set in grim lines; his white curly hair seemed to stick out a little farther from his scalp.

"Stay down, Uncle Martin." Michael let go of the old man and placed a hand on his shoulder. "We're going to get you out of here."

Hollowell nodded to them all, though to Lilia it seemed his gaze lingered a fraction longer on Jasper and the twin nanoblades he held. "Thank you."

Michael motioned to Lilia. "Start—"

Hollowell cut him off. "I saw the Ambassador die," he said in a querulous voice. "Where is Aiden?"

"Kedis isn't dead, and neither is Grandfather," Michael assured him, gesturing to the table beside them. "They're both under there."

Hollowell blinked as he registered Kedis's feet sticking out from beneath the tablecloth, looking faintly taken aback. "Ah." The querulous note faded from his voice. "Excellent. I am…glad to hear it."

"Yeah." Lon shot him a tight smile as he flipped the tablecloth up and reached down to grab Kedis's legs. He nodded to both Aiden and Renner before glancing back over his shoulder at Hollowell. "We're going to get all of you out of here, Uncle Martin. Don't worry."

Hollowell shook his head. "Getting out of here is the least of my worries. I was more afraid—"

It was time.

Heart thudding in her chest, Lilia thrust her hands out in front of her. She caught a puzzled look from Jasper out of the corner of her eye, but ignored him. It took all of three seconds to sift through the various coordinates she had to different places in the hospital and settle on the main hall on Grandfather's floor.

"—the Ambassador would escape."

Something about those words and their curiously satisfied tone struck Lilia as odd. On the verge of opening the portal, she paused long enough to turn her helmeted head toward Hollowell—

—just in time to watch the old man draw a shining blade from thin air and lean forward to casually run Jasper through.

# CHAPTER 99

AIDEN knelt beneath the table with Corporal Renner—he refused to think of it as cowering—even if he felt beyond old and helpless to provide any assistance in their current situation. The two of them hunkered awkwardly around Kedis's unconscious form. It was dim enough that Aiden had nearly sat on the Ambassador's chest when Michael unceremoniously pushed him under the table. The smell of blood, sweat, and burned flesh filled the rapidly warming air trapped beneath the long tablecloth. It felt like the whole galaxy had narrowed down to this tiny space.

Part of his brain still floundered, unable to accept that everything had gone so horribly wrong. The rest of his brain started processing and analyzing things in an attempt to contrive some sort of solution. Anything to make sense of the situation.

What could Freedom's Children possibly hope to gain from an attack now? The trade agreement was signed. It was too late for—Aiden exhaled slowly, his vision traveling past the shadowy white tablecloth in front of him as his mind put pieces together.

*All they can do now is create chaos.* Yes, it was too late for the Mastermind and his followers to stop the trade agreement from being signed. But that did not mean they had to give up and roll over.

*Oh, no. There are still all kinds of mayhem they can cause to make us— and the Galactic Union—regret our decision.*

Was it vindictive? Absolutely. Would it be effective? Aiden shook his head. Only time would tell.

Corporal Renner started muttering under his breath, effectively breaking Aiden's trance. The soldier was leaning over Kedis's body, a bandage pressed to the Ambassador's face.

Aiden cleared his throat. "How may I be of service?"

The younger man looked up sharply, and in the dim light, Aiden read the helpless frustration in his face.

"I don't know. Sir," he tacked on belatedly. "He needs a doctor. I—" Renner broke off, a muscle in his jaw twitching, and bent his head over the Ambassador again.

Aiden pressed his lips into a thin line as he considered the unconscious man. From the moment Kedis had revealed his presence at the Closing Ceremonies Gala, everything seemed to have fallen into place for him smoothly and easily. Now, it appeared the Ambassador's meteoric rise had come to a sudden and abrupt end.

Hushed voices floated through the tablecloth. The dearly-familiar sound of his grandchildren both relieved him and made his stomach clench with fear. Once again, they stood between him and danger. *Should this not be the other way around?*

He had honored—even welcomed—Michael and Derek's desire to be part of his staff, but moments like this brought him up sharply against the stark reminder that they would lay down their lives for him and he was currently helpless to do anything about it.

Renner stuck his head out from the tablecloth and said something in Tarynian. Wright cut him off, and the corporal withdrew beneath the table again, scowling.

A moment later, Aiden tilted his head to one side as he thought he heard the words, "Martin Hollowell." He blinked, and his old heart began to pound a little faster. Had Martin been trapped here too?

Scant moments later, though to his screaming joints it felt more like hours, Aiden heard Martin's familiar rumbling voice. Another faint wave of relief crashed through him. Martin, at least, was safe.

Aiden heard Martin ask about him and Michael's response, and then a wave of brighter light hit their little cave as someone lifted the edge of the tablecloth. Lon appeared, and nodded to them both before reaching down for Kedis's legs.

Beyond Lon, Hollowell was saying, "I was more afraid the Ambassador would escape."

Aiden frowned. Those words…and that tone…*That is strange.* He opened his mouth to ask his old friend what he meant, but at that moment Hollowell produced a sword from nowhere and impaled Lieutenant Wright.

The sound of his granddaughter's heartbroken scream shattered the stillness.


For a heartbeat, Lilia's brain refused to believe what her eyes told her. She watched in astonished horror, along with Kevin, Michael, and Lon, as Hollowell twisted the blade in Jasper's chest and then withdrew it in a smooth motion. The blade emerged wet with blood. Jasper's blood.

An involuntary scream ripped from her throat. It wasn't a conscious reaction; it was something primitive and instinctive, something from a part of her that realized what had happened while the rest of her was too shocked to believe it. "NO!"

Jasper looked stunned. Gray eyes wide, he looked from Hollowell down to his chest and back with impossible slowness, as though he was moving at one quarter speed. Then he slumped forward on his knees.

He would have collapsed flat on his face, still holding Lilia's nanoblades, had she not lunged forward and caught him.

The scene dissolved into chaos.

Michael threw himself sideways to tackle Hollowell, but the old man sprang to his feet with surprising agility and danced back, nanoblade at the ready. Michael shifted to place himself between Hollowell and the rest of them.

Sliding one arm beneath Jasper's arm and around his back to support him, Lilia stripped the nanoblades from his grip with her gloved free hand before the impossibly sharp blades could hurt him. They clanged to the floor. "Jasper. Jasper!"

Jasper pressed a hand to the wound, blood already seeping through his fingers to soak his black uniform jacket. Body armor didn't stand a chance against a nanoblade. His face was already rapidly losing color, his skin going pale against his golden hair.

Lon clutched Kedis's feet, gaping at the man they'd considered family all their lives. "Why? Why would you do that?"

"It had to be done." Dark eyes blazing, Hollowell spread his hands. The soft golden light from the sconces above glinted off his blade. It had a simple hilt and cross guard, nothing fancy. "In time, you will see. We will rid the Coalition system of scum like them." He nodded to Jasper's slumped form and Kedis's unconscious body.

Hot tears threatened to blur her vision; she furiously blinked them away. No time for the luxury of tears now. A couple escaped anyway and dripped down her cheeks behind her facemask.

Jasper was dying.

It didn't take a medical genius to see it. If by some miracle Hollowell had missed his heart, the wound was too close. He was losing blood too fast; she wouldn't be able to save him. Not by herself. She simply didn't have the equipment.

*The hospital. I have to get him to the hospital.* It was his only chance.

"Lil—Lil—ia." Jasper tried to say her name, but it came out in a choked gurgle. Blood frothed at the corners of his mouth.

Her heart wrenched. *Oh, God, please don't let him die. Please, please, please, Lord, don't let him die.* She wanted to kiss him, but her facemask was in the way and there wasn't time to dematerialize it.

Instead, she put a gloved finger to his lips. "Hush. Don't talk." Then, carefully, she lowered him to the floor and thrust her hands out in front of her again. "Lon!"

Lon conquered his astonishment and whipped his head around to look at her. He comprehended her intentions in an eyeblink; she read his acknowledgment in the sudden hardening of his green eyes.

Ignoring Hollowell and the gaping hole his impossible betrayal had punched in her gut, Lilia focused on the coordinates to the hospital. A pinprick of a portal sphere appeared in the air before her. She threw her arms wide and it bloomed to full size in a matter of seconds, a rush of displaced air ruffling the tablecloths around them.

Hollowell looked at her and a spasm of fury contorted his face. She had never, in all her years, seen him direct such an angry, hateful look at anyone, least of all her. "No!"

"Hurry!" Lilia gritted her teeth. "I won't be able to hold it for long."

"Come on!" Lon lifted Kedis's legs and pulled. The rest of Kedis's body emerged from beneath the table as Aiden and Renner heaved him forward, both bent over awkwardly to avoid bumping their backs into the underside of the table.

"I've got him," Renner grunted, shunting Aiden aside as he got a better grip under Kedis's armpits.

Lon stepped backward into the portal without a second thought, carrying Kedis's legs, and Renner followed with the rest of them. They vanished. *Please, God,* Lilia prayed, *don't let that portal have opened far off the floor.*

She looked at Aiden. "Grandfather! Go!"

Aiden knew he should follow his grandson through the portal, but his body refused to cooperate. His feet stayed glued to the floor, his eyes stuck to his old friend. "Martin? What are you doing?"

The first glimmers of the truth hit him—a horrifying truth—and his voice broke. "What have you *done?*"

"I've done what needed to be done, old friend," Hollowell snarled. "I've done what no one else had the courage to do—including you." He looked at Michael. "Get out of my way."

Michael shook his helmeted head. "I can't do that."

Hollowell simply shrugged. "You were warned."


Lilia watched in horror as gray nanites seeped through Hollowell's clothing and from the pores of his exposed skin to form defense-mode armor. *Uncle Martin is a Guardian?*

No. That couldn't be right, could it? She didn't think the NCDC accepted candidates that old. No. This…this was something else.

"Stand aside, boy," Hollowell commanded with a flick of his blade. "This is between your grandfather and me."

"No." If anything, Michael's armored form seemed to stand a little taller.

*That helmet and the way he talks…*Hollowell's voice wasn't distorted, but the cadence was the same. Lilia sucked in a sharp breath. "*You're* the Mastermind."

Hollowell turned his helmeted head toward her, and even though she couldn't see his eyes, she felt his burning gaze. "I see your nanites are still functional." He shook his helmeted head. "You should have joined me. You will regret that decision."

The portal still hummed between Lilia's hands. She continued to hold it open, but her wrists had begun to tingle and that odd sense of urgency hovering on the edge of her consciousness grew stronger. *Not. Much. Longer.* Time was slipping away from them—from *him.*

Her eyes flicked down to Jasper's still form, sweat breaking out on her forehead beneath her helmet. Her armor tried to compensate. "Mike! You've got to get Jasper out of here. Please!"

Even if she could manage to lift Jasper's dead weight, it wasn't possible for her to both hold the portal open and get him through it at the same time. And if they ran out of time and the portal closed?

*No.* She couldn't even bring herself to *think* it.

"You've lost your mind, child. Better to let him die," Hollowell snarled, taking a menacing step forward. "It's too late. There will be no saving him."

Michael tilted his nanoblade, holding the old Representative at bay, while their grandfather continued to stand frozen beside the table.

"Mike!" A hysterical note slid into her voice; danger bells were going off inside her head. "Please!"

All at once, Aiden seemed to break free of the spell binding him in one place. He surged forward and bent down to seize Jasper beneath the arms. With a strength Lilia hadn't thought he possessed anymore, he hauled Jasper up to a sitting position and shoved him across the short distance separating them from Lilia and the portal.

They were almost out of time. *Grandfather can't do that alone!* "Michael!" Lilia shrieked.

Her oldest brother weighed his choices in a split-second—and leaped back toward Aiden and Jasper.

Hollowell roared with fury and lunged after him, but Michael was younger and his reflexes were faster. He reached Aiden first and helped his grandfather heave Jasper through the portal. Just before the three of them vanished, he shouted, "Lilia, get out of here!"

Something in Lilia's head was *screaming*—a shrill, mechanical warning.

They disappeared just as something *sparked* in both of her wrists, exploding with a muffled *pop*. The portal winked out of existence, creating a little breeze. Lilia's gloved hands went numb.

"NO!" Hollowell bellowed.

He lunged for Lilia now, intending to impale her with his nanoblade, but she shot sideways on her hoverdisc toward her abandoned blades. Her fingers didn't work, but she used her wrists to scoop the blades up and soared a few meters into the air before whirling to face the Glo'Stean Representative. Pressing the hilts of her nanoblades to her chest, she prayed he wouldn't attack her until she could use her hands again.

"All this time it was you?" Anger and grief mixed with betrayal and shock, threatening to choke her with a torrent of overwhelming emotion. "All those attacks, all those people who've been hurt, the assassination attempt on Grandfather—*you* were behind them!"

Hollowell looked up at her, an imposing figure in gray nano-armor wielding a nanoblade. He looked like a Guardian, right down to the green Glo'Stean insignia over his heart. Lilia swallowed, setting her jaw. *But he's not a Guardian.*

He was—had been—their friend. She'd grown up considering him family. And now…to learn he was the mysterious figure behind so many terrible things? It was almost too much to take in. It *was* too much to take in.

Hollowell lowered his nanoblade. "I am willing to give you one last chance to change your mind, my dear. I was young once—I remember what it is like to be infatuated with someone. Put that boy out of your mind, put all those hormones and that emotion aside, and *think* about what I am offering."

He waved his gloved free hand. "The Tarynians have terrorized us for too long. A trade agreement will not change that. *You* have seen the destruction they've wrought. I know you haven't forgotten Coral Island."

No, she would never be able to forget that day. Lilia swallowed again, dimly aware that she stood on the edge of another precipice—this one as precipitous as the one she felt she had stood on with Jasper.

She straightened on her hoverdisc, sinking down far enough to put them at eye level, though a space a handful of meters wide still separated them. Her fingers had begun tingling. "What you've done isn't any better than what they did on Coral Island." She shook her helmeted head. "You and your people have killed and injured Glo'Stean citizens who were unfortunate enough to get in your way. How are you any better than the Tarynians?"

"If you fraternize with the enemy, certain consequences are to be expected."

The cold, matter-of-fact way in which Hollowell spoke the words, coupled with distant screams and shouts, sent ominous chills down Lilia's spine. She dematerialized her facemask so he could see her face—the face of a child he had watched grow up into a young woman. "*I've* fraternized with the enemy. I helped Lon get Kedis in to see the Triumvirate. Why are you offering me a second chance?"

Hollowell paused a beat, as though considering this, and then he held one hand out to the side, palm up. "Because I made you."

# CHAPTER 100

*B*ECAUSE *I made you.* Those words rolled through Lilia's mind, leaving terrible implications in their wake like ripples expanding out from a stone thrown into a lake. Realization—horrible realization—washed over her, but she had trouble accepting it. "What?"

Hollowell dropped his hand. "I chose you, Lilia. Just like I chose your brothers, and your friend Holt, and others throughout the NCDC. I saw qualities in you that I knew we would need for the future—for the fight to save our worlds from the Tarynians."

"*You're* the reason we're nano-genetic anomalies?" Lilia felt like she'd been kicked in the stomach. She'd known it had to be an external cause—Nob had discovered as much—but to learn for sure? And to learn who was responsible? She had never, in her wildest dreams, imagined anything like this.

"I made you," Hollowell repeated. "It would be foolhardy to allow the NCDC the opportunity to dismiss any of you." He paused. "I did not expect you to have already discovered your transporter—much less how to use it."

Lilia didn't even know how to respond to that. Her now-recovered fingers found the hilts of her nanoblades; she gripped them so tightly it felt like her gloves and the hilts had fused together.

"This is your last chance, Lilia. Join me and all your…indiscretions…are forgiven." Hollowell held out a hand, finally choosing to dematerialize his facemask. His face held the kindly expression he always wore when he interacted with any of her family. "You are a bright, intelligent young woman with your whole future ahead of you. We need your help. Join your brothers and sisters in Freedom's Children and fight for the Coalition's freedom. For our people's freedom."

Lilia pressed her lips into a thin line, considering his words. Thoughts darted through her mind, almost too fast to process. *Join him—and he uses you to bring your brothers in. Join him—and you condone what he did to Grandfather, what he's done to you and everyone else.*

Join him—and everything Birch ever said about her and her brothers being traitors would be true.

Just not the way any of them had ever imagined.

It took courage to speak, but once Lilia began, the words flowed easily. "You've *murdered* people in the name of freedom, Uncle Martin." She shook her head at him. "How is that any different from what the Tarynians have done all these years?"

The old Representative's expression hardened into stone. "I warn you, young lady, you spurn my offer at your peril."

Lilia took a deep breath and let it out slowly. She stood on the edge of another precipice—and this time she didn't jump.

She forced herself to loosen her grip on her nanoblades. "Then, Uncle Martin, I'm afraid you're going to have to kill me. Because I'll have to answer to God one day for what I've done in my life, and I can't stand before Him and say I helped you do this."

In that moment, as he looked at her, Hollowell's face became an alien mask. His features were familiar, and yet Lilia did not recognize the man beneath. "Very well then." His voice was ice cold, his tone as sharp as a nanoblade. "You've made your choice."

Lilia braced herself for him to attack her, but he only waved a gloved hand. She had a split-second to realize he was beckoning to someone *behind* her and whirled just in time to see four gray-clad figures on hoverdiscs swooping down toward her. They had apparently been hovering in the middle of the atrium, awaiting orders. Nanoblades flashed in their hands.

*Lovely.* Lilia gritted her teeth. One against four. *Not good odds at all.*

"You will regret this," Hollowell said over his shoulder as he turned away, materializing his facemask again. He pulled a hoverdisc from his ISF, expanded it, and dropped it to the floor before stepping aboard and floating away.

Part of Lilia wanted to chase after him, to keep him from escaping and bring him to justice. The rest of her knew she had bigger problems. *Which is exactly what he wanted.*

She had her nanoblades, but a good chunk of her nano-armor and ISF were frozen for the next hour. And even if she *could* access all of her ISF, Jasper had her carbine.

*Jasper.*

A sharp pain pierced her chest. *Oh, God, please let him live.* Desperate prayer said, she pushed thoughts of Jasper away.

Surviving this fight would take every bit of her focus.

One of the four not-Guardians dove toward her, nanoblade held to the side as though intended to slice Lilia in two. The figure was slight—another woman, Lilia guessed.

*She has to know she won't pierce my nano-armor that way.*

But then, did it really matter what *one* of them intended? All this woman had to do was keep Lilia busy and one of her friends could come in for the kill.

Lilia zipped sideways, dropping down and around in a tight circle that brought her sharply to the rear of her would-be attacker. The move would only afford her a few seconds' advantage, but—

Her attacker didn't react as quickly as she should have. The woman took too long to bring her hoverdisc around. Her movements were choppy and slightly uncoordinated instead of smooth and graceful.

Lilia's eyes widened and then narrowed behind her visor. This not-Guardian, at least, did not appear to be terribly familiar with flying—or fighting, for that matter—on a hoverdisc.

*Oh, good.*

In flying, at least, Lilia had the advantage.

*Looks like our rescue mission to Lanx and getting bounced all over the Coalition had an upside after all.*

Fighting on a hoverdisc was another matter entirely.

Lilia saw an opening—and took it. Before the other woman could complete her turn, she surged forward and rammed both of her nanoblades into the woman's side. With that kind of force behind them, her nanoblades pierced the not-Guardian's armor and ran her through as though her insides didn't exist.

The not-Guardian screamed—a horrible, pain-filled keening sound that threatened to turn Lilia's knees to jelly. She set her jaw, remorseless, and withdrew her blades in one fluid motion. She then arced around in time to block a fierce blow from one of the not-Guardian's enraged companions, a tall, lean man.

The woman she'd wounded—probably killed—collapsed to her knees on her hoverdisc, clutching her sides. Her nanoblade clattered to the pearlescent floor below.

Another of the not-Guardians, a man around Erik's build, zoomed over to the dying woman's side and slid one arm around her shoulders and another under her knees. He shot off in the direction Hollowell had disappeared, carrying the woman in his arms with her feet dangling in the air, the hoverdisc still attached.

That brought Lilia's opponents down to two. Smiling grimly behind her facemask, she settled her nanoblades into a defensive position. It was awkward, fighting on a hoverdisc, but it could be done.

The remaining two not-Guardians—the tall man and another woman around Lilia's height—both let loose a stream of profanity in Glo'Stean and zipped forward to batter away at her in turns. Lilia dodged several of their ferocious blows, deflected several more, and shot backward just in time to keep the woman from taking a chunk out of her hoverdisc.

She found herself insanely grateful for all those years she'd practiced fencing with her brothers. They'd taught her how to defend herself against multiple attackers. *I never thought I'd actually have to do it.*

Her opponents closed in on her—and one of the man's blows landed on her arm. Her nano-armor protected her, but stinging pain still shot up her arm. It was bad enough that she almost lost her grip on her nanoblade.

Biting back a cry of pain, Lilia jammed her left booted heel down onto her hoverdisc's rear acceleration panel while simultaneously slamming the booted toes of her right foot onto the forward acceleration panel. She dropped four meters like a rock, temporarily taking herself out of the fight, and then shot backwards and up to soar toward the male not-Guardian at an angle calculated to put force behind the blow to come.

She was counting on him not being able to turn fast enough to avoid her.

He didn't.

Lilia stabbed him through the back, driving her left nanoblade through his heart and out the other side of his armor. He made a terrible gurgling sound. She soared up and backwards again to put space between them, whipping her blade out of his torso as she went.

The man fell to his knees on his hoverdisc, but overbalanced and tipped over. His nanoblade slipped from his suddenly limp fingers as he dangled upside down in midair, his feet still attached to his hoverdisc. He didn't move. Blood began to run down from his upper torso and drip off the top of his helmet.

That left just one of Hollowell's not-Guardians.

The woman snarled at Lilia, fury vibrating from her armor-clad figure like an almost tangible thing, but she approached more cautiously this time. She glided around Lilia in a circle, searching for an opening. Unlike most of her companions, she seemed a little more at home on a hoverdisc. The NCDC insignia above her breast was Glo'Stean blue.

The screams and rush of noise from the crowd of panicked guests had begun to fade. Lilia didn't have time to wonder if it was because they were finally able to escape the Dome, or because Freedom's Children had murdered most of them.

The not-Guardian zoomed toward Lilia head-on as though she was going to attempt to run her through, but feinted at the last second. She attacked from the side instead. Lilia parried with one blade and jabbed at the not-Guardian with the other.

The woman slid to the side and brought an elbow down on Lilia's left forearm, hard enough to make Lilia' cry out and drop the nanoblade she held in that hand. At the same time, the woman slammed her helmeted head into Lilia's.

Her helmet protected her from the brunt of the blow, but Lilia's head still snapped back with the unexpected force. She gritted her teeth and broke away from the woman in a short downward spiral that took her toward her nanoblade. She scooped it up from the floor and arced around to face her opponent again.

She blinked.

The not-Guardian was…fleeing?

The woman had cocked her helmeted head to one side as though listening to something she didn't understand, and then, all at once, she abruptly swung around and shot towards one of the doorways into the hall surrounding the atrium. As she went, the not-Guardian held her nanoblade out to the side like she was preparing to slice through something—and a sudden jolt of understanding struck Lilia like an impactor bolt.

*She's not running away—she's been sent to kill people!*

The Mastermind's—Hollowell's—doing. Lilia had taken out most of his team; he'd decided to change tactics.

Lilia set her jaw in grim lines. *Because he knows I won't let people die if I can help it.* Resolve raced through her veins even as nausea swirled in the pit of her stomach. Sinking into a crouch on her hoverdisc, she jammed her foot down on the forward acceleration panel and surged forward. In a matter of seconds, she had crossed the pearlescent Dome floor in pursuit of the not-Guardian.

She slalomed through the doorway into the hall after the woman, only to find the left side of the hall was empty. Lilia immediately performed a tight somersault-and-twist that brought her up facing the right side of the hall in time to catch a glimpse of the not-Guardian rounding the curved edge of the hall ahead of her. She surged forward again, flying for everything she was worth, her nanoblades tucked against her sides like skis.

Sounds from the tail-end of the frightened, panicked crowd still trying to escape via the accelevator bank and the stairway exit echoed down the hall as the not-Guardian raced toward them. *You won't lay a finger on them,* Lilia promised her silently. *I won't let you.*

Without warning, the not-Guardian suddenly slowed and plunged her nanoblade into the wall, using it to help swing herself around at a ninety-degree angle through a doorway back into the Dome. The nanoblade sliced through the wall in the process, but it served its purpose.

Lilia was so startled she almost didn't slow down in time. *What is she doing? Where is she going?* She performed the same maneuver, though her attempt was a little wobbly, and streaked back into the Dome after the woman.

The not-Guardian flew straight up to the center of the atrium's curved, latticed ceiling, thrust her nanoblade into it, and carved out a giant circle. She promptly zipped sideways to avoid the entire chunk of plastiglass and latticework as it fell free to crash on the atrium floor far below. She then shot a look over her shoulder at Lilia that radiated smugness, even through her facemask and visor, and shot up to vanish through the hole she'd just made.

Baffled, Lilia streaked after her. She didn't hear someone shouting her name from one of the walkway openings, didn't see her brother Derek leaning over the railing and waving his arms at her. Her attention was solely focused on the not-Guardian. She soared up to the hole.

# CHAPTER 101

IT didn't take Kevin long to cut holes through three of the Pearl's floors. Not with the adrenaline humming through his veins, fueling him with purpose—a purpose that required most of his concentration and didn't leave time for wondering things like how the rest of his family was faring.

Or how all the other guests still trapped in the Dome above them were faring.

Every rustle of fabric, every footstep, every thud and thunk of sections of cut flooring and ceiling seemed magnified and made his heart pound faster. Sweat beaded on his forehead, trickled down his skin. They would be in deep trouble if they ran into more than two of Freedom's Children's not-Guardians.

Two, he could probably handle, but not more than that.

He didn't want to die here any more than Chesnee, his wife, or their security detail.

Kevin had left Chesnee's jacket crammed into a desk drawer in an interior office two floors below the kitchen. He figured they could always send somebody back for it later.

The Admiral hadn't seemed to mind. He was more fascinated by their escape method.

When Kevin cut through to the fourth floor, they found themselves in another interior office. Kevin had no idea who it belonged to, though several holos of a smiling older couple with dark hair and golden skin hovered above the golden wood desk.

Large and spacious, the office made up for its lack of windows by having a holoscreen that covered the entire length of one wall. It was currently set to display the sun setting over the ocean. Two of the other walls were taupe, and the third wall, which faced the holoscreen, had been painted in dark gold.

Shelves of knickknacks from around Glo'Stea—pieces of driftwood, ethereal pieces of glasswork, shells, and the occasional interesting rock—were zigzagged on the walls. A pale blue couch stood beneath one of these sets of zigzagged shelves. Admiral Chesnee helped his wife over to this couch. The smell of fear and Mrs. Chesnee's perfume mixed with the scent of exotic flowers and a hint of sea breeze that pervaded the Pearl—a decidedly odd combination.

Kevin glanced at the couple as he crossed plush taupe carpet to the office door. All things considered, Sylvia Chesnee was handling their current situation fairly well. Her beautiful golden-brown face was pale and bloodless, and she had a death grip on her husband's arm, but she hadn't lost her head and gone into hysterics.

Kevin had to give her credit for that.

Chesnee, his wife, and their security detail all tensed as Kevin palmed the door release. The door slide aside almost soundlessly, and Kevin carefully checked the hall beyond. Yet again, he wished fervently that his nanites weren't frozen and that he had access to his ISF. His scanner would have come in exceedingly handy right about now.

Thankfully, the hall was empty. Just like the last three floors.

Touching the door panel again, Kevin turned back to the others. "Looks clear. The stairs should be close."

Laying Erudita's nanoblade on the desk, he extracted his comlink from his pocket and pulled up the Pearl's schematics again. Diaz and Taft both crowded around him. The other four men split to guard both the office door and the entry hole Kevin had created in the ceiling.

Out of the corner of his eye, Kevin saw Chesnee make a slight motion, as though the Admiral intended to rise and join them, but he glanced at his wife and seemed to think the better of it. Kevin turned his attention back to the blue lines of the schematics hovering in the air above his comlink.

"We're here." He pointed to a spot. "The stairs are here." He moved his fingers a few centimeters to the left. "Southwest side of the building."

"Not far," Taft said thoughtfully. He jabbed a finger at the schematics. "They won't be expecting anyone to be down here."

"Maybe not," Diaz interjected, "but what's to stop them from watching the stairs like they are all of the accelevator banks?" He didn't fold his arms across his chest, but he might as well have. His expression was tight, his dark eyes grim and mistrustful. "We'd be just as trapped."

Kevin started to respond, but Taft beat him to it. "The stairs have too many access points." The older man shook his head. "There's no way these terrorist have the manpower for something like that." He looked from Kevin to Diaz to Chesnee and back. "The stairs will work."

"Plus, we don't have to go all the way to the lobby." Kevin wanted to be sure to point that out. "Time is on our side, not theirs. The police and probably the entire Glo'Stean Resistance are converging on the Pearl right now."

He met Mrs. Chesnee's eyes, making sure to sound confident as he added, "All we have to do is hold out a little while longer, and we can do that barricaded in an office five or six floors down from here."

"You're also assuming they haven't rigged explosions at all the stair entrances," Diaz said mulishly.

Taft shook his head a second time. "Too much manpower, not enough time. Even for an attack as well planned as this one, that's too much."

Diaz held up his hands in surrender. "I hope you're right." His voice was desert-dry. "For all our sakes."

Chesnee chose that moment to speak. "Captain Diaz, while I appreciate your concern on our behalf, I agree with Taft and Captain Strong. We have escaped this massacre—"

*For now*, Kevin thought. A glance at Diaz told him the Tarynian soldier was thinking the same thing.

"—and the prudent thing to do is to sit tight and wait for backup." The Admiral paused, a wry smile curving his lips. "Even though I confess part of me would rather just storm the lobby and get everyone out of here."

This drew answering smiles and a few grim snorts from the rest of his security detail. Beside him, Mrs. Chesnee even mustered a weak smile.

Once again, Kevin's fingers itched to reach into his ISF. He pushed the feeling aside—wallowing in frustration wouldn't help anyone—and picked up Erudita's nanoblade again. He looked around the office. "Everyone ready?"

Receiving confirming nods from the Chesnees and all six members of their security detail, Kevin squared his shoulders and swept a hand toward the office door. "Onward."

As he led the way out of the office and down the hall toward the stairs, Kevin gripped the hilt of Erudita's nanoblade a little tighter. *This will work*, he told himself. *Taft is right—Freedom's Children doesn't have the manpower to keep an eye on all the stairs.*

An ugly thought crossed his mind. *What if they've taken over the main security control center?* He had to take a deep breath to quell the sudden churning in his stomach.

*Doesn't change anything.* Even if Freedom's Children had access to all the cams throughout the Pearl and they'd already figured out what Kevin was doing, they still had to send not-Guardians after them. That would take time.

*Time they don't have.* Kevin forced himself to go cold and calm. *All we have to do is hold out a little while longer.*

# CHAPTER 102

IN the split-second between when he and Renner plunged into the portal carrying Kedis's unconscious form between them and when they emerged, Lon experienced a burst of panic. *Please, God, don't let this be one of the portals that opens two meters off the floor.*

It wasn't.

Lon felt like he was falling for a mere two heartbeats before his foot hit solid ground. He took another step backward, tightening his grip on Kedis, and watched Renner emerge from the portal. He then kept going. *Have to get out of the way.*

He'd gone through the portal, trusting Lilia to get them as close to help as she possibly could, and at first glance he thought she'd transported them to a church. A large stained glass window rose behind the rippling portal, with a small altar in front of it that held an arrangement of flowers and a few candles. Behind them, rows of maple wood pews with green velvet cushions stretched to the back of the room.

Lon blinked, his eyes adjusting to the dimmer light, and realized they were actually in a chapel. A *hospital* chapel, judging from the small, sparse look of things. "Oh, praise Jesus," he breathed.

Before he could do more than look around for the exit, Michael and their grandfather stumbled out of the portal sphere, awkwardly carrying Wright between them. The lieutenant was unconscious, his skin deathly pale.

An unpleasant chill jolted Lon straight to his bones. *He won't last much longer.*

"Good girl," Michael said grimly, as he took in their surroundings. He looked at their grandfather. "We're in Atalia, at the hospital you were in after the Gala bombing."

Lon thought he would have preferred to be off Glo'Stea entirely, but at least they were out of Jamal. Catching Renner's eye, he nodded to the door. "Come on."

Together, they carted Kedis across the chapel and Lon bumped the door release with his shoulder. It had barely slid aside when they staggered through it and out into a wide hall with beige walls and doors set into it at regular intervals.

"Help!" Lon shouted. "We need medical attention! Help!"

The startled faces of two doctors and a couple of nurses who had been passing turned toward them, as well as the expressionless silver countenance of a multi-armed med 'bot. As soon as they registered Kedis's mangled, unconscious form, they converged on the three of them, deluging Lon and Renner with rapid-fire questions.

The noise grew even louder when Michael and Aiden appeared with Wright's limp body.

In the midst of the chaos, Lon looked over his shoulder at the chapel entrance. He fully expected to see his sister come hurtling through at any second in search of Wright, but she didn't appear. A terrible sinking feeling filled his stomach.

Heedless of the chatter of the doctors and nurses around him, Lon climbed to his feet and rushed back into the chapel. The portal had disappeared—

—and Lilia was nowhere in sight.

Stark horror flooded Lon. He tried to swallow, but his mouth had gone bone dry. *She's still at the Pearl.*

Facing Hollowell—who had apparently lost his *mind*—alone.


Though the doctors recognized Michael as a Guardian, the fact that his identcard was trapped in his frozen ISF was a problem. Aiden swiftly took control of the situation with the consummate skill that came from long years of dealing with squabbling politicians and clamoring media crews, though something deep inside him was screaming in pain. He showed his identcard and calmly identified himself before succinctly laying out what had happened. He then strongly suggested the hospital send security up to keep an eye on Kedis and Wright.

It was only as he watched the doctors rush the two wounded Tarynians away on floating stretchers, both of them trailed by Lon and Renner, that Aiden allowed the past few minutes to begin to sink in. The wordless screaming inside his head continued. Martin Hollowell—a man he had called his best friend for more than three decades—was the head of Freedom's Children.

His best friend had threatened his grandchildren.

His best friend had attempted to have him killed.

His best friend was taking on the G.U. and the entire Coalition in a cold, calculated bid for revenge.

Aiden struggled to breathe; it felt like a steel band was squeezing his chest. Black spots danced before his eyes. The world began to fade.

Dimly, he heard Michael's voice. "Grandfather, I think you'd better sit down."

Someone asked a question in Glo'Stean and Michael answered, but Aiden registered none of it. His gaze had turned inward, his mind replaying every conversation he and Hollowell had shared over the past few months. Cast in the light of this new revelation, some of his friend's words—and actions—took on an entirely new meaning.

"Oh, Martin," he murmured as Michael led him to the surgery waiting room and pressed him into a chair. "What have you done?"

One thought finally penetrated his shocked haze. Blinking as he returned to himself, Aiden twisted in his seat to seize Michael's armored forearm. "Lilia. Where is she?"

He could not see Michael's expression through his smooth gray facemask, but he heard the wince in his grandson's voice as he answered, "She didn't make it through the portal before it closed."

Aiden felt cold. "She is trapped with Martin."

"I wouldn't say 'trapped', exactly." Michael shook his helmeted head. "The Dome is big enough that she should be able to escape him. And don't forget—Derek and Kevin are still there too."

"But their nanites are frozen, are they not? She cannot contact either of them?"

Michael sucked in a deep breath and let it out all at once, his broad, gray-armored shoulders slumping. "No."

Aiden clenched his fists in frustration, then slowly unclenched them and looked down at his hands. His skin had that old, papery look that reminded him of his own grandparents, dotted with the occasional liver spot. *How did I ever get so old?*

Old…and useless.

He tipped his head back to stare up at the white ceiling without really seeing it. Words and motives were his arena, his area of expertise, and yet he had just found himself completely blindsided. "'I broke bread with that man for thirty years and never saw this coming," he said softly.

Michael placed a gloved hand on his shoulder. "None of us did."

Aiden suddenly chuckled—a harsh, mirthless sound. "I can see the look on Dion Pamos's face now. He is in for a shock."

The entire Triumvirate was in for a shock. Aiden pressed a shaking hand over his eyes, still chuckling mirthlessly. After a moment, he sobered. "Pray Kedis lives. I do not know what the Coalition's future will hold if he dies."

# Chapter 103

LILIA popped up through the hole in the top of the Dome and hovered there for a second, suspended in midair. She and Jasper had looked at Jamal's cityscape from the observation walkway; now she was part of it. A few stars twinkled in the dark sky above, visible even though the city's bright glow made it difficult to see the rest. Below, Jamal stretched out around the Pearl, a latticework of glowing different-colored lights with streets and roads running through it like orderly veins and arteries.

A handful of silver-pale police craft had converged on the Pearl, blue and red lights flashing wildly. They hovered around the top of the capitol building, spotlights blazing, obviously intending to keep any other craft from attacking.

*They have no idea what they're up against,* Lilia thought grimly. The Mastermind—Hollowell—had planned this too well. Those men and women wouldn't do a bit of good. *Except maybe to help get the wounded to a hospital.*

Hospital. *Jasper.* Her heart ached again; she ruthlessly tamped it down. No time for sentiment now.

The top of the Pearl itself glowed with a faint pink-gold light from within, making it easy for Lilia to spot her quarry. The not-Guardian was gliding along the curved side of the Pearl like a dark bead of water, headed down. Unfortunately, this also made Lilia visible as well.

*Why is* she *still visible?* A sudden wave of unease washed over Lilia *If she's got armor, surely she's got stealth-mode. Why isn't she using it?*

Did the not-Guardian *want* her to follow? Was this some kind of a trap?

Lilia bit her lip. Probably, but what could she do except follow? She couldn't just let the other woman escape—if that was even what she was doing.

Amplified voices shouted at the pair of them from the nearest police hovercraft as the police registered they were there. Lilia ignored them, jamming her booted foot down on her forward accelevator panel again. The shouted warnings faded into the distance, lost in the rush of wind as she shot down after the not-Guardian. *Where is she going?*

Dropping into a crouch to minimize her profile, Lilia pushed herself harder and faster, skimming along the Pearl's rounded surface at an angle calculated to shorten the distance between herself and the not-Guardian. The other woman might have had a head start, but Lilia intended to catch up.

She was less than five meters from the not-Guardian when the other woman unexpectedly twisted around on her hoverdisc and fired an impactor bolt at her.

Lilia broke right, but she wasn't quite fast enough. The crackling glob of energy grazed the top of her left shoulder. Pain radiated from the spot; she ground her teeth together in frustration. *So much for making it out of here with functioning nano-armor.*

Not to mention she was now glued to her hoverdisc for the next six hours.

*At least you* have *nano-armor*, she reminded herself. It could be worse.

Her target let out a wild laugh and shifted to face front again.

Narrowing her eyes in concentration, Lilia put on a burst of speed. They were three-quarters of the way down the Pearl's curved side now, rapidly approaching the manicured grounds that surrounded the capitol building. The not-Guardian's flight leveled out for a stretch, before she abruptly dropped into a steep glide.

With a shock that made the hairs on her arms stand up beneath her armor, Lilia realized where the not-Guardian was headed—straight for the Pearl's main entrance. The massive double doors beneath the portico roof, with their gorgeous lacy network of gold and plastiglass, were still open

Behind her visor, Lilia's violet eyes widened for a second before narrowing suspiciously. *What is she planning on doing? Kill anybody who makes it outside the lobby?*

It was the logical conclusion, but…Lilia had already been wrong once about the not-Guardian's motives. *Why would they kill everyone now when they could have taken them all out in the Dome?*

Hollowell *could* have killed them all—she knew that full well. That he hadn't meant he only wanted specific targets dead. At least one of those was Ambassador Kedis; she hadn't been able to identify any other bodies.

Her feeling of unease increased, but she couldn't stop now.

They were still high enough that Lilia could see the beautiful garden that lay before the white-columned portico, its roof upswept at each end like graceful wings, that formed the Pearl's elaborate main entrance. Warm golden light from the decorative glowposts spilled across the garden's paths, flower beds, bushes, and trees, and reflected off the water canals lining the paths. It illuminated the giant fountain, turning the water spraying from the trio of laughing dolphins' mouths into showers of gold.

The atmosphere would have been perfect for a quiet, romantic walk—except for the angry shouts echoing across the distance from the protesters lined up along the gleaming white fence encircling the Pearl's grounds. The Glo'Stean Resistance fighters in sea-blue lined up on the other side of the fence offered answering shouts.

Media crews lingered around the garden's edge, waiting to cover the end of the evening. The honor guard of Resistance fighters maintained their positions lining the pristine white stone walkway from the Pearl's main entrance to the curb, stoic despite the muggy evening air.

Without warning, a portal opened above the garden. It swelled to a massive size in a matter of seconds and disgorged a sleek, predatory armored skimmer with a camouflage blend exterior finish that allowed it to fade into its surroundings.

The not-Guardian did not change her flight path, but pumped a victorious fist in the air.

Behind her facemask, Lilia's mouth dropped open. Not only was that the biggest portal she'd ever seen, but…*That's a Hawk!*

Hawks were all-terrain, armed, and armored skimmers used by the G.U. across Glo'Stea and also in the occupied portion of Lanx.

They were fast, highly maneuverable, and deadly. Somehow, Freedom's Children had gotten their hands on one.

Frightened cries mixed with the shouting and chanting from the protestors. The Resistance fighters guarding the fence, the media crews, and the honor guard exclaimed loudly and pointed.

As everyone in the vicinity watched, the portal collapsed in on itself. The Hawk immediately swiveled around to face the main gate…and fired a torpedo. The gate and security checkpoint—along with the Pearl Security personnel who had been inside—vanished in a massive explosion. Gouts of fire lit the night air.

"No!" Horror flooded Lilia; she unconsciously slowed a fraction.

The Hawk swiveled back around to face the Pearl, debris still falling from the sky. The media crews had scattered; some of them flattened themselves on the stone walkway and covered their heads, while others took refuge inside the garden, as though the bushes and decorative trees would somehow protect them. A handful of the more intrepid reporters among them immediately began broadcasting live.

The Resistance fighters guarding the Pearl's main entrance recovered quickly. Most of them retreated toward the white-columned portico, while the rest drew pistols and covered their comrades, opening fire on the Hawk. Their laserfire only splashed harmlessly against its shields.

Lilia realized what would happen next a split-second before it actually did. A scream rose in her throat as the Hawk's gunner sprayed the Resistance fighters on the stone walkway with a deadly barrage of golden laser bolts. A number of the men and women in sea-blue uniforms fell, never to rise again.

The not-Guardian Lilia was chasing whooped loudly and dove toward the remaining Resistance fighters, her nanoblade at the ready.

Beyond the white fence and smoking remains of the main gate, a fierce, bloodthirsty cheer rose from the crowd. They surged forward, overwhelming the Resistance fighters lining the fence, and streamed across the Pearl's grounds like a dark, destructive mass.

Cold chills rolled down Lilia's spine as she realized the not-Guardian's plan. She didn't intend to cut down guests *escaping* from the Pearl—she intended to make sure the crowd of angry protestors got *in*.

The crowd of angry protestors that had just morphed into an angry mob—a crazed, mindless, conscienceless mass with hundreds of arms and legs, bent on harming everyone in its path and destroying everything in its wake.

Lilia had faced both Hawks and Tarynian soldiers in the past several years, but at this moment, she thought this was the scariest thing she had ever encountered. People engulfed in mob mentality did things they would never ever have done if they were alone.

*Oh, God, help us,* she thought as she dove after the not-Guardian again.

She hadn't flown more than a couple of meters when she caught a flash of movement out of her peripheral vision to her right. She reacted instinctively, whipping her nanoblades around to defend herself against an oncoming attack.

It never came. Instead, a familiar voice shouted, "Whoa, whoa, whoa! It's me!"

It took a second for her brain to register who was flying beside her. "Erik!?"

Her fellow Guardian crouched on his hoverdisc, still clad in his tuxedo. He held his nanoblade in one hand, and wore his laser carbine in its sling. His blond head was bare; drying blood smudged on one cheek. He gave her a feral smile. "Was startin' to wonder if I'd catch up to ya."

Lilia wanted to ask how he'd even know she was out here, but they didn't have time—or Nancom. She pointed to the not-Guardian and the remaining Resistance fighters. "She's going to kill them so the mob can get in!"

Erik comprehended the entire situation in an instant—and made his choice with the swift precision he had honed from years of serving in the Sonela police force's bomb division. He pointed his nanoblade toward the not-Guardian. "You take her out an' I'll—" he swung his nanoblade around to point at the Hawk, "—take care of that."

"What?" Lilia gaped at him behind her visor. "Erik—that thing has armor *and* shields!"

"I know." That feral smile appeared on Erik's face again. "Watch me. Actually," he added hastily before Lilia could say anything else, "don't watch me. Help *them.*" He pointed down at the beleaguered Resistance honor guard.

Erik then peeled away from Lilia and streaked toward the Hawk, shouting a battle cry that echoed in his wake.

Lilia watched him go for only a second before she snapped back to reality and resumed her chase. She frantically flew after the not-

Guardian, who had almost reached the portico. "Don't. You. Dare!" she shouted at the woman's armor-clad back.

The Resistance honor guard clustered under the portico's up-swept roof saw the not-Guardian coming for them and tried to fling themselves out of her flight path. Most of them made it; one man did not. The not-Guardian cleaved him in two like she was slicing butter with a hot knife and kept going. Spurting blood from severed arteries, the upper and lower halves of the dead man collapsed to the white stone walkway. A red stain rapidly spread beneath him.

A cry of rage ripped from Lilia's throat. "NO!"

She barreled after the not-Guardian, who climbed into the air at a sharp angle that took her closer to the Pearl's globe-like surface. At the last second, the woman decided she would drop back down to make another pass at the honor guard. Her flight path peaked at the top of a high arc and then she swung back down toward the Pearl's main entrance like a pendulum. Her deadly nanoblade glinted in the lights from the beautiful garden below.

That proved to be a mistake.

*You should have run, lady.* Setting her jaw, Lilia braced herself as she turned herself into a human battering ram and shot straight toward the other woman, one nanoblade extended.

The not-Guardian tried to dodge, apparently under the impression she could outmaneuver Lilia…but she hadn't taken Lilia's speed into account. She couldn't get out of the way in time.

Lilia slammed into the not-Guardian six meters above the walkway in front of the portico and knocked her backwards, away from the Resistance fighters below. The collision rattled both their teeth and drove all the air out of their chests. Lilia had intended to impale the other woman on her nanoblade, but the not-Guardian managed to twist slightly to one side at the last second and avoided the blade.

The tip of her nanoblade scored a deep gash in the armor shielding Lilia's ribcage, but Lilia didn't even register it. She had a half-second to realize her plan had backfired before the other woman rallied.

Regaining control of her hoverdisc, the not-Guardian jammed her heels down on her rear acceleration panels to stop Lilia from pushing her backwards any longer. Their flight slowed and ground to a halt as the two women grappled in mid-air.

If Lilia had thought dueling on a hoverdisc was tricky, hand-to-hand combat was even worse. Particularly since she was still trying to hang on to both of her nanoblades. The fact that she was glued to her hoverdisc meant the not-Guardian couldn't knock her off, but it also meant kneeing her opponent in the stomach was out of the question.

The not-Guardian didn't have this issue.

Demagnetizing one of her boots, she brought that knee up into Lilia's stomach. At the same time, she shoved Lilia away with her free hand—hard.

Lilia doubled over, gasping, still clutching her nanoblades, and slowed. The woman seized her opportunity to escape. She shot around Lilia and streaked down, back on target to eliminate more Resistance fighters and clear the way for the approaching mob.

"No!" Lilia arced around, still breathless and doubled over. She straightened, forcing herself to breathe, and shot after the not-Guardian again. *I can't let her kill them!*

Stark reality slapped her in the face—this time, she was too far behind to catch up.

# Chapter 104

LILIA clamped her jaw shut in helpless fury as she watched the other armor-clad woman swoop down toward the Pearl's main entrance, nanoblade held to the side, ready to cut down more Resistance fighters.

Without warning, Erik slammed into the not-Guardian from the side. The force of his impact drove them both into one of the white marble columns holding up the portico's upswept roof. When Erik pulled back, a nanoblade protruded from the woman's armored chest.

Lilia sucked in an astonished breath. *He did it.*

He'd succeeded in stopping her before she killed anybody else.

Erik withdrew his nanoblade in one swift motion and the not-Guardian's limp body slid down the marble column, leaving a crimson streak. She tipped sideways to hang upside down from her motionless hoverdisc. Her helmet banged against the column and then she was still, a gray shadow against the white marble.

It was only then that Lilia remembered the Hawk. Jolting, she looked wildly around—

—just as the Hawk's pilot fired at Erik. He barely managed to zip out of the way; the globs of golden energy struck the motionless not-Guardian instead. Smoke rose from her armor and the marble column behind her.

If Erik hadn't killed her, she was dead now.

"Get out of the way!" Erik flapped his free hand at Lilia. "I think I ticked him off!" He shot into the air and broke right.

*No kidding,* Lilia wanted to shout back, but there wasn't time.

She dropped three meters with stomach-losing speed and broke left as the Hawk, its pilot apparently enraged by the death of the not-Guardian, fired burst after burst of golden laser bolts toward the spot they had just occupied. Each shot missed its target; they pounded the portico's columns instead, leaving smoking, charred black holes in the white marble.

*We've got to keep him from targeting those guards!* Lilia thought frantically, crouching on her hoverdisc again as she soared up and away from the Pearl's entrance. She had never missed Nancom more than in this moment. *Somehow, we have to distract him long enough to—*

The Hawk stopped shooting.

The sudden absence of laser bolts spitting in their direction raised the hairs on the back of Lilia's neck beneath her armor. *Why did he stop?*

It could only mean something bad.

She arced back around to see what was happening—and finally registered the rushing, roaring sound flooding her ears. Though filtered by her helmet's auditory modulator, it was still loud and frightening. Out of the corner of her eye, she spotted Erik floating fifteen meters above the ground on the other side of the portico, but her eyes had more pressing things to take in.

Her blood ran cold. The mob was nearly upon them.

In a minute, at most a minute and a half, the first wave of angry protestors would reach the Pearl's main entrance.

Lilia sucked in a sharp breath. *This is not good.*

A quick glance down toward the Pearl's main entrance told her that doors were still open. The surviving Resistance fighters were retreating back toward the portico, obviously intending to take up position at the security checkpoint just inside the lobby and prevent the mob from getting in.

As she watched, four members of one of the media crews broke from where they had been crouched in the garden beside the dolphin fountain and raced toward the Pearl's main entrance. All four of them abruptly skidded to a halt at the edge of the portico, looking horrified. They immediately backed away and fled, apparently deciding they were better off taking their chances in the garden. One man tripped over his shoes and fell to the pavement, but he scrambled gracelessly to his feet and kept running.

An instant later, Lilia saw why.

So did Erik.

A broad-shouldered figure clad in dark gray nano-armor emerged at a dead run from the Pearl's massive double doors and immediately began laying about with a nanoblade. The surviving Resistance honor guards fell, one after another, with each broad sweep of his blade.

"NO!" Erik bellowed.

He and Lilia both converged on the portico, but the last of the surviving Resistance fighters were dead before they had flown more than a handful of meters.

Lilia screamed wordlessly at the murderer in nano-armor, a potent mix of grief, rage, and frustration welling up inside her. She and Erik had saved those men and women from one not-Guardian… only to watch them die at the hands of another.

Their deaths affected Erik the same way. Ignoring the Hawk, ignoring the mob that was nearly upon them, he raised his own nanoblade and shot toward the not-Guardian like a laser bolt. Every line and muscle in his body radiated grim fury.

Intent on slaying the honor guard, the not-Guardian didn't see him coming in time. He had barely turned, gleaming blade in hand, when Erik plowed into him. The two men tumbled through the open double doors into the security checkpoint in a tangle of arms, legs, nanoblades, and a hoverdisc.

That rushing, roaring sound grew louder. A handful of voices rose above the others. Instigators, perhaps.

Lilia risked a glance over her shoulder at the Hawk, but its guns remained silent. Unease prickled across her skin, but it was swallowed up by a larger, much more pressing concern.

The oncoming mob.

Quelling the panic threatening to choke her in the face of such overwhelming odds, Lilia bit down hard on her lower lip and tried to think.

What could they do? What could *she* do? Sure, she was a Guardian, but a Guardian whose armor, ISF, and Nancom were all inoperable for the next few hours.

*I can't fight them off all by myself.*

Even if she could, the merest *thought* of the kind of body count that would leave behind sent her mind instinctively skittering away to protect itself.

Then, like a lightning bolt from above beamed directly into her brain, Lilia remembered something. *The security doors.* Michael had gone over the Pearl's main security measures with them that afternoon before they departed the hotel. It seemed a lifetime ago.

She could have slapped herself for not remembering sooner.

*That* was why the Hawk had stopped shooting at them. The pilot didn't want to risk triggering those doors.

Those highly-reinforced secondary security doors, perfect for keeping out an angry mob.

Lilia didn't hesitate. She dropped into a steep glide, tightening her grip on her nanoblades again.

Below and behind her, part of the mob was still clashing with the surviving remnants of the Resistance fighters who had been lining the fence encircling the Pearl. It was only a matter of time before those remaining fighters were completely overwhelmed. Their line was broken and they were vastly outnumbered.

It was too late for them, but it wasn't too late to save the Pearl from being overrun. Not yet.

Lilia zoomed through the Pearl's main entrance, passing from hazy evening darkness to the golden solar-powered brightness of the lobby inside. Sharply cutting left to avoid passing through the security matrix, she flew up and over the metal-and-plastiglass railing ringing the security checkpoint and skidded to a short, violent halt in front of the security control center.

She'd barely stopped moving before she located the door panel for the main entrance and slapped it.

Nothing happened.

Lilia hit it again.

Still, nothing.

Across the massive lobby, with its sea blue walls and aquamarine floor, Erik and his opponent were still brawling. Lilia couldn't tell who was winning…and she didn't have time to find out.

Erik had spotted her, however, and it didn't take a genius to figure out what she was trying to do. "What are you waitin' for?" he shouted, ducking a wild blow from the male not-Guardian that nearly lopped off his head. "Shut the doors already!"

Lilia tried the door panel a third time, out of desperation, but she already knew it wouldn't work.

The Mastermind—Hollowell—had planned for this too. Somehow, one of his sleeper minions had disabled the door locks.

Gloved fingers skimming over the control panel, Lilia searched for the override panic button for the security doors. Her heartbeat quickened as she slapped it. A dialogue box popped up, informing her that a login code was required before she could continue, and her stomach sank all the way to her toes.

"Lilia!"

"It won't work!" she shouted back, frantically searching the control panel for something—anything—else. "They've disabled it!"

"Have to—" Erik blocked a knee his opponent attempted to thrust into his gut, "—trigger it—" he rammed an elbow into the not-Guardian's armored throat, "—manually!"

*Manually?* Dismay mixed with horror washed over Lilia. How in the galaxy was she supposed to do that?

Abandoning the useless security control desk, she flew back toward the still-open doors. Her hoverdisc skimmed along a few centimeters above the floor's aquamarine surface. That rushing, roaring sound flooded through the doors—the sound of a giant, crazed monster descending on Glo'Stea's capitol building.

A handful of red laser bolts shot toward her as she settled into a defensive stance in the middle of the doorway. It was difficult, given that her boots were still glued to her hoverdisc. Most of laser bolts missed, but several of them splashed against her nano-armor.

Lilia ignored them. Her heart thudded in her chest; her mouth felt as dry as the sand on Kyman's windless beach. She was completely exposed, backlit spectacularly by the light from the crystal chandelier hanging in the lobby. Light glinted off her twin nanoblades.

*Oh, God, help us. Please. I don't want to do this.*

The dead bodies of the Resistance honor guard lay where they had fallen beneath the portico roof. The once-pristine white walkway now ran red with their blood.

The last thing Lilia wanted to do was add to it.

She raised one nanoblade a little higher, tried to swallow.

Footsteps thudded against the walkway; shouts and angry cries swelled to a frenzied crescendo. She could *see* the seething mass of humanity outside now, crowding toward the Pearl's main entrance.

Inside her armor, sweat trickled down from her armpits. With her nanites frozen, her armor couldn't compensate for her body heat. How long could she hold the mob off before either backup arrived or they completely overwhelmed her too?

"Lilia!"

Focused as she was on her upcoming melee, Lilia almost didn't register Erik's shout. He had escaped his opponent long enough to fly closer to the main entrance.

"Get out of the way!" he hollered, waving a frantic hand toward her before pulling something out of his tuxedo jacket pocket with his other hand. He chucked it toward the door.

It only took Lilia a split-second to realize what he'd thrown.

A grenade.

Her violet eyes widened in shock, but she didn't waste time trying to turn around. Stomping both heels down on her hoverdisc's rear acceleration panels, she shot backwards just as the grenade hit the floor in front of the double doors and exploded.

The force of the explosion pushed her backwards, a few fragments of shrapnel hammering against the front of her armor.

Chunks of aquamarine flooring rained down on the lobby, mixed with bits of shrapnel. Sensing smoke and fire, the lobby's sprinkler system turned itself on, spraying a fine anti-inflammatory mist down over everything.

Lilia had instinctively raised an arm to shield her face, still clutching her nanoblades, She now lowered her arm to see the gleaming surface of the reinforced security doors forming an impenetrable barrier between the lobby and the mob at the main entrance.

Clearly, the security doors hadn't liked Erik's grenade.

She glanced toward the nearest one-way window in the curved lobby wall, but of course it was too dark to see anything beyond it. She looked back at Erik, who was still kneeling on the floor. His blood-streaked face was split in a wide grin. "You just happened to have a grenade in your pocket?"

"Hey." He shrugged, still grinning. "Figured I'd better be ready for anythin'. At least now we don't have to worry about bein' overrun."

The knot of tension in Lilia's stomach started to ease, but before she could do more than exhale in relief, a cold, furious voice rang across the lobby's aquamarine floor.

"You think you've won?"

She and Erik both spun to face the not-Guardian, who was picking himself up off the floor. He'd been close enough to be caught in the blast radius as well.

"You haven't won," the man continued in Glo'Stean, raising his blade. "Not even close. You think those—" he nodded to the security doors, "—will stop us? We've got a Hawk out there."

Erik made a show of looking over his shoulder. "Yeah, I think they'll stop you."

"This is the Pearl." Lilia took up a defensive stance, both nano-blades at the ready. "The police are already here. It's only a matter of time before—"

"Before what?" the not-Guardian interrupted rudely. "Before they drive the Hawk off?" He snorted loudly. "I'd like to see them try. After all these years the Tarynians have used them to oppress us, it's time they were on the receiving end."

"Hey." Erik took a step forward, whirling his nanoblade through the air. "It's not just Tarynians you've hurt today. Look around—you and your Mastermind are hurtin' your own people."

The not-Guardian shrugged gray-armored shoulders, stepping to one side to keep Erik in full view. "Collateral damage is to be expected. And, really, should we mourn the loss of those who have collaborated with the enemy?"

"You've crossed the line into fanaticism," Lilia said sharply. She shook her helmeted head. "All of you have."

"True freedom comes with a price." The man shrugged again. "Unfortunately that price is usually blood."

"Lay down your nanoblades an' surrender," Erik commanded.

"You don't have anywhere to go," Lilia added.

The not-Guardian tilted his helmeted head to one side. "Actually…I do."

*What?* Lilia and Erik darted confused glances at each other, but before either of them could speak, a portal sphere swirled into existence on the other side of the lobby. It expanded in size and just hung there beside the sea-blue wall, about twenty meters from the not-Guardian.

At the sight of it, a rush of pure fury coursed through Lilia. "Oh, so now you're just going to leave?" She waved one of her nanoblades toward the reinforced security doors. "What about your friends out there?"

The not-Guardian didn't even bother following her gesture. Behind his visor, his eyes were glued to the portal. "They'll manage." He took off across the aquamarine floor at a dead run.

*Oh, no, you don't.* Lilia was flying after him before he'd taken more than two steps. Her eyes narrowed in concentration. He was *not* going to murder all of those people and then disappear through a portal.

Not if she could help it.

Erik shot after her, and together they closed in on the not-Guardian.

Lilia stretched out a nanoblade toward the not-Guardian, but he suddenly danced sideways. At the same second, Lilia registered something small and dark flying out of the portal toward them. Her subconscious recognized it as a threat before her conscious mind realized what was happening.

A grenade.

And Erik didn't have a helmet.

Lilia didn't hesitate. She threw herself sideways into Erik, wrapping herself around him and shielding his head as they tumbled to the floor. He grunted in surprise, but there wasn't time for him to do anything else.

The not-Guardian dived into the portal just as the grenade bounced once on the floor, rolled over to the wall, and exploded.

Lilia had a second to realize that had definitely been more powerful than your average grenade before several heavy chunks of wall slammed down onto her and Erik.

The world went black.

# CHAPTER 105

EVEN before someone canceled the comm jamming and restored communication throughout the Pearl, Kevin knew something else had gone terribly wrong. The longer he and the Chesnees and their security detail stayed holed up in the office he had chosen, the stronger that feeling of dread grew. He couldn't shake it; it became a monster gnawing away at the pit of his stomach.

The interior office he had selected for their temporary hideout belonged to a lower-level member of the Pearl's staff. It was smaller, with cream walls and a sea-blue carpet, and the holoscreen on the wall opposite the desk was only a meter square. It, too, depicted a beach at sunset.

Kevin wasn't sure if that was because everybody around here loved ocean sunsets, or because the Pearl had some sort of building-wide default setting for holoscreens in interior offices.

The office did boast a small brown settee that matched the wide desk; Admiral Chesnee had ensconced his wife on it. Mrs. Chesnee sat very still the entire time they were waiting; the only movement her fingers as she twisted her hands together in her lap. Chesnee, too, said very little, and his security detail followed his lead.

Kevin found it a relief not to be forced to make small talk—particularly as the minutes wore on and his sense of disaster grew stronger. Erudita's nanoblade in one hand and his comlink in the other, he leaned a shoulder up against the office door, all of his physical senses attuned to the world beyond their small refuge. Without his scanner, they were blind to any impending attacks until they actually happened.

Taft, Diaz, and the other four men took up positions around the room, ready for a possible attack from any direction. Kevin suspected that up until recently, an attack through a ceiling or floor probably hadn't been as high on their radar screen.

The sound of his comlink chiming startled all of them.

Heart lodging in his throat, Kevin looked down at the display. It was Derek. He didn't dare let himself relax. "Yes?"

"Are you all right? Where are you?"

The instant he heard his brother's voice, Kevin knew his fears were justified. Something was terribly wrong. Derek's usually pleasant, calm tone held a wild edge.

Kevin clutched his comlink tighter. "I'm fine. What's wrong?"

Derek ignored the question. "Where are you?"

"I'm—" On the verge of answering, Kevin hesitated. He was acutely aware of everyone's eyes on him. Despite the fear and anxiety tying his stomach into knots, he had a responsibility as a Guardian to Admiral Chesnee and his wife.

"Is it over?" he asked instead. "Did Freedom's Children—"

"They're all gone. They did as much damage as they could and then disappeared through a bunch of portals. Took their wounded with them."

Though contained, the timbre of his brother's voice held a rough, raw edge that told Kevin it probably wouldn't take much to push Derek over the edge. He swallowed; it had been a while since he last heard his brother so angry. "Any prisoners?"

"None," Derek said flatly. "Freedom's Children didn't leave anybody living behind. Other than the woman Mike said you captured. Pearl Security is *not* happy about it."

Kevin winced, his mouth twisting into a frown. "She's dead. I'll explain later." His eyes darted to Taft, who met his gaze without flinching. The man had no regrets there, obviously.

Derek made a frustrated sound in the back of his throat, but otherwise let Kevin's statement pass without comment. This only served to further cement Kevin's certainty that something was terribly wrong. "Where are you?" Derek asked again.

Kevin clenched his jaw. *Duty first,* he reminded himself. Shooting Chesnee what he hoped was a reassuring look, he said, "I'm with Admiral Chesnee, his wife, and their security detail."

"Admiral Chesnee made it out alive?" The tiniest flicker of relief lightened Derek's voice.

When Chesnee just looked at Kevin, his gaze sober and considering, Kevin said, "Yeah. He and his wife are both okay."

"Good. The Triumvirate will be very glad to hear that." A pause ensued, during which Kevin heard only muffled conversation, and then Derek said, "Malik Thane wants to know where you are. He's sending a contingent of his security personnel to escort the Admiral back to his hotel."

Kevin frowned. "Malik Thane? Isn't he—"

"Guy Caradoc is dead, Kev, and nobody knows where his second-in-command is right now. Everything is a mess. Nobody even knows yet exactly how many people are dead or wounded."

The monster in the pit of Kevin's stomach was back again, gnawing away with renewed vigor. Derek sounded so *ragged.* Words burned on the tip of his tongue, but he forced himself to wait.

Closing his fingers around his comlink, he looked instead at Chesnee. "Admiral, Director Thane wants to send men to take you and Mrs. Chesnee back to your hotel."

Beside Kevin, Taft and Diaz looked to Chesnee as well. The air inside the small office seemed suddenly charged with electricity. After all their waiting around like trapped animals, now was the chance for action.

Chesnee nodded curtly, indicating his approval. On the settee next to him, his wife reached over to clutch his arm.

Kevin exhaled, relieved that the Admiral wasn't going to be difficult. He didn't think he could take that on top of the last few hours. He spoke into his comm again. "The Admiral sends his thanks."

"I'll inform Director Thane."

"Derek—" Kevin couldn't contain himself any longer. Words poured out of him; he didn't care if Chesnee, Taft, Diaz, or anyone else heard him. "What's happened? Is everybody okay? My nanites are frozen and I can't contact anyone."

"Mike, Lon, and Grandfather are fine." That ragged note was back in Derek's voice, as though he, too, had been holding himself together until they'd gotten through this official business with Chesnee.

Kevin waited with baited breath, every nerve on edge and every muscle taut. His stomach churned with anxiety. *What about Lilia?*

"Kev…" Derek's voice broke. "Lilia is—Lilia's been hurt."

*Lilia's been hurt.*

The words rolled through Kevin's mind like the rumble of thunder before the start of a torrential downpour. For a second, his mind refused to accept them, refused to process the shape and sound of them. Then terrible understanding dawned, and he froze in place as though struck by lightning.

His mouth was desert-dry; he had to swallow twice before he could force words out. "How bad is it?"

"Pretty bad. She's unconscious and they can't get her armor off."

The bottom dropped out of Kevin's stomach, taking the gnawing monster along with it. A knot formed in his throat, all but choking him.

Before he could find words again, Derek continued, "Holt's been hurt too—we're taking both of them to the hospital."

Kevin jolted in shock, uncaring that everyone was watching him. "Erik's been hurt too?"

"Yeah. We just found them—they were both buried under rubble."

*Rubble?* Kevin blinked. "What *happened?*"

"I don't know exactly." Fatigue and frustration flooded Derek's voice. "All I know is that there was an explosion in the lobby and the two of them were caught in it.

"An *explosion?* In the *lobby?*" Kevin felt like he was two steps behind, struggling to catch up and make sense of everything. He blinked, rubbing the back of the hand that held Erudita's nanoblade against his temple.

"Look, I'll explain everything when I see you. Thane's men will be there soon—get down here as soon as you can."

Kevin took a breath. "Okay."

"Give me a call and I'll tell you where to meet me," Derek said, before ending the call.

Kevin's hands were shaking as he slid his comlink back into his pocket. He breathed once, twice, and scrubbed his free hand through his dark hair. He then turned to face the Chesnees and their security detail. "Director Thane's men will be here shortly."

He had to force himself to stand still—he wanted nothing more than to charge out of the office and storm down to the lobby as fast as he could. Belatedly, he realized his grip on Erudita's nanoblade was so tight his fingers were going numb.

"Who has been hurt?"

The soft, feminine voice shattered the heavy, charged stillness permeating the office after his comlink call.

Startled, Kevin looked at Mrs. Chesnee, to find her regarding him with dark, concerned eyes. It was the first time he'd heard her speak since the Dome. The knot in his throat swelled; it took effort to say, "My sister. And our friend."

"I am sorry to hear that." Mrs. Chesnee paused. "She is a lovely girl, your sister."

Kevin simply nodded; further conversation was beyond him just now. His mind began racing, sifting through every horrible scenario that could have resulted in Lilia and Erik ending up in the lobby. *How did they even get* down *there?*

# CHAPTER 106

AFTERWARD, Kevin didn't remember much of the time between when he spoke to Derek and when Thane's men arrived. All he knew was that it seemed to take an eternity; he felt like he aged years in those silent, stretched-out minutes.

When a sharp knock sounded on the door, Kevin tensed along with everyone else. He nodded to Taft and Diaz in turn before reaching over to tap the door panel. He braced himself in the middle of the doorway, borrowed nanoblade at the ready.

The door slid aside to reveal a completely unexpected figure at the front of a squad of tuxedo-clad security guards. Kevin blinked, taken aback. "*Birch?*"

Alan Birch stared back at Kevin, his expression grim. His lower lip was split, his angular face bruised and streaked with blood, and his black ponytail was askew. His tuxedo was rumpled and torn in several places. Clearly, he'd been involved in the fight against Freedom's Children.

At the last second, a flicker of something that could almost have been resigned amusement showed on his face. "Strong."

"Thane sent *you?*"

"I volunteered." Birch's icy green gaze slid past Kevin to scan the office beyond before he shook his head slightly. "It figures you would be in the center of this."

Any other day, Kevin would have bristled and demanded to know what that was supposed to mean. Now, he let it slide. He had far more important things to worry about. He remained blocking the door. "You have any proof the Director sent you?"

As though he'd been expecting this, Birch made a show of carefully reaching into his breast pocket and extracting a comlink. He tapped in a command and extended the small device to Kevin.

As Kevin took it, a tiny holograph of Malik Thane's head and shoulders appeared in the air. The older man looked harried and exhausted, but he arched a haughty red eyebrow at Kevin. "I trust you know who I am, Captain Strong?"

"I know who you are."

"Good. Then you'll have no issues standing down and allowing Mr. Birch to escort Admiral Chesnee and his wife to safety."

"No, sir."

"Glad to hear it." Thane's holograph abruptly disappeared as he ended the holo-call.

"Satisfied?" Birch held out a hand for the comlink; Kevin dropped it into his palm.

In lieu of answering, Kevin turned toward Chesnee. "Admiral, this is Alan Birch. He's a Guardian and also works in security at the Internal Affairs Tower in the Four Towers in Sonela."

"I'm a division *head* of security in the Internal Affairs Tower," Birch said coolly.

Kevin ignored him, urgency thrumming in his veins. Pointing to Taft and Diaz in turn, he introduced them to Birch. He then stepped over to the settee, where the Admiral and his wife both rose to meet him. "Admiral, I—"

"Go." Chesnee nodded to the door. "We'll be fine." He glanced from Kevin to Birch and back before holding out a hand to Kevin. They shook. "Thank you."

"Yes, thank you." Mrs. Chesnee extended a hand to him as well, a relieved smile gracing her beautiful features. "And tell your sister I will be thinking of her."

Kevin bowed his head; that awful knot had tightened in his throat again. He nodded to Taft and Diaz in turn, shot a quick nod to the other members of their security team, and crossed to the door.

Just before he crossed the threshold, he met Birch's eye. "Take care of them."

For once, Birch answered without his customary smirk. "I will." He paused, as though he wanted to add something, but then seemed to think the better of it. Instead, he jerked his chin toward Erudita's nanoblade. "That's not yours."

"No, it's not." Kevin didn't follow his gaze. "I'll be making a report to the NCDC on it."

"That should be interesting."

Kevin didn't bother to reply. Brushing past Birch, he exited the office and turned left to stride down the hall. He waited until he turned the corner at the other end to break into a dead run.

Lilia was hurt. Erik, too.

Panic and terrible fear clawed at him with icy fingers. What kind of explosion could they possibly have been involved in?

He found the closest accelevator bank and punched the button for 'down'.

While he waited, he fumbled for his comlink. "Derek, where are you? I'm on my way."

The accelevator's silver doors opened; he dashed inside.

"Still in the lobby," his brother answered tersely. "Apparently, there's now a mob outside and it's making evacuating the Pearl difficult."

*A mob?* Kevin blinked. "This just keeps getting better and better. Lobby," he told the accelevator, and it obligingly began to descend.

"You don't know the half of it." A pause. "I have to go."

"Okay. See you in a minute."

Kevin leaned against the accelevator's back wall, trying to get a hold of himself. His imagination continued to run rampant, churning out terrible expectations of what he would find when he reached the lobby.

The accelevator doors had barely started to slide apart before Kevin was shimmying his way through the widening gap. His heart thudded in his chest, that awful anxiety constricting his breathing.

At the sound of the accelevator's arrival, a knot of men in navy-blue uniforms turned to face him. All four of them took one look at him and drew weapons.

"Halt," one of them demanded, a stocky man with red-brown skin and sleek black hair. "Drop your weapon and put your hands on your head!"

*Weapon?* Kevin looked blankly down at his hand; he'd almost forgotten he was still clutching Erudita's nanoblade.

For a second, he considered disobeying. He discarded the idea as foolish, despite the surge of adrenaline pumping through him, urging him to action. He wasn't wearing his helmet, and one of these guys might just go for a head shot if he didn't cooperate. Besides, he knew he must look half-wild with worry and fear.

Letting Erudita's nanoblade clang to the floor, Kevin turned both hands palm-up in a conciliatory gesture. "Hi."

He reigned himself in, forcing himself to sound calm and rational instead of slightly unhinged. "My name is Kevin Strong. I'm a Guardian. I've been summoned to the lobby," he tipped his head past them down the hall, "by Derek Strong. Also a Guardian, and my brother."

The four men exchanged darting glances, and then one of them turned away, touching the comlink in his ear. A brief, hushed conversation later, he turned back to regard Kevin with still-suspicious eyes. "You've been cleared to pass." He jerked his head down the hall. "Take a right at the intersection and keep going straight."

"Thanks." Kevin bent long enough to scoop up his discarded nanoblade and the knot of security personnel stepped aside to let him pass. He made three strides before his walk turned into a run again.

He emerged into the massive, airy lobby, but parts of it bore little resemblance to the way it had looked when everyone arrived earlier that evening.

Thin gashes marred the center of the floor where Glo'Stea's seal had been embedded, and the beautiful main doors beyond the security checkpoint had been replaced by a sleek set of security doors. The floor in front of those doors was blackened and pitted from an explosion of some sort. Debris—broken bits of marble and who knew what else—had rained down in an impressive radius.

Several body bags littered the floor around the security checkpoint, beside sticky pools of dark red blood. Dead Pearl Security personnel, most likely. A small group of Jamal police officers mixed with more Pearl Security personnel guarded the bodies.

Kevin swallowed, a muscle in his jaw tensing, but his gaze traveled past them. The people on the floor were dead and past saving; his sister and Erik were still alive.

*Please, God, let them still be alive.*

Kevin's eye was drawn to the site of another explosion off to the side of the hall. A large, roundish hole had been blown in the side of the sea-blue wall. Chunks of wall with blackened edges littered the aquamarine floor. And beside that awful-looking hole…

*Oh, God.* Kevin's heart stuttered in his chest as he caught sight of Derek standing beside two floating stretchers holding motionless bodies. One wore a tuxedo, the other was clad completely in nano-armor. Derek looked pale and miserable. Four emergency medical technicians—three men, one woman—with bright yellow crosses on their pale blue jackets stood around the stretchers, their heads bent together as though they were in the midst of a fervent discussion.

Breaking into a run again, Kevin sprinted across the lobby. "Derek!"

At the sound of his name, Derek's head snapped up, a look of pure relief flashing across his face. He turned to the EMTs and Kevin heard him say, "My brother's here. We'll help you."

Kevin skidded to a halt beside them as the woman, medium height with short black hair, pale skin and almond-shaped dark eyes, nodded to her colleagues. A name tag emblazoned on her uniform above her heart read, *Kino*. "You go see what else you can do. Hicks and I will take care of these two."

The other two EMTs moved off without a word and Kino and Hicks—who was a tall, rail-thin young man with a dark brown skin, curly black hair, and a compassionate face—took charge of the hoverstretchers. Kino jerked a thumb over her shoulder. "You're sure there's no way to get this stuff off?"

Kevin followed the gesture to the stretchers and his heart seized in his chest. Erik lay on one of the stretchers, his face covered in so much blood and dust it was hard to tell what had happened to his head. And beside him…

He moved up to the stretcher with almost dreamlike steps, dimly aware of Derek patiently explaining that a Guardian had to be conscious to dematerialize nano-armor. He'd know that nano-armor-clad figure anywhere. Lilia'd had her facemask and helmet to protect her, but she lay motionless on the stretcher. A fine layer of dust covered parts of her armor; Kevin's heart seized again as he took in the ugly gash along her ribcage. *She's been fighting for sure.*

A hand shaking his shoulder brought him back to reality. Derek tipped his head toward the hall Kevin had just exited. "Come on. They're adding Lilia and Erik to the ambulance queue."

Kevin suddenly remembered the mob. "What about the mob? How are we going to—"

"Between Jamal's police and the Glo'Stean Resistance, they're getting the mob under control." A muscle twitched in Derek's jaw. "They've been sending people to local hospitals for the past half an hour. Supposedly, it's safe."

"Okay." Kevin nodded, still feeling like he was in a surreal sort of dream. Belatedly, he realized the growing pain in the fingers of his left hand was because his hand was beginning to cramp from his death grip on Erudita's nanoblade.

He extended the weapon hilt-first to his brother. "This is evidence. You wouldn't happen to still have a working ISF, would you?"

# Chapter 107

LILIA dreamed she stood in a long tunnel with sandy gray rock walls and a smooth stone floor. Strips of ancient glowpanels dialed down to their lowest setting were embedded in the tunnel ceiling's rocky surface at regular intervals, providing faint illumination. The cool air smelled of dust.

Hazy recognition dawned—she was in the underground tunnel system beneath Quinton, Lanx's capital city. What was she doing down here? Lilia looked down at herself, taking in the filmy sapphire blue folds of her evening gown. And what had possessed her to come down here wearing *this*?

A voice called her name; she turned to find Jasper standing behind her. He wore his black tuxedo and the grin she'd spent so long denying that it had any effect on her. Still smiling, Jasper stretched a hand out to her.

Lilia smiled back, instinctively, and started to walk toward him, but her feet refused to move. Her smile slipped as searing pain shot up her right leg and down her right arm, which hung limp at her side. She struggled to make her feet cooperate, but her shoes seemed to have melded to the tunnel floor.

Panicked, she stretched out her left hand to Jasper for help, but he didn't move. He just stood there smiling, hand still extended toward her.

Without warning, a nanoblade pierced his chest from behind. A widening patch of crimson blood stained his white shirt beneath his tuxedo jacket.

Lilia screamed.

Jasper made a choked little sound and looked down…and then his gaze rose to meet hers. His gray eyes were full of betrayal and accusation. When he spoke, blood trickled out of the corner of his mouth. "You could have saved me. You didn't."

Lilia stopped screaming long enough to protest that she'd done everything she could, but it didn't matter. Jasper fell to his knees and then slumped face-first on the tunnel floor, the Mastermind's nanoblade protruding from his back.

Screaming his name, Lilia struggled to free herself and reach him before it was too late. She clawed at the folds of her skirt with her good hand, trying to get to her stupid shoes, but her skirt, too, seemed to have melded to the tunnel floor.

A sudden *crack* drew her attention to the left, where the sandy gray wall abruptly split. Water trickled out, first a few drops, and then a small stream that turned the dust coating the tunnel floor into rivulets of mud. Within seconds, the crack widened under the pressure of the water behind it and the stream became a roaring waterfall.

Dark, foaming water began to flood the tunnel. It was strangely hot, instead of cold, and the spray tasted of salt. In a matter of seconds, it had covered Jasper's motionless body.

"No! Jasper!"

Lilia kept screaming, even though her throat now burned and her voice had become hoarse. She fought to get to Jasper, but she still couldn't move. She couldn't do anything but stand there, thrashing, as the dark water now swirled up around her hips and rose to engulf her chest.

She barely had time to gulp in a breath before the hot, rushing force of water swallowed her whole.

Lilia couldn't *breathe*.

Panicked and terrified, she thrashed in the water, helpless to save Jasper or herself. She couldn't move, she couldn't breathe…

They were both going to die here.

She thought she could hear him calling her name.

*Lilia. Lilia.*

She thrashed harder, fighting the water. She needed air. *He* needed air. She—

Jasper's voice changed, lightening in timbre. "Lilia…Lilia… wake up!"

Lilia regained consciousness with a start, still screaming and flailing wildly, to find herself stretched out flat and something obstructing her face. Painfully bright light shone down on her, temporarily blinding her. Searing pain still engulfed her right arm and raced up her leg from her right foot.

Completely disoriented, she scrabbled frantically to clear her face with her good hand. *Can't breathe, can't breathe, can't breathe.*

Hands caught her hand, stilling her frantic movements, and a voice cut through her panic.

"Lilia, Lilia, it's okay! You're okay."

She knew that voice.

*Kevin.*

"Can't—breathe," she wheezed. Her chest burned, heaving with every labored attempt to expand her lungs, which only increased her panic. Her head felt like someone was using it for drumming practice.

"It's okay, Lil. Just calm down." Her brother's hands tightened around her fingers. "You need to calm down."

"She is hyperventilating." This from an unfamiliar voice, one with a metallic tinge.

"I can see that."

The painfully bright light dimmed as a figure bent over Lilia. *Kevin.* She could just make out his face through her watering eyes. He still held her hand in a tight grip.

"Lilia. We need you to dematerialize your armor. Can you do that?"

Dematerialize her…armor? Lilia blinked, and a fraction of her disorientation faded.

Armor.

Helmet.

Facemask.

Her heartbeat began to slow as understanding washed over her. *That* was why it felt like something was covering her face. *I'm still wearing my helmet and facemask.*

She frowned. *Why* was she wearing—

Memories returned in a rush, though they were fixed and oddly unmoving, like a slideshow of holo stills.

The mob.

The lobby's security doors.

Erik and the not-Guardian.

Jasper—*Jasper*—with Martin Hollowell's nanoblade through his chest.

Her own chest constricting again, Lilia sat bolt upright—or tried to. Kevin stopped her before she made it more than a few centimeters off of whatever she was lying on—a hospital bed?—but he had to let go of her hands in the process.

"Jasper!" she gasped, the searing pain in her arm and leg temporarily forgotten. "The Mastermind stabbed him!" Her gloved fingers gripped the front of Kevin's white shirt; he had discarded his tuxedo jacket. "Is he—"

"He's in surgery," Kevin said quickly. "That's all I know."

*Surgery.* He was still alive. The Mastermind hadn't succeeded in killing him.

Such a powerful wave of relief washed over her that Lilia nearly went limp. Her grip on her brother's shirt loosened, her lips moving in a silent prayer of thanksgiving.

He wasn't dead.

*Thank you, Jesus. Thank you, thank you.*

Another memory suddenly jolted Lilia, draining the blood from her face behind her facemask.

The portal.

The *grenade* that not-Guardian had dropped just before he disappeared through said portal.

Her hand fisted into her twin's shirtfront again. "Erik! The grenade! Is he—"

"He's going to be fine." Kevin tried to smile, though the expression was worn around the edges. He looked exhausted, but he didn't seem to mind the death grip she had on him. "Couple of broken bones and he hit his head, but it could have been worse."

He shook his head slightly. "Erik said you tackled him right before the explosion. He's not very happy about it."

*I remember that.* Lilia blinked, and let go of her brother's shirt before hissing through her teeth as a wave of pain crashed over her. Concern for Jasper and Erik had kept it at bay, but now she broke into a cold sweat beneath her armor. Closing her eyes, she collapsed back on the bed and focused on breathing through the pain.

The way her chest hurt every time she inhaled or exhaled, it took a moment for her to be able to speak again. "He wasn't—wasn't wearing a helmet."

"Yeah, I figured. Told him that even as hard as his head is, you still probably saved his life."

Lilia wanted to smile at that, but the pain was intensifying. She writhed on the bed, unable to help herself, even though the slightest movement made everything hurt worse. Nausea churned her stomach.

"She needs to lie still," the metallic voice said again. "Movement will exacerbate her injuries."

"Hey, hey, calm down." Kevin bent over her and gently put his hands on her shoulders. "You've got a broken arm, a couple of cracked ribs, and your foot—" His voice wavered; he had to clear his throat.

Even in her agony, Lilia registered that hesitation. She forced her eyes open, better prepared for the bright light, and demanded through gritted teeth, "My foot?"

A silver med 'bot appeared in her field of vision, next to Kevin. It had a human-shaped head with a built-in headlamp, four spindly arms and a long, rectangular torso. "You—"

"It's pretty badly broken, Lil," Kevin interjected, cutting the 'bot off before it could finish. Hands still on her shoulders, he tipped his head toward the foot of her bed. "They pulled you and Erik out from beneath a pile of debris."

Lilia started to nod, but stopped immediately—the motion made her throbbing headache worse. Tears burned the backs of her eyes as she shut them against the light. The sharp medicinal smell filling the room—she guessed she must be in the hospital—didn't help her nausea.

"Lil, they can't give you anything for the pain or even *do* anything to help you until you dematerialize your armor." Kevin audibly swallowed, his next words hopeful. "Can you?"

*Can I?* Lilia would have laughed, if she hadn't hurt so badly. It took everything she had to open her eyes and say, "No. Frozen."

Kevin's face fell. He swallowed again, a muscle in his jaw twitching. "I'm so sorry."

*Me too,* Lilia wanted to say, as the throbbing pain in her body intensified. She closed her eyes again, groaning, tears leaking out to stream down toward her ears beneath her facemask.

"Oh, God," she heard Kevin say softly, "please give her relief from the pain. Please help her make it through this."

Darkness danced around the edges of her vision. Lilia embraced it willingly.

The next few hours were filled with bouts of unconsciousness punctuated by brief bursts of consciousness. The throbbing pain was an ever-present companion, making Lilia moan even while asleep. Kevin stayed by her side the entire time, holding her good hand.

Derek arrived eventually; at one point Lilia opened her eyes to find him sitting beside her bed next to Kevin. Every time she awoke, both of her brothers prodded her to see if she could dematerialize her armor.

It was a relief to everyone when Lilia could finally command her nanites to retreat back into her sweat-soaked skin. She slumped limply on the hospital bed, clad in only her panties and the upper half of her truncated evening gown, welcoming the cooler air. The med 'bot immediately swept in to administer pain medication.

"Oh, my God," Kevin said softly.

*That* didn't sound good. Lilia opened her eyes to slits to peer at her brother, who was staring down at her feet. She started to ask what was wrong, but at that second she became aware of a cool sensation traveling through her veins, making the agony fade. Extreme exhaustion followed in its wake.

Keeping her eyes open suddenly seemed to take a monumental amount of energy. *Whatever it is can't be that bad, can it?*

"We need to get her into surgery," she heard the med 'bot said crisply, "or—"

The rest of the 'bot's sentence faded into oblivion.

# Chapter 108

GILES Chesnee wanted nothing more than to leave Glo'Stea in his shuttle's afterburners and return to the familiar environs of the *Winds of Change*, but he knew it would have to wait. He and Sylvia couldn't leave the planet until he'd heard from Kedis. And so far, the Ambassador wasn't answering his comlink.

It was hopefully nothing. Just Kedis putting politics—in this case, taking a terrorist attack and turning it to his advantage—ahead of little things like letting the other highest-ranking representative of the Galactic Union on Glo'Stea know he was still breathing.

Swallowing his ire and doing his best to ignore the worry twisting his insides, Chesnee sat back against the luxurious black leather seat of the skimmer that was whisking them away from the Pearl. He was still in his shirt-sleeves; there had been no time to retrieve his uniform jacket from its hiding place. Sylvia sat beside him, while Captain Diaz and Birch occupied the seats facing them. Birch had replaced Taft, sending the man instead to the front passenger seat of the skimmer behind them.

On the verge of searching his comlink for Captain Strong's comm details—the young Sta'Gloan was a more likely source of information at this point—Chesnee paused as Birch's comlink chimed softly.

The dark-haired man answered and listened in silence before responding with an affirmative. The blood and bruises on his face took his already grim features and turned them into something almost savage. He maintained admirable control of his features, though once or twice his eyes widened in surprise at something he heard.

Chesnee watched him with narrowed eyes. He was still not entirely sure what he thought of Alan Birch.

It was impossible to miss the man's dislike of anyone from the Galactic Union, though Birch covered it with a thin veneer of civility. He had coolly and efficiently escorted Chesnee, Sylvia, and their security detail through the Pearl to the underground parking garage, where he had bundled them into different skimmers from the ones in which they had arrived and they had taken off.

Beside Chesnee, Sylvia curled just a little closer to him, tangling her fingers with his. His lips tilted in a small smile. His wife looked exhausted and her makeup was smudged, but she was still as beautiful as she had been at the evening's start.

Chesnee then cast a wary glance through the skimmer's tinted windows. They had just cleared the Pearl's security perimeter, but the streets on this side of Glo'Stea's capitol building looked remarkably empty. He could guess why; like a stream of flowing water, the bulk of the mob had chosen the path of least resistance.

Across from him, Birch slid his comlink back into his pants pocket and cleared his throat. "I regret to inform you, Admiral Chesnee, that for security reasons we will not be returning you to your hotel tonight."

*Security reasons?* Chesnee lifted an eyebrow. "Is that so?" He gestured over his shoulder to the Pearl vanishing into the darkness behind them. "Is your Director Thane concerned that the mob may attempt to storm my hotel?"

A muscle in Birch's jaw tightened. "Something like that."

Ah, well. It was probably to be expected, after tonight. Chesnee looked down at Sylvia to see how she was taking this news. She met his gaze, her dark eyes solemn and wide.

"We will, of course," Birch continued, "return all of your belongings to you as soon as possible. At the moment, however, your safety is paramount." He looked like the words left a bad taste in his mouth.

"Understood." Chesnee waved a hand; the temporary lack of their belongings was a nuisance and an inconvenience, but hardly the end of the galaxy. "In that case, take me to Ambassador Kedis."

Birch did not miss a beat. "I'm afraid I can't do that. Sir."

The temperature in the skimmer abruptly nosedived, the atmosphere growing tense. Chesnee fixed Birch with an icy stare carrying the full weight of his rank as an Admiral in the Galactic Union StarFleet. "And why, Mr. Birch, is that?"

Birch met his gaze without flinching. "Ambassador Kedis is no longer on Glo'Stea."

"Excuse me?" Those words caught Chesnee off-kilter; they were probably the last thing he had expected to hear. "What do you mean Ambassador Kedis is no longer on Glo'Stea?"

Birch's expression suddenly looked like he had just swallowed something foul-tasting. "The Ambassador was wounded tonight, Admiral, and due to the extent of his injuries, he was immediately evacuated to Sonela General on Sta'Gloa."

The bottom dropped out of Chesnee's stomach. Kedis, wounded? *Damn it all, Giles, you were supposed to keep that foolhardy young man in one piece.*

Straightening his shoulders, Chesnee fixed Birch with a glare that had terrified more than one subordinate over the years. "Why am I only learning of this now?"

For his part, Birch refused to be cowed. "Because Director Thane only informed me of it now, Admiral." He indicated his comlink.

Chesnee wanted to growl and ask why Thane hadn't seen fit to inform him any sooner, but he reigned himself in. Though perhaps temporarily satisfying, it would be a pointless endeavor—Birch was only a lackey, after all. Instead, he asked, "How bad is it?"

"I believe he was shot in the head."

Sylvia gasped at this, recoiling instinctively.

Chesnee clenched his jaw, his eyes boring into Birch and willing him to continue.

The young Sta'Gloan man lifted one shoulder in the barest of shrugs. "From what I understand, it is a miracle he survived at all."

"And instead of stat-flighting him to the local hospital, your Directors saw fit to send him off-world?" Chesnee didn't even try to hide his derision.

Birch's green eyes flashed and he opened his mouth to retort, but seemed to the think the better of it at the last second. He swallowed—hard—and when he did speak, his voice was cool and controlled. "They didn't fly the Ambassador to Sta'Gloa, Admiral. They used the transporter."

Chesnee stilled. *The transporter.* That thought hadn't even crossed his mind. A fraction of his fury ebbed. "I—ah—suppose that *would* be a faster means of getting him there."

If they really had to take Kedis all the way to *Sta'Gloa*. Something about that was off, but he couldn't put his finger on it.

"I also understand that Lon Strong went him." Birch looked like he had tasted something disgusting again. Obviously, he did not care much for Captain Strong.

Chesnee filed that away for future reference. In the meantime, the tension tying his guts into knots eased. "He did? That is excellent news."

He wasn't sure he'd ever be able to say he *trusted* a citizen of the Coalition exactly, but at the very least Lon Strong had proved he didn't want Kedis dead. And if he was still with Kedis, he would most definitely be an *excellent* source of information.

Chesnee did not miss the way Birch's upper lip curled slightly in disgust before the younger man mastered his expression.

On the seat beside Birch, Diaz continued to look deeply suspicious. His dark brow had been furrowed in suspicious concern since the Dome; Chesnee wondered idly if his subordinate's face might get stuck that way.

"Where *are* you taking us?" Sylvia fixed questioning eyes on Birch, her slender fingers tightening their grip on her husband's hand. She held up her free hand. "And, please, Mr. Birch, don't say 'someplace safe'. I've had quite enough of political smooth-talking from Ambassador Kedis."

Her soft, yet blunt words apparently caught Birch off-guard. He blinked at Sylvia, his green eyes widening for a second before he inclined his head ever so slightly in acknowledgment.

Acknowledgment of what, Chesnee remained uncertain, but a thrill of pride in his wife still ran through him.

"My instructions are to deliver you to Director Vance's secure safe house," Birch said. "It's not that far; we'll be there soon."

For the span of two eyeblinks, Chesnee wondered if his auto-translator was functioning correctly. "Did you say you're taking us to a *safe house?*"

He made sure to speak clearly and enunciate each word, just in case *Birch's* autotranslator was the one malfunctioning.

"That's correct, Admiral. Chief Minister Vance's safe house. Director Thane and Director Talon both thought that would be best."

"Absolutely not." The words emerged with no conscious thought, but Chesnee meant every syllable. He leveled Birch with his weighty stare again. "We are not going to a safe house."

He shook his head slightly. "You will either take us to the transporter and send us to Sta'Gloa as well, or else you will deliver us to my shuttle at the spaceport and I will return to my flagship."

For the first time, Birch seemed at a loss for words. Eyes wide, he opened and closed his mouth twice before he finally spoke. "Admiral, I'm afraid that is—"

Chesnee held up a finger. "Do not tell me it is out of the question." His expression darkened. "I am well aware you are only the messenger, Mr. Birch. Contact your Directors of Security immediately. I wish to speak to them.

Birch looked like he would very much like to argue, but Chesnee was pleased to see he was smart enough to realize when he had been defeated. He swallowed hard and then wordlessly tapped his comlink.

Beside him, Diaz's dark expression lightened; he covered his mouth with one hand to hide a smile.

It was a holo-call, and Thane answered almost immediately, his head and shoulders coalescing in a tiny holograph above Birch's comlink. Birch did not give the redheaded man time to do more than bark a harried question before he said, "Admiral Chesnee wishes to speak to you, Director."

He then passed the comlink across the skimmer to Chesnee without another word.

Chesnee considered this another point in Birch's favor. Taking the comlink, he offered Thane's holographic figure a thin, mirthless smile.

"Admiral Chesnee," Thane began, with a real effort at civility.

"We are not going to your safe house, Director." Chesnee kept his voice pleasant, but implacable. He laid Thane's options out for him in a few concise sentences and waited.

Beside him, Sylvia squeezed his fingers in silent approval.

To his credit, Thane did not sputter or flail—not exactly, anyway. His civility, however, cooled considerably as he regarded Chesnee.

Kedis would have used that to his advantage somehow, but Chesnee didn't care. He knew from the sour look on Thane's face he'd already won this battle.

"I appreciate your desire to see to Ambassador Kedis's safety and swift recovery," the Director began cautiously, "but I am afraid travel via the transporter is out of the question tonight."

"And why is that?"

"The transporter was also targeted by Freedom's Children and may have suffered some damage."

Chesnee raised an eyebrow. "You managed to send the Ambassador through."

Thane's face went strangely blank, as though he wasn't quite prepared for this statement, but he covered quickly. "That was something of a miracle, Admiral—and we were desperate." He paused. "The Ambassador's injuries are quite severe."

"I wouldn't know." Chesnee gave the younger man a stern look. "And that is something I ought to know, don't you think, Director Thane?"

Thane had the grace to look abashed. "A great deal has transpired in a very short span of time this evening, Admiral. Forgive us for failing to flow information through the proper channels fast enough."

It didn't take a politician to see through *that* statement. Chesnee continued to stare at the Sta'Gloan Director of Security. "Like you, Director, I have superiors I must report to. I am returning to my flagship, but I will be sending several members of the Ambassador's retinue to Sta'Gloa, along with my personal security detail."

He expected that to be the end of it, but to his surprise, Thane rallied.

"Admiral, believe it or not, we are doing our best to keep you, your wife, and your men alive."

"Are you expecting these terrorists to have staked out my shuttle?"

"Not…exactly."

That slight hesitation confirmed Chesnee's niggling feeling that something about tonight's attack was…off. Cold, heavy resolve settled in his gut. "I think you had better tell me what is really going on, Director."

Thane hesitated again. "This channel is not secure."

*To hell with that*, Chesnee wanted to respond, but he held himself in check. "Then you can fill me in once I reach my shuttle."

He could tell Thane still wasn't happy.

"Admiral…" The younger man seemed to be choosing his words very carefully. "There is a chance that Freedom's Children could…attack…your shuttle by means undetectable by your crew. They could…compromise…your shuttle's integrity for space travel."

Unlike anything else Thane had said thus far, *that* gave Chesnee pause. "You mean by using nanoblades?"

Thane looked pained to admit it, but nodded. "That is correct."

Chesnee considered for a few seconds, his thoughts racing as fast as his battlecruiser at full speed. "Are your concerns also related to how these terrorists bypassed your security tonight?"

This time, Thane seemed to anticipate the question. "I can neither confirm nor deny that."

"I see." Chesnee glanced around the skimmer's interior, his gaze flicking from Birch and Diaz, who both tried to hide rapt, curious expressions, to his wife. He returned his gaze to Thane. "It is imperative that I return to my flagship, Director, but I do not wish to place myself or anyone else in unnecessary danger. Surely there is another option?"

*Kedis*, he thought grimly, *would be proud.*

Thane had apparently been considering this himself, because it didn't take him long to come up with an answer. "You can use my yacht, Admiral." One corner of his thin mouth lifted in the barest of smiles. "I traveled to Glo'Stea for the treaty signing via the transporter, but I had my pilot fly here just in case."

*His own yacht?* Chesnee just barely managed to keep the surprise he felt from showing on his craggy face. "Many thanks, Director."

"I'll instruct Mr. Birch to take you to the spaceport. You shouldn't draw too much attention in the section where my ship is berthed, but we'll be careful just the same." Thane paused. "I will also send you everything I have on the Ambassador's current medical situation."

"That would be appreciated." Chesnee didn't bother telling him he intended to talk to Lon Strong. Instead, he passed the comlink back to Birch.

The younger Sta'Gloan man listened in silence before responding with an assurance that he would take care of everything. He immediately issued orders for their two skimmers to change course, and they headed around through Jamal's dark streets to the spaceport.

Chesnee spent a few moments composing mental reports, strategizing what he would tell Admiral Riley. He rubbed his temples, feeling the first stirrings of a throbbing headache.

Even wounded, Kedis was *still* causing trouble.

*The Senate will not be happy about this.* The only upside was that the trade agreement was signed first. That Kedis was still alive—so far—was also a plus, but when you came right down to it, Chesnee wasn't convinced the Senate would care as much about Kedis as they did the peace treaty.

In that respect, politics reminded him of certain military strate-
gies. Sometimes, there were acceptable casualties.

His mouth set in a grim line, Chesnee pulled out his comlink
again and tapped a name. "Captain Strong? This is Admiral Chesnee.
We need to talk."

# Chapter 109

A steady beeping, like a mechanical heartbeat, penetrated the warm cloud of emptiness cradling Lilia. It was familiar, reminding her that whoever it was monitoring was still alive. *Still alive.* A knot of tension inside her relaxed a little.

Those words were a good thing, though just this second she couldn't quite recall why.

Still half-asleep, Lilia let her mind drift, but then she frowned. Something terribly important niggled in the back of her mind. She couldn't sleep right now, she had to wake up and check on—

*Jasper!*

Lilia inhaled sharply, her eyes flying open, and tried to sit up. Her eyes refused to focus; all she saw at first was a dim white blur. Before she could wonder where she was, she felt a firm hand grip her shoulder and hold her in place.

At the same time, a familiar voice said, "Hey, kid, calm down."

"Erik?"

It took a few blinks to get her eyes to focus properly, but then Lilia found herself staring up at Erik Holt's concerned face. Blond stubble covered his jaw, the left side of which bore a dark bruise. He had exchanged his tuxedo for his preferred white shirt, brown vest, and pants, and a quick-heal cast covered his right forearm from elbow to wrist.

"Yeah, it's me." Erik gave her a wry look, his brown eyes full of concern. "You're not exactly supposed to be movin' around right now. If I let go, will you behave?"

Lilia nodded, though even that slight movement made the world swim around her. Dimly, she registered she was lying propped up on a narrow hospital bed. She had to be in the hospital—that sharp medicinal smell mixed with the strong scent of disinfectant was too distinctive to be anything else.

"Promise?"

She forced herself to speak. "Yes." Her voice emerged as a hoarse whisper.

"Okay." Releasing her shoulder, Erik eased himself back into his chair beside her bed. He jerked his chin toward something to her right. "Want some water?"

Water sounded fantastic—Lilia realized suddenly that she was absolutely parched. She gave him a ginger nod and had to close her eyes again.

"Okay." Erik leaned over to pour her a cupful; she heard the clink of ice.

Lilia drew in a breath, noticing that though her chest still ached it wasn't as bad as before, and opened her eyes. Without moving her head, she sent her gaze sweeping around the room. She was in a private room with pale mauve walls, a holo of magenta and pink flowers on the wall facing her, and beige curtains pulled across the windows to her right. A bank of machines stood around the head of her bed, monitoring her vitals.

"Here ya go." Erik leaned forward to put a straw to her lips with his good hand and she took several eager sips.

Thirst temporarily slaked, she managed a small smile. "Thank you."

Erik nodded and set the cup off to the side.

Lilia then glanced down at herself to take stock of her situation. Bandages wrapped around her chest, peeking out of the neckline of her pale pink flowered hospital gown. A quick-heal cast just like Erik's encased her right forearm.

*Oh, my God...*

Kevin's voice floated through her mind and she glanced at her feet, frowning. What had he been—

Lilia choked on her own spit.

Her left leg was covered by a blanket, but her right leg was propped up in a sling. A bare foot poked out from behind specialized bandages wrapped around her right ankle—bandages she recognized from her days working at medcenters on Glo'Stea.

They only used those kinds of bandages on amputated limbs that had been fitted with replacement mechanical parts.

For the span of a few heartbeats, Lilia just stared at her foot, her brain unable to process the full implications of the information her eyes were relaying. Then, violet eyes wide, lips parted in horror, she looked at Erik. "What—what—"

Words failed her; the rest of her sentence died in her throat. She could only shake her head, fluttering her left hand in a mute, helpless gesture.

For his part, Erik looked like he wanted to throw up. Face twisted into a grimace, he lurched to his feet and began pacing back and forth across the room. He moved with a limp, favoring his left leg, but where Lilia ordinarily would have asked how badly he was hurt, her mind was a hazy blank.

"It shouldn't be me tryin' to explain this." Erik shot her an equally helpless look, running a hand over his short blond hair. "Kevin was supposed to be here."

Lilia just continued to stare at him, uncomprehending.

Erik finally took a deep breath, obviously bracing himself, and turned back to face her. He came to stand behind his chair, gripping the back of it with his good hand.

"Kid…when that grenade went off an' we got buried in all that debris from the wall, it—well…it crushed your foot." Erik swallowed, his grip tightening on the chair. In that moment, he looked ten years younger—and scared.

"Your boot protected you a little, kept your foot from bein' smashed flat like a pancake, an' your armor kept it from swellin' too bad for a while, but—" He swallowed again. "They couldn't save it."

He nodded to the end of the bed. "Your foot was too badly mangled."

His words, hesitant and apologetic, washed over Lilia, and then receded, leaving scattered fragments in their wake.

*Crushed…boot protected you a little…couldn't save it…too badly mangled.*

It was only when her chest began to ache for a different reason that Lilia realized she'd forgotten to breathe. She forced herself to inhale. *Breathe in.* She exhaled. *Breathe out.*

Erik was talking again, a jumbled rush of words, but Lilia didn't hear any of it. A rushing, roaring sound filled her ears.

*Breathe in.*

*Breathe out.*

She couldn't stop staring at her new prosthetic foot. Dimly, as though the memory was playing behind dark glass, she recalled pain in her leg following waking up in the emergency room after the explosion. Excruciating, nauseating pain.

That pain was gone now, though Lilia wasn't sure how much of that was from the medication no doubt still pumping through her body. She curled her fingers around the rough edge of her hospital blanket and breathed in that antiseptic smell. It seemed hard to believe—if she hadn't recognized those bandages, she probably wouldn't have noticed it so soon.

A hysterical laugh tried to burble up in her throat, but it died in a choked little cough. *Could I really* not *have noticed I'd lost a foot?*

She'd lost a *foot.*

A heavy weight settled down on Lilia's shoulders, pressing her into her hospital bed, as those words formed in her mind.

*I lost a foot.*

She sucked in a deep, shuddering breath. At first glance, her replacement foot didn't look any different from her real foot. The skin covering it was the same pale cream tone as her own, the toes looked like her own. Even a second glanced didn't reveal anything out of the ordinary.

Lilia squinted at her feet, a tiny spark of hope lighting inside her. *Maybe Erik's wrong. Maybe* I'm *wrong and those bandages don't mean a thing.*

She tried to wiggle her toes.

Nothing happened.

Dull shock flooded her this time, bringing with it a wave of disappointment so crushing and devastating that it clogged her throat and brought tears to her eyes.

*I lost a foot.*

It was only then that she realized she was shaking.

Just then, the door to her room burst open and Kevin barreled in. A corner of Lilia's mind noted that Erik must have Nancommed him.

Erik promptly slid out from behind the chair to make room for Kevin, retreating to the back wall, where he stood with his arms folded across his chest and his face set in a grim, haunted expression.

"Lilia, hey." Kevin leaned over her bed to rest a large hand on top of hers. His skin was warm in comparison, and like Erik, he wore street clothes. "Sorry I wasn't here when you woke up. I was in the caféteria."

He looked so guilty that a hint of amusement poked fragile tendrils through the miasma of devastation swamping Lilia. "It's okay." Her voice emerged sounding hoarse and rusty again. "You have to eat."

Kevin had needed to eat, of that she was suddenly quite sure. He looked as exhausted as she felt. Dark smudges lined his eyes, his dark brown hair looked like it hadn't seen a comb in a couple of days, and he needed a shave. Dark stubble coated his jaw.

"Are you okay?" both siblings asked at the same time.

At the back of the room, Erik snorted and shook his head.

Kevin opened his mouth, but Lilia beat him to it. "You first."

"I'm fine." Kevin scrubbed a hand through his already-crazy hair. "Just tired." He managed a small smile threaded with almost giddy relief. "I'm better now that I know you're okay."

"Okay?" Lilia's voice cracked. She waved a hand toward her right leg, tears burning the backs of her eyes. "Apparently, I lost a foot."

Kevin's gaze followed her movement and he winced in sympathy, but then his expression firmed into hopeful resolve. "It could have been worse, Lilia. You could have been killed."

"Or lost your whole leg," Erik put in.

Lilia didn't look at him; her attention was solely fixed on her brother. Intellectually, she knew he was right—it could have been much, much worse.

But that was small consolation to the part of her wailing internally like a small child at her loss.

Kevin swept forward to engulf her in a gentle—but firm—hug. "It's going to be okay."

Behind him, the door flew open again to admit a silver med 'bot.

"Please, sir," the 'bot said in its faintly metallic tone, "I must ask you to step aside so I can examine my patient."

*Jasper.*

A small surge of adrenaline pumped through Lilia at the thought of him, making her heart monitor pick up speed. She opened a Nancom channel to Kevin, rejoicing in the fact that it worked again, and ignoring a concerned cluck from the med 'bot. [Is Jasper okay?]

For a second, Kevin's exhaustion faded—he looked like he wanted to laugh. Then he shook his head. [You've got a one-track mind, Lil, that's for sure.]

[Kev—]

[As far as I know, he made it through surgery.]

Relief curled through Lilia, but she didn't let herself relax yet. [How bad—]

[—is it?] Kevin gave her a minute shrug. [I don't have any details yet. Sorry.] A shadow flitted over his face, but before he could voice his thoughts, the 'bot began speaking again.

"—are you feeling, Miss Strong?"

Blinking, Lilia turned her head from her brother to regard the 'bot standing patiently beside her bed. She shook her head dumbly; she wasn't even sure how to answer that.

Kevin and Erik both stepped out into the hall as the 'bot ran through its post-surgery checkup procedures. They didn't take long, but Lilia was still exhausted by the time the 'bot finally finished. Some of her exhaustion was physical, but she was emotionally and mentally worn out as well.

"Dinner will be served shortly," the 'bot said as it turned to leave. "I will return in a while to check on you. In the meantime, rest."

Lilia just nodded, sinking back into her pillow. She turned her head to the side and stared blankly at the beige curtained window. She was so tired; dealing with reality seemed to have taken everything she had right now.

She heard the door open again, but her eyes were already growing heavy. By the time someone—presumably Kevin—settled into the chair beside her bed, she was asleep again.

This time, she didn't dream.

# CHAPTER 110

KEVIN sat slumped in the surprisingly comfortable chair beside his sister's hospital bed, his hands clasped in front of him as he listened to the slow, steady cadence of her breathing. He wasn't surprised to find Lilia asleep again after the med 'bot finally departed. The shock of learning she'd lost a foot on top of everything else that had happened in the past twenty-four hours was enough to overtax anybody.

It did feel strange to be on this side of the hospital bed, though. Kevin stared down at the white tile floor, worn from countless feet sitting in this chair just like he was, and thought back to those days he'd spent in a bed like this one after the explosion at the Opening Ceremonies Gala a few months earlier. He shuddered, a chill running down his spine.

He'd almost lost an eye then.

Last night, Lilia had lost a foot.

Slowly, Kevin lifted his gaze to contemplate his sister's prosthesis. The hospital's med 'bots had assured both him and Derek that Lilia would be just fine. Recovery rates for amputees were almost a hundred percent.

Kevin was grateful to hear that, but he still felt shaken to his very core. His brush with severe injury had given him pause, reminded him that being a Guardian didn't make them invulnerable.

Lilia's injury had completely shattered whatever illusion of safety remained.

He'd known their nano-armor could only protect them from so much, but it took this to really pound it home.

Sighing, Kevin sat up and stretched his arms over his head. His back gave a satisfying 'pop'. He was contemplating pouring himself a glass of water—his sister certainly wasn't going to drink it at the moment—when his comlink buzzed softly in his pocket.

He almost ignored the call—their comlinks had all blown up with people trying to get a hold of them again for interviews and whatnot—but he knew he couldn't take the risk that it was actually important.

One glance at the display and his stomach tightened with anticipation.

He wasn't surprised—he'd known this would be coming at some point.

It was a message from Jayce's private comlink, the one he'd procured just to talk to Kevin and Lilia. He'd had it on him when he jumped through the portal Lilia had opened to save him from the not-Guardians coming to kidnap him.

*Can you talk yet? What is going on?*

Kevin frowned. Jayce—or, more likely, Nob, using Jayce's comlink—had messaged him after the news about the Pearl broke, but Kevin hadn't had time to do more than say he'd have to explain later.

*Looks like 'later' has finally arrived.*

Kevin drummed his fingers absently on his thigh, still thinking. He reached for the water pitcher sitting on the tray beside Lilia's bed, poured himself a glass, and drank half of the icy water in one fell swoop. Wincing as the cold water froze its way down his throat, he made a decision.

Derek was out in the hall, quietly triaging their grandfather's calls and messages. He had refused to leave the hospital yet, but Kevin knew it was only a matter of time before he had to head back to Sonela. For one thing, Derek couldn't deal with sensitive matters in a busy hospital hallway, and for another, their grandfather was going to need him.

*Better take my chance while I can.*

Kevin opened a Nancom channel to his brother. [Hey, can you sit with Lilia for an hour? I've got to leave for a while.]

His brother responded almost immediately. [Let me guess. Nob?]

[And Jayce.]

[Got it. Give me a moment and I'll be there.]

[Thanks.]

Kevin then Nancommed Erik. [Meet me back up here, will you? We need to go talk to Nob.]

Erik responded in the affirmative and Kevin drained the last of his water, resisting the urge to jump up and start pacing the hospital room again. He instead sent Jayce and Nob a quick message to let them know he and Erik would be there shortly.

A few moments later, Derek slipped through the door, with Erik right behind him. Kevin immediately vacated the chair and Derek took his place.

"Comm me before you leave so I can make sure we're clear." Derek indicated the room with a sweep of his fingers.

"Thanks."

Materializing his gloves, Kevin held his hands out in front of him, toward the end of Lilia's bed where there was more room. He focused on the nanites comprising the transporter embedded in his wrists and thought about the coordinates to Nob's apartment. A portal sphere blossomed in the air before him, sending a wave of displaced air out on all sides.

Kevin widened his hands, expanding the portal until it was big enough for them to pass through. Beside him, Erik gingerly stepped onto his hoverdisc, which he had just expanded and dropped to the floor, and flew into the portal. He vanished without a sound.

Kevin didn't bother with his own hoverdisc, though he knew he probably should have gotten it out of his ISF. With a nod over his shoulder to Derek, he plunged into the portal.

He landed less than gracefully on the other side, stumbling a few steps on the carpet in the center of Nob's living room.

"I do have neighbors," Nob said dryly, from where he stood framed in the doorway leading to his tiny kitchen. He looked tense and just a little bit harried.

"Sorry," Kevin said as he straightened and let the portal collapse.

Erik floated a meter away on his hoverdisc, having not had time to dismount yet.

Jayce sat on the couch, his thin face more pinched and haunted than it had been the last time Kevin had set eyes on him. Kevin frowned. *What's wrong with him now?*

"How is your sister?" Jayce asked without preamble.

Kevin blinked at him in surprise. "She'll be all right. It could have been worse."

Jayce's brown eyes skimmed over Erik, cataloging his obvious injuries. "What about you?"

"Oh, I'll live." Erik waved the fingers of his good hand flippantly. "It'll take more than that to do me in." He limped over to an armchair and sank into it.

Kevin raised an eyebrow at him, but didn't bother to say anything. They had far more important matters to deal with and nowhere near enough time.

Jayce nodded, his expression already going distant.

"What *happened?*" Nob demanded, still standing in the doorway. "Half of the reports coming out of Glo'Stea since last night have said one thing and the other half completely contradict them. Kedis is still alive, right?"

"He's still alive." Kevin exchanged a dark look with Erik. Where did they even begin?

"They opened portals into the Pearl, didn't they?"

It wasn't a question.

Startled, they all turned to look at Jayce.

The redheaded scientist fixed blazing brown eyes on Kevin, his hands tightening into fists. "That's how Freedom's Children bypassed Pearl Security, didn't they?" He shook his head slightly. "It's the only explanation that makes any sense."

From the doorway, Nob made a sound of agreement.

Kevin exchanged another look with Erik before he locked his hands behind his head and began pacing the small living room. "They did. The Triumvirate is still trying to piece everything together, but I'll tell you what we do know."

Nob was swearing softly by the time Kevin and Erik finished. He shook his head, looking thoroughly disgusted. "The worst part is, now the NCDC—not to mention the Tarynians, and God only knows who else—know that Lilia can somehow open portals herself."

"Yeah." Kevin ran a hand over his face. "There wasn't any way around that."

"And Representative Hollowell *stabbed* Lieutenant Wright?" Nob shook his head again. "That definitely did not make the news."

"With a nanoblade," Kevin said grimly. "According to Lon, anyway. Grandfather doesn't have much familiarity with nanoblades, but he knows it wasn't an ordinary fencing blade."

"Why?" It was Nob's turn to begin pacing. "Why would a Glo'Stean Representative have a *nanoblade?*" He was shaking his head again. "If it wasn't his, where did he get it? And if it *was* his, where in the galaxy did he *keep* it?"

From his seat in an armchair, Erik raised a hand. "He could have gotten it from one of the not-Guardians, although—" he frowned, "—that doesn't explain *how.*" He shrugged. "It's either that or the old man is a Guardian."

*...old man is a Guardian...* Kevin blinked, Erik's words triggering something in his brain. His breath stilled in his chest. *That can't be right.*

"Strong?" Nob had stopped pacing and was staring at him, his dark eyes burning with a sudden, intense curiosity.

"Uh…" Kevin struggled to find words; he felt like he'd just knocked his own world off its axis. "I—uh—"

"What's the matter with you?" Erik straightened in his chair, frowning at him.

Kevin looked around the apartment living room, but didn't really see any of them. He scrubbed a hand through his dark hair before clasping the back of his neck. "I—uh—just remembered something Lilia said while she was in the emergency room."

The room seemed to be closing in around him; for a second, he thought he might pass out. He felt the blood drain from his face.

It couldn't be true.

"What?" three voices demanded together.

"I—" Kevin shook his head helplessly. "I don't think she was in her right mind. It doesn't make any *sense.*" Months of frustration colored his tone.

*Except,* whispered a voice in the back of his mind, *that it* does *make sense.*

It made a terrible, horrible kind of sense—and his brain was only just beginning to grasp the implications.

"For cryin' out loud, don't leaves us in suspense," Erik complained. "Not after everythin' that's happened."

Kevin bit his lip hard enough to draw blood; the taste of copper jolted him back to reality. Swallowing, he took a deep breath. "In the emergency room, Lilia told me the Mastermind stabbed Jasper."

Dead silence greeted these words; he saw confusion on all of the other men's faces.

"I know for a fact that it was Uncle Martin." Kevin spread his hands. "So either my sister was very confused—"

"Or else she had reason to believe Martin Hollowell *is* the Mastermind," Nob finished grimly.

Kevin gave him a slow, reluctant nod. "Exactly."

"What?" Erik looked taken aback—and deeply disturbed. "Are you tryin' to tell me a *Glo'Stean Representative* is the *Mastermind?*"

"I'm just telling you what she said." Kevin shrugged defensively.

"It's certainly a possibility." Nob spared Erik a glance before turning his attention back to Kevin. "We need to talk to your sister."

"Trust me," Kevin held up a hand, "as soon as she's up for it, we will."

"I knew somebody at the top had to be involved."

Jayce's quiet voice startled all of them. Kevin, Nob, and Erik shifted to look at him, but the scientist had already leaned back against the couch and was staring up at the ceiling. His face took on a faraway look, as though his brain was hard at work processing everything and spinning out theories and possibilities.

Kevin opened a joint Nancom channel to Nob and Erik and tipped his head slightly toward the scientist. [How is Jayce holding up?]

[Not well.] Nob's mouth flattened into a thin line. [He's starting to climb the walls.]

[Can't say I'm surprised.] Erik lifted his good shoulder in a shrug.

Nob returned to his spot in the doorway, leaning up against the doorjamb and folding his arms across his chest. [We're going to have to do something soon—put him to work and give him something to occupy his mind, or he's going to end up driving *me* crazy too. And that's if I don't wake up one morning and discover he's flown the coop.]

The grim tone of the older Guardian's mental voice gave Kevin pause. He supposed it was to be expected—after all, Jayce was in hiding and unable to work, his colleagues were missing, and everyone the man knew and loved thought he was dead.

Not to mention he'd just learned that somebody in the Triumvirate was possibly behind it all.

Kevin gave Nob a quick nod. [We'll figure something out.]

[Soon.] Nob's gaze landed on Jayce, tense and considering. [He's in danger of doing something stupid—like attempting to contact Freedom's Children and offer to trade himself for Dr. Lang.]

Kevin and Erik both winced. [Yeah,] Erik drawled, [that'd be a problem.]

Nob's eyes flicked back to Kevin. [I don't like this. We need to know what Lilia knows as soon as possible.]

[I know.] Kevin scrubbed his hand through his hair. [Also, we need to tell my grandfather Jayce isn't dead.]

When both of the other Guardians turned incredulous looks on him, he just shrugged. [We can't keep him hidden forever, and Grandfather may be able to help us figure out what to do with him. Or the best place to hide him.]

Erik looked skeptical, but didn't say anything.

Nob's expression turned grim. [Maybe.] He glanced at Jayce and they all followed suit. [But not until we talk to your sister.]

# CHAPTER 111

Uncle Martin is the Mastermind.

Those words repeated themselves over and over inside Lilia's mind, interspersed with his voice snarling, *Because I made you.*

*I made you.*

Lilia stared blankly at the wall opposite her hospital bed. She hadn't told her brothers yet. There hadn't been time, for one, and besides, she didn't know *how*. She had been the only person present to hear those fateful words. Would they even believe her?

She barely believed it herself.

It seemed so incredible. Just another surreal moment in what had been a completely surreal evening.

And yet…the more she thought about it, the more the scattered jumble of pieces they'd been collecting for months began to fit together. Slowly, a picture began to come into focus. Fragmented and blurry, yes, but a picture nonetheless.

A fine shudder wracked Lilia's body; she wrapped her arms around herself, suddenly cold.

The Mastermind had handpicked them—her, her brothers, Erik, and others.

*Uncle Martin* had handpicked them.

*Uncle Martin* had tried to recruit them into Freedom's Children.

Lilia swallowed, a sudden bout of nausea twisting her insides and threatening to send her lunch back up into her lap.

*Uncle Martin* had tried to kill their grandfather.

A hundred different memories rushed through her brain at hyperspeed, tumbling over each other.

Uncle Martin having dinner with their family at the Mansion in Marina when she and Kevin were tiny.

Uncle Martin, standing by to offer silent support at their grandmother's funeral.

Uncle Martin, standing by that terrible day when they thought they were laying Lon to rest.

Uncle Martin, visiting Aiden in the hospital after the explosion at the Opening Ceremonies Gala.

*Uncle Martin*, with his kind smile, kind eyes, and kind words, while the entire time he'd been plotting his best friend's murder and the takeover of the Coalition.

Lilia did retch then. She barely managed to grab a plastic container off her tray in time before she lost the entire contents of her stomach. When she was finished, she wiped her face with a napkin and lay back on her bed, pale and shaking.

The smell of her own vomit nearly set her off again, but she took a few deep breaths and managed to quell the nausea. She tapped the call button with a trembling finger and waited for a med 'bot.

The silver 'bot arrived fairly quickly. It whisked away the mess and tutted over her for a moment before saying in a chipper voice, "How do you feel now?"

In response, Lilia shrugged. "I'm alive." Her glance fell on her prosthetic foot before skipping away.

A knock sounded on the door. Kevin stuck his head in and gave Lilia a bright smile. "Good morning."

Despite the heaviness pressing down on her, Lilia managed a return smile. It *was* good to see a dear, familiar face. "Morning."

Kevin entered the room and plopped down in the chair next to her bed, rubbing his hands together. He looked at the med 'bot. "What's on the agenda for today?"

"It is time for you, Miss Strong, to learn to use your new foot."

Lilia didn't bother to hide her grimace. *Oh, this is going to be fun.*

The 'bot turned its silver-white photoreceptors on Lilia, looking strangely expectant. "Can you wiggle your toes?"

Lilia rolled her eyes at it. "Of course I can't wiggle my toes. That," she pointed to her prosthetic, "is not my foot."

Even as the words left her mouth, she knew they were childish. People all over the Coalition—all over the *galaxy*—suffered amputations on a regular basis, were fitted with prosthetics, and went on with their lives. She knew it wasn't the end of the world, but it sure as hell felt like it right now.

The 'bot nodded sympathetically, an entirely human reaction programmed into its subroutines. "Denial is not an uncommon reaction in situations like this. Your body and mind will, however, adapt in time."

Moving down to the end of the bed, the med 'bot gently unwrapped one of the bandages swathing Lilia's ankle to reach a tiny access panel. "In actuality, you can't wiggle your toes yet because your foot has not yet been properly calibrated."

*Calibrated. Right.* Lilia blinked; that actually made sense. She had to take another deep breath, however, as a wave of dizziness washed over her. The fact that a part of her body had to be *calibrated* still felt overwhelming.

She and Kevin watched in equal parts fascination, amazement, and horror as the med 'bot extended one of its hands toward her foot and a tiny cable popped out from the end of a fingertip. The 'bot attached this cable to the tiny access panel and waited.

For a few seconds, the only sounds in the room were Lilia's shallow breathing and the not-so-steady mechanical counterpart of her heart monitor. Finally, the med 'bot fixed her with its silver-white photoreceptors and said in a gentle, encouraging voice, "Try wiggling your toes again."

Lilia felt foolish—how was she supposed to move something that wasn't actually there anymore?—but she obeyed.

Nothing happened.

Her stomach clenched in disappointment.

In that instant, she saw a snapshot of what her future would look like if she couldn't even control a prosthetic foot. She'd be doomed to travel everywhere on old-fashioned crutches, or else be confined to a hoverchair like her grandfather still needed to use on occasion.

The med 'bot emitted a thoughtful hum. It made another tiny adjustment and then focused on Lilia again. "Miss Strong, I know losing a limb is a difficult thing—"

*How can you know?* she wondered abruptly. *You're a machine.*

"—but you will be all right. Ninety percent of patients who receive mechanical replacement limbs report that in time they forget the limbs were not originally their own." The med 'bot waved one of its two left arms. "You must allow your mind to make the mental connection to this new part of your body."

Lilia opened her mouth to protest, but the 'bot continued evenly, "You received a nanite infusion from the Nanotech Coalition Defense Corp and had to allow your mind to make a connection to those nanites in order to control them. This—" it waved both of its left hands toward her foot, "—is the same concept."

*The same concept…*

Those three words seeped into Lilia's brain, and a tiny ray of bright hope pierced her gloomy disappointment. She thought back to those first few hours training with Neela in the NCDC's headquarters in Jamal, learning how to use her nano-armor. She'd initially had trouble commanding her nanites, but she had eventually overcome it.

*It's the same concept.*

Narrowing her eyes at her new foot in determination, Lilia took a deep breath and willed her toes to move. She imagined she could *feel* the neural pathways in her brain reconnecting to the space beyond her ankle, where her new foot had been grafted to her leg.

Her big toe twitched, and then all five of her new toes wiggled back and forth.

A broad grin stretched across Lilia's face. Excitement flooded her, giving her enough adrenaline that she had the sudden urge to hop out of her bed and do a little jig.

"Yes!" Beside her, Kevin pumped a fist in the air. He turned shining violet eyes on her. "You did it!"

They shared a happy smile, and then Lilia looked expectantly at the med 'bot. "Now what?"

The 'bot ran her through a few more exercises, things like flexing her foot and waving it around in a circle, before it finally told her she could get out of bed and attempt to put weight on her foot.

Lilia wet her lips, suddenly nervous again. She looked at her brother.

Kevin offered her an encouraging smile. "You can do it."

Lilia lifted her chin, resolve solidifying in her veins. *Yes, I can.* Throwing back the blanket covering her legs, she gingerly swung her legs over the side of the bed.

"Go easy," the med 'bot cautioned her. "You have been in bed for the past couple of days."

Lilia nodded in acknowledgment, but didn't speak. Her entire attention was focused on her feet. Her left foot was covered in a slim hospital thermal sock, but her new right foot was bare.

As the balls of her feet made contact with the tiled floor, she expected to feel its firm surface against her new foot.

She didn't expect to feel *cold*.

Her startled intake of breath made Kevin jump; he immediately leaned forward, hand outstretched toward her. "Are you all right?"

She nodded quickly, her eyes still glued to her feet. "The floor's cold—I can *feel* it."

"That is an excellent sign." The med 'bot sounded quite pleased with itself.

Lilia pressed both feet flat to the floor, amazed and astounded at the sensations traveling through her newly-formed neurological pathways. She hadn't expected her prosthetic to actually *respond* like a real foot.

"Here." Kevin rose from his seat and held out his hands to her.

"No." Lilia waved him off, shaking her head. "Thanks, Kev, but I need to do this."

She took a deep, bracing breath, and then pushed off the bed and stood.

She wasn't quite sure what she'd expected—pain and uncomfortableness from putting weight on something alien to her body, perhaps?—but she felt surprisingly…normal.

"Good job." The med 'bot inclined its silver head in a nod. "Now, take a step. Don't overthink it—just let your body move naturally."

That proved a little harder to accomplish. Lilia felt hyperaware of her foot, and part of her brain started stressing over whether or not she would be able to command it to behave properly. *Don't overthink this*, she reminded herself.

Resolutely, she focused on the door to the hygiene unit instead.

She took one tentative step, followed by another.

Elation surged through her, along with a wave of relief so powerful her knees almost buckled. *I'm walking.*

Lilia made it all the way to the hygiene unit door and carefully pivoted to face Kevin and the med 'bot. Her brother was beaming; even the silver 'bot seemed to somehow exude satisfaction.

"I can walk." Lilia's voice cracked on the last word; she had to swallow and clear her throat. Her emotions were apparently all over the map and they hadn't bothered to consult her about it.

"I knew you could do it, Lil. You're going to be just fine."

She nodded, unable to restrain a giddy smile, and turned to the med 'bot. "Now what?"

The silver 'bot held up one of its four hands. "We will keep you for observation another hour or two to ensure your foot has integrated with your nervous system properly and then you will most likely be released."

Lilia exhaled in a rush. "Oh, thank God."

She was more than ready to go home.

Her legs were a little shaky as she sank back down onto her bed; she was grateful to be sitting down again. The past couple of days had taken more out of her than she realized. The med' bot checked her vitals again and then departed.

"I can't wait to go home." Lilia looked at Kevin, smiling, but the smile died on her lips as she took in his suddenly somber expression.

He looked troubled, his dark eyebrows knitting together in a frown.

Unease stirred in her gut. "Kev? What's wrong?"

"Lilia..." he began slowly. "I didn't remember it until now, but earlier—when we first got you to the hospital..." He hesitated, still frowning at her, his eyes full of concern. "You said the *Mastermind* stabbed Wright."

*Did I?* Lilia's gaze drifted past him as she tried to think back. She couldn't remember.

"The thing is..." Kevin continued cautiously, "according to Grandfather and Michael, *Uncle Martin* stabbed him." He shook his head, looking green around the edges. "I still can't believe that, but..." He trailed off with a helpless little shrug.

*I see.* Lilia took a deep breath, settling back against her pillows. She frowned slightly. For whatever reason, neither Grandfather nor Michael had told Kevin Uncle Martin had admitted to being the Mastermind. *Have to deal with that later. For now...this is it.*

She hadn't known how she was going to tell her brothers everything...this was as good an opening as any. She might as well start with the person who knew her best.

She had to take two more breaths before she could quell the nausea suddenly churning her stomach and actually force out words. "Kev, I know it's going to sound crazy, but Uncle Martin *is* the Mastermind. He told me himself."

Her words hung in the air between them; there was no going back now.

"He's been behind everything. Freedom's Children, the assassination attempts on Grandfather…all of it." She swallowed, tasting bile. "And now I don't know what to do."

Kevin was silent for a long, long moment. At last he stirred. "We'll figure it out. One way or another, we'll figure it out."

"I hope so." Lilia bit her lip. "Because I'm afraid this has the potential to start another war. I'm—" she took a deep breath, "I'm afraid that's what Uncle Martin *wants*."

# EPILOGUE

HANDS clasped behind his back, Martin Hollowell stood by a thick, heavily-reinforced window in the large stone room that had been set aside as his office in Freedom's Children's headquarters on the island of Meloran. He was seldom here; his work as a Representative kept him busy on Sta'Gloa most of the time.

But not today.

He was high enough that he had a view of the ocean through a gap in the jungle. A storm was moving in, as evidenced by the way tree branches whipped back and forth and choppy, white-capped waves rippled on the water's gray surface in the distance.

Hollowell clasped and unclasped his hands, relishing the feel of his nano-armor gloves. He wore full defense-mode armor, sans helmet and facemask. It felt good to be in uniform—a uniform he could usually only display here.

They had a fight on their hands, and he was ready for it.

The smell of his favorite tea wafted through the room, but his mind was too far away to register it.

It had been two days since their successful attack on the Pearl. Two days, and no one had attempted to arrest him yet, or even question him, beyond verifying he had survived the attack.

Hollowell pursed his lips. Obviously, Aiden Monroe, Michael Strong, and Lilia had yet to tell anyone he was the Mastermind. Either that, or they *had*…and no one had believed them.

He thought the former more likely. Particularly since it was only Sunday, and the Triumvirate was dealing with deaths and injuries.

This holding period would not last, however. Within the next few hours or the next day, Aiden would share what he knew with certain members of the Triumvirate, and then he, Hollowell, would need to act accordingly.

Hollowell stared out at the moody sea, his dark gaze not so much seeing it as seeing *through* it. He hadn't planned on revealing he was the Mastermind this early, but the moment had presented itself when Lilia put the pieces together and he had not hesitated.

Besides, he had never intended to stay hidden forever. The time was soon approaching when the entire Coalition would know him as the man fighting to free them from the Galactic Union. He could feel it in his old bones.

Hollowell's mouth twisted into a frown. That Lilia had flat-out rejected his offer—to his face—was…disappointing, to say the least. He had expected better from her and her brother.

They would need to be punished for that.

All that *time* he had poured into cultivating a relationship with them over the years.

All the money he had invested in them—paying Dover to alter their nanites, among other things.

The sound of a comlink chiming interrupted his brooding. Hollowell turned away from the window to glance at his large desk, made from gleaming red-brown jungle wood. It was empty save for his datapad, a tray with a teapot and teacups, and two comlinks. The device currently chiming was his secondary comlink.

Crossing to the desk, Hollowell materialized his facemask and helmet and enabled his voice synthesizer. Then he answered the comlink. "Yes?"

"You wanted to talk to me, boss?"

"Yes. It's in regards to the *Talia* and her captain and crew."

"I did what you said, boss. Told Ibaka to back off and leave 'em alone for now."

"Well, I am now rescinding that order." Hollowell's voice was very cold. "It is time Kevin and Lilia Strong learn that one cannot simply say 'no' to an offer from Hesperia."

A pause greeted these words as his top lieutenant in the Glo'Stean branch of Hesperia Shipping carefully considered them. "Are you sayin' you want them…eliminated?"

A tempting thought, but one that would ultimately serve no purpose other than to hurt Aiden Monroe. And while making Aiden pay was tempting, he had bigger things in mind.

Hollowell shook his head, even though his lieutenant couldn't see him. "No. I don't want a repeat of the Holt incident. What I want is for you to apply pressure to them until their only options are either to shut down their business or else take you up on your generous offer."

"I see. That can be done."

"Then do it." Hollowell turned back to face the window again, glimpsing his masked reflection. "Is Nigel still comfortably in the dark?"

Liam Nigel was the president and founder of Hesperia. He was a brilliant man and had done a fantastic job of managing all three branches of his business as it flourished and expanded—but not brilliant enough. He had no idea Hollowell had been subverting certain smugglers for years, using them to smuggle secret cargos inside and outside the Coalition.

Smuggling within smuggling. So simple, and yet so elegantly complex at the same time. Hollowell loved it.

"Completely oblivious, sir. Nothing's changed on that front. He has no reason to be suspicious of anything."

"Good. Keep it that way."

Freedom's Children would need to maintain its sources of supplies—not to mention income—over the coming months.

"Anything else?"

"Not now. Keep up the good work."

Ending the call, Hollowell tossed his comlink back on his desk and dematerialized his facemask and helmet. He stepped over to the window again, rubbing his chin thoughtfully as he considered his next move.

He needed to return to Sonela, he decided after a moment. He had received a memo stating the Triumvirate would be holding an emergency session in two hours. Emergency elections needed to be held to replace Representatives who had been killed, and an interim Glo'Stean Director of Security needed to be appointed to replace Guy Caradoc.

Aside from that, it would be just another pointless emergency session in which his colleagues would scramble to look like they were actually accomplishing something in the face of chaos.

Hollowell smirked, a sense of satisfaction flooding him. The hard part for him would be trying not to laugh at the absurdity of it all. Of course, if Aiden talked, the afternoon would go much differently. He needed to ensure he had an escape route.

Casually, he reached into his ISF by his left hip and withdrew his gleaming nanoblade. The blade was straight, seventy centimeters long, with a simple silver hilt and guard. He examined it for a long moment, turning the blade this way and that to catch the light.

This blade had tasted Tarynian blood.

He had never used it on a living being before, but the nanoblade had sunk as effortlessly into the lieutenant's back as it pierced anything else. Hollowell smiled slightly, recalling the look of mingled shock and horror on Aiden and his grandchildren's faces. Lilia's expression, in particular, stood out to him.

He tapped the flat of his blade with a gloved finger. *Let that serve as her punishment for fraternizing with the enemy.*

With any luck, his goddaughter would learn from this error and be more guarded in the future.

His expression turned to granite. *That is a lesson most of the Triumvirate needs to learn as well.*

The memory of Lilia opening a portal came to him next, and Hollowell scowled. He hadn't anticipated the twins learning they even *had* transporters, much less how to *use* them.

This development would force him to change his plans ever so slightly. True, he had taken precautions in the event this happened… but if he was brutally honest with himself, a large part of him had not actually believed it *would.*

Despite the anger and frustration curling through him, Hollowell couldn't help a flicker of pride. *This* was precisely why he'd chosen the twins for inclusion in Freedom's Children in the first place.

Their conviction, their courage, their intelligence and willingness to act…

They were bright and, despite everything, he had hopes that he might yet be able to sway them to his side.

Hollowell scowled again. *Not without some punishment for the very poor choices they have been making of late.*

His thoughts turned again to Lilia and the portal. *If she has figured it out, it's a safe assumption her brother has as well.*

Not a certainty, but he wouldn't lay odds on Kevin remaining oblivious. Nor on Lilia keeping something of this magnitude from him.

Hollowell stared out at the patch of gray, white-capped ocean again, casually resting the flat of his nanoblade on his armored shoulder. It would be nice to know exactly how long the twins had been aware of their transporters, but he supposed in the end it didn't really matter. The important thing was making sure his plans from here on out took this new variable into consideration.

He shook his head. *The best laid plans…*

They weren't supposed to have found out about the transporters until he told them himself. It was supposed to have been a crowning moment. Now it was an aggravating edge they possessed.

*I wonder if they've told Aiden about them yet.*

Hollowell snorted softly to himself. Now *there* was an interesting question.

He considered it for a moment, turning it over in his mind to examine all the various facets, before he concluded he simply didn't know. Along with their brother Lon, the twins had had their independence for several years now—though that time was a mere drop in the bucket compared to the years he and Aiden had under their belts—and it was entirely possible they felt capable of handling something like this themselves.

Hollowell's eyes narrowed thoughtfully. *After all, isn't that what they did with Kedis?* They had shielded their grandfather from that information until the end.

He gave himself a slight shake, banishing thoughts of the twins in the process. Transporters or no transporters, he would have plenty of time to deal with them later.

Briskly, Hollowell returned his nanoblade to its crimson-and-black sheath in his ISF. It was an elegant weapon—not to mention an excellent source of income for Freedom's Children—but not his most effective weapon by a long shot.

No, his best weapon was his mind. Years of planning and strategizing were about to come to fruition.

Years of carefully-laid plans and carefully building a foundation.

Years of biding his time and waiting for the right moment.

Years of gathering a group of like-minding people from across the Coalition to guard against exactly what had taken place—the Triumvirate finally giving in and bowing to the Tarynians.

Hollowell gritted his teeth, his breath emerging in a hiss as he glared past his reflection in the plastiglass window. The very thought of it still made his blood boil.

He forced himself to relax. The doctor kept reminding him to mind his blood pressure. The thought of *that* nearly made him laugh too. Really, that somebody as ice-cold as he was now should have high blood pressure?

Hollowell allowed himself a grim smile. Well, it couldn't be helped.

He flattened a gloved hand against the plastiglass. The Triumvirate had sown the proverbial wind—and they were about to reap the whirlwind.

He would personally make sure of it.

# ACKNOWLEDGEMENTS

Writing *Freedom's Children* was definitely an adventure. In the three years it took me to finish the story, I got married had two babies, and have another one on the way. (That's probably *why* it took me three years…) I am so blessed to have family and friends encouraging me along the way.

Special thanks go to my husband, Tim Williams, for all your prayers and encouragement. I really appreciate everything you do for me. Especially your understanding of the fact that sometimes I just need to write down what the voices in my head are saying… ::grin::

Thanks also go to my family, for your continual support and encouragement.

Connie Trapp and Hannah Hedges, for being such helpful, insightful beta-readers. Y'all caught things I missed, and I'm grateful.

Thanks also to Lori, Kimberly, Heather Stearns, Kimberly Richie, Sherry Mosley, Heather Brown, Veronica, Justin and Chelsea Stevens, Kendrah, Meta Clark, Bonnie Lamb, Karleine Justice, Kitty Perkinson, my Aunt Janie, various friends at church, and many, many others.

# About the Author

An avid science fiction and mystery fangirl, E.R. Paskey writes across several genres and is the author of eleven books, including her Christian science fiction series, *The Guardians*. She currently lives in Southern Indiana with her husband and their five children.

You can find her website at www.erpaskey.com.

Made in the USA
Monee, IL
15 March 2022

92603453R00430